S. B. Smith

Elements of ecclesiastical law

Vol. II

S. B. Smith

Elements of ecclesiastical law
Vol. II

ISBN/EAN: 9783741194689

Manufactured in Europe, USA, Canada, Australia, Japa

Cover: Foto ©Andreas Hilbeck / pixelio.de

Manufactured and distributed by brebook publishing software
(www.brebook.com)

S. B. Smith

Elements of ecclesiastical law

ELEMENTS

OF

ECCLESIASTICAL LAW.

COMPILED WITH REFERENCE TO

THE SYLLABUS, THE "CONST. APOSTOLICAE SEDIS" OF POPE
PIUS IX., THE COUNCIL OF THE VATICAN AND
THE LATEST DECISIONS OF THE
ROMAN CONGREGATIONS.

ADAPTED ESPECIALLY TO THE DISCIPLINE OF THE CHURCH IN THE
UNITED STATES.

BY

˙REV. S. B. SMITH D.D.,

FORMERLY PROFESSOR OF CANON LAW, AUTHOR OF "NOTES,"
"COUNTER-POINTS," "THE NEW PROCEDURE,"
"COMPENDIUM JURIS CANONICIS,"
ETC., ETC.

VOL. II.

ECCLESIASTICAL TRIALS.

*Thoroughly revised according to the Instruction "Cum Magnopere" and the
"Third Plenary Council of Baltimore."*

FIFTH EDITION

NEW YORK, CINCINNATI, AND CHICAGO:

BENZIGER BROTHERS,

PRINTERS TO THE HOLY APOSTOLIC SEE.

1892.

Nihil Obstat,

H. GABRIELS, S.T.D.,

Censor Deputatus.

Imprimatur,

✠ MICHAEL AUGUSTINUS,

Archiepiscopus Neo-Eboracensis.

Datum NEO-EBORACI,
Die 29 APRILIS, 1887.

LETTER FROM CARDINAL SIMEONI.

S. Congregazione di Propaganda,

Roma, li 12 Maggio, 1883.

Rev.^{DE} Domine

Secundum volumen operis a te conscripti cui titulus "Elements of Ecclesiastical Law," obtuli tuo nomine Ssmo Dño Nostro, qui benigne illud excepit atque acceptum habuit, tibique Apostolicam benedictionem impertire dignatus est.

Alterum exemplar enunciati operis ad me transmissum valde gratum mihi fuit, atque tibi plurimas ago gratias, teque hortor ut quam tibi Deus Optimus Maximus ingenii vim concessit, in utilitatem Catholicae Ecclesiæ impendas.

Interim fausta omnia a Domino tibi adprecor.

D. T.

Addictus

IOANNES CARD. SIMEONI PRÆFECTUS,

✠ D. Archiep. Tyren., *Secret.*

PREFACE.

IT is now over five years since we published the first volume of these *Elements*. The reader will naturally ask himself why we should have allowed so long a time to elapse before issuing the second volume. Our chief excuse is the difficulty of the task. There are perhaps not many persons who have an idea of the arduous nature of our undertaking. Canonists all agree that the matter—ecclesiastical judicature—of which the present volume treats is by far the most difficult and complicated portion of all ecclesiastical law. Schmalzgrueber[1] says: "Est hic liber" (the second book of the decretals of Pope Gregory IX., which treats of ecclesiastical trials) omnium aliorum librorum juris canonici difficillimus, et maxime utilis."

This difficulty is heightened, in our case, by the peculiar circumstances under which we write. Ecclesiastical trials in criminal and disciplinary causes of ecclesiastics are to be conducted in the United States in the manner laid down by the Instruction of the Sacred Congregation de Propaganda Fide, issued July 20, 1878. This Instruction authorizes certain departures from the prescriptions of the sacred canons concerning ecclesiastical trials. It permits a simpler, easier, and less intricate mode of procedure. Yet it gives but the general features of the proceedings. Now, what are the principles which must guide the ecclesiastical judge and the canonist in filling up this sketch or outline? Evidently no others than those which are contained and embodied in the

---

[1] Lib. 2, Prooem.

sacred canons, the decrees of œcumenical councils, and the constitutions of the supreme pontiffs, as interpreted and applied by the approved canonists of every age and every clime.

The common law of the Church—and we mean not merely its letter, but also its spirit—must therefore be, so to say, the mirror before which our peculiar mode of procedure must be placed, considered, and studied. This law alone furnishes the correct key of the Instruction. Hence, throughout this volume, the peculiar trial as prescribed for this country by the Instruction of July 20, 1878, is everywhere and in all its details compared with the canonical trial as established by the sacred canons. The points of agreement as well as of divergence between the one and the other are carefully pointed out and explained.

The present volume is divided into two Parts. The first treats of ecclesiastical trials in general: namely, of the judicial power of the Church; of the *personnel* of ecclesiastical courts: of the judge and our Commissions of Investigation; of plaintiffs and defendants, procurators and advocates; of the nature, various kinds, and force of judicial proofs. The Second Part discusses ecclesiastical trials in particular—that is, chiefly the various stages and formalities of ecclesiastical trials, both ordinary and extraordinary, civil and criminal, and matrimonial. Particular attention is paid everywhere to our form of trial, and it is explained in all its details.

We are happy to call attention to the fact that their Eminences Cardinals Manning and Newman, the greatest lights of the Church in England at the present day, have been graciously pleased to approve of the first volume of this work.

S. B. S.

St. Joseph's Church, Paterson, N. J.,
Feast of the Assumption of the Blessed Virgin, 1882.

PREFACE TO THE SECOND EDITION.

NEARLY two years have elapsed since the first edition of the present volume became exhausted. We have delayed this new edition, chiefly on account of the new legislation relative to judicial proceedings, which has taken place since that time.

The procedure laid down by the S. C. de Prop. Fide, in its Instruction of July 20, 1878, and the subsequent authentic explanations, had not fully attained the end for which it had been enacted. It was, indeed, a judicial proceeding, and yet not a canonical trial. Hence, it created some uncertainty when there was question of carrying out its principal details.

In 1884, the Holy See, wishing to remedy this inconvenience, and to provide a mode of proceeding which would be in every respect adequate to the regular administration of justice, issued the Instruction *Cum Magnopere*. This document, which had been already discussed in the conferences held at Rome, in 1883, between some of the cardinals of the Propaganda and our archbishops, outlines and prescribes the mode of proceeding, which shall be observed in future by Ordinaries before they can inflict preventive or repressive punishments. This procedure is a canonical trial, in the strict sense of the word, as we show in our *New Procedure*, or methodical explanation of the Instruction *Cum Magnopere*.

Yet this same Instruction *Cum Magnopere*, in Art. XII.,

allows, by way of dispensation, the Instruction of 1878 to remain in force *ad interim* in those dioceses where the *curia* cannot as yet be canonically established. Accordingly, there are at present a number of dioceses, especially in the West and South, where the procedure outlined and prescribed in the Instruction of 1878 still obtains, and will continue to obtain for some time to come.

Besides, the procedure laid down in the Instruction of 1878 is in force all over England, was recommended for Ireland by the Plenary Synod of Maynooth, and is, we believe, also adopted or observed in Scotland.

Hence we have retained, in this new edition, the principal explanations of and references to the proceedings as conducted by Commissions of Investigation. However, we have also given due weight to the procedure as prescribed by the latest Instruction, *Cum Magnopere*, which we explain and refer to in many places.

Moreover, we give, in this new edition, an accurate outline of the trial or procedure in matrimonial causes, as made obligatory, throughout the United States, by the recent Instruction, *Causae Matrimoniales*, issued by the S. C. de P. F. in 1884, and embodied by the *Third Plenary Council of Baltimore* in its acts and decrees.

In the Appendix, we subjoin the full text of this Instruction, as also of the Const. *Dei Miseratione* of Pope Benedict XIV. concerning matrimonial causes.

We refer with no ordinary pleasure to the gracious letter of His Eminence Cardinal Simeoni, Prefect of the Propaganda, printed on the front page of this volume. We also return sincere thanks for the many other commendatory letters kindly sent us by Prelates and Priests, not only from this country, but also from Europe.

PATERSON, N. J.,
    Aug. 15, 1887. }

PREFACE TO THE FOURTH EDITION.

In this new edition, besides correcting several inaccuracies, we have added some important supplementary notes. We call especial attention to the supplement on the *Expenses of Ecclesiastical Trials, both in the first instance and on appeal.* This subject is still new in this country; yet the Instruction *Cum Magnopere* of the S. C. de Prop. Fide, Article 44, has already brought up the question several times, to our own knowledge, during the course of ecclesiastical trials, and will make its consideration more urgent every day.

PATERSON, *Feb.* 17, 1890.

PREFACE TO THE FIFTH EDITION.

THIS new edition has been carefully revised and amended; some important changes and additions have been made. The question, mooted in Nos. 838, 839, whether witnesses can or should be examined *in the presence of the accused or of the party against whom they testify*, and whether they can and should be *subjected to cross-examination*, is pretty fully discussed in Appendix XI., specially added in the present edition. Then again, in Appendix XII., the *dies fatales* in EXTRAJUDICIAL appeals are explained.

We have also added, in the new Appendix XIII., a careful review of the modern practice and teaching of the Church concerning the various kinds of oaths, as taken or administered in or out of judicial proceedings. An important correction has also been made on p. 374, n. 1413, with reference to matrimonial causes.

PATERSON, N. J., January 20, 1892.

BOOK II.

ON ECCLESIASTICAL JUDICATURE, OR OF JUDICIAL PROCEEDINGS, CIVIL AND CRIMINAL, IN ECCLESIASTICAL COURTS.

(DE JUDICIIS ECCLESIASTICIS.)

---

685. We shall divide this book into two parts: the first will treat of ecclesiastical judicature in general; the second will discuss the same subject in particular.

PART I.

OF ECCLESIASTICAL JUDICIAL PROCEEDINGS, CIVIL AND CRIMINAL, IN GENERAL.

686. Under this heading we shall speak of the nature and various kinds of judicial proceedings; of the various persons intervening at them, namely, of the judge, plaintiff and defendant, procurators and advocates; of the competency of the court; and of judicial proofs.

CHAPTER I.

WHAT IS MEANT BY JUDICIAL PROCEDURES OR TRIALS AND HOW MANY KINDS ARE THERE?

687. *Nature of judicial proceedings.* In every trial or forensic procedure there must be 1, a decision (*sententia*), regarding (a) a thing (*res*) or right (*jus*) belonging to a person, or (b) a punishment incurred by him according to law. Hence all trials or processes consist in the application of the

law to the fact. Therefore each trial or process resolves itself into a syllogism, of which the major is the nature of the law applying to the case; the minor the fact to which the law is to be applied, the conclusion, the sentence of the court or judge.[1] From this it will also be seen that the subject-matter of trials or judicial proceedings is essentially only a *litigious matter*. In other words, only questions or matters of law, about which two parties dispute,—*v.g.*, how far a person is entitled to some right or liable to some punishment,—can form the subject-matter of judicial proceedings. Hence questions that are merely theoretical or speculative or scientific—*v.g.*, whether the sun moves—cannot be the object of trials.[2]

688. 2. A judge (*judex*) or a person lawfully appointed to pronounce the sentence or give the decision, and, moreover, vested with power to execute it, that is, possessed of jurisdiction *in foro externo*.[3] From this it will be seen that every judge proper has the power not only to pronounce sentence (*potestas judicandi, notio*), but also to enforce it by penalties. We observe, however, with Devoti,[4] that this coercive power is not always attached to the *potestas judicandi* or *notio;* for there are judges—*v.g.*, arbitrators—who have only the *notio*, that is, merely the power to render a decision, but not to enforce it. However, these are judges only in a broad sense. Perhaps it might be said that members of Commissions of Investigation in England and the United States may, in a similar broad sense, be called judges. We say "in a similar broad sense," but not "in the same broad sense"; for although these commissioners have exclusive charge of the trial, or hearing of the case, their sentence or opinion, unlike that of arbitrators, is only consultative, and not binding upon the bishop, who alone can pronounce and enforce the final sentence.

[1] Salzano, vol. iv. p. 19.
[2] Craiss., n. 5476.
[3] München, Canonical Trials, vol. i. p. 6.
[4] Lib. iii., tit. ii., § 3; and tit. xvii., § 5.

689. 3. A plaintiff or quasi-plaintiff (*actor, quasi-actor, accusator, denuntiator*), namely, the person who sues or prosecutes—*i.e.*, demands that justice be done him, or a due punishment inflicted upon another. This plaintiff must be a distinct person from that of the judge, according to the axiom: " Nemo potest esse simul accusator et judex." However, the judge can, upon rumor or fame reaching him of the commission of a crime, summon before his tribunal the parties whom fame charges with the deed. and if upon due trial he finds them guilty, pronounce sentence. In this case, common fame (*fama communis*) itself supplies the place of the plaintiff, in fact, is considered the plaintiff, as Pope Innocent III. says: "Non tanquam idem sit accusator et judex, *sed quasi denuntiante fama, vel deferente clamore.*"[1] But in no case can the judge proceed merely on his own private knowledge of the offence.[2] Hence, as Schmalzgrueber[3] says, in every trial there must be a plaintiff, distinct from the judge, either in a literal or at least metaphorical sense.

690. 4. A defendant (*reus*), namely, a person of whom something is demanded or upon whom it is asked that a punishment shall be inflicted.

691. 5. Finally, it is necessary that the case be discussed or argued (*causae disceptatio*)—*i.e.*, that the plaintiff submit his proofs, and the defendant be allowed to defend himself.

692. This is all that is required by the law of nature for trials or judicial proceedings, ecclesiastical or secular. All other formalities (*solemnitates judicii*), even prescribed on pain of nullity, are necessary not because of the nature of processes, but solely from positive law. To understand this better, it must be borne in mind that, so far as their substance or essential elements are concerned, trials hold of the law of nature itself and are based upon it. For, considering the state of fallen human nature, litigations must frequently

[1] Cap. Qualiter et quando 24, De accusat. (v. 1).   [2] Craiss., n. 5478.
[3] Lib. 2, tit. 1, n. 16.

occur. It is therefore indispensable that there should be certain persons who can, in such cases, put an end to dis. putes and give each one his due. Now, evidently, this cannot be done by the contending parties themselves, nothing being more repugnant to right reason than that a person should be judge in his own cause. Hence it is necessary that tri. bunals or courts be established by public authority for the adjudication and settlement of causes.

693. We said, *so far as the substance or essential elements of trials are concerned;* for the mode of conducting trials—that is, the various formalities (*solemnitates judicii*)—have been established by human positive law. Hence, as we have already seen, the demand of the plaintiff, the citation of the defendant, the discussion of the cause,—*i.e.*, the submitting of proofs by the plaintiff, and the defence by the defendant, the sentence of the judge,—are required by the natural law to constitute a trial. For they pertain to the substance of trials, and are of such a nature that without them the cause could not be properly tried. The various other formalities, as we have shown, owe their origin to positive human law.[1] In the beginning trials or judicial proceedings were naturally informal. But as suits or litigations grew more numerous, it became necessary to establish a certain fixed mode or order of proceeding in these discussions or trials. This order or method of procedure in a particular case is styled process or trial, which may be, as we shall see, either ecclesiastical or secular.[2]

694. From what has been said, it follows: 1. A trial or process, considered in its essential elements,—*i.e.*, those which, as we have seen, are required by natural law,—is, properly speaking, defined to be "the sentence of the judge in regard to the demand of the plaintiff against the defendant, pronounced after due discussion or argument of the case."[3] Viewed

---

[1] Schmalzg., lib. 2, t. 1, n. 4.   [2] Salzano, vol. iv., p. 19.   [3] Craiss., n. 5481.

with regard to the formalities established by positive law, a process or trial is "the sentence. etc., pronounced by the judge, after the case has been argued or tried, *according to the method prescribed by law.*"[1] 2. In no trial or judicial proceedings (and this holds, as a matter of course, also of ecclesiastical trials; for we are now speaking in general of ecclesiastical and secular trials), even though only summary, can those things be omitted which form the substance of trials. For they are based upon the natural law, against which no custom can prevail.[2] 3. Supreme rulers (the Pope for the Church) can personally or through others omit those formalities of trials which are prescribed by positive law, but not those which derive from the law of nature.

695. Every trial or process, as we shall see further on, may be said to have three stages: the beginning, the middle, and the end; that is, the introduction of the cause into court, the trial proper, or hearing of the argument of plaintiff and defendant; the sentence.[3]

696. *Division.*—Trials or judicial proceedings are divided chiefly, 1, into ecclesiastical and secular. An ecclesiastical trial (*processus canonicus, judicium ecclesiasticum*) is that which takes place before the ecclesiastical judge as such, and is defined to be "the sentence which the ecclesiastical judge passes on a demand or accusation made by the plaintiff against the defendant, after the case has been duly argued before him, in the manner and form presented by the law of the Church." This "manner and form" are given in detail in the second book of the Decretals.

* The present mode of conducting ecclesiastical trials in the United States, in criminal and disciplinary causes of ecclesiastics, is laid down in the recent Instruction *Cum Magnopere*, issued by the S. C. de Prop. Fide, in 1884, and

---

[1] Cf. Ferraris, v. Judex, Novae add., n. 1.
[2] Schmalzg., l. c., n. 4. [3] Craiss., n. 5483, nota 1.

inserted in the Acts of the *Third Plenary Council of Baltimore.*
The trial outlined and prescribed in this Instruction is a
canonical summary trial. In those dioceses where, owing to
Papal permission, this Instruction is not yet introduced, the
Instruction of 1878, together with the Response *Ad Dubia*,
and the declarations of Art. XII. of the Instruction *Cum
Magnopere*, remains in force *ad interim.*[1]

697. 2. Into civil and criminal. Criminal trials are those
where crimes are punished; civil, where there is question,
not of punishing offences, but of deciding other disputes.[2]
This division applies to ecclesiastical as well as secular trials.
Further on we shall describe more fully the nature of criminal and civil trials in ecclesiastical courts.

698. 3. Into ordinary (*judicium ordinarium, solemne, plenarium*), where all the formalities prescribed by law are observed; and extraordinary (*processus summarius, judicium
extraordinarium*), where many of the formalities ordained
solely by positive law can be omitted. We say, *by positive
law;* for those which are required by the law of nature must
be retained even in summary trials.[3]

699. 4. Into petitory and possessory. Petitory trials or
processes (*judicium petitorium*) are those where there is question (a) of the ownership (*proprietas rei*, as distinguished
from *possessio rei*)—*i.e.*, just title or claim to a thing, *v.g.*, to a
field, an ecclesiastical benefice or office, the right of election;
(b) or of some right *in re* or *ad rem*, *v.g.*, the right resulting
from a mortgage or other security or pledge given, or from
heirship. Possessory trials, on the other hand, are those in
which the parties contend solely about obtaining, retaining,
or recovering *possession* of a certain object (*res*) or right (*jus*).
The difference therefore, between petitory and possessory
trials is that in the former the plaintiff asks that his title or
claim be declared valid or just; in the latter, he merely de-

[1] Conc. Pl. Balt. III., n. 297, 298.   [2] Our Counter-Points, n. 55, 56.
[3] Reiff., l. 2, t. 1, n. 41.

mands possession of the object or right, or that he be not disturbed in his quiet possession, or that the object having been lost by or taken from him be restored to him.[1]

Possessory trials (*judicia possessoria*) are subdivided (*a*) into *judicia immissionis*, that is, those where the parties seek to *obtain* possession, *v.g.* where an ecclesiastic, also with us, who has made the *concursus*, and finds that his competitor is appointed, appeals against the appointment ; (*b*) *judicia manutentionis—mandatum de manutenendo*—or those where a person asks to be allowed to *retain* peaceful possession, and therefore not to be disturbed in his possession, *v.g.* where a rector, whom the bishop attempts to deprive of his parish, appeals to the higher superior, and asks that he be not disturbed in the possession of his parish ; (*c*) *judicia reintegrationis* or *judicia spolii*, or those where a person asks to be *restored* to the possession of an office or other thing which has been taken from him, *v.g.* where a rector who has been actually dispossessed of his parish appeals to the higher superior, and asks to be reinstated.[2]

700. 5. Into those of the first and second instance (*judicia primae et secundae instantiae*), according as it is allowed to appeal to a higher tribunal or not.[3]

701. 6. Into trials *bonae fidei* and *stricti juris*. A trial is *bonae fidei* when the law allows the judge a certain equitable discretionary power in determining what is due to the plaintiff. It is *stricti juris* when the law does not give the judge this power, but obliges him to confine himself, in his sentence, strictly to what the parties have submitted, or what is specified in the law in regard to the matter under dispute. All those trials or actions which are *bonae fidei* are enumerated in the Roman law.[4]

---

[1] Schmalzg., lib. 2, t. 12, n. 30.   [3] De Angelis, l. 2. t. 12, n. 17.
[2] Craiss., n. 5489.   [4] §§ 28, 29, 30, Instit. De Actionibus.

CHAPTER II.

702. Protestants contend that the Church is but a corporation or imperfect society, not a perfect society or Sovereign State; that she has only the power of suasion, not of external jurisdiction, and is therefore possessed of no judiciary power proper. It is moreover falsely asserted by many, that what judiciary power the Church has ever exercised, she has done so only by consent of the secular power.

703. Against these and other errors of a similar kind we lay down the following proposition: "The Church is possessed of an external forum for the exercise of judicial power, properly so called." What is to be proved here is not precisely the power to make definitions of faith, or enact disciplinary laws binding on all the faithful, or even the judiciary power *in foro poenitentiae;* but that the Church can establish courts or tribunals of its own, where judges appointed by it have power to try and pass sentence upon certain ecclesiastical causes in such a manner that persons accused or sued are bound even in conscience to appear before them (if properly cited), and may be compelled by the judge, both by censure and temporal penalties, to appear and undergo the sentence pronounced against them.

704. We will now prove our thesis: first, from theological reason; next, from S. Scripture; finally, from the practice of the Church. The argument from reason is as follows: We have already shown that the Church, being a supreme, perfect, and independent society, and not a mere corporation, is

vested with power to make laws obligatory on all its members, and also the power to enforce them, even by punishments.[1] Now these very powers necessarily include another, a third, namely, the judiciary power, which forms at once the natural outgrowth of the legislative power and the necessary condition of the coercive.[2] We say, first, *the natural outgrowth of the legislative power;* for the latter would be imperfect and useless if it did not include the judiciary power—*i.e.*, the power to apply and enforce the law in a particular case, whenever a dispute arises as to its meaning and application. We say, secondly, *and the necessary condition of the coercive;* for, when there is question of inflicting an ecclesiastical punishment, the following mode of procedure, flowing as it does from the very nature of the case, must evidently be observed. The offence must be first brought to the notice of the ecclesiastical superior; the latter must then obtain certainty as to whether it has been committed or not. In other words, the offence must be proved; consequently the defence as well as the prosecution must be heard. Then only can sentence be justly passed and punishment inflicted on the delinquent. Therefore the exercise of the coercive power can be just only when it is preceded by the exercise of the judicial power.[3] In other words, punishments are as a rule unjust, when imposed without a previous trial. For, as we have seen, trials, so far as concerns their substantial parts, hold of the very law of nature. That is, natural law itself ordains that, as a rule, no punishment shall be inflicted except upon due observance of the substantial formalities of trials.

705. The Sacred Scriptures also show that the Church is vested with judicial power. Thus, our Lord, in laying down the rule that a deliquent should be first reproved privately, and next before witnesses, adds: " If he will not hear them,

---

[1] Supra, n. 183–186 and 201–204.   [2] Fessler, The Canonical Trial, p. 9.
[3] Fessler, l. c.; Bouix, De Jud., vol. i., p. 31.

tell the Church"—*i.e.*, the rectors or superiors of the Church ;
" and if he will not hear the Church, let him be to thee as the
heathen and the publican ;"[1] that is, let him be cut off from
the Church, or excommunicated, and treated as excommunicated.   Here, then, the Church is given the power to
excommunicate.   This is placed beyond doubt by the verse
immediately succeeding: " Amen, I say to you, whatsoever
you shall bind upon earth, shall be bound also in heaven."[2]
For, as the illustrious Bishop Fessler,[3] Secretary to the Vatican Council, explains, the phrase " to bind " means the same
as to excommunicate or punish.   Now, as we have seen,
ecclesiastical, no less than secular punishment, can, as a rule
at least, be justly inflicted only when a trial or hearing of the
cause has preceded.   Hence the power to excommunicate or
punish necessarily presupposes the right and duty to hear or
try the cause.   In fact, in the above quotation from Sacred
Scripture we have all the essential elements of a trial or judicial proceeding, namely, the judge, the accuser, the accused,
the hearing or argument, the sentence and its execution.[4]

706. Again, to continue the argument from Sacred Scripture, St. Paul threatens to come to the Corinthians " with a
rod,"[5] and expressly tells them that he has power to punish
all disobedience, when he says: " Having in readiness to revenge disobedience."[6]   In fact, he made full use of this power
in passing sentence of excommunication upon the incestuous
Corinthian,[7] and Hymeneus, and Alexander.[8]   Now, as was
already observed, the power to punish necessarily presupposes the judicial power—that is, the power to hear the
cause, or to ascertain by a trial whether the offence has been
committed or not.   We observe here, by the way, that the
case of the incestuous Corinthian, being notorious, needed
no further investigation or trial, prior to sentence.[9]   Finally,

---

[1] Matth. xviii. 17.   [2] Ib., v. 18.   [3] l. c., p. 12.   [4] Cf. Bouix, l. c. p. 30.
[5] 1 Cor. iv. 21.   [6] 2 Cor. x. 6.   [7] 1 Cor. v. 3, sq.
[8] 1 Tim. i. 19, 20.   [9] Fessler, l. c., p. 14.

St. Paul tells his beloved Timothy, Bishop of Ephesus, *Against the priest receive not an accusation, but under two or three witnesses.*[1] Here we have all the essential elements of a trial: the accused; the judge, in the person of Timothy ; the hearing of the cause, as indicated by the deposition of the witnesses, etc. St. Paul, moreover, points out how trials are to be begun.[2]

707. The practice of the Church confirms our thesis. As a matter of fact, the Church exercised this judicial power from the very beginning. We have already seen the action of St. Paul. Space permits us to mention but one more instance. Toward the end of the second century Montanus began to broach his heresy. Several synods were held, in which his teaching was carefully examined and found to be heretical. Thereupon sentence was passed upon him and his adherents, cutting them off from the Church. Here, then, we have all the essential constitutive parts of a trial, the sentence being preceded by a careful investigation or hearing of the cause.[3]

708. From what has been said, we infer : 1. The Church is clothed with judicial power proper; that is, she can have tribunals of her own, to hear or try causes, before giving decisions or inflicting punishments. 2. Consequently, she can compel persons, even by penalties, to appear before her tribunals and obey the sentence of her courts. Otherwise her judicial power would be useless. 3. This judicial power was given her, not by secular rulers, but by God Himself. In fact, St. Paul, in passing sentence upon the incestuous Corinthian, expressly states that he does so *with the power of our Lord Jesus,*[4] or as he elsewhere says, *according to the power which the Lord hath given me.*[5]

709. Here, in conclusion, it may be asked, what causes

[1] 1 Tim. v. 19.   [2] Fessler, l. c., p. 15.   [3] Fessler, l. c., p. 17.
[4] 1 Cor. v. 4.   [5] 2 Cor. xiii. 10.

pertain to the ecclesiastical forum ?   For the answer, we refer to n. 204-207, and to n. 478.   From the principles there
laid down, it follows that among other causes those fall under
the ecclesiastical judicial forum which relate to the appointment of prelates or inferior ecclesiastics ; the conferring of
orders; religious profession; the validity of marriages or
betrothals; certain crimes, such as heresy, apostasy, schism,
simony, and the like ; the rights and duties of ecclesiastics, as
such ; etc.[1]

[1] Cf. Schmalzg., l. c., n. 6.   See also above, Vol. I , n. 456, *sixth* edition,
where the latest decision of the S. C. de Prop. Fide is given respecting ecclesiastics suing other ecclesiastics, in secular courts, even in matters not purely
ecclesiastical.

CHAPTER III.

710. The principal persons who necessarily take part in a trial, and without whom there can be no trial, are the judge (*judex*), the plaintiff or accuser (*actor, accusator*), and the defendant (*reus*). The other persons who usually intervene either assist (a) the contending parties, as advocates, procurators or agents, and witnesses, or (b) the judge; as assessors and counsellors, auditors and referees, notaries and secretaries or clerks, messengers or constables.[1] We shall now, in the following articles, treat of these various persons.

ART. I.

Of the Judge.

711. The judge (*judex*) is the person who presides by public authority at the trial, and, so to say, acts as the mediator between the contending parties, by deciding the matter in dispute, according to law. In other words, the judge is a person who is vested with legitimate power to hear and pronounce upon litigious causes.[2] The ecclesiastical judge is a person who has this power in regard to ecclesiastical causes or matters.

712. *Various kinds of ecclesiastical judges.*—Ecclesiastical judges are divided chiefly, 1, into those who hold by divine right (*jure divino*), as the Pope, over the entire Church, and

---

[1] Cf. Schmalzg., l. c., n. 13.   [2] Schmalzg., l. c.; Craiss., n. 5540.

in regard to all ecclesiastical causes; the bishops, when they judge collectively with their head, the Roman Pontiff. Whether, however, bishops are judges *jure divino*, each in his own diocese,—that is, whether they, in the case, hold immediately of God—is, as we have shown, a controverted question.[1] The other ecclesiastical judges hold only by ecclesiastical or positive law.

713. 2. Into those who may exercise the judicial power, individually or singly (*judices singulares*); and those who can do so only collectively—that is, in a body, as the Roman Congregations of Cardinals.[2] Commissions of Investigation in the United States and England may also be classed with these judicial bodies, though only improperly, as they are judges only in a broad sense.

714. 3. Into ordinary (*judices ordinarii*) and delegated (*judices delegati*) judges. The former have judicial power by virtue of their office. As a rule, they can delegate their judicial power to others—that is, authorize others to act as judges for them. We say, *as a rule;* for vicars-general, though ordinary judges, cannot delegate their judicial powers to others. The latter are those who act as judges, not in their own name, but only in the name or stead of others. They are delegated (*a*) either by the law (*delegati a jure*); thus bishops are frequently authorized by the Council of Trent to act as judges in place of the Holy See; (*b*) or by a person having ordinary judicial authority (*delegati ab homine*).

715. 4. Into judges proper (*judices proprie dicti*), or those appointed by the competent authorities; and judges improperly so-called, namely, arbitrators (*arbitri*), or those chosen by the litigants themselves to decide the case. Arbitrators are chosen by the contending parties either with entire freedom or by command of the law. The former are called voluntary (*arbitri voluntarii*), the latter necessary or compulsory arbi-

---

[1] Supra, n. 242, 250. [2] Bouix, De Jud., vol. i., p. 122.

trators (*arbitri necessarii*). Necessary arbitrators have juris-diction not merely by the consent of the parties choosing them, but also by law or statute. Hence they are judges proper; their sentence passes into *res judicata* (unless sus-pended by an appeal), and admits of an appeal.[1] An instance of necessary arbitrators is given in the Cap. 39, De Off. Jud. Del., where Pope Gregory IX. ordains, that when a judge is challenged as suspected, arbitrators shall be chosen to decide whether the exception or challenge is justified by sufficient cause. Voluntary arbitrators have no jurisdiction, according to the Roman or civil law, and are not, therefore, judges in the strict sense. The reason is that they receive the power to adjudicate upon the cause submitted to them solely from the mutual agreement of private parties, namely, the litigants, who cannot confer any judicial authority proper. However, by the law of the Church, as interpreted by custom, the decision of voluntary arbitrators gives the right to make an exception or to institute proceedings in the ecclesiastical courts.[2] Persons who are chosen as arbitrators may accept or decline the office. But once they accept, they are bound, and may even be compelled by the superior, to fulfil the duties devolving upon them.[3]

716. 5. Into judges *a quo* and judges *ad quem*. See vol. 1., p. 425, sq.

717. The various judges in the Church are the Supreme Pontiff, Patriarchs, Primates, Metropolitans, Bishops, and prelates having quasi-episcopal jurisdiction. There are, moreover, various other judicial tribunals, namely: 1. The sacred congregations or Commissions of Cardinals and other Roman tribunals; 2. Legates, Nuncios, and Apostolic Visi-tors; 3. Synodal Judges chosen in each diocese to adjudicate causes committed to them by the Holy See; 4. Vicars-gen-

---

[1] Cf. cap. 39, De Off. Jud. Del. (i. 29); cap. 14, De Rescript. (i. 3).
[2] Devoti, lib. 3, tit. 17, § 5. [3] Devoti, l. c., § 10.

eral, whose jurisdiction, though ordinary, may be restricted by the bishop;[1] 5. Other judges, appointed extraordinarily by the Holy See, or by bishops or other prelates for particular cases—*i.e.*, not to act as judges permanently, but merely in a certain case.[2]

718. *Who can be appointed an ecclesiastical judge?* All those who are not disqualified by nature or by law. Now the following persons are disqualified by nature—*i.e.*, by reason of certain mental or bodily defects: Those who are deaf or dumb, or permanently insane, or under the age of puberty,—*i.e.*, under the age of fourteen (*impuberes*),—or deficient in knowledge (*illiterati*). All these are evidently wanting in those physical and mental requirements which are necessary to a judge.[3] By law—*i.e.*, canon law—the following persons are chiefly incapacitated: Those who are infamous (*infames*), whether by law (*infamia juris*) or by fact (*infamia facti*), as heretics, schismatics, excommunicates, perjurers, etc.; 2. Slaves; 3. Women; 4. Minors under the age of twenty, though if the parties consent they can be chosen judges at the age of eighteen complete.[4] Finally, lay persons cannot be appointed judges for ecclesiastical causes, except by the Pope. They can, however, be assessors in ecclesiastical courts.[5]

719. *Q.* What is required in a judge that his sentence may be valid?

A. I. That he have competence in the case; in other words, that the case fall under his jurisdiction. Of this point, however, we shall speak more at length further on under the heading " The Competent Tribunal or Forum."

720. II. That there be no circumstances on account of which the law declares the sentence null and void. Hence,

[1] Cf. supra, n. 620. 627.   [2] Bouix, l. c., p. 123; Craisc., n. 5548.

[3] München, Canonical Trials, vol. i., p. 67; Soglia, Inst. Jur. Priv., § 202.

[4] Cap. Cum Vigesimum 41, De Off. Jud. Del. (i. 29).

[5] Cap. Statutum 11, § Assessorem, de Rescript. in 6° (i. 3).

1. Nobody can be judge or assessor in the same cause in which he previously acted as advocate.[1] The reason is that, considering the frailty of human nature, such a person could scarcely feel inclined to give a judicial sentence different from what he formerly defended as just.[2] 2. Nor can a judge pronounce sentence validly in a cause if as a private person he is engaged in a similar case, whether in the capacity of plaintiff or defendant. For it would justly be presumed that he would judge in the case as he himself would wish to be judged by others in his own case. This prohibition is also conformable to natural law.[3]

721. 3. Much less can any one, as a rule, be judge in his own cause—*i.e.*, in causes between the judge himself and his subjects, or where he is himself directly interested, *v.g.*, in the case of an injury inflicted upon himself. We say, *as a rule;* for there are certain exceptions. They are as follows: 1. The judge who is supreme—*i.e.*, has no superior, namely, the Pope —can be judge in his own cause,[4] though it were better and more conformable to natural law to commit the cause to arbitrators or other judges, ordinary or delegated.[5] 2. Where there is question of matters pertaining to the exercise of voluntary jurisdiction. 3. If the fact—*v.g.*, the injury to the judge —is notorious. 4. Where the matter does not directly and principally affect the person of the judge, but his church or dignity, though canonists say that even in this case the judge can be objected to as suspected, because of his presumed leaning or attachment to his church or dignity.[6] 5. When there is doubt whether the jurisdiction of the judge extends to the case brought before his tribunal; for, in this case, the judge can, as a rule, declare whether he has jurisdiction or not. This is evident from the Roman law adopted by canon law:

[1] Cap. Postremo 36, De Appell. (ii. 29).   [3] Schmalzg., l. ii., t. i., n. 17.
[2] Cap. Causam 18, De Judic. (ii. 1).
[4] Arg., cap. 12, De Judic. (ii. 1); ex l. et hoc 41 ff., De Haer. Inst.
[5] Schmalzg., l. c., n. 18.   [6] Ib., n. 19.

"Praetoris" (*judicis*) *" est aestimare an sua sit jurisdictio."* [1] The reason is that in this case the judge cannot be said to judge in his own cause, since he does not derive any personal benefit or satisfaction from his decision. We say, *as a rule ;* for in three cases the judge cannot decide whether or not he has jurisdiction in the case, namely, 1, when a defect is objected to him affecting his own person—*v.g.,* that he is excommunicated, infamous, or incapable of having jurisdiction ; 2, when he is challenged as suspected, unless the challenge is frivolous ; 3, if the judge, whose jurisdiction is called in doubt, would receive a notable benefit by trying the cause.[2]

722. Is a judge competent, from the fact that he is so considered, although in reality he has no jurisdiction : in other words, are the acts and sentence of a judge valid, who is reputed to be competent, or vested with jurisdiction, but who in reality has none ? We have already sufficiently answered this question above, n. 223–226.

723. *Q.* What are the general duties or obligations of judges?

A. 1. They must have sufficient knowledge. A judge who pronounces an unjust sentence, because of a want of sufficient knowledge, commits a mortal sin, and is bound to make restitution to the party injured. Hence a judge destitute of the necessary learning cannot be absolved in confession, unless he resigns his office, or has a firm purpose of so doing.[3] Moreover, if a judge finds he has made a mistake, even though without any grievous fault on his part, and thus injured one of the litigants, he is bound to correct it, or hinder its effects, if he can do so without incurring a bad name. He may try to rectify his mistake, *v.g.,* by telling the injured party to appeal, or by suggesting other suitable remedies.

724. 2. A judge sins mortally by deferring without just

[1] L. 5 ff., De Jud. (v. 1); ex l. unica, C. Si Quis Imp. Maled. (ix. 7).
[2] Schmalzg., l. c., n. 19 (4).　　　　[3] S. Thomas, 2. 2, q. 66, art. 2.

cause the hearing of cases for a very notable time; and he is bound to make restitution to the injured party for all damages and expenses caused by the unjust delay.[1]

725. 3. Both by divine and ecclesiastical law, a judge is forbidden to accept gifts from the litigants.[2] A judge who accepts gifts of considerable value is not only guilty of mortal sin, but also bound to restore them. Nor can he be released from this obligation by the remission of the parties from whom he received the money or present. This is expressly enacted by Pope Boniface VIII., as follows: " Si quid autem contra Constitutionem praesentem" (judex ecclesiasticus)" receperit, ad ipsius restitutionem integram teneatur: nulla eorum, quibus restitutio facienda fuerit, remissione ullatenus profutura eidem."[3] In like manner, persons giving or receiving anything for the obtaining of a favor, or of justice from the Holy See, formerly incurred *ipso facto* excommunication, and that reserved. We say, *formerly;* for this censure is not mentioned in the Const. Apost. Sedis of Pope Pius IX., and is therefore no longer in force. If the above persons—namely, those giving or receiving presents in the case—are ecclesiastics, they are deprived, even at present, of all their offices and benefices.[4] However, if the ecclesiastical judge has no fixed stipend or suitable means of support, he can demand an honorary from the litigants.[5]

726. 4. The judge is the guardian or custodian, not the arbitrary controller, of the law. Hence he must take the law as it is, and give his decision in accordance with it. Now, in civil causes, he must as a rule pronounce sentence according to the more probable opinion. We say, *in civil causes;* for in criminal causes the accused should be pronounced not guilty, unless his crime is proved beyond a doubt or to a

---

[1] Ferr., V. Judex, n. 32.
[2] Exod. xxiii. 8; Deut. xvi. 19; Can. Judices 23, et Can. Jubemus 126, Caus. 1, q. 1.   [3] Cap. Statutum 11, De Rescript., in 6° (i. 3).
[4] Craiss., n. 5564.   [5] Ferr., V. Judex, n. 45.

certainty. We said also, *as a rule;* for certain grave civil causes are placed on an equal footing with criminal causes, and the sentence, in their case, must be given upon proofs which give not merely a greater or less degree of probability, but certainty. Thus full and complete proof is needed, of the nullity, in order that a marriage which has been contracted may be declared invalid. Where, all things considered, the judge finds that both the litigants have equally probable opinions in their favor, or that equally strong arguments or proofs militate in favor of each of the contending parties, he should, in civil causes, divide the object equally between the parties, or advise a compromise, or arbitration.[1] If however, in the case, one of the parties has *bona fide* possession of the object in dispute, decision should be given in his favor, according to the *Reg. juris* 11, *in* 6° : " Cum sunt partium jura obscura, reo favendum est potius, quam actori ;" and the other *Reg. juris* 65, *in* 6°: " In pari delicto vel causa, potior est conditio possidentis." And this holds even when the arguments or proofs favoring the plaintiff are more probable than those favoring the defendant, or the one in actual possession of the controverted thing, provided the reasons militating in favor of the latter are really probable or good.[2] An exception, however, must be made in favor of privileged causes, namely, marriage (as we have just seen), dowers, and testaments.[3] Because the law of the Church expressly declares that when in these causes the proofs are equally strong or probable on both sides as *pro* and *con*, judgment is to be given in favor of the validity of the marriage, testament, dower, etc.[4]

727. 5. As a rule, the judge must pronounce sentence according to the evidence or testimony submitted—*secundum allegata et probata.*[5] But is he bound to do so, even when

---

[1] Ferr., l. c., Nov. Add., n. 10.   [2] Craiss., n. 5567.   [3] Ferr., l. c., n. 54.
[4] Cap. Ex Litteris 3, De Prob. (ii. 19).   [5] Ex Can. Judicet 4, Caus. 3, q. 7.

his own private information or knowledge is to the contrary ? The question is disputed. There are three opinions. The first, that of St. Thomas,[1] affirms universally. The second denies universally. The third, which Ferraris[2] calls more probable than the other two, distinguishes and holds that the judge can and should pronounce sentence according to the *allegata et probata* in civil, and also in those criminal causes (*causae criminales minores*) where the punishment to be inflicted is merely a pecuniary fine, dismissal from office, etc., but not in graver criminal causes, or those where the punishment of death or mutilation is to be inflicted. As the Church never inflicts the penalty of death or mutilation, it would follow from the third opinion that the ecclesiastical judge in the case must always pass sentence in accordance with the evidence, or *secundum allegata et probata*, even against his own certain private knowledge, save in the case where he would have to oblige a woman to live with a man not her husband. Whatever opinion a person may choose to follow, it is certain that the judge, in the case, is bound to do all in his power to procure the acquittal (*v.g.*, by closely questioning the witnesses, endeavoring to find reasons for dismissing the charge)[3] of an accused person, whom of his own private knowledge he certainly knows to be innocent ; and that, if he cannot succeed in doing this, he should, if possible, send the case up to the higher judge.[4]

728. *Q.* Can a judge pronounce an accused person guilty, who by the juridical evidence is not proved guilty, but whom, of his own private knowledge, he certainly knows to be guilty?

A. He cannot. For, as we have seen, a judge is bound, as a rule, to pronounce sentence, not according to his own private information, but *secundum allegata et probata.* Hence

---

[1] 2. 2, q. 64, art. 6, ad. 3.   [2] V Judex, n. 60.
[3] Ferr., l. c., n 63.   [4] Craiss., n. 5570.

he cannot condemn any person, unless the latter has been juridically proven guilty. This principle is very lucidly explained by St. Thomas,[1] as follows: "Sed contra est quod Ambrosius dicit super psalterium, *Bonus judex nihil ex arbitrio suo facit, sed secundum leges et jura pronuntiat.* Sed hoc est, judicare secundum ea quae in judicio proponuntur et probantur. Ergo judex debet secundum hujusmodi judicare, et non secundum proprium arbitrium." He then lays down this conclusion: "Cum judicium ad judices spectet, non secundum *privatam*, sed *publicam* potestatem, oportet eos judicare, non secundum veritatem, quam ipsi, ut *personae privatae noverunt;* sed secundum quod ipsis, ut personis publicis, per leges, per testes, per instrumenta et per allegata et probata res innotuit."[2]

729. *Q.* Is the above principle—namely, that ecclesiastical judges must pronounce sentence *secundum allegata et probata* —also applicable to Commissions of Investigation in the United States and England? In other words, are Commissions of Investigation in the United States and England obliged to make up their verdict or opinion, on the merits of the cause submitted to them for investigation,[3] according to the *allegata et probata?*

A. We feel inclined to answer in the affirmative, and that on the principles laid down by St. Thomas. For as the Angelic Doctor says: " Judicare pertinet ad judicem, secundum quod publica potestate ; et ideo informari debet in judicando, non secundum id quod ipse novit tanquam privata persona, sed secundum id quod sibi innotescit tanquam personae publicae. Hoc autem innotescit ei . . . in particulari negotio aliquo" (judicio aliquo) " per instrumenta et testes, et alia hujusmodi legitima documenta, quae debet sequi in judicando, magis quam quod ipse novit tanquam privata persona."[4] However, it might be objected that Commissions of Investi-

---

[1] 2. 2, q. 67, art. 2.
[2] l. c.
[3] Instr. S. C. de P. F., 20 Julii, 1878, § 9.
[4] l. c., 2. 2, q. 67.

gation in the United States and England are not judicial bodies proper, as they do not and cannot pronounce the final sentence, but merely give their verdict or opinion on the case, which the bishop, who is the judge, is at liberty to disregard ; that, consequently, the reasoning of St. Thomas does not apply to these Commissions. The objection does not seem to us well taken. For the S. C. de Prop. Fide, in its reply to the *Dubia* or questions proposed by bishops of the United States, concerning the meaning of the Instruction of July 20, 1878, on Commissions of Investigation, expressly declares that these Commissions do exercise judicial functions, as the investigation or trial is committed to them exclusively. So far, then, as concerns the trial or hearing of the cause, the Commissions of Investigation take the place of the judge proper, or bishop ; this part of the judicial proceedings having been intrusted to them, as is stated in the Response *Ad Dubia.* Hence they form an integral part of the Bishop's Court, act as judges, so far as concerns the investigation, and are bound to follow the same rules which the judge proper would be obliged to observe if he conducted the trial personally. What, therefore, St. Thomas says above of judges, also applies to Commissions of Investigation. Again, the opinion or verdict of the Commission forms the basis for the sentence or action of the bishop, and in case of appeal, also of the superior to whom the appeal is made. Now, as we have seen, the judge (in our case, the bishop, or on appeal, the metropolitan) can, as a rule, base his decision only on juridical proofs—that is, he must decide *secundum allegata et probata.*

730. But it may again be objected that the trial or hearing of the cause before the Commission of Investigation is not a canonical trial proper or *processus canonicus;* that, consequently, neither the Commission of Investigation nor the bishop need decide *secundum allegata et probata,* but may act upon private information. This objection also seems to us

destitute of a solid foundation. For that the proceedings or functions of Commissions of Investigation are judicial, is too obvious to admit of dispute, and is, moreover, expressly defined by the Propaganda, in its reply *Ad Dubia*, when it says: " Ex quibus patet officium Consiliariorum *judiciale* quidem esse, cum instructio" (the trial or hearing of the cause) " sit iisdem commissa." Consequently the Commissioners and the bishop *act as judges*, each in his own sphere. Now St. Thomas, as we have seen, lays down the principle that whenever superiors proceed *as judges*, they are bound to decide *secundum allegata et probata.* Moreover, canonical trials are, as we have shown, divided into ordinary and summary or extraordinary. Now in the latter many of the formalities prescribed for the former may be omitted. Yet will any one on that account say that in summary or extraordinary trials the judge need not decide *secundum allegata et probata ?*

731. Finally, it seems scarcely necessary here to say that the very object and aim of all judicial proceedings is to prevent the judge from acting on his own private information, and thus being led into error. Hence we conclude that as Commissions of Investigation exercise judicial functions, the hearing of the cause being committed to them, and as their opinion or verdict forms the basis of the sentence of the bishop, they should, in making up their verdict,[1] be guided, not by their private information, but by what has been juridically proved. However, if the private knowledge or information of a member of the Commission of Investigation conflicts with that juridically obtained, he can and should make use of his private knowledge in order to examine the testimony more closely, so as to discover its defectiveness.[2]

732. How are delegated judges appointed? or how are

---

[1] Cf. Instructio S. C. de P. F., 20 Julii, 1878, § 9.   [2] Cf. S. Thomas, l. c.

judges appointed by delegation? We have already sufficiently answered this question above, under n. 227, 228.

733. Who can be appointed delegated judges? or upon
whom can judicial power be delegated? The answer has
already been given above, under n. 231–235. We here but
add that an ordinary judge—*v.g.*, a bishop—can delegate
causes of his court not only to a person subject to him, but
even to one not subject to him ; in other words, a bishop can
authorize a person not belonging to his diocese, and therefore not subject to him, to act as judge in his stead. The
latter, however, cannot be compelled to accept the office,
while a subject can.[1]

734. *Q.* How can and should delegated judges proceed
when several (two or more) are appointed to take cognizance
of the same cause?

A. We premise : They are appointed (*a*) either *in solidum*,
(*b*) or only *simpliciter*, (*c*) or in such manner that if all cannot
hear the cause together the rest can do so. We now answer:
1. If they are appointed *in solidum*,—that is, if in the letter of
their appointment the following or a similar formula is used
" Ut omnes, *aut* duo, *vel* unus mandatum exequantur, aut
exequatur" ; in other words, if the formula of appointment
expressly states that the cause may be heard and decided
either by all of the delegated judges, *or* by two, *or* even by
one of them, then there is room for prevention,—*i.e.*, preoccu-
pation or anticipation,—so that if one of them has begun to
hear or try the cause without the others, the latter cannot
interfere or take part in the proceedings, save in case the
delegated judge who began to hear the cause is hindered
from proceeding by infirmity or other cause, or maliciously
refuses to go ahead.[2] Hence, in this case, each one of the
delegated judges can individually or by himself, and without

---

[1] Ex Cap. Pastoralis 28, De Off. Jud. Del. (i. 29). Schmalzg., h. t., n. 16.
[2] Cap. 8, De Off. et Pot. Jud. Del. in 6° (i. 14).

the others, hear the cause, as the *Cap*. just quoted expressly declares: "Ipsorum quilibet injunctum potest libere adimplere mandatum."[1]

735. 2. If they are appointed, not *in solidum*, but *simpliciter*, and without the above or other similar clause empowering them to act or proceed separately: in other words, if the instrument of their appointment simply states that a certain cause or causes are committed to them, and does not state in express or equivalent terms that they can proceed individually or separately, then they must proceed collectively, and in a body; and one cannot hear the cause without the others, even where one of them is legitimately hindered or has died. Otherwise the proceedings are *ipso jure* null and void, except when the letter of appointment states differently. Thus Pope Alexander III. says: "Cum causa duobus committitur, sententia unius non tenet."[2]

736. 3. If several are appointed to hear the same cause, in these or similar words: "Ut si omnes interesse nequiverint, reliqui mandatum exequantur,"[3] they must indeed proceed collectively or in a body ; but if one or the other of them is absent by reason of a legitimate excuse, the rest can proceed without the absentee, provided the excuse of the absent member be properly communicated—*v.g.*, by the absentee in person, or by letter or messenger from him, or in some other canonical manner—to the remaining delegated judges; otherwise—*i.e.*, without such notification—the latter cannot proceed; and if they, nevertheless, do proceed, their acts are null and void. But if any one of them refuses to attend, where it is possible for him to be present,—*i.e.*, where he is not lawfully hindered,—the rest can proceed as soon as they have.certain or undoubted information of the refusal on the part of their colleague. The latter commits a grievous sin

---

[1] Cf. Schmalzg., l. l., tit. 29, n. 17.

[2] Cap. 16, De Off. Jud. Del. (i. 29). Schmalzg., l. c.

[3] Cap. 21, De Off. Jud. Del. (i. 29).

by his action.' For the rest in the above cases, as in all cases where a matter is to be adjudicated by several persons collectively, the opinion of the majority is to be followed; in other words, the majority decides. When the votes are equally divided, recourse must be had to the su. perior from whom the delegation emanated.'

737. *Q.* Whether and in what manner the foregoing principles apply to Commissions of Investigation in the United States and England?

A. We premise: 1. These Commissions, as established in the United States by the S. C. de Prop. Fide, July 20, 1878, for the adjudication of criminal and disciplinary causes of ecclesiastics, are composed of five, or where so many cannot be had, of at least three members, who must be priests of the highest integrity, and, as far as possible, learned in canon law.' 2. That these Commissions must proceed collectively, is plain from the *Instructio* quoted.' Hence, too, it is expressly provided in said *Instructio* that each and every member of the Commission shall be invited to the proceedings, and that by letter.' 3. The vote of the majority decides or rules, and that not only in regard to the final opinion or verdict,' but also all interlocutory sentences—*i.e.*, all intermediate steps, resolutions, or proceedings.

738. We now answer: 1. It is certain that in all cases where a member absents himself without legitimate cause, which he is bound to communicate to the other members of the Commission,—*v.g.*, by letter or messenger,—he commits a mortal sin, being guilty of disobedience or contempt (or at least indifference and carelessness) of a grave command of the Holy See, which, in establishing these judicial councils or bodies for this country, has at least impliedly ordained that each and every member shall attend the proceedings of the

---

¹ Cap. 21, cit. ² Bouix, De Jud., vol. i., p. 151.
³ Instr. S. C. de P. F., 20 Julii, 1878, § Itaque.
⁴ Cf. Ib., § 9. ⁵ Ib., § 3. ⁶ Cf. Ib., § 9.

Commission. The reason is thus given by Pope Celestin III., in speaking of delegated judges: "Illa fuit antiqua sedis apostolicae provisio, ut hujusmodi causarum recognitiones, duobus, quam uni, tribus quam duobis, libentius delegaret, cum integrum sit judicium, quod plurimorum sententiis confirmatur." [1] In fact. it is clear that the superior, in charging several persons to take cognizance together of the same cause, does so precisely because he has greater confidence in the combined action and opinions of all than of some only.

739. 2. But are the proceedings invalid in case some of the members absent themselves from the meetings of the Commission? They are not, in case at least three members are present, as we shall presently show. But what if less than three attend? We distinguish. In causes or matters which fall, properly speaking, under the competence of the Commission,—that is, which must, before decision is rendered by the bishop, be brought before the Commission,— three members at least must be present at all the proceedings in the case, and, upon the conclusion of the trial or hearing, give their verdict or opinion on the case. Otherwise the proceedings are null and void, and the subsequent action or sentence of the bishop invalid and of no effect. Thus the Instruction of the S. C. de Prop. Fide of July 20, 1878, speaking of the case of dismissal, expressly says: "Quod si de alicujus Rectoris Missionis remotione agatur, nequeat ipse a credito sibi munere dejici, *nisi tribus saltem praedictae Commissionis membris per Episcopum ad causam cognoscendam adhibitis, eorumque consilio audito.*" [2] Hence if, during the course of an investigation or trial in such causes, the number of commissioners attending the proceedings should be reduced to less than three, whether by death, resignation, challenge, or otherwise, others must be appointed to fill up the number,[3] and meanwhile all proceedings suspended.

---

[1] Cap. 21, cit. [2] Instr. cit., § Quod si.
[3] Cf. Instr. cit., § Electi Consiliarii; cf. Ad Dubia, § Extra Synodum.

740. 3. When there is question of other causes not necessarily to be brought before the Commission of Investigation, it is plain that the proceedings are not invalid, nor even, at least theoretically speaking, illicit, if less than three members of the Commission attend. For in these cases the Commission would act or obtain competence by the consent of the litigants, who may agree to allow a less number than three to sit upon the case. We say, *theoretically speaking;* for it is evident from the whole tone of the *Instructio,* dated July 20, 1878, of the S. C. de P. F., and also from the practice of the Sacred Congregation of referring all cases whatever to the Commissions of the respective dioceses where the cause originates, that the Holy See desires all cases whatever of dispute among ecclesiastics to be submitted in the first instance to the Commission.[1] Of course this applies, with us, at present only to those dioceses where Commissions of Investigation still exist, by permission of the Holy See. For outside of these dioceses, the Instruction *Cum Magnopere* of 1884 is now in force.

741. In connection with this matter it need scarcely be said that Commissions of Investigation in the United States or England cannot proceed to take cognizance of a cause, save upon being convened by the bishop (*sede vacante,* administrator), to whom alone belongs the initiative.[2] But when once convened by the ordinary according to §3 of the above Instruction, the Commission itself, acting under its president, determines whether, when, and how often future meetings or sessions are to be held in the hearing of a case.[3] Of course if the bishop should unjustly refuse to call the Commission together, an appeal lies against such refusal, just the same as in the case of any other grievance. For as Pope Alexander III. says: " De appellationibus *pro causis minimis interpositis,* volumus te tenere, quod eis, pro quacunque levi

---

[1] Cf. Instr. cit., § Commissionis ita; § In Causis Cognoscendis.
[2] Instr. cit., § 3 Locum.   [3] Instr. cit., § 10 Quod si ulterior.

causa fiant, non minus est, quam si pro majoribus fierent, deferendum:" [1]

742. *Q.* Can a delegated judge proceed to take cognizance of the cause before he has received the rescript or letter of his appointment or delegation?

A. He cannot. If he, nevertheless, does so, his acts are null and void.[2] Nay, the letter of appointment must be shown in its authentic form to, and a copy of it given, the contending parties when they appear before the delegate. Otherwise they are not bound to obey him.[3] The reason is, among others, that nobody is presumed to have judicial power in a place but the ordinary judge of such place, unless the contrary is proved. Yet there are some exceptions. Thus: 1. A delegate of the Pope need not show his letter of appointment if the litigants and the ordinary are willing to take his word for it. 2. Persons delegated by an ordinary, inferior to the Pope, can prove their appointment or delegation by witnesses, and not merely by their letters of appointment. 3. If the contending parties have commenced proceedings before the delegate, prior to being shown his letters of appointment, the proceedings are valid, because the parties have thus waived their right of seeing the letters.[4]

743. *Q.* How far does the power of a delegated judge extend?

A. Speaking in general, the power of a delegated judge is to be measured from the authority of the superior delegating and the wording of the mandate or commission, so that if the delegate goes beyond his mandate, his acts are null and void.[5] He does not, however, go beyond his mandate if he takes cognizance of or decides those matters or questions which, though not directly committed to him, are

---

[1] Cap. 11, De Appell. (ii. 28); supra, n. 444. [2] Cap. 12, De Appell. (ii. 28).
[3] Cap. 31, De Off. Jud. Del. (i. 29); cap. 24, De Rescript. (i. 3).
[4] Schmalzg., l. i., tit. 29, n. 27.
[5] Cap. 32, 37, De Off. et Pot. Jud. Del. (i. 29); Schmalzg., h. t., n. 28.

nevertheless connected with or accessory to the matter or cause delegated to him. In other words, he can, even though this be not expressly stated in his commission, do all those things or has all that power, without which he could not properly perform the office assigned to him. The reason is that a person who authorizes another to do something, by that very fact empowers him also to use all the means neces- sary or conducive to the end to be attained.[1] Thus Pope Alexander III. expressly says : " Quia ex eo, quod causa sibi " (delegato) "committitur, super omnibus, quae ad causam ipsam spectare noscuntur, plenariam recipit potestatem."[2] Hence, even though it be not mentioned in the mandate, the delegated judge can, among other things, (*a*) cite the parties, and compel them by penalties to appear before him ;[3] (*b*) he can—*v.g.*, where the parties cited object that he has no juris- diction to try the case, because, for example, the letters of his appointment are null and void—declare whether he has jurisdiction or not.[4]

744. *Q.* Do the principles just given apply also to Com- missions of Investigation in the United States?

A. They do, in the sense now to be explained. We need scarcely observe that the powers of these Commissions are to be determined by the Instruction of the S. C. de P. F., dated July 20, 1878, and by the subsequent answer *Ad Du- bia*, of the same Congregation, and by Art. XII. of the In- struction *Cum Magnopere* of 1884. According to these docu- ments, Commissions of Investigation are charged with the hearing of certain kinds of causes, exclusive of the cita- tion of the defendant and the definitive sentence, which are reserved to the bishop.[5] If the above Instruction it- self could have left any doubt upon this head, the deci-

---

[1] Schmalzg., l. c., 2. 31.   [2] Cap. 5, De Off. Jud. Del. (l. 29).

[3] Cap. 4, De Off. Jud. Del. (l. 29).

[4] Ex. cap. 33. De Rescript. (l. 3); Schmalzg., l. c., n. 34.

[5] Instr. cit., § Commissionis ita; § In Causis Cognoscendis.

sions of the Propaganda *Ad Dubia* have certainly removed it. For the Propaganda expressly says that the hearing of the cause is committed to these Commissions. Its words are: "Cum instructio sit iisdem commissa." [1] Hence, according to the principles above laid down by us, these Commissions have all those powers, without which they could not fully and properly hear and examine the causes or matters brought before them, and that even though such powers are not expressly mentioned in the above Instruction of the S. C. de P. F., or its decisions *Ad Dubia*. Hence also, so far as concerns the hearing of the cause, or its full and complete investigation, this power extends not merely to the naked ascertaining of facts, but also to the mode or means of ascertaining them. In other words, they have power to determine, or rather apply, those questions of ecclesiastical law which come up in, and are incidental to, or connected with the hearing of the cause. Otherwise, they could not try the cause properly. This is also inferable from the fact that the above Instruction calls the Commission a "Consilium quoddam *judiciale*," [2] and directs that as far as possible its members should be canonists, or learned in canon law.[3]

These principles apply equally to Commissions in England. For they also, being empowered to hear the causes of rectors permanently appointed, which involve dismissal, are, by that very fact, authorized to do all those things without which they could not properly hear the cause.

745. *When and how does the jurisdiction of a delegated judge lapse?* The answer has been already given.[4] When does a member of a Commission cease to be such? The answer is indicated in the above Instruction.[5]

[1] Ad Dubia, § Ex quibus. [2] Instr. cit., § In Causis Cognoscendis.
[3] Ib., § Itaque SSmo. [4] Supra, n. 378, 379.
[5] Instr. cit., § Electi Consiliarii; supra, n. 407.

Art. II.

Of the Plaintiff (actor, accusator) and the Defendant (reus).

746. Under this heading we shall treat of two questions:
First, What persons are admissible in ecclesiastical courts as
plaintiffs or defendants. Secondly, Can a person be compelled to appear before the ecclesiastical judge, either as
plaintiff or defendant?

747. 1. *What persons are disqualified from acting as plaintiffs or defendants?*—As in secular, so in ecclesiastical courts,
not all persons can appear as plaintiffs or defendants or have
a standing in court (*persona standi*), some being incapacitated
by the natural law, others by the ecclesiastical, others by
both. Now, what persons are chiefly excluded from acting
as defendants or plaintiffs in ecclesiastical courts? 1. *Infants,*
or those who have not yet attained the use of reason;
*persons of unsound mind (furiosi, amentes); the deaf, the dumb,
and prodigals.* These persons being unable to defend their
rights, cannot personally be plaintiffs or defendants. We
say, *personally;* for their guardians can sue and be sued in
their stead.[1] It may, however, be doubted at present whether
this still holds of those deaf or dumb persons who, by our
new methods of instruction, have learned to understand
others, and make themselves understood by them. In the
case of prodigals, the rule certainly holds in civil matters.
Whether it does also in criminal causes, is not so clear.[2]

748. 2. *Those who are under the age of puberty.* Persons
under the age of puberty (*impuberes*)—*i.e.*, under fourteen,—
cannot indeed be plaintiffs or defendants personally; but a
guardian (*curator ad litem*) is to be appointed for them by the
judge (we speak here of the ecclesiastical judge, namely, the
bishop, vicar-general, etc.), or they may, if above the age of

[1] L. Gerere 1, § 2, sufficit ff., de Adm. et per. tut. (26. 7); Schmalzg., lib. 2,
t. 1, n. 23. [2] Bouix, l. c., pp. 168, 169.

infancy, be allowed by the judge to select their own agent (*procurator*) themselves.[1] There are, however, some exceptions to this rule. Thus, in criminal causes, children or wards may be admitted as plaintiffs if otherwise the crime could not be proved. For the public good demands that crimes shall not remain unpunished.[2] It is certain that *minors—i.e.*, persons above the age of fourteen, but under the age of twenty-five, may in spiritual causes, or those connected with them, either personally or by an agent appointed by them, implead and be impleaded.[3]

749. 3. *Women*, with certain distinctions.—Thus, religious women, even though not under enclosure, as most of the sisterhoods in the United States, cannot even with their own consent appear in any cause whatever personally in court, ecclesiastical or secular, whether as plaintiffs, defendants, or witnesses.[4] We say, *appear personally;* for where it is necessary to receive their testimony, the judge should either go in person, or send a deputy to the convent, and take their deposition there.[5] As to other women,—*i.e.*, secular women, —they should not in civil causes be compelled to appear personally in court (we speak of the ecclesiastical court). We say, *compelled;* for if they choose, they may in such causes sue or be sued in person, and not merely through procurators. In criminal causes, however, they are not permitted to act as plaintiffs or rather accusers,[6] save (*a*) in order to prosecute an injury inflicted upon them or others belonging to them; (*b*) where the public good demands it; (*c*) or the cause is such as to require their personal presence.[7] We said, *to act as plaintiffs;* for when they are accused of an atrocious crime, they can be compelled to appear in court as defendants.[8]

---

[1] Cap. Si annum 3, de Judic. in 6° (ii. 1).   [5] Schmalzg., l. c., n. 25.
[2] Cap. Si annum, cit.   [4] Cap. Mulieres 2, de Judic. in 6° (ii. 1).
[3] Arg. ex cap. Mulieres, cit.   [6] L. 8 ff., de Acc. et inscr. (48. 2).
[7] Schmalzg., l. c., n. 30.   [8] Nov. 134, cap. 9.

750. 4. *Persons under major excommunication.*[1] Here we must distinguish between those excommunicates who are to be shunned (*vitandi*), and those who need not be avoided (*tolerati*). I. It is certain that those who are to be shunned cannot as a rule (1) act as plaintiffs. We say, *as a rule;* for there are several exceptions. Thus, such excommunicates can, among other cases, act as plaintiffs (*a*) when they wish to prove that the excommunication inflicted on them is, *ipso jure*, null and void; not, however, when they merely desire to show that it is simply unjust, though valid. For, in the latter case, they would first have to be absolved from the excommunication before they could be allowed to proceed.[2] (*b*) In all cases where it is necessary. (2) They can, as a rule, be admitted, nay, compelled, in any cause whatever, to appear in court as defendants.[2] We say, *as a rule;* for when they appear *voluntarily,*—*i.e.*, without having been cited, either generally or specially,—and for their own benefit as defendants, they should be rejected.[3] II. An excommunicate who need not be shunned can be admitted as plaintiff, provided neither the opposing party nor the judge objects. He may appear as defendant, even when he does so of his own free will or for his own benefit, if the opposing party and the judge consent.[4]

751. 5. *Regulars*, in the sense now to be explained. We observe, we speak here only of members of religious orders of males; for of religious communities of females we have already spoken.[6] Regulars who are professed may be considered, either individually or collectively. Taken individually, regulars cannot, as a rule, appear in a court, ecclesiastical or secular, except by permission of their superior. The reason is, that by their profession they become dead to the world, cease to be *sui juris*, and are placed on the same foot-

---

[1] Cap. 7, de Jud. (ii. 1).
[2] Ex cap. 1, de Rescript., in 6° (i. 3); Schmalzg., l. c., n. 34.
[3] Ex cap. 7, cit. [4] Schmalzg., l. c., n. 33. [5] Craiss., n. 5605. [6] Supra, n. 750.

ing as sons still under the control of their father, who cannot, as a rule, act in court without the consent of their
father.[1] We say, as a rule. For the exceptions we refer to
Schmalzgrueber.[2] But can the religious of a monastery,
taken collectively, appear in court as plaintiffs or defendants?
In other words, can a monastery or religious house (the
same applies to churches and other ecclesiastical corporate
bodies) as such implead and be impleaded? As monasteries
and churches are moral persons, vested with various rights,
they must evidently have the right to sue and be sued,
though this cannot be done, except through certain persons,
to whom the law of the Church has committed the duty of
acting as plaintiffs or defendants in the name of the church
or monastery.[3] Now to what persons has the law of the
Church committed this duty? As a rule, to the prelate of
the monastery, at least with the consent of the monks, and
to the prelate of the church, at least with the consent of the
chapter.[4] Thus Pope Innocent III. says: "Cum ex officio
suo teneantur" (abbates, praelati) "Congregationum suarum
negotia procurare."[5] By prelates are here meant (*a*) bishops
in respect to their cathedral church: (*b*) prelates having
quasi-episcopal jurisdiction in a church where there is a
chapter; (*c*) the chief superiors of religious orders, namely,
abbots and superiors-general, and generally provincials and
local superiors, according to the rules of their order. By
the common law of the Church, abbesses and other lady
superiors of religious female communities can, in matters of
their respective houses, appear in ecclesiastical courts as
plaintiffs or defendants by procurators or agents, in the
same manner as prelates of regulars.[6]

[1] L. 8, C. de Bonis, quae lib. (v. 61); cap. 3, de Jud., in 6° (ii. 1).

[2] l. c., n. 38.   [3] Bouix, de Jud., vol. i., p. 177.

[4] Can. 9, caus. 18, q. 2; cap. Edoceri 21, de Rescript. (i. 3); Craiss., n.
5607.   [5] Cap. Edoceri, cit.

[6] Cap. 2, de his quae a prael. (iii. 10); Glossa, in hoc cap., v. Continebatur;
Schmalzg., l. c., n. 40.

752. *Q.* To whom pertains by the common law of the Church the right to appear as plaintiff or defendant when there is question of the rights and property of parish churches?

A. To the parish priest, as is inferred from the above cap. *Edoceri.* Because, by the common law of the Church, the parish priest also is vested with the administration of the rights and property of his parish. This must not, however, be understood to the exclusion of the bishop. For the latter has cumulative power over all the churches of his diocese not exempt from his jurisdiction. *A fortiori,* rectors of parishes in the United States cannot act in the case to the exclusion of the bishop. What has been said of parish priests applies also to rectors of hospitals and other charitable or religious institutions. Observe that in the above question we say, *by the common law of the Church;* for a great deal depends, in this matter, upon custom and concordats.[1]

753. II. *Can a person be compelled to appear against his will as plaintiff or defendant?* The defendant certainly can; and if he refuses to appear he may be proceeded against, even though absent, and condemned, if found guilty upon due investigation or trial. But, as a rule, no one can be compelled to appear against his will as plaintiff, whether in civil or criminal causes. Thus the Roman law adopted by the Church says: "Invitus agere vel accusare nemo cogatur."[2]

754. *Q.* Can a plaintiff or defendant be compelled to appear *in person?* Or, are they always free to appear by proxy—*i.e.,* by an agent or procurator?

A. 1. The Sovereign Pontiff can certainly compel the parties to appear *personally,* and not merely through agents. The same applies to Papal delegates when they have a special mandate to that effect.[3] For while it is true that the law of

---

[1] Schmalzg., l. ii., t. 1, n. 40; cf. Bouix, l. c., p. 181.

[2] L. Unic. C., Ut nemo inv. ag. vel acc. cog. (iii. 7).

[3] Ex cap. Juris 1, de Jud., in 6° (ii. 1); Glossa, in h. c., v. Speciale.

the Church, as we shall see, allows litigants to appear in court by proxy,[1] it is also certain that the Pope is not bound by this law.[2] 2. The other judges (we speak of ecclesiastical judges) cannot, as a rule, compel persons to appear personally in court.[3] We say, *as a rule;* for there are several exceptions, namely, (*a*) where the cause is criminal and the punishment to be imposed is corporal, or considered greater than exile. In all other criminal causes the defendant and, *a fortiori*, the plaintiff may appear by proxy or procurator. (*b*) If it is specially necessary to examine the personal qualities of the parties.[4] (*c*) Where the truth or facts of the case can be better elicited or understood by the personal statement of the plaintiff or defendant.[5] (*d*) When the indications of the guilt of the accused are so strong as to give well-grounded hope that the truth will be more easily ascertained by his presence, his looks, his answers, etc. Several other exceptions are given by Schmalzgrueber.[6] In a word, the judge may compel litigants to appear in person whenever he has grave cause to think that the truth will thereby be better ascertained.[7] Without such grave and sufficient cause,—*i.e.*, except where it is necessary, as stated,—the ecclesiastical judge, inferior to the Pope, cannot summon the parties to appear in person against their will; and if he nevertheless does so, his act is null and void.[8] Moreover, the cause for citing the party to appear in person must be stated in the citation. Otherwise the party cited can suppose there is no sufficient cause, and disobey the citation.[9]

755. *Q.* Do the principles just laid down in regard to the personal appearance in court apply also in the United States to plaintiffs and defendants summoned before Commissions of Investigation?

[1] Cap. 2, de Proc. (i. 38).
[2] Cap. Juris, cit.; ibi Glossa, v. Juris esse.
[4] Ex l. 2, C. de his qui ven. aet. imp. (ii. 45).
[6] l. c., n. 47. [7] Bouix, l. c., p. 186. [8] Cap. Juris, cit.
[3] Schmalzg., l. c., n. 45.
[5] Cap. 14, de Jud. (ii. 1).
[9] Bouix, l. c.

A. We see no reason why they should not. For the Instruction of the S. C. de P. F., of July 20, 1878, says nowhere that the defendant or other parties must appear in person. Consequently, unless it is expressly stated in the citation that the accused must come in person, and the cause therefor given, it would seem that he has the alternative of appearing either in person or by proxy. Of course, according to the above principles, he can be summoned and compelled to appear in person before the Commission, whenever this is thought expedient or necessary. Moreover, it is nearly always in the interest of such defendant to be personally present at the proceedings, even when he is represented by a procurator.

Art. III.

Of Procurators or Agents.

756. Sometimes it will happen that a person does not wish or is unable to defend his rights *in person.* Hence, as in secular so also in ecclesiastical courts, litigants can, as we have seen, appear either in person or by a procurator (in secular courts, *attorney*).

757. What, then, is a procurator? Speaking in general, a procurator (*procurator*) or agent is a person *qui aliena negotia mandato domini administrat,*[1] or one who transacts business for, or acts in the name of, another. In other words, and to speak more fully, a procurator is one who is appointed by another (called the principal), unwilling or unable to attend personally to his own affairs, to manage in whole or in part, in his absence, these affairs, whether they be judicial or extrajudicial.[2] Hence a procurator differs (*a*) from an advocate, because the latter merely assists a client who is present, while the former takes the place of the prin-

---

[1] L. 1 ff. de Procurat. (iii. 3).　　　[2] Schmalzg., l. i., t. 38, n. 1.

cipal himself, who is absent; (*b*) from a guardian (*curator, tutor*), since the latter is appointed not by the ward or minor, but by the law, magistrate, or deceased testator, while the former is deputed by the principal himself.

758. *Various kinds of Procurators.*—How many kinds of procurators are there? 1. Some are judicial (*procurator judicialis, ad lites, ad judicia*), others extrajudicial (*procurator extrajudicialis, ad negotia extra judicium tractanda*), according as they are deputed for judicial matters, or matters not of a judicial nature. We speak here chiefly of judicial procurators. 2. Both judicial and extrajudicial procurators may be either general (*procurator generalis*) or special (*procurator specialis*), according as they are appointed either for (*a*) *all* extrajudicial affairs, or *all* judicial causes, (*b*) or only for a certain affair, or a determinate judicial cause. 3. A general procurator may be appointed either *cum libera,*—*i.e.,* with full power or freedom to act for his principal in all causes or matters,—or only *simpliciter,*—*i.e.,* without such full power.[1] 4. Some are appointed *simpliciter cum aliis,*—*i.e.,* in such a manner as to be obliged to act jointly with others; others, *in solidum.* Where two or more procurators are appointed *simpliciter* for the same affair or judicial case, they cannot proceed individually, but must act conjointly. But if they are deputed *in solidum,* each can act separately from the others, in the manner prescribed by Pope Boniface VIII.[2] Here we may observe that the law of the Church does not restrict a person to one procurator, but allows him to appoint several for the same cause. (Ex cap. 6, De Proc., in 6°.) 5. Finally, there are principal procurators (*procuratores principales*) and mere substitutes (*procuratores substituti*), according as they are appointed either by the principal himself or merely by his procurator.

759. *Q.* Who can appoint a procurator for himself?

---

[1] De Angelis, l. i., t. 38; t. i. p. ii., p. 352. [2] Cap. 6, de Procurat. in 6° (i. 19).

A. As a general rule, any person whatever, who is not forbidden by law, can appoint a procurator to act in his stead, and that even though he be present himself. The reason is that everybody can do through others what he can do in person, unless the law forbids it.[1] Now by the law of the Church persons under major excommunication are forbidden to appoint procurators to act for them as plaintiffs in judicial proceedings, for the reason that they cannot themselves act as such in person.[2] We say, *as plaintiffs;* for they not only can, but should, appoint procurators to act as defendants for them. For the other persons who are disqualified, see Schmalzgrueber, l. c., n. 4.

760. *Q.* What persons can be appointed procurators?

A. All those who are capable of managing affairs, and are otherwise not expressly excluded by law. Now the law of the Church excludes as procurators *ad lites* or in judicial matters, among other persons, (*a*) those who are under major excommunication, (*b*) or not yet twenty-five years old.[3] Laymen may be appointed procurators in spiritual causes, provided they exercise a *simplex ministerium,* but no jurisdiction or administration proper.[4]

761. *Q.* In what causes or matters can procurators be appointed to act for others?

A. In all causes, where it is not expressly prohibited by law. For, as canonists say, the *edictum de procuratore constituendo est prohibitorium.* Hence the rule holds, in our case, that whatever is not expressly forbidden, is granted. And this is true of judicial causes,—*i.e.,* matters adjudicated in court,—as well as of extrajudicial affairs.[5] We say, *where it is not expressly forbidden by law.* Now, does the law of the Church, in some cases, expressly forbid the appointment of

---

[1] De Angelis, l. c., p. 353. [2] Supra, n. 751; cap. 15, de Proc. (i. 38).
[3] Cap. 5, de Proc. in 6° (i. 19).
[4] Cap. 1, de Procurat. in 6° (i. 19); De Angelis, l. c., p. 355.
[5] De Angelis, l. c., p. 356.

a procurator, whether for extrajudicial or for judicial causes? Space permits us here to answer only in regard to procu- rators for judicial causes. Concerning these, it may be said that the law of the Church makes no exclusion what- ever ; in other words, canon law does not forbid a principal to be represented in the ecclesiastical courts by a procura- tor, in any cause whatever, civil or criminal. As to civil causes, this is certain. As to criminal causes, it is true, as we have seen,[1] that where the punishment to be inflicted is corporal, or greater than exile, no procurator can be ap- pointed. But, as De Angelis[2] observes, ecclesiastical courts do not inflict death or mutilation. Hence, procurators are to be admitted before ecclesiastical courts in all criminal causes, namely, where dismissal from parish or benefice, ex- communication, suspension, and the like, are to be inflicted.[3] However, it must not be forgotten that, as we have already said,[4] the judge (we speak of the ecclesiastical judge) can for just cause command the personal appearance of the princi- pal, and thus exclude the procurator.

As to the application of these principles to contending parties in the United States, also before Commissions of In- vestigation, see n. 755.

762. *Q.* How are procurators appointed?

A. The procurator for the plaintiff must on pain of nul- lity, as a rule, have a mandate or authorization (called in secular courts, power of attorney).[5] This mandate should state the name of the principal or appointer of the procurator appointed, of the plaintiff against whom, and of the judge be- fore whom the proceedings are instituted ; the nature of the matter or cause entrusted to the procurator, the day and year. Finally, the principal should state that he will ratify whatever is done by the procurator.[6] We have said, *for the*

---

[1] Supra, n. 754.   [2] L. c., p. 360.   [3] Ex cap. 5, De Procur. (i. 38).
[4] Supra, n. 754.   [5] Ex cap. 4, De Proc. (i. 38).   [6] De Angelis, l. c., p. 361.

plaintiff; for, absolutely speaking, a person may act as procurator for an absent *defendant*, even without an express authorization. We say, moreover, *as a rule;* for there are several exceptions, namely, among others: 1. Where the procurator is one who is accustomed to act as procurator for parties, and brings with him the documents or papers relating to the case ;¹ 2. If he acts for others in a cause where he is a co-principal—*i.e.*, where he is jointly interested with them.² Here it must be observed that in all cases where a procurator acts without an express mandate, whether it be for a plaintiff or defendant, he must give security that the principal will ratify whatever has been done, or, to use a technical phrase, *debet cavere de rato.*³

763. *Powers of Procurators.*—Whatever the procurator does within the limits of his mandate is valid, whether it be beneficial or injurious to the principal, according to the rule: "Qui facit per alium, est perinde ac si faciat per se ipsum." Again, the judicial procurator becomes the *dominus litis,* and that, generally speaking, as soon as the *litis contestatio* has taken place ;⁴ or where the procedure or trial is summary, and no *litis contestatio* required, as soon as he has begun to act in the principal matter, or has taken the first steps in the cause.⁵ Once he has become the *dominus litis,* he can appoint a substitute. We say, *the judicial procurator becomes the dominus litis;* in other words, he takes the place and assumes the responsibilities of the principal himself. Hence, the citations and the like are to be directed to him, and not to the principal.⁶ Herein, by the way, we again see how a procurator differs from an advocate. The latter, as such,—*i.e.*, unless he acts also as procurator,—never becomes the

---

¹ Cap. 34, De Off. Del. (i. 29).
² L. Commune 2, C. De Cons. ej. lit. (iii. 40).   ³ De Angelis, l. c., p. 362.
⁴ Reg. 72 Juris, in 6 (v. 12); Devoti, l. 3, t. 3, § 4.
⁵ Cap. 1, De Procur., in 6° (i. 19).   ⁶ De Angelis, l. c., p. 354.
⁷ Leur., For. Eccl., l. i., t. 38, q. 1010.

dominus litis, but merely assists him ; hence the mandates of the court (in our case, the ecclesiastical court) are never directed to him, but to his client, or the latter's procurator.

764. *Q.* How does the office of a procurator expire?

A. Chiefly as follows: 1. By the mutual consent of the principal and his procurator, and that even *re non amplius integra,* though without prejudice to a third party. 2. By revocation of the power of attorney or procurator.[1] The revocation, however, once the *res* is no longer *integra,* is valid only when made for just cause, which must, moreover, be approved by the judge when there is question of judicial procurators.[2] 3. If the principal wishes to conduct the cause himself.[3] For the other modes, see Schmalzgrueber, l. c., n. 42–48.

765. *Q.* What special remarks apply to procurators of communities, or ecclesiastical corporations, such as monasteries, convents of nuns, colleges of students, and confraternities?

A. Individuals, as we have seen, may as a rule plead their causes personally—*i.e.,* act personally as plaintiffs or defendants in ecclesiastical courts. But moral bodies, or communities, are obliged to do so by proxy, and consequently must appoint procurators, who are called *syndici,* to prosecute and defend their rights in ecclesiastical courts. Otherwise, as is evident, these bodies could not prosecute their rights at all. For it is practically impossible for an entire body—*i.e.,* for all the members of such body—to act collectively or simultaneously in such matters. A community or corporate body can appoint not merely one, but several procurators for itself. Where several are appointed, each one is considered as appointed *in solidum,* even though this is not expressed in the mandate, contrary to what happens in the case of proc-

[1] Cap. 2, De Proc., in 6° (l. 19).
[2] L. Post litem 17 ff., De Procurat. (iii. 3); De Angelis, l. c., p. 366.
[3] Cap. 8, l. c., in 6°.

urators of individuals.[1] These procurators or *syndici* are chosen by election—*i.e.*, they are elected by the community or corporation they are chosen to represent. All the members of such community or corporation, who have the right to vote, must be called to the election. However, it is sufficient that two thirds of all the voters are present.[2] A majority vote elects. In some religious orders, however, the procurator is simply appointed by the superior, not elected. The right to appoint the procurators of convents of nuns belongs, *de jure ordinario*, to the bishop. We say, *de jure ordinario;* for sometimes, either by the act of foundation, or custom, or the Rule as properly approved, it belongs to the nuns themselves, or even to laics.[3] As to procurators under the Instruction *Cum Magnopere*, see our *New Procedure*.

ART. IV.

Advocates (Advocati).

766. When contending parties are unable to settle a disputed matter in an amicable manner, and are consequently about to bring the case into court (in our case, ecclesiastical court) for adjudication, the first step to be taken by them is the selection of an able advocate (as they rarely plead their cause themselves); so much so, that when a party, owing to poverty, or the power, position, or authority of the opposing party, or other cause, is unable to procure an advocate, the ecclesiastical judge (for we speak of ecclesiastical courts) is bound to obtain or appoint one for him, as is enacted by Pope Honorius III.[4]

767. Now, an advocate (*advocatus, patronus causae, orator, causidicus;* in secular courts, lawyer, counsellor-at-law) is one who conducts the case in court for a client present, and

---

[1] Schmalzg., l. i., t. 39, n. 5; cf. supra, n. 758 (4).

[2] L. 3 ff., Quod cujusc. univ. nom. (iii. 4).

[3] Craiss., n. 5641.   [4] Cap. 1, De Off. Jud. (i. 32); Reiff., l. i., t. 37, n. 1.

assists him by his counsel, authority, and otherwise.[1] To act as advocate (*postulare*), therefore, means to discuss the merits of the case—*i.e.*, to explain in court, or before the judge or judicial body composing the court, the arguments, whether of law or fact, militating in favor of one's client.[2] The office of an advocate is called by canonists *munus publicum et honorificum.* Consequently, only able and esteemed persons are allowed to exercise it.[3] The difference between advocates and procurators has already been sufficiently explained by us, in the preceding article on procurators.

768. *Q.* Who can be or act as advocate in ecclesiastical courts?

A. All those who are not expressly prohibited by canon law. The reason is, that the *edictum de postulando* (*i.e.*, of acting as advocate) is *prohibitorium*, no less than that *de procuratore constituendo.*[4] Now, what persons are expressly excluded by the law of the Church? Chiefly these: 1. Persons who are notably infamous. They can, indeed, act as advocates for themselves, but not for others.[5] Persons who are infamous indeed, but not *notably* so, can be advocates, not only for themselves, but also for their relatives, minors and wards, but not for anybody else.[6] 2. Excommunicates;[7] for, as we shall see when we come to speak of censures, they are cut off from association with the faithful, even in forensic or judicial matters. 3. Monks or regulars, except in favor of their monastery, and, even then, only with the consent of the superior.[8] The Franciscans or Friars Minor, however, are an exception even to the latter privilege; for they cannot act as advocates for their monastery, even with the consent of their superior.[9]

[1] Schmalzg., l. l., t. 37, n. 2; De Angelis, l. l., t. 37, n. 1.
[2] Reiff., l. c., n. 4.   [3] Ib., n. 6.   [4] Ib., n. 8.
[5] Leg. 1 ff., De Postulando (iii. 1).   [6] Ib.
[7] Cap 8., De Sent. Excom., in 6° (v. 11).
[8] Cap. 2, De Postul. (l. 37).   [9] Clem. Exlvi 1, De V. S., § Proinde (v. 11).

As to whether secular ecclesiastics can be advocates, we shall see below. It is not necessary here to say that nuns or sisters cannot be advocates. For women, and *a fortiori* nuns, are, generally speaking, disqualified for this office.[1] 4. A judge cannot be advocate in the same cause in which he is to act as judge.[2] 5. Those who are not sufficiently versed in the law.[3] In order to exclude persons who are ignorant of the law or otherwise unfit, the secular courts at the present day allow only those to act as advocates who have passed the prescribed examination and received the requisite diploma. In ecclesiastical courts, however, no such examination or diploma is required by the general law of the Church.[4]

769. We say, *by the general law of the Church;* for by particular or local law such examination or diploma, or at least a simple approbation, may be necessary. Thus, in fact, so far as concerns us, the S. C. de P. F., in its answer to the questions (*dubia*) addressed to it, concerning the meaning of the Instr. of July 20, 1878, and in the Instr. *Cum Magnopere,* Art. XXX., expressly declares that the advocate should be approved by the bishop. It is scarcely necessary to observe, in passing, that this approbation cannot be refused arbitrarily. For the S. C. de P. F., in the above answer *Ad Dubia,* gives the accused rector (and by implication all other defendants or plaintiffs, as the case may be) the full right to choose his own advocate, subject only to the approval of the bishop. The words of the Sacred Congregation are: "*Liberum cuique Rectori est alium Sacerdotem ab Episcopo tamen approbandum secum habere coram Consilio,* sive ad simplicem adsistentiam, sive ad suas animadversiones aut defensionem exhibendam."[5] Hence the right of the bishop to approve cannot be used in such a manner as to destroy the right of the rector

[1] L. 1 ff., cit. [2] L. 6, C. de Postul. (II. 6). [3] L. 2 ff., tit. cit.
[4] Bouix, De Jud., vol. i., p. 237; De Angelis, l. c., n. 2.
[5] S. C. de P. F., Ad Dubia, § iv.

or defendant to choose an advocate. In other words, the approbation can be refused only for solid reasons—namely, (*a*) when the advocate is ignorant of the law of the Church; (*b*) or has a bad reputation; (*c*) or in the cases already mentioned under n. 768. The best mode of settling disputes that may not unfrequently arise on this head would seem to be to adopt the plan at present in vogue in most of the ecclesiastical courts of Europe—that is, to have a fixed method by which able ecclesiastics will be *permanently* approved as advocates, so that, when occasion offers, a rector will be able to select an advocate from this number without being obliged to ask for the bishop's approbation.

770. *Q.* Can secular ecclesiastics act as advocates in ecclesiastical courts?

A. We premise: 1. We say, in our question, *secular ecclesiastics ;* for we have already seen that monks, and consequently regular ecclesiastics, cannot be advocates.[1] 2. We say, secondly, *in ecclesiastical courts*, thus leaving out the question whether they can do so also in secular courts— which is of no particular consequence in this country, where ecclesiastics never aspire to such positions. 3. Again, a distinction must be made between secular ecclesiastics who are *priests*, and those who are only in inferior orders—namely, deacons, subdeacons, and those in minor orders.

771. Having premised this, we now answer: All canonists agree that secular ecclesiastics, even though in sacred orders, provided they be not yet priests, can freely act as advocates and procurators in ecclesiastical courts. The only question is: Can priests also do so? There are two opinions: the common opinion, followed, among others, by Schmalzgrueber,[2] Reiffenstuel,[3] and Bouix,[4] is, that they cannot, except in four cases, namely, (*a*) in their own causes— *i.e.*, for themselves; (*b*) for their church; (*c*) or persons re-

[1] Supra, n. 768 (3).
[2] L. i., t. 37, n. 18.
[3] L. i., t. 37, n. 10.
[4] De Jud., vol. i., p. 203, sq.

lated to them, to the fourth degree of consanguinity ; (*d*) or for *personae miserabiles*, such as the poor, orphans, widows.[1] This opinion is founded chiefly on the cap. 3, *De Postul.*, which says : " Cum sacerdotis sit officium nulli nocere, omnibus autem velle prodesse, nonnisi pro seipso . . . sibi licitum est postulare." One of the reasons assigned by the advocates of this opinion is the one intimated in the above *caput* —namely, that a priest, by acting as advocate even in ecclesiastical courts, would be instrumental in inflicting pain and penalties upon others—*i.e.*, upon those of the opposing party, which is not in harmony with his priestly office.

772. The affirmative is, however, held by such eminent canonists as Benedict XIV.,[2] De Angelis,[3] and others. Thus Pope Benedict XIV. expressly says : " Saeculari autem clerico minorum ordinum, etiam Beneficiato, item subdiacono" (et diacono), " *immo sacerdoti*, Jus ipsum canonicum permittit ut se advocatos in tribunalibus quidem ecclesiasticis libere exhibeant." In fact, the above cap. 3, which those who hold the negative on this question quote in their favor, and which *prima facie* seems certainly in their favor, can be construed to mean that priests are forbidden to act as advocates in *secular*, but not in ecclesiastical courts. Besides, as Bouix[4] himself well remarks, it is far more proper, and becoming the priestly dignity that a priest cited before the bishop's tribunal should be defended by an advocate who is a priest, rather than by an inferior ecclesiastic, or even a layman, whom he would nevertheless have to employ as his advocate in case he were forbidden to select his advocate from among his fellow-priests. Moreover, as De Angelis[5] says, nobody can be better adapted than ecclesiastics or priests to act as advocates in ecclesiastical tribunals, particularly by reason of the nature of the questions there

---

[1] Cap. 1. 3, De Post. (l. 37).   [2] De Syn., l. 13, c. 10, n. 12.
[3] L. l., t. 37, n. 2.   [4] L. c., p. 204.   [5] L. c., p. 343.

tried and decided—namely, of ecclesiastical law, in which ecclesiastics are supposed to be well versed. Moreover, this view is in full accord with the more recent decisions of the Holy See. Thus, the Sacred Congregation de Prop. Fide ordains in Art. XXX. of the Instruction *Cum Magnopere* of 1884: "Qua die causa proponetur, inquisito fiet facultas defensionem suam per alium *sacerdotem* suo nomine in scriptis exhibendi." *The Third Plenary Council of Baltimore*, n. 302, also enacts: "Defensorem, qui semper sit vir ecclesiasticus . . . sibi eligendi accusato jus est."

773. Here the question may be asked: Can and should an advocate be allowed to assist a defendant (or, as the case may be, a plaintiff) before a Commission of Investigation in the United States, not only when there is question of the dismissal of a rector, but also in other cases—*v.g.*, where there is question merely of suspending or otherwise punishing an ecclesiastic, even though he be not a rector? The reason of the question is, that the above declaration of the Propaganda speaks only of rectors, not of other priests or ecclesiastics.

774. We are of opinion that all ecclesiastics whatever, whether they be rectors or not, who are defendants (the same holds of plaintiffs) before a Commission of Investigation, in criminal or disciplinary, or even purely civil, causes or matters, have a right to be assisted by an advocate. For, as we have seen,[1] the *edictum de postulando* is *prohibitorium*. Hence, by the general law of the Church, an advocate is to be admitted before ecclesiastical tribunals *in all causes whatever*, where it is not *expressly* prohibited by law. Now, by the law of the Church, the admission of an advocate, at least for the defendant, is not only *never* refused, but is positively required. Thus De Angelis[2] expressly writes: "Advertimus non esse confundendam positionem procuratoris *cum defen-*

---

[1] Supra, n. 768.   [2] L. l., t. 38, n. 5, in fine.

sione advocati, quae nunquam negatur, immo *positive exigitur.*"
This holds true in such a manner that where a litigant cannot procure an advocate, the judge, as we have seen,' is
bound to provide one for him;' so much so, that the litigant
or defendant cannot be condemned for contempt or *in contumaciam* so long as he has not been able to find a suitable
advocate. Time must be given him until he has found an
advocate, or, if he cannot do so, until the court has appointed
one for him.' Moreover, as it is allowed in ecclesiastical
courts to have several procurators, as we have shown, so
also, it seems, is it permitted to have several advocates for
the same cause, especially for the defence, which should
never be impaired.

775. Hence, by the general law of the Church, every
defendant before a Commission of Investigation in the United
States, no matter whether he be a rector or not, whether the
cause be criminal or not, has a right to an advocate. But
is this right, guaranteed though it is by the general law,
restricted by the S. C. de P. F., in its declarations to the
Dubia of American bishops? We think not. It is true that
the Propaganda, in the above declarations, mentions only
rectors as having the right to select an advocate. But it is
also true that this same Sacred Congregation, in its Instruction of July 20, 1878, distinctly intimates that the proceedings as prescribed in the case of rectors shall serve as a
model for the other cases.' Besides, the assistance of an
advocate is one of the best means of defence. Now, by the
above Instruction the defendant is to have the full right
(*facta ipsi plena facultate*) of defending himself. So far, then,
from excluding advocates in the cases under discussion, the
Sacred Congregation plainly admits them.

776. *Duties of Advocates.*—While, as we have seen, the

---

[1] Supra., n. 766.   [2] L. 1, § 4, Ait Praetor ff., De Postul. (iii. 1).
[3] Cap. 1, Ut lite non cont. (i. 6); Schmalzg., l. i., t. 37, n. 17.
[4] Instr. S. C. de P. F., 20 Julii, 1878, § Commissionis ita; § In causis cogn.

advocate's is an honorable and public office, it has also grave obligations annexed. These duties have reference either to the cause undertaken or the honorary. I. *Duties of advocates with regard to the management of the cause.*—1. An advocate must have the proper knowledge. And he is guilty, speaking in general, of a grievous sin if he under takes a case without sufficient learning. 2. He cannot engage in a case which he knows to be unjust or bad.[1] If he nevertheless does so knowingly or through culpable ignorance, he is bound to compensate both his client (unless he informs him of the injustice of his cause) and the opposing party for any damage or loss they may have sustained. This rule, however, admits of an exception in favor of defendants in criminal causes. For it is always lawful to defend an accused person, also in ecclesiastical courts, even when the advocate knows him to be guilty. The reason is, that the accused is never obliged to suffer punishment unless he is juridically convicted. Hence he can either personally or through an advocate try to evade punishment till properly convicted.[2] 3. It is not, however, required that he should be *certain* of the justice of the cause; otherwise he could never engage in any cause, since nearly all causes brought before judicial tribunals proceed from doubtful facts or matters. It is, therefore, sufficient that the cause should have good or probable reasons in its favor.

777. 4. Once he has undertaken a case he should defend or conduct it faithfully. Hence (*a*) he should diligently study both the facts and the law in the case, so as to be fully prepared when he appears before the judge.[3] And if, through his want of skill or diligence, he loses the case, he is bound in conscience to compensate his client.[4] (*b*) He should not reveal the secrets or proofs of his client to the opposing party. Hence he cannot be advocate for both parties in the

---

[1] L. 14, C. § Patroni (iii. 3).
[2] L. 14, § 1, Patroni, C. de Judiciis (iii. 1).
[3] Craiss., n. 5648.
[4] Schmalzg., l. i., t. 37, n. 17.

same cause. (*c*) He should cite no false law nor wrongly interpret a true law; nor should he make use of any false arguments or documents to sustain his case; nor should he produce false or corrupt witnesses. Otherwise he is guilty of the *crimen falsi.*[1] He can, however, employ arguments and the like resting on mere probability. (*d*) In court he should not indulge in personalities. His arguments should be based upon laws and facts, rather than upon invectives against or abuse of the opposing party.[2] (*e*) Finally, he should conduct the cause to the end, or to the final sentence, and not give it up against the will of his client.[3] Lastly, an advocate (we speak of ecclesiastical advocates) who is approved by public authority as advocate, cannot, if the judge requires him to do so, refuse without just cause to undertake the case of one who is unable to secure an advocate.

778. II. *Proper honorary.*—It is certain that ecclesiastical advocates, no less than secular, can demand a fee for their services, and that even though no agreement to that effect has been made beforehand. For, as the cap. 16, De Praescr., says: "Nemo suis stipendiis cogatur militare."[4] Hence, before undertaking a case, he can make a contract with his client as to the honorary to be given him. Where a fixed honorary is established by law or custom, the advocate should not go beyond it. Where no such fee is fixed by law or custom, he can demand what is regarded by good men a fair compensation, considering the amount of his labor, his position, his ability, and the difficulty of the case.[5]

779. Can the advocate make an agreement with his client, obliging the latter to pay him, over and above the ordinary fee, also a special honorary (called *Palmarium* by canonists) if he wins the case? He can do so *after* the case

---

[1] L. 14, C. cit.   [2] L. 6, § 1, Cod. de Postul. (il. 6).
[3] L. 13, § 9, Cod. de Judic.
[4] Schmalzg., l. c., n. 12; De Angelis, l. c., n. 3, p. 348.
[5] L. 1, § 10 ff., De extr. cogn. (50. 13).

is finished, provided always that this *palmarium* or special
fee be moderate.[1]   But he cannot do so, according to
Schmalzgrueber,[2] *before* the case is finished.   Finally, he cannot enter into a contract with his client, binding the latter
to give him, as his fee, a share or part (*quota litis*) of what
will be adjudicated to him in case of his gaining the cause.[3]
Note, what has been said thus far of ecclesiastical advocates
affects, of course, also ecclesiastical advocates before Commissions of Investigation in the United States.

ART. V.

*Of Auditors, Assessors, Fiscal Promoters and Advocates, Secre-
tarics or Clerks, and Messengers of Ecclesiastical Courts.*

780. Of these officials of ecclesiastical courts we shall
speak later on, under the head of episcopal curias.

We also refer the reader to our treatise entitled *The New
Procedure, or a full and clear explanation of the Instruction
" Cum Magnopere," issued by the S. C. de P. F. in* 1884.   Fr.
Pustet & Co., New York, 1887.

---

[1] Ib., § 12.   [2] L. c., n. 13.   [3] De Angelis. l. c., p. 349.

CHAPTER IV.

OF THE COMPETENT ECCLESIASTICAL TRIBUNAL
(*De Foro Competente Ecclesiastico*).

781. In ecclesiastical no less than in secular courts, when judicial proceedings are about to be commenced against any person, it is of paramount importance to find out which is the *forum competens*, or what particular tribunal has competence in the case. In other words, it is necessary to ascertain the tribunal to which the accused or defendant belongs. For the general rule is that the plaintiff (in criminal causes, the accuser or prosecution) must follow the forum to which the defendant is subject.[1] Hence, even where the plaintiff belongs to a different forum from that of the defendant, he has to institute proceedings before the latter's forum. Consequently, it is sufficient for a judge, in order to be competent to try a cause, to have jurisdiction over the defendant, and it is not necessary for him to have jurisdiction also over the plaintiff. All this follows from the maxim : *Actor sequitur forum rei*, which applies both in civil and criminal causes.[2] By the competent ecclesiastical forum, we therefore mean the tribunal of the ecclesiastical judge to whose jurisdiction the defendant in a cause is subject. Hence, that ecclesiastical judge is the competent judge (*judex competens*), to whose jurisdiction the defendant is subject, or before whom the case can be tried.[3]

782. It will be seen that the question now under consideration is not, whether an ecclesiastical court or judge has,

---

[1] Cap. 5, 8, De for. comp. (ii. 2); L. Juris 2, C. de jurisd. om. jud.(iii. 13).
[2] L. in criminali 5, Cod. (iii. 13).   [3] De Camillis, vol. iii., p. 15.

speaking in general, power or competence to try causes.
For every ecclesiastical judge, by the very fact of his being
a judge, has such power, in general. The question therefore
is : Has such judge the power to try or hear this or that
particular cause, or is he competent in this or that case ?
The question, therefore, who is the competent ecclesiastical
judge in a cause, is the same as this one : Before what ecclesiastical judge or tribunal is the case to be heard and decided ?

783. *Various ways in which an ecclesiastical court becomes
competent—i.e., has power to try a cause.*—In how many ways
does an ecclesiastical court or judge become competent to
adjudicate a cause?   In other words, in how many ways can
a person belong to the forum of an ecclesiastical judge, and
be, therefore, triable by him?   1. *Ordinarily,* in these four
ways—namely, by reason (*a*) of domicile or the parties ; (*b*)
of contract ; (*c*) the crime committed ; (*d*) the location of the
thing or object in dispute.   These ways are thus enumerated
by Pope Gregory IX. : "Ratione delicti, seu contractus,
aut domicilii, sive rei de qua contra possessorem causa
movetur, forum regulariter quis sortitur." [1]   2. *Extraordinarily,* in the following ways : (*a*) by delegation ; (*b*) prorogation ; (*c*) compromise or arbitration ; (*d*) counter action ; (*e*)
connection of causes.   There are consequently, altogether,
eleven ways or modes in which an ecclesiastical judge becomes competent in a cause, and in which, therefore, a person is justiciable by him.   We shall now briefly explain each
mode.

784. I. *Competence by reason of domicile.*—It is certain that
a person falls under the competence or forum of, and is
therefore triable by, the ecclesiastical judge or court of the
place where he has his domicile, and that in all causes, civil
or criminal.[2]   Nay, this *forum domicilii* has concurrent juris-

---

[1] Cap. Licet 20, De For. Comp. (ii. 2).
[2] Cap. 20, cit. ; L. Cives 7, C. De Incolis (x. 39); Schmalzg., l. ii., tit. 2, n. 15.

diction or competence with all the other ecclesiastical courts, so that, even where a person is justiciable out of his own domicile,—namely, as we shall see, in the place where he has committed a crime, or made a contract, or the object in dispute is situate,—he can nevertheless be tried also by the court of his domicile, provided one of the other courts has not yet taken up the case.[1] This court of domicile can proceed to try a person even when he is out of the place of his domicile. For it can summon him to appear; and if he contumaciously refuses to appear, proceed against him, as being in contempt.[2] Nor can it be objected that such citation is executed or served on the defendant out of the territory (*v.g.*, diocese of bishop) of the judge issuing it. For this serving of the citation, whether by messenger or registered letter, is purely a ministerial act, and not an act of jurisdiction.[3] This court or forum, therefore, is justly called the natural, ordinary, and chief forum of defendants. It has full and general competence, and can try persons, as we have seen, even for crimes committed out of their domicile.

785. What has been said applies to domicile proper (*domicilium stricte dictum*). Does it also hold true of quasi-domicile?[4] We must distinguish here between crimes or acts which are committed in one's quasi-domicile, and those which are perpetrated out of it. Now, it is certain that a person may be tried and sentenced by the judge of his quasi-domicile for crimes committed or contracts made *in such quasi-domicile*. Whether this holds also in the case of crimes committed or acts done *out of such quasi-domicile*, is controverted. In common with Reiffenstuel,[5] Schmalzgrueber,[6] and others, we hold the affirmative.[7]

---

[1] Reiff., l. ii., t. 2, n. 28.   [2] Cap. 3. 8, De Dol. et Cont. (ii. 14).

[3] Ex cap. Romana 1, De For. Comp. in 6° (ii. 2); Reiff., l. c., n. 30.

[4] For the definition of and difference between domicile and quasi-domicile, see supra, n. 650.   [5] L. c., n. 39.

[6] L. c., n. 17.   [7] Ex l. Sciens 2, C. Ubi de crim. agi op. (iii. 15).

786. We observe here, that as Rome is the home or fatherland of all Catholics, ecclesiastics (and even laics, in ecclesiastical causes) can, when in Rome, be tried there, in the first instance, even though they have not acquired a domicile or quasi-domicile there, nor committed the offence or act there.[1] This holds true, even at present, notwithstanding that the Council of Trent[1] ordains that all ecclesiastical causes shall in the first instance be tried and decided only by the ordinaries of places. Because the Roman tribunals are "ordinaries of places" for all Catholics, and, therefore, not excluded by the above Tridentine enactment.[3] Hence, a defendant cannot object to being tried in the Roman Curia, in the first instance. He may, however, if he has come to Rome for some just and necessary cause, ask to be allowed to return home, and plead before his ordinary.[4]

787. II. *Competence by reason of contract.*—The next mode of falling under the competence of an ecclesiastical judge is by reason of contract (*ratione contractus*). For, if a person makes a contract in a place, he becomes, as a rule, triable, so far as concerns the contract, in such place, even though he has no domicile or quasi-domicile there.[5] Observe that the word contract, or agreement, is here used in its widest sense, and, consequently, means not only contracts, or agreements proper, but also quasi-contracts, and every other action from which springs an obligation.[6] We say, *as a rule;* for there are a few exceptions. Thus, the contracting parties are not triable by the judge of the place where the contract was made, if they agreed that, in case of difficulties arising out of the contract, the trial should take place elsewhere—*v.g.*, before the judge of the domicile. As a rule, therefore, the judge of the place where the contract was

---

[1] Cap. 20, De For. Comp.   [1] Sess. 24, c. 20, De Ref.
[3] Craiss., n. 5689.   [4] Schmalzg., l. c., n. 27.
    [5] Cap. Licet 20, cit.; cap. Romana, cit., § 3; L. 19, § 2, Proinde ff., De Jud.
(v. i.).   [6] L. Omnem 20 ff., De Judic. (v. 1); Reiff., l. c., n. 81.

made, or the obligation contracted, has full power to try an ecclesiastic, even though a stranger, who has entered into a contract there, provided the latter has not yet left the place or territory of the judge of contract, or provided (in case he has already left) that he was cited to appear in court before he left.[1] We say, *provided the latter*, etc.; for if he has left before being cited, the judge of contract cannot proceed in any other way against him, than by putting his opponent in possession of his goods or possessions, if he has any, in the place of contract; but he cannot inflict any other punishment upon him.[2]

788. What has been said of the competence of the ecclesiastical judge *ratione contractus*, applies also to matrimonial causes,—namely, when a question arises as to whether the marriage was celebrated according to the law of the Church, or before the *proprius parochus*, or with the necessary witnesses, or the proclamations.[3]

789. III. *Competence by reason of the location of the object.*— It is certain that a person falls under the competence of an ecclesiastical judge, or forum, by reason of the location of the object which is the subject of the dispute (*forum competens ratione rei sitae*); so that a person may be tried by the judge of the territory where the object in question is situate,[4] even though he is otherwise in no way under his jurisdiction.[5] This is true, (*a*) not only with regard to immovable property or real estate, but also movable property, or personal estate, provided the latter (*i.e.*, the personal estate) remains permanently, or at least for some time, in the place, and is not there merely *in transitu ;* (*b*) even when the party is not in the territory or place. For, in the latter case,—*i.e.*, where the party has left the territory,—the judge can cite him to appear, as though he were still in the place, and, if he

---

[1] Cap. Romana, cit., § 3. [2] Cap. cit.; Reiff., l. c., n. 95.
[3] Prael. in Sem. S. Sulp., tom. 3, n. 658. [4] Cap. 3. 20, De For. Comp. (ii. 2).
[5] Reiff., l. c., n. 98; Schmalzg., l. c., n. 49.

contumaciously refuses to appear, he can also put the complainant in possession of the object in controversy. Note, however, that only a real, not a personal, action can be brought against the defendant in the case.[1] In other words, the defendant comes under the competence of the ecclesiastical court by reason of the *res sita*, only so far as concerns his goods, not his person, as we have already intimated.[2] The judge, therefore, of the place where the object is located cannot pass a sentence or issue any mandate which would directly affect the person of the defendant (*v.g.*, he cannot excommunicate or suspend him), but only decree that the thing or property in dispute be given the complainant.[3]

790. Observe that by the *res sita* are also meant ecclesiastical benefices. Hence, where, *v.g.*, an ecclesiastic has two benefices, one in his own diocese, the other out of it, he is triable, so far as the latter benefice is concerned, by the bishop of the diocese where it is situate.[4]

791. *Competence by reason of crime—"Forum competens ratione criminis."*—The law of the Church is that a person falls under the competence of, and is therefore justiciable by, the ecclesiastical court or judge of the territory or place where he has committed the crime, even though he be otherwise in no sense subject to him.[5] In fact, it is eminently proper that crimes should be punished where they have been committed, partly to deter others from doing the same, and partly also because the proofs of guilt can be more easily obtained there.[6]

792. *Q.* How can the ecclesiastical judge of the territory where the crime was committed proceed against the person perpetrating the crime?

---

[1] L. Actor 3, C. Ubi in rem. actio (iii. 19).   [2] Supra, n. 787.

[3] Ex cap. Romana, cit.; Schmalzg., l. c., 51, 53.

[4] Cf. Prael. S. Sulp., l. c., n. 658; Devoti, l. 3, t. 4, § 16.

[5] Cap. 14. 20, De For. Comp. (ii. 2); L. quaestiones 1, et l. Sciens 2, § qua in C. Ubi de crim. (iii. 15).   [6] Schmalzg., l. c., n. 59.

A. We distinguish : The delinquent is at the time either actually in the place or territory where he committed the crime, or he has left it, and that either before or after he was cited to appear before the *judex delicti.* In the first case,— *i.e.,* where the delinquent is still in such territory,—the ecclesiastical judge—*v.g.,* bishop of the diocese—of this territory has full power to try and punish him, so much so that he can even pass sentence of dismissal from benefice or ecclesiastical office where the nature of the crime warrants it, and that even though the benefice is situate in another place.[1] We say, *pass sentence of dismissal;* for the execution of this sentence of privation belongs to the judge or bishop of the diocese where such benefice or office is.[2]

793. In the second case,—that is, where the delinquent has indeed left the place, but was, prior to leaving, cited by the judge of such place or territory,—it is certain that the latter can proceed against him even in his absence; so that if the defendant refuses contumaciously to obey the citation and appear for trial, the judge or bishop can proceed against him as in contempt—that is, he can, besides punishing him for contempt, proceed with the trial even in the defendant's absence, and if he find him guilty, inflict punishment—*v.g.,* suspension, excommunication — upon him. Nay, he may even decree dismissal from benefice or office,[3] though, as we have just seen,[4] where such office or benefice is out of his district, he must remit the execution of such decree to the bishop of the diocese where the benefice is located.

794. In the third case,—namely, where he had left before he was cited,—no personal action *(actio personalis)* can be brought against him before the judge of the territory or district where he committed the deed. For, as Pope Boniface VIII. says: *Extra territorium jus dicenti non parcatur*

[1] Cap. Postulasti 14 (il. 2); Reiff., l. c., n. 48; Schmalzg., l. c., n. 61.
[2] Schmalzg., l. c., n. 60 (3).
[3] Cap. Proposuisti 19, De For. Comp. (il. 2).   [4] Supra, n. 792.

impune.[1] We say, *no personal action;* that is, the judge cannot, as we have seen in the case of *judex rei sitae,*[2] inflict any
punishment directly affecting his person, such as suspension.
But an *actio realis* lies against him before such judge—*i.e.,*
this judge can issue decrees depriving the absent defendant
of his goods or possessions located in the said judge's district.[3] The reason is that the defendant who has left the
place before having been cited remains subject indeed to the
judge of that place so far as his goods located there are concerned, but not so far as his person is concerned. Moreover,
the defendant in the case may, upon the requisition or
request of the *judex delicti,* be compelled by the bishop or
ordinary of his domicile or place where he actually lives at
the time, and that even by censures, to appear before the
ordinarius delicti for trial. And if he appears, the *judex
delicti* can proceed both against his person and his goods.[4]
But if he does not appear, he can, even in this case, be proceeded against, though only so far as his goods are concerned.

795. We observe that where the crime was begun in one
territory or diocese and consummated in another, it is the
more probable opinion that the delinquent may be tried and
punished by the judge or bishop of either place; in such
manner, however, that the ordinary who has first taken up
the case has the exclusive right to continue and finish it.
This right is called the *jus praeventionis—i.e.,* the right of
anticipation.[5]

796. *General remarks regarding the above four modes of
having competence.*—From what has been said, it follows that
the only competent judge, in the first instance, of ecclesiastics, even though only in minor orders or tonsure, in all
ecclesiastical causes, civil or criminal, is their bishop or
ordinary. By the latter is meant, as we have seen, and in

---

[1] Cap. 2, de Const., in 6° (il. 1).   [2] Supra, n. 789.   [3] Schmalzg., l. c., n. 61.
[4] Ex Clem. Pastoralis 2 (ii. 11); Reiff., l. c., n. 61; Prael. S. Sulp., l. c., n.
657.   [5] Reiff., l. c., n. 75.

the manner explained, the bishop or ordinary of the place (*a*) where an ecclesiastic has his domicile or quasi-domicile; (*b*) or where the contract or obligation was entered into; (*c*) or the crime committed; (*d*) or the object in controversy is situate; (*e*) finally, the Roman Curia. Again we observe, that of all these courts or judges the bishop or ordinary of the domicile has the fullest power, and is, in fact, the ordinary forum of ecclesiastics. The Roman Curia, as we have seen, is considered the *judex domicilii* for all Catholics of the whole world.

797. Besides these four ways in which a person may fall under the competence of an ecclesiastical judge, there are, as we have seen, several others of minor importance. The first is by *delegation*, which we have already sufficiently explained.[1]

798. The second is by *prorogation* (*prorogatione jurisdictionis*) or by the *consent of the parties*. This prorogation is defined the extension of the jurisdiction or competence of a judge beyond its limits,—*v.g.*, to persons or causes which otherwise do not fall under his jurisdiction,—made by the consent of the parties voluntarily submitting themselves to him.[2] It is certain that in ecclesiastical courts parties may in many cases agree upon a judge otherwise incompetent in their particular case.[3] It is true that, according to the Council of Trent, the ordinary, as judge in the first instance, has the right to call before his tribunal all ecclesiastical causes of his diocese, whether the contending parties be seculars or ecclesiastics. But from this it does not follow that he must necessarily do so.[4] Hence, not only the laity,[5] but also the clergy,[6] may even at present, in ecclesiastical causes, agree upon an ecclesiastical judge, to whom they are

[1] Supra, n. 226 sq.   [2] Ex l. 1 et 2 ff. de Judic. (v. 1); Reiff., l. c., n. 122.
[3] Ib.; Craiss., n. 5660.   [4] Schmalzg., l. c., n. 145.
[5] Cap. Nullus 3, de par. et al. par. (iil. 29).
[6] Cap. Significasti 18, de for. comp. (ii. 2).

otherwise not subject, *provided it be with the consent of their own ordinary.*

799. In order that the prorogation may be valid, certain conditions are required. They are chiefly: 1. The judge whose jurisdiction is to be extended to the case must have some jurisdiction. For it is evident that where there is no jurisdiction it cannot be extended. 2. This jurisdiction which is to be extended to a case must be of the same kind with that which is requisite in the case. Thus, if the cause is criminal, the judge whose jurisdiction is to be extended must have criminal, not merely civil, jurisdiction. Otherwise, there would be not merely prorogation, or extension of competence, but a conferring of new jurisdiction, which private persons cannot do.[1] 3. The parties must freely and knowingly consent to the judge.[2] 4. The judge, whose jurisdiction is to be extended, must have not merely delegated, but ordinary jurisdiction, or at least delegated jurisdiction *ad universitatem causarum*, which is placed on a like footing with ordinary jurisdiction.[3]

800. Hence we think that in the United States ecclesiastics in one diocese could, with the consent of their bishop, submit their cause for trial and adjudication to the bishop and Commission of Investigation of another diocese. For it seems that Commissions of Investigation are *delegati ad universitatem causarum*, in regard to the hearing of causes.

801. The third extraordinary way of falling under the competence of, and being triable by, an ecclesiastical court, otherwise destitute of competence in the case, is by compromise or arbitration (*competentia per compromissum*). Speaking in general, there are two kinds of arbitrators—arbitrators in the strict sense, and arbitrators in a broad sense.[4] By an arbitrator in the broad sense of the term, we mean

---

[1] Schmalzg., l. c., n. 144.
[3] Cap. 40, de Off. jud. del. (i. 29).
[2] L. 2 ff. de Judic.
[4] Schmalzg., l. i., t. 43, n. 1.

any worthy person selected to settle some matter or question. Arbitrators proper, (*arbitri*), or in the strict sense of the term, of whom we here speak, are those worthy and competent persons who are chosen either by direction of ecclesiastical law, or by the agreement of the parties, to take cognizance of, and pronounce sentence upon, the matter in dispute, in such manner that the parties are bound to abide by their decision.[1] The chief differences between arbitrators proper and arbitrators in a broad sense are two: 1. The former should observe in their proceedings the formalities prescribed for judicial proceedings ; for they act as judges. The latter settle the matter *ex aequo et bono*, and even without the observance of the formalities required in judicial proceedings. 2. The sentence of arbitrators proper, even though unjust,[2] must, as a rule, be accepted as final, and obeyed, save where they were chosen by direction of the law ; whilst that of arbitrators, in the wide sense, may simply have that force or weight which the opinion of a worthy person would possess.[3]

802. Arbitrators proper, as is evident from the definition, are of two kinds—necessary and voluntary. Necessary arbitrators (*arbitri juris, arbitri necessarii*) are those who are chosen, indeed, either by the judge or the parties, though necessarily—*i.e.*, in cases where the law of the Church not only allows, but positively commands it. Now, in what cases does the law of the Church prescribe that arbitrators be chosen to settle the dispute or cause ? Chiefly in the following: 1. Where an ecclesiastical judge is challenged or objected to as suspected. In this case the law of the Church is, that the judge cannot himself take cognizance of this challenge, but that arbitrators must be selected to do so.[4] 2. Where an ecclesiastic has a dispute or controversy with

---

[1] Reiff., l. l., t. 43, n. 5; De Angelis, l. i., t. 43, n. 1.
[2] L. Diem 27 ff. de recep. qui arb. rec. (iv. 8).   [3] De Angelis, l. c.
[4] Cap. 39, de Off. jud. del. (i. 29); cap. 11, de Off. jud. del., in 6 (i. 14).

his own bishop. The law of the Church directs that such dispute be settled by arbitrators chosen by both parties.[1]

803. Voluntary arbitrators (*arbitri voluntarii, arbitri compromissarii*) are those who are chosen not of necessity,—that is, not because the law so directs,—but by the free consent of the contending parties. Necessary arbitrators differ from voluntary chiefly (*a*) in that the former have jurisdiction, and also a certain coercive power.[2] Hence they can, like judges proper, cite the parties, compel the witnesses to appear, etc. The latter have merely what is called *notio* or *mera cognitio causae*,[3] but no jurisdictional or coercive power, and, consequently, can indeed hear the cause and pronounce sentence, but cannot compel the parties or witnesses to appear. The reason of the difference is, that necessary arbitrators are appointed by the law or the superior. Now, either of the latter can and is presumed to give jurisdiction to the arbitrators. Voluntary arbitrators, on the other hand, are selected solely by the will of the parties, who neither have nor consequently, can give jurisdiction.[4] (*b*) From the sentence or award of necessary arbitrators, as we have seen, it is *always* allowed to appeal; from that of voluntary, it is not permitted, as a rule, to appeal. (*c*) Again, a person can be compelled to act as necessary arbitrator,[5] but not as voluntary.

804. An arbitrator, in the proper sense, especially if he is a necessary arbitrator, does not differ greatly from a judge proper,[6] but is, in fact, in most respects considered a judge, in the true sense of the word. We say, *does not differ greatly;* for there are some differences. Thus, a judge can execute his sentence, while an arbitrator cannot, but must leave the execution of his sentence to the ordinary judge having competence in the matter.[7]

---

[1] Can. Si Clericus 46, C. 11, q. 1; De Angelis, l. c., n. 2.
[2] Ex cap. 39, de Off. del.   [3] L. 5 ff., de Re jud. (42. 1).   [4] Schmalzg., l. c., n. 3.
[5] Cap. 61, de Appell.   [6] L. 1 ff. de Recep. qui, etc. (iv. 8).
[7] L. Cum antea 5, C. de Recep. arb. (ii. 56).

805. *Q.* Who can be appointed arbitrators?

A. Generally speaking, all persons whatever, unless they are expressly excluded by law. Nor does it matter whether they are private individuals or public officials.[1] Now, by the law of the Church, the following are chiefly excluded: 1. Regulars, except where there is question of the good of their monastery, and even then they can act only with the consent of their superior. The reason is the same as that on account of which they are forbidden to act as procurators or judges. 2. Laymen, in ecclesiastical causes, unless they are specially authorized by the Holy See, or chosen with the permission of the superior conjointly with an ecclesiastic.[2] Whether a layman can be chosen as an arbitrator in the broad sense, is controverted. Schmalzgrueber[3] holds the affirmative; De Angelis[4] the negative. 3. Finally, a person who is excommunicated as *vitandus.*[5] It is allowed to choose one or more persons to arbitrate in the same cause. If several are selected, it is more advisable to make the number uneven,[6] so that in case of disagreement there can be a majority. It is, however, not forbidden to make the number even.[7] The majority decides,[8] unless it was specially agreed among the contending parties that the verdict of the arbitrators must be unanimous.[9]

806. *Q.* What causes or matters can be submitted to arbitrators freely chosen by the parties?

A. We premise: We do not here speak of causes which *must,* as we have seen,[10] be submitted to arbitration, but only of those which *may* be submitted. We now answer: All causes whatever which are not expressly excepted by law. By "law" we here mean the law of the Church, or the civil law of the Romans as adopted by the Church. Now by this

---

[1] Schmalzg., l. c., n. 11. [2] Cap. 8, 9 (l. 43). [3] L. c., n. 13.
[4] L. c., n. 4. [5] Cap. 39, de Sent. exc. (v. 39).
[6] Cap. 1, de For. comp. (l. 43); Schmalzg., l. c., n. 11. [7] Cap. 12, l. c.
[8] Cap. 1, in 6° (i. 32). [9] De Angelis, l. c., n. 8. [10] Supra, n. 802.

law the following causes are excepted: 1. Criminal causes,
when criminally tried or prosecuted;[1] 2. Matrimonial
causes,[2] when there is question of the validity of the marriage;[3] 3. Causes or questions relating to appointments to
ecclesiastical offices or benefices, except, however, when the
ecclesiastical superior consents or the ordinary himself is
chosen arbitrator;[4] 4. Causes which have been decided by
a sentence that has passed into *res judicata;*[5] 5. Causes that
redound to the prejudice of the Holy See;[6] 6. Major
causes, and those specially reserved to the Holy See.[7]

807. *Powers and Duties of Arbitrators.*—1. The power of
those arbitrators who are chosen freely (*arbitri compromissarii*), and not necessarily, is neither greater nor less than
what is given them by the parties in the compromise or
agreement, or by the judge. For, says the Roman law, *id
venit in compromissum, de quo actum est ut veniret.*[8] Thus,
before a voluntary arbitrator, no counter-action (*reconventio*)
can be instituted,[9] unless the contrary be expressed in the
agreement.[10] Nor can such counter-action be brought even
before a necessary arbitrator when the latter is chosen to
settle, not the whole case, but merely a particular issue or
question—*v.g.*, whether the judge is suspected. But if the
necessary arbitrator be chosen to decide the whole cause,
—which happens, *v.g.*, in controversies or disputes between
a bishop and one of his ecclesiastics,—a counter-action lies
before him.[11]

808. 2. The arbitrators, even though voluntary, and even
though this is not expressly stated in the compromise or
agreement, can, like delegated judges, take cognizance of
questions or causes which are, so to say, intrinsically or

---

[1] Cap. Causa 9, de In int. rest. (i. 41).   [2] Ib.

[3] Schmalzg., l. c., n. 16 (2).   [4] Ex cap. 10 (i. 43).   [5] Cap. 11, l. c.

[6] Cap. 5, l. c.   [7] Ex cap. Causa, cit.

[8] L. 21, § Plenum ff. de Rec. qui, etc. (iv. 8); De Angelis, l. c., n. 6.
Schmalzg., l. c., n. 26.   [9] Cap. 6 (i. 43).

[10] Schmalzg., l. c., n. 17.   [11] Can. 46, C. 11, qu. 1; De Angelis, l. c., n. 6.

necessarily connected with or incidental to the principal cause in such manner that they cannot well decide the latter without at the same time pronouncing upon the former.[1] Thus they can decide exceptions, both dilatory and peremptory; what comes within the agreement or arbitration,[2] etc.

809. 3. Where nothing else is said in the agreement, the mode of procedure to be observed by the arbitrators is nearly the same as that observed in trials or judicial proceedings. For arbitrations resemble judicial processes. Thus the Roman law, adopted by the Church, says: " Compromissum ad similitudinem judiciorum redigatur."[3] We say, *where nothing else is said in the agreement;* for the parties choosing the arbitrator (we speak of voluntary arbitrators) can, and usually do, by mutual agreement establish the form of procedure or trial to be followed.[4]

810. *Effects of the Decision or Award of the Arbitrators.—* Are the parties always obliged to abide by the decision or award (*laudum*) of arbitrators? We must distinguish between arbitrators proper and arbitrators in a wide sense. The decision of the latter, if unjust, need not be complied with by the aggrieved party, but may, when proved to be unjust, be corrected or modified according to the estimate of a good and competent person.[5] As to arbitrators proper, we again distinguish between voluntary and necessary arbitrators. Against the decision or award of the latter it is, as we have seen, always allowed to appeal.[6] But against the award of voluntary arbitrators, whether it be just or unjust, it is not, as a rule, permitted to appeal.[7] The reason is, that a person who of his own free-will submits his case to arbitrators, has only to blame himself if he is thereby injured.

811. We said, *as a rule;* for there are several exceptions. Thus the decision of voluntary arbitrators need not be

---

[1] Ex cap. 5, 21, de Off. del.
[2] L. 1 ff. (iv. 8); cap. 6 (i. 43).
[3] Supra, n. 801. [4] Supra, n. 803.
[5] De Angelis, l. c.
[6] Schmalzg., l. c., n. 26.
[7] Ib.; L. 27 ff. de Rec. qui rec. (iv. 8).

obeyed by the aggrieved party (*a*) if the arbitrator violated any of the conditions of the arbitration agreement.' For, as we have seen, voluntary arbitrators have no power beyond that agreed upon by the parties choosing them. (*b*) Where the decision is contrary to the sacred canons. (*c*) If the arbitrator was deceived or bribed by the opposing party. (*d*) When the injustice of the decision is notorious. (*e*) When the injury inflicted by the decision is of an extraordinarily grave character. Because in this as in the preceding case, fraud or deceit is presumed.' We have said, *of an extraordinarily grave character;* for whether it is lawful to refuse to abide by the decision, if the injury is grave indeed, but not extraordinarily so, is controverted. Schmalzgrueber,' with most canonists, holds that once the sentence of the arbitrators is accepted or acquiesced in by the parties (*quando arbitrium homologatum est a partibus*), either expressly or tacitly,—*v.g.,* by not appealing within ten days,—it can no longer be modified, on the plea of grave injury.

812. Finally, an ecclesiastical judge or court obtains competence by what is called *continentia causae,* or the connection or bearing which one cause has with or upon another.' Thus, a judge can take cognizance of, and decide all questions or matters which in the course of the trial come up incidentally to, or in connection with, the main cause or question at issue, in such manner that the one cannot be well decided without the other. This holds of delegated as well as ordinary judges,' and it is needless to add, also of Commissions of Investigation, both here and in England, so far as the trial, exclusive of final sentence in such causes, is concerned. The rule is based on the general principle, that when a person is empowered to proceed in a cause or causes, he is, by that very fact, implicitly authorized to do whatever is necessary or expedient to the discharge of his duty.

---

¹ Cap. 6 (i. 43).   ² De Angelis, l. c., n. 10.   ³ L. c., n. 36.
⁴ L. 10, C. de Jud. (iii. 1).   ⁵ Reiff., l. 2, t. 2, n. 145.

CHAPTER V.

ART. I.

Judicial Proofs, in General.

813. When the defendant, upon being duly summoned, appears in the ecclesiastical court (also before Commissions, where they still exist), and denies the charges or allegations made against him, it becomes necessary to prove them ; otherwise they fall to the ground, according to the maxim: "Actore non probante, reus absolvitur." We shall therefore speak of judicial proofs, and that, first, in general ; next, in particular.

814. A proof (*probatio*) in general is the demonstration or establishment of a disputed or controverted matter by lawful means or arguments. Proofs are of two kinds : judicial, or extrajudicial. A judicial proof (*probatio judicialis*) is defined a judicial act, by which the judge is convinced of the certainty of a disputed thing or fact, and that either through documents, or witnesses, or proper arguments.[1] A judicial proof, therefore, is that which is made in court, or before the judge ; an extrajudicial, is that which is made out of court, or not before a judge sitting in or holding court.[2] A judicial proof is either full or perfect (*probatio plena*)—namely, when it fully and clearly establishes or demonstrates, in court, an alleged fact or statement, and thus enables the judge to pronounce sentence, without further investigation ; or it is in-

---

[1] Schmalzg., l. ii., t. 19, n. 1.   [2] Reiff., l. ii., t. 19, n. 9.

complete or imperfect (*probatio semiplena*)—namely, when it establishes as probable, though not as certain, the fact or affair on trial before the judge.[1] In other words, a full proof is one that makes the judge or court certain of the fact or matter in dispute; an incomplete one is that which leaves him in doubt.

815. How many kinds of full proof are there? Chiefly these: 1. The testimony or deposition of two witnesses, who are above all suspicion or objection, on one and the same point. 2. A public instrument, or other authentic writing, having the force of a public instrument. 3. The presumption which is called *juris et de jure*. 4. The oath taken by one of the litigants, upon the demand of the opposing party. 5. Confession of the accused. 6. Evidence or notoriety of the fact.[2] The chief effect of a full proof is that sentence has to be pronounced in accordance with it.[3] In other words, the judge is bound to pass judgment *secundum allegata et probata*.[4] Hence he should either condemn the defendant, if the plaintiff has fully proved the charges or allegations, or absolve him if the allegations are not fully sustained.

816. What are the chief kinds of incomplete proofs? 1. The deposition (*a*) of one witness (*b*) or of several singular witnesses (*testes singulares*)—i.e., of several witnesses, each of whom testifies to a different point, (*c*) or even of two witnesses who testify on the same point, but who are not above all suspicion. 2. A private writing or instrument. 3. Comparison of handwriting, where there is a doubt as to the writing. 4. Probable presumptions. 5. Fame or current report. 6. The supplementary oath.[5]

817. Can two imperfect proofs (*probationes semiplenae*) constitute a full proof? 1. It is certain that they cannot (*a*) in criminal causes;[6] because in such causes the proofs

---

[1] Schmalzg., l. c., n. 10; Devoti, l. 3, t. 9, § 3.   [2] Schmalzg., l. c., n. 10.
[3] Reiff., l. c., n. 190.   [4] Can. Judicet 4, C. 3, q. 7.
[5] Schmalzg., l. c., n. 14.   [6] Supra, n. 726.

must be, as canonists say, clearer than the noonday sun —
luce meridiana clariores.[1] (*b*) In matrimonial causes, when
there is question of the validity of a marriage already contracted. (*c*) In civil causes of a grave character.[2] 2. With
these exceptions, two imperfect proofs can make a full
proof if they are joined together and tend to the same end,
even though they be of a different kind—such as, one witness
together with the oath; presumptions in conjunction with
common fame.[3]

818. From what has been said, it follows that judicial
proofs must, as a rule, be full and conclusive (*probatio plena*).
This is inferred by canonists from these words of the Justinian
code: "Judices oportet imprimis rei qualitatem *plena
inquisitione discutere.*"[4] Nay, such full and complete proof
is required even *jure divino*, as appears from these words of
our Lord : "In ore *duorum* vel *trium* stat omne verbum."[5]
We say, *as a rule;* for there are some exceptions. Thus (*a*)
the testimony of but one witness is full proof, when his
deposition is beneficial to another person and does not hurt
anybody.[6] Thus the testimony of one witness is sufficient
to establish the fact that a person has been baptized or that a
church is consecrated.[7] (*b*) Again, an imperfect proof is sufficient in summary causes which are of but little moment and
not prejudicial to any one. By summary causes we mean
causes that are tried summarily, or where a person is empowered to proceed *summarie ac de plano.* We have just
said, *which are of but little moment*, etc.; for in summary
causes which are of graver importance and may seriously
prejudice others, the proofs must be full and conclusive.
Thus Pope Clement V. says: "Non sic tamen Judex litem
abbreviet" (in processu summario) "quin *probationes neces-*

---

[1] L. 25, C. de Probat. (iv. 19); Bouix, de Jud., vol. i., p. 305.
[2] Supra, n. 726. [3] Schmalzg., l. c., n. 16, 17. [4] L. 9, C. de Jud. (iii. 1).
[5] Matth. xviii. 16; Reiff., l. c., n. 57. [6] Can. 110, de Consecr. dist. 4.
[7] Glossa in cap. 1, de Test. v. nisi juratus.

sariae . . . admittantur." [1]   We conclude, therefore, with Reiffenstuel [2] that full proof (*probatio plena*) is required also in summary and extrajudicial proceedings when there is question of inflicting an irreparable damage. These principles, it would seem to us, apply also to proceedings before Commissions of Investigation in the United States. Finally, (*c*) imperfect proofs are sufficient when a cause is committed to a judge in such a manner that he may proceed *sola facti veritate inspecta.* [3]

819. Upon whom rests the *onus probandi*, or burden of proof, in judicial proceedings before ecclesiastical courts? Generally speaking, upon the plaintiff; [4] so much so, that where the latter has not sufficiently proved his allegations, the defendant must be acquitted, even though he has said nothing whatever in his defence. [5] This holds both in civil and criminal causes, and also when the judge proceeds *ex officio* by way of inquiry—that is, without any accuser or denouncer. For in this case the judge or bishop, or his prosecuting official (so far as concerns this official in the United States, see the Instruction of the S. C. de Prop. Fide, *Quamvis*, July 20, 1878, § 2, and also the later Instr., *Cum Magnopere* of 1884, Art. XIII.), is bound to prove the charges or allegations. [6] We have said, *generally speaking;* for sometimes the burden of proof rests with the defendant—namely, among . other cases, (*a*) when the presumption of the law is in favor of the plaintiff; (*b*) when the defendant makes an exception [7] —*v.g.*, when he objects that the judge is not competent. For in this case he becomes the plaintiff, so far as the exception is concerned. [8]

[1] Clem. Saepe 2, De V. S. (v. 11.)   [2] L. c., n. 65.
[3] Ib., n. 68.   [4] Ex L. 2 ff. de Prob. (xxii. 3); L. 1, C. de Prob. (iv. 19).
[5] Cap. 36, de Jurejur. (ii. 24).   [6] Bcuix, l. c., p. 306.
[7] L. 9. 19 ff. de Probat.   [8] Devoti, l. 3, t. 9, § 2.

Art. II.

Of Judicial Proofs in Particular.

1. *Of Confession (De Confessione).*

820. Canonists, following the order of the Decretals, usually treat of confession before they enter upon the discussion of the other proofs. The reason is that where a defendant, in a proper manner, acknowledges the truth or justice of what is alleged against him, no further proof is needed, and the plaintiff or prosecuting party is relieved of all necessity of submitting further proofs.

821. Confession (*confessio*), as here understood, is the acknowledgment by a person, in or out of court, of the truth and justice of what is charged or asserted by the opposing party.[1] As will be seen from this definition, confession is divided into judicial and extrajudicial. Judicial confession (*confessio judicialis*) is that which is made in court (*in jure, in judicio*)—i.e., before the competent judge and during the trial or judicial proceedings. Extrajudicial (*confessio extrajudicialis*) is that which takes place out of court.[2] Whether and when the accused, if interrogated by the judge as to his guilt, is bound to answer, we shall discuss later.[3]

822. What is the chief effect of a judicial confession? Judicial confession is justly termed the queen of proofs, being the most perfect of all proofs. Hence it ends the trial, and relieves the plaintiff or prosecuting party of the necessity of giving further proofs. For there can be no better proof than that which proceeds from one's own

[1] Schmalzg., l. ii., t. 18, n. 1.   [2] Reiff., lib. ii., t. 18, n. 4.
[3] Cf. Schmalzg., l. c., n. 3.

mouth.[1]   However, in order that it may have this effect, it
should be possessed chiefly of these qualities: 1. It should
be made by a person who is twenty-five years old ;[2] 2. with
entire liberty, not from fear; 3. from certain knowledge—
that is, not from error or want of deliberation;[3] 4. in court
(*in jure*)—that is, before the competent judge while holding
court.   We say, first, *before the judge ;* hence a confession
made before an arbitrator, in the broad sense, is not judicial.
But that which is made before arbitrators in the proper
sense, whether they be voluntary or necessary, is a judicial
confession.   The reason is that arbitrators proper take cognizance of matters like judges proper.   We say, secondly,
while holding court ; for the confession is not considered as
made in court (*in jure*) simply because it is made before the
judge, but only when it is made before him while holding
court.[4]   5. During the trial (*in judicio*).   6. With clearness
and definiteness.[5]

823. What are the chief effects of extrajudicial confession ?
Before answering directly, we observe that we speak of
extrajudicial confession, *as properly proved.*   In other words,
it must first be lawfully shown—*v.g.*, by two witnesses who
were present when the confession was made,[6] or by writing
—that the confession really took place.   Otherwise, if a person denies that he has ever made the confession imputed to
him, it will have no weight whatever, until the opponent
proves that it has really been made.[7]   We now answer
directly.   In civil causes an extrajudicial confession constitutes full proof, if it is made in the presence of the adversary,
and is at the same time specific—*i.e.*, expresses the origin or

---

[1] Cap. 2, de Capell. mon. (iii. 37); cap. 10 (iii. 2); cap. 24 (v. 11); Schmalzg.
l. c., n. 20.

[2] L. 6 ff., de Conf. (42. 2).   [3] Can. 1, c. 15, q. 6.

[4] L. un. C. de Confessis; L. 11 ff. de Just. et jur. (i. 1); Reiff., l. c., n. 7.

[5] Schmalzg., l. c., n. 10-16; Devoti, l. 3, t. 9, § 4.

[6] Cap. 23. de Testibus.   [7] Reiff., l. c., n. 36.

cause of the obligation; *v.g.*, if it is worded thus: I owe Titius $100, by reason of a loan he gave me.' In criminal causes, such confession constitutes, indeed, a grave presumption, but not full and sufficient proof.' Hence the accused in the case cannot be convicted or condemned on such confession.'

ART. III.

2. *Of Witnesses (De Testibus)*.

824. When the truth or facts in a case cannot be elicited by the confession of the defendant, recourse must be had to other proofs. Of these, the testimony of witnesses is the most important, as well as the one most frequently employed. Speaking in general, witnesses (*testes*) are persons made use of to show the truth of a thing which is being disputed. There are three kinds of witnesses: judicial, instrumental, and testamentary, according as they testify in judicial proceedings, or attest an instrument, or a will.' Judicial witnesses, of whom alone we here speak, are persons worthy of belief, lawfully called or summoned to testify in court, or before the judge holding court, on the facts or questions in dispute.'

825. *Q.* Who can be witnesses in ecclesiastical courts, also in the United States?

A. The rule is that all persons can act as witnesses who are not expressly excluded by law.' By "law" we here mean (*a*) the natural law; (*b*) the positive law. The latter consists of canon law proper, and of the Roman or civil law, as adopted by the Church. Who, then, are excluded by the

---

[1] Cap. 14, de Fide instr. (ii. 22); Reiff., l. c., n. 37.
[2] Ex cap. 25, de Rescript. (i. 3). [3] Schmalzg., l. c., n. 28.
[4] Schmalzg., l. 2, t. 20. n. 1.
[5] Soglia, l. 4, § 39. vol. ii., p. 293 (ed. Vecchiotti).
[6] Cap. 1, de Test. (ii. 20); Glossa, ib. v. idonei.

law of nature? All those who are deprived of the use of reason, such as madmen, lunatics, imbeciles, infants, etc.[1] Who are disqualified by positive law—*i.e.*, the law of the Church? Some are disqualified absolutely, others only in part—namely, so far as concerns certain persons or causes. We proceed to treat of both classes.

826. What persons are absolutely (*i.e.*, in all causes, civil and criminal) disqualified by the law of the Church? Chiefly three classes: 1. Those who labor under a defect of age—namely, persons under the age of fourteen (*impuberes*).[2] 2. Those who have certain bodily defects. Thus, as a rule, those who are blind, deaf, or dumb, are disqualified.[3] 3. Those who are defective, so far as their character or morals are concerned—namely, (*a*) those who have been bribed, (*b*) or hired to give testimony.[4] (*c*) Those who are infamous (*infames*), whether by law or by fact.[5] The exceptions are given by Schmalzgrueber.[6] (*d*) Those who are under judicial investigation for crime. For they cannot, so long as their cause is pending and their innocence not shown,[7] act as witnesses in criminal causes. (*e*) Those against whom a grave offence is objected and proven by the opposing party, even though they had not before been prosecuted for or judicially convicted of such offence.[8] (*f*) Perjurers.[9] (*g*) Persons under major excommunication.[10] A distinction, however, is to be made between excommunicates who are to be shunned (*vitandi*), and those who are not to be avoided (*tolerati*). The latter can be admitted as witnesses by the judge, provided the opposing party does not object. But the former must be rejected, even though no objection is made against them by the opponent.[11] (*h*) Finally, persons

[1] Schmalzg., l. c., n. 3.
[2] Can. Testes 1, c. 4, q. 3; L. 19 ff. de Testibus.
[3] Schmalzg., l. c., n. 7.
[4] L. 3 ff. de Test.
[5] Cap. 47, de Test.
[6] L. c., n. 17.
[7] Cap. 56, de Test.
[8] Cap. 54, de Test.; München, l. c., vol. i., p. 132.
[9] Cap. 54. cit.
[10] Cap 38, de Test.; cap. 8, de Sent. exc., in 6°.
[11] Schmalzg., l. c., n. 26.

who are very poor, and of low station in life, by reason of their being presumed to be liable to being easily bribed.[1] Where, however, they bear a good reputation, this suspicion or presumption does not hold.

827. What persons are disqualified by ecclesiastical law, as witnesses, *only in part—i.e.*, only in regard to certain causes or persons? We observe that of those persons who are disqualified only in part, some are forbidden to testify *in favor of*, others *against* certain persons; others in certain causes. Who, then, are forbidden to testify in favor of certain persons? 1. Parents in favor of their children, and *vice versa;*[2] because their mutual love renders their testimony suspected. There are, however, exceptions to this rule, which may be seen in Schmalzgrueber.[3] 2. Brothers and all other relatives, whether by consanguinity or affinity, to the fourth degree exclusive;[4] members of the same household, such as domestics, cannot, as a rule, testify in favor of each other; because, as the can. 12, c. 3, q. 5, says: "Propinquitatis vel familiaritatis ac dominationis affectio veritatem impedire solet."[5] Where, however, these persons are of a specially good character, so that it may be safely assumed that they will tell the truth, without regard to their feelings, or where they are the best, or even only persons, who can testify on a certain matter,—*v.g.*, as to the age, relationship, or legitimate birth,—their testimony is admissible. Other exceptions may be seen in Schmalzgrueber.[6] 3. Advocates and procurators, in matters concerning their clients or principals.

828. Who are chiefly prohibited from giving testimony *against certain persons?* 1. Accomplices or associates in crime cannot testify against each other,[7] except (*a*) where the crime necessarily supposes accomplices—*v.g.*, fornication;

---

[1] Can. Si testes 3, c. 4, q. 3; L. 3 ff. de Testibus   [2] L. 9 ff. de Test.
[3] L. c., n. 30.   [4] Schmalzg., l. c., n. 31.   [5] Cf. cap. 24, de Test.
[6] L. c., n. 30, 32, 36.   [7] Cap. 10, de Test.

(*b*) in what are called *crimina excepta*, such as simony. However, even where the testimony of an accomplice is received,
it is to be regarded as that of a low, infamous, and suspected
person.[1] 2. Nor can an enemy testify against his enemy;[2]
nor Jews, pagans, and heretics against Catholics;[3] chiefly
because of their supposed hatred against the latter.[4] 4. Nor
laics against ecclesiastics, in criminal causes, and that partly
because of the supposed antipathy, or even hostility, of the
former to the latter, but especially because of the respect
due the ecclesiastical state.[5] This is the rule, which, however,
has its exceptions. Thus a lay person can testify against
an ecclesiastic where there is question (*a*) of the crimes
called *crimina excepta,*—namely, heresy, simony, and high trea-
son ; (*b*) and of other scandalous and notorious crimes—*v.g.*
theft ; (*c*) where there are no ecclesiastics who have a knowledge of the facts; (*d*) where a lay person's interest, temporal or
spiritual, is involved. Thus a parishioner can testify against
his parish priest, because it is to his spiritual interest to have a
good rector.[6] However, even in this case, a laic is not regarded as a witness *omni exceptione major*, unless his testimony
is fully corroborated by a witness who is an ecclesiastic. 5.
Finally, persons who are united by some special tie, whether
of relationship, or duty, or business, cannot testify against
each other.[7] Thus, parents cannot testify against their children ; nor near relatives against each other ; nor advocates
against their clients; nor intimate friends against their
friends.[8] The reason is, chiefly, that the Church wishes those
bounds which so greatly influence human intercourse, and promote the welfare of society, to be respected and kept sacred.[8]

[1] Schmalzg., l. c., n. 41.
[2] Cap. 13 et 19. de Accus. (v. 1); L. 17, C. de Test. (iv. 20).
[3] Can. 24 et 26, c. 2, q. 7.   [4] München, Can. Trials, vol. l., p. 131.
[5] Cap. 3, in 6° (iii. 23); cap. 33 (ii. 20).
[6] Schmalzg., l. c., n. 50.   [7] Can. 3. c. 4, q. 3; L. 6, C. de Test.
[8] München, l. c., p. 141.   [8] Ib.; Schmalzg., l. c., n. 51.

829. Who are prohibited from being witnesses *in certain causes*, and what are these causes? 1. Minors under the age of twenty cannot testify in criminal causes,[1] while, as we said above, those under the age of fourteen cannot testify in *any cause*. 2. Ecclesiastics and religious cannot be witnesses against laics or even other ecclesiastics in secular courts, *in causa sanguinis*.[2] We say, first, *in secular courts;* for they can testify against seculars, and also, *a fortiori*, against other ecclesiastics, in ecclesiastical courts, and that even in criminal causes. We say, secondly, *in causa sanguinis*[3]—that is, in causes or trials where there is question of inflicting the penalty of death or of bodily mutilation.[4] For in civil causes, or even in criminal, which are either civilly tried *or* not punishable by death or bodily mutilation, ecclesiastics may be witnesses before the secular courts, provided it be with the leave of their bishop.[5] They may, moreover, be witnesses in these courts, even *in causa sanguinis*, for the defence—that is, for the purpose of showing the innocence of the accused. Finally, they can testify in such courts even without the bishop's consent, in matters relating to testaments, instruments, and contracts of laics.[6]

830. 3. Women cannot, as a rule, be witnesses in ecclesiastical courts in criminal causes.[7] The reason is, that a woman is, by her very nature, inconstant and changeable. Hence, as Pope Gregory I. says, "Varium et mutabile testimonium semper foemina producit."[8] We say, *as a rule;* for sometimes women, as well as other objectionable witnesses, can testify in criminal causes—namely, (a) in regard to what are called *crimina excepta;*[9] (b) where the testimony of men cannot be had; (c) where the judge proceeds *ex officio* by way of

---

[1] L. 20 ff. de Test. [2] Ex can. 9, c. 11, q. 1; Glossa., ib. v recipiat.
[3] München, l. c., p. 133. [4] Reiff., l. c., n. 170. [5] Can. 2, c. 14, q. 2.
[6] Schmalzg., l. c., n. 55. [7] Can. 17, c. 33, q. 5.
[8] Cap. Forus 10, de V. S. (v. 40): Glossa, ib. v. non foemina, et v. varium.
[9] Supra, n. 828.

inquiry, or *per modum inquisitionis;* (*d*) for the purpose of showing the innocence of the accused ; (*e*) where the crime is being tried civilly.[1] Observe, even when women are admitted, their testimony is always to be regarded as that of witnesses not above all suspicion.[2] We say, secondly, *in criminal causes;* for in civil causes their testimony is admitted.[3]

831. Nobody can be witness in his own cause[4]—namely, in a cause in which he is interested in such manner that if he testifies he will be benefited, and if he does not, he will suffer, whether in his honor, feelings, property, etc.[5] Hence the following persons are chiefly excluded : 1. Those who have a cause similar to that in which they are to testify;[6] 2. A judge in a cause which he adjudicates or has adjudicated;[7] 3. Procurators or advocates in causes which they represent or defend.[8] Whether and when bishops and other ecclesiastics can be witnesses in causes relating to the churches of which they have charge, see Reiffenstuel.[9]

832. We observe here that the witnesses whom we have enumerated as disqualified in part—*i.e.,* in regard to certain persons or causes—may indeed be allowed to testify even out of the cases already incidentally mentioned—*v.g.,* if the opposing party does not object, or if the facts can thereby be more fully elicited. But their testimony is always to be regarded as that of *testes minus idonei,* or witnesses not above all suspicion ; and consequently the testimony of two such witnesses does not constitute full proof, but only a presumption.[10]

833. How many witnesses are required in order to prove a thing? Two witnesses are, as a rule, requisite and sufficient, provided they are above all suspicion or objection,

---

[1] Schmalzg., l. c., n. 56.   [2] Ib., n. 52.   [3] Cap. 3 et 22 et 33, de Test.
[4] L. 10 ff. de Testibus; L. 10, C. eod.   [5] Schmalzg., l. c., n. 62.
[6] Cap. 20, de Test.   [7] Can. 1 et 2, c. 4. q. 4; cap. Forus, cit.; cap. 40, de Test.
[8] Cap. 4, de Test.   [9] L. c., n. 197.
[10] Schmalzg., l. c., n. 52; München, l. c., p. 136.

and are *contestes—i.e.*, agree in their testimony.[1] We say, first, "are, as a rule, *sufficient;*" for there are cases where the Church prescribes a greater number. Thus, in matrimonial causes, where there is question of dissolving a marriage because of the impediment of impotency, the latter must be proved by the oath of both the husband and wife, and of seven relations or neighbors.[2] We say, secondly, "are, as a rule, *required;*" for, generally speaking, one witness, even though he be above all suspicion, and clothed with the highest dignities, does not constitute full proof.[3] The reason is that a single individual may easily be deceived or led into error or corrupted. This rule holds good not only by virtue of ecclesiastical, but even of divine law, according to the words of our Lord: "That in the mouth of *two or three witnesses* every word may stand."[4] Hence no statute, custom, or law, even of the Pope, can establish the contrary.[5] So far as criminal causes are concerned, this rule has no exceptions whatever, even at the present day. Hence in such causes the testimony of at least two competent witnesses is always required for conviction.[6] As to the sense in which one witness is sufficient in causes of solicitation, see below, n. 1650.

834. In civil causes (we speak, of course, of civil causes pertaining to the ecclesiastical forum), however, two witnesses are not always necessary. Thus one witness is sufficient, 1, in favorable matters or causes which do not redound to any one's prejudice or injury—*v.g.*, where it is doubted whether a church is consecrated, or a dying person has asked for the confessor, or whether a person is baptized, or has the legitimate age for the reception of holy orders. 2. In matrimonial causes, when there is question of hinder-

---

[1] Can. Si testes 3, c. 4, q. 3; cap. 4 et 23, de Test.; L. 12 ff. De Test.: L. 9, Cod. de Test. [2] Cap. 5 et 7, de Frig. et malef. (iv. 15).

[3] L. 12 ff. cit.; L. 9, Cod. cit.; cap. 10, 23, 28, de Test.

[4] Matt. xviii. 16, cf. Deut. xvii. 6; ib. xix. 6; Reiff., l. c., n. 249.

[5] Schmalzg., l. c., n. 69. [6] Bouix, de Jud., t. i., p. 311.

ing a marriage from being contracted on account of an annulling impediment.[1] 3. Where an official or public minister testifies to an act performed by himself—*v.g.*, a notary concerning an instrument made by him ; a bishop in regard to his official acts ; a rector or parish priest respecting baptisms or other official acts performed by him.[2] 4. The testimony of *one expert* is sufficient, if more than one cannot be easily consulted.[3]

835. We said, thirdly, *provided they are above all suspicion or objection ;*[4] hence the witnesses must be such that no objection whatever can be made against them, whether in regard to their person or their deposition. The objections that may be urged against their persons have been already explained by us above.[5] Those which may be advanced against their depositions or testimony are chiefly : 1. That they did not give a sufficient cause for the facts testified to by them ; 2. That they did not agree in their testimony : 3. That they testified, not from their own personal knowledge, but merely from hearsay : all of which we shall explain further on.[6] We said, fourthly, *and are contestes— i.e.*, agree, etc.; this phrase we shall explain below.

836. *Q.* How are the depositions of witnesses to be received, or how are witnesses to be examined ?

A. 1. The plaintiff or prosecutor (*v.g.*, according to the Instruction of July 20, 1878, Art. II., the bishop's official ; according to the Instruction *Cum Magnopere*, Art. XIII., the *procurator fiscalis*'), or the defendant who wishes to produce the witnesses, gives the latters' names to the judge, auditor, or Commission of Investigation where this body still exists. The judge, auditor, or Commission then summons them to

---

[1] Cap. 22, de Test.
[2] Ex cap. 19, de Appell. (ii. 28); ib., Glossa, v. suus nuntius.
[3] Schmalzg., l. c., n. 70.   [4] Supra, n. 833.
[5] Supra, n. 825 sq.   [6] Cf. Schmalzg., l. c., n. 71 ; infra, n.
[7] Instr., 20 julii, 1878, § 2, Instr. *Cum Magnopere*, Art. XIII.

appear and give their testimony, allowing them a reasonable time to refresh their memory and prepare for their testimony.   Here it may be asked whether a witness is worthy of belief (*fide dignus*) when he comes into court, or appears before the Commission, where this body still exists, and testifies, without having been cited by the judge to do so?   We distinguish.   Such a witness has either been asked to give testimony by the plaintiff or defendant, or he has presented himself without being thus asked, simply out of alleged love of justice or truth.   In the first case, he cannot be rejected.   In the second, his testimony is, as a rule, suspected, and by no means above all suspicion.   The reason is chiefly, that such a one shows a singular leaning and affection toward the person in whose favor he wishes to testify, and is consequently objectionable.[1]   We said above, *then the judge summons them.*   This must not be understood in the sense that the judge should always issue a formal summons, or, as it is called in our secular courts, a *subpœna.*   The phrase means that the judge either allows the party to produce the witnesses, or issues a formal citation either where the witnesses are unwilling to come at the sole request of the parties, or where it is customary for the judge always to cite the witnesses.[2]

837. 2. The rule is that before the witnesses are allowed to give their testimony the party against whom they are produced must be cited to be present, so as to be able to object against the admission of the witnesses if he wishes. Otherwise the testimony will be of no force whatever. Thus Pope Gregory IX. says: "Ecce admonendus est semper adversarius, ut ad audiendos testes veniat."[3]   The reason is that, generally speaking, a person must always be called to be present in court, when anything which concerns

---

[1] Schmalzg., l. c., n. 77; Reiff., l. c., n. 415.

[2] L. 3, § fin. ff. de Test. ; Reiff., l. c., n. 414.

[3] Cap. In nomine Dñi 2, de Test.; L. 19, Cod de Testibus.

his interests is there transacted.[1] Again, if he were not allowed to be present he would be deprived of the right to object against the admission of the witnesses. Now no one should be despoiled of any lawful means of defence.[2]

838. But it will be asked: In what sense has the party against whom the witnesses are produced the right to be present at their admission? The decretal *In Nomine Domini*, just cited, seems clearly to state that the party has the right to be present during the entire examination of the witnesses. Nevertheless canonists, following the Glossa,[3] commonly hold that he can be present only when they take the oath prior to giving their testimony, and not at the examination itself. For they say with the Glossa, according to the cap. 52, De Test., and the l. 14, C. de Test., the witnesses are to be examined apart from the parties.[4] (See Appendix XI.)

839. We say, *canonists commonly*, etc.; for there are very able canonists—*v.g.*, Devoti,[5] Craisson,[6] Todeschi[7]—who maintain that the opposite party has a right to be present also at the examination itself, and not merely at the taking of the oath. In fact, the decretal *In Nomine Dñi* repeatedly says that the party must be cited to come and *hear* the witnesses—" venire et *audire* testes." And, on the other hand, the decretals which require the witnesses to be examined *singillatim* or separately or in secret may very well be explained to mean that they should be examined apart from each other, or not in each other's hearing, lest they might enter into collusion. Hence it does not follow that they must be examined in the absence of the opposing party. This confronting of the witnesses with the party against whom they testify is at present the rule in all secular courts in the United States and elsewhere, and is introduced into some ecclesiastical courts in Europe,—*v.g.*, in France,—and

[1] L. 47 ff. de Re jud.
[2] Reiff., l. c., n. 419.
[3] In cap. 2, de Test., v. audire.
[4] Reiff., l. c., n. 421; Schmalzg., l. c., n. 83.
[5] L. 3, t. 9, § 18.
[6] N. 5714.
[7] Man. ii. 20, § 3.

is also permitted in the ecclesiastical courts of the United States,—*v.g.*, Commissions of Investigation,—provided the Commission judges it prudent and the witnesses are willing.[1]

840. 3. The witnesses must give their testimony under oath. In other words, they must, prior to deposing, swear that they will tell the truth, the whole truth, and nothing but the truth, and that they are not moved by hatred, friendship, favor, or their own interest, but solely by love of truth ;[2] and that they will not reveal their deposition to either party before its publication. This last promise is, of course, made only where the parties are excluded from the examination.[3] This oath is so necessary, that witnesses who do not depose under oath, even though they be ecclesiastics, or regulars, or high dignitaries, are not to be believed to the prejudice of a third party. Thus Pope Honorius III. says: " Nullius testimonio, quantuncunque religiosus existat, nisi juratus deposuerit, in alterius praejudicium debet credi."[4] In fact, what could be better calculated to make witnesses tell the truth than the fear and reverence inspired by the sanctity of the oath.

841. This law requiring witnesses to take the oath holds so strictly, that it is obligatory (*a*) even in summary causes; (*b*) on all witnesses whatsoever, no matter of what station, dignity, or excellence of character; (*c*) in such manner that no law or custom can generally allow of witnesses deposing without the oath. For such law or custom would be unreasonable, nay, opposed to the very law of nature, since it would open the door to many calumnies, falsehoods, and great corruption of the witnesses.[5] We said *generally;* for there are some exceptions. Thus, by custom or statute, certain persons, of great probity of character or in high dignity,

---

[1] Instr. S. C. de P. F., 20 Julii, 1878, § 12, Consentientibus.
[2] Cap. 5. 17, de Test.; Glossa, in c. 17, de Test., v. juramentis.
[3] Schmalzg., l. c., n. 87. [4] Cap. 51, de Test.; L. 9 et 18, C. de Test. (iv. 21).
[5] Reiff., l. c., n. 478; Schmalzg., l. c., n. 89.

may be—in fact, are in many places—allowed to depose without the oath. The reason is, that in their case there can be no danger of fraud, subornation, or perjury. Again, the oath may be omitted if both the parties—*i.c.*, the plaintiff and defendant—consent.[1]

842. The oath is to be administered in the presence of the judge or his deputy, who previously, with becoming dignity and uncovered head, admonishes the witnesses of the gravity of an oath, and the penalty of taking a false oath.[2] As we have already seen, the opposing party (the same holds of the other party) has a right to be present while the oath is being administered to the witnesses, and to present its objections against the admissibility of the witness.

843. In the ecclesiastical courts of the United States, as established in conformity with the latest Instruction of the S. C. de Prop. Fide, *Cum Magnopere* of 1884, the witnesses are bound to depose under oath, as is expressly stated in Art. XVIII. of this Instruction. In England, for reasons given below, n. 1345, witnesses before Commissions of Investigation do not take the oath. Can the oath be administered to witnesses before Commissions, with us, where the latter bodies still exist? According to the Instruction of 1878, it cannot.[3] But the Instruction *Cum Magnopere*,[4] by the fact that it prescribes the oath for the members of Commissions, where the latter are still in existence, would seem to allow of the oath also for witnesses. Whatever may be said, the Propaganda, to show the great importance it attaches to the oath, ordains in the Instruction of 1878, immediately after the words "non requiratur juramentum," as follows: "si testes ipsi non renuant, et se paratos esse declarent ad ea quae detulerint, juramento, data occasione, confirmanda, *fiat adnotatio hujusmodi dispositionis in actis.*"[5]

---

[1] Cap. 39, de Test.; ib., Glossa, v. remittantur.

[2] Schmalzg., l. c., n. 86.   [3] Instr. cit., § 11, Singull.

[4] Cf. Soglia, vol. ii., p. 295, ed. Vecch.   [5] Instr. cit., § 11.

In other words, the Sacred Congregation, in places where the civil law forbids ecclesiastics to administer oaths, finding it impossible or imprudent to enforce the letter of the law in this matter, wishes its spirit to be carried out.

844. 4. After the witnesses have taken the oath, they are examined, or give their testimony. Here three questions present themselves : First, How are they to be examined? second, On what matters? third, How should they depose? Let us briefly treat of each. *First,* How are witnesses to be examined? They should, as a rule, be examined (*a*) by the judge himself.[1] In the ecclesiastical courts of the United States, as constituted by the Instruction of the Propaganda, dated July 20, 1878, the witnesses are examined by the president of the Commission of Investigation, or by the other commissioners through the president.[2] (*b*) In the place where the court holds its sittings (*in jure, in loco judicii*), though where the witnesses are ladies, or nuns, or persons of distinction, or unable to come into court by reason of sickness or other hindrance, the judge or his deputy (in the ecclesiastical courts of the United States, as established by the Propaganda in 1878, at least two members of the Commission[3]) shall take the testimony at the house of the witnesses, with all the formalities which would have to be observed if the deposition were taken in court—*i.e.,* the contending parties would have to be summoned to be present, etc.[4]

845. (*c*) The testimony should be taken down by the notary very carefully, and, as far as possible, word for word.[5] In difficult causes, in order to prevent any error in the record, many eminent canonists say it is advisable to allow, besides the notary, two worthy and discreet persons to be present and take minutes or notes of the examination.[6]

---

[1] Ex L. 3 ff. de Test.; Nov. 60, cap. 2.   [2] Instr. cit., § 11, Singuli.
[3] Instr. cit.. § 15, Quod si testes.
[4] Cap. 2, de Jud.. in 6° (ii. 1); Reiff., l. c., n. 504.
[5] Cap. 37 et 52, de Test.; Reiff., l. c., n. 508.   [6] Reiff., 1. c., n. 501.

(*d*) When the witness has finished his testimony, it should be
read for him, especially if he desires it, by the notary, so that
he may see whether he has been rightly understood, and also
that he may correct whatever he may have said erroneously
or inconsiderately.' (*e*) Finally, he should be cautioned to
keep silence regarding his deposition.

846. *Secondly,* On what matters should witnesses be examined? 1. First, certain general questions (*interrogatoria
generalia*) should be put to them—namely, what their age is,
their occupation, whether they have any interest in the case,
whether they are enemies or friends of the party for whom
they are about to testify, and the like. 2. Next they should
be examined on the cause itself—that is, not only on the principal facts in the case, but also on all the particulars or circumstances; on the time, place, persons, etc. Thus Pope
Innocent III. says: "Mandamus quatenus recipias testes
quos utraque pars . . . duxerit producendos, ac eos diligenter examinari procures; et de singulis prudenter inquirens,
de causis videlicet, personis, loco, tempore, visu, auditu,
scientia, credulitate, fama, certitudine, cuncta plene con-
scribas."* Hence they are to be interrogated, among other
things, not only whether they know the facts in the case,
but also how they came to know them—namely, whether
they were eye or ear witnesses, etc. In other words, they
should be asked to give reasons for their statements.

847. Here we observe, that the judge (we speak of the
ecclesiastical judge) cannot, either in civil or criminal causes,
ask any leading question (*quaestio suggestiva*)—that is, a question so framed as to indicate the answer desired—*v.g.*, Did
you see Titius killing Caius on such a day and in such a
place?' Hence the examination of the witnesses must be by
general questions, ascending gradually to the more particular
matters or facts in the case. The same holds true of the

---

¹ Schmalzg., l. c., n. 96.   ² Cap. 37, de Test.   ³ Reiff., l. c., n. 516–519.

examination of an *accused* in criminal causes. Hence the judge—or, as the case may be, the Commission of Investigation, with us—should not at once ask the accused, *v.g.*, whether he killed Caius. But he should begin by first asking general questions—*v.g.*, whether he knows Caius, or was present when he was killed; whether he had any quarrel with him, and thus gradually come to the crime itself.[1]

848. *Thirdly*, How should a witness give his testimony? 1. In person and orally, not merely in writing. The law of the Church expressly says: " Testes, per quamcunque scripturam testimonium non proferant, sed praesentes de his, quae noverunt et viderunt, veraciter testimonium dicant."[2] The reason is, that the judge, especially in criminal causes, is greatly aided in estimating the value of the testimony, by the countenance, behavior, etc., of the witness.[3] 2. His testimony should be clear, definite, and certain, not vague or doubtful. Hence, if he speaks doubtfully,—*v.g.*, if he says, " I believe, I think, unless I am mistaken, if I remember correctly," etc.,—his testimony should be rejected. 3. Finally, he should adhere to his testimony, not vary or change, now saying one thing, then another; much less should he contradict himself.[4]

849. *Q.* What are *testes singulares ?*

A. Witnesses are called (*a*) concordant (*contestes*) when they agree in their testimony; that is, when they testify concordantly to one and the same fact—*v.g.*, that they saw Titius killing Caius in such a place and at such a time; (*b*) singular (*testes singulares*), when they testify to two different acts or facts, so that each one is, so to say, alone in his testimony. This singularity or disagreement may regard (*a*) the material facts in the case—*v.g.*, if one of the witnesses testifies that Titius stole a cow, another that he stole a horse

---

[1] Reiff., l. c., n. 528.   [2] Can. Testes 15, C. 3, q. 9; et Can. 3, C. 5, q. 2.
[3] München, l. c., vol. i., p. 146.
[4] Reiff., l. c., n. 313; Schmalzg., l. c., n. 102.

(*b*) the quantity—*v.g.*, if one asserts that Titius stole a hundred, another only five dollars; (*c*) the quality—*v.g.*, if one says that the horse sold to Sempronius was lame, another that he was sound; (*d*) time and place—*v.g.*, where one witness states that the crime was committed on such a day, another on another day, etc.[1]

850. *Q.* Now, do singular witnesses prove anything?

A. We premise: Witnesses may be singular or disagree in three ways. *First*, by directly contradicting each other in regard to the same fact—*v.g.*, when one of them says the theft was committed in such a place or at such a time, another in another place or at another time. *Secondly*, by testifying to two different acts or occurrences, which, however, converge to one central or main fact—that is, tend to prove one and the same thing—if one deposes that he saw Titius stealing the horse, another that he heard Titius confessing he had stolen the horse. Here, as is manifest, while the depositions refer to two different specifications, they nevertheless help each other in proving the same crime or *corpus delicti*. *Thirdly*, by testifying to two different acts or facts having no connection with or opposition to each other, and consequently not tending to prove the same thing—*v.g.*, if one says Titius murdered Caius, another that he killed Sempronius.[2]

851. We now answer: Witnesses of the first kind, no matter how numerous, even though there were a thousand, prove nothing whatever.[3] In fact, when we said above[4] that two witnesses constitute full proof, we added, *provided they agree in their testimony*. In regard to witnesses of the second class, a distinction must be drawn between civil and criminal causes. In civil causes they sometimes constitute full proof (*probatio plena*), sometimes only half or imperfect

[1] Reiff., l. c., n. 283.   [2] Reiff., l. c., n. 288; Schmalzg., l. c., n. 105.
[3] Cap. 9, de Probat. (ii. 19); Schmalzg., l. c., n. 106.   [4] Supra, n. 833.

(*probatio semiplena*); in other words, a sufficient number of such witnesses—*v.g.*, two—sometimes establishes a thing fully, sometimes only imperfectly, just as though they agreed in each and every particular.[1] In criminal causes, however, they do not constitute full proof, but merely a presumption.[2] The reason is that in these causes the evidence must be as clear as the noonday sun, and in every respect perfect, full, and unobjectionable.[3] Hence, in criminal causes, two or more witnesses who in any way disagree do not suffice for conviction. This holds, of course, also in the United States, for the simple reason that every person is entitled to be considered innocent until he is fully, clearly, and juridically proven guilty. Witnesses of the third class, no matter how numerous, constitute only an imperfect, not a perfect proof.

852. *Q.* What is the force of the testimony of contradictory witnesses (*testes contrarii*)?

A. A witness may be contradictory in two ways: by contradicting (*a*) himself, or (*b*) other witnesses. In the latter case it is important to see whether the contradictory witnesses have been produced by one and the same party or by different parties. Where they are produced for and by the different parties,—namely, some by and for the plaintiff, others by and for the defendant, and are equal in number on both sides—in other words, where the number of witnesses denying is equal to the number affirming a thing, sentence must be pronounced, other things being equal, in favor of the accused or defendant, except in the causes of marriage, dower, liberty, etc.[4] Where they are produced by the same party,—*v.g.*, by the plaintiff,—we must again distinguish: Either this party produces but two witnesses, and these contradict each other; or he produces a greater number, of

---

[1] Arg. ex l. 16, Cod. de Poenis (9. 47): Schmalzg., l. c. [2] Reiff., l. c., n. 307.
[3] L. 25, Cod. de Probat. (4. 19); Can. 39, c. 2, q. 7. [4] Ex cap. 3, de Probat.

whom two or more agree in their testimony. In the first
case, the two witnesses prove nothing whatever; in the
second, the testimony of the two concordant witnesses constitutes proof, though it is manifest that their testimony if
weakened by the contradictory assertion of their fellow-
witnesses.[1] Coming now to the case of a witness contra
dicting himself, it is certain that the testimony of a witness
who expressly contradicts himself in his judicial deposition
is of no value whatever,[2] unless he forthwith corrects himself.[3]

853. *Q.* Do hearsay witnesses (*testes de auditu alieno*)
prove anything?

A. We premise: 1. By hearsay witnesses (*testes de auditu
alieno*) we mean those who depose that they have heard the
facts from others worthy of belief.[4] Contradistinguished
from these witnesses are what are called *testes de scientia*—
that is, witnesses who testify of their own personal knowledge; in other words, witnesses who testify to what they
have learned through their own senses—*v.g.*, by their eyes or
ears. Thus a witness who testifies that he *saw* Titius killing
Caius or *heard* him blaspheming, is a witness *de scientia*.[5]
2. Now, by the law of the Church, only those are proper
and competent witnesses who belong to the latter class, or
who have received the knowledge of the facts in the case
through their own senses, and not from others. This is clear
from the Can. Testes 15, C. 3, Q. 9, where Pope Callistus,
writing to the Bishops of France, says: "Nec de aliis causis
vel negotiis dicant" (testes) "testimonium, nisi de his, *quae
sub praesentia eorum acta esse noscuntur.*" The very title
of this canon is: "Testes non dicant testimonium nisi de his
quae *praesentialiter* et veraciter noverunt."

854. We now answer: Hearsay witnesses are not wit-

<hr/>

[1] Schmalzg., l. c., n. 107; Reiff., l. c., n. 322 sq.
[2] Can. 3, q. 9; et can. 23, q. 7; cap. 34, de Appell   [3] Cap. 7, de Test. cog. (il. 21)
[4] Reiff., L c., n. 346.   [5] Ib., n. 342.

nesses in the proper sense, and, no matter how numerous, do not, as a rule, prove anything, but constitute at most a presumption.[1] This applies more particularly to criminal causes. For in these causes hearsay witnesses not only do not prove anything, but do not even constitute a presumption against the accused. For, as we have frequently said, in criminal causes the proofs must be altogether certain and unobjectionable.

We have said, *as a rule;* for there are some exceptions. Thus, among other cases, hearsay witnesses are admissible also in criminal causes: (*a*) in matters which are difficult of proof, *v.g.*, in occult crimes;[2] (*b*) for the defence of the accused.[3] See also the Instruction *Cum Magnopere*, Art. XX.

855. What is meant by the *publicatio attestationum?* When the examination of the witnesses is finished, a day is appointed by the judge on which the depositions, together with the names[4] of the witnesses, are read in the hearing of the contending parties—namely, the plaintiff and defendant. This is called *publicatio attestationum*, or the communication of the depositions and testimony to the parties. Both the litigants must be cited to be present at this act. The reason is, that the parties must always be cited whenever anything which affects them or is likely to be prejudicial to them is transacted in court. After the publication of the testimony, the judge, at the request of the parties, is bound to give them a copy of these depositions, as taken down by the notary, in order to enable them to except to the testimony if they wish.[5]

856. Here the question arises: What objections or exceptions can be made against witnesses after their depositions have been published or read before the parties? We distinguish between three kinds of exceptions: 1. Some, as we have seen,[6] regard the *persons* of the witnesses—*v.g.*, when it

---

[1] Reiff., l. c., n. 360. [2] Ib., n. 369. [3] Schmalzg., l. c., n. 112.
[4] In causes of heresy the names of the witnesses are not made known.
[5] Schmalzg., l. c., n. 116. [6] Supra, n. 825–833.

is objected that the witness is disqualified because of his enmity, bad reputation, etc. 2. Others have reference to the *mode of examination—v.g.*, when it is objected that the witnesses have not been examined under oath (where the oath is obligatory), or not apart from each other.[1] 3. Others, finally, relate to the testimony itself—*v.g.*, when the objection is raised that the testimony is vague, indefinite, contradictory, not to the point, etc.[2]

857. We now answer: Exceptions of the third class—namely, those which are advanced against the testimony itself—can evidently be made only after the publication of the testimony, for the simple reason that this testimony does not become known (in case the parties are not allowed to be present at the examination of the witnesses)[3] to the parties before that time. Exceptions of the second class—that is, exceptions against the mode of examination—can be made, as appears from the nature of the case, partly before and partly after the publication. But exceptions of the first class, or exceptions against the persons of the witnesses, must, as a rule, be made before the publication of the depositions; in other words, they must be made when the witness, as we have seen,[4] is about to take the oath, prior to deposing.[5] The reason is chiefly, that there is ground to fear that after the witness's deposition becomes known, the party against whom he has testified, being irritated by the adverse testimony, will maliciously try to invent causes of suspicion against the witness.[6]

858. We have said, *as a rule;* for there are three cases where exceptions can be made against the persons of the witnesses, even after the publication of their testimony—namely, 1. where the defendant or accused has, prior to the examination of the witness, or the publication of his testi-

---

[1] Supra, n. 836–844. [2] Supra, n. 846–849. [3] Cf. supra, n. 840, 841.
[4] Supra, n. 837. [5] Cap. 31, de Test. [6] Schmalzg., l. c., n. 128, 129.

mony, reserved, as is now usually done, the right to make such objections. 2. If the facts upon which the objection is based—*v.g.*, the fact that the witness has been bribed, is infamous, etc.—become known to the defendant only after the publication of the testimony. 3. Where the defendant gives under oath a reasonable excuse for not having sooner made the objection ; nay, when there is question of absolute disability of the witness—*v.g.*, where the witnesses are excommunicates *vitandi*, or infamous by law, he can object to them, even though he does not allege any excuse under oath, as just stated.[1] *Note.*—It is advisable, as a rule, to object first against the deposition or the mode of examination of the witness, and only afterwards, if the force of his testimony cannot be otherwise broken down, against his person.[2]

859. We observe that, ordinarily, exceptions against a witness do not hinder his being admitted and examined, the judge being vested with discretionary power to defer his decision on the exception to the end of the trial.[3] The reason is, that during the progress of the trial it may become apparent that there is sufficient other evidence, exclusive of that of the witnesses in question, to enable the judge to decide the cause, and that, consequently, it is useless to dispute about the admissibility of the objectionable witnesses.[4] We say, *ordinarily ;* for there are some exceptions, of which the following are chiefly to be noted : 1. Where a defect or disability is objected to a witness, which is notorious, or at least can be proved without delay ;[5] 2. Where there is a presumption of law against the witness ; 3. Where the witness is accused of being a deadly enemy of the person against whom he is produced ;[6] or that he is *excommunicatus vitandus.*[7]

860. Can witnesses be compelled to testify in eccle-

[1] Ex cap. 31, cit., de Test. (ii. 20); Schmalzg., l. c., n. 129.
[2] Schmalzg., l. c., n. 135. [3] Auth. Si Testes, Cod. de Test.
[4] Schmalzg., l. c., n. 136. [5] Cap. 7, de Test.
[6] Authent., cit. [7] Cap. 2, de Excep., in 6°.

siastical courts?   They can, and that by censures—namely,
excommunication in the case of laics, and suspension, excommunication, and dismissal in the case of ecclesiastics.   Pope
Alexander III. thus lays down the law, which is still in force:
" Mandamus quatenus testes ab alterutra partium in suae
assertionis testimonium invocatos, ne veritatem occultent,
diligentius moneas et inducas.   Si autem odio vel gratia,
vel timore se subtrahant, *eos ad ferendum testimonium* . . .
ecclesiastica districtione compellas."[1]   However, before recourse is had to compulsory measures or censures, suasion
should be employed, as is evident from the above decretal of
Alexander III.[2]   Where censures have to be resorted to,
they must be preceded by the usual warning or *monitio
canonica.*[3]   We observe, however, that it is scarcely advisable
at the present day to make use of censures to compel witnesses to testify in ecclesiastical courts.   For these penalties,
as Card. Soglia[4] says, are not unfrequently disregarded by
the laity.

861. Do the above laws, authorizing ecclesiastical courts
to compel witnesses to testify, and that even under pain of
censure, apply also in the United States?   They do, at least
per se.   The reason is, the common good requires here, as
elsewhere, that the ecclesiastical judge should have power
to compel witnesses to testify, " ne veritas occultetur, et ne
malus ut bonus aestimetur."[5]   We say, *per se;* for it is manifest, for the reason given already, that it were hardly advisable to resort to compulsion or censures in this country.
Hence, also, the Instruction of the S. C. de Prop. Fide,
July 20, 1878, ordains that where witnesses are unwilling to
come and testify before the Commission of Investigation,

---

[1] Cap. 1, de Test. cog. (ii. 21); cf. ib., cap. 2, 3, 4, 5, 6, 7, 8, 9, 10, 11; L.
16 et 19, C. de Test. (iv. 20); Reiff., l. 2, t. 21, n. 2; Schmalzg., l. 2, t. 21,
n. 1.

[2] Cf. cap. 3, de Test. cog.   [3] München, l. c., vol. i., p. 140.
[4] Inst., vol. ii., p. 295, ed. Vecch.   [5] Reiff., l. c., n. 5.

the latter body shall appoint at least two of its members to go to the witnesses for the purpose of obtaining all the information possible. Here are the words of the Instruction: "Quod si testes nolint . . . Consilio assistere . . . duo saltem ex Consilio deputentur, qui testes adeuntes . . . relationem suae investigationis, ad Consilium deferant . . ." [1]

862. But in case it were deemed advisable to compel witnesses to testify before our Commissions of Investigations, the mode of procedure would seem to be this: The Commission having the right to summon witnesses,[2] has also the right and duty to declare them contumacious,—*i.e.*, in contempt of the Commission, in case they refuse to appear, without alleging any reasonable excuse, and to report this contumacy to the bishop, whose right and duty it is to inflict upon the recalcitrant witnesses the proper ecclesiastical censures, after due warning. As to compelling witnesses to testify under the Instruction *Cum Magnopere*, see our *New Procedure.*

ART. IV.

3. *Of Instruments.*

863. The next species of proofs is called instruments (*instrumenta, documenta*). By instruments we here mean any writing drawn up or produced for the purpose of proving something.[3] They are divided into public and private. A public instrument (*instrumentum publicum*), in the strict sense of the word, is one which is drawn up (*a*) by public authority—that is, by a public official, or person authorized by law, namely, by a notary; (*b*) with the requisite formalities.[4] We say, *in the strict sense;* for in a broad or general sense all instruments which have public authority, and consequently all authentic private instruments, are considered

---

[1] Instr. cit., § 15, Quod si testes. [2] Ib., § 10, Quod si ulterior.
[3] Schmalzg., l. ii., t. 22, n. 1; Devoti, l. 3, t. 9, § 20.
[4] Ex cap. 2, 6, de Fid. instrum. (ii. 22); Reiff., l. ii., t. 22, n. 7.

public instruments.[1] We say, moreover, *with the requisite formalities.* Now, what formalities are chiefly required in a public instrument proper? 1. It should begin with the invocation of the name of God, thus: In the name of God, Amen; or, In the name of the Most Holy Trinity. 2. It should be properly dated—that is, give the day, the month, and year of our Lord when the document was written. 3. It should, moreover, state the name of the reigning pope, and supreme civil ruler; the place—*i.e.*, not only city or town, but also house and street—where the transaction mentioned in the instrument took place. 4. The names also of the witnesses who were present when the transaction which the instrument records took place. Two witnesses are at least required. It is not, however, necessary that the witnesses should themselves sign the instrument, it being sufficient for the notary to mention their names in the document. 5. The notary himself must sign his name to the instrument, which should not contain any abbreviations.[2]

864. Public instruments in the proper sense of the word are divided (*a*) into protocols (*protocolla*)—that is, rough drafts or minutes of a transaction, which are afterwards written out in a fuller, clearer, and more orderly manner; (*b*) transumpts (*transumpta*)—that is, the protocols as written out in the full manner just stated, provided they (that is, the transumpts) are original and authentic.[3]

865. Private instruments (*instrumenta privata*) are those which are written *either* by a private person, *or* without the prescribed formalities.[4] They are divided into authentic and non-authentic. Authentic private instruments (*instrumenta privata authentica*) are those which are written indeed by private persons, but (*a*) are attested or signed by competent witnesses, (*b*) or bear an authentic seal, (*c*) or are authenti-

---

[1] Reiff., l. c., n. 6, 14, 16.   [2] Reiff., l. c., n. 17-29; Schmalzg., l. c., n. 13.
[3] Schmalzg., l. c., n. 2.
[4] Ib., n. 36; Kutschker, Eherecht, vol. v., p. 871; München, l. c., p. 162.

cated in some other customary lawful manner. The following are authentic private instruments: 1. All judicial acts
(*acta judicialia*)—that is, the minutes and records of judicial
proceedings written by persons appointed by the court,
even though not notaries.[1] 2. Writings taken from the files
of public archives—*v.g.*, episcopal or diocesan archives.
3. Writings drawn up indeed by private persons, but bearing
a public or authentic seal—*v.g.*, of a bishop, or corporation
having the right to use a seal. 4. Writings or letters of
private persons, which are subscribed by three, or sometimes
only by two, witnesses still living, and verifying their signature.[2] 5. Parochial registers of baptisms, marriages, etc.
Non-authentic private instruments (*instrumenta privata non-
authentica*) are those writings or letters of private persons,
which are not authenticated in the above manner, as ordinary letters.[3]

866. *Force of instruments.*—A public instrument—a protocol as well as a transumpt—constitutes of itself, and without any other corroborative evidence, full proof, either in
favor of or against the party producing it, until the contrary
is proved, provided the original and not merely the copy be
produced.[4] We say, *protocol as well as*, etc. Here we
observe that some canonists contend that the protocol, being
but an inchoate instrument, does not constitute full proof.
However, the contrary opinion is more commonly held. We
say, moreover, *of itself*, etc.; that is, one instrument of this
kind has the same force as two concordant and unexceptionable witnesses.[5] We say, again, *until the contrary is proved;*
for even public officials may commit fraud or error. Hence,
when such deception or error is proved, the instrument loses
its force or authority. We say, finally, *provided the original,*
etc.; for credence or belief is not easily given to a copy,

[1] Ex cap. 11, de Prob. (ii. 19). [2] Ex cap. 2, de Fid. instr. [3] Reiff., l. c., n. 143.
[4] Ex cap. 1, 2, de Fid. instr.; L. 15, C. de Fid. instr. (iv. 21.
[5] Cf. cap. 10, de Fid. instr. (ii. 22).

except it be lawfully or properly taken from the original by a public person.[1]

867. What has been said concerning the force of public instruments proper, applies also to authentic private instruments. For, as we have seen above,[2] these latter writings have the same force and effect as public instruments proper.[3]

868. But a non-authentic private instrument constitutes, generally speaking, full proof (*a*) only against the writer himself, and that (*b*) provided he acknowledges it as his own or as written by himself, (*c*) or when (in case he denies having written it) the authenticity or genuineness is *proved;* otherwise the instrument proves nothing.[4] We say, first, *provided he* (the writer) *acknowledges it as his own;* for such an acknowledgment, when made in writing, even though extrajudicial, has the force of a judicial confession.[5] We say, secondly, *when, in case he denies*, etc.; for if the alleged or presumed writer denies that he wrote the letter, or consented to its being written, the adversary on producing the letter or instrument must prove it—*v.g.*, by comparison of handwriting, or by competent witnesses who testify that they were present and saw him write the letter. Three such witnesses are required.[6] We say, finally, *only against the writer himself;* and in this respect public and authentic private instruments differ from non-authentic private instruments. The latter constitute proof, as a rule, only against the writer, and not in his favor nor against a third party; while the former prove either for or against their writer or a third party.[7]

869. *Production of instruments during the trial.*—To pro-

---

[1] Cap. 1 et 16, de Fid. instr. (ii. 22) ; Soglia, ed. Vecch., vol. ii., p. 296; Schmalzg., l. c., n. 22-36.

[2] Supra, n. 863.   [3] Reiff., l. c., n. 14 et 16.

[4] L. 5, C. de Prob. (iv. 19); ex cap. 2, de Fid. instr.; Reiff., l. c., n. 158, 170.

[5] L. 26 ff. Depositi (16. 3); Reiff., l. c., n. 170, 173; Schmalzg., l. c., n. 77.

[6] Reiff., l. c., n. 163.   [7] Ib., n. 12, 174.

duce an instrument (*producere instrumentum*) or document or writing, is to submit it to the court or judge for the purpose of proving an allegation. This production can take place, ordinarily, only after the *litis contestatio* or making of the plea, or where no formal *litis contestatio* is required, after the act which is construed as the *litis contestatio*. The reason is, that proofs of whatever kind—whether by witnesses or otherwise—cannot, generally speaking, be submitted to the court before the plea.[1]

870. Is a litigant bound to show his instruments to the opposing party? We distinguish between the plaintiff or prosecution and the defendant or accused. It is certain that the plaintiff or prosecutor is obliged to exhibit his instrument to the defendant; but the latter is not, as a rule bound either in civil or criminal causes to communicate his documents to the plaintiff or prosecution.[2] The reason, among others, is that the defendant or accused is an unwilling party to the trial, and appears merely to defend himself, not to cause any damage to another person. Hence it is not strange that the law (we speak of canon law) should be more favorable in this, as in similar matters, to the defendant or accused.[3]

871. We said, "is not, *as a rule*, bound;" for there are some exceptions. Thus the accused or defendant must show his instruments to his opponent—*v.g.*, (a) where the instruments do not belong exclusively to him (*i.e.*, defendant), but are common property.[4] Thus the judge or notary is bound to show all the acts or minutes of the trial to any of the interested parties, and, consequently, also to the plaintiff or prosecution, even to the prejudice of the defendant. For

[1] Ex cap. un, de Lit. cont.; cap. 1 et seq., ne lit. non cont.; Reiff., l. 2, t. 19, n. 142 sq.

[2] Cap. 1, de Probat. (ii. 19); cap. 5, de Fid. instr., L. 7 ff. de Testibus; L. 1 et 4, Cod. de Eden. (ii. 1); Schmalzg., l. 2, t. 19, n. 42.

[3] Schmalzg., l. c., n. 42; München, l. c., vol. i., p. 168.

[4] Cap. 12, de Fid. instr.; ib., Glossa, v. Communium.

these acts are public or common property.[1] (*b*) Again, where the defendant submits an instrument to prove an allegation which is in his favor, he must submit it to his opponent. For he is privileged against being obliged to produce his instruments only as against himself—*i.e.*, when they are simply to be used by his adversary as against him.[2]

872. How is an instrument to be shown to the opposing party? Where, in accordance with the rules just laid down, a party is obliged to show (*edcre instrumentum*) his documents to the other party, it is done in the following manner: The party who is to show the document first presents it to the judge or court. It is then read in its entirety before the judge or his deputy and the opposing party, who is then allowed to take a copy of so much of the paper as relates to the matter under discussion, provided the paper treats of different matters, and not simply of the one which is in controversy.[3] Where the instrument treats exclusively of the matter in dispute, the opponent is allowed to copy the whole document.[4] Of course, it is manifest that the opponent, who demands to see the instrument, must be cited to be present in court on the day appointed by the judge for its production, just as the opposing party is to be summoned to be present at the admission of witnesses. Again, we observe that the original must be produced in court, since belief is not usually given to a copy.[5] The person submitting the paper need not, however, leave the original to the judge or court, and thus expose himself to the danger of losing it. It is sufficient for him to exhibit the original in the manner stated, and allow a copy to be taken.[6]

873. *Q.* Can instruments be impugned or called in question? And if so, in how many ways?

[1] L. 2, C. de Edendo (ii. 1); Reiff., l. 2, t. 22, n. 249.
[2] Schmalzg., l. c., n. 44.   [3] Cap. 5, de Fid. instr.
[4] Reiff., l. 2, t. 22, n. 238 sq.; Schmalzg., l. 2, t. 22, n. 84.
[5] Cap. 1, de Fid. instr   [6] Reiff., l. c., n. 236.

A. They can, and that chiefly in two respects—namely, (*a*) either as not genuine, (*b*) or as containing false statements. Thus, first, a paper becomes suspected as having been forged, and consequently its genuineness may be called in question—*v.g.*, when it is not drawn up with the requisite formalities (when there is question of public instruments), or not properly authenticated.[1] Secondly, even where an instrument is conceded to be genuine, it may be attacked as containing misrepresentations, or even false statements, totally at variance with the real facts of the case. For it is plain that the writer of an instrument or paper, even though he is a public official,—*v.g.*, a notary, or secretary of the court, —may, either inadvertently or maliciously, misrepresent the transaction recorded by him.[2] Consequently, where it is shown—*v.g.*, by competent witnesses[3]—that the paper or instrument, even though genuine, and not forged, or interpolated, does not state the truth in any essential point, it loses all its force and authority.[4]

ART. V.

4. *Presumptions (Praesumptiones).*

874. The next kind of proofs are presumptions (*praesumptiones*). A presumption is a reasonable conjecture or inference in regard to a doubtful matter, based upon signs or indications, which usually lead very near the truth.[5] Schmalzgrueber's[6] definition comes to the same. He says: "A presumption is a conjecture or opinion based upon some probable sign or indication, and submitted as proof, or assumed by the judge in proof of a doubtful matter."[7] Presumptions,

---

[1] Cap. 6, de Fid. instr.
[2] Cap. 10, de Fid. instr.
[5] Todeschi, Man. du Droit Can., l. 2, t. 23, n. 1, p. 151.
[6] L. 2, t. 23, n. 1.
[3] München, l. c., p. 165.
[4] Cf. Reiff., l. c., n. 286.
[7] Cf. Reiff., l. 2, t. 23, n. 3.

therefore, constitute what is called in civil law circumstantial evidence. In fact, the word *praesumptio* comes from the two words *prae* and *sumptio*, which mean the taking a thing for granted or to be true prior to or without being directly and positively proved. Presumptions do not establish or prove a thing or fact directly, but only inferentially.

875. *Division.*—Presumptions are divided into *praesumptiones hominis* and *juris*, according as they come from persons or from the law (in our case, canon law). Hence a presumption is personal or of man (*praesumptio hominis*) when it is derived from personal observation—namely, when a person from certain signs or circumstances infers something, or assumes a thing to be true, until the contrary is proved.[1] This personal presumption is (*a*) either *rash* (*praesumptio temeraria*) —namely, when it proceeds from slight or frivolous reasons, and then it is called suspicion, rather than presumption ; (*b*) *probable, reasonable, or grave* (*praesumptio probabilis*),— namely, when it arises from conjectures or signs, capable of persuading a prudent person; in other words, when it is based upon signs or facts which are very frequently connected with what is presumed—*v.g.*, if a woman is suspected of unchastity, because she is frequently seen alone with young men, especially if it be in solitary places. (*c*) *Violent* (*praesumptio violenta, vehemens*), when it is based upon several signs, or even one sign or fact, which points very strongly and forcibly to the fact presumed, in such manner as to leav , morally speaking, no doubt as to the thing presumed. Such is the presumption that fornication was committed, "si solus cum sola, nudus cum nuda, in eodem lecto sunt deprehensi.**

876. A presumption is legal or of the law (*praesumptio juris*) when the law itself infers something from certain circumstances or contingencies. The difference between the *praesumptio hominis* and the *praesumptio juris* is that in the latter

[1] Schmalzg., l. c., n. 4.   * Schmalzg., l. c. n. 5.

case the law itself (in our case, canon law) enacts or directs that from certain facts or circumstances the existence of some other fact is to be inferred, while in the former case the inference or conjecture is based on the reasoning of the judge.[1]

877. The *praesumptio juris* is subdivided into (*a*) the simple presumption of law—namely, that which holds a thing to be true, not absolutely, but only till the contrary is proved, and therefore admits of proof to the contrary ; (*b*) the *praesumptio juris* ET DE JURE, or that which holds a thing to be absolutely true, in such a manner as not to admit, generally speaking, of proof to the contrary.[2] Instances of both kinds of presumptions of law are found in various parts of the decretals. We shall give only a few. Thus the law of the Church, by simple presumption, takes it for granted (*a*) that a person born and brought up among Christians is baptized;[3] (*b*) that one who is seven years old has the use of reason.[4] In like manner, the law of the Church takes it for granted, by presumption which is *juris et* DE JURE, that a woman who has lived for a year and a half spontaneously with a man whom she married compulsorily, has freely consented to the marriage.[5]

878. *Effects of presumptions.*—The effect of a simple presumption of law (*praesumptio juris tantum*) is that a thing is held to be true until the party against whom it stands proves ‚the contrary. Hence it causes the burden of proof to fall upon the latter, so that, unless he overthrows the presumption by sufficient proof to the contrary, the facts against him are considered true,[6] and sentence may be pronounced accordingly, at least in civil causes. The effects of a *praesumptio juris et de jure* are, among other things, 1, that it causes the fact presumed to be taken as completely true or proven, and therefore ordinarily excludes any proof tending to show the

---

[1] Ib., n. 7; Kutschker, l. c., vol. v., p. 830. [2] Schmalzg., l. c., n. 7.
[3] Cap. 3, de Presbyt. non. bapt. (3. 43). [4] Cap. un. de Desp. impub., in 6°.
[5] Cap. 21, de Spons. (iv. 1); Schmalzg., l. c., n. 9. [6] Ex cap. 2, 4, de Prob,

contrary.[1]   We say, *ordinarily;* since there are a number of exceptions, for which see Schmalzgrueber.[2]   2. It deprives the party against whom it militates of the right of appealing. For this party is regarded as both convicted and as having made a judicial confession.[3]   3. Sentence may be pronounced in accordance with it.

879. A *praesumptio hominis*, when violent, constitutes in civil causes, at least when not of too great importance, full proof, so long as the contrary is not proved, and therefore sentence can be pronounced in accordance with it.[4]   We say, " in civil causes, *at least where they are not of too great import-ance;*" for, as we shall presently see, mere presumptions, even though violent, do not constitute full proof in criminal causes, nor in civil causes of a grave nature ; the latter being placed in canon law, owing to the gravity of their character, on an equal footing with criminal causes.[5]

880. *Q.* Do mere presumptions suffice for the conviction and condemnation of an accused person in criminal causes?

A. We said above, that both simple presumption of law [6] and violent presumption of man,[7] so long as the contrary is not established, authorize a judge to pass sentence according to them, *in civil causes*, at least, when the latter are not of a very grave character.   The question therefore arises : Do mere presumptions, even though very strong and violent, suffice for conviction and condemnation, also in criminal causes ?   There are four opinions.   The first, which is held by such eminent canonists as Pirhing, Engl, Bouix, denies that an accused can be convicted or condemned on mere presumptions or circum-stantial evidence, even though violent, and contends that he is to be absolved in the case, from the very fact that no posi-

[1] Cap. 30, de Sponsal.   [3] L. c., n. 12.

[2] Ex l. 2, C. Quor. appel. non rec. (vii. 65).

[4] Ex cap. 2, 12, et 13, de Praes. (ii. 23); Reiff., l. c., n. 37, 61; Schmalzg. l. c., n. 6.

[5] Reiff., l. c., n. 62.   [6] Supra, n. 878.   [7] Supra, n. 879.

tive or direct proof exists against him. The second, which is directly opposed to the first, affirms, provided the presumptions are violent.and give moral certainty. The third holds the mean between the two foregoing, and contends that mere presumptions, even though violent, do not indeed suffice for conviction or condemnation, but yet authorize the judge to inflict upon the accused a light penalty—lighter than that which would have been imposed upon him had he been properly convicted. The fourth is that of Schmalzgrueber, who holds, 1, that the presumption which is called *juris et de jure* suffices for conviction and condemnation; 2, that other presumptions, even though very strong or violent (*praesumptiones violentae, vehementes*), do not suffice; 3, that presumptions, whether of law or of man, when they are most violent or exceedingly vehement (*praesumptiones vehementissimae*), and based upon signs or circumstances which are, ordinarily speaking, always connected with the crime, and are consequently, morally speaking, sure and undoubted indications of the crime, suffice for conviction and condemnation, especially in the case of crimes which are of an occult.nature and can be proved only with difficulty. For, these presumptions, not less than the testimony of two unexceptionable witnesses, constitute a moral certainty, which should suffice.[1] Moreover, if this theory were not admitted, these occult crimes could scarcely ever be punished.

881. Bouix, as we have said, holds the first opinion—namely, that mere presumptions, no matter how violent, do not suffice. For, as he says, the presumptions always leave a doubt as to the guilt of the accused. Now the law of nature, as well as the law of the Church, requires that where there is a doubt, sentence of condemnation should not be passed in criminal causes. Thus the law of the Church demands that, in these cases, the proofs must be of the fullest,

---

[1] Schmalzg., l. c., n. 18 sq.

clearest, and most undoubted kind—clearer than the noon-day sun. The *Can. Sciant cuncti* 2 ' says : " Sciant cuncti accusatores, eam se rem deferre debere . . . quae" (sit) "instructa *apertissimis documentis*, vel indiciis ad proba-tionem *indubitatis*, et *luce clarioribus* expedita." Again, Pope Innocent III., speaking of a person accused of ·heresy, expressly enacts : " Propter solam suspicionem" (praesump-tionem), " *quamvis vehementem*, nolumus illum de tam gravi crimine condemnari." ' Hence Reiffenstuel ' concludes : " Ex solis praesumptionibus, *quamvis vehementibus*, nemo in causa criminali condemnandus est." For it is better, as the Roman law adopted by the Church says, "impunitum relinquere facinus nocentis, quam innocentem damnare." ' It must be observed, however, that those who advocate this opinion, except those presumptions which leave no doubt whatever as to the crime committed—*v.g.*, where a wife, whose husband has been absent a year, is found *enceinte*. But, as Bouix ' observes, such presumptions should be called direct proofs rather than presumptions.

882. *Q.* Can two or more presumptions be combined so as to make full proof?

A. i. They can, in civil causes, at least when the latter are not of a very grave nature. Hence, in these causes, two pre-sumptions combined constitute full proof, provided each of them constitutes of itself a half or imperfect proof,' as is the case with reasonable personal presumptions.' . 2. They can-not, in criminal causes ; for, as Reiffenstuel ' remarks, in these causes, " requiruntur probationes *indubitatae, ac luce meridiana clariores.*" Now, as the same author continues, even a num-ber of presumptions, though combined, always leave a certain doubt. Bouix ' teaches the same when he says : " In quibus" (causis criminalibus) "duae pluresve semiplenae probationes

¹ Caus. 2, Q. 8.   ⁷ Cap. 14, de Praes. (ii. 23).

³ L. c., n. 63.   ⁴ L. 5 ff. de Poenis (48. 19).   ⁵ L. c., p. 330.

⁶ Reiff.; l. c., n. 75.   ⁷ Ib., n. 34.   ⁸ Ib., n. 77.   ⁹ L. c., p. 305.

non sufficiunt ad condemnandum." In like manner, two presumptions combined do not produce full proof in matrimonial causes as against the validity of a marriage already contracted, nor in general in civil causes of a grave character.

883. *A few of the rules governing presumptions.—Rule I.* The presumption is always in favor of the validity of an act performed. Hence such act is to be considered as valid and done in the proper manner until the contrary is proved.[1] *Rule II.* In the United States, and wherever the Tridentine decree *tametsi* is not promulgated, a man who has had carnal intercourse with his betrothed—*i.e.*, with a woman whom he had previously promised to marry—is presumed *in foro externo* to have acted *cum affectu maritali*, and consequently cannot be allowed to desert her, since he is considered as having contracted and consummated marriage with her. Nay, this presumption is so strong, that it excludes any proof to the contrary, and is therefore a *praesumptio juris et* DE JURE.[2] Hence, even though such a man subsequently contracted another marriage *in facie ecclesiae—i.e.*, publicly and with all the ceremonies of the Church—this marriage would be null and void.

884. *Rule IV.* From the past the future is presumed.[3] Thus it is presumed that a person who has been good in youth will be good when older. Again, a person who has been chaste in youth is presumed chaste in old age. So also it is presumed that a person who has been bad in the past will be the same in the future. In fact, the maxim is: "Semel malus, semper praesumitur esse malus,"[4] unless the amendment of life is clearly established. *Rule V.* Every person is presumed good unless the contrary is proved.[5] *Rule VI.* Neighbors are presumed to know what has happened in their neighborhood.[6]

---

[1] L. Si post 4, C. de Juris et facti ignor. (i. 18); Reiff., l. c., n. 91.

[2] Cap. 30, de Sponsal. (iv. 1); ib. Glossa, v. *Is qui*, v. *Contra praesumpt.;* Schmalzg., l. c., n. 24.   [3] Cap. 6 et 9, de Praesumpt.

[4] Reg. 8 Juris, in 6°.   [5] Cap. fin. de Praes.   [6] Cap. 7, de Praesumpt.

ART. VI.

The Oath as a Proof (Juramentum litis decisorium).

885. It often happens that litigants can establish or prove their case but imperfectly, not fully, because their proofs are incomplete—*v.g.*, when they have only one competent witness, etc. In these cases recourse is frequently had to the oath for the purpose of deciding the matter or cause, which otherwise would have to remain undecided. Hence this oath is called (a) *decisive* (*juramentum litis decisorium*), because its effect is to decide the case or end the dispute; (b) supplementary (*juramentum suppletorium*), since it supplies the want of complete ordinary proofs, or fills up the gaps in the evidence submitted; (c) purgative (*juramentum purgatorium*), because, when taken by an accused, it purges him of all suspicion of guilt. (See Appendix XII.)

886. As will be seen, this oath must not be confounded (a) with the oath taken by witnesses prior to deposing, as it is taken by the litigants themselves—that is, by the plaintiff or defendant; (b) nor with the oaths called respectively *juramentum calumniae, malitiae* and *veritatis dicendae*, which are indeed taken by the litigants themselves, but not for the purpose of staking the decision of the cause upon them, but simply to pledge themselves to act in good faith, not maliciously, and to say the truth during the trial.[1]

887. This decisive oath is divided into judicial and extra-judicial, according as it is taken in or out of court (we speak of ecclesiastical courts) or judicial proceedings. The decisive extrajudicial oath is defined to be that oath which one of the contending parties, voluntarily or by agreement, tenders to the other out of court, on condition that he will abstain from all further judicial proceedings if it is taken.[2] As is

---

[1] Reiff., l. 2, t. 24, n. 12 sq.
[2] Ex l. Jusjurandum 17 ff. de Jurejur.(xii. 2); Schmalzg., l. 2, t. 24, n. 10.

evident, this oath is made use of (*a*) before the matter has been brought into court; (*b*) by those parties who, having insufficient proof, and fearing the expenses of a trial, are anxious to end the dispute without judicial proceedings.

888. The party to whom this extrajudicial oath is tendered is entirely free to agree to take it or not. But once it has been taken its effect is to decide the matter, since it is regarded in the light of a transaction or settlement between the parties.[1] Thus a person who, upon having the oath tendered him, swears, *v.g.*, that he owes the other party nothing, gains his case, and acquires the same right as if he had obtained a judicial decision in his favor, or settled the matter with his opponent. This holds so true, by the law of the Church, adopting in this respect the Roman law, that if the cause were afterwards brought before the judge, he would be obliged, as a rule, to decide in favor of the one who took the oath. For in the case the judge could not inquire into the justice or merits of the cause itself, but simply whether the oath was taken, and under what agreement. Having ascertained this, he would have to ratify the agreement and subsequent oath.[2] Some canonists do not, however, admit that this oath cuts off recourse to judicial proceedings and finally settles the matter in dispute.[3]

889. What is the decisive judicial oath? As we have seen, the decisive extrajudicial oath is resorted to out of judicial proceedings. Sometimes, however, the oath is made use of to decide causes, even in the course of judicial proceedings or the trial—namely, when it is found that the proofs are not sufficient to determine the matter. In this case the oath is called judicial, and is divided into (*a*) simply judicial (*b*) and necessary or compulsory. It is called simply judicial (*juramentum judiciale*) when offered by one of the

---

[1] L. 2 ff. de Jurejur. [2] L. 5 ff. de Jurejur., § 2; Schmalzg., l. c., n. 20, 21.
[3] Cf. Reiff., l. c., n. 134.

litigants themselves to the other, not indeed by order, but yet by approval of the judge, on condition that if he takes it he shall gain the case, without any further judicial proceedings.[1] The party to whom it is offered, with the approval of the judge, cannot without just cause refuse to take it, unless he prefers to tender it in turn to the opponent who first tendered it.[2] If he refuses to do either, without just cause, he loses the case. We say, *without just cause;* for there are many reasons why he may decline to take both the simple judicial oath and the necessary oath. Thus, he may decline where he has already fully proved his case. The judge may also excuse him if he sees fit.[3] Once taken, it has the effect of full proof, so that sentence should be pronounced for the one who has sworn. It has, moreover, the force of a compromise or settlement, and of *res judicata*, and consequently excludes the right of appeal.[4]

890. The decisive judicial oath is called necessary (*juramentum necessarium*) when the judge himself, having taken cognizance of the cause, and finding the proofs insufficient, tenders it to one of the litigants. It is called necessary, both because the judge is obliged to tender it when requested to do so by one of the parties, or even sometimes *ex officio*, and because the party to whom it is tendered cannot refuse to take it without just cause, nor can he in turn offer it to the opponent.[5] Again, this oath, as will be observed, is tendered by the judge himself either *ex officio* or at the request of one of the parties, while the others are tendered by the parties themselves to each other. Finally, it may be administered for two purposes: (*a*) to complete insufficient proofs ; (*b*) and to purge an accused of all suspicion of guilt.[6]

891. In what causes can the necessary judicial oath be

[1] Schmalzg., l. c., n. 24.
[2] Cap. 36, de Jurej. (ii. 24).   [3] Schmalzg., l. c , n. 31.
[4] L. 2 ff. de Jurejur. (xii. 2), Soglia, ed. Vecch., vol. ii., p. 208.
[5] Reiff., l. c., n. 139; Schmalzg., l. c., n. 40.   [6] Schmalzg., l. c.

tendered by the judge? As a rule, in all causes whatever which are not specially excepted. Now what causes are excepted? Chiefly the following: 1. All criminal causes when tried criminally, not merely civilly. The oath may, however, be tendered in these causes to the accused for the purpose of establishing his innocence, though not to the plaintiff or prosecuting party in support of the charges, or as a means of completing his proofs otherwise incomplete. The reason of the latter conclusion is that in criminal causes, as we have repeatedly said, the prosecuting party must sustain his charges fully and completely; in other words, the proofs against the accused must be of the fullest, clearest, and most convincing kind, so as to leave no doubt of the guilt.[1] Now this cannot be said to be the case with imperfect proofs even when supplemented by the oath.[2] We said: *The oath may, however, . . . be tendered to the accused for the purpose of establishing his innocence.* This holds, of course, only when the charges against him have been already imperfectly proven. For where they have not been sustained at least imperfectly, or to some extent, the accused, even though he has not yet said a word in his defence, cannot be compelled to purge himself from the charges by an oath, but is simply to be absolved or declared not guilty.[3]

892. 2. All causes imperilling the reputation of a party (*causae famosae*); in other words, those causes where a person who is condemned becomes infamous—*v.g.*, causes of theft, usury, etc. However, in these causes, as in criminal causes, the oath can be tendered to the defendant to purge himself from suspicion, but not to the plaintiff in completion or supplement of his imperfect proofs.[4] 3. Civil causes of a very grave nature. For they are, as we have seen, placed on the same footing with criminal causes.

---

[1] L. fin., C. de Probat.   [2] Schmalzg., l. c., n. 47.
[3] Cap. 36, de Jurej.; ib. Glossa, v. probatione.
[4] L. 6 ff. de His qui not. (iii. 2).

893. 4. Matrimonial causes, where there is question of dissolving or sustaining a marriage already contracted. These causes may be said to come under the foregoing head, being civil causes of a very grave character. When, however, there is question of a marriage *about to be contracted*, the oath can be tendered to a person bearing a good name, who has imperfectly proven the existence of an impediment.[1]

894. The chief effects of this necessary oath are: 1. The party to whom it is tendered by the judge cannot offer it to the opponent or refuse to take it except for just cause. And if he refuses without just cause he loses the case.[2] 2. Once taken, it perfects the imperfect proofs, so that sentence must be pronounced in favor of the one who took it. From this sentence, however, it is allowed to appeal, and that, in case new documents are discovered, even after the lapse of ten days.[3]

Important practical observation.—We have said (n. 891) that the oath in question may be administered to the accused for the purpose of establishing his innocence. This, however, does not appear to apply any longer. For Pope Benedict XIII., in the Roman Council held in 1725,—which though not a general Council has nevertheless, by reason of custom, obtained the force of a general law in regard to the oath to tell the truth,—strictly forbids the *juramentum veritatis dicendae* to be in future administered to the accused when examined as principal in his own cause. It is true that the *juramentum veritatis* is, strictly speaking, different from the *juramentum decisorium*. But it is also true that the reason why Benedict XIII. forbade the former applies equally to the latter. His reason was to prevent perjury on the part of the accused. We say *as principal;* for he may be sworn when he testifies *as a witness for or against others.*

[1] Ex Cap. 34, de Jurejur.; ib. Glossa, v. absoluto; Schmalzg., l. c., n. 51.

[2] Cap. 36, de Jurej.; ib. Glossa, v. a te; L. 12, C. de Rebus cred. (iv, 1).

[3] L. 31 ff. de Jurejur (xii. 2); Schmalzg., l. c., n. 56.

PART II.

OF ECCLESIASTICAL JUDICIAL PROCEDURE, IN PARTICULAR.

895. Under this heading we shall speak, 1, of the organization or *personnel* of the episcopal and metropolitan courts of justice; 2, of ecclesiastical trials, both ordinary and extraordinary, in criminal causes; 3, of ecclesiastical trials in civil causes.

CHAPTER I.

ORGANIZATION OF THE BISHOP'S COURT OR TRIBUNAL FOR THE EXERCISE OF JUDICIAL POWER, ALSO IN THE U. S.

. (*De Curia Episcopali.*)

896. Where the common law of the Church obtains, the bishop's court or judicial tribunal is composed, 1, of the bishop or his substitute, the vicar-general, as judge; 2, frequently, also, of assessors and auditors, who act as counsel to the judge; 3, of a fiscal promoter or prosecuting advocate; 4, of a notary or chancellor, or clerk; 5, of a messenger, who delivers the citations or other orders of the court. We shall briefly describe the rights and duties of each of these officials. For the organization of the *Curia* under the Instruction *Cum Magnopere*, see our *New Procedure*.

ART. I.

Of the Judge.

897. We have already spoken at sufficient length of the ecclesiastical judge.[1] We shall here add but a few remarks.

[1] Supra, n. 711 sq.

The bishop is the ordinary judge of the first instance, for his diocese. Hence his judicial tribunal constitutes the court of the first instance, for all ecclesiastical causes whatever, of his diocese. In other words, all causes belonging to the ecclesiastical forum must, before being appealed to the higher ecclesiastical judge, be first tried, or taken cognizance of, and decided by the ordinary of the diocese, or his representative.[1]

898. From this rule, however, the following cases are excepted: 1. Where canon law expressly directs that the matter shall be tried before the Holy See; 2. Where the Pope, in view of peculiar circumstances, deems it proper to reserve the hearing or decision of the cause to the Holy See. In this case, however, a special rescript, signed by the Holy Father himself, is necessary.[2] 3. Where the ordinary has not terminated the cause within two years, at the latest, from the time the action was instituted or the proceedings begun. 4. Where both the ordinary and the contending parties agree to have the case tried directly before the Holy See.[3]

899. The bishop, being the ordinary judge of his diocese, can adjudicate causes—*i.e.*, preside at trials or the hearing of causes, and pass sentence—either in person or through others. As a rule, bishops in Catholic countries try or hear causes, not in person, but through their vicars-general. It may therefore be said that in these countries vicars-general, generally speaking, preside at all ecclesiastical trials, in the bishop's stead. Of course the bishop is not restricted to allowing the vicar-general to act for him in these matters; he may also delegate or authorize others to sit as judges in his stead, in particular cases, or even in a certain kind of

---

[1] Conc. Trid., sess. 24, C. 20, de Ref.

[2] Ib.; cf. Molitor, Kanonisches Gerichtsverfahren, p. 212.

[3] S. C. C., 4 Aug., 1691, ap. Richter, Can. et Decret., p. 319; Phillips, Compend., § 179.

causes—*v.g.*, in all criminal causes.[1] The latter, however, would be only delegates, and consequently appeals would lie from them to the bishop. The vicar-general, on the other hand, is a "judex ordinarius," and forms one and the same court with the bishop, and therefore appeals from him must be made, not to the bishop, but the higher superior.[2]

In England, and in those dioceses of the United States where the Commissions of Investigation still exist *ad interim*, the hearing of the cause, that is, the procedure from the citation of the accused to the final sentence exclusive, is conducted by these Commissions. The bishop, however, both in England and with us, retains the exclusive right to pronounce the final sentence.

ART. II.

Auditors of the Bishop's Court—Commissions.

900. There are two kinds of auditors: some are judges in the proper sense of the term—namely, the auditor of the apostolic chamber (*auditor camerae apostolicae*), and the auditors of the *Rota* (*auditores Rotae*); others—namely, those of episcopal and archiepiscopal courts—are not judges, but merely officials or persons to whom a cause is either in whole or in part committed, in order that, having diligently examined its merits, they shall report the entire affair to the judge for his decision.[3] These auditors have indeed jurisdiction so far as the hearing or taking cognizance of the cause is concerned, so that they can summon the parties, admit witnesses, proofs, etc. but they have no jurisdiction so far as the final sentence is concerned, and consequently they cannot pronounce definitive sentence, unless they have been especially empowered to do so.[4] Hence they may be

---

[1] Molitor, l. c., p. 268; Bouix, de Jud., vol. i., p. 469. [2] Molitor, l. c., p. 264.
[3] Ex Cap. 27, de Off. jud. del. (i. 29); Craiss., n. 5758.
[4] Schmalzg., l. 2, t. 1, n. 15.

compared to the referees or masters in chancery of the secular courts of the United States.

901. It will also be observed that there is a striking resemblance between these auditors and our Commissions of Investigation, who, while charged with the entire and exclusive hearing of the cause, cannot pronounce final sentence, but must simply report the whole case, together with their verdict, to the bishop, whose sole privilege it is to pass final sentence, and that either in conformity with or opposition to the advice or report of the Commission.

902. According to the common law of the Church, the judge or bishop is not obliged to appoint any auditors for his court. There are, however, cases where it may be expedient for the bishop to appoint an auditor for his vicar-general (where the latter sits in court, in the bishop's stead, as is the case nearly all over Europe)—*v.g.*, (*a*) where the number of causes is too great to be expedited in proper time by the vicar-general alone ; (*b*) where the vicar-general is not versed in canon law. The jurisdiction of these auditors is delegated, not ordinary.[1]

903. Is it allowed to appeal from an auditor? It is, 1, when he acts as a judge proper ; 2, when he is justly suspected by the parties—that is, when there are good reasons for believing that he is biassed against the parties.[2] That this holds also of Commissions of Investigation in the United States, we shall show a little farther on.

ART. III.

Assessors of the Bishop's Court—Are Commissions of Investigation in the United States Assessors of the Bishop's Court ? In what sense?

904. Assessors (*assessores*) are persons appointed to assist the judge by their advice, in the hearing of causes and the

---

[1] Cap. 27, de Off. jud. del. (i. 29).   [2] Bouix, de Jud., vol. i., p. 461.

conduct of judicial proceedings. Hence they are also called counsellors (*consiliarii*) of the judge.[1] By the common law of the Church, assessors have no jurisdiction. For their office consists simply in giving advice to the judge, who is not bound to follow it.[2] We say, *by the common law of the Church;* for, by particular law, they may possess jurisdiction. Thus, it is certain that where, as we have seen, vicars-general ordinarily preside at trials in place of the bishop, the latter may for the hearing of certain kinds of causes—*v.g.*, criminal causes—associate with his vicar-general one or more assessors, whose advice he is bound to follow. The assessors in this case would of course be associate judges, and not mere advisers.[3]

905. Who can appoint assessors? As a rule, any judge can appoint assessors for himself, whose right and duty it will be to sit by the judge when holding court, participate in all the proceedings, advising the judge, etc. The reason is, that no one is forbidden to take counsel of others. Hence, too, the vicar-general, in places where he acts as judge for the bishop, can select assessors for himself, unless the bishop has reserved the appointment to himself.[4]

906. Can assessors be challenged as suspected? They can, and if the judge does not admit the challenge, he can himself be objected to as suspected. The reason is, that by giving advice to the judge they naturally influence his decision, and thus become instrumental in inflicting a grievance upon the party. Hence the party who has just cause for suspecting the assessor can object to his acting as assessor.[5]

907. From these principles it will be seen that members of Commissions of Investigation in the United States (the same holds true of those in England) may be challenged when there is just cause for suspecting, *v.g.*, that they are

---

[1] L. 5 ff. de Offic. adsess. (i. 22); L. 1, C. h. t. (i. 51).
[2] L. 1 ff. h. t.; L. 1, C. h. t.   [3] Bouix, l. c., p. 467.
[4] Bouix, l. c., p. 468.   [5] Bouix, l. c., p 469.

biased against the parties, or otherwise unfavorably disposed towards them. These Commissions are, in fact, established by the Holy See as the official advisory boards of bishops in criminal and disciplinary causes of ecclesiastics.[1] Hence the members of these bodies or judicial committees are expressly called assessors of the bishop.[2] Their advice or report, submitted to the bishop in the manner laid down by the Instruction of the Propaganda,[3] forms part of the authentic records of the cause tried, and therefore has to be always inserted among the acts, and must have, as it is intended by the Holy See that it should have, the greatest weight both with the bishop and, in case of appeal, with the judge of appeal. If, therefore, it is allowed to challenge as suspected assessors who have no jurisdiction whatever, it seems certain that, *a fortiori*, members of our Commissions of Investigation who are clothed with jurisdiction for the hearing of the cause can be excepted to by parties who have just reasons for suspecting them. These grounds, however, of suspicion are not presumed, but must be proved, as we shall show.

ART. IV.

Collegiate form of the Bishop's Court—The Bishop's Court in the United States, as established by the S. C. de Prop. Fide on July 20, 1878.

908. Can the bishop, by virtue of the general law of the Church, make his court or judicial tribunal consist of a college of judges,—that is, of a number of judges,—who shall be bound to proceed collectively and decide the case by a majority of votes? In other words, can he enact, for instance, that his court shall consist of his vicar-general and one or more assessors or associate judges, who shall, like the

---

[1] Instr. S. C. de Prop. Fid., 20 Julii, 1878, § Commissionis ita.
[2] S. C. de P. F., Ad Dubia, § Ex quibus patet.   [3] July 20, 1878, § 9, Quibus

vicar-general himself, have a decisive, not merely a consultative vote? He certainly can, as we have already said.[1] For as the bishop has the power, if he wishes, to preside at the trial and pass sentence in person, associate with himself, and that in all causes whatever, associate judges, having a decisive, not merely a consultative, vote, so he can evidently appoint such associate judges for his vicar-general,[2] or other judge appointed by him.[3] In reality, the law of the Church not only permits but greatly favors such colleges or bodies of judges, on the ground that conclusions or decisions arrived at by several persons are of more weight and soundness than those reached by a single individual.[4]

909. As a matter of fact, the Holy See has in recent times set a praiseworthy example in this respect. For in 1831 it enacted that in all the dioceses of the Pontifical States the court of the bishop for the adjudication of criminal causes of ecclesiastics should consist of the ordinary and four other judges. In Rome the court of the vicariate or cardinal vicar-general of the Pope for the diocese of Rome is made up of the cardinal-vicar and four other prelates.[5]

910. *Present organization of the bishop's court in the United States.*—We have, in the above lines, described the collegiate form of the bishop's court as authorized by the common law of the Church. We now come to our own ecclesiastical courts. In 1884, the S. C. de Prop. Fide issued the Instruction *Cum Magnopere* for this country. It determines the manner in which our ecclesiastical courts are to be organized in future, and in which they must proceed in hearing and deciding criminal and disciplinary causes of ecclesiastics. This Instruction is obligatory all over the country, and has, therefore, superseded that of July 20, 1878. Accordingly in most of our dioceses the Instruction of 1884 is

---

[1] Supra, n. 904.   [2] At least, for the hearing of a certain class of causes.
[3] Molitor, l. c., p. 269.   [4] Cap. 21, de Off. jud. del. (i. 29).
[5] Bizzarri, Collectanea, pp. 192, 193 ; Bouix, l. c., p. 470.

now in force. In some of our dioceses, however, the Instruction of 1878 and the response *Ad Dubia* still obtain
by Papal dispensation, in the manner pointed out in the Instruction *Cum Magnopere*.[1] In those dioceses where the Instruction of July 20, 1878, is still in force, the bishop's court
has the following collegiate form or organization: It consists of five priests, or where so many cannot be had, at
least of three, who shall constitute a Commission of Investigation. They are appointed by the bishop, *in* and *with the
advice of the Synod.* In England, they are presided over
by one of their own number. This was the case also here
till 1884, when the Instruction *Cum Magnopere* enacted that
the bishop should in future be the president of the Commission.[2] The members once appointed hold office till the
next synod, when they may be confirmed or others appointed
in their stead.[3] If a vacancy should occur in the *interim*, the
bishop can fill it without the advice of the diocesan synod,
though it is becoming that he should consult the other members of the Commission.[4] To this Commission belongs
entirely and exclusively the trial or hearing of the cause
which falls under their jurisdiction or competence. The
mode in which the trial or judicial proceedings are to be
conducted before these Commissions is outlined in the
Instruction of the Propaganda establishing these judicial
colleges or councils. After the members of the latter bodies
have fully and thoroughly investigated or tried the cause in
the manner prescribed by said Instruction, and obtained all
possible light on the subject, and received all the available
testimony, they enter into consultation in order to discuss
the case and exchange views with each other. If upon consultation it is found that a majority of the members believe
the facts to be sufficiently proven, each member writes out
his opinion *in extenso*, together with the reasons upon which

[1] Art. XII. [2] Art. XII. [3] Supra, n. 407.
[4] Instr. S. C. de Prop. Fide, 20 Julii, 1878, § Electi Consiliarii ; S. C. de P.
F., Ad Dubia, § 2 Electio Consiliariorum ; ib., § Extra synodum.

it is based.[1] These opinions, together with all the other records of the case, are then delivered to the bishop, to enable him to pass final sentence. Consequently the bishop remains the sole judge in the proper sense of the term, the final decision of the cause being reserved exclusively to him.

911. The Commissioners may be said to be both auditors and assessors of the bishop. Auditors, because they not merely advise the bishop or the judge, but are entrusted with the entire conduct of the trial or hearing of the cause, and have consequently jurisdiction for the hearing of the cause. Assessors, because their opinion or verdict, as submitted to the bishop, has not the force of a decision of the cause, but merely of advice to the bishop.[2]

ART. V.

Diocesan Promoter and Advocate (Promotor fiscalis).

912. Another official usually attached to the bishop's court is called the promoter or procurator of the fisc (*promotor*, or *procurator* or *advocatus fiscalis*). This official is called in our secular courts prosecuting attorney, city counsel, district and state attorney, attorney-general. By the ecclesiastical fisc (*fiscus ecclesiae*) we here mean the property, things, and rights relating to the public good and interest of the Church. As the secular fisc is a secular corporation, so the ecclesiastical fisc—*v.g.*, the diocese as such— is an ecclesiastical corporation or moral person, having, in general, all the rights of physical persons. Hence, we say, the ecclesiastical fisc or the diocese enters into engagements, makes contracts, sells, buys, pleads and is impleaded, etc. But it is manifest that a moral person, or to speak more precisely, an ecclesiastical juridical person, cannot act of itself,

[1] Instr. cit., § 9, Quibus omnibus.
[2] S. C. de P. F., Ad Dubia, § 3 Votum a Consilio; ib., § Ex quibus.

and is therefore unable personally to institute judicial proceedings or act as plaintiff or defendant to defend and secure
its rights.   Hence it is necessary that somebody be appointed whose duty it shall be to act for the fisc or diocese
in judicial proceedings.   The person appointed to do so is
called the fiscal, or, in the case of a diocese, diocesan promoter.

913. Hence a promoter or prosecuting attorney of the
bishop's court is an official lawfully appointed to guard and
promote the rights of the diocese or diocesan fisc, and act
as plaintiff or defendant in its stead.[1] As will be seen from
this definition, the duties of the diocesan attorney or promoter consist chiefly, 1, in prosecuting criminal offences
before the ecclesiastical tribunal, or bishop's court (in the
United States, before Commissions of Investigation) ; for the
good of the Church and of the diocese evidently requires
that crimes shall be punished ; 2, in acting as the representative of the diocese, and therefore as plaintiff or defendant in
judicial proceedings, where the rights, prerogatives, property,
etc., of the diocese are involved.[2] Consequently, he is not only
the prosecuting attorney, but in general the procurator or
attorney for the diocese in all judicial proceedings or litigious matters.

914. By whom and how is the diocesan promoter appointed? He can certainly be appointed by the bishop.
But, in case no appointment has been made by the bishop,
or the appointee of the bishop is hindered from discharging
his office, it would seem that the vicar-general (when acting
as judge), or other judge delegated by the bishop, can appoint a promoter.   The reason is, that, as a rule, the judge
should provide a procurator or attorney or advocate for a
party that is in need of one, and cannot himself procure
one.   Now, this is plainly the case with the ecclesiastical

[1] Leur., For. Eccl., l. 3, t. 21, q. 460, n. 1.
[2] Bouix, l. c., p. 471; Craiss., n. 5770.

fisc or diocese. The promoter is removable *ad nutum.* When about to enter upon his office, he must take an oath to perform his duties faithfully.[1]

915. *Q.* Is it obligatory, by the common law of the Church, to appoint a diocesan attorney?

A. Prior to the year 1880 the question was controverted, some canonists holding the affirmative, others the negative. Those who maintained the affirmative argued thus: The Roman law prescribes that in all proceedings against a defendant the fiscal promoter shall be cited, and that on pain of nullity of sentence which may be passed on the defendant.[2] The Roman law, therefore, takes it for granted that these attorneys must be appointed. As the sacred canons are silent on this head, and do not enact the contrary, this Roman or civil law must be regarded as adopted by the canon law. For it is a rule of canon law, that where the latter is silent, or does not expressly enjoin the contrary, the Roman or civil law holds also in the ecclesiastical forum.[3] Those who held the negative contended that the Roman law on this head was never adopted by the Church, and that prosecutors were sometimes appointed in ecclesiastical courts simply because of particular custom or local practice, and not because of any general law of the Church.

916. We have said, *prior to the year* 1880. For the Instruction of the S. C. EE. et RR., June 11, 1880, makes it absolutely necessary to appoint a prosecutor in every *Curia.* The Instruction *Cum Magnopere* (Art. XIII.) imposes the same obligation for the United States. Sometimes the number of causes is so great, that the diocesan promoter is unable to attend to them alone and unaided. In this case he can associate an ecclesiastical advocate with himself, who is on that account called fiscal

[1] L. 5, C. (x. 10).   [2] Ex l. 1, C. de Sent. adv. fisc. (x. 9); Bouix, l. c., p. 475.
[3] Cap. 1 (v. 32); Bouix, l. c., p. 19.

advocate (*advocatus fiscalis*). It depends upon the bishop, however, whether the promoter can select him at his discretion, or only from among the number of those approved for this office.[1]

ART. VI.

Diocesan Promoter in the United States, under the Instruction of the S. C. de P. F., July 20, 1878.

917. This Instruction of the Propaganda, which prescribes the mode of procedure in criminal and disciplinary causes of ecclesiastics, and which is still in force in some of our dioceses, requires that when a matter or cause has been or is to be brought before the Commission of Investigation, the bishop shall depute his vicar-general, or some other priest, to draw up a full statement of the case, supported by proofs, against the defendant or accused, and read it before the Commission, and be subject to cross-examination by the latter body. The words of the Instruction are: "Re ad Consilium delata, episcopus vicario suo generali, vel alii sacerdoti ad hoc ab ipso deputato committat, ut relationem causae in scriptis conficiat, cum expositione investigationis eo usque peractae, et circumstantiarum quae causam vel ejusdem demonstrationem specialiter afficiant."[2] And again: "Relatio causae legatur coram Consilio ab episcopi officiali, qui etiam ad interpellationes respondebit a praeside vel ab aliis Consiliariis per praesidem faciendas ad uberiorem rei notitiam assequendam."[3] It will therefore be seen that this official of the bishop takes the place of the diocesan promoter spoken of in the preceding article. His status, therefore, before the Commission of Investigation is not that of an advocate, or even judge, but simply of plaintiff or defendant for the diocese. He is therefore, placed on the same footing with the accused or defendant, so far as judicial proceedings are concerned.

[1] Boulx, l. c., p. 476.   [2] Instr. cit., § 2, Re ad.   [3] Ib., § 6, Relatio causae.

ART. VII.

Notaries or Chancellors—Secretary of Commissions of Investigation in the United States.

(De Notariis et Cancellariis).

918. A notary (*notarius, actuarius, tabellio, protocollista, cancellarius*) is a person appointed by public authority in order that acts written by him may have public authority, or be worthy of belief.[1] Notaries are either ecclesiastical or secular, according as they are appointed by the ecclesiastical or the secular power. Ecclesiastical notaries are again divided into apostolic (*notarii apostolici*)—that is, those appointed by the Holy See—and episcopal—or those named by bishops. Apostolic notaries are subdivided into notaries simply, and prothonotaries.[2]

919. Can ecclesiastics and regulars be appointed notaries? By the written common law of the Church, all secular ecclesiastics who are in sacred orders[3]—nay, according to the more probable opinion, even those who are merely in minor orders, and without a benefice—and all regulars are forbidden to act as notaries, not only in secular courts and causes, but also, according to the more probable opinion, in ecclesiastical courts and causes,[4] except (*a*) in causes of faith,[5] (*b*) and where the notary is appointed by the Holy See, such appointment being equivalent to a derogation of the above written law of the Church.[6] We say, *by the written common law ;* for the general practice or custom makes it lawful, also at present, to appoint ecclesiastics, even though in sacred orders, notaries, though only for acts of the ecclesiastical authority, and not for secular courts or matters. In fact, not only in the United States, but all over the world, the chan-

---

[1] Bouix, l. c., p. 479.
[2] Cap. 8, Ne cleric. vel monach. (iii. 50).
[3] Cap. 11, de Haeret. in 6° (v. 2).

[4] Cf. supra, n. 526.
[5] Ib. Glossa, v. clericis in sacris.
[6] Bouix, l. c., p. 482-487.

cellors of bishops are ecclesiastics, nay, usually priests. In truth, considering the present state of society, it seems far more becoming that ecclesiastics, not laymen, should be appointed notaries for ecclesiastical matters and in ecclesiastical courts.[1]

920. By whom are notaries for ecclesiastical causes to be appointed? Strictly speaking, and *ex jure proprio*, only by the Pope. For the Pope alone can enact something which is altogether contrary to the general law of the Church. Now, the enactment that the writing of one man—the notary—shall of itself constitute full and complete evidence, is certainly wholly opposed to all law.[2] However, by virtue of custom, based upon the consent, at least tacit, of the Sovereign Pontiff, notaries can be appointed also by bishops —nay, even by generals and provincials of religious orders for the criminal causes of religious subject to them.[3] Observe, what has been just said with regard to the appointment of notaries (*notarii*) applies also to chancellors (*cancellarii*) or secretaries (*actuarii*). For the writings or instruments signed or attested by these chancellors or secretaries have the same force and authority as those of notaries proper.[4]

921. Can lay notaries act validly in ecclesiastical and spiritual causes? We distinguish lay notaries who are appointed, or at least admitted, as notaries in the ecclesiastical courts, and for spiritual or ecclesiastical matters, by the ecclesiastical authorities, from those who are appointed solely by the secular power. As to notaries of the first kind, there can be no difficulty. For it is certain that laymen can be, nay, are sometimes laudably appointed notaries by the bishop for ecclesiastical matters and his ecclesiastical court.[5] In regard to notaries of the second class, it seems, considering merely the rigor of the law, that they cannot validly exercise the office of notary in ecclesiastical causes or matters.

---

[1] Ib., p. 493.   [2] Bouix, l. c., p. 497.   [3] Ferraris, v. notarius, n. 21.
[4] Bouix, l. c., pp. 481, 500.   [5] Bouix, l. c., p. 493.

The reason is, that the secular power has no jurisdiction over such causes or matters, and consequently cannot make a law whereby instruments made by notaries created solely by itself shall have full authority also in the eyes of ecclesiastical judges. Such a law would be an act of ecclesiastical jurisdiction, and therefore a usurpation on the part of the secular ruler.

922. We said, first, *considering merely the rigor of the law ;* for, as a rule, these notaries may at least, by virtue of general custom, act validly as notaries, also in the ecclesiastical forum, and in ecclesiastical matters, until prohibited by the bishop from doing so. This seems to follow manifestly from the following decree of the Council of Trent :[1] "Whereas the unskilfulness of notaries causes very many injuries, . . . the bishop . . . may by actual examination search into the competency of all notaries, even though created by apostolic, imperial, or royal authority ; and if such notaries be found incompetent, . . . he may forbid them . . . to exercise that office in ecclesiastical and spiritual affairs." Here the Council of Trent plainly takes it for granted that notaries created solely by the secular power can validly exercise their office also in ecclesiastical matters. For the Council authorizes bishops to forbid them to act as notaries in ecclesiastical affairs only when they are found incompetent or unworthy.[2] We said, secondly, *as a rule ;* since causes of canonization are excepted. For these latter causes, notaries created by the Apostolic See are absolutely required.

923. It happens not unfrequently in this country, that ecclesiastics have instruments or documents relating to ecclesiastical causes and affairs drawn up, or certified by a notary public or other official appointed solely by the civil power. Here it is to be observed that, where this is done for just cause,—*v.g.,* where no ecclesiastical notary is at hand or

---

[1] Sess. 22, c. 11, de Ref.   [2] Boulx, l. c., p. 504.

accessible,—a notary public who is a Catholic should as far as possible be employed. For the custom above mentioned, authorizing lay notaries appointed solely by the civil power to act as notaries also in ecclesiastical matters, seems to have had reference only to Catholic notaries appointed by Catholic princes at a period when the Church and state were in mutual concord and harmony.[1] Observe, also, that an instrument validly drawn up by a notary is of full authority—*i.e.*, constitutes of itself full proof—not only in the place where it was made, but everywhere.[2]

924. *Q.* Is the ecclesiastical judge bound to make use of a notary, chancellor, or secretary, both in ordinary or solemn, and in extraordinary or summary, trials or judicial proceedings?

A. He is. This is expressly ordained in the decretal *Quoniam* issued by Pope Innocent III., in the General Council of the Lateran, held in 1215. His words are: "Statuimus ut tam in ordinario judicio, quam extraordinario, judex semper adhibeat aut publicam (si potest habere) personam, aut duos viros idoneos, qui fideliter, universa judicii acta conscribant."[3] This law is still in force, having never been revoked. Hence a secretary or notary, or where he cannot be had, two trustworthy persons, must intervene at all judicial proceedings or investigations, even though of the simplest kind,[4] of ecclesiastical courts or tribunals, and consequently also at trials or proceedings before Commissions of Investigation in the United States and England. This holds so strictly, that the records or minutes or acts of the proceedings have no authority, and are not worthy of belief, even though they are signed or attested by the judge, unless they are written and signed by a secretary, or, in his absence, two trustworthy persons. Thus the *Cap. Cum a*

---

[1] Cf. Bouix. l. c., p. 505.

[2] Ib., p. 508.

[3] Cap. Quoniam 11, de Probat. (ii. 19).

[4] München, l. c., vol. i., pp. 65, 77.

nobis says: " Districtius inhibemus, ne unius judìcis, quantaecunque fuerit auctoritatis, verbo credatur." [1]

925. The object of this law, therefore, is to have an authentic and reliable record of what has taken place, and that in the interest of all the parties concerned—namely, the plaintiff, defendant, judge, etc. Hence it is the duty of the secretary to take accurate and faithful minutes of the entire proceedings—namely, of citations; of dilatory motions, or delays asked and granted ; of challenges against the judge; of exceptions taken by the parties; of the complaint or accusation of the plaintiff, and the answer of the defendant; of interrogations or positions, or specifications of charges ; of the testimony of the witnesses ; of the production of instruments, etc., etc. All this is expressly set forth in the above decretal of Pope Innocent III. The latter says : " Fideliter universa judicii acta conscribant; videlicet citationes, dilationes, recusationes, exceptiones, petitiones, responsiones, interrogationes, confessiones, testium depositiones, instrumentorum productiones, interlocutiones, appellationes, renunciationes, conclusiones, et caetera quae occurrerint, competenti ordine conscribendo, loca designando, tempora et personas." [2] The notary or secretary should, on being appointed, take an oath, though not on pain of the nullity of his acts, to discharge the duties of his office faithfully. As to secretaries under the Instruction *Cum Magnopere*, see our *New Procedure.*

Art. VIII.

Judicial Messengers (Nuntii judiciales).

926. As in secular, so also in ecclesiastical courts, messengers (*pedelli, cursores, apparitores ;* in our secular courts they are called constables, marshals, sheriffs, etc.) are offi-

[1] Cap. 28, de Test. (ii. 20). [2] Cap. 11. de Prob. cit.; ib. Glossa, v. citationes, etc.

cially employed to execute the orders of the judge or court, to summon the parties or litigants to trial—*i.e.*, serve the citation on the parties, deliver the messages of the court, etc.[1]   In the United States, as elsewhere, citations and notifications of the ecclesiastical court are to be in writing, and served upon the contending parties either by its official messenger, if there is one attached to the court, or by any trustworthy person, or by registered mail.[2]   When the letter containing the citation or notification is sent by registered mail, a proof is at once had of its delivery.   For the recipient of a registered letter is obliged to sign and give to the mail-carrier or post-office official a receipt of the delivery of the letter, which receipt is transmitted to the sender.

Q. How are citations and notifications made according to the Instruction *Cum Magnopere ?*

A. For the answer, see our *New Procedure*, or Commentary on the Instruction *Cum Magnopere*, Chap. II., Art. XIV.

[1] Schmalzg., l. ii., t. 1, n. 14.
[2] S. C. de P. F., 20 Julii, 1878, § 4; Cum Magnopere, art. xiv.

CHAPTER II.

OF THE ARCHBISHOP'S COURT OF JUSTICE, ALSO IN THE UNITED STATES.

(*De Curia archiepiscopali.*)

927. *Organization or personnel of the archbishop's court, where the common law of the Church obtains.*—Besides the episcopal jurisdiction which an archbishop has in his own diocese, he possesses also, as we have shown elsewhere,[1] a metropolitan jurisdiction over his suffragan bishops and their subjects. For the exercise of this metropolitan jurisdiction archbishops usually establish a special tribunal, distinct from that charged with the exercise of the jurisdiction of the archbishop's own diocese. However, though this metropolitan tribunal is generally distinct from the diocesan court or tribunal proper of the archbishop, it is, nevertheless, in form and construction similar to it. In other words, it is composed of the archbishop as primary ordinary judge; of his vicar-general as vice-judge—that is, secondary ordinary judge; of a fiscal promoter, a secretary, and the other customary officials.[2]

928. *Present organization of the archbishop's court in the United States.*—Where the Instruction of the S. C. de Prop. Fide of July 20, 1878, is still in force, the archbishop's court with us, for the hearing and adjudication of criminal and disciplinary causes of ecclesiastics appealed to it from a diocese of the province, is formed or organized in the same manner as the archbishop's diocesan court for these causes. Hence this metropolitan tribunal is composed of the archbishop or his vicar-general as judge, and of the Commission of Investigation as a board of assessors to whom belongs

[1] Supra, n. 530 sq.   [2] Bouix, l. c., p. 516.

exclusively the trial or investigation of the case appealed.[1]
From the principles above laid down, it is evident that the
metropolitan may establish two distinct Commissions of Investigation—one for the hearing of causes of his own diocese,
another for the adjudication of causes appealed to him from
his province.

929. We have already seen that it is allowed to appeal to
the metropolitan both from judicial and extrajudicial grievances; that the archbishop may hear these appeals either in
person or through his vicar-general or other person; that in
Catholic countries he does so, as a rule, not personally, but
through his vicar-general. Of course, archbishops in the
United States may also allow their vicars-general to act for
them in this matter,—that is, to receive appeals and convene
the Commission of Investigation, by whom the appeal is
heard or tried,—and upon the conclusion of the investigation
or hearing of the appeal by the Commission, pass sentence
or decide the appeal.

In those dioceses, however, in which the recent Instruction of the S. C. de Prop. Fide, *Cum Magnopere*, has been introduced, the archbishop's court or *curia* for the hearing
and deciding of criminal and disciplinary causes of ecclesiastics appealed to it, consists of the archbishop, his vicar-
general, or other person delegated to that effect, as judge;
of the diocesan prosecutor, and of the secretary.

930. Hence it may be asked: Can the archbishop appoint
one and the same vicar-general to exercise diocesan as well
as metropolitan jurisdiction? We reply in the affirmative;
nay, unless the archbishop determines otherwise, the vicar-
general appointed by him is to be considered as vested both
with the diocesan and metropolitan jurisdiction. When,
however, he appoints one vicar-general for the exercise of
the diocesan, and another for that of the metropolitan juris-

---

[1] Cf. Instr., S. C. de P. F., 20 Julii, 1878, § 17, Si vero.

diction, it may be somewhat disputed whether either of them can be regarded as vicar-general, in the proper sense of the term, or whether each in the case is not simply a delegate. The reason is, that neither of them would seem to have that universal jurisdiction, morally speaking, which a vicar-general ought to possess.[1] Hence the safer course for the archbishop will be, not to limit the jurisdiction of his vicars-general to diocesan or metropolitan matters, especially as he can always, without restricting their jurisdiction, order the one to confine himself to diocesan, the other to metropolitan, causes or matters.[2]

931. When is it allowed to appeal from the suffragan to the metropolitan, and what are the effects of such an appeal? Both questions have already been sufficiently answered by us: the first in Nos. 444, 449, 452, 531; the second on pages 426 and 427 of the first volume of this work. See also the Instruction *Cum Magnopere* of 1884, and our commentary on it, entitled *The New Procedure in Criminal and Disciplinary Causes of Ecclesiastics in the United States.*

---

[1] Supra, n. 620.   [2] Craiss. n. 5791.

CHAPTER III.

(Processus Criminalis Ordinarius.)

932. By an ordinary or formal canonical criminal trial (*processus ordinarius, solemnis, judicium plenarium*) is meant that mode of procedure for the punishment of crime where all the prescribed formalities, both essential and non-essential in the sense above explained,[1] are accurately observed.[2]

SECTION I.
Various Modes of beginning Canonical Criminal Trials.

933. A formal canonical criminal trial can be initiated or take place in four ways: 1, by way of accusation; 2, of denunciation; 3, of inquiry;[3] 4, and of exception. Let us briefly explain each of these modes.

·ART. I.

Mode of procedure by way of accusation (Processus per viam accusationis).

934. This method consists in this, that a person charges another with a crime before the competent judge and in a lawful manner, and assumes the obligation of proving his charge, and that for the purpose of having the offender pun-

---

[1] Supra, n. 692, 693. [2] Ib., n. 698; Craiss., n. 5789.
[3] Cap. 16, de Accus. (v. 1); Cap. 31, de Simon. (v. 3).

ished, and thus satisfying the demands of justice.[1] According to the positive law of the Church, the accusation or criminal charge has to be made in writing. We say, *positive law;* for, by custom to the contrary, it can be made also orally, at the present day, provided it be taken down in writing by a public notary or official.[2]

935. The charge (*libellus*) should be properly drawn up —that is, it should express the names of the judge before whom the accusation is made, of the accuser and accused, the nature of the crime, the place, year, and month of its commission.[3] Moreover, by the positive common law of the Church, it should be signed by the accuser, who by this signature pledges himself to prove the charges, or if he fails to do so, to suffer the same punishment (*poena talionis*) which the accused would have incurred had he been found guilty.[4] Of course this *poena talionis* or retaliative punishment was not incurred unless it appeared that the accuser had falsely and maliciously made the accusation. We said, *by the positive common law of the Church;* for it is the opinion of most canonists that the law of the *poena talionis* has been, at least generally speaking, abrogated by custom to the contrary, and is no longer in force, at least generally.[5]

936. It will be observed that the procedure by way of accusation, as above described, was surrounded with many difficulties. The *rôle* of an accuser was a perilous one, owing to the fact that he was bound under the pain of retaliation (*poena talionis*) to prove his charge. Hence, few were found willing to undertake the dangerous task of an accuser; and those who did undertake it acted mostly from feelings

---

[1] Reiff., l. 5, t. 1, n. 5; Schmalzg., l. 5, t. 1, n. 21; Craiss., n. 5800.

[2] Bouix, de Jud., vol. ii., p. 5.

[3] L. Libellorum 3 ff. de Accus. et inscript. (48. 2).

[4] Ib., § 2 item; L. 7 ff. eod. tit.; Cap. 16, de Accus. (v 1).

[5] Schmalzg., l. 2, t. 1, n. 23; Stremler, l. c., p. 83; Craiss., n. 5802, cf. tamen Bouix, l. c , p. 33.

or motives of revenge or private interest. Thus it came to pass that many crimes remained unpunished.

937. For these and other reasons of a similar kind, Pope Innocent III., the greatest canonist and lawgiver of his age, established the modes of procedure by way of denunciation and inquiry, as ordinary modes of procedures, or as trials which should be ordinarily made use of. We say, *as ordinary modes;* for before the time of this Pope these modes had indeed existed, but only as extraordinary modes of procedure. Yet the mode of procedure by way of accusation was not abolished by this Pontiff. For, in his celebrated decretal *Qualiter et quando,*[1] he expressly enumerates this method, as approved and lawful. Nevertheless, it soon fell into almost total disuse; so that at present the usual mode of procedure is by way of inquiry.

938. Hence it may be asked whether the mode of procedure by way of accusation is unlawful at present? We think not, at least so far as its substance is concerned. For it has never been abolished by any positive law, or by custom. Not by any positive law; for it is certain that no such law exists. Nor by custom to the contrary. For the custom above referred to—namely, the disuse into which the procedure by accusation has fallen—is simply one of preference for the trial by way of inquisition, not one reprobating that by way of accusation. Hence this latter mode may still be resorted to, especially where the accuser has an interest in the punishment of the delinquent; nay, as Bouix remarks, there may be cases where it is far better and more effective than its more favored rival—the trial by inquiry.[2]

939. The effects of a criminal charge or accusation may be viewed chiefly so far as they concern either the judge or the accused. The judge, upon receiving a criminal charge, can and should proceed to take cognizance of the case. The

---

[1] Cap. 24, de Acc. (v. 1).   [2] Bouix, l. c., vol. ii., p. 30; Stremler, l. c., p. 84.

effects upon the accused are the same as in the case of procedure by way of inquiry or denunciation, which will be described farther on.

940. Can a person, in the ecclesiastical court, be again accused of and tried for a crime for which he has been once already tried, and either found guilty and condemned or not? He cannot, generally speaking.[1] The law of the Church herein but imitates the clemency of God, who, once He has forgiven the sin, does not allow it to be revived again for punishment.[2] We said, *generally speaking;* since there are some exceptions, for which see Reiffenstuel, l. c., n. 42 sq.

941. Can a criminal action or accusation be extinguished in the ecclesiastical court by prescription? In other words: Is it forbidden to accuse or try a person for a crime after a certain time has elapsed from the time the offence was committed? It is, by the Roman law, adopted by the sacred canons. Now, by the Roman law, no person could be accused of or tried for sins of the flesh, five years after the offence was committed;[3] nor for other crimes, twenty years after the offence was perpetrated.[4] Custom, however, does not at present observe this law, and seems to allow of a crime being prosecuted in ecclesiastical courts at any time.[5]

ART. II.

Mode of procedure, or beginning criminal trials, by way of denunciation (Processus per viam denunciationis).

942. By denunciation, we here understand the manifestation of a crime made to the superior by a person who does not assume the obligation of proving the charge. The latter

---

[1] Cap. 6, de Accus.; Glossa, ib.; L. 6 ff. Nautae, § 4 (4. 9).
[2] Can. 23, 29. q. 4; Reiff., lib. v., t. 1, n. 41.
[3] L. 29, § 5 ff. Ad leg. Jul. de adult. (48. 5).
[4] L. 12, C. ad leg. Corn. de falsis (9, 22).   [5] Schmalzg., l. 5, tit. 1, n. 121.

clause shows how denunciation differs from accusation. A person who denounces another may have two objects in view: first, to have the offender simply reprimanded by the superior as a father; second, to have him punished by the superior in the capacity of ecclesiastical judge. Hence there are two kinds of denunciation—paternal (*denunciatio evangelica, fraterna,* etc.) and judicial (*denunciatio judicialis*). The denunciation is evangelical, when the delinquent, having as a rule been charitably admonished, but without effect, is denounced to the superior as a father, not indeed to be punished, in the strict sense of the word, but to be corrected paternally.[1]

943. Judicial denunciation, which is here chiefly under discussion, is that which is made to the superior or bishop in his capacity of ecclesiastical judge, in order that he may proceed against the offender judicially, and punish him.[2] This judicial denunciation, therefore, serves as a basis for judicial proceedings against the offender, while the evangelical cannot, generally speaking, serve as such basis.

944. *Q.* What crimes can be judicially denounced?

A. 1. Those which common fame reports as having been committed, and that even when the person who makes the denunciation is not able to suggest or indicate to the judge any other proofs of the guilt. The reason is, that common fame is of itself sufficient to authorize the judge to inquire into the guilt of the alleged delinquent—*i.e.,* to begin the process of inquiry against him.[3] 2. It is controverted whether an occult crime, even though provable, can, generally speaking, be judicially denounced. Those who hold the affirmative contend that the publicity of the crime, or defamation, is required, only when the judge proceeds by way of inquiry, and that *ex mero officio,* but not when he pro-

---

[1] Soglia, vol. ii., p. 299, ed. Vecch.
[2] Reiff., l. c., n. 83; Schmalzg., l. c., n. 151.   [3] Bouix, l. c., p. 44.

ceeds upon a denunciation, or at the instance of another person. For, in the latter case, the person denouncing takes the place of the accuser or of common fame.[1] Those who hold the negative, say that the judicial denunciation is not, strictly speaking, a distinct and separate mode of procedure, but serves rather as a means, or an occasion for beginning proceedings by way of inquiry; that, consequently, as defamation is necessary for the process of inquiry, so also it is requisite for the trial by denunciation. Thus the *Glossa*[2] expressly says: "Si vero procedat judex ad petitionem alicujus procurantis inquisitionem . . . cognoscet prius judex utrum " (denuntiatus) "*sit infamatus*, et postea procedet super iis quae denuntiata sunt; alias non procedat, *nisi primo constet quod infamatus sit.*" . . . Hence, say the advocates of this opinion, the ecclesiastical judge cannot, as a rule, proceed judicially against a person, upon a mere judicial denunciation, unless there exists also defamation. Bouix[3] holds that this applies even when the diocesan promoter, or prosecuting official, makes the denunciation or complaint. Of the two above opinions, the negative seems the safer.[4] However, whether the first or second opinion is held, it is certain that in some few cases an occult crime can be denounced—namely, where it would inflict a grave injury upon a community or a third party.[5] 3. It is certain that a crime which is occult, and at the same time not provable, cannot, as a rule, be judicially denounced. The reason is that the denunciation in the case would be worse than useless. For it would simply result in the defamation of the accused, while the judge could not condemn him, as in the supposition the crime could not be proved.

945. How should the judicial denunciation be made? Nearly all the formalities prescribed for the trial by way of

---

[1] Reiff., l. c., n. 88; Schmalzg., l. c., n. 157.
[2] In cap. 24, de Acc., v. ad inquirendum. [3] L. c., p. 79.
[4] Cf. München, l. c., vol. i., p. 489, n. 6, 7. [5] Reiff., l. c., n. 89.

accusation, must be observed and that on pain of nullity. Hence, as in the trial or process by way of accusation, so in the trial by way of denunciation, it is necessary : 1. That the denunciation be made in writing, which should contain the name of the judge, of the person denouncing, and the person denounced ; the nature of the offence ; the place and time where and when it was committed ; the day when the denunciation was made. 2. That the person making the denunciation name the witnesses, and point out or indicate to the judge the other proofs—*v.g.*, instruments—in his possession, so as to enable him to determine whether the denunciation can be sustained or not, and, consequently, whether it should be received or rejected. Here we see one of the differences between denunciation and accusation. In the trial by way of denunciation, the denouncer is not bound to prove his charges, but simply to indicate the proofs to the judge ;[1] in the trial by way of accusation, the accuser must prove the charges.

946. *Q.* What are the chief effects of a judicial denunciation, (*a*) upon the judge, (*b*) the person denouncing, (*c*) and the person denounced ?

A. 1. As regards the judge, the effect is that he is bound to inquire into the alleged offence, and begin judicial proceedings against the alleged offender—*v.g.*, to summon and examine witnesses, etc.[2] 2. The denouncer, as we have seen, must name the witnesses and place the judge in possession of the other proofs alleged by him to exist. If he is convicted of having knowingly and maliciously made a false denunciation, he should be punished as a calumniator ; nay, even where he merely fails to give proper proofs, even though no malice be shown, he is *presumed* to be a calumniator, and should be punished as such until he has proved his innocence.[3] Among the punishments which may, ac-

---

[1] Reiff., l. c., n. 96.   [2] Nov. 17, cap. 3; Reiff., l. c., n. 125.
[3] Cap. 2, de Calumn. (v. 2); ib. Glossa, v. Calumniandi.

cording to law, be inflicted upon calumniators, the following is noteworthy, as being still in force: Where an ecclesiastic is found guilty of having calumniated another ecclesiastic, he should be deprived of his ecclesiastical office and benefice.[1]

947. 3. Generally speaking, the person denounced cannot, pending the denunciation, be promoted to ecclesiastical dignities or benefices, or to sacred orders.[2] The same holds true of a person against whom judicial proceedings by way of accusation and inquiry are pending. The reason is that while a person is not considered guilty by the mere accusation, or judicial denunciation or inquiry, he is nevertheless thereby lowered in the estimation of others. Observe that a judicial denunciation, accusation, or inquiry only hinders a person from being appointed to an office, etc., as stated, but not from the exercise or administration or jurisdiction of an office or dignity already possessed. Hence a bishop or other ecclesiastical superior, accused or denounced by his subjects or others, is not thereby, as a rule, prohibited from continuing the exercise of the powers of his office. We say, *as a rule;* for the following two cases are excepted: 1. The prelate or superior in the case cannot, pending the denunciation, exercise his jurisdiction with regard to the particular matter or cause which is the subject of the denunciation;[3] 2. A prelate denounced of wasting or dilapidating ecclesiastical goods or property, remains, pending the case, suspended from the administration of such property.[4]

948. *Note.*—At the present day judicial denunciation, in the proper sense of the word, is but rarely resorted to. In fact, private individuals now scarcely ever use the right given them by the sacred canons to make a judicial denunciation, except where their private or personal interests are

---

[1] Cap. 1, de Calumn.; Reiff., l. v., t. 2, n. 4 sq.
[2] Ex cap. 4, de Accus.; Reiff., l. v., t. 1, n. 130 sq.
[3] Ex cap. olim 26, de Accus.   [4] Cap. 27, de Accus.; Reiff., l. c., n. 139.

at stake. In all other circumstances, judicial denunciations proper are, at present, made only by the bishop's official or diocesan promoter.[1]

949. *Of canonical or legal denunciation.*—Some canonists divide denunciation into evangelical, judicial, *and canonical.* Strictly speaking, however, the canonical is a species of the judicial denunciation. For the sake of greater clearness, we shall here briefly explain what is meant by this canonical denunciation. By it we mean the denunciation which the sacred canons prescribe in certain cases for the common good.[2] Now the law of the Church imposes the obligation of denouncing chiefly: 1. Impediments to marriages, to the reception of sacred orders, to the promotion to ecclesiastical dignities and benefices. 2. Heretics and apostates; those who aid and abet them, or read, keep, or sell their works. 3. Confessors who demand of their penitents the name of the accomplice.[3] 4. Confessarios sollicitantes ad turpia occasione vel praetextu confessionis.[4] 5. Members of secret societies. 6. Bishops and other superiors, parish priests, etc., who are guilty of excess, or maladministration of their office. The reason is that the common good requires that unworthy superiors shall be corrected, and, if obstinate, removed from their office. However, not all are indiscriminately entitled or bound to denounce delinquent superiors, but only those who are directly concerned—that is, the subjects.[5] Thus the right as well as duty of reporting the bishop's excesses to Rome belongs only to his ecclesiastics; that of informing on delinquent rectors of congregations, to these congregations.[6]

950. From the above cases it will be seen that the canonical denunciation is established for the purpose of averting

[1] Stremler, l. c., pp. 93, 106.
[2] Stremler, l. c., p. 97.
[3] Const. Apostolici, Bened. XIV.
[4] Bened. XIV., Const., 1 Jun., 1741.
[5] Can. 45, 46, 47, 48, Caus. 2, q. 7.
[6] Schmalzg., l. c., n. 166.

spiritual injury from a community or private individual.[1] However, as Stremler[2] observes, the obligation of making the denunciation in some of the above cases can scarcely be said to exist any longer. In fact, crimes committed against the Catholic Church have unhappily become so common, that it is well-nigh impossible for the Church to punish the offenders. We observe, moreover, with Stremler,[3] that anonymous denunciations should be rejected as calumnious, and utterly unworthy of belief.[4]

ART. III.

Process or Trial by way of Inquiry (Processus per viam Inquisitionis).

951. The mode of procedure in criminal causes—which, as we have seen,[5] is at present in use in ecclesiastical courts, even to the exclusion of the trial by accusation—is by way of inquiry or investigation. Before the time of Pope Innocent III. this process was resorted to but rarely, and only in extraordinary cases. The ordinary way of procedure was by accusation. This learned Pope, as already intimated, brought the trial by way of inquiry into prominence, and from his time it began to be substituted for the trial by way of accusation. At the present day it has come to be the usual and commonly adopted mode of procedure in ecclesiastical courts.[6] The mode of procedure to be followed by our bishops in hearing and deciding criminal and disciplinary causes of ecclesiastics, as prescribed by the S. C. de Prop. Fide, both in its Instruction of July 20, 1878, and in its recent Instruction *Cum Magnopere* of 1884, is also by way of inquiry. Thus the Instr. of July 20, 1878, calls the asses-

---

[1] Reiff., l. c., n. 147.   [2] L. c., p. 102.   [3] Ib., p. 100.
[4] S. C. I., 10 Martii, 1677 ; Ferraris, v. denunciatio, n. 1 et 50.
[5] Supra, n. 937.   [6] Schmalzg., L c., n. 172.

sors, Commissions of *Investigation*, and the Instr. of 1884 says
" processus instruitur *ex officio*."

952. What then is here meant by inquiry (*inquisitio*)? To
inquire into, means, grammatically, to search into, investigate,
examine into, and find out by careful examination, etc. In
jurisprudence, it signifies the searching into a matter, not as
done by everybody, but only by the *judge ;* nay, it expresses
not every act of investigation even of a judge, but only that
which is made by him *in criminal matters*—that is, for the
purpose of discovering crimes and criminals.[1] Hence the
inquiry or investigation, as here understood, is, speaking in
general, the act of the bishop or ecclesiastical judge lawfully
seeking to discover crimes or criminals.[2]

953. There are three kinds of inquiry : A general, a
special, and a mixed. The inquiry is *general* (*inquisitio generalis*), when the ecclesiastical judge or superior inquires in
general, and without naming any specific crime or criminal,
whether either in his whole diocese or some part of it any
crimes are committed, or the laws of the Church or statutes
of the diocese violated ; *special* (*inquisitio specialis*), when both
the crime and the criminal are specified—namely, when the
judge examines whether a certain person (*v.g.*, Peter) has
committed a certain crime (*v.g.*, slander) ; *mixed* (*inquisitio
mixta*), when (*a*) either the crime to be inquired into is specified, but its author is uncertain and not specified—*v.g.*, when
the judge inquires thus : Who has committed this murder? (*b*) or *vice versa*, when the presumed offender is expressed, but the offence not specified—*v.g.*, if the inquiry is :
Has Peter committed any crime or violated any law ?[3] Each
of these kinds of inquiry may be paternal or judicial, according as its object is either simply the paternal correction of
the offender or his punishment.

[1] Bouix, de Jud., vol. ii., p. 60
[2] Reiff., l. 5, t. 1, n. 149; Schmalzg., eod. n. 172.
[3] Schmalzg., l. c., n. 174 sq.; Stremler, l. c., p. 138.

954. *Q.* Can the ecclesiastical judge or superior proceed against any one by way of inquiry without previous ill-fame?

A. We premise: 1. The inquiry is either general, or special, or mixed. 2. Again, the ecclesiastical superior or judge proceeds (*a*) either absolutely *ex officio*, or *ex mero officio*—that is, without being officially requested to do so by any one, thus acting at the same time as judge and plaintiff or prosecutor, (*b*) or *ex officio* indeed, but at the instance of a third party—namely, either of a private person or the public prosecutor. 3. Finally, the inquiry is either paternal or judicial.[1]

955. We now answer: 1. The rule is that the superior or judge, when proceeding absolutely *ex officio*, cannot institute a special judicial inquiry against any one who has not been previously designated by public opinion, fame, or report, as the party guilty of the crime for which the inquiry is to be instituted.[2] This is certain and beyond controversy, and follows from the principles above laid down.[3] This is proved from the decretal *Inquisitionis* 21, de Acc., where Pope Innocent III. expressly says: "Ad haec respondemus nullum esse pro crimine, super quo *aliqua non laborat infamia, seu clamosa insinuatio non praecesserit*, propter dicta hujusmodi puniendum: quinimmo super hoc depositiones contra eum recipi non debere, cum inquisitio fieri debeat solummodo super illis, de quibus *clamores aliqui* praecesserunt." The same is clear also from the decretal *Qualiter et quando*,[4] issued by the same Pope, in the Lateran Council held in 1216. This decretal says: "Sicut accusationem legitima debet praecedere inscriptio, sic et . . . inquisitionem *clamosa insinuatio praevenire*."

956. This holds so true, that, unless a previous public report exists of the guilt, not even the sworn testimony of two

[1] Bouix, l. c., p. 61.
[2] Cap. 21 et 24, de Acc.; Schmalzg., l. 5, t. 1,,n. 196; Reiff., l. c., n. 173.
[3] Supra, n. 944. [4] Cap. 24, de Acc.; cf. cap. 19, de Acc. (v. 1).

or more witnesses, who depose that they saw the party com
mit the crime, suffices to authorize the judge to proceed to a
special judicial inquiry against any one.[1] The reason is, that
the crime in the case, being known only to two or three, is
still occult; and consequently should not be made public
by the inquiry. Hence it is necessary that the report of a
crime committed by a person be diffused through the
greater part of the neighborhood or community in which
the delinquent lives.[2] In fact, the ecclesiastical judge should
not proceed to the punishment of crimes, save upon public
knowledge or information. Now, the knowledge of a crime,
which is neither derived from common fame, nor something
equivalent to it, is not public knowledge. Therefore, etc.
Again, a person could justly complain that an injury was
done him if he were subjected to such inquiry without any
previous current report of his alleged guilt. For by such
inquiry he would come to be suspected of crime, and
grievously suffer in his reputation or good name.[3]

957. We said above,[4] *the rule is;* for there are certain
exceptions, as appears from the sacred canons and the common opinion of canonists. The following are the exceptions
—that is, the cases—where no previous ill-fame is required
for a special judicial inquiry: 1. When a person has confessed his crime in court.[5] 2. When the crime has been
committed in court—*v.g.*, if a witness makes a false statement
before the judge. Observe that these two cases can scarcely
be said to be exceptions to the rule given. For the occult
crime in the case becomes notorious, *notorietate juris*, from
the very fact of its being thus confessed or committed in open
court.[6] 3. In crimes of heresy, apostasy, or other very great
crimes which are very injurious to the common welfare of
the faithful. In these crimes the ecclesiastical judge can

[1] Cap. 21, de Accus.; cap. 24, de Acc.; ib. Glossa, v. ad inquirendum.
[2] Schmalzg., l. c., n. 197.   [3] Ib., n. 196.   [4] Supra, n. 955.
[5] Cap. 1, in 6° (v. 1).   [6] Bouix, l. c., p. 70.

proceed to a special judicial inquiry when there are grave suspicions, even though there be no public report. 4. When the crime tends directly to inflicting an injury upon a third party, whether it be a private individual or a community. 5. When there are very strong indications of guilt—*v.g.*, when a person keeps up a familiar intercourse with the criminals who are known as such, or has fled to avoid appearing in court. For these and similar acts take the place of public report. 6. When the person against whom the inquiry is made is present and does not protest, where the judge proceeds to a special judicial inquiry without previous public opinion. The reason is that the supposed delinquent thus tacitly waives his right, and therefore can blame nobody but himself,[1] if the judge proceeds without common fame.

958. Where the judge, out of these cases, proceeds to a special judicial inquiry, without previous defamation, his acts and judicial proceedings are not only illicit, but invalid, and that in such manner that even where the guilt is subsequently fully and canonically proved in the trial, the guilty party cannot be convicted or condemned.[2] *Note.*—We observe with Bouix,[3] that the above law of the Church, requiring previous public report or common fame, has not been abrogated either by the Council of Trent or by any other subsequent Papal enactment, and is therefore in full force at the present day.

959. *Q.* Is previous ill-fame or public report also requisite when the judge institutes a special judicial inquiry *at the instance of a third party?*

A. We premise: This third party, as we have seen, is either a private individual or the public official appointed to prosecute crimes. We now answer: There are two opin. ions. The negative holds that no previous defamation or common fame is required, even when the denouncer is a

---

[1] Schmalzg., l. c., n. 207.
[2] Cap. 21 et 24, de Acc.; Schmalzg., l. c., n. 198.   [3] L. c., p. 71.

private person, and, *a fortiori*, when he is the public or diocesan promoter.[1] This opinion, at least so far as the public
promoter is concerned, is the one more commonly followed
by canonists.[2] The reason on which this view is based is,
that the denouncer in the case takes the place of common
fame. The affirmative, which is maintained by very able
canonists, such as Bouix[3] and Craisson[4] among the more
recent authors, seems, however, grounded upon strong arguments. In fact, the decretals above cited,[5] which are, as we
have noted, still in force, point unmistakably to the necessity
of previous public report in all cases where a special judicial
inquiry is to be instituted, even though at the instance of a
third party, whether it be a private person or public official.

960. Of course the exceptions given above,[6] apply here
also, even though the affirmative be adopted. However, as
has been observed, most of these exceptions can scarcely be
called exceptions, since their very nature involves publicity
at least of the law. Bouix grants at most that the only cases
where the ecclesiastical judge seems justified in proceeding
without previous common fame are those where the interests
of a third party, who is innocent, are directly injured by the
occult crime. For the interests of a third innocent party
should be protected rather than the reputation of an occult
criminal. He holds that where the crime is injurious only
to the delinquent himself, and not to a third party, there must
always be previous defamation. In illustration of this view
he adduces the following example: Suppose one or two
persons know that a parish priest who enjoys a good reputation is guilty of some occult crime, which, however, does not
redound to the spiritual injury of his flock. Here it is
manifest that to institute a special judicial inquiry, and thus

---

[1] L. Ea quidem 7, C. de Acc. (9. 2); Reiff., l. c., n. 176; Schmalzg., l. c.,
n. 204.

[2] Ap. Bouix, l. c., p. 79.   [3] L. c., p. 79–84.   [4] N. 5857.

[5] Cap. 16, 19, 21, 24, de Acc. (v. 1).   [6] Supra, n. 957.

divulge the crime, would cause great scandal, and weaken the faith of many; and it is evidently better to permit the secret sin of one, than to cause, by its divulgation, the spiritual ruin of many.[1] From all that has been said, it is clear that the safest policy is to proceed only upon previous common report.

961. *Q.* Is previous common fame or defamation necessary for a general inquiry?

A. We premise: 1. It is certain that bishops can and should, in their episcopal visitation of the diocese, make a general inquiry into offences—*v.g.*, whether in the parish visited any crimes are being committed.[2] 2. The general inquiry may be either paternal or judicial. Bishops usually make it in a paternal manner.

962. We now answer: 1. No previous common fame or defamation is required when the inquiry is paternal. When it is judicial there are two opinions. Some deny universally. Others—*v.g.*, Bouix[3] and Craisson[4]—distinguish thus: When, it is altogether general, referring to the whole diocese,—*v.g.*, when the bishop inquires whether any crimes are committed in the diocese,—no previous public report is needed. But it is requisite, when the inquiry is somewhat particular—*v.g.*, when the bishop examines whether crimes are committed in a certain monastery or even parish. Because such investigation would injure the reputation of such place.

963. Observe that the judge or superior (we speak always of the ecclesiastical judge or superior) should inform those whom he interrogates whether he proceeds judicially or only paternally. The reason is that witnesses are not only not bound, but are forbidden to reveal the occult author of a crime, where the judge proceeds judicially against him, unless there is previous defamation. And this

---

[1] Bouix, l. c., p. 83
[3] L. c., p. 89.
[2] Conc. Trid., sess. 24, c. 3, de Ref.
[4] Man., n. 5853.

holds even where the crime can be fully proved by witnesses, and even when the judge interrogates under oath.
The witnesses can answer with a mental restriction that they
do not know.   Much less is the occult guilty party, when
interrogated by the judge, obliged to confess, so long as the
crime is occult.   For the judge has no right to interrogate
in regard to occult cases.   This holds true except (*a*) where
the crime has not yet been committed, but is about to be
committed, (*b*) or where it is being continued, (*c*) or where a
grave injury results to a third party, which cannot be easily
averted   except   by   judicial   intervention.   In these cases
the person interrogated should reveal the delinquent, even
though his crime be altogether occult, and he has not been
defamed, in order that the judge may thus be enabled to
prevent the sin or injury by opportune remedies.[1]

964. *Q.* Is previous common fame or defamation necessary also for a mixed judicial inquiry?

A. It is, when the inquiry is special with regard to the
author of the crime, and general as to the crime—*v.g.*, when
it is made thus: Has Titius committed a crime?   Hence
the Roman or civil law, followed by the Church, says: "Qui
quaestionem habiturus est, non debet specialiter interrogare
an Lucius Titius homicidium fecerit; sed generaliter, quis
id fecerit."[2]   It is not, when the inquiry is general as to the
person, and special only as to the crime—*v.g.*, when it is
made thus: Who has committed this murder?[2]

965. *Nature and conditions of common fame, where it is
indispensable prior to a judicial inquiry.*—So far, we have seen
when previous defamation or common fame is required,
when not.   Let us now go a step farther and ask: What kind
of common fame is necessary in the cases where it is required
previous to a trial by inquiry?   The law of the Church

---

[1] Schmalzg., l. c., n. 195.   [2] L. 1 ff. de Quaest., § 21 (48. 16).
[2] Reiff., l. c., n. 169, 170.

expressly requires, 1. That the common fame or report shall originate with persons of probity and worthy of belief, not with malicious persons or slanderers. 2. That it shall reach the ears of the superior, not merely once, but often.' 3. It must, moreover, be spread, not only among a few persons, *but the greater part of the neighborhood or community.* Thus the *Glossa*' says: "Quia fama loci requiritur, non fama aliquorum." 4. When the ecclesiastical judge proceeds at the instance of a third party, whether it be a private individual or the public prosecuting official, the existence of defamation or common fame must be, moreover, juridically established. This conclusion, however, is not admitted by all canonists. For, as we have seen,' there are some who hold that no defamation, and, *a fortiori*, no canonical proof of its existence, is required, when the judge proceeds at the instance of another party. When the judge proceeds *ex mero officio*, previous common fame must indeed exist, and the judge must, moreover, be certain of its existence; but he need not, at least absolutely speaking, formally and juridically establish this fact—*i.e.*, the existence of the report.' We say, *absolutely speaking;* for the person against whom the inquiry is directed may deny that there is defamation, or at least that it has the requisite conditions; and he may, if the judge decides against him on this point, whether expressly or tacitly, appeal to the higher superior; and then the judge *a quo* is obliged to establish the existence of the report, fully and juridically, before the judge *ad quem.*' Hence it is safer for the judge, in all cases, even when he proceeds *ex mero officio*, to have the existence of the defamation juridically established.

966. Here it may be asked: How is the existence of common fame proved? It is established, like all other ex-

' Cap. Qualiter 24, de Acc. (v. 1).   ' In cap. 21, de Acc., v. dicta procorum.
' Supra, n. 959.   ⁴ Reiff., l. c., n. 192; Bouix, l. c., p. 91.
⁵ Reiff., l. c., n. 193; München, l. c., vol. i., p. 493, n. 8.

ternal facts, chiefly by the testimony of witnesses. This testimony should go to show, not precisely that the crime was committed by such a one, but that many persons or the greater part of the community say or believe that such a crime was committed by such a person. Next, the witnesses, upon being asked, should give the names of the persons among whom the common report exists, so that the judge may know whether they are worthy of belief or not.[1]

967. In order that the ecclesiastical judge may be able to proceed to a special judicial inquiry, besides previous common fame or defamation, it is necessary that the body of the crime (*corpus delicti*) or the main criminal act be established. In other words, before the judge proceeds to inquire who has committed the crime, he must assure himself that the crime itself has been really committed.[2] Thus the Roman law, followed by the Church, says: " Item illud sciendum est, nisi constet aliquem esse occisum, non haberi de familia quaestionem. Liquere igitur debet, scelere interemptum, ut Senatus-consulto locus sit."[3] And this holds true even where the accused has confessed his guilt.[4]

968. But how is the body of the crime or the *corpus delicti* to be established? We must distinguish between those crimes which are *facti permanentis*—that is, those which leave some traces behind; *v.g.*, murder, incendiarism—and those which are *facti transcuntis*, that is, those which leave no vestige behind ; *v.g.*, blasphemy, contumely, slander, magic, etc. When the crime is *facti permanentis*, the judge must generally obtain a *clear and undoubted* knowledge of the *corpus delicti*—namely, by ocular inspection. In other words, the judge must either go in person, or send somebody else for him, to the place where the crime was committed, and view the *corpus delicti*,—*v.g.*, the murdered body, the ruins

[1] Glossa in cap. 24, de Acc., v. ad inquirendum; München, l. c.
[2] Bouix, l. c., p. 100.
[3] L. 1 ff. de Scto. Silan., § 24.   [4] Schmalzg., l. c., n. 212.

of the burned house, etc. If the crime is *facti transeuntis*, it is sufficient for the judge to base his knowledge of the *corpus delicti* upon presumptions and conjectures.[1]

969. As will be seen, the steps of the trial or process by way of inquiry, which have been thus far considered, precede and lead to the main or real trial or inquiry itself, and may therefore be termed the preliminary investigation or trial.[2] The object of this preliminary investigation is to see whether there is sufficient evidence to warrant the judge to proceed against the alleged offender. Its character, therefore, is the same as that of preliminary examinations, which take place in our secular courts. In fact, as will be easily seen, the formalities of trials in vogue in secular courts, all the world over, have many things in common with those of ecclesiastical courts.

970. *The main part of the trial by inquiry, or the real trial properly speaking.*—When the preliminary investigation has been closed or finished, and the judge finds that the facts disclosed warrant him to proceed against the accused, the real trial or the main proceedings begin. The various steps or stages of these proceedings will be fully described further on, when we come to discuss them *ex professo*, in their proper places.[3] Here we shall but indicate them. The first step to be taken is the citation of the accused. Next, the latter must be shown the charges made against him, the depositions and also names of the witnesses, so that he may be able fully to defend himself.[4] His defence must be admitted ; and he must be given the fullest latitude in defending himself. We observe, that in causes of *heresy* the names of the witnesses may be withheld, especially where it is feared that, if made known, the witnesses will suffer grave harm or injury, and be deterred from testifying, or at least testifying

---

[1] Ib., n. 216.   [2] Cf. Stremler, l. c., p. 159.   [3] Infra, n. 982 sq.
[4] Cap. 24, de Acc.; Reiff., l. c., n. 208 ; Schmalzg., l. c., n. 214.

correctly.[1] We observe, moreover, that the charges—which, as we have just seen, must be communicated to the defendant—must be specific, not merely general, and must therefore give the circumstances or details of the crime—namely, the kind or species, the place and time when and where the crime was committed. The reason is, that the knowledge of these particulars enables the accused to defend himself better.[2]

971. Are all these formalities obligatory *sub poena nullitatis* of the process or trial? They are. Hence, if any of them are omitted,—*v.g.*, if there is no previous defamation, where it is required for the trial, or if the citation is omitted, or even where the order in which these formalities follow each other is inverted,—the trial or proceedings are null and void ; provided the accused, being present, protests or excepts.[3] We say, *provided the accused, etc. ;* for if the accused is present, and does not protest, the proceedings are valid, even though some of the requisite formalities are omitted.[4]

972. *Q.* Are the above formalities obligatory, *sub poena nullitatis*, also in proceedings before Commissions of Investigation in the United States ?

A. We premise : The formalities here meant are the ascertaining of the *corpus delicti*, the existence and proofs of defamation or common fame, the citation of the defendant ; the informing him, in detail, of the charges and specifications, as well as of the testimony of the witnesses, and all other evidence ; the hearing of his defence.

973. We now answer: They are, at least so far as their substance is concerned. For they are either expressly or impliedly prescribed by the S. C. de P. F., in its Instruction of July 20, 1878, establishing Commissions of Investigation

---

[1] Reiff., l. c., n. 209; Schmalzg., l. c., n. 214.   [2] Reiff., l. c., n. 210.
[3] Cap. 17 et 22, de Acc. (v. 1).   [4] Cap. 1, 2, de Acc., in 6° (v. 1).

in the United States, and are, moreover, enjoined by the very law of nature, in every judicial proceeding, formal or informal. As regards the law of nature, we have already seen that it requires these substantial formalities. So far as the above Instruction is concerned, it enacts expressly that the accused shall be cited;[1] that the charges shall be fully and clearly communicated to him;[2] that he shall be given full power to defend himself;[3] that, consequently (by implication), the testimony, as also the names of the witnesses, and all other evidence, be made known to him. Moreover, by implication, the Instruction prescribes that what has been said concerning the necessity of previous defamation or common fame be observed. We said, *at least as far as their substance is concerned;* for the *manner* in which these essential formalities are to be observed according to the sacred canons need not always be carried out with us, *sub poena nullitatis,* though it is laudable to adhere even to this manner, as far as practicable. The reason is, that while the proceedings before our Commissions of Investigation are indeed judicial in their character,[4] they do not constitute canonical trials, in the strict sense of the term.[5] Of course, the formalities in question, so far as the summary trial will allow of them, are obligatory *sub poena nullitatis* in all trials which are conducted in accordance with the Instr. *Cum Magnopere* of 1884.

974. *Note.*—It is worthy of note, that publicity is excluded from ecclesiastical trials, even though solemn or formal. Hence, as Stremler[6] very justly remarks, it is a deplorable error, caused by ignorance of the sacred canons, to pretend that in order to avoid scandal it is necessary to suppress or omit the formalities of canonical trials, and to adjudicate all criminal causes of ecclesiastics extrajudicially or *ex informata conscientia—i.e.,* without any judicial formali-

---

[1] Instr. cit., § 4, Per litteras.   [2] Ib.   [3] Ib., § 7, Deinde.
[4] S. C. de P. F., Ad Dubia, § iii., *Ex quibus.*
[5] S. C. de P. F., Instr. cit., § 5, *Convenientibus.*   [6] L. c., p. 162.

ties whatever. For, as the same author continues, it is very possible or feasible to give an accused ecclesiastic a regular or formal canonical trial without any publicity, in such manner that no one, save the parties directly concerned,—namely, the judge, the accused, and the witnesses,—need know of it. Of course this applies also to our trials as conducted before Commissions of Investigation, as is, moreover, clearly indicated by the S. C. de P. F. itself, in its above Instruction, when it directs that the bishop shall admonish the members of these Commissions (and *a fortiori*, all others who may be present at the proceedings) to keep silence in regard to what they may hear in the course of the proceedings.[1] This privacy or secrecy of the proceedings is evidently prescribed chiefly for the benefit of the accused, lest his reputation should otherwise be unnecessarily injured.

Art. IV.

Mode of Procedure by way of Exception (*Norma Procedendi per viam Exceptionis*).

975. The right of the defendant to take exceptions—that is, to protest against or object to the judge, accuser, witnesses, or the proceedings themselves, whether in whole or in part—being a legitimate means of defence, forms part of ecclesiastical trials. Now from such objections or challenges or protests, made in court or during the trial, a new cause or issue arises incidentally, which must be adjudicated according to the prescriptions of the sacred canons.[2] Now, as we shall see, it may happen that the exception of the defendant is based upon a criminal charge made then and there against the judge, informer, witnesses, etc. Thus it is evident that crimes may be brought into court by way of exception. The latter is therefore one of the means of

---

[1] Instr. cit., § 5, *Convenientibus.*　　　　[2] Bouix, l. c., p. 107.

instituting or beginning criminal trials in ecclesiastical courts.[1] It seems, therefore, proper, that we should here briefly explain the mode of procedure by way of exception.

976. By an exception we here mean an objection or protest made by the defendant against the judge, the accuser, denouncer, informer, or witnesses, for the purpose of disabling these parties from acting respectively as judge, accuser, or witnesses, or even (where a crime is objected against them) for the purpose of having them punished.[2] From this definition it will be seen that there are two kinds of exceptions: 1, criminal (*exceptio criminalis*)—namely, when a crime is objected; 2, civil (*exceptio civilis*), when a disability is objected, which is not culpable. We shall here speak only of criminal exceptions, and that only so far as they give rise to a new though incidental cause or trial, since we shall treat of exceptions, especially civil, more fully later on.

977. A criminal exception can be made in two ways: civilly and criminally. It is made civilly when a crime is objected to the judge, opponent, witness, etc., not in order that he may be punished according to canon law, but merely that he may be excluded from acting as judge, witness, etc., in the case. It is made criminally, on the other hand, when the accused or defendant objects a crime,—*v.g.*, to a witness or opponent,—not simply for the purpose of having its author rejected as a witness, etc., but, moreover, in order that punishment may be inflicted upon him for his crime by judicial sentence. To this kind of exception another bears a strong resemblance—namely, that by which an ecclesiastic, who has been appointed to a prelatic, episcopal, or other ecclesiastical dignity, or to an ecclesiastical benefice or office, is charged with or accused of a crime which, by the sacred canons, is an obstacle to his consecration, ordina-

---

[1] Reiff., l. c., n. 233. [2] Ib., n. 234.

tion, or installation.[1] This exception is also called a quasi-exception. For an exception proper is one which is made only by a *defendant*, whereas this exception can be advanced also by others.[2]

978. *Q.* What should the ecclesiastical judge do when the defendant makes a criminal objection or exception civilly?

A. He should, before all else, that is, before proceeding with the trial of the main cause, adjudicate upon—*i.e.*, hear and decide—the exception.[3] And if he finds it sustained by sufficient evidence, he should exclude the parties against whom the exception was taken from acting as plaintiffs, witnesses, etc. But if the exception is not fully established by the defendant, upon whom rests the burden of proof, as he becomes the plaintiff, for the purpose of the exception, the judge should, by an interlocutory decision, decree, or resolution, reject it as frivolous and frustrative, and thereupon continue with the trial of the main issue, as though no exception had been taken.[4]

979. Can a person—*v.g.*, the plaintiff, opponent, or witness, against whom the defendant has entered a criminal exception or protest civilly, and established it by full proof—be punished by the judge for the crime thus proved? He cannot, generally speaking. He can only be rejected either as plaintiff or witness, or as acting in another capacity. The reason is that the judge should, in proceeding, and in pronouncing sentence, adapt himself, or conform to, or comply with, the intention or petition of the party making the complaint or exception. Thus the cap. 31, *de Sim.*,[5] expressly says: "Juxta judicii formam, sententiae quoque forma dictetur." And the *Glossa*,[6] commenting on these words, remarks: "Et ita judex" (ecclesiasticus) "semper secundum finem, ad quem quis agit, formabit sententiam."

[1] Schmalzg., l. c., n. 243.   [2] Bouix, l. c., p. 109.
[3] Cap. 1, de Ord. cogn. (ii. 10); ib. Glossa, v. Cognoscendum.
[4] Bouix, l. c., p. 110.   [5] L. 5, t. 3, Decret.   [6] Ib., v. Formam.

Now the end of a criminal protest or exception made civilly is simply to repel the party protested against from acting as witness, etc., but not to punish him. We said, *generally speaking;* since there are a few exceptions to this rule, for which see Schmalzgrueber, l. c., n. 246.

980. *Q.* How should the judge (ecclesiastical) proceed when a defendant makes a criminal objection criminally, not merely civilly ?

A. As such an exception partakes of the nature of a formal criminal accusation or charge, the proceedings should be nearly the same as those of criminal trials *per viam accusationis*, already described.[1] If the person making the exception succeeds in proving it, the opponent or plaintiff, witness or other party, against whom it has been proven should not only be rejected as plaintiff or witness, etc., but, moreover, punished according to the sacred canons, as though he had been convicted on a separate trial. However, if the accused who has made the exception fails to sustain it, he does not incur the *poena talionis*, or retaliatory punishment, since consideration is shown him on account of the provocation under which he acts.[2] *Note.*—As we shall see further on, criminal exceptions, whether made civilly or criminally, can be made also in trials or proceedings before Commissions of Investigation in the United States and in England.

981. Many canonists here add a fifth kind of ecclesiastical trial—namely, that which is followed when the crime is *notorious (processus ex notorio).* But, as we shall treat of this procedure later on, we shall not dwell on it here further than to remark, that while no trial need be given the offender where his crime is notorious, yet certain judicial formalities are required to ascertain whether the crime is really notorious.

[1] Bouix, l. c., p. 111.   [2] Schmalzg., l. c., n. 250.

SECTION II.

The different Stages and Formalities of Ordinary or Solemn Criminal Trials (Processus Criminalis Ordinarius) in Ecclesiastical Courts— Formalities of Ecclesiastical Trials in the United States.

982. Having shown how criminal causes are introduced into the ecclesiastical court, or how ecclesiastical criminal trials are begun also in the United States, we shall now describe the various stages or formalities of the trial itself. Here it is well to repeat, that unless the trial is conducted according to the forms prescribed by the law of the Church (which law, for criminal and disciplinary causes of ecclesiastics in the United States, are the Instructions of the S. C. de P. F. *Quamvis* of July 20, 1878, and *Cum Magnopere* of 1884[1]), the proceedings are null and void.[2] It is therefore exceedingly important for all concerned to know these requisite formalities. Moreover, it is evident that unless judicial proceedings are conducted with order and method, they will end in confusion, rather than a knowledge or demonstration of the facts in the case.

983. Trials may be divided into three parts or principal stages. The first runs from the beginning or opening of the case to the contestation or defendant's plea, which is called *litis contestatio*, exclusive, and may be termed the preliminary trial, of which we have already spoken;[3] the second, from the plea to the definitive sentence; the third, from the final sentence to the end of the cause, or the execution of the sentence.[4] Accordingly, we shall divide this section into three articles. We speak here solely of *criminal* trials in the ecclesiastical courts. As, however, *civil* trials in the

[1] Supra, n. 972.

[2] Supra, n. 971; L. 4, C. de Sent. et Interl. omn. jud. (vii. 45); cap. 22, de Rescript. (i. 3); ib. Glossa, v. Juris ordine.

[3] Supra, n. 969.   [4] Soglia, l. iv. cap. 3, § 30, ed. Vecch.

ecclesiastical courts—of which we shall treat later—have many things in common with criminal ecclesiastical trials, we shall, in the course of the present section, explain as occasion offers, certain questions which refer peculiarly to civil trials in ecclesiastical courts. This will conduce to greater clearness, and at the same time obviate the necessity of repeating the same remarks when we come to treat of ecclesiastical civil trials. For similar reasons, we shall also set forth in this section the peculiar formalities of trials before Commissions of Investigation, here and in England, as occasions present themselves, though we are fully aware, as we have already several times stated, that these trials are not strictly canonical trials. It is plain that by showing where this peculiar ecclesiastical trial differs from, and where it agrees with, the canonical trial proper, we shall better illustrate the nature and characteristics of both.

ART. I.

The Steps or Stages of formal Criminal Trials, from the beginning or opening of the Cause to the Plea exclusive—Application of the Principles here laid down to Trials in the United States.

984. The first step in the trial usually consists in tendering to the judge the written accusation, called *libellus*, or bill of complaint, by which both the judge and the accused are informed of the nature of the charges made. Next the judge issues the citation summoning the defendant to appear and answer the charges preferred against him. If the latter wilfully disobeys the citation, he becomes guilty of contempt. If he obeys and appears in court, he may, before giving a direct answer to the charge, make various protests or exceptions, either against the action itself, or the mode of procedure, or the judge, or witnesses, etc.; or he may even make a

counter-charge against the plaintiff. Hence, in this article, we shall treat, under separate headings, of the " libellus," the citation, contumacy and its effects, exceptions—especially those made against the judge, and counter-charges.

§ 1. *On tendering to the Ecclesiastical Judge the written Criminal Charge (de Libelli Oblatione).*

985. If the procedure is by way of accusation (*processus per viam accusationis*), the accuser should, before all else, hand to the judge the written accusation or bill of complaint (*libellus accusationis*).[1]   This is the first step in the trial by way of accusation.   In like manner, if the procedure is by way of denunciation (*processus per viam denuntiationis*) or by way of inquiry (*per viam inquisitionis ad instantiam alicujus*) instituted at the request of a third party, the first act is the presenting to the judge the written denunciation, or denunciatory bill of complaint (*libellus denuntiatorius*), signed by the person making the denunciation, or demanding the inquiry, whether he be a private person or a public official—*v.g.*, the bishop's promoter or prosecuting official.   To this denunciatory bill of charges should be appended a list of the witnesses or documents by which the charge is to be sustained.[2] If the procedure is by way of inquiry, conducted by the judge altogether *ex officio*,—that is, not at the instance of a third party (*per viam merae inquisitionis*),—the first step is that the judge should assure himself of the existence of public fame, in the manner laid down above.[3]   Before proceeding to the citation, therefore, the judge should examine witnesses and gather all the information he can, to ascertain the existence of defamation.   Where he proceeds to a special judicial inquiry, he must moreover, according to many canonists, juridically verify the existence of common fame after he has received the denunciatory bill.[4]   Here we remark, that when the

---

[1] Supra, n. 935 sq.   [2] Supra, n. 945.   [3] Supra, n. 965 (4).   [4] Ib.

judge has received the bill of accusation or denunciation, and finds it properly drawn up, he is bound to proceed against the alleged offender. For he is the public official appointed for the purpose of rendering justice to all.' Finally, where the procedure is by way of exception, the person excepting must, before anything else, give the judge the bill of exceptions, or of the charges on which the exception is based.

986. From what has been said, it is plain that the handing to the judge the written charge or bill of charges is the first step, except when the judge proceeds *ex mero officio.* But as a matter of fact, the trial by inquiry is rarely if ever instituted, except at the instance of a third party—namely, of a private individual, or the diocesan prosecuting official, who draws up, and tenders the bill to the judge, in the name of the diocese.' Hence it may be said that, as a rule, the first step of a canonical trial is the tendering of the bill to the judge.

987. In our secular courts, all over the United States, no offender can be put on trial on a criminal charge until a bill of indictment has been found against him by the grand jury. The language of the Federal Constitution is, " that no person shall be held to answer for a capital or otherwise infamous crime, unless on a presentment or indictment of a grand jury." The various State constitutions include all criminal charges. The number of the members of a grand jury is usually fifteen, and generally twelve out of the fifteen must concur, in order to sustain an indictment. As to the weight of evidence required, the rule is, that they ought not to find a bill unless the evidence be such as, if uncontradicted, would induce them on the trial to convict. The trial itself takes place before the petit jury.'

988. What then is meant by the *libellus* or bill of com-

' Bouix, l. c., p. 139.   ' Bouix, l. c., p. 141.   ' Walker, p. 713 sq.

plaint, in ecclesiastical causes? It is a short writing or written statement, setting forth clearly the demand of the plaintiff or prosecution, and the reasons therefor.[1] It is divided (*a*) into simple or summary (*libellus simplex* or *summarius*), or that which states the case in a summary manner; (*b*) articulate, specific, or itemized (*libellus articulatus*), or that which gives the complaint or charge under distinct and separate heads or specifications or counts; (*c*) civil and criminal, according as the cause is civil or criminal.

989. *Q.* How should the bill of complaint or *libellus* be drawn up?

A. It should consist of three parts: the statement of the facts in the case; the reasons for the demand; the conclusion, or statement of what is asked of the judge. The first part—the narrative of the facts in the case—should chiefly give (*a*) the name of the judge before whom the case is to be tried; (*b*) the name of the plaintiff, (*c*) and of the defendant; (*d*) the facts in the case, with the necessary circumstances or details; and if the cause is a civil one, what and how much is due or asked. (*e*) In a criminal bill, besides the above particulars, the place where, the year and month when, the crime was committed should be given; otherwise the process or trial is null and void, even though the opposing party does not protest.[2] We say, *criminal bill;* for in a civil bill the designation of the time and place is not generally required. How the second part of the *libellus*—that is, the reasons or grounds on which the complaint is based—is to be formulated, see Schmalzgrueber, l. c., n. 3. How should the third part or the conclusion of the bill (*conclusio libelli*) be worded? At the end of the bill the plaintiff should clearly state or specify what he demands of the defendant, and consequently what he wishes the judge to adjudicate or award to him. This part of the bill is of great importance.

---

[1] Supra. n. 935; Schmalzg., l. 2, t. 3, n. 1.   [2] L. libellorum 3 ff. de Acc. (48. 2).

For, as we have seen, the judge, in civil causes, cannot award more to the plaintiff than is asked by him.[1] This conclusion is necessary only in civil, not in criminal causes. For in the latter the law itself decides what penalty is to be inflicted, and hence it does not become the plaintiff to suggest what penalty the judge should inflict. Here we remark, by the way, that when the judge has received the bill of complaint he should carefully examine it, and thus inform himself of the nature of the case. He should, moreover, communicate it to the defendant, and either give him a copy or allow him to make a copy. Finally, he should give the latter sufficient time to prepare to plead, or reply as to whether he will contest the case or not—say about twenty days.[2]

990. *Q.* Is a bill of complaint necessary in all ecclesiastical trials or judicial proceedings?

A. It is, generally speaking, necessary, and that on pain of nullity of the proceedings, in all formal or solemn canonical trials, civil and criminal; so much so, that it cannot be remitted even by the parties themselves.[3] We say, *in all formal trials;* for in extraordinary trials—that is, where the judge proceeds *ex notorio,* or *ex informata conscientia,* or summarily, especially where the cause is of little importance— no *libellus* is needed;[4] since in this case it is sufficient that the demand of the plaintiff be made verbally before the judge, and be immediately thereupon inserted among the acts of the cause, so that if the defendant wishes he may have a copy of it.[5] We said, moreover, *generally speaking;* for even in ordinary or formal canonical trials the bill of complaint may sometimes be dispensed with. Thus, as we have already seen, it is not required in formal or ordinary trials *per viam merae inquisitionis—i.e.,* when the judge pro-

---

[1] Bouix, l. c., p. 148.
[2] Auth. offeratur. C. de Lit. cont. (3. 9); Schmalzg., l. c., n. 10.
[3] Cap. 1, de Lib. oblat. (ii. 3); ib. Glossa, v. Libellum.
[4] Clem. saepe 2, de V. S. (v. 11).   [5] Ib., § Verum quia; Schmalzg., l. c. n. 11.

ceeds altogether *ex motu proprio* or *officio*.[1] Several other exceptions are given by Schmalzgrueber, l. c.

991. Can the bill of complaint be changed or amended once it has been given to the judge? We observe, the bill is said to be *changed* when something is altered in it which pertains to its substance. It is *amended* when some defect or obscurity is corrected, or something added to or taken from it which does not affect its substance, in such manner that neither the complaint itself or the demand made, nor the grounds upon which it is based, are changed. Now canonists agree that the bill may be amended during the trial until the final sentence is to be pronounced, on condition, however, that the expenses incurred by the defendant, by reason of the defective bill, be refunded to him. A person can amend his bill in various ways—*v g.*, by explaining what is obscure; by correcting slight mistakes of form, such as names, dates, places; by adding those things which have occurred after the *litis contestatio*.[2] On the other hand, it is not allowed, either in civil or criminal causes, to change—*i.e.*, substantially to alter—the bill after the *litis contestatio*.

§ 2. *Visitation or Inspection of the Corpus Delicti.*

992. The visitation of the *corpus delicti* is the next step. Where the crime, as we have seen, is *facti permanentis*, the judge or other person deputed by him may personally visit and view the physical traces of the crime—*v.g.*, the ruins of a burned house.[3] *Observation.*—The steps thus far described— namely, the filing of the bill, the ascertaining or proving of defamation, the visitation of the body of the crime, etc.—con- stitute what is called the preliminary trial or investigation (*processus informativus*). They have all been sufficiently explained already. For the sake of greater clearness, how-

---

[1] Schmalzg., l. c., n. 12.   [2] Schmalzg., l. c., n. 13.   [3] Supra, n. 967.

ever, we shall here briefly recapitulate what has been said regarding this preliminary trial or investigation. First, the object of this preliminary trial is either to verify or ascertain the existence of common fame, or to see whether there exists against the accused at least imperfect proof of guilt or *probatio semiplena*, so as to warrant the judge to proceed to the citation.[1] Second, no preliminary investigation is needed when the judge proceeds by way of accusation (for the reason given below), which, however, is now rarely the case. Third, where the existence of public report has been juridically proved or otherwise sufficiently ascertained, and consequently where there has been a preliminary investigation in regard to the existence of public opinion, the judge need not further inquire whether there exists also incomplete proof of guilt. For, by the law of the Church, the existence of common fame is of itself a half or imperfect proof. We say, *need not;* for in practice it is advisable for the judge always to see whether besides the *fama* there is also at least some other imperfect proof of guilt. Fourth, where no previous common fame is required, the judge must institute a preliminary investigation to find out whether there is at least imperfect proof of guilt or grave suspicion. For, as was already observed, a person who is cited as a defendant in a criminal cause becomes thereby suspected of guilt among the people. Now the law of nature itself dictates that no one shall be thus treated without a sufficient cause—*i.e.*, without sufficient grounds for believing him guilty.

993. This reasoning evidently applies also to criminal proceedings, and *a pari* to disciplinary proceedings partaking of the nature of criminal, before Commissions of Investigation in the United States. This is, moreover, confirmed by the fact that our trials before Commissions of Investigation partake of the nature of a canonical trial or process by

---

[1] Craisson, Man., n. 5886.

inquiry, though they are not strictly the same. From what has been said, it follows that, practically speaking, the preliminary trial or investigation, both as to the common report and sufficient proof of guilt, should in most cases; even with us, precede the citation of the accused. It is desirable to make this investigation as full as possible.[1]

§ 3. *Citation of the Accused—As made also in the United States (Citatio Rei).*

994. The next step is the citation of the accused. When at the end of the preliminary trial or investigation the judge finds there is not at least an imperfect proof of guilt, he should command that ulterior proceedings be stopped. But if he finds there is full proof, or at least imperfect proof, he should proceed to the citation of the accused.[2] No preliminary investigation, as we have seen, is needed when the procedure is by way of accusation. For in the latter case it is the duty of the accuser, not of the judge, to see whether there is sufficient ground to proceed to the citation.

995. In the United States, besides the requisite preliminary investigation, the Commission, where it still exists, shall not be convened, and the citation shall not issue, save in the following contingency : " Ad commissionem investigationis non recurratur, nisi prius clare et praecise exposita ab episcopo causa ad dejectionem finalem movente, ipse rector missionarius malit rem ad consilium deferri quam se a munere et officio sponte dimittere."[3] The condition here required for the citation applies not only in cases where there is question of dismissal from office, but also where (*a*) a censure, whether of suspension, excommunication or interdict, or (*b*) a grave disciplinary correction, is to be imposed.[4] Hence,

---

[1] Bouix, l. c., vol. ii., p. 154.   [2] Bouix, l. c., p. 157.
[3] Instr. S. C. de P. F., 20 Julii, 1878, § 1 Ad commissionem.
[4] Ib., § In causis cognoscendis. Cf. S. C. de P. F., Ad Dubia, § 1, Instructio.

before the bishop proceeds to convene the Commission, prior to and for the purpose of inflicting dismissal, or a censure or a grave disciplinary correction, he should clearly, distinctly, and concisely inform the accused of the charges or allegations pending against him, and leave him the alternative of voluntarily accepting the bishop's proposals or terms, or of being tried before the Commission. Out of the above cases—that is, in purely civil causes falling under the ecclesiastical forum—the rule in question need not be necessarily observed, though even then it is laudable to follow it. For the S. C. de P. F., in its Instruction, already quoted, of July 20, 1878, plainly intimates its desire that all, even civil, causes be brought before the Commission, before the bishop passes sentence on them. Thus the words of the above Instruction " Commissionis ita constitutae PRINCEPS erit officium criminales atque disciplinares . . . causas . . . cognoscere," [1] and " In causis cognoscendis, iis PRAESERTIM, in quibus de rectore . . amovendo agatur . . Commissio hanc sequetur agendi rationem" [2]—seem manifestly to contain an implied recommendation that the office and duties of the Commission be extended to other cases besides criminal and disciplinary.[3]

996. We now proceed to the citation. The citation is the legitimate act whereby a person, by command of the judge, is called into court for trial. Thus the Roman laws, from which the definition is derived, says: "In jus vocare est juris experiundi causa vocare." [4] It is divided chiefly: 1, into verbal and real; 2, simple and peremptory. The citation is verbal (*citatio verbalis*) when the judge sends a messenger or official (in our secular courts, sheriff or constable) to the accused, to notify him, either orally or in writing, that upon a certain day he is to appear in court, or before

---

[1] Instr. cit., § Commissionis.   [2] Ib., § In causis.   [3] Supra, n. 740.
[4] L. 1 ff. de In jus. voc. (ii. 4); Schmalzg., l. ii., t. 3, n. 16.

the judges for trial. The real citation (*citatio realis*) is that
by which the person cited is apprehended or arrested. The
verbal citation, which can also be sent by mail or letter,
instead of by a messenger of the court, is subdivided into
private and public. It is private when it is served upon or
sent to the defendant in a private manner and without any
publicity. It is public when made in a public manner or
before the whole community—namely, by public announce-
ment or notification posted in a public place or inserted in
a newspaper. The citation, as prescribed in the Instructions of the S. C. de P. F. of July 20, 1878, and of 1884, is
private, being sent by letter, delivered or served through the
mail, or by messenger of the bishop's court.[1] However, we
think—*v.g.*, where a defendant conceals himself—a public
citation could be made also in this country, provided, as we
shall see, there is a real necessity for so doing.

997. Next, the citation is simple or peremptory. It is
simple (*citatio simplex*) when the judge simply commands the
accused to appear on a certain day, without threatening to
refuse the defendant any further time or delay in case of his
non-appearance. It is peremptory (*citatio peremptoria*) when
it is worded in such a manner as to impose the obligation of
appearing on a certain day without fail, and without further
citation. The simple citation does not render the person
contumacious if he fails to appear, save when it is repeated
three times. This is the common law of the Church. In
the United States, by the Instructions of the S. C. de P. F.
of July 20, 1878, and of 1884, the simple citation, when made
twice and disobeyed, constitutes contumacy or contempt of
court.[2] But if the citation is peremptory, the person cited
becomes contumacious or guilty of contempt if he fails to appear on the day fixed, and that without any further citation,
the one peremptory citation being sufficient. However, in

---

[1] Instr. cit., § 4, Per litteras.   [2] Instr. cit., § 8, Si contingat.

order that the citation, when made but once, may be per-emptory, it must, 1, expressly say that it is made peremp-torily, or something equivalent to this—*v.g.*, that the citation is one for all; that if the person cited fails to appear at the time specified the judge will nevertheless proceed with the case and pronounce sentence after due investigation of the cause. Thus the Roman law, adopted by the Church, says: "In peremptorio autem, comminatur is, qui edictum dedit, *etiam absente parte diversa cogniturum se, et pronuncia-turum.*"[1] 2. It must, moreover, grant the person cited as much time for appearing as should intervene between the three simple citations—namely, at least thirty days. For between each of the three simple citations a period of ten days should elapse.[2] By custom, however, this term may be prolonged or shortened, but cannot be abridged in such manner as to leave the party cited insufficient time. And if the time fixed is too short, the person cited can appeal; and the higher superior to whom the appeal is made, having heard the complaint and decided it to be just, should annul whatever may have been done by the inferior judge pending the appeal.[3] The judge has the right to issue a peremptory citation in the place of three (with us, two) simple ones, whenever, in his judgment, the nature of the case, the cir-cumstances of persons, places, and time, warrant it.[4]

998. As a rule, the citation should be made privately ; for it were evidently wrong to injure the reputation of the de-fendant by a public citation, unless there is sufficient reason for the publicity. We say, *as a rule ;* because, as we have just noted, the citation may be made in a public manner,—that is, by public notice,—either posted in a public place, as the doors of the cathedral, or published in a newspaper,

[1] L. 71 ff. de Judic. (v. 1); Schmalzg., l. c., n. 16 et 19.
[2] L. 68, 69, 70 ff. de Jud. (v. 1).
[3] Cap. 1, de Dilat. (ii. 8); cap. 24, de Off. et pot. jud. del. (i. 29).
[4] L. 72 ff. (v. 1).

where there are sufficient reasons for so doing—that is, where it is necessary ; in other words, where the accused could not be cited in any other manner [1]—*v.g.*, where his residence is not accessible to the messenger bearing the citation with safety ; or where he lives out of the territory of the judge issuing the citation; where he maliciously hides himself, or hinders the citation from reaching him, even by letter.   Observe that the right to issue a public citation—*i.c.*, by public notice—belongs only to ordinary judges and delegates of the Holy See.[2]   Moreover, before a public citation can be issued, a summary investigation or trial should take place, in order to prove that there is a sufficient justification for making the citation publicly.   In other words, it must be shown, upon this investigation, that the accused has fled, or is hiding, or is hindering the citation from reaching him,[3] etc.

999. We have just said that the citation may be made by public notice or in a public manner when the accused is out of the territory of the judge issuing the citation.   This needs some explanation.   The citation of a person who is outside the territory of the judge citing, can take place in three ways: First, by a messenger (and *a fortiori* by letter, especially when registered) sent by the judge issuing the citation. This mode of citing is valid, as it is not an act of jurisdiction in another judge's territory, but merely the execution of a jurisdictional act.   Second, by the judge of the place where the accused is at the time.   This second way of citing is carried out as follows : The judge issuing the citation writes to the judge of the place where the accused is, and requests him to execute or serve the citation on the accused, through his own officials.[4]   Third, by a notification, posted in the

---

[1] Ex Clem. 1, de Jud. (ii. 1); Extrav. Rem non novam, de dol. et cont.; Reiff., l. 2, t. 3, n. 76.   [2] Schmalzg., l. c., n. 18.   [3] Ib.

[4] Cf. cap. Romana 1, § 3 Contrahentes, de For. comp., in 6° (ii. 2); Bouix, l. c., p. 161.

neighborhood of the place where the accused is at the time. Circumstances must determine in which of the first two ways the citation is to be made. But it should not take place in the third way—namely, publicly—unless it cannot be made in any other manner.[1]

1000. *Necessity of citation.*—Generally, the citation of a person absent is so necessary that its omission invalidates, *ipso jure*, every other juridical act or proceeding in the case.[2] This applies not only to ordinary or formal canonical trials, but also to summary or informal.[3] It holds in the United States[4] as well as elsewhere. Nay, not even the sovereign can dispense with the citation. For it pertains to and is part of the defence, and is consequently guaranteed by the law of nature itself, since nobody should be condemned without having had a hearing.[5] We say, *generally;* there being some exceptions. They are chiefly: 1. Where the crime is so notorious that no defence whatever is possible.[6] Yet, practically speaking, as we show elsewhere in this volume, it is now scarcely advisable to proceed, even in notorious causes, without a trial preceded by due citation. 2. Where the accused, knowing that he is about to be tried, appears before the judge without being cited, and answers to the charge—*i.e.*, pleads in the case. For by this voluntary appearance in court he tacitly acquiesces in the omission of the citation. We say secondly, *of a person absent;* since, if the person to be cited is present in court, whether fortuitously or otherwise, and declares himself willing and ready to go on, without any formal citation, the latter is evidently not required, on the grounds just now stated,

[1] Schmalzg., l. c., n. 23.
[2] Can. 2. 4, C. 3, Q. 9; Clem. Pastoralis 2, de Sent. et re jud. (ii. 10).
[3] Reiff., l. 2., t. 3, n. 67.
[4] Cf. Instr. S. C. de P. F., 20 Jul., 1878, § 4, Per litteras.
[5] Reiff., l. c., n. 68; Schmalzg., l. c., n. 15.
[6] Can. Manifesta 15, C. 2, Q. 1; cap. cum Olim 12, de Sent. (ii. 26)

according to the maxim: " Volenti non fit injuria.' These
principles apply, of course, also to the citation in the United
States as prescribed in the Instruction of the S. C. de P. F.,
July 20, 1878, and in the Instruction *Cum Magnopere* of 1884.

1001. *Contents or tenor of the citation.*—The citation, in
order to be lawful and valid, also with us, must generally
state, 1, the name and surname of the judge issuing the citation ;[1] 2, of the accused, or person to be cited ;[2] 3, of the
plaintiff or the party at whose request the citation is issued.
The object of this is to enable the accused to know (*a*) who
is his opponent, and thus to prepare better for his defence,
and also (*b*) whether the citation is issued by the judge of his
own accord—*ex motu proprio*—or at the instance of a third
party. For in private causes, or those which concern private utility,—*i.e.*, the interest of private persons only,—the
judge cannot validly issue a citation, save at the instance of
a third party.[3] We say, *in private causes;* for in matters
which affect the public welfare or good of the Church, and
where he proceeds *ex officio*, the ecclesiastical judge can cite
without being requested to do so by a third party.[4]

1002. 4. The cause for which the citation is issued, and
that in criminal and disciplinary as well as civil causes. The
object of this is to inform the accused of the charges or
nature of the case, so that he may deliberate what to do, and
come prepared to defend himself.[5] Many canonists hold it
is sufficient to express this cause in a general way ; yet, as
Schmalzgrueber[6] observes, it is more advisable to state the
charges or cause in a clear and determinate and specific
manner. Hence, also, it is very advisable for the judge to
enclose in the citation a copy of the charges, or bill of complaint (*libellus*), if there is any, instead of waiting until the
defendant appears in court on the day fixed by the citation,

[1] Ex L. 2 ff. Si quis in jus vocat. (ii. 5).   [2] Ex cap. 34 et 36, de Rescrip. (l. 3).
[3] Ex cap. 19, de For comp.   [4] Reiff., l. ii., · **·**, n. 59; Schmalzg., l. c., n. 20 (4).
[5] Can. Si primates 4, C. 5, Q. 2.   [6] L. c. (6°).

to communicate the charges, or bill of complaint to him. For in the latter case, a new delay will have to be granted the defendant to enable him to prepare his defence, while in the former case this delay need not be given.'

1003. As will be seen, it is in accordance with these principles that the S. C. de P. F., in its Instruction of July 20, 1878, determining the mode of procedure or conducting trials, in the United States, in criminal and disciplinary causes of ecclesiastics, enacts; " Per litteras etiam rectorem missionarium, de quo agitur, ad locum et diem constitutum ad Consilium habendum advocet, *exponens, nisi prudentia vetat, uti in casu criminis occulti, causam ad dejectionem moventem per extensum,* monensque ipsum rectorem ut responsum suis rationibus suffultum ad ea praeparet, quae in causae expositione vel jam antea oretenus, vel nunc in scriptis relata fuerint."[2]

1004. 5. The place where the trial or proceedings are to take place. 6. Finally, the day or time for appearing in court. This time must be suitable or convenient for the accused.[3]

1005. *What else is required for the validity of the citation?* 1. That it be issued by a judge having authority to do so. However, the judge need not issue it personally, but may authorize another person to do so for him.[4] 2. It must be properly executed—that is, it should be served on the defendant *in person,* where he can be found.[5] If he cannot be found, it should either be served on his procurator or agent, if he has any, or be left at the house, with the domestics or members of his family, or if none can be found, with neighbors; and if even this cannot be done, the citation may be affixed to the house where the defendant generally resides.[6] Finally, if he maliciously hides himself, or in any way, either

---

[1] Cap. 2, de Dilat.; Reiff., l. c., n. 61; Schmalzg., l. c., n. 24.
[2] Instr. cit., § 4, Per litteras.   [3] Reiff., l. c., n. 63.   [4] Ib., n. 49.
[5] Ex cap. 3 et 10, de Dol. et cont. (ii. 14).   [6] Schmalzg., l. c., n. 25 (5°).

personally or through others, hinders the citation from reaching him, or if he has no fixed residence and it is not known where he can be found, or if his residence, where he has any, is not accessible to the messenger with safety, the citation, as was seen, can be made by public notice or edict.[1] This public citation, however, should be resorted to only as a last means, when no other way is practicable.

1006. From the above, it is plain that it is expedient to execute—*i.e.*, to serve or deliver—the citation by means of a messenger appointed for that purpose. For he will be able, in case the defendant attempts to deny having received the citation, to prove its delivery or execution.[2] However, especially where custom has it, it may be executed—*i.e.*, delivered—by mail.[3] In the United States it certainly may be executed—*i.e.*, served or sent or delivered by mail.[4]

1007. 3. Finally, the fact that the citation has been executed—that is, served on the defendant in one or other of the above ways—should also with us be carefully recorded, and that on pain of nullity of citation, among the minutes or acts of the proceedings, so that it may appear that the citation was properly made ;[5] otherwise, the accused, in case he refuses to appear, cannot be adjudged or considered contumacious. For no one can be punished as contumacious unless he is juridically convicted of contumacy. Now a person cannot be juridically convicted of contumacy unless it be juridically—*i.e.*, by the minutes or acts of the case—shown that he did, at least presumptively, receive the citation.[6] Hence it is advisable that, in the United States, when the citation is sent by mail, it be sent by registered mail: as thus a proof of its delivery or execution is at once had in the re-

---

[1] Cap. 3, cit., de Dol. et cont. (ii. 14); Clem. cap. 1. (ii. 1).
[2] Schmalzg., l. c., n. 25.   [3] Craiss., n. 5899; Prael. S. Sulp., n. 666.
[4] Instr. S. C. de P. F., 20 Julii, 1378, § 4, Per litteras; ib., § 8.
[5] Ex cap. 11 (ii. 19); Schmalzg., l. c. (7°).   [6] Reiff., l. c., n. 51.

ceipt which the post-office officials require of the recipient and forward to the sender of the letter.

1008. *Q.* What are the effects of a citation legitimately made?

A. Chiefly these: 1. The person cited is bound to appear, unless he has a just excuse.[1] 2. The *litis pendentia* ensues— that is, pending the trial, or cause, nothing new can be done. Thus the law of the Church says: "Cum lite pendente, nihil debeat innovari; litem quoad hoc pendere censemus, postquam . . . citatio emanavit."[2] The *Glossa*, commenting upon the word *innovari* in this passage, gives an instance of such innovation: "Quod" (scilicet innovare) "fieret, si possessor privaretur possessione." Hence, once the citation has been issued and executed, no change should be made in the status of the person on trial which is injurious to his interests. Thus, for instance, an ecclesiastic who is under investigation or on trial should not, pending the investigation, be deprived of his office, parish, or benefice.[3] 3. It extends the jurisdiction of the judge, so that the defendant is obliged to appear before him for trial, even though he has meanwhile become subject to another judge.[4] 4. It perpetuates the jurisdiction of a delegated judge in such manner that it does not expire with the death of the judge delegating. For, once the citation has been issued, the matter or cause is no longer *a res integra—i.e.*, untouched.[5]

1009. These effects follow only upon a citation which is legitimate and valid. For when it is invalid it produces no effect whatever, except it be afterwards made valid—*v.g.*, by the appearance of the person cited, as was seen,[6] which appearance would imply a tacit consent in the omission of the citation.

---

[1] Cap. 5 (i. 6).   [2] Clem. 2 (ii. 5).   [3] Schmalzg., l. 2, t. 16, n. 6.
[4] L. 19 ff. de Jurisd. (ii. 1).   [5] Cap. 20, de Off. del.   [6] Supra, n. 1000.

§ 4. *Contumacy or Contempt of Court (De Contumacia).*

1010. By contumacy or contempt of the ecclesiastical court, as here understood, is meant, in general, any act of stubborn or obstinate disobedience to the judge. We say, *stubborn*, etc.; because contumacy does not consist in an act of simple disobedience, but an act of disobedience coupled with obstinacy or stubbornness, and therefore implying contempt of the authority of the judge. Hence, *per se*, a person is guilty of contumacy only by refusing to obey the commands of the judge when reiterated or given peremptorily. Accordingly, the law of the Church is that the simple citation must be repeated three times (in the United States, twice) before the party who is cited and refuses to appear can be adjudged guilty of contempt.[1] This disobedience may be committed not only with reference to the citation—namely, by refusing to appear upon a due citation; but, in general, in relation to any order of the judge—namely, by any act of disobedience to the judge or court (also Commission of Investigation where this body exists), in the legitimate exercise of his judicial authority during any part of the trial, investigation, or judicial proceedings.[2]

1011. At present we shall confine ourselves chiefly to that contumacy or disobedience which consists in the failure or refusal on the part of the person duly cited to obey the citation and appear in court or before the judge on the day specified in the citation. This contumacy is of two kinds: true and presumptive. Contumacy is true (*contumacia vera*) when the citation has been served upon the defendant in person, so that there can be no doubt of its having reached him,[3] or (in case the citation has not been delivered to him in person) when it is otherwise *certain* that the citation has

---

[1] München, Canonical Trials, vol. i., p. 227.
[2] Ex cap. 3 et 6, de Dol. et cont. (ii. 14); Reiff., l. 2, t. 14, n. 45 sq.
[3] Reiff., l. 2, t. 14, n. 58 sq.

reached him, and when, notwithstanding these facts, the person cited fails to appear before the judge, and that without any sufficient excuse.[1]

1012. Contumacy, on the other hand, is presumptive (*contumacia ficta seu praesumpta*) when it is doubtful whether the citation has come to the knowledge of the person summoned—namely, when the citation has not been served upon him in person by a messenger, but was, *v.g.*, sent by mail (not registered), or left at his house, or made by public edict or notification. In this case, if the person summoned does not appear at the time specified, he becomes presumptively contumacious. For the law of the Church violently presumes that the citation, in the case, has certainly become known to him.[2]

1013. *Causes excusing from `contumacy.*—There are many causes which exempt the person summoned from the obligation of appearing in court, and consequently also from contempt for not coming. The following are some of them: 1. Ill-health. 2. Important business or other serious occupations.[3] 3. Citation to a higher tribunal.[4] 4. Bad weather.[5] 5. Unsafety of the place to which the party is cited. 6. The want of an advocate.[6] That these and similar reasons excuse from contumacy is so true, that if the judge (we speak of the ecclesiastical judge) pronounces sentence against a person who is prevented from appearing by a legitimate or just excuse, such sentence is *ipso jure* null and void, provided the judge was at the time aware of the excuse. But if he was ignorant of it, the sentence should be revoked, and the party thus condemned reinstated in his position occupied by him before the sentence.[7]

---

[1] Ex l. 53 ff. de Re jud. (42. 1).

[2] Extrav. com. cap. un. Rem non novam, de dol. et cont. (ii. 3); Schmalzg., l. 2, t. 14, n. 38.

[3] L. 53 ff. de Re jud. (42. 1).   [4] L. 54 ff. l. c.   [5] L. 2 ff. Si quis caut. (ii. 11).

[6] Schmalzg., l. c., n. 42.   [7] L. 6 et 7 ff. de In integr. rest. (iv. 1).

1014. *Q.* What are the effects or penalties of contumacy on the part of the *plaintiff*, and what is the mode of procedure against him for contempt or disobedience?

A. We premise: Not merely a defendant or an accused person, but also a plaintiff, may become guilty of disobedience or contempt. Now a plaintiff may be guilty of contempt in various ways—*v.g.*, if, after having lodged a complaint before the judge, he nevertheless refuses to appear and prosecute it, though commanded to do so by the judge. For although nobody is obliged to act as plaintiff against his will before he has made an accusation, yet, once he has preferred the charge, he can be forced to prosecute it,[1] and that on pain of being considered and punished as a calumniator.

1015. We now answer: If the plaintiff does not appear at the proper time,—*i.e.*, on the day fixed in the citation of the defendant,—he should be cited in the same manner in which the defendant is cited. If he does not appear after the first or second simple citation, he is to be condemned to pay all the costs of the trial, and also of the defendant.[2] If he fails to appear after the third citation, the judge can, if the defendant so demands, and that even though no *litis contestatio* has taken place, go on with and try the cause, in the absence and to the detriment of the plaintiff, and pronounce final sentence, in accordance with the evidence, either for or against the plaintiff. We say, *and to the detriment;* for it is evident that this absence will redound to the injury of the plaintiff, whose interests are thus not properly represented. We say moreover, *if the defendant so demands;* because the defendant may, if he choose, simply demand that he himself be definitively absolved, on the strength of the maxim: " Actore non probante, reus absolvitur."[3]

1016. *Q.* What is the mode of procedure against a *defendant* for contumacy?

---

[1] Reiff., l. c., n. 80.   [2] L. 79 ff. de Jud.   [3] Schmalzg., l. c., n. 45.

A. Some canonists,—*v.g.*, Engel, whom Bouix' seems to follow—assert that contumacy on the part of a defendant is equivalent to juridical confession and conviction of the crime charged; that, consequently, an accused who is in contempt may without any further proof or trial be forthwith condemned as guilty of the offence of which he stands accused.' Against these canonists, we hold it as certain with Reiffenstuel,' Schmalzgrueber, München,' and others, that neither true nor presumptive contumacy is tantamount to a full proof of the crime or to a *probatio plena delicti,* for which a person is on trial. Therefore, neither of them constitutes a juridical confession or conviction of guilt. Consequently, contumacy, whether real or presumed, does not dispense with the necessity of a trial, and of juridically proving the guilt, but has among other effects simply this, that the trial or investigation can now go on, in the absence of the accused, just as though he were present. Thus the Roman law, as adopted by the Church, expressly says: " Et post edictum peremptorium impetratum, cum dies ejus supervenerit, tunc absens citari debet: et sive responderit, sive non responderit, *agetur* de *causa, et pronunciatur:* non utique secundum praesentem, sed interdum vel absens, si bonam causam habuit, vincet." ' Schmalzgrueber distinctly says: "Ob solam enim contumaciam reus, actore non probante, causa cadere non debet."' (Conc. Pl. Balt. III., n. 313.)

1017. *Application of these principles to the United States.—* From what has been said, it is manifest that if with us a defendant or accused person is guilty of contumacy, true or presumptive, the judge, auditor, or Commission cannot, in the absence of the accused, omit the hearing of the cause and dispense with the trial, and forthwith make up their verdict

---

' De Jud., vol. ii., p. 558 sq. ' Ap. München, l. c., vol. i., p. 408, note 4.
' L. 2, t. 14, n. 143, 145, 150, 151. ' Can. Trials, vol. i., p. 408, 409.
' L. 73 ff. de Jud. (v. 1), et l. 13, C. de Jud. (iii. 1); cap. 4, de Dol. et cont.
(il. 14). ' L. c., n. 51, 54.

or opinion on the whole case, finding the accused guilty, without any trial, of the charges made against him, solely on the ground of his contumacy. All that the court therefore can do is to examine whether the accused is really guilty of contumacy, and, if so, to declare him guilty of it, and then to proceed with the trial or hearing of the main cause, in the absence of the accused, just as though he were present, and find him guilty or not guilty, according to the evidence submitted during the investigation.

1018. *Observation.*—Canonists usually observe that in ordinary or formal canonical trials, whether of civil or criminal causes, the ecclesiastical judge cannot as a rule go on with the trial and pronounce final sentence, in the case of a defendant in contempt, except when the contumacy or disobedience takes place *after the litis contestatio.*[1] The reason is that in formal trials no witnesses can be allowed to testify (the same holds of other proofs), and consequently no trial can take place and no final sentence passed, until after the *litis contestatio* has taken place. This is expressly stated in the heading of the sixth title of the second book of the Decretals, which heading, having full sense by itself, has the force of law. The words are: " Ut lite non contestata, non procedatur ad testium receptionem, vel ad sententiam definitivam." We have said, *in ordinary or formal canonical trials ;* for when the proceedings are summary, no *litis contestatio* is needed, as we shall see, and therefore, in summary trials, the judge can go on with the trial, even if the contumacy of the accused occurs before the *litis contestatio.*[2] We have said, secondly, *as a rule ;* for in some cases the trial can go on, even though it is an *ordinary* trial, without any *litis contestatio.* These cases are, chiefly : 1. Where the judge proceeds *ex mero officio,* and not at the instance of another, *per viam inquisi-*

---

[1] Cap. 4, de Dol. et cont. (ii. 14); ib. Glossa, v. Utpote.
[2] Cap. 8, de Dol. (ii. 14); Schmalzg., l. 2, t. 6, n. 2.

ionis, to a special judicial inquiry against a person charged with crime.[1] 2. Where there is question of criminal charges against ecclesiastics, especially when in charge of souls. For there is, in such cases, evident danger to souls, in delay. Schmalzgrueber,[2] however, adds that where there is question of depriving ecclesiastics of their benefices, offices, or pastoral charge, the order to be followed is this: First, the defendant in contempt should be punished for his contempt —*v.g.*, by excommunication. Secondly, however, the trial or hearing of the cause should be suspended for one year. 3. If after the lapse of one year, during which the defendant has been under excommunication, he does not appear, then let the trial be resumed and final sentence of deposition or dismissal be pronounced, if he is found guilty.

1019. With all deference to Schmalzgrueber, we venture to say that this order need not necessarily be followed, but that, especially where there is grave reason for the contrary, the judge, particularly in the United States, may, without waiting a full year, proceed with the trial and pronounce sentence, according to the evidence elicited during the proceedings before the Commission of Investigation. Moreover, in the United States, the trial before the Commission of Investigation is not a formal trial, but partakes of the nature of proceedings which are summary, and moreover *per viam inquisitionis*. Consequently, no formal *litis contestatio* is required with us. Hence our Commissions can go on with the trial, even when the contumacy happens before the *litis contestatio* or its equivalent has taken place.

1020. *Q.* What are the chief effects or penalties incurred by an accused person, also in the United States, for contumacy?

A. We premise: While, as we have just seen, contumacy is not equivalent to guilt, and while, therefore, no accused

---

[1] Schmalzg., l. c., n. 3. [2] Ib., n. 10.

person can be forthwith convicted of the crime of which he stands charged solely because he is contumacious, yet it is also plain that contumacy is itself punishable as such, apart from the question of the guilt or innocence of the defendant in contempt. For it is an act of stubborn disobedience or resistance to the lawful authority of the judge, and is therefore considered a crime, though, of course, in a defendant it frequently has extenuating circumstances, since it often proceeds rather from fear than any real disregard or contempt of the judge's authority.

1021. We now answer: 1. The first effect of contumacy is, as we have seen, that it authorizes the judge (with us, also the auditor, or the Commission) to proceed with the trial or hearing of the case in the absence, and therefore to the detriment, of the accused. For, though absent, he is considered present at the trial: "Quia," as the Roman law, adopted by the Church, says, "contumacia pro praesentia est."[1] 2. The second effect or penalty of the defendant's contumacy, true or presumed, is, that it constitutes a presumption of guilt against the accused.[2] But, as we have seen, presumptions, no matter how numerous, do not suffice for conviction in criminal causes, even with us. Hence, if, aside from this presumption, the prosecution (with us, the diocesan prosecutor, or where there are Commissions, the priest appointed by the bishop, according to the Instruction of the S. C. de Prop. Fide, July 20, 1878, § 2) produces merely additional presumptions or grounds for suspicion, but not direct and positive proof, there can be no conviction in criminal causes, or even grave civil causes, and the judge will have to declare the charges or allegations not proven.

1022. 3. The third effect or penalty is that a pecuniary fine—the amount of which is discretionary with the judge—

[1] L. 2, C. Ubi de crim. agi op. (ill. 15); ib. Auth., Qua in prov.
[2] München, l. c., p. 408.

may be imposed upon an accused who is guilty of true contumacy.[1] 4. The fourth effect or penalty is that an accused who is in contempt can be excommunicated for such crime of contempt.[2] And if he obstinately remains under excommunication for one year, he becomes suspected of heresy, and may be proceeded against as such.[3] Observe, however, that as excommunication is the greatest penalty in the Church,[4] it should not be resorted to until the lesser punishments—*v.g.*, first pecuniary fines, then suspension from office or benefice—have been vainly tried.[5] 5. Finally, a defendant, guilty of true contempt, loses the right to appeal, so that he cannot appeal against a final or definitive sentence pronounced against him in his absence.[6] We say, *true contempt*; for presumed contempt does not deprive of this right.

1023. *General remarks in regard to these penalties.*—1. Before proceeding to punish any one for contempt, the judge (auditor, or as the case may be, Commission) should first declare him in contempt.[7] For it were unjust to punish a person for contempt before the latter has been juridically established.[8] In other words, the contempt must first be juridically (though only in a summary manner) proven and declared before any penalty can be inflicted for it. Hence, also, a new citation should be issued for this purpose, summoning the accused to show why he should not be punished for contempt.[9]

1024. Where there are Commissions of Investigation, the citation to the accused to appear for trial is issued by the bishop.[10] But it pertains to the Commission to examine

---

[1] L. 2 ff. Si quis in jus voc.; Reiff., l. c., n. 137.
[2] Cap. 3, Ut lit. non. cont. (ii. 6); cap. 8, de Dol. (ii. 14).
[3] C. Trid., sess. 25, c. 3, de Ref.   [4] Can. 17. C. 24, Q. 3.
[5] C. Trid., l. c.; L. Relegati 4 ff. (xlviii. 19).
[6] L. 13, C. de Jud. (iii. 1); L. 73 ff. (v. 1).   [7] Ex cap. 6, de Dol. (ii. 14).
[8] Reiff., l. 2, t. 14, n. 122.   [9] Schmalzg., l. 2, t. 14, n. 55.
[10] Instr. cit. S. C. de P. F., § 4.

whether the accused has been disobedient to this citation, and therefore whether he is in contempt or not; and upon full proof of such contumacy, to find or declare the party guilty of contempt. When the Commission has found a person guilty of contempt, it pertains to the bishop to inflict the proper penalties for such contempt or disobedience.

1025. 2. The second general remark is that, generally speaking, the judge cannot proceed against a party in contempt, save at the instance or demand of the opposing party.[1] We say, *generally speaking;* for when the judge can and does proceed *ex officio*, or at least *ex mero officio*, or if he wishes simply to impose a pecuniary fine for the contempt, he can proceed of his own accord. We have just said, *at least ex mero officio;* because where the judge proceeds *ex officio* indeed, but yet at the instance of another,—*v.g.*, prosecuting official,—it may be doubted whether he can act of his own accord.[2] The safest way, therefore, is for the auditor or the Commission, where this latter body still exists, to take cognizance of the contempt, and for the bishop to inflict the penalty therefor, only at the instance of the official appointed by the bishop *pro causa*. München[3] contends that in criminal trials both the plaintiff or prosecution and the defendant must be present in person, not merely by procurators. .

§ 5. *Exceptions (Exceptiones).*

1026. After the citation has been issued, and the accused comes into court, he may, without joining issue, and before entering upon the cause, or into the merits of the charges, make various exceptions or objections, which either throw the case altogether out of court or at least delay it.[4] By an exception (*exceptio*), therefore, we mean an allegation, pro-

---

[1] L. 68, 69, 70 ff. de Jud. (v. 1); Schmalzg., l. c., n. 55.
[2] Reiff., l. c., n. 66.   [3] L. c., p. 394, n. 10.   [4] München, l. c., p. 398, n. 2.

test, or objection made by the accused, which either retards or entirely repels the action brought against him.[1] As will be seen from this definition, exceptions are divided chiefly into peremptory and dilatory. Peremptory exceptions (*exceptiones peremptoriae, perpetuae*) are those which quash the accusation or charge—*i.e.*, throw it altogether out of court. They are also called perpetual, because they permanently and forever extinguish the action or accusation.[2] The exceptions of this kind may be reduced to three heads: 1. Those which show that the alleged foundation of the complaint or charge never existed—*v.g.*, if a person objects or excepts that an act said to have been done, was not done; or that what is alleged to have been donated, agreed upon, or bequeathed, was never donated, agreed upon, or bequeathed.[3] 2. Those which demonstrate that the action or cause has become extinct—*v.g.*, by compromise, prescription, by having been already definitively adjudicated. 3. Finally, those where a person objects or protests, for instance, that he has acted from fear, or compulsion, or error, etc.[4]

1027. Dilatory exceptions (*exceptiones dilatoriae, temporales*) are those which do not quash, but merely defer the action for a time.[5] There are various kinds of dilatory exceptions. For some of them regard, 1, the judge—*v.g.*, if the defendant objects that the judge is suspected, for instance, either because of his enmity to the defendant or his friendship for the plaintiff; or is without jurisdiction in the case, or ignorant of the law; or otherwise disqualified—*v.g.*, by defect of body or mind or birth—to perform his duties as judge. 2. Others relate to the person of the plaintiff (prosecuting party, in criminal causes) or his procurator or agent —*v.g.*, if a defendant objects that the agent has no man-

---

[1] Ex l. 2 ff. de Except. (44. 1).
[2] Inst., iv. 13, § 9; l. 3 ff. de Except; Reiff., l. 2, t. 25, n. 8.
[3] Schmalzg., l. 2, t. 25, n. 4.   [4] Inst., l. iv., tit. 13, §§ 1-10.
[5] Inst., iv. 13, § 10; l. 3 ff. de Except. (44. 1).

date. 3. Again, some have reference to the accused himself, or defendant; *v.g.*, where the latter complains that he has been *spoliatus,—i.e.*, despoiled,—in other words, unjustly deprived of his rights by the plaintiff or prosecutor, and therefore asks to be reinstated in his rights, before he is obliged to plead in the cause or answer the complaint. 4. Others relate to the time and place, mode of procedure, etc., of the trial or judicial proceedings—*v.g.*, if a person protests that the place is unsafe; that the time granted him for appearing is too short; that the prescribed formalities of the trial have not been or are not being observed. 5. Finally, others concern the cause itself—*v.g.*, where a person objects that the charge or accusation or complaint (with us, *v.g.*, the charge drawn up by the diocesan prosecutor, or where Commissions of Investigation still exist, by the bishop's official[1]) is too obscure, vague, doubtful, etc.[2]

1028. Not unfrequently an exception which seems *prima facie* just is in reality groundless. Hence from the defendant's right to make exceptions follows the right of the plaintiff or prosecution to reply to or rebut them. To the latter's reply the defendant may rejoin, and *vice versâ* the plaintiff may surrejoin, and so on, until both parties have exhausted their arguments. Lest, however, this should proceed *ad infinitum*, the judge may put a limit to the discussions. From this it will be seen also that perfect equality should exist before the law or judge between the plaintiff or prosecution and defendant; that what is allowed to one—*v.g.*, the prosecution—should be allowed to the other; nay, the defendant should always be treated more liberally and generously than the plaintiff or the prosecution.[3] Lest, moreover, too much delay be caused, the proceedings in the case of exceptions— that is, in the making, proving, and trial of exceptions—are

[1] Instr. S. C. de P. F., 20 Jul., 1878, §§ 2 et 6.   [2] Schmalzg., l. c., n. 5.
[3] Reg. 71, in 6°; l. Invitus ff. de Reg. jur.; Reiff., l. 2, t. 25, n. 1.

always conducted in a summary manner, even when the trial during which they are made is ordinary or solemn.[1]

1029. *Q.* Can exceptions be made also in summary canonical trials, and in trials before the Commissions of Investigation in the United States, and in England?

A. Reasonable and legitimate exceptions must be admitted, not only in ordinary or solemn canonical trials, but also in summary.[2] The reason is, that reasonable objections belong to and are part of a just defence, which is given all defendants by the very law of nature.[3] Hence no accused person should ever be denied the right of taking proper exceptions, even in summary proceedings.[4] It is true that Pope Clement V.[5] enacts that in summary proceedings the judge should reject exceptions ; but, as the Glossa[6] and canonists explain, this is to be understood only of frivolous objections, not of reasonable.

1030. From what has been just said, it is plain that the right of making exceptions obtains also in proceedings before Commissions of Investigation in the United States. In fact, this right, being part of a just defence, is guaranteed by the law of nature itself, and is moreover clearly granted the accused, in the Instruction of the S. C. de P. F., dated July 20, 1878, where this sacred congregation provides that full liberty shall be given the defendant to defend himself.[7]

1031. *Q.* At what stage of the proceedings are the exceptions to be made and proved?

A. A distinction must be made between dilatory and peremptory exceptions. 1. Dilatory exceptions should, as a rule, be made and proved before the *litis contestatio—i.e.,* before the accused enters his plea; or, speaking of places,

---

[1] München, l. c., p. 259.
[2] Cap. 13, de Off. del. (i. 29); ib. Glossa, v. Nullae.
[3] L. Praetor 1, § 27 ff. de Vi, et de vi arm. (43. 16).
[4] Reiff., l. c., n. 101.   [5] Clem. Saepe 2, de V. S. (v. 11).
[6] In Clem. cit., § Amputet.   [7] Instr. cit., § 7, Deinde.

where there are Commissions of Investigation, before he submits to the Commission his answer to or refutation of the
charges or statement made against him by the bishop's official.[1] We say, *as a rule;* for there are some exceptions to this
rule.   Thus, among other dilatory exceptions, the following
can be made *after* the contestation of the cause (*v.g., after* the
defendant has given in his answer before the Commission): 1.
Where the defendant reserves to himself the right to make
other exceptions.   He must, however, specify or name them,
as it is not sufficient for him to say in general that he reserves
the right to make other exceptions.   2. If after the *litis contestatio* (*v.g.,* after the defendant's answer has been read before
the Commission) an exception arises anew,[2] or becomes
known or provable only then.[3]   3. If the exception is made
immediately after the contestation.   For it is a general rule,
that whatever is done immediately after another act, is considered part of it, and as forming one whole with it.[4]   4.
Where the exception has for its object a grievance which is
continuous.[5]

1032. We have said, *and proved;* since exceptions must be
fully and completely proved by the person making them;
otherwise they have no effect whatever.[6] For the party or
defendant who makes an exception becomes the plaintiff, so
far as his objection is concerned; and therefore the burden
of proof lies upon him.[7] From what has been said, it is evident, as we have already shown elsewhere,[8] that when exceptions are made, whether dilatory or peremptory, it becomes
the duty of the judge (that is, of the bishop, vicar-general, auditor, or also Commissions of Investigation where
they still exist) not to proceed with the case itself until
he has first heard the proofs in support of the exceptions and the answer of the opponent thereto, and pro

[1] Instr. cit. § 7, Deinde.   [2] L. 11 ff. de Except. (44. 1).
[3] Cap. 24, de Except. (ii. 25).   [4] L. 40 ff. de Reb. cred. (12. 1).
[5] Schmalzg., l. c., n. 22.   [6] Ib., n. 32.   [7] L. 19 ff. de Probat.   [8] Supra, n. 978.

nounced these exceptions either just or unjust by an inter-locutory sentence.[1] This holds so strictly, that if the judge acts differently it is lawful to appeal against his action, even at present ; and whatever he has done in the case after this appeal should be annulled as an attentate.[2] Of course the above does not apply in the case of peremptory exceptions, which are, as we shall presently see, made after the main cause has been finished and decided by a final sentence.

1033. 2. Peremptory exceptions should, generally speak-ing, be made after the *litis contestatio.*[3] The reason is that these exceptions, if proved, quash the accusation or com-plaint. But no action can be quashed before it has a juridical existence, or before it is in court. Now an action is brought into court by the contestation.[4] When we say, *after the litis contestatio,* we mean that they can be made at any time after the contestation till the final sentence[5] (with us, in proceed-ings before Commissions of Investigation, from the time the accused begins to reply to the statement of the bishop's offi-cial, till the final sentence of the bishop).

1034. We say, *generally speaking ;* for some peremptory exceptions may be made *before* the contestation of the cause : —*v.g.,* the exception of prescription; those exceptions whose truth is notorious; or the exception of *res judicata,* or of com-promise.[6] The reason is that the cause being barred by pre-scription, or, as the expression is in our secular courts, by the statute of limitation, or having been terminated and settled by compromise or final sentence, should not be revived or begun anew.[7] Some peremptory exceptions may even be made after the final sentence has been pronounced—*v.g.,* the ex-ception that the sentence is null and void, and in general those exceptions which have reference to the final sentence

---

[1] Cap. 19, de Jud. (ii. 1).

[2] Ex leg. 9, C. de Except. (viii. 36).

[3] Glossa, in cap. 12, de Except. (ii. 25), v. In dilatoriis.

[4] Cap. 1, de Lit. cont., in 6°.

[5] Schmalzg., l. c., n. 32.

[6] Schmalzg., l. c., n. 23.

[7] Reiff., l. c., n. 47.

or its execution.' *Note.*—As a rule, the exception, whether dilatory or peremptory, must be made, not by the judge, but by the defendant. Otherwise the latter is considered as having waived his right of so doing. Again, exceptions, whether dilatory or peremptory, should be made in writing, but can also be made *viva voce*, provided they are recorded on the minutes or in acts of the cause.'

§ 6. *Exceptions against the Judge.*

1035. As the exceptions which are made against the judge himself are made and proved and decided in a manner altogether peculiar, and different from that in which the other exceptions are decided, we shall discuss them here under a separate heading. Before giving the mode of procedure in these exceptions, we shall, for the sake of greater clearness, make a few prefatory remarks. 1. As we have already seen, the exception against the judge is always a dilatory, not a peremptory one. For the effect of such an exception is not to extinguish the action or complaint, but merely to transfer its adjudication to another judge. 2. The exception against the judge may be either against his competence— namely, that he has no jurisdiction in the case, or against his judicial integrity—namely, that he is suspected. 3. It is certain that a judge otherwise competent in the case can nevertheless be challenged or objected to, solely because there is reasonable ground for suspecting his integrity in rendering justice in the case.' For, as Pope Celestin III. says: "Ipsa namque ratio dictat quod suspecti et inimici judices esse non debent."'

1036. 4. The Pope cannot be objected to as suspected, since his exalted position places him above all suspicion. But all other ecclesiastical judges, both ordinary, such as

---

' Reiff., l. c., n. 52; Schmalzg., l. c., n. 24.   ' Schmalzg., l. c., n. 29.
' L. 16, C. de Jud.   ' Cap. 41, de Appell. (ii. 28); Can. 15, C. 3, Q. 5

bishops, and delegated, and even judges of appeal, such as metropolitans, can be challenged as suspected;[1] nay, even a college or collective body of judges—*i.e.*, a number of judges acting collectively or as a moral body—can be challenged. Hence also, as we have already seen, both individual members and the entire body composing a Commission of Investigation, with us, may be challenged as suspected, because, among other reasons, they take the place of the judge (bishop) so far as concerns the hearing of the cause.

1037. 5. The legitimate reasons for challenging a judge as suspected are chiefly the following: (*a*) If there is ground for believing him to be hostile to the defendant, which can be presumed if he has made threats against him, or refused to show him the ordinary signs of courtesy or benevolence; (*b*) When he has a special affection for, or particular relations with, the opponent of the person making the challenge— *v.g.*, if he is a relative, master, colleague, or particular friend of the opponent. (*c*) If he has a particular bias in favor of the cause—*v.g.*, if he has acted as advocate in the same case ; or if he has, as a private person, a similar cause pending before another judge. The reason is that it is presumed he will pass sentence in the same way as he wishes the other judge to do in his own case.[2] In general it must be observed that it is left to the arbitrators selected, as we shall presently see, to decide what is a just cause for challenging a judge as suspected. For it is their right and duty to decide not only whether the facts exist, but also whether they are sufficient to authorize the rejection of the judge.[3]

1038. *Q.* What is the mode of procedure when the judge is challenged or objected to?

A. When the judge is excepted to as incompetent,—*i.e.*, as not possessed of jurisdiction in the cause,—he himself has

---

[1] Ex cap. 41 et 61, de Appell. (il. 28); Schmalzg., 1. 2, t. 28, n. 135.
[2] Schmalzg., l. c., n. 138.   [3] Ib., n. 137.

the right to pronounce upon the exception, or decide whether or not he has jurisdiction.[1] If he is challenged, however, as suspected, the following is the mode of procedure prescribed by the Church or the sacred canons. 1. The person challenging must state the specific or precise cause of the challenge or suspicion, and that in writing, and to the judge himself who is challenged.[2] 2. The cause of the suspicion is not, however, to be tried and decided by the judge himself who has been challenged (lest he may thus seem to act as judge in his own cause, which is forbidden[3]), but must, as a rule, be committed to arbitrators for decision.

1039. 3. The mode of appointment of these arbitrators is this: Where there is a plaintiff, distinct from the judge,— *v.g.*, where the trial is by way of accusation or denunciation —two arbitrators are selected by mutual agreement of the plaintiff and defendant, if they can agree upon two. If they cannot agree upon any two, the plaintiff selects one and the defendant the other. Where the judge proceeds *ex officio*, as in the trial by way of inquiry (the trial in the U. S., as prescribed by the Instr. of July 20, 1878, and by the Instr. *Cum Magnopere* of 1884, partakes of the process of inquiry), and where, consequently, there is no plaintiff distinct and separate from the judge, the selection or appointment of the arbitrators should be made in the manner just given, by the judge who is challenged and the party challenging. This is certain in the case of a judge proceeding absolutely *ex officio* —*i.e.*, not at the instance of a third party; *v.g.*, the diocesan promoter or prosecuting official.[4] Whether, in case he proceeds at the instance of the promoter (see Instr. *Cum Magnopere*), the appointment of one of the arbitrators belongs to the latter official—who is, so to say, the plaintiff—or to the bishop or judge, we do not feel competent to decide.

---

[1] Supra, n. 721. [2] L. 16, C. de Jud. [3] L. unic. C. Ne quis in sua caus. jud. (lil. 5).
[4] Instr. S. C. de P. F., July 20, 1878, § 2.

1040. 4. If the two arbitrators thus chosen cannot agree upon a decision as to the cause of the suspicion, they should choose a third one. Whatever two of these three arbitrators decide, shall be binding. 5. If the arbitrators decide that the cause or reason upon which the challenge is based is insufficient or not proven, the judge challenged will then proceed with the case as though he had not been challenged. If, however, they pronounce the cause of the challenge legitimate and proven, the challenged judge cannot proceed with the case, but should either transmit it to the superior tribunal, or delegate it, with the consent of the person challenging, to some other person. This can be done even before recourse is had to arbitration.[1] The mode of procedure above outlined, was established by Popes Celestin III.[2] (1195) and Innocent III.[3] (1216), and is still in force.

1041. What are the rights and duties of these arbitrators? They can and should take cognizance of, and pronounce solely on, the cause or grounds of the challenge or suspicion, and not on the merits of the main cause or issue during the trial of which the challenge is made. For this purpose they can cite witnesses and compel them to testify; admit exceptions against the persons or depositions of the witnesses; etc., etc.[4] They should decide, as we have seen, upon two questions: First, one of law—namely, whether the cause of the suspicion, as alleged, is one which, according to the law of the Church, or the opinion of prudent and good men, would justly render the judge suspected. Second, the other of fact—namely, whether the cause is proved to exist in reality.[5]

1042. *Application of the above principles to the United States.*—That it is allowed also with us to object against an ecclesiastical judge as suspected, there can be no doubt. For, as we have seen,[6] the right to make exceptions of this

---

[1] Schmalzg.,l. c., n. 142. [2] Cap. 41, de Appell. (ii. 28).

[3] Cap. 61, de App. (ii. 28). [4] Schmalzg., l. c., n. 141.

[5] Supra, n. 803, 808; Bouix, de Jud., vol. ii., p. 182. [6] Supra, n. 1030.

kind forms part of a just defence, which is given by the law
of nature, and is, moreover, expressly granted by the Instructions of the S. C. de P. F. *Quamvis* of July 20, 1878,[1] and
Cum Magnopere of 1884, Art. XXVII.. It is certain that the
bishop, with us, as elsewhere, can be challenged. We have,
moreover, seen that members of Commissions of Investigation may also be objected to. Where the bishop, with us, is
objected to, the mode of procedure is plain enough; since
the principles above laid down seem easy of application.
For the bishop either transmits the whole or main cause to a
higher ecclesiastical tribunal, or, with the consent of the
challenger, delegates it to some other ecclesiastic for adjudication, or the cause of the challenge is submitted to arbitrators, chosen as stated above. That the bishop cannot himself decide the allegations upon which the challenge is based,
is clear from the fact that the law of the Church, forbidding
the challenged judge to take cognizance of the challenge, is
founded upon the natural law, as Pope Celestin III. intimates,[2] which obtains also with us, independently of the
question whether canon law fully obtains in this country.

1043. *Mode of procedure when a member of a Commission of
Investigation is challenged, with us, as suspected.*—This question
seems to us difficult of solution. Is the issue or question,
whether the reasons alleged for challenging a member of a
Commission are well-founded and sufficient, to be decided
by the bishop or by the Commission, without any recourse to
arbitration, or is it to be committed to arbitrators, as above
explained; and if so, how are these arbitrators to be chosen?
By the defendant and the bishop or the latter's prosecuting
official? Or by the defendant and the Commission—or at
least the member of the Commission who is challenged?
Before answering directly, we beg to say that the only safe
way in which, it seems to us, a satisfactory answer can be

---

[1] Instr. cit., § 7, Deinde.   [2] Cap. 41 (ii. 28).

given, is by a decision of the Holy See. The organization of our ecclesiastical courts, according to the Instruction of the S. C. de P. F., dated July 20, 1878, is somewhat different from that established by the common law of the Church, and resembles in many ways that of secular courts in this country and elsewhere, which are composed of a judge and a jury. Hence it is not easy to arrive at certain conclusions.

1044. In the absence of any authentic decision of the Holy See, and without wishing to forestall such decision, we venture to lay down the following inferences: 1. We said above, "that, *as a rule*, the grounds for the challenge of a judge must be referred to arbitrators. From this rule there are three exceptions—*i.e.*, cases where the reasons for the challenge need not be submitted to arbitrators, but may be taken cognizance of by others. These cases are: I. Where the judge challenged is a delegated judge, and where the judge who delegated him is easily accessible, or not too far away, the cause of the challenge is taken cognizance of, not by arbitrators, but by the judge delegating.[1] So a challenge against a judge delegated by the bishop is decided by the bishop, and not by arbitrators. In like manner, it may be argued, when a member of a Commission of Investigation, with us, is challenged, the cause of the challenge should be taken cognizance of by the bishop, and not by arbitrators. However, against this it may be said that members of Commissions are indeed appointees, but not delegates of the bishop, but rather delegates of the Holy See, or, *a jure*, like synodal judges, since they are clothed with jurisdiction, not by the bishop, but by the law,—*i.e.*, the Instruction of the S. C. de P. F., of July 20, 1878. Now, the reasons upon which a challenge against a delegated judge are based are to be decided by the judge who delegated him only when this delegating judge is near at hand, so as to cut off delay. When

---

[1] Cap. Si contra 2, de Off. del., in 6° (i. 14).

he is far off, as the Holy See is with regard to the United States, the decision is to be left to arbitrators. Moreover, as we shall see in the case of vicars-general, the judge or bishop delegating cannot try the challenge, but must refer it to arbitrators, when he is himself suspected. Now, it may happen from various reasons that when a Commissioner is suspected the bishop may also become suspected.

1045. II. The second exception is where the vicar-general acting as judge is challenged. In this case the challenge is decided by the bishop, not by arbitrators,[1] unless the bishop is himself suspected.[2] From this again it may perhaps be inferred that the bishop, and not arbitrators, has the right to hear the challenge made against a member of a commission. Against this conclusion it may, however, be objected that the decision of the challenge, in the case of the vicar-general, belongs to arbitrators, and not to the bishop, if the latter is himself suspected. Now, according to Bouix,[3] practically speaking, the bishop may always be considered suspected when his vicar-general is so regarded, and *vice versâ*. In like manner it may perhaps be reasoned, when a member of a Commission is suspected, the bishop who appointed him becomes frequently, *eo ipso*, also suspected, and therefore incompetent to try the challenge.[4]

1046. III. The third exception is where two delegates (the same holds where more than two are appointed[5]) are appointed by the Holy See (the same holds of delegates appointed by others[6]), with the clause, *Quod si ambo non potestis, unus seu alter procedat*—*i.e.*, in such manner that if both or all cannot proceed in the cause, then the other or others can proceed. In this case, when one of the delegates is challenged as suspected, the challenge is tried and decided, not by arbitrators, but by the other delegate or delegates not challenged,

---

[1] Cap. Si contra cit.   [2] Schmalzg., l. 2, t. 28, n. 140.   [3] De Jud., vol. ii., p. 184.
[4] Cf. Leur., For. Benef. Tr. de Vicario-gen., Q. 90 et 91.
[5] Glossa, in cap. 4, in 6° (i. 14), v. Ex duobus.   [6] Glossa, ib. v. A Sede Ap.

so that the latter may know whether he or they can go on without the colleague challenged. This law, however, does not apply to two or more delegated judges appointed in such a manner as to be obliged to proceed collectively, so that one cannot proceed without the other. In the latter case, the challenge against one of the judges must be referred to and decided by arbitration.[1]

1047. From this third exception it may perhaps be argued that from the fact that in the United States a Commission of Investigation—supposing it to consist of five members—is empowered to proceed in a cause so long as three members remain qualified or unchallenged,[2] it follows that in case the fourth or even fifth member is challenged it becomes the right and duty of the other three or (in case only one member is challenged) four members who are unchallenged, to take cognizance of and decide the challenge, so that they may know whether their colleague has become disqualified or not, and whether consequently they can proceed in the cause without him. But, it may perhaps likewise be further reasoned, if only two (or less) members remain unchallenged (no matter whether the Commission consists of five or only three members), the challenge must be referred to and decided by arbitrators; for two cannot proceed validly (of course, in causes where the Commission must be convened), and therefore have no right to inquire whether they can go on or not without their colleagues. Besides, it may further be said, as these two cannot proceed alone, they are like a number of delegates or judges appointed collectively for a cause without the clause, "quod si non omnes possunt, alter procedat," and consequently recourse must be had to arbitrators.

1048. Note, however, we say "it is the right and duty of the three or four unchallenged Commissioners *to take cogni-*

---

[1] Cap. Si contra cit.
[2] Instr. S. C. de P. F., 20 Julii, 1878, § Quod si.

sance of the challenge;" for although, according to the view just explained, the challenge is to be *proved* before the members who are unchallenged, it is nevertheless to be proposed or made before the whole body, inclusive of the member challenged, as the *Glossa*[1] explains in the case of challenged delegates.

1049. Q. By whom are the arbitrators to be chosen in the United States, supposing that the challenge is referred to arbitrators?

A. 1. One, of course, by the defendant making the challenge; the other by the member of the Commission challenged, or perhaps by the priest appointed by the bishop to conduct the prosecution of the cause.[2] For, as we have seen,[3] where the judge proceeds *ex officio*, and there is consequently no plaintiff distinct from the judge, the judge himself who has been challenged appoints the second arbitrator. Now, with us, the procedure is *ex officio*, and the Commissioner who is challenged, together with the rest of the Commission, represents the judge or bishop, and therefore has the appointment of the second arbitrator. We say, however, *or perhaps by the priest*, etc.; the reason of this conjecture is, that the proceedings of the judge or Commission, where a promoter or prosecuting official intervenes, are *ex officio* indeed, but yet not absolutely or strictly so; that, consequently, as this official seems to a certain extent to occupy the position of a plaintiff, it may perhaps be his right to name the second arbitrator.

1050. 2. If the two arbitrators cannot agree as to the existence or reasonableness of the cause alleged for the challenge, they should select a third one, as stated above.[4] Should the arbitrators decide (and they should proceed sum-

[1] In cap. Si contra, v. Probari.
[2] Instr. S. C. de P. F. cit., § 2, Re ad consilium.
[3] Supra, n. 1039.   [4] Supra, n. 1040.

marily) that the challenge is well taken,—*i.e.*, legitimate and
proved,—the decision of the arbitrators must be communicated to the bishop (at least where only two Commissioners
remain unchallenged), who will thereupon appoint another
priest to act on the Commission (at least, where otherwise
the Commission would consist of less than three members),
for that particular case, in the place of the challenged member of the Commission. The latter does not cease to be a
member, but is simply disqualified to sit in the particular
case of the person by whom he has been challenged.

1051. Again, a member of a Commission, when objected
to, may save the necessity of recourse to arbitrators by voluntarily giving up his place for that particular case. And
as the acts of the Commission are valid, provided three
members remain qualified and conduct the proceedings, the
bishop need not necessarily appoint any other priest to fill
the place of the challenged member, provided three members remain. Should, however, the bishop determine to
appoint a temporary member to fill the place of the one challenged (which he is bound to do when less than three remain
unchallenged or qualified), he would be obliged to appoint
one who would not be objectionable to the challenger.[1]

1052. *Q.* When is the objection or challenge against the
ecclesiastical judge to be made?

A. Before the *litis contestatio*, and within twenty days
after the bill of complaint or charges (with us, the charge
drawn up by the *procurator fiscalis*, or where there are Commissions of Investigation, by the bishop's official[2]) has been
presented to the accused or defendant. Thus the Roman
law, adopted by the Church, says: "Offeratur ei qui vocatur
in judicium libellus; et exinde . . . viginti dierum gaudeat
induciis, quibus deliberet . . . an recuset eum" (judicem).[3]

[1] Ex cap. 61 (ll. 28).   [2] Instr. S. C. de P. F., 20 Jul., 1878, §§ 2 et 4.
[3] L. offeratur 1, C. de Lit. cont. (lll. 9).

We say, "before the *litis contestatio* or plea." For the exception or challenge against the judge belongs to the class of exceptions called dilatory exceptions, which, as we have seen,[1] must generally be made or proposed before the contestation of the cause. Nay, the exception against the judge has this peculiar characteristic, that it should be proposed before any other dilatory exception.[2] The reason is, that a person who submits any other dilatory exception before he challenges the judge, is presumed to have accepted the judge, by allowing the exception to be tried before him, and thus to have waived his right of challenge.[3] As shown, however, above,[4] this exception, like dilatory exceptions in general, may sometimes be made *after* the contestation.

1053. Finally, we remark, that as exceptions are the legitimate weapons of defence,—*arma reorum*,[5]—and therefore guaranteed by natural law itself, it follows that if the judge refuses to admit an exception properly made, it is allowed to appeal (also with us, in proceedings before Commissions of Investigation, and in trials conducted according to the Instruction *Cum Magnopere*) at once against such refusal.[6]

1054. What are the chief effects of the challenge against the judge? After the challenge or recusation has been proposed, and pending its decision, the judge should not, unless the challenge is manifestly frivolous, proceed with or do anything further in the main cause; otherwise his acts will be attentates, as though done after an appeal had been interposed. Consequently, these acts, or rather attentates, must before all else be revoked by the superior judge. It is, however, a controverted question whether they are *ipso jure* null and void, or only subject to being declared void by the higher judge.[7]

[1] Supra, n. 1031.   [2] L. 13, C. de Jud. (8. 36); Reiff., l. c., n. 12.

[3] Glossa, in cap. 12 (ii. 25), v. In dilatoriis; Glossa, in cap. 20 (ii. 26), v. Subeundo.   [4] Supra, n. 1031; Schmalzg., l. c., n. 133.

[5] Glossa, in tit. de Except. [6] Reiff., l. c., n. 82. [7] Schmalzg., l. c., n. 144.

§ 7   *Of Ecclesiastical Countersuits or Charges, also in the United States* (*De Mutuis Petitionibus*).

1055. Sometimes the defendant, having received the *libellus* or bill of complaint brought against him by the plaintiff, demands in turn something of the plaintiff, and having presented a bill of complaint to the judge, also institutes an action against the plaintiff himself. This counter-action (*reconventio*) is called in canon law *mutua petitio*, because the reciprocal demand or complaint of the defendant causes two mutual or reciprocal complaints or actions to arise. What, then, is meant by a counter-complaint or *mutua petitio* or *reconventio?* It is an act whereby the defendant, having received and read the libellus or complaint (with us, in trials before Commissions of Investigation, the statement *pro causa*, sent the defendant with the citation ') of the plaintiff, in turn makes a demand upon or complaint against him, and that before the same judge and during the same trial.' Observe that the plaintiff, so far as concerns the counter-complaint brought against him by the defendant, becomes subject to and is triable by the judge in the case, even though he would otherwise not fall under the latter's jurisdiction.'

1056. *Q.* In what causes is a defendant allowed to institute a counter-action, or make a counter-charge, in ecclesiastical tribunals?

A. Generally speaking, in all causes which are not expressly excepted by law—*i.e.*, by the sacred canons, or by the Roman law as adopted by the sacred canons. Speaking in particular, a counter-action may be instituted (*a*) in all civil causes; (*b*) not only in formal or solemn trials, but also in sum-

---

[1] Instr. S. C. de P. F. cit., §§ 2, 4.
[2] Ex. cap. 2, de Mut. pet. (ii. 4); L. 14, C. de Jud. et Interl. (vii. 45); Schmalzg., L. 2, t. 4, n. 1.   [3] Reiff., l. 2, t. 4, n. 5.

mary causes—*i.e.*, in causes where the mode of procedure is summary ;[1] (*c*) even where the subject-matter of the counter complaint is of an entirely different nature from that of the plaintiff's action or complaint.[2]

1057. We said above, *in all civil causes.* We now ask: Can a counter-charge be made by a defendant *in a criminal cause?* We distinguish between four kinds of criminal causes : 1. Either a person who stands civilly charged with a crime wishes in turn to accuse the plaintiff or prosecution criminally of a crime ; 2, or, one who is criminally charged desires to make a criminal counter-complaint civilly ; 3, or a person who is accused civilly wants to bring a civil counter-action ; 4, or, finally, a defendant who stands criminally accused of crime wishes also in turn to accuse his accuser or opponent criminally.

1058. In the first case, the counter-charge or complaint is allowed. Because a criminal cause is privileged and takes precedence of any civil cause. Hence, in the case, the civil cause of the plaintiff cannot be tried or decided until after the criminal charge made by the defendant has been adjudicated.[3] In the second case, no counter-complaint is admissible ; since the criminal complaint, being of greater importance (as the common good of the Church requires that crimes shall be punished), takes precedence of the civil.[4] In the third case, the defendant can bring a counteraction. In the fourth case, the defendant cannot, generally speaking, prefer a counter-charge. In other words, in a purely criminal cause,—*i.e.*, where a defendant stands criminally, not merely civilly, charged with a crime,—the defendant or person so accused cannot, generally speaking, bring a criminal

---

[1] Ex Clem. 2, de V. S., § Verum de.

[2] L. Praeses 1 ff. de Var. et extraord. cognit.; Schmalzg., l. c., n. 9.

[3] L. 3, C. de Ord. cognit. (3. 8); Schmalzg., l. c., n. 11.

[4] L. 4, C. de Ord. cogn.; L. Consensisse 2 ff. de Jud. (5. 1), § 5, Sed et si agant.

counter-complaint against the plaintiff or prosecution. Thus Ulpianus elegantly says: " Si quis reus factus est, purgare se debet : nec ante potest accusare quam fuerit excusatus. Constitutionibus enim observatur, ut non relatione criminum, sed innocentia reus purgetur." [1]

1059. We said, speaking of the fourth case, *generally speaking;* for even in purely criminal causes a person may institute a counter-criminal complaint, in ecclesiastical courts, chiefly in these cases: 1. Where he prosecutes or asks redress for injuries inflicted upon himself or persons belonging to him. 2. Where the counter-charge is of a graver character than the accusation of the plaintiff or prosecution.[2] 3. Where the crimes are interlinked or connected with each other. In this case, any crime whatever, even though much less serious than that with which the person making the counter-complaint stands charged, can form the basis of the counter-charge. 4. Finally, a defendant can prefer a criminal counter-charge of any kind whatever, before an ecclesiastical judge who has jurisdiction over both parties, the plaintiff as well as the defendant—*v.g.*, if both belong to the same bishop.[3]

1060. *Q.* In what other causes is it forbidden to make counter-complaints ?

A. Chiefly in these: 1. In causes of appeal. In other words, when a case has been appealed, the judge of appeal cannot allow any new counter-charge or complaint to be made before him, in the trial of the appeal. For the rule is, that he cannot permit any entirely new issue to arise during the appeal, but should confine himself to what was advanced during the trial in the first instance. 2. In causes of spoliation or unjust deprivation (*in causis spolii*) ; that is, in causes where a person complains of having been unjustly deprived of a right or possession,—*v.g.*, an ecclesiastical office or benefice,—and asks to be reinstated. In such cases the person

---

[1] L. 5 ff. de Publ. Jud. (48. 1).   [2] L. 19, C. (9. 1); Can. 2, C. 3, Q. 11.
[3] Schmalzg., l. c., n. 11.

against whom the complaint of spoliation or unjust deprivation is made cannot make a counter-complaint, but must,
before all else, reinstate the complainant, and then, but not
before, can the latter be compelled to answer any counter-
charge made against him.   3. The plaintiff, against whom a
counter-complaint has been made, cannot in turn also institute a counter-charge, lest there be no end to litigations. For
it is the plaintiff's duty to embody all his grievances or
charges in his original complaint or charge.[1]

1061. *Q.* What are the effects of a counter-action?

A. Chiefly these: 1. That it extends or, so to say,
stretches the jurisdiction of the judge (*prorogatio jurisdictionis*); because the plaintiff against whom the counter-
complaint is instituted becomes subject to the judge before
whom the counter-complaint is made, in such manner, that
even though he does not otherwise fall under this judge's
jurisdiction,—*v.g.*, if the judge is a bishop, and the plaintiff
in the case is an ecclesiastic belonging to the diocese of a
different bishop,—he nevertheless, so far as the counter-
complaint is concerned, becomes subject to and triable
by such judge.[2] 2. That both cases—*i.e.*, the complaint
of the plaintiff and the counter-complaint of the defendant—must be tried simultaneously, and adjudicated or
decided by one and the same sentence. The mode of this
simultaneous procedure is this : After the defendant has received the plaintiff's bill of complaint, and the latter in turn
that of the defendant's counter-complaint, the latter must
first put in his plea (*litis contestatio*) to the plaintiff's bill, and
then the plaintiff his plea to the defendant's counter-complaint.
Thus the *litis contestatio* is effected both in regard to the complaint and the counter-complaint. Then follows the trial,
which should be so conducted that both cases are tried hand
in hand, or simultaneously, and decided by the same sentence.[3]

---

[1] Schmalzg., l. c., n. 10.   [2] Ib., n. 12.   [3] Ib.

1062. At what stage of the proceedings is the counter-complaint to be made, in order that it may have the above two effects? In the beginning of the trial, or at least immediately after the *litis contestatio*, and before the litigants proceed to any other judicial act.' The counter-action may indeed be instituted after the *litis contestatio*, and at any time during the trial. But, in such case, it will have but the one effect of extending the judge's jurisdiction, but not that of simultaneous trial.'

1063. *Application of the above principles to the United States.*—That the principles laid down above in reference to counter-complaints are, in the main, applicable also in the United States,—*v.g.*, to proceedings or trials before Commissions, where they still exist,—there seems to be no reason to doubt. For, as we have seen, counter-complaints are admissible in summary causes. Now, our trials before Commissions of Investigation partake of the nature of summary trials or causes. Again, counter-charges, as is plain, are one of the means or weapons of a legitimate defence. But, the latter, as was seen, is expressly guaranteed by the Holy See in our trials.' *A fortiori*, counter-complaints are allowed under the Instr. *Cum Magnopere* of 1884.

ART. II.

Various Stages of Regular or Ordinary Canonical Criminal Trials, from the Litis Contestatio to the Final Sentence exclusive.

§ 1. *Of the Plea or Contestation of the Cause, also in the United States (De Litis Contestatione).*

1064. Thus far we have spoken of those acts which, so to say, precede the trial strictly speaking. We now come to those judicial acts or proceedings which constitute the pro-

---

¹ Cap. 1, de Mut. pet. (ii. 4); Clem. 2, de V. S. (v. 11).
² Schmalzg., l. c., n. 13. ³ Instr. S. C. de P. F., July 20, 1878, § 7.

cess or trial proper. Of these, the first is the contestation of the cause (*litis contestatio*),—called in our secular courts, the plea or joining of issue,—by which the trial is in reality begun. When the defendant, having been duly cited, and having received the *libellus*, comes into court or before the judge, it becomes the duty of the plaintiff to repeat before the judge the allegations contained in his statement or bill of complaint. To this the defendant must plead or answer. If he simply and unqualifiedly admits the plaintiff's allegations, the cause is by that very fact or confession terminated in the plaintiff's favor.

1065. But if he denies them, either in whole or in part, and is willing to repel or refute them in court—*i.e.*, contest the case—rather than yield, the cause is said to be contested (*lis contestata*), or the issue joined. Hence the contestation of the cause consists in the plaintiff's (prosecution's) affirmation or statement, and its denial or contradiction by the defendant, made in court or before the judge (*in jure*), preliminary to the trial proper. Thus Pope Gregory IX. says: " Cum . . . per petitionem in jure propositam, et responsionem secutam, litis contestatio fiat." [1] We say, "in court—*in jure ;*" for both the plaintiff's statement and the defendant's answer or plea must be made *in jure*—*i.e.*, in court, not out of it.

1066. *Q.* Is the contestation of the cause required in all ecclesiastical trials ?

A. It is, as a rule; and that in such manner that if it is omitted in formal or ordinary canonical trials, the whole trial or entire proceedings are null and void, [2] even though the judge or litigants should consent to its omission. In fact, it is the basis, corner-stone, or foundation of the whole trial. Its object is to fix clearly the points of dispute or con-

---

[1] Cap. un. de Lit. cont. (ii. 5); cf. Reiff., l. 2, t. 5, n. 2, 5.
[2] Ex cap. un. de Lit. cont.; cap. 1, 2, Ut lit. non cont. (ii. 6); Reiff., l. c., n. 3.

test between the contending parties. Now, as is evident, in order to avoid confusion, it is very useful, nay, even necessary, apart from the law of the Church, to have the points or questions at issue—that is, the complaint or charge which is to be tried—clearly stated or laid down in the very beginning of the trial or proceedings, so that there will remain no doubt whatever as to the question at issue.[1] Otherwise, it will easily happen that neither the plaintiff (or prosecution) nor the defendant will know precisely what is the object of the trial, and will consequently simply lose their time and money.[2] For this reason also, it is plain that while, as we shall presently note, no formal *litis contestatio* is requisite in certain causes, yet something similar or equivalent to it is always needed. (Schmalzg., l. 2, t. 5, n. 3.)

1067. We said above, *as a rule;* for there are several exceptions. Thus no formal contestation is necessary in the following cases: 1. In summary causes or trials.[3] We say, *necessary;* for it *may* take place. 2. In appeals; because the contestation made before the judge or court of the first instance is sufficient.[4] 3. In notorious causes; for no formality whatever is required in these causes. 4. In causes adjudicated before the Pope. 5. In all causes where no *libellus* is required.[5] Observe that in these cases, where no formal contestation is requisite, the first judicial act, which would otherwise take place immediately after the *litis contestatio*, is considered as and has the force of the *litis contestatio*.[6]

1068. Is the *litis contestatio* required not only in civil, but also in criminal causes? It is; though in this case the cause is said to be contested—*i.e.*, the *litis contestatio* takes place when the judge in the examination preliminary to the trial, or at its opening, interrogates the accused as to his guilt, and

---

[1] Molitor, Eccl. Trials of Ecclesiastics, pp. 148, 149.
[2] Cf. Permaneder, Manual of Canon Law, p. 502.
[3] Clem. 2, de V. S. (v. 11).　[4] Cap. 58, de Appell.　[5] Schmalzg., l. c., n. 4.
[6] Glossa, v. Absentia, in cap. 1, de Elect., in 6 (i. 6); Reiff., l. c., n. 4.

the latter denies it, in whole or in part.[1] Whether and when the accused is bound to confess his guilt in answer to the judge's questions, will be seen later.

1069. *Q.* Is a formal contestation of the cause required in proceedings or trials as conducted before Commissions of Investigation in England, and some parts of the U. S.?

' *A.* It is not. The reason is, that these proceedings are summary, and moreover do not constitute a canonical trial or process in the strict sense of the term. We said in our question, *formal;* for, as we have seen, something similar or equivalent to a plea or contestation is required in every trial, no matter of what kind, and consequently also in proceedings before our Commissions of Investigation. In other words, in all ecclesiastical trials or judicial proceedings, whether they be canonical trials proper or not, and consequently also in proceedings or trials, with us, as established by the S. C. de P. F., in its Instruction of July 20, 1878, care should be taken that, in civil causes, the point or matter in dispute, and in criminal causes the charges against the accused, be clearly and fully defined and stated before the trial begins.[2] Thus confusion and delay will be avoided. Hence also it would be well for the vicar-general or other priest acting as the bishop's representative, to draw up the statement or charges against the defendant, to be read before the Commission of Investigation, in this manner: First, let him give, in his paper, a summary statement of the charges and specifications, or if there is question of civil causes, an outline or epitome of the case. Next let him take up the charges and specifications, one by one, and fully and clearly prove them, by the testimony of witnesses, documents, etc., etc. The accused or defendant should likewise, in his defence before the Commission, clearly and categorically answer the official's statement. All extraneous matter should, of course, be carefully eschewed.

[1] Bouix, de Jud., vol. ii., p. 192.   [2] Cf. Instr. S. C. de P. F. cit., § 4, Per litteras.

§ 2. *Positions and Articles* (*Positiones, Articuli*).

1070. The so-called positions and articles are akin to the contestation of the cause, and as a rule follow immediately after it. To a certain extent, they serve the same purpose as the contestation—namely, to fix clearly the questions at issue, or the charges to be proved. What, then, is meant by positions and articles? Positions (*positiones*) are certain brief and concise or categorical questions, assertions, specifications or counts, pertaining to the cause on trial, which one of the litigants (usually the plaintiff, and in criminal causes the diocesan prosecuting official) submits to the judge, with the request that the other litigant (usually the defendant) be compelled to answer categorically yes or no, or whether he admits or denies them, and that for the purpose of being relieved from the burden of proving those points or specifications that are admitted by the opponent.[1]

1071. Positions may be made either in the form of questions, or positive affirmations or assertions. The following is a specimen of a position in the form of a positive statement: I affirm or charge that thou, Titius, the defendant, hast killed Caius; that thou didst perform the deed on such a day, in such a place, with a sword; that thou didst know him to be an ecclesiastic, etc., etc. The following, on the other hand, is a sample of an interrogative position: Did you, Titius, kill Caius? Did you kill him at such a place, etc.; did you not know him to be an ecclesiastic, etc.?[2] Those positions which are denied by the opponent, and which consequently must be proved by the one who has submitted them, are called articles (*articuli*), the others simply positions.

1072. From what has been said, the object and utility of positions will at once be seen. For if the diocesan prose-

---

[1] Glossa, in cap. 1, de Confessis, in 6° (ii. 9), v. Statuimus; Schmalzg., l. 2, t. 5, n. 5; Bouix, de Jud., vol. ii., p. 207.   [2] Cf. Glossa, cit.

cuting official, for instance, proposes ten such specifications
or categorical questions, and the defendant admits six, and
only contends that four are false, it will be necessary to
prove only the four, as the other six are established or
proved by the defendant's own confession, which is the best
possible proof.

1073. *Do these positions and articles still obtain, also in the
United States?* By virtue of the positive canon law these
positions and articles (in criminal causes they are called
chapters or *capitula*) still obtain and form part of canonical
trials, even though not solemn or formal, but merely summary.[1] We say, *positive canon law;* for, as Bouix,[2] Craisson,
and other canonists testify, these positions are no longer
formally in use, at least in a number of ecclesiastical courts,
having been abolished by legitimate custom to the contrary.
Observe we say, *formally in use;* for they are still informally
or substantially in vogue ; since the judge, in examining the
litigants or the accused, in the preliminary hearing, substantially puts at the present day the same questions as would be
embodied in positions.[3] In this informal way they certainly
also may be, in fact are, employed with great advantage in
trials or proceedings before Commissions of Investigation
in the United States.

§ 3. *Oaths administered in Ecclesiastical Trials to the Principals or Litigants themselves.*

1074. *Note.*—In speaking of the positions and articles,
before the oaths taken by the litigants, we have somewhat
anticipated the course of the trial. For one of the oaths, of
which we shall now treat, is taken immediately after the contestation, and directly before the positions and articles are
submitted.[4] Again we observe, that the oaths, of which we

---

[1] Clem. Saepe 2, de V. S. (v. 11); cap. 1, 2 in 6° (ii. 9); Bouix, l. c., p. 210.
[2] L. c.   [3] Molitor, l. c., p. 251.   [4] Ex cap. 2 in 5° (ii. 9).

here speak, are taken by the litigants themselves,—both plaintiff, or prosecution, and defendant,—but not by the witnesses. The oath administered to the latter is altogether different. We shall now briefly describe the oaths in question.

1075. The nature and character of these oaths will be best understood by simply describing the course of procedure. After the contestation has taken place, and before any testimony is taken,[1] the litigants—that is, both the plaintiff, or prosecution, and defendant—are put under oath; in other words, the plaintiff swears that he has begun and continues the cause in good faith, and without malice or chicanery (*calumnia*), and the defendant that he contests it, believing he has a right to do so. This oath is called *juramentum calumniae*, the word *calumnia* meaning here, or in judicial matters, deceit or chicanery. This oath is general in its character and application—that is, it refers to all the acts of the litigants in the course of the entire trial. In other words, by it the parties pledge themselves to act in good faith during the whole trial. Hence this oath is justly defined to be that by which the litigants swear that they have begun and will prosecute or continue their cause in good faith and without *calumnia*—*i.e.*, chicanery or wiles.[2]

1076. The oaths called respectively *juramentum veritatis* and *juramentum malitiae* are akin to the oath of *calumnia* just described. By the *juramentum veritatis* the parties—*i.e.*, the plaintiff or defendant—swear they will tell the truth in a particular matter or point coming up during the trial. By the *juramentum malitiae* they swear they will not act maliciously in this or that instance. The difference between the *juramentum calumniae* and the oaths *veritatis* and *malitiae* is apparent from their respective definitions. The *juramentum calumniae* is general and refers to the whole cause, and is

[1] Schmalzg., l. 2, t. 7, n. 1.
[2] L. 1, 2, C. de Jurej. prop. cal. (ii. 59); cap. 1, de Jur. cal. (ii. 7); ib. Glossa, v. Calumnia; Schmalzg., l. c., n. 2.

therefore taken at the beginning—*i.e.*, immediately after the *litis contestatio*—and only once. The other two are particular,—*i.e.*, refer only to this or that act during the trial,—and may therefore, and are, taken during any part of the trial, and as often as occasion requires.

1077. It is certain that both the oaths of *calumnia* and *malitiae* are now entirely obsolete in ecclesiastical courts, being no longer taken. The oath to tell the truth is still in use in ecclesiastical courts, though it can no longer be administered in criminal causes to the accused when criminally examined. This was enacted by Pope Benedict XIII. in the Roman Council held in 1725.[1] Although this council is but a provincial council, and therefore not obligatory out of the Roman province, yet its prohibition is observed everywhere, and can be considered as a common law of the Church.[2] Neither can the oath (*juramentum veritatis*) be administered to a defendant in grave civil causes; since the latter are, in canon law, placed on an equal footing, owing to their gravity, with criminal causes. In proceedings or trials before our Commissions of Investigation, none of the above oaths is administered either to the defendant or the plaintiff, or the bishop's official who represents the plaintiff or prosecution in criminal causes.[3]

§ 4. *Of Delays which occur during the Trial (De Dilationibus).*

1078. After the contestation has taken place and the oath of *calumnia* been administered (where it is still in use), and the positions put and answered, the litigants usually ask for a delay, or for time to make out their case. In other words, the plaintiff or prosecution generally asks for time to complete his proofs, etc., and the defendant for time to prepare his defence. Nay, delays may and do occur even

---

[1] Tit. 13, cap. 2.   [2] Craiss., n. 5931.
[3] Arg. ex Instr. cit., S. C. de P. F., July 20, 1878, § 11, Non requiratur.

previous to the contestation. Hence this seems to be the proper place to say a few words in regard to delays that may happen in judicial proceedings, also before our Commissions of Investigation.

1079. What are judicial delays? As here understood, a judicial delay is a just, proper, or sufficient interval or space of time granted to the plaintiff (prosecution) or defendant for the purpose of enabling him to prepare for and perform some judicial act more conveniently.[1] Of these delays (*dilationes judiciales*) some are given, 1, by the law—*i.e.*, by the law of the Church, or the Roman law as adopted by the Church, or by statute, or also by custom, and are called legal delays (*dilationes legales*). Thus ten days are granted by the sacred canons for appealing against a sentence, so that it may not pass into *res judicata*.[2] 2. Others take place by the mutual consent of the contending parties. They are styled conventional delays (*dilationes conventionales*), and are, within due bounds, allowed by the Church.[3] 3. Others, finally, are given by the judge, and termed *dilationes arbitrariae*—*i.e.*, delays granted at the discretion of the judge, according as circumstances may demand.[4]

1080. Delays may occur during any stage of the trial. Hence they are divided into three kinds, according as they happen (*a*) during the first part of the trial or proceedings—*i.e.*, from the citation to the contestation inclusive; (*b*) or during the second part—namely, from the contestation (or its equivalent) to the pronouncing of final sentence exclusive; (*c*) or during the third and final stage—*i.e.*, from the sentence till its execution.[5] We shall now explain these three classes.

1081. I. *Delays which occur before the contestation.*—These delays refer directly or indirectly to the defendant's appear-

---

[1] Reiff., l. 2, t. 8, n. 2.   [2] Cap. 15, de Sent. et re jud. (ii. 27).
[3] Cap. 28, de Off. jud. del. (i. 29), § Cum autem; ib. Glossa.
[4] L. 72 ff. de Jud. (v. i.); cf. Reiff., l. c, n. 11–14.   [5] Reiff., l. c., n. 10.

ance in court, upon due citation, being conceded to a person who for just cause either cannot or need not appear before the judge at the time, place, or in the manner specified in the cita. tion. Of these delays, some are citatory, others deliberative, others finally recusative. Citatory delays (*dilationes citatoriae*) are those which are given a defendant, who is cited, to enable him to appear in court on the day specified in the citation. By the general law of the Church, as we have seen, ten days must intervene between each of the three simple citations, or thirty when there is but one peremptory citation. This rule, however, is subject to certain modifications. For, where there is just cause, this time may be prolonged or limited by the judge, provided always that the defendant has sufficient time not only to appear, but also previously to deliberate upon the case, consult advocates, experts, etc. Otherwise another delay would have to be granted for deliberation, and if refused by the judge, there would be just cause for appeal.[1]

1082. Deliberative delays (*dilationes deliberatoriae*) are those which are allowed the defendant after the bill of complaint or charges has been served upon him, for the purpose of enabling him to consider whether he will contest the case or not. A delay of twenty days is conceded by the common law of the Church for this purpose.[2] Sometimes, however, no such delay is granted—namely, when the person cited has been fully instructed as to the nature of the complaint by the letters of citation;[3] *i.e.*, where these letters are accompanied by a copy of the libellus or complaint, or by a specific statement of the complaint or charges.[4]

1083. From this it is apparent that, as a rule, these deliberative delays, preceding the trial, cannot always be claimed in the United States. For the oft-quoted Instruc.

---

[1] Cap. 1, de Dilat. (ii. 8); Schmalzg., l. c., n. 7. [3] Novella 53, cap. 3, § 1.
[2] Cap. 2, de Dilat. (ii. 8). [4] Ib. Glossa, v. Plene.

tion of the S. C. de Prop. Fide, dated July 20, 1878, ordains
that except where prudence forbids it, as in the case of
occult crime, the bishop shall send to the accused, together
with the citation, a full and specific statement of the charges
or complaint, which will enable the latter to understand the
nature of the case fully. Here are the words of the Instruction: " Per litteras etiam rectorem missionarium . . . advocet,
exponens nisi prudentia vetat, uti in casu criminis occulti,
causam ad dejectionem moventem, per extensum."¹ We
say, *as a rule;* since, if the time fixed in the citation for
appearing is not sufficiently long to enable the accused to
consult advocates and prepare his defence, or if the statement *pro causa* sent the accused is not sufficiently clear, full,
and explicit, a further reasonable delay ought to be granted.'
Otherwise the defendant has legitimate cause for appeal.'
Moreover, where, as in the case of an occult crime, the citation with us, need not and is not accompanied by a full and
specific statement of the charges,' the accused, on appearing
before the Commission of Investigation in obedience to the
citation, must be fully informed of the charges, and given
time to prepare his defence.

1084. Finally, recusative and dilatory delays (*dilationes
recusatoriae, dilatoriae*) are those which are given for the
purpose of enabling the parties to submit and prove their
recusative and other dilatory exceptions.

1085. II. *Delays which are granted after the contestation to
the sentence.*—These delays are called probative (*dilationes
probatoriae*), and are defined to be those which are conceded
to each of the litigants to prove his case—namely, to the
plaintiff or prosecution to obtain witnesses, and in general
to prepare the proofs of the complaint or charges; to the
defendant to enable him to get ready for the defence—*i.e.,*

¹ Instr. cit., § 4. Per litteras.   ² Ex cap. 3, de Dilat. (ii. 8).
³ Ex cap. 1, de Dilat. (ii. 8); cf. Schmalzg., l. c. n. 7.   ⁴ Cf. Instr. cit., § 4.

to obtain witnesses, documents, etc.[1]   The duration of a probative delay, as established by the common law of the Church, is as follows: Where the proofs or instruments or witnesses to be produced are in the same province (with us, State) in which the trial takes place, three months are granted; where they are in a different province (with us, a different State of the Union) which is near by, six; when abroad, or at a great distance, nine months.[2]   However, at the present day, the duration or length of these delays (the same holds of all other legal delays—*i.e.,* delays given by the law itself) is left in a certain measure to the discretion of the judge, provided always that the defendant be equally favored with the plaintiff—*i.e.,* that as much time or delay be given to the defendant as is given to the plaintiff or prosecution, especially as the law always favors the accused or defendant more than the plaintiff.[3]   We say, *in a certain measure;* we mean that the judge can limit or prolong these delays, for cause, but not arbitrarily.[4]

1086. In criminal causes (the same holds of grave civil causes) the accused can be granted a second and a third probative delay to enable him to prepare for his defence, but the prosecution only a second.[5]   The reason is, that if ever the defendant should be more favored than the plaintiff or prosecution, it should be in criminal causes, where he has so much at stake, and where, consequently, every facility should be afforded him for defending himself.[6]   Besides, the prosecution has always this advantage, that it can select its own time, and begin the criminal procedure only when it is perfectly ready and has collected all the necessary proofs; whereas the defendant has no such advantage.

1087. *Application of the preceding principles to the United States.*—The above principles concerning delays apply in a

---

[1] Cap. 1 (ii. 8); L. 1 et 2, C. de Dilat. (iii. 11).   [2] L. 1, C. de Dil.
[3] Reg. 32, Jur. in 6°; Schmalzg., l. c., n. 13.   [4] Glossa, in cap. 1, de Dil., v. Plene.
[5] L. 10 ff. de Feriis (ii. 12).   [6] Schmalzg., l. c., n. 15.

measure also to proceedings or trials before our Commissions of Investigation. It is true that these trials are of a summary character, and that in summary causes or trials the judge should cut off all avoidable and unnecessary delays.[1] We say, *avoidable delays;* for reasonable delays must be granted even in summary trials,[2] and consequently also in proceedings before our Commissions of Investigation. In fact, these delays, when reasonable, form part of a just defence, which can never be refused. We have just said that in summary causes the judge should endeavor to prevent all avoidable delays. Hence, also, it is ordained in the Instruction of the S. C. de P. F., dated July 20, 1878, that in this country the bishop shall send to the accused, together with the citation, a full and specific statement of the charges,[3] and that the accused shall come before the Commission with his defence already prepared, at least as far as possible, so as to avoid all unnecessary delay. When, therefore, a defendant, in a trial before our Commissions of Investigation, finds it useful, even after the prosecution has closed,—*i.e.*, where the bishop's official has read the statement *pro causa* and submitted his proofs,—to ask for a delay, or even several delays (*v.g.*, where the defendant has not been fully informed beforehand of all the charges against him), to prepare more fully for his defence, his request should be granted by the Commission.

1088. III. *Delays granted from the sentence to its execution inclusive.*—These delays are of three kinds: 1. Those which are given to enable the parties—prosecution and defence—to prepare their final summing up (*dilationes allegatoriae*). For the judge (we speak always of the ecclesiastical judge), having heard all the testimony on both sides, should, before he proceeds to pass final sentence, ask the parties whether

---

[1] Clem. Saepe 2, de V. S. (v. 11).
[2] Ib. Glossa, v. Amputet, et v. Dilatorias.   [3] Instr. cit., § 4, Per litteras.

they wish to submit or say anything else; and if either answers in the affirmative, a delay of thirty days is given him
by the judge to prepare his final arguments.[1] This delay
may be repeated three times. 2. Those which are granted
to the parties to enable them to appear in court and hear the
final sentence pronounced (*dilationes definitoriae*). 3. Finally,
those which are conceded to enable the party condemned to
execute or carry out the provisions of the sentence (*dilationes
exccutoriae.*)[2] These latter are allowed only in çivil causes;
for in criminal causes the execution of the sentence is not
usually delayed. Four months are generally allowed in
civil causes to execute the sentence.[3]

1089. *What are the effects of delays?* The chief effect is
that, pending the delay, the office of the judge is inoperative,
or wholly at rest, so far as concerns the matter in which the
delay has been given, and nothing is to be done or changed
in this respect until the delay has expired;[4] any attempt to
the contrary being *ipso jure* null and void.[5] Finally, we
observe that delays are given, as a rule, at the request of the
litigants; though the judge may and should grant them himself *ex officio*, when he deems it necessary. Moreover, no
delay whatever should be granted by the judge to either the
prosecution or defence, except in the presence of both parties, and upon due proof being given that there is sufficient
reason for the delay.[6]

1090. *Of judicial holidays.*—Speaking on the subject of
judicial delays, we subjoin a few remarks in regard to the
so-called *feriae*, which partake of the nature of judicial delays. By *feriae* are here meant those days on which judicial
acts or proceedings are forbidden, and therefore delayed.
They are divided into sacred and profane. The former are
those which are instituted by the Church for the worship of

---

[1] Auth. Jubemus, C. de Jud. (iii. 1).   [2] Schmalzg., l. c., n. 21.
[3] Cap. 26, de Off. del.   [4] L. 3, C. de Dilat. (iii. 11).   [5] Reiff., l. c., n. 77.
[6] L. 1, 4, C. de Dilat.(iii. 11); cf. Schmalzg., l. c., n. 12.

God and in honor of the saints. Such are the Sundays and holidays of obligation.[1] The latter are those which are established by the secular power for the temporal wants or benefit of the people. Thus, according to the Roman law, the time of harvest—usually from July to August—and the time of vintage—generally from September to October— were judicial holidays in the secular courts[2]—*i.e.*, they were days on which no one could be compelled to go to trial, lest he should thus be disabled from reaping his harvest.[3] These profane or secular judicial holidays naturally vary in different countries. Our legal holidays in the United States partake of the character of judicial holidays.

1091. What are the *feriae* or holidays on which judicial proceedings are forbidden in ecclesiastical courts? 1. All the sacred holidays; that is, all the holidays of obligation established by the Church—namely, all Sundays and holidays of precept.[4] The law of the Church is that on these days all judicial proceedings are, as a rule, so strictly forbidden, that if they nevertheless take place they are *ipso jure* null and void, even though the litigants should consent to them. We say, *as a rule;* for where necessity (*necessitas*) or justice (*pietas*) demands otherwise,[5] judicial proceedings can take place, in ecclesiastical courts, on those days.[6]

1092. 2. Even on all secular holidays,—that is, holidays instituted formerly by the civil government of the Roman empire,—judicial proceedings were forbidden by the Church, in her courts, under pain of nullity. On certain profane holidays, however, the Church allowed judicial proceedings in her courts, provided the parties consented.[7] For there were two kinds of legal holidays : (*a*) Those instituted for

---

[1] Cap. 9, de Feriis. (ii. 9); L. 2 et 3, C. de Dilat.
[2] Cf. Schmalzg., l. 2, t. 9. n. 17.   [3] L. 1, 3 ff. de Feriis; L. 2, C. de Feriis.
[4] Cap. Conquestus 5, de Feriis (ii. 9); Schmalzg., l. 2, t. 9. n. 6.
[5] Cap. Conquestus cit.; ib. Glossa, vv. Necessitas, pietas.
[6] Reiff., l. 2, t. 9, n. 36.   [7] Cap. Conquestus cit.

the wants or direct utility of the people—namely, the harvest and vintage season.   On these days judicial proceedings
could take place validly if the parties consented, since these
days were established for their direct benefit, and could
therefore be given up by them.   (*b*) Those which were established to commemorate some public event—*v.g.*, a battle
won.   On these latter legal holidays judicial proceedings
could not take place, even by consent of the litigants.
Whether, at present, the Church adopts the legal holidays of
the various countries of the world as judicial holidays for
her courts, we do not feel competent to decide, though we
feel inclined to answer in the affirmative.

1093. The above rules concerning *feriae* or judicial holidays apply also to summary trials or proceedings, though
with regard to the latter trials, Pope Clement V. allows that
they may take place, and that without the consent of the litigants, on the rustic holidays, or during the harvest and vintage season, but not on other legal holidays, nor on the holidays of the Church.[1]   From all this it seems to follow that
proceedings or trials before Commissions of Investigation in
the United States, though of a summary character, cannot
take place on Sundays and feasts of precept, except in the
cases of *necessitas* or *pietas* spoken of above.   Nay, it is even
doubtful whether they can take place on our legal holidays.

§ 5. *Order to be observed by the Ecclesiastical Judge when, in
the Hearing of the same Cause, several Questions come up for
Decision (De Ordine Cognitionum).*

1094. When the contestation has taken place, and the
oath of *calumnia* been administered, and the usual delays
granted, the parties proceed to prove their case.   In other
words, the taking of the testimony to prove the cause is the

---

[1] Clem. Saepe 2, de V. S. (v. 11); Reiff., l. c., n. 44.

next step of the trial. However, as we have seen, it will frequently happen that, prior to the submitting of testimony in the main cause, a defendant makes various exceptions, which in turn often give rise to two or more incidental questions or causes, to be decided by the judge in the same cause. Again, the defendant may bring a counter-complaint against the plaintiff; and thus two main or principal causes, connected indeed, but yet distinct, present themselves for decision. These questions must be decided or disposed of in a certain order; otherwise confusion will follow. We shall therefore follow the order of the decretals, and treat of this matter before we proceed to discuss the taking of testimony in the main cause.

1095. *Q.* Which of the several questions or causes arising from the exceptions of the defendant or otherwise, during the same trial, must be discussed or decided first by the judge?

A. We have already in part answered this question incidentally when we spoke of exceptions,[1] especially that of recusation,[2] and of counter-complaints.[3] We shall now add the following: 1. That question or cause should be first tried and discussed or decided, upon the decision of which the other one depends.[4] Among the various illustrations of this principle we will mention that given in the cap. 5, de Renunciat. Here Pope Clement III. (an. 1189) lays down the rule, that where an ecclesiastic asks to be reinstated in his benefice, and where the opposing party objects to the reinstatement on the ground that the plaintiff had voluntarily resigned the benefice, the ecclesiastical judge should first take cognizance of the question as to whether the resignation had really taken place, and that voluntarily, not through fear or force. For it is evident that if the objection were sustained—*i.e.*, if it were shown that the plaintiff had

---

[1] Supra, n. 1031.   [2] Ib., n. 1035 sq.   [3] Ib., n. 1054 sq.
[4] Cap. 1, 3, de Ord. cogn. (ii. 10); L. 16, 17, 18 ff. de Except.

voluntarily resigned—he could no longer ask to be rein
stated.[1] For the same reason, all exceptions, whether dilatory or peremptory, should be tried before the main cause—
with this difference, however, that dilatory exceptions must
not only be tried, but also decided, before the main cause;
while peremptory, according to many canonists, must indeed
be tried, but need not be decided, before the principal cause.[2]

1096. 2. When a criminal and a civil cause come together,
and each is to be tried separately as a main cause, not
merely as an incidental cause or counter-charge, the rule is
that the criminal cause, being the more important, is to be
tried before the civil.[3] We say, *and each is to be tried separately as a main cause;* for when a criminal cause comes up
incidentally in a civil cause,—*v.g.*, by way of exception,—and
vice versâ, when a civil cause arises incidentally in a criminal
cause, then the judge should try both causes simultaneously,
and decide them by one and the same sentence.[4]

1097. 3. In the question of spoliation (*causa spolii*),
namely, when the defendant, or person against whom the
plaintiff has brought an action, in turn complains or objects
that he has been spoliated (*spoliatus*) by the plaintiff, that is,
unjustly stripped or deprived of some property or right,—it
is asked whether this objection should be tried and decided
first, that is, before the action brought previously by the
plaintiff? Before answering, we shall give a brief explanation of what is here understood by spoliation. By spoliation (*spolium, spoliatio*) we here mean the most grievous
crime by which a person is despoiled (*spoliatus*) or stripped
of something belonging to him.[5] Canonists agree that this
is a most grievous crime, and exceedingly odious in the eyes
of the law of the Church. Schmalzgrueber calls it *gravis-
simum et frequentissimum facinus.*

---

[1] Reiff., l. 2, t. 10, n. 8.   [2] Schmalzg., l. 2, t. 10, n. 7.   [3] L. 4, C. de Ord. Judic.
[4] L. 3, C. de Ord. jud.   [5] Devoti, l. 3, t. 11, § 6.

1098. Two things are required to constitute spoliation—namely, first, that a person has had possession or quasi-possession of a thing; secondly, that he has been unjustly deprived of it.' Spoliation, as here understood, is committed not merely when a person is dispossessed violently or by force, but also when he is deprived of a thing by deceit, fraud, or without just cause, or arbitrarily.' Thus an ecclesiastical judge—*e.g.*, a bishop—is guilty of spoliation if he deprives an ecclesiastic of his office, parish, or benefice without a manifest and sufficient cause, established by due trial or judicial proceedings.'

1099. Again, spoliation is committed, not only in corporal or temporal goods, movable and immovable, but also in spiritual things—that is, in rights. Hence spoliation, as here understood, is taken in its widest signification, so that whoever is unjustly stripped of a thing or right possessed by him is considered as despoiled or *spoliatus.* Thus a husband who is rashly deserted by his wife,' as also a wife who is unjustly put away by her husband,' is said to be despoiled—namely, of the respective marriage rights. In like manner, as we have already seen, an ecclesiastic who is unjustly removed from his office, parish, or benefice, or even unjustly obliged to resign it, is regarded as despoiled.' Thus, also, a rector in the United States, even though not irremovable, would be despoiled, at least in a broad sense, if he were dismissed without trial, as prescribed by the Instruction *Cum Magnopere* of 1884, and by the Instruction of July 20, 1878, where the latter is still in force, or if he were even transferred against his will, without grave and sufficient cause.'

1100. Having explained what is meant in canon law by

---

¹ Cap. 10, de Off. jud. del. (l. 29); cap. 16, de Rest. spol. (ii. 13).
² Can. 3, C. 3, Q. 1; München, l. c., vol. i., p. 354.
³ Cap. 7, de Rest. spol. (ii. 13). ⁴ Cap. 8, de Rest. spol. (ii. 13).
⁵ Cap. 10 (ii. 13). ⁶ Cap. 2, 3, 7, de Rest. spol.; cf. Devoti, l. c., § 7, nota 2.
⁷ S. C. de P. F., Ad Dubia, § i., Episcopi vero curent ; Instr. *Cum Magnopere*, Art. XLV.

spoliation, we now return to the question put above under No. 1097.   Where a plaintiff, or the prosecution, institutes an action or judicial proceedings against a defendant,—*v.g.*, where a bishop prefers criminal charges against an ecclesiastic for the purpose of punishing him,—and the latter, *i.e.*, defendant, interposes the plea or exception of spoliation, that is, complains that the plaintiff, *v.g.*, the bishop, has despoiled him, or unjustly removed him from his place, should this plea or exception of spoliation be tried and decided first—*i.e.*, before the action brought by the plaintiff? Before answering, we observe that it is plain that we speak here of the exception of spoliation as coming up incidentally in a cause on trial, and not as a separate and independent cause or action.

1101. We now answer. We must distinguish. The defendant in the case interposes the plea of spoliation either in the form of an exception, for the purpose of nonsuiting the plaintiff,—*i.e.*, of throwing his case out of court,—or in the form of a counter-action or counter-complaint, having for its direct object the restitution of the thing taken by the plaintiff, or, speaking, *v.g.*, of the removal from a parish, the reinstatement of the person despoiled.[1]   In the first case, the defendant making the exception of spoliation must be heard first, and having proved his exception, is not obliged to answer the plaintiff or prosecution until he has been reinstated by or received restitution from the latter.[2]   This holds true even where the plaintiff's complaint was that he was despoiled by the defendant.   For the position of a defendant in a cause is always more favorable than that of the plaintiff or prosecution.[3]

1102. We said, first, *and having proved the exception ;* for, so far as concerns the exception, the defendant making it

---

[1] Cap. 2, de Ord. cogn. (ii. 10).   [2] Cap. 2, 4, de Ord. cogn. (ii. 10).
[3] L. 125 ff. de Reg. jur. (50. 17); cf. Schmalzg., l. 2, t. 10, n. 15.

·becomes the plaintiff, and therefore assumes the burden of proof. The exception of spoliation must be proved, according to the common law of the Church, within fifteen days after it has been made.[1] We said, secondly, *the defendant is not obliged to answer until he has been reinstated.* This is the only direct effect of the exception of spoliation. For an exception has for its direct object simply the quashing or delaying of the complaint, and nothing else.[2] Hence restitution or reinstatement does not follow directly, but only indirectly ; in other words, the plaintiff must first reinstate the defendant, who excepts and proves spoliation, before he can continue or pursue his action, and thus reinstatement becomes the *conditio sine qua non* of his right to prosecute or sue the defendant.

1103. In the second case—namely, where a defendant interposes the plea of spoliation against the plaintiff in the form of a counter-charge, and for the direct purpose of being reinstated, and where the plaintiff's action is also for spoliation—two main causes or *mutuae petitiones* arise, and both causes must be tried simultaneously, and decided by one and the same sentence. Note we said, and *where the plaintiff's action is also for spoliation—i.e.*, where a plaintiff charges a defendant with spoliation, and the latter in turn makes a counter-charge that he was also spoliated by the plaintiff. Both actions in the case—that is, the action of the plaintiff and the counter-action of the defendant—must be for spoliation.[3] For if the action of the plaintiff is alone for spoliation, and that of the defendant for some *gravamen* other than spoliation, or if, *vice versâ*, the counter-action of the defendant is for spoliation and the action of the plaintiff for some injury other than spoliation, then the complaint of spoliation must be adjudicated first.

---

[1] Cap. 1, de Rest spol., in 6° (ii. 5).   [2] Cap. 2, cit.; Reiff., l. 2, t. 10, n. 19.
[3] Ex cap. 2. de Ord. cogn. (ii, 10).

1104. Besides the above two ways, there is a third way of complaining of spoliation—namely, where a person who has been spoliated prefers the charge of spoliation by way of a separate and independent action or cause, and not merely incidentally by way of exception or counter-action. What is the mode of procedure in this case? The general rule is, that the person spoliated must be reinstated or receive restitution before all else, provided it is really shown or lawfully proved by him that the spoliation has taken place.[1] We say, *before all else;* hence the person spoliated is not obliged to answer, nor can the judge hear any objection or counter-complaint (except, as we have just seen, that of spoliation) interposed by the defendant or spoliator until the complainant has been reinstated. This holds, as a rule, even when the objection interposed by the defendant charged with spoliation is that the complainant had no valid title or claim to the thing, or, speaking of benefices, that he was not canonically appointed,[2] or that he is guilty of crime.[3] Hence, generally speaking, none of these objections or complaints can be heard or tried, until the person spoliated has been fully reinstated, or received restitution.[4]

1105. An apposite illustration of this teaching is given in the decretal *Conquerente* 7, de Rest. spol. (ii. 13). A certain ecclesiastic named Renaldus complained to Pope Alexander III. that the Archbishop of Canterbury had illegally dismissed him from his parish without due trial or judicial proceedings—*juris ordine non servato.* The archbishop, it seems, sought to justify himself on the ground that the ecclesiastic in question had been guilty of crime. The Pope, however, ordered that if the ecclesiastic's complaint were true, the archbishop should at once reinstate him in his

---

[1] Can. 1, 2, 3, C. 3, Q. 1; cap. 4, de Ord. cogn.; cap. 5, 6, 7, de Rest. spol. (ii. 13); L. 1, § 31 ff. (xliii. 16).   [2] Cap. 5, de Rest. spol. (ii. 13).
[3] Cap. 6, de Rest. spol.   [4] Cap. 5, 6 (ii 13); Schmalzg., l. 2, t. 13, n. 27, 28.

parish, and allow him to govern it in peace; that only after the reinstatement had taken place could the archbishop, if he had anything against the cleric, prefer his charges before the Pope's delegate in the proper judicial manner.[1]

1106. This decision shows two things: 1. That the rule above given—to wit: A person spoliated must before all else be fully restored to his rights—applies not only to corporal or temporal possessions, but also to spiritual things, such as parishes, benefices, ecclesiastical pensions or annuities, the right of electing ecclesiastical superiors, bishops, etc. 2. That this rule holds not only when a person or an ecclesiastic has been despoiled by a private person, but also when he has been spoliated by his bishop proceeding without observing the proper judicial forms—*v.g.*, when he is deprived of his parish without sufficient cause duly established by a proper trial.[2]

1107. We said above,[3] *the general rule is;* for there are some exceptions. Thus, speaking of spiritual causes, this rule—namely, that a person spoliated must before all else be reinstated—does not apply, 1, where it is *notorious* that the person or ecclesiastic spoliated of his benefice had no valid title to it—*v.g.*, because he is a heretic, and therefore incapacitated for any benefice.[4] 2. Nor even where there is a strong presumption that he has obtained his ecclesiastical benefice without any title at all, or with a vicious one. For by reinstatement in these cases a person would be put in possession of a benefice without a canonical appointment, against the Regula I. de Reg. jur., in 6°: "Beneficium ecclesiasticum non potest licite sine institutione canonica obtineri." In both these cases the person spoliated would have to prove his title before he could be reinstated. 3. Nor does the rule stated apply in cases—whether they regard matters strictly

---

[1] Cf. Reiff., l. 2, t. 13, n. 56.
[2] Supra, n. 1104.
[3] Reiff., l. 2, t. 13, n. 55.
[4] Schmalzg., l. c., n. 67.

spiritual, or any other matter whatever falling under the
competence of the ecclesiastical judge—where the person
spoliated waives his right—that is, consents to the non-
enforcement of the rule. For the rule was made in favor of
the person spoliated, and therefore can be renounced by him
if he chooses.[1] And this is true, even when the person
spoliated consents, not expressly, but only tacitly—*e.g.*, by
not protesting, when the judge allows the spoliator to go
on with his case, before he reinstates the person spoliated.[2]

§ 6. *Examination of the accused, also in the United States.*

1108. After the preliminary questions—that is, the various
exceptions—have been decided, and the contestation has
taken place, and the usual delays have been granted, the chief
part of the trial, the taking of testimony, begins. Sometimes, however, as we have seen, the plaintiff or prosecution
(with us, the bishop's official appointed to act as the prosecution[3]) is released, either in whole or in part, of the necessity of producing proofs, by the confession of the accused—
that is, by his admitting, in whole or in part, the charges and
specifications (*positiones, articuli, capitula*) upon which he is
examined or interrogated by the judge, either *ex officio* or at
the instance of the prosecution. Where the trial is by way
of inquisition, the charges and specifications, together with
the proofs obtained in the preliminary investigation, should
be shown the accused, also with us, as soon as he comes into
court upon due citation, unless they have been made known
to him beforehand. He is then asked by the judge whether
he admits or denies them. This interrogation of the judge,
and the negative answer of the defendant, constitute, as we

---

[1] Ex cap. 12, de For. comp. (ii. 2); ib. Glossa, v. Pacto privatorum; Reiff.,
L. c., n. 73.   [2] Cap. 1, de Rest. spol. (ii. 13).

[3] Instr. S. C. de P. F., 20 Jul., 1878, § 2, Re ad.

have seen,[1] in formal canonical trials by way of inquisition, the contestation of the cause.[1]

1109. This examination of the accused, as made prior to the taking of the testimony, and for the purpose of relieving the prosecution of the necessity of proving their case, need not take place in summary criminal trials, nor in proceedings before our Commissions of Investigation. We say, *need not ;* for it *may* take place, at this stage of the trial, even in proceedings before our Commissions of Investigation, provided, as we shall see, there are strong proofs of guilt, warranting such examination. Apart from this, however, the law with us is, that the accused, after having made or read his defence, and during the time he produces his proofs, is subject to cross-examination by the members of the Commission, through its president.[1]

1110. We therefore ask : Is the accused (we speak of course of criminal causes), when examined by the judge (with us, either by the bishop or, as the case may be, by the Commission of Investigation), whether in the beginning of the trial or during its progress, bound to confess his guilt? We must distinguish between three cases—namely, (*a*) when it is apparent that the judge examines lawfully ; (*b*) unlawfully ; (*c*) when it is doubtful whether or not he examines lawfully. Where the judge examines unlawfully, it is certain that the accused is not bound to answer or confess his guilt, if he be guilty. For the judge in the case exceeds the limits of his authority, and consequently acts simply as a private person. Now when does the judge interrogate unlawfully or *non servato juris ordine ?* Chiefly in these cases: 1. Where no public report, or at least no imperfect proofs, of the guilt of the accused exist, or where such common fame or imperfect proofs are not juridically established.[4] Hence the judge can-

---

[1] Supra, n. 1068.
[3] Instr. cit., § 7.
[2] Cf. Bouix, de Jud., vol. ii , pp. 192, 201.
[4] Stremler, l. c., p. 166.

not interrogate the accused in regard to occult crimes,[1]—
i.e., those crimes which are not public, either by common
fame, or quasi-public, that is, provable in court.[2] For occult
crimes should not be made public.[3] 2. Where the judge
does not make known to the accused the proofs, suspicions,
witnesses, depositions, etc., that exist against him. For in
this case the accused cannot know whether the judge interrogates juridically—*i.e.*, lawfully—or not, and therefore is not
bound to answer. For he is obliged to answer only when
it is certain that the judge interrogates lawfully. Moreover,
the judge, by interrogating the accused unlawfully, commits
a mortal sin, being the cause of the latter's defamation.[4]

1111. Where it is doubtful whether the judge interrogates
lawfully or not, the accused is not bound to confess his
guilt or to answer; for where there is a doubt, the axiom
holds: " Melior est conditio possidentis."[5]

1112. Where, however, it is apparent or certain that the
judge interrogates lawfully or *servato juris ordine,—v.g.*, where
the public report, or at least the half proof of guilt, is established,—the general opinion of canonists is that the accused is
bound to answer and confess his guilt, at least if the penalty
to be inflicted is not very serious. But what if the penalty is
of a grave character—*v.g.*, loss of entire property, or, in the
case of an ecclesiastic, dismissal from his parish, which is the
means of his support, and is therefore equivalent to loss of
entire property? There are two opinions: one affirms, the
other denies, that the accused is bound to answer or confess
his guilt. The negative opinion, as explained by Stremler,[6]
is, that unless the guilt is fully proven, or at least susceptible
of being completely proved, the accused is not bound to answer or confess his crime, even where the judge interrogates
lawfully. This opinion is probable, and may certainly be

[1] Reiff., l. 2, t. 18, n. 156.   [2] Cap. Qualiter et quando, de Accus.
[3] Can. Erubescant, Dist. 32.   [4] Relff., l. c., n. 159.
[5] Schmalzg., l. 2, t. 18, n. 3.   [6] L. c., p. 168.

followed by confessors, especially where the accused cannot be persuaded to confess his guilt. The chief reasons upon which this opinion is based are : (*a*) that no human law, such as the command of the judge, binds under grave inconvenience. (*b*) Again, nobody is obliged to testify against a relative, if a serious evil should be the consequence. Now, no person is a nearer relative to one's self than such person is to himself. (*c*) Finally, it would seem repugnant to the very law of nature to oblige an accused party to complete, by his confession, the proofs of his own guilt, and thus become instrumental in inflicting upon himself a grave penalty.[1]

1113. On the other hand, those who hold the affirmative, which is the more probable opinion,[2] contend that the judge has the right, nay, the duty, of interrogating the accused, and of finding out by all lawful means who are the guilty parties, especially as the good of the Church requires crimes to be punished; that therefore the accused has the correlative duty to answer and confess his guilt (if he is guilty), when juridically or lawfully interrogated by the judge, even though a grave punishment should be the result. However, the supporters of the negative opinion answer, that from the right and duty of the judge (we speak of the ecclesiastical judge) to interrogate, the duty of the accused to confess his guilt does not follow, just as it does not follow that because the judge has a right to imprison a defendant the latter has no right to evade imprisonment if he can.

1114. However, even those who hold the affirmative admit that the accused is not bound to answer *ad mentem judicis* or confess, if the offence was but a material one—that is, if the accused was excused from mortal sin, owing, *v.g.*, to want of deliberation. They concede, moreover, that the accused need not confess an external circumstance or occurrence, if this avowal would cause him to be suspected of a

---

[1] Fermosin. Rubr. de confessis, Q. 5, nn. 18, 19. Col. Allobr., 1741.
[2] Schmalzg., l. 2, t. 18, n. 3.

crime of which he is otherwise innocent. Thus the accused who is asked whether at such an hour he was in such a place, may deny it (even though he was there) if he foresees that from his affirmative answer the judge will infer that he has committed the deed.[1]

§ 7. *Manner of submitting the Proofs in Ecclesiastical Courts, also in the United States—The Trial Proper—Mode of conducting the Prosecution and the Defence.*

1115. When the accused denies the charges and specifications, either wholly or at least substantially, it becomes necessary for the prosecution to produce before the judge whatever proofs he may have in support of his charges. These proofs, as we have seen, consist of instruments, documents, etc., and chiefly of the depositions of witnesses.[2] It is scarcely necessary to remark here, that the burden of proof rests upon the prosecution. Consequently, where the latter (also in the United States) fails to submit good and sufficient proofs, the defendant may simply content himself with denying the charge. He need not prove his innocence, as that is presumed, until the contrary is clearly established.

1116. We have already dwelt at sufficient length upon the nature and force of the various judicial proofs.[3] Here we shall confine ourselves to the manner in which both the prosecution and defence produce their proofs for or against the cause. As the testimony of witnesses constitutes the chief and most important kind of proofs, we shall here speak mainly of the manner in which witnesses are produced and examined in court. Much has been already said on this head above, under Nos. 836 sq., to which we refer the reader. It only remains for us to add a few remarks.

1117. *Mode of producing and examining witnesses, whether*

---

[1] Stremler, l. c., p. 168.   [2] Supra, n. 815 sq.   [3] Supra, n. 820 sq.

for or against the cause, where the common law of the Church obtains on this head.—Witnesses, as we have seen,[1] must be examined one by one, and apart from each other. They can, at least, if the judge deems it proper or where it is the custom, be confronted with the party against whom they testify; in other words, the opposite party, whether it be the prosecution or defendant, can be allowed, at least, at the discretion of the judge, to be present at the examination. We say, *at least;* for, as we have shown above,[2] there are two opinions: one denies,—and this is the common opinion,—the other affirms that the common law of the Church permits the confrontation of the witnesses with the party against whom they testify. Owing to this fact, the custom was introduced into some ecclesiastical courts of confronting witnesses with the opponent—at least where the judge thought it proper. In the larger number, however, of these courts the more common opinion of canonists was followed, and no confrontation was allowed, except in extraordinary cases. As both modes may be and are followed,[3] we shall separately discuss the manner of examining the witnesses in both cases.

1118. *Mode of examining the witnesses, where the witnesses are not confronted with the party against whom they are testifying.—Observation.*—Where the defendant or accused is excluded, *i.e.*, not confronted with the witnesses, the prosecutor must also be excluded—*i.e.*, he must not be allowed to be present at the examination of the witnesses. Hence also, in proceedings before Commissions of Investigation, the bishop's official who acts as promoter or prosecutor cannot be allowed to be present at the examination of witnesses unless the same right is also conceded to the defendant. Having made this observation, we now proceed to discuss the question. Where the litigants—*i.e.*, the prosecutor and defendant—are excluded from the examination of the witnesses, the prosecutor, before

---

[1] Supra, n. 839.   [2] Supra, n. 838, 839.   [3] Cf. Craiss., n. 5714, 5944, 5945.

the beginning of the examination, submits to the judge a
written list of the questions or interrogatories on which he
wishes the judge to examine the witnesses for the prosecution, and the defendant in like manner hands to the judge
a similar list of questions on which he requests the judge to
cross-examine the witnesses.

1119. In order that the accused may be able to know
what questions to hand to the judge for cross-examination,
he must of course know the questions submitted by the
prosecutor. Hence the judge, after having received the
prosecutor's interrogatories for the direct examination, com-
municates them to the accused, so as to enable him to frame
his cross-questions and hand them to the judge. This
applies also to proceedings before Commissions of Investigation in the United States, when the Commission does not
think it prudent or when the witnesses are unwilling to
allow the confrontation.[1]

1120. When both the prosecutor and the defendant have
handed in their interrogatories or questions the judge proceeds to examine the witnesses, first on the questions and
cross-questions submitted by the prosecutor and defendant,
and then on the facts of the case in general. On the conclusion of the examination he proceeds, on a day fixed for that
purpose, to the publication of the entire testimony and proceedings in the case : that is, he causes the testimony of the
witnesses examined by him, as just described, together with
all the other evidence and acts in the case, to be read before
the parties—prosecutor and defendant, and gives the accused
a copy of the entire evidence and all the acts, so as to enable
him to prepare for his defence.

1121. This is called *publicatio attestationum—i.e.*, the communication of the prosecution's evidence to the accused.[2] It
is also termed *publicatio processus offensivi*, for the reason that

---

[1] Instr. S. C. de P. F., 20 Jul., 1875, § 12, Consentientibus. [2] Craiss., n. 5939.

hitherto or up to the present stage of the proceedings the prosecution has mainly acted, and the defence has as yet not begun, properly speaking, and the publication of the evidence is intended chiefly for the benefit of the accused. Hence the judge, if requested, must give the accused a copy of the entire proceedings or acts,—*i.e.*, of all the testimony and minutes of the case,—so as to enable him to prepare for his defence. The witnesses for the defence are examined in the same way, as we shall see.

1122. *Mode of procedure, according to the common law of the Church, when the litigants—the prosecution and defence—are allowed to confront the witnesses.*—The above is the mode of procedure when the litigants are not allowed to confront the witnesses. Where, however, the contending parties are permitted to be present at the examination and to hear what the witnesses say, the prosecutor and the defendant may themselves or personally examine the witnesses, though as a rule only through the judge. We say, *though . . . only through the judge;* for, by the common law of the Church, witnesses must be examined and cross-examined by the judge himself, and not directly by the prosecution or defence, or their respective advocates.[1] We say, moreover, *as a rule;* since, where there is a just cause, the judge may allow or depute others—*v.g.*, the parties themselves or their advocates —to examine the witnesses. This holds also of the examination of witnesses before Commissions of Investigation where they exist.[2] From what has been said, it follows as a matter of course, that in this mode of examination the parties or litigants need not hand the judge a list of their questions and cross-questions, as they do when they are excluded from the examination, or not allowed personally to examine the witnesses. It follows, moreover, that a publication of the testi-

---

[1] Ex Nov. 60, cap. 2; Schmalzg., l. 2, t. 20, n. 93.
[2] Cf. Instr. S. C. de P. F. cit., §§ 11, 12.

mony, etc., is scarcely necessary in the case, as the parties, having been present at the examination, are fully aware of what transpired. However, the defendant should be given a copy of the depositions and proceedings if he requests it, as this will the better enable him to prepare for his defence.

1123. We must here call attention to certain things which are peculiar to the examination of witnesses when the trial is by way of absolute inquiry (*ex mero officio*)—*i.e.*, where there is no promoter or bishop's official, or other person to prefer and prove the charges, and where, consequently, the bishop or judge must himself collect and prefer and establish the charges. In this case, the judge, before beginning the trial,—*i.e.*, before proceeding to the citation of the accused,—should first be sure that the requisite defamation or common fame exists, as without such fame he cannot even validly cite the accused; he should also gather all the information, facts, and proofs possible in the case, so that, before he cites the accused, he may have in his possession full, or at least imperfect, proofs of the guilt. The fuller this preliminary information or trial is, the better will it be.[1]

1124. When the bishop or judge has completed this inquiry, which is called the preliminary inquiry for the judge's information (*processus informativus, processus pro informatione curiae*), and finds that the evidence in hand warrants it, the citation is issued. When the accused appears in obedience to the citation, he should at once be informed of the charges and specifications, and also of the proofs existing against him. If he acknowledges his guilt, sentence may be pronounced forthwith. If he denies it, and moreover refuses to declare that he accepts or regards the witnesses, as examined in the preliminary investigation, as lawfully examined,[2] the bishop or judge must formally and in court examine all the witnesses over again, and that in the manner and with the

---

[1] Bouix, de Jud., vol. i., p. 154.   [2] Craiss., n. 5942.

formalities described above.[1] Upon the conclusion of this examination, the publication takes place, as above stated. Where the accused denies the guilt, but is willing to accept the examination of the witnesses in the preliminary investigation as legitimate, or where he has been allowed to be present at the preliminary investigation and examination of the witnesses, and cross-examine them, no repetition of the witnesses' testimony need take place; but a copy is simply given the accused of the entire testimony and proceedings or acts, to enable him to prepare for his defence.

1125. The preliminary investigation or inquiry, here spoken of, takes place, only when the judge proceeds by way of inquiry and denunciation, but not when he proceeds by way of accusation. Because in the latter case the accuser binds himself to produce the necessary proofs. Hence the judge is relieved from the necessity of finding sufficient proofs of guilt, so as to warrant him to proceed to the citation. Consequently, in the trial by way of accusation, the witnesses are not examined before the citation, to see whether there is common report, and sufficient proof of guilt to warrant the citation. This examination takes place only in the usual course of the trial—*i.e.*, after the citation of the accused.

1126. In connection with this matter, we observe that what has been said of the publication of the testimony of the witnesses applies equally to all the other kinds of evidence or proofs submitted by the prosecution. In other words, whatever evidence or proof is advanced by the prosecution must be communicated to the defendant for his defence. Thus if instruments, documents, or letters are submitted as proofs, a copy of them must be furnished to the defendant.[1]

1127. As this communication of all the evidence of the prosecution is a necessary condition and part of a legitimate

---

[1] Supra, n. 836 sq.; n. 1117 sq.; n. 1122 sq.
[2] Cap. 11, de Prob. (ii. 19); München, l. c,, vol. i., p. 273, n. 7.

defence, and therefore forms substantially part of all trials, formal or summary, it must also substantially take place in trials in the United States as conducted before our Commissions of Investigation. This is apparent from the following words of the Instruction of the S. C. de P. F., of July 20, 1878:[1] "Per litteras, etiam rectorem . . advocet" (episcopus) "exponens . . causam ad depositionem moventem, per extensum." The same is also inferable from these words of the above Instruction: "Facta ipsi" (reo) "plena facultate ea omnia in medium afferendi . . quae ad propriam defensionem conferre possunt."[2] For this full liberty of defending himself implies necessarily that the accused shall be fully informed as to the evidence that stands against him. Otherwise, how defend himself! Here we note, that not only the depositions but also the names of the witnesses must be communicated to the defendant, also with us, except of course where the confrontation has taken place.

1128. *Manner of conducting the defence (processus defensivus)—i.e., examining witnesses, etc., for the defence—according to the principles of the common law of the Church.*—After the publication of the evidence, as above stated, the real defence, or the *processus defensivus*, begins, properly speaking.[3] Not only positive and human, but also natural and divine law, gives the accused the right to defend himself.[4] It is, moreover, a principle of the Roman or civil law, incorporated into the canon law, that whatever is allowed the prosecution or plaintiff must *a fortiori* be conceded to the defence or the accused. "Non debet," says the Roman law, "licere actori, quod reo non permittitur."[5] And again: "Cui damus actiones, eidem et exceptionem" (defence) "competere multo magis quis dixerit."[6] Not only, therefore, are the prosecution and defence placed on a footing of perfect

[1] § 4, Per litteras.
[2] München, l. c., vol. i., p. 279, n. 14.
[3] L. 44 ff. de Reg. jur. (50. 17).
[4] Ib., § 7, Deinde.
[5] Bouix, de Jud., vol. ii., p. 222.
[6] L. 156 ff. de Reg. jur (50. 17).

equality, but the defence must even be given the preference or advantage. Consequently, as the prosecution has full liberty to prove its charges, so must the defendant, *a fortiori*, have the fullest liberty to disprove them and defend himsell. Thus the Instruction of the S. C. de P. F., of July 20, 1878, applying these principles to the United States, says: " Facta ipsi " (rectori missionario seu reo) *"plena facultate* ea omnia in medium afferendi . . quae ad propriam defensionem conferre possunt."[1]

1129. How, then, is the defence to be conducted? The accused has the right (also with us, as is expressly stated in the two Instructions of 1878 and of 1884) to produce, and the judge is obliged to hear and examine, all arguments, documents, witnesses, and proofs whatsoever, that the accused wishes to produce in his defence. For this purpose, the accused, either in person or through his advocate, first draws up a written outline of the defence,—*i.e.*, a written statement setting forth the various heads or points of the defence (*articuli defensorii*),—and promising to produce the requisite witnesses, documents, etc., in proof of each and every head or article of the defence. Next, this writing is given to the judge on the day set down for the defence, and it forms the basis and frame of the entire defence or defensive proceedings.[2]

1130. The following is a specimen of the manner in which this statement is drawn up by the defendant's advocate: 1. That the crime was committed, not by the accused, but by a certain person called N. 2. That the accused was during such a month, or on such a day, and at such an hour at C., a village five miles distant from the place where the crime was committed, and remained at C., *v.g.*, from 7 A.M. to 10 P.M. This defence is commonly called an *alibi* in our secular courts. 3. That N., one of the witnesses for the prosecution (*pro causa*),

---

[1] Instr. cit., § 7, Deinde. [2] Boulx, l. c., p. 223.

is under excommunication, a perjurer, infamous, an enemy of his client, etc. 4. That R., another witness for the prosecution, belongs to a faction or party or clique opposed to his client, and that after his examination he said he had stood well by his friend. 5. That Y., the accuser or plaintiff, is a drunkard, liar, etc. At the conclusion of these and other heads of the defence the advocate adds that he will produce the proper witnesses, documents, and other proofs, one after another, in succession, to prove each of the above articles or heads of the defence.[1]

1131. After this written outline of the defence has been handed to the judge, the latter assigns the defence a day (either the same day, if the parties are ready, or another) on which they must begin to present their witnesses, documents, and other proofs, by which they wish to establish the above heads of the defence. If the witnesses for the defence refuse to come spontaneously, at the request of the accused, they should be summoned to appear by authority of the judge. On the day appointed, the accused or his advocate should produce his proofs in the following manner: He should take up the heads of the written defensive outline, one by one, in succession, and prove each one separately. When he has produced all the evidence in his possession—witnesses, letters, etc.,—to prove the first head of the defence, he proceeds to the next, proving it fully, and then to the third, and so on.[2] The witnesses for the defence are examined in the same manner as those for the prosecution.[3] The other proofs, such as letters, documents, submitted by the defence, are similarly examined.

1132. As the defendant was allowed to cross-examine (usually through the judge, sometimes in person) the witnesses for the prosecution, and offer objections to the other evidence submitted against him, so also is the ʼplaintiff or

---

[1] Bouix, l. c., p. 579.   [2] Cf. Bouix, l. c., p. 580.   [3] Supra, n. 837.

diocesan prosecutor (*promotor fiscalis ;* with us, bishop's official appointed to present the case to the Commission) now
permitted to cross-examine the witnesses for the defence,
either through the judge (with us Commission, or as the
case may be, bishop) or in person, and reply to and endeavor
to break down any other evidence that may have been produced by the defence.   To enable him (prosecutor) to do so,
he must either be allowed to be present at the examination
of the witnesses for the defence (where this privilege was
granted to the defence), or informed of the interrogatories
upon which they are to be examined.

1133. To this replication by the prosecution (*replicatio*),
the accused or his advocate may again answer (*duplicatio*),
and produce further proofs, such as witnesses, letters, etc.,
in support of his answer or rejoinder.   In like manner, the
prosecution has the right to reply to and try to overthrow
the defendant's rejoinder, and *vice versâ ;* and so on until both
the prosecution and the defence have exhausted all their respective proofs or arguments.[1]   In fact, in criminal causes no
limit can be placed to the replies or presentation of testimony,
etc., on the part of the defence. Of course the prosecution has
a corresponding right always to submit rebutting testimony.[2]

1134. *Summing up by the parties.*—When the accused has
finished his defence, and declares that he has no further
defence to make, a day (either the same day or another) is
appointed by the judge on which the parties will sum up
their case, and the judge pronounce sentence. On the day
fixed, the parties—the plaintiff or diocesan promoter on the
one hand, and the accused on the other, together with their
respective advocates—having appeared in court, the defendant's advocate, or the defendant in person, if he wishes to
conduct his own defence, is allowed to speak first and sum
up the case. Speaking in general, the defendant or his ad-

---

[1] L. 2 ff. de Except. (xliv. 1); München, l. c., vol. i., p. 281.
[2] Bouix, l. c , vol. ii., p. 223.

vocate should, in his speech, endeavor to show that from the evidence submitted during the trial it is clear, 1, that the alleged crime was committed by nobody; 2, that if it was perhaps committed, the fact was not sufficiently proved; 3, that even admitting gratuitously that it had been committed, it was shown on the trial that the defendant was not its author; 4, that even though it had not been sufficiently proved that the defendant was innocent, yet neither had it been proved that he was guilty; for the trial had been conducted without the proper formalities, or the witnesses had made contradictory statements, or, in general, the proofs adduced were of little or no account, etc. 5. Finally, even though it had been conclusively shown that the defendant had committed the alleged crime, yet the offence was only a material, not a formal one, as it had not been proved that there was malice and premeditation. Hence the defendant must be declared not guilty.[1]

1135. Next, the plaintiff or diocesan promoter (with us, bishop's official) is permitted to speak or sum up, either personally or through his advocate. Then the defendant or his advocate may reply, and *vice versâ*. These speeches may continue as long as the judge thinks proper, or as custom allows. The last speech is always made by the defence. When the parties have finished summing up the case, the judge may proceed to pronounce sentence.

1136. *Procedure in England and some parts of the United States, before Commissions, in the examination of witnesses and admission of proofs, both for the prosecution and the defence.* —The course of the defence, as laid down in the Instruction of the S. C. de P. F., of July 20, 1878, is substantially the same as that of formal canonical trials above described. After the prosecution—*i.e.*, the vicar-general or other priest appointed by the bishop to act as diocesan prosecutor,[2] or

---

[1] Bouix, l. c., p. 587.   [2] Instr. cit , § 2, Re ad Consilium.

his advocate—has read before the Commission of Investigation the written statement of the charges and specifications, submitted the requisite evidence to sustain the charges, and answered the questions put by the Commission, the defendant or his advocate begins the defence properly speaking. We say, *properly speaking;* for improperly or incidentally the defence runs through the whole trial, and is begun, *v.g.*, already as soon as the accused cross-examines the witnesses for the prosecution. This, however, is only, as is plain, an ʹincidental defence. The defence proper, with us, begins when the accused or his advocate reads before the Commission a written statement or answer to the charges preferred by the bishop's official.[1]

1137. This answer is drawn up and signed by the defendant's advocate, or by the defendant himself if he wishes to conduct his own case in person. It forms the basis of the entire defence, and should therefore be a complete outline of the defence, as above described.[2] Next, either on the same day, or on a subsequent day or days fixed by the Commission, the defence have the right to take up, one after another, the heads of their answer, and to present consecutively any proofs, such as witnesses, letters, etc., they wish, in support of each and every point or head of the defence, as given in the written statement read before the Commission, as above described.[3]

1138. This right cannot be limited by the Commission of Investigation. Hence the defendant or his advocate cannot be compelled to present his witnesses or documents, etc., to the Commission on the same day on which he reads his statement or general answer. Sufficient and proper time must be given him to produce his witnesses, etc., one after another, and without undue hurry or inconvenience. This is clearly implied in these words of the oft-quoted Instruc-

[1] Instr. cit., § 7, Deinde.   [2] Supra, n. 1129-1131.   [3] Supra, n. 1131.

tion of July 20, 1878 : " Facta ipsi " (reo) " plena facultate ea omnia in medium afferendi, intra tempus tamen a Consilio determinandum, quae ad propriam defensionem conferre possunt." [1]

1139. The manner in which the defendant's witnesses are examined is the same as that in which the witnesses for the prosecution are questioned.[2] Now the latter are examined by the Commission, one by one, apart from each other, and first in the absence of the accused.[3] Next, if the Commission judge it prudent, and the witnesses consent, they are re-examined in the presence of the accused, who can cross-examine them through the president of the Commission.[4] Of course, when the witnesses are unwilling or the Commission deems it inexpedient to allow them to be confronted with the accused, it is apparent from what has been said that the latter must be permitted to hand in to the president of the Commission, in writing, any questions upon which he wishes and requests the witnesses of the prosecution to be cross-examined by the Commission.

1140. The witnesses for the defence are examined, as we have said, in the same or a similar manner. Hence they are examined first in the absence of the prosecution—*i.e.*, the bishop's official appointed for this purpose, or his advocate;[5] and only when the Commission thinks it proper, and the witnesses for the defence consent, can the prosecution be allowed to be present and cross-examine the witnesses through the president of the Commission. Of course, where the prosecution are not allowed to be present at the examination of the defendant's witnesses, they have the right, just as the defendant had in reference to the prosecution's witnesses, to hand to the Commission written questions or interrogatories to be put to the witnesses by the president of the Commission.

---

[1] Instr. cit., § 7.   [2] Ib., § 13. Eadem.   [3] Ib., § 11, Singuli.
[4] Ib., § 12, Consentientibus.   [5] Instr. cit., § 2, Re ad.

1141. The accused may again reply to what the prosecution may have advanced in their cross-examination or otherwise. The bishop's official or promoter, or his advocate, may in turn be permitted to answer again, and *vice versâ.* The last production or presentation of evidence is always made by the defendant. From what has been said, it is evident that the defendant in the United States, as elsewhere, in order to be able to defend himself properly, must receive, not only from the bishop, a full statement of the charges, etc., before the trial, but also from the Commission a copy of all the acts and proceedings which have taken place from the beginning of the trial down to the time when he begins his defence proper—*i.e.,* all the proofs advanced by the prosecution—namely, depositions of witnesses, letters, etc., as also the minutes of the Commission.[1]

1142. When the defendant or his advocate has exhausted all the means of defence at his command, and moreover expressly declares that he has no further defence to make, the Commission proceeds to the final stage of the trial or investigation, and appoints a day (either the same day or some other) on which it will hear the final arguments or summing up of the parties, and enter into consultation on the results of the trial, prior to making up its report to the bishop.[2] On the day appointed, the defendant or his advocate speaks first, and sums up the case for the defence. Next follows the promoter appointed by the bishop, or the promoter's advocate. The latter in turn is followed by the defendant or his advocate, and so on. The defendant or his advocate always makes the last speech, as already stated. This final summing up by the parties forms an integral part of a legitimate defence, and therefore it would seem that it cannot be forbidden by the Commission.[3]

1143. Next the Commission proceeds to deliberate and

[1] Cf. Instr. S. C. de P. F. cit., §§ 2, 7, 12. [2] Instr. cit., §§ 9, 14.
[3] Cf. Instr. cit., § 7, Deinde.

make up its decision on the case, in the following manner: After the summing up by the parties, the Commission, either immediately, or on a subsequent day set apart by it, goes into consultation. Here the members of the Commission first carefully go over the evidence of the prosecution and defence, discuss among each other its force, authenticity, etc. Having carefully weighed all the testimony before them, they proceed to vote, and if a majority finds the accused or defendant guilty or not guilty, or, speaking of civil causes, the facts proved or not proved, each member will write out his opinion or verdict in accordance with his vote, together with the reasons therefor.[1] In order to enable the members to write out their opinions at leisure, the Commission may adjourn to another day. On the day fixed, the Commission reassembles, and the members will then compare their written opinions with each other, for the purpose of ascertaining whether they correspond with the vote, and also to enable them to make opportune corrections, at the suggestion of their fellow Commissioners.[2] The best way would seem to be that each member should read his opinion to the other members.

1144. Afterwards the acts of the proceedings (*acta in Consilio*)—*i.e.*, all the documents, letters, depositions of witnesses, and also the minutes kept—are filed or arranged, or put in order by the bishop's official or promoter (unless this has been already done during the course of the trial), signed by the president in the name of the Commission (unless this has been already done during the course of the trial), and handed to the bishop, together with the written opinions or verdict of the Commission, either by the president of this body or its secretary.[3]

1145. By the *acta in Consilio*[4] are meant not only the minutes of the proceedings kept by the secretary of the

---

[1] Instr. cit., § 9, Quibus.   [2] Ib.   [3] Instr. cit., § 9, Quibus.   [4] Ib.

Commission, but also all steps taken by or before the Commission, such as the issuing of citations, interlocutory decisions, resolutions, etc.; also all documents whatever—*v.g.*, letters, depositions of witness, etc., etc.—submitted to the Commission, whether by the prosecution or defence.[1] All these are first signed and thus authenticated by the president of the Commission, in the name of the latter body, before they are delivered to the bishop.[2] Where the Commission holds more than one meeting, it may be advisable to have the minutes of the previous meeting (*acta judicii*) read, corrected, approved or adopted by the Commission, and signed by the president at each subsequent meeting. In like manner, the various documents relating to the cause itself, such as letters, proofs, etc., may be signed by the president of the Commission at each meeting, as they are presented.

1146. The above phrase of the Instruction of the Propaganda, of July 20, 1878, *all the documents . . . are filed . . . by the bishop's official or promoter (acta in Consilio ab episcopi officiali redigantur)*, has given rise among some of our ecclesiastics to two different opinions. One affirms that the bishop's official—*i.e.*, the vicar-general or other priest appointed by the bishop to act as promoter or prosecutor—is thereby charged to act as secretary or notary for the Commission, and therefore to keep the minutes, etc. The other opinion, which seems to us the true one (we say it with all deference and submission to any future decision of the Holy See), denies this, chiefly on the following grounds: 1. The bishop's official in the case is entrusted with the duty of drawing up a full and specific statement of the charges against the accused.[3] To this end he must naturally gather all the available information, proofs, and witnesses for the prosecution, in order to be able to substantiate the charges to be preferred by him against the accused before the Commission.

---

[1] Cf. Reiff., l. 2, t. 1, n. 185.
[2] Instr. cit., § 9, Quibus.
[3] Instr. S. C. de P. F. cit., § 9.
[4] Ib., § 2, Re ad Consilium.

He is charged with the office of reading this statement to, and consequently of preparing the charges before, the Commission, and of establishing or proving them before this body.[1] Upon him devolves, therefore, in every sense of the word, the duty and office of a diocesan promoter or prosecutor.

1147. Now, is not the position of so interested a party as that of the prosecution or plaintiff wholly incompatible with that of a notary or secretary, whose duty it is to write out impartially the minutes relating both to the prosecution and defence, and who should, therefore, be entirely disinterested in the matter? Could it be supposed that the Propaganda, considering the bias and natural inclination of human nature, would allow the prosecutor, who by his very office becomes one of the contending parties, to write out the minutes relating not only to the prosecution, but even to the opponent? Would it not be unreasonable to deny that grave suspicion must attach to the acts or minutes drawn up by a party so directly concerned in the cause? Do not all laws, secular and ecclesiastical, prescribe that the notary shall have no interest, direct or indirect, in the matter or case for which he acts as notary or secretary.

1148. 2. Moreover, shall it be said that the prosecutor or bishop's official, by being allowed to act as secretary of the Commission, shall have the right to be present at all the meetings of the latter body, and thus, *v.g.*, confront the witnesses for the accused, whereas the latter may be excluded from the meetings where the prosecutor's testimony is presented? Or that he shall have the custody of, and therefore free access to, all the documents of the defence, even before the time for their publication arrives? Would this not be giving every possible advantage to the prosecution and every possible disadvantage to the defence? whereas the law of the

---

[1] Cf. Instr. cit., § 6, Relatio.

Church is that the defence shall not only be placed on a footing of equality with the prosecution, but always given the advantage.

1149. 3. However, it might be objected that Pope Benedict XIV., speaking of synodal judges, with whom our Commissions of Investigation are expressly compared by the S. C. de P. F. in its answer *Ad Dubia,*[1] explanatory of its Instruction of July 20, 1878, says that they cannot appoint a notary or secretary of their own, but must take one of those who are appointed by the bishop. Those who hold the negative, answer this objection by saying that it does not refer to this country at all; that it applies merely to places where, as in Europe, the bishop appoints several permanent notaries, not to act as his secretaries or chancellors, but as notaries indiscriminately for all persons in ecclesiastical causes, just as secular notaries are appointed by the secular power in this country. That the view of Pope Benedict XIV. does not apply to our country, seems apparent from the fact that with us, as in France, there are no other notaries but the secretaries or chancellors of bishops, or others appointed by the bishop for this or that matter. Now, as the annotator of Reiffenstuel says, these notaries or officials, being removable *ad nutum,* cannot in certain causes or matters win the full confidence of the subjects, lay or clerical, of the bishop. We add with the same writer, that there seems no reason why two or three ecclesiastical notaries should not be permanently appointed for each diocese.[2]

1150. 4. Again, the phrase *acta in Consilio ab episcopi officiali redigantur,* means simply to arrange or put on file the acts and documents, but not to act as secretary, or take down the minutes. Bouix[3] uses this same phrase in the sense just explained. 5. Finally, the bishop's official in our

---

[1] S. C. de P. F., Ad Dubia, § ii., Electio Consiliariorum.
[2] Annotat. VIII., in tom. iii. ap. Reiff., vol. iii., pp. 609, 610: Parisiis, 1866.
[3] De Jud., vol. ii., p. 594.

case is supposed to be the vicar-general. For the words of the Instruction plainly indicate that only where there is sufficient reason for it shall another priest, and not the vicar-general, act as the diocesan promoter or prosecutor. Now, it could hardly be supposed that the Propaganda wished to impose the onerous duty of a secretary upon such a dignitary as the vicar-general. Hence it would seem that the Commission of Investigation has the right to appoint its own secretary or notary. This, in fact, is the custom with us, at least in many dioceses.

1151. *Nature of the opinion or verdict rendered by the Commission of Investigation.*—In this matter, both the Instruction of the S. C. de P. F., dated July 20, 1878, and its supplementary declarations *Ad Dubia* are explicit. This verdict or opinion is not a final judicial sentence, but resembles the verdicts given by the juries of our secular courts. It is an advice given to the bishop by the Commission, in a solemn manner, and with a full knowledge of the whole case. It cannot, therefore, but have great weight with the bishop, and, in case of appeal, also with the superior to whom the appeal is made. For it must always be filed among the acts of the cause and trial, and therefore forms part of the official documents, which on appeal must be forwarded to the judge of appeal. Yet the bishop is not bound to follow this verdict. He is free, absolutely speaking, to pronounce the final sentence—*v.g.*, of condemnation, even where the Commission has not found the accused guilty.[1] We say, *absolutely speaking;* for practically it will rarely happen that the bishop will pronounce sentence against the advice or opinion of the Commission.

---

[1] Cf. Instr. cit., § Commissionis ita; S. C. de Prop. F., Ad Dubia, § iii. Votum a Consilio datum.

Art. III.

Proceedings in formal Canonical Trials, and also in Trials before Commissions of Investigation in the United States, in Criminal Causes, from the Final Sentence to the end.

1152. When the defence rests, or declares that it has no further defence to make, it but remains for the judge to pronounce sentence, and thus put an end to the controversy or trial. We shall therefore now briefly speak of the final sentence, its execution, and appeals from it.

§ 1. *Nature and Division of Judicial Sentences—Interlocutory Sentences.*

1153. A judicial sentence (*sententia*), speaking in general, is the decision of the judge in the matter or case on trial, or in the controversy brought before his tribunal.[1] There are two kinds of judicial sentences : interlocutory and definitive. Interlocutory sentences (*sententiae interlocutoriae*) are decisions given by the judge during the course of the trial,—*i.e.*, at any time or stage of the trial between the beginning and the end,—not on the merits of the cause itself, or of the main question under litigation, but on some incidental matter or question—*v.g.*, on the admissibility of witnesses or other evidence ; on the propriety of granting the parties longer delays or time to prepare, etc. Hence any decision, command, or resolution of the judge pertaining to the case or trial, which is made between the beginning and the end of the trial,— that is, from the citation to the final sentence exclusive,—is, properly speaking, an interlocutory sentence.[2]

1154. We say, *from the citation*, etc.; for a decision given by the judge on an incidental matter, before the citation or after the final sentence, is not, properly speaking, an inter-

[1] Schmalzg., l. 2, t. 27, n. 17. [2] Reiff., l. 2, t. 27, n. 14.

locutory sentence, but only a quasi-interlocutory sentence. And it is to be borne in mind that the prohibition to appeal from interlocutory sentences applies only to interlocutory sentences proper, but not to quasi-interlocutory sentences.[1]

1155. Interlocutory sentences are subdivided into simple and mixed. A simple interlocutory sentence is one which remains strictly within the limits of an interlocutory sentence, and therefore does not affect the cause itself, or the main question at issue, in such a manner as to virtually end it. Decisions of this kind are those by which the judge grants further delays, or commands the parties to be present in court on a certain day, to produce their proofs,[2] etc. A mixed interlocutory sentence (*sententia interlocutoria mixta, vel habens vim definitivae*) is one that goes farther, and does not merely touch on or decide an incidental point, such as the admissibility of witnesses, but materially affects the main cause itself, in such a manner as to virtually decide it.[3] We say, *virtually;* for although such a sentence does not formally terminate the cause, yet it does so indirectly, or, as we have said, virtually. Hence such a sentence is called an interlocutory sentence having the force of a final.

1156. Such, *v.g.*, are the following decisions: (*a*) All decisions which preclude the hope of any other decision in the same court or instance—*v.g.*, where the judge decides that a person can or cannot appeal ; that the appeal is given up or abandoned by the appellant.[4] (*b*) Any decision by which a fine is imposed, (*c*) or a person is commanded to give or do something ; (*d*) or by which the judge decides that he has no competence in the case,[5] (*e*) or adjudicates one of the substantial points of the controversy or main cause ;[6] (*f*) admits or rejects a peremptory exception ; (*g*) or decides that the plaintiff or prosecution has sufficiently proved his case,[7] etc.

---

[1] Reiff., l. c., n. 15.   [2] Ib., n. 16.   [3] Ex l. 9, C. de Sent. et interl. (vii. 45).
[4] Reiff., l. c., n. 18.   [5] Ferraris, v. Appellatio, art. 4, n. 7.
[6] Ex l. 39 ff. de Minor. (iv. 4).   [7] Schmalzg., L 2, t. 27, n. 18.

1157. Interlocutory sentences differ from final chiefly as follows: 1. *As to their form.* For a final sentence should be pronounced with certain formalities (as we shall see further on), while an interlocutory can be pronounced summarily, and without any judicial formalities. 2. *As to their stability ;* for the judge can, as a rule, revoke or amend an interlocutory sentence, but not a definitive.'

1158. 3. *As to the right of appealing.* For from a final sentence it is always allowed to appeal, except in a few specified cases, given above.' While at present an appeal from an interlocutory sentence is permitted only (*a*) when the interlocutory sentence has the force of a final sentence ; (*b*) or if it inflicts a grievance which cannot be remedied by a final sentence,' or by an appeal from a final sentence.' We say, *at present ;* for, according to the common law of the Church, as it stood before the Council of Trent, and is laid down in the *corpus juris canonici*,' it was allowed, generally speaking, to appeal from all interlocutory sentences whatever. But the Council of Trent ' restricted this right in the manner just stated.

1159. Now when is an interlocutory sentence considered as having the force of a final sentence, or inflicting an injury or grievance which cannot be redressed by a final sentence, or by an appeal from a final sentence, so as to admit of an appeal, even at the present day ? I. An interlocutory sentence is regarded *as having the force of a final sentence,* and therefore admits of an appeal, chiefly in these cases: 1. When counts or articles or specifications of the defendant, or, as the case may be, of the complainant or prosecution, are unjustly admitted or unjustly rejected by the judge or court.

---

[1] Schmalzg., l. c., n. 20.   [2] Supra. n. 445 sq.

[3] Cf. cap. 59, de Appell. (ii. 28); ib. Glossa, in casum.

[4] Cf. cap. 12, de Appell. in 6° (ii. 15); ib. Glossa, in casum.

[5] Cap. 12, de Appell. (ii. 28).

[6] Sess. 13, cap. l., de Ref.; sess. 24, cap. 20, de Ref.

2. Where witnesses are rejected ; or when there is question of admitting or rejecting witnesses. 3. Where any other kind of proof—*v.g.*, instruments, documents, letters, etc.—offered in evidence is rejected. 4. Where the time given a person to prepare or produce his proofs is so short as to make it difficult or well-nigh impossible for him to be ready at the time fixed. 5. If the judge imposes the burden of proof upon the wrong person. 6. When peremptory exceptions are decided by an interlocutory sentence. 7. Hence, also, when the judge pronounces himself competent or incompetent. 8. Where the judge refuses to furnish the defendant (or, as the case may be, the complainant or prosecution) with a copy of the minutes, acts of the case and of the proceedings, and of the proofs.[1]

1160. It is evident that upon the interlocutory decisions in the cases just enumerated depends in a measure the final sentence or decision of the main cause. For if the judge, *v.g.*, refuses to admit important witnesses or documents, or excludes part of the case, he thereby virtually decides the whole case against the person whose witnesses, etc., he rejects, as the nature of the final sentence depends materially upon the evidence submitted.[2] Hence, too, interlocutory decisions of this kind are properly said to have the force of a final sentence.

1161. II. An interlocutory sentence is considered *as inflicting an injury that cannot be remedied* by a final sentence, or by an appeal from a final sentence, chiefly : 1. Where the judge decrees that a bodily penalty, such as imprisonment, shall be inflicted. 2. Where a censure, such as suspension, is to be imposed ; and in this case the appeal, as we have seen,[3] if interposed before the censure is fulminated, has a suspensive effect. It is plain that in both these cases the

---

[1] Ferraris, v. Appellatio, art. iv., n. 33–48.
[2] Cf. ib., Novae add., n. 4.   [3] Supra, n. 446.

ecclesiastical judge could not, in any subsequent final sentence, or in proceedings of appeal (if the case were appealed to him), redress or undo the injury inflicted by the previous imprisonment or censure.[1] 3. Where dismissal from one's office or parish is decreed; and in this case the appeal has a suspensive effect. 4. Where a person is excluded from a public office—*v.g.*, a parish—because of alleged infamy.[2]

1162. From this it will be seen that interlocutory sentences which have the force of a final sentence, or inflict an irreparable gravamen, are in many respects placed on an equal footing with final sentences proper.[3] We observe here that the restriction of the Council of Trent, prohibiting appeals from interlocutory sentences except in the above cases, extends only to appeals against interlocutory sentences *as pronounced in the course of a trial or of judicial proceedings*, but not to appeals from extrajudicial acts or grievances.[4] For from the latter—*i.e.*, extrajudicial grievances—it is always allowed to appeal, whether they partake of the nature of final acts and sentences, or only of interlocutory.[5]

1163. Finally, we shall state a few of the formalities peculiar to appeals from interlocutory appeals: 1. They must express the cause of the appeal—that is, they must state the *gravamen* against which the appeal is made.[6] 2. The complaint must be reasonable, not frivolous.[7] 3. The litigant or party who considers himself aggrieved by an interlocutory ruling, mandate, or resolution of the judge cannot appeal immediately against such ruling, but must first make the objection—*i.e.*, except to or protest against the ruling—before the judge himself who has made it; and only when the judge rejects the protest, even though he does so only tacitly,—*v.g.*, if he goes on with the trial with-

---

[1] Cf. cap. Super eo 12, de Appell. in 6° (ii. 28); Ferraris, l. c., Novae add., n. 16.
[2] Ferraris, l. c., art. 4, n. 44 sq.   [3] Schmalzg., l. c., n. 21; Reiff., l. c., n. 24.
[4] S. C. C. ap. Ferraris, l. c., n. 32.   [5] Supra, n. 444.   [6] Ferraris, l. c., n. 10.
[7] Our Elements, vol. i., p. 426.

out heeding the exception or protest,—can the aggrieved party appeal to the higher judge.[1]

1164. *Interlocutory sentences of ecclesiastical courts in the United States, as established by the Instructions of the S. C. de P. F., July* 20, 1878, *and* 1884.—In those dioceses where the latest Instruction of the S. C. de Prop. Fide, *Cum Magnopere* of 1884, is already carried into effect, the *compilatio processus* or the conduct of the trial may be entrusted by the bishop to a competent ecclesiastic.[2] The latter is called *auditor* or *Actorum Redactor*.[3] It is the right and duty of this auditor, as we explain in our *New Procedure*, or *Explanation of the Instruction " Cum Magnopere,"* to preside over the whole trial or hearing of the cause, both informative and probative, in the manner laid down in the above Instruction. Consequently it becomes his duty to give the necessary interlocutory decisions during the course of the trial. In other words, one of his functions is to decide all incidental questions or matters that may come up during the proceedings.

1165. Where there are Commissions of Investigation, as in England, and in some parts of the United States, the final sentence is indeed reserved exclusively to the bishop; but the hearing of the cause from the citation to the final sentence exclusive, is committed to these Commissions,[4] who are, with us, presided over at present by the bishop or vicar-general,[5] but in England by one of their own members.

1166. Consequently, where there are Commissions of Investigation, these bodies are empowered to pronounce interlocutory decisions, that is, to decide incidental questions arising in the course of the proceedings conducted by them. In other words, the Commission, being charged with the exclusive right to hear the causes above mentioned, has

---

[1] Cap. 63, de Appell. (ii. 28); Schmalzg., l. 2, t. 28, n. 69 ; Ferr., l. c., n. 15.
[2] Instr. *Cum Magnopere*, Art. XII.   [3] Conc. Pl. Balt. III., n. 299.
[4] Instr. 1878, § Quod si ; S. C. Ad Dubia, § 3, Votum.
[5] Instr. *Cum Magnopere*, Art. XII.

alone the right and duty to grant delays, admit exceptions, etc.[1] As the Commission is an ecclesiastical corporation, and therefore proceeds as a body corporate, in the hearing of causes, it follows that all its interlocutory sentences are rendered by the vote of the majority, and not by its president alone. Hence the interlocutory sentences of our Commissions of Investigation are those resolutions of the Commission which are passed either tacitly or expressly, by a majority of its members, in regard to incidental matters, questions, or facts connected with the cause on trial.

1167. Here it may be proper to observe that Commissions of Investigation must on the one hand allow both the defence and the prosecution full liberty to make out their case, and yet on the other cut short all such delays and procrastinations as are evidently resorted to for the purpose of evading the ends of justice.[2]

1168. What has been said concerning appeals from interlocutory sentences of the ecclesiastical judge proper, seems to apply also to appeals from the interlocutory decisions of Commissions of Investigation. The question, however, may be asked, whether, in case of an appeal being made from the interlocutory sentence of a Commission of Investigation, such appeal is to be made to the bishop, of whose tribunal the Commission forms part, or to the higher judge —that is, the Metropolitan or Holy See? We think the appeal must be made to the Metropolitan or Holy See. For although the Commission of Investigation is a judicial body, vested with judicial power, not by the bishop, but by law,— that is, by the Instruction of the S. C. de P. F., dated July 20, 1878,—and distinct from the bishop or judge proper, it is nevertheless a branch or part of the bishop's court, and in this respect morally identified with him. Hence the interlocutory decisions of the Commission are regarded as decisions

---

[1] Cf. Instr. cit., § 7.   [2] Cf. Instr. cit., § Commissionis ita; ib., §§ 6, 7, 15.

of the bishop's court. The appeal against them, therefore, should be made in the same manner in which they would have to be made if they emanated directly from the bishop himself—that is, they must be made to the Metropolitan or Holy See. Nor can it be objected, that as the appeal from a person or judge delegated must be directed to the judge delegating, so also from the Commission to the bishop. We deny the parity. The Commission is not delegated by the bishop, but is clothed with ordinary power.

§ 2. *The Final Sentence (Sententia Definitiva).*

1169. Having spoken of interlocutory sentences, we come now to sentences in the proper sense of the term, and which are, properly speaking, the subject-matter of this whole arti- cle—namely, final or definitive sentences. A definitive sen- tence (*sententia finalis, definitiva*) is one by which the judge pronounces upon or decides the case itself, or the main issue of the trial, and not merely an incidental point, or some ques- tion arising incidentally during the proceedings.[1] It should be, 1, either absolutory—that is, it should absolve the accused of the crime charged against him ; 2, or condemnatory—*i.e.*, declare him guilty, and condemn him to the proper punish- ment ; 3, or, finally, it may be merely declaratory—that is, it need not condemn the accused, but may simply declare that he is guilty of the crime charged, and has incurred the pun- ishment inflicted *ipso jure* by the law itself. It will be seen that in this third case the judge does not impose the penalty, but merely declares that the accused has committed a crime, for which the law itself inflicts the penalty *ipso facto*. Hence, too, the effect of a declaratory sentence is retroactive,—*i.e.*, takes effect from the moment the crime was committed,— and not merely from the time the declaratory sentence was pronounced.[2]

[1] Reiff., l. 2, t. 27, n. 9.   [2] Schmalzg., l. 2, t. 27, n. 18.

1170. What is chiefly required on the part of the judge (we speak, of course, of the ecclesiastical judge) in order that he may pronounce sentence lawfully? 1. He must have competence in the case ; 2, be not publicly excommunicated ; 3, he must be prudent and learned in the law ;[1] 4, he should not be animated by personal motives, such as dislike, hatred ; 5, nor act with levity. He should give the parties a full and fair trial, and carefully and impartially weigh the evidence.[2]

1171. What is principally requisite on the part of the sentence itself, in order that it may be canonical? 1. The sentence should be absolute, not conditional. Hence this sentence is invalid: I condemn Titius, if he has been proved guilty. 2. It should be clear and determinate, not vague or obscure, or uncertain ;[3] otherwise it is null and void.[4] 3. As a rule, it should be conformable to the bill of complaint or *libellus (conformis libello)*—that is, it should not decide any other matter, nor pronounce upon any other demand, than that which is contained in the bill of complaint, and which was consequently the subject of the trial.[5] We say, *as a rule ;* for there are some exceptions. Thus the rule holds only in civil, but not in criminal causes. Nay, in criminal causes it is not necessary for the prosecution to demand, in its bill of complaint, that a certain fixed penalty be inflicted upon the accused. For, if the accused is found guilty, the judge should impose the penalty which the law decrees for the offence, or if the law leaves it to the judge's discretion, the penalties he thinks proper.[6]

1172. 4. It should be conformable to law or *conformis juri* —*i.e.*, in harmony with the sacred canons. Now a sentence can be contrary to law in two ways: *First*, because it is against the disposition of the law (*contra jus constitutionis*) ;

---

[1] Novella 82, Praefat.   [2] Schmalzg., l. c., n. 27.
[3] § Curare 32, Inst. de Action. (iv. 6).   [4] L. 3, 4, C. de Sent. quae sine (7. 46).
[5] Clem. Saepe 2, § Verum, de V. S. (v. 11); München, l. c., vol. i., p. 211, n. 9.
[6] Reiff., l. c., n. 84.

in other words, because the judge decides otherwise than is decreed by law or established by custom—*v.g.*, if he decides that an ecclesiastical election made by suspended ecclesiastics is valid. For the law of the Church expressly declares that an election by suspended ecclesiastics is null and void.[1] All sentences of this kind are *ipso jure* null and void, and may be disregarded. Nor is it necessary to appeal from them, since they are not considered as having been pronounced at all.[2]

1173. *Secondly*, because it is against the right of any one of the litigants (*contra jus litigatoris*)—namely, when the judge wrongfully refuses by his sentence what the contending party has sufficiently proved to be due him. This sentence, though unjust so far as concerns the merits of the case, is nevertheless valid until it is revoked by the superior judge, on appeal.[3]

1174. How is the sentence to be pronounced, or what other conditions are chiefly necessary, in order that it may be canonical? 1. The litigants should be cited to hear the sentence, and that where the trial preceding the sentence was formal or ordinary, by three simple citations or one peremptory citation. This holds so true, that if one of the contending parties is not cited for sentence, the latter is null and void.[4] This applies even in the case of interlocutory sentences, which are of such a nature as to inflict a serious gravamen upon the absent party.[5] We said, *where the trial . . . was formal;* for in summary trials the parties must indeed be cited to hear the sentence: yet one simple citation is sufficient.[6] As the proceedings or trials before Commissions of Investigation partake, as we have frequently ob-

---

[1] Cap. 16, de Elect. et elect. pot.(i. 6).

[2] Cap. 1, de Sent. (ii. 27); ib. Glossa, v. Sententia.   [3] Reiff., l. c., n. 76.

[4] Ex Clem. Pastoralis 2, de Sent. et re jud. (ii. 11); L. 7, 8, 9, Cod. Quomodo et quando judex (vii. 43).

[5] Schmalzg., l. c., n. 50.   [6] Clem. Saepe 2, de V. S.

served, of the nature of canonical summary trials, it would seem proper that when the trial before the Commission is over, the bishop should fix a day for sentence, and cite the parties to hear it.

1175. Now what is to be done where the party has been cited indeed for sentence, but fails to appear on the day appointed for pronouncing sentence? If he is contumaciously absent,—that is, if he refuses to appear without sufficient cause,—sentence may be validly pronounced in his absence.[1] If he fails to appear, not through contempt, but for just reasons, these reasons are either known to the judge or not. If they are, the judge cannot validly pronounce sentence in the absence of the party.[2] If they are not, the sentence, if pronounced, is indeed valid, but must be revoked when the party that was absent proves that the absence was caused by good reasons.[3]

1176. 2. It should, on pain of nullity, be pronounced after due trial, conducted with the prescribed formalities.[4] These formalities differ, of course, according to the various kinds of trials. Hence, where the judge should proceed by a formal or solemn canonical trial, he must observe, in the course of the trial, all the formalities prescribed by the sacred canons for such trials. Otherwise the trial and subsequent sentence are null and void. Hence the different stages of the trial, such as the bill of complaint, the citation, etc., must be carefully conducted in the manner laid down by the sacred canons.

1177. Where, on the other hand, the judge (we speak always of the ecclesiastical, not secular judge) can proceed by an extraordinary trial,—that is, either summarily, or *ex notorio*, or *ex informata conscientia*, or *sola facti veritate*

---

[1] L. 8, C. tit. cit. (vii. 43). [2] L. 7, C., l. c.

[3] Cap. 18, de Sent. (ii. 27); ib. Glossa, v. Cum Bertholdus.

[4] Cap. 24, de Sent. (ii. 27); ib. Glossa in v. Ex alia justa causa; Leg. 4, C. de Sent. et interl. (vii. 45).

inspecta,—he must observe the formalities peculiar to each of these kinds of proceedings. Here, by the way, we observe, that when a judge is authorized by the superior judge —*v.g.,* a bishop by the Pope—to proceed in a matter or case "sola facti veritate inspecta," he is not bound to observe all the forms of a summary trial. For the power to proceed " sola facti veritate inspecta" is one by which the judge is empowered to proceed even in a simpler manner than in summary causes, as he can dispense with all the formalities established by positive law, though not with those based upon natural law.[1] This power is usually given only in cases of little importance.

1178. In the United States, the *curia,* as established by the Instruction *Cum Magnopere* of 1884, or the Commissions, where they still exist, are obliged to observe the formalities prescribed respectively in the Instruction of the S. C. de P. F. of July 20, 1878, or of 1884; otherwise the trial and subsequent sentence of the bishop would be null and void.[2] And here we remind the reader of what we have already said,[3] that where the sentence is clearly against the sacred canons or legitimate custom—*v.g.,* where the requisite formalities of trials are omitted, as just stated; or where a judge is incompetent or publicly excommunicated, the sentence is *ipso jure* void, and of no effect whatever.

1179. 3. In ordinary or formal canonical trials, the sentence should be pronounced by the judge sitting (*sedens pro tribunali*), not walking or standing, or in any other posture;[4] otherwise the sentence is invalid. We say, *in formal trials;* for in summary trials it is not necessary that the judge should be seated when he pronounces sentence;[5] he may occupy any posture he chooses. 4. It should, as a rule, be in writing, and be read from the manuscript by the judge himself.[6] We say,

---

[1] Reiff., l. c., n. 82.   [2] Cf. Schmalzg., l. c., n. 52.   [3] Supra, n. 1172.
[4] Cap. ult., de Sent, et re jud., in 6°; nov. 82, cap. 3; Reiff., l. c., n. 61.
[5] Clem. 2, de V. S., § Sententiam.   [6] Cap. ult., de Sent., in 6°.

as a rule; for in matters of little importance it need not be written ; and, moreover, judges of high dignity—*v.g.*, bishops —can have it read and published through others. 5. It should be pronounced in a public place; nay, in the case of an ordinary judge, as a rule, in the place where he is accustomed to hold court. We say, *as a rule;* for the bishop may hold court and pass sentence, either personally or through others, in any part of his diocese.[1]

1180. 6. It should be pronounced on the day and at the hour appointed in the citation for the sentence ; otherwise the sentence is null and void, as if it had been pronounced against a party not summoned for sentence.[2] 7. It should not be pronounced on Sundays, and holidays of obligation.[3]

1181. 8. Generally speaking, the judge need not embody or state in his sentence the cause or reasons therefor.[4] We say, *generally speaking;* for the following, among other cases, are excepted from this rule: (*a*) criminal causes;[5] (*b*) especially where a censure—that is, excommunication, suspension or interdict—is inflicted. Thus Pope Innocent IV. (in the Council of Lyons held in 1245) expressly says: " Quisquis" (judex ecclesiasticus) "igitur excommunicat . . . causam excommunicationis expresse conscribat, propter quam excommunicatio proferatur . . . et haec eadem in suspensionis et interdicti sententiis volumus observari."[6]

1182. Hence in these cases the bishop or ecclesiastical judge (also in the United States) is bound to state in his sentence the cause—that is, the crime or criminal act—for which he inflicts the censure or penalty, in order that it may appear whether such cause—*i.e.*, crime—is sufficiently grave to justify the imposing of the censure or penalty. Nor is it sufficient for the bishop or judge to state this cause in a general way—*v.g.*, by saying: I hereby suspend Titius for

---

[1] Cap. 7, de Off. ord., in 6°.   [2] Schmalzg., l. c., n. 58.   [3] Cap. 1, de Feriis.
[4] Cap. Sicut 16, de Sent. (ii. 27).   [5] Schmalzg., l. c., n. 61.
[6] Cap. Cum medicinalis 1, de Sent. excom., in 6° (v. 11).

good and valid reasons.   He must specify the particular
crime or criminal act on account of which the punishment
is inflicted.   Hence he should formulate his sentence—*v.g.*,
thus : I hereby excommunicate Titius, because he is contumacious, having failed to appear before me, although duly
cited ; or : I suspend Titius, because he is guilty of drunken-
ness.'

1183. This law holds so strictly, that if the ecclesiastical
judge, in violation of it, inflicts a censure without expressing
the crime or cause therefor, the superior to whom an appeal
is made should forthwith, unhesitatingly, and without first
inquiring into the justice or merits of the appeal, revoke the
censure and sentence, and moreover in other ways punish
the inferior judge.' The same holds true where the judge
pronounces sentence of excommunication by word of mouth,
not in writing ; or where he refuses to deliver a copy of his
written sentence to the person censured, within a month,
though requested to do so.' Hence it does not seem that
the sentence, pronounced in violation of the above conditions,
is *per se* invalid—at least where no protest or appeal has been
made.   It is however subject to being—nay, should be forthwith annulled by the higher judge, on appeal.' Hence in
this case, as in most other cases, the aggrieved party should
be careful to protest or appeal, lest he should appear to consent to the grievance, and thus render valid what otherwise
would not be sustained.'

1184. (*c*) Finally, where the superior, having been appealed
to in a case, reverses the sentence of the inferior judge (we
speak always of the ecclesiastical judge), he should in his decision give the cause or reasons therefor, and that in order
to shield or protect, as far as possible, the honor of the in-

---

' Glossa, in cit. cap. Cum medicinalis, v. Causam.
' Cap. Cum medic. cit.; ib. Glossa, v. Difficultate.   ' Ib.
' Glossa, ib. v. Cum medicinalis.   ' Cf. Reiff., l. c., n. 103.

ferior judge.[1] Examples of this rule are given in the cap. 10, de Fid. instr. (ii. 22); cap. 14, de Priv. (v. 33); cap. 18, de Sent. (ii. 27). In all these places, the Popes, in reversing the sentences of inferior judges, that had been appealed to them, always state the reasons why they reversed said sentences.[2]

§ 3. *Chief Effects of the Final Sentence—Res Judicata.*

1185. The chief effect of the final sentence is, that where the person who loses the case, or is condemned, has not appealed within the time fixed by ecclesiastical law,—namely, ten days,—the sentence becomes *res judicata ;* that is, the cause or litigation comes absolutely to an end, and the sentence acquires such force and authority that it must be regarded as truth,[3] and can no longer be reversed, and the person condemned who may wish to appeal against it can no longer be heard.[4]

1186. By *res judicata* in the proper sense of the word, therefore, canonists commonly mean the final sentence or judgment itself, not indeed as soon as it is pronounced, but only when *de facto* it has not been suspended by an appeal, and cannot, owing to the lapse of the ten days allowed for appealing, be any longer suspended.[5] We say, *in the proper sense of the word ;* for in a broad sense the cause itself, or controverted matter, which has been decided by the final sentence, is also styled *res judicata.*[6] A judgment or sentence, therefore, is said to have passed into *res judicata* when its effect is not and cannot be any longer suspended.

[1] Glossa, in cit. cap. Cum medicinalis, v. Exprimantur.

[2] Cf. München, l. c., vol. i., p. 210.

[3] Thus the Roman law, adopted by the canon law, says: " Res judicata pro veritate accipitur."—Reg. 207 ff. de Reg. jur.

[4] Cap. 13, 16, de Sent. (ii. 27); Reiff., l. c., n. 107; Leur., For. Eccl., l. 2, t. 27, Q. 965, Resp. 1°.

[5] Reiff., l. c., n. 105; Schmalzg., l. c., n. 62.   [6] Schmalzg., l. c.

1187. It is therefore pertinent to ask: When, or at what particular time, does the sentence pass into *res judicata ?* As a rule, the sentence becomes *res judicata* when the person condemned acquiesces in it, whether expressly—*v.g.*, by declaring himself ready to pay, or asking for time to pay, the sum of money to which he is condemned ; or tacitly—*v.g.*, by not appealing within ten days.

1188. We say, *as a rule ;* for the following among other cases are excepted : 1. Where the sentence is *ipso jure* null and void—*v.g.*, if pronounced by a judge not having competence in the case ; or if it is in open violation of the sacred canons or lawful custom.   In these cases the sentence may be disregarded altogether, just as though it had never been pronounced.   No appeal is therefore necessary.   For such a sentence has no effect whatever, since it has no validity. 2. When the sentence is based upon false evidence, such as spurious instruments, corrupt witnesses ;[1] provided however it is proved that the judge was influenced by or based his sentence upon this false evidence.[2] 3. If the sentence is grounded upon mere presumptions.   In this case the sentence can always be reversed as soon as the contrary is established by real proofs, and not mere presumptions. 4. Where the sentence is based upon the testimony of experts. In this case it does not become *res judicata,* but can, as a rule, be revoked at any time as soon as the expert's testimony is proved to be incorrect, either by clear evidence or the testimony of abler experts.   We say, *as a rule ;* the exception is where both the contending parties have agreed upon the expert.[3]

1189. 5. When the sentence decides upon the validity or invalidity of marriages, it does not become *res judicata,* but may always be revoked whenever it is shown to be erroneous.[4]   6. If the sentence is based upon error, or insufficient

---

[1] Cap 9, de Test. (ii. 20).   [2] Cap. 22, de Sent. (ii. 27); ib. Glossa, v. Secut.
[3] Reiff., l. c., n. 134.   [4] Cap. 9, h. t. (ii. 27).

motives, it is *ipso jure* null and void, and does not pass into *res judicata*, and therefore can always be reversed, provided this error or insufficient cause is expressly stated, or appears in the sentence. 7. When the sentence inflicts a censure—namely, excommunication, suspension or interdict. For although a person under censure cannot appeal, properly speaking, after ten days, he can at any time, by way of recourse, complain of the injustice of the sentence. Consequently he should be heard always, if he asks for absolution from the censure, and wishes to prove the injustice of the sentence.[1]

1190. What other effects, besides that of *res judicata*, has a definitive sentence? They may be reduced to three heads, some of which regard the judge; others the matter itself, or cause decided ; finally, others the litigants. I. *Effects as to the judge.*—He cannot revoke or change his final sentence (the same holds of an interlocutory sentence having the force of a final sentence), even when he sees it is manifestly unjust, except where the sentence is *ipso jure* null and void.[1] This holds even before the sentence has passed into *res judicata*—that is, before the lapse of the ten days allowed for the appeal.[2] The reason is, that having pronounced final sentence, he is *functus officio*, and has no further jurisdiction in the case. We say, *except where the sentence is "ipso jure" null and void;* since such sentence is no sentence at all, and the judge who has pronounced it is regarded as not having pronounced it at all. Hence he is not thereby *functus officio*, and still retains jurisdiction in the case, until he pronounces a valid sentence. Hence he can himself revoke or change a sentence of his which is *ipso jure* invalid, though it is more becoming that the superior judge should do so.

1191. II. *Effects upon the litigants.*—These effects are

---

[1] Cap. 36, de Off. Iud. del.; cap. 48, de Sent. excom.; Schmalzg., l. c., n. 65 (4).
[2] Leg. 55 ff. de Re jud.   [3] Schmalzg., l. c., n. 78.

chiefly the following: 1. If no appeal is interposed within ten days, the litigants must obey the judgment. 2. As far as the accused or defendant is concerned, he acquires, if he has been absolved or declared not guilty, the right to oppose the exception of *res judicata* to any future action brought against him in the same matter, which exception is a bar to any such future action.[1]

1192. III. *Effects as to the cause itself or matter decided.*— As we have already seen, the effect of a final sentence, which has passed into *res judicata*, is that the trial or cause is wholly ended, and cannot be tried over again by a higher judge, as there is no appeal in the case. For the law of the Church presumes, by what is called *praesumptio juris et de jure*, that the sentence against which no appeal has been interposed is just, and that both as a mark of respect to the authority of the judge, and because of the tacit consent of the party who is condemned, implied in his not appealing. The Roman law, adopted by the Church, is, that a person who does not appeal tacitly consents to and ratifies the sentence pronounced against him.[2] Of course, what we have said here with regard to the effect of a final sentence, in regard to the cause decided, does not apply to the cases enumerated under No. 1178, where the sentence does not pass into *res judicata*, and therefore produces no effect, even when no appeal is made.

§ 4. *Execution of the Sentence.*

1193. After the judge (ecclesiastical) has pronounced sentence he should also see that it is carried into effect or executed. By the execution of the sentence we mean the judicial act by which the victor or person who gains the cause is actually or *de facto* given that which was *de jure*

---

[1] L. 4 ff. de Except. rei jud. (xliv. 2); Reiff., l. c., n. 146.
[2] L. 4 C. de Sent. quae sine (vii. 46); Reiff., l. c., n. 108.

obtained by him through the sentence.[1] We say, first, *judicial act;* because it belongs to the trial or judicial proceedings in the case, and forms, so to say, the final act or consummation of the whole cause. We say, secondly, *by which the victor*, etc.; to show the difference between the sentence and its execution. For by the sentence the victorious party obtains his rights by words or orally, while by the execution he acquires them in fact or reality. Hence the execution of the sentence may be briefly said to be the carrying into effect what was decreed by the sentence.

1194. Now, when should the sentence be executed? Before answering, we premise: Some sentences do not stand in need of a separate execution, but carry their execution with themselves; while others must be executed, otherwise they have no effect whatever.[2] Sentences of the first kind are chiefly those, 1, which inflict a censure, whether of excommunication, suspension, or interdict. The reason is, that such a sentence produces its effect of itself, and without any other agency. 2. Those sentences which absolve the accused. For the accused, by the very fact of his being absolved, obtains what he contended for during the trial. 3. Where the sentence does not require the person who is condemned to do a positive action, in order to undergo the punishment imposed by the sentence, but merely commands him to abstain from doing something—*v.g.*, where a person is deprived of his active or passive vote in an ecclesiastical election. In all other cases—*v.g.*, where the ecclesiastical judge imposes a pecuniary fine, or dismissal from office or benefice, etc.—the canonical execution must follow the sentence.[3]

1195. We now answer: 1. In civil causes or actions (we speak, of course, of civil causes pertaining to the ecclesiastical forum) the sentence pronounced by the judge cannot

[1] Schmalzg., l. c., n. 93.
[3] Boulx, de Jud., vol. ii., p. 239.

[2] Schmalzg., l. c., n. 93.

be executed immediately, but it is necessary to wait at least ten days. The reason is, that before the lapse of ten days the sentence does not pass into *res judicata;* nay, it is allowed to appeal from it within that time.[1] We say, *in civil causes;* for it was formerly disputed whether this held also in criminal causes. Abbas and others held the affirmative.[2] The reason they gave was, that in criminal causes a person has even more at stake than in civil causes, and should therefore be allowed at least as much in the one as in the other.[3] Of course they excepted those criminal causes which do not admit of an appeal,—*v.g.*, where the guilt is notorious.[4] Others held the negative, and said in consequence, that it would be necessary, in criminal causes, for the condemned person to appeal at once, if he wished to have the execution of the sentence suspended.[5]

1196. We say, *formerly it was disputed;* for, at present, the question is settled. Thus the Instruction *Cum Magnopere* of 1884 expressly enacts in Art. XXVIII., that the sentence cannot be executed within the ten days allowed for appealing.

1197. By whom is the sentence to be executed? Not by the contending parties themselves,—*i.e.*, the victorious party, —but by the judge, and that by the same judge by whom the sentence was pronounced, at least if he be an ordinary judge. We say, *if he be an ordinary judge;* for in the case of a delegated judge canonists distinguish between delegates of the Pope and delegates of inferior judges—*v.g.*, of bishops. It is certain that delegates of the Holy See can themselves execute their sentence, either personally or through others, and that within a year from the time it was pronounced.[6] We say, *or through others;* hence a papal delegate can command a bishop to execute his sentence.[7]

---

[1] Cap. 15, de Sent. (ii. 27).
[2] Ap. Reiff., l. c., n. 162; Leur., For. Eccl., l. 2, t. 27, Q. 983, Resp. 4°.
[3] Ex l. 6 ff. de Appell. et relat. (xlix. 1).   [4] Cf. supra, n. 445 sq.
[5] Bouix, l. c., p. 240.   [6] Cap. 9, 26, 28, de Off. del. (i. 29).
[7] Reiff, l. c., n. 169.

1198. It is disputed whether delegates other than papal —*v.g.*, delegates of bishops—can execute their sentence without a special mandate to that effect. Schmalzgrueber,[1] following the Glossa,[2] holds the affirmative, on the ground that according to the cap. 5, de Off. del. (i. 29), a person or delegate to whom is committed the hearing of a cause receives, by that very fact, full power in all matters referring to such cause, and therefore also to execute the sentence. The same cannot be said of arbitrators, whether voluntarily (*arbitri compromissarii*) or necessarily (*arbitri juris*) chosen by the contending parties. They can only pronounce sentence, and are bound to leave its execution to the ordinary judge.[3]

1199. *A fortiori*, neither can Commissions of Investigation in the United States execute their verdict. For they are not judges proper, but only assessors or auditors of the bishop, or in a certain sense arbitrators appointed by the law, whose office expires, so far as a particular case is concerned, as soon as they have given their opinion on the case, in the manner prescribed by the Instruction of the S. C. de P. F., July 20, 1878, § 9. Hence also the supplementary Instruction issued by the same Sacred Congregation[4] expressly states that the pronouncing (and by implication the executing) of the final sentence pertains solely to the bishop.

1200. By whom is the sentence to be executed when the case has been appealed? By the judge from whom or by the judge to whom the appeal has been made? We distinguish: The sentence of the inferior judge is either reversed or confirmed by the judge of appeal. In the first case, the execution belongs to the judge of appeal. In the second, the question is disputed. According to Schmalzgrueber,[5] the common and approved opinion of canonists holds, 1, that where the judge of appeal confirms the sentence of the in-

---

[1] L. c., n. 95.   [2] In cap. 4, de For. comp. (ii. 2), v. Ipsius solicitudine.

[3] Cap. 4. de For. comp.; Schmalzg., l. c., n. 95.

[4] Ad Dubia circa modum, § iii., Votum.   [5] L. c., n. 96, 97.

ferior judge only tacitly or indirectly,—that is, where he does not take cognizance of the cause appealed, but simply declares that the time for appealing has lapsed, or that the appeal has been abandoned, and that, consequently, the case has not devolved upon him by the appeal,—the sentence is to be executed by the judge from whom the appeal has been made; 2, that, however, if the judge of appeal, upon due trial or hearing of the cause appealed, expressly pronounces the sentence of the inferior judge to be just (*i.e.*, decides *male appellatum, et bene judicatum*), and thus directly confirms it, he can himself execute it.[1] The reason is, that by the appeal properly made, entertained, and decided, the jurisdiction in the case was suspended, or taken away from the inferior judge, and transferred to the superior, or judge of appeal.

§ 5. *Expenses of Ecclesiastical Trials—By whom to be paid, also in the United States.*

1201. The expenses occasioned by trials in ecclesiastical courts, also with us, may be of two kinds: voluntary and necessary. The voluntary or optional (*expensae voluntariae, delicatae*) expenses are those which are incurred over and above what is necessary—*v.g.*, a very liberal honorary to the advocate. The necessary are those outlays without which the trial cannot be well or properly carried on by the party, such as a moderate fee for the advocate, the ordinary travelling expenses of the litigant or his witnesses.

1202. The law of the Church is that in trials before the ecclesiastical judge the party succumbing should never indeed be condemned to pay the voluntary expenses of the victor, but that he should be condemned to defray the necessary, if he rashly entered upon the cause or trial, whether as plaintiff (prosecution) or defendant.[2] This holds not only in civil,

---

[1] L. 32, § 5, Sane, C. de Appell. (vii. 62).
[2] Cap. 2 et 5, de Dol. et cont. (ii. 14); L. 13, § 6, Sive autem, Cod. (iii. 1).

but also in criminal causes,[1] and that whether they are
ushered in or tried by way of accusation, denunciation or
inquiry, or exception. However, in purely criminal causes
a distinction should be made between the plaintiff or prosecution and the defendant. The latter is never considered
rash for defending himself. For nobody can blame him for
using all lawful means of escaping punishment, even though
he is guilty. Hence he cannot, in any case, be condemned
to pay the costs. With the former, the case is different, and
he can be obliged to pay the costs.[2]

1203. We say, *if he* RASHLY *entered upon the cause;* because
a person who does not rashly go to trial cannot be condemned to pay the expenses. Now a person is considered
as having rashly entered upon a trial or cause, not only when
he does so from malice or deceit, but also when he does so
imprudently and unadvisedly—*i.e.*, without due diligence
and examination of the matter, and without taking proper
advice.[3]

1204. But, on the other hand, a person is not regarded as
having rashly (*temere*) entered upon a cause when he has a
sufficient reason for believing in the justice of his cause—*v.g.*,
if he took the advice of canonists, and was informed by them
that his cause was just.[4] We observe here that the judge is
bound to condemn the party who loses the case to pay the
expenses of the victor only when the latter so asks, either
expressly or tacitly.[5] Again we note that the judge can at
times condemn one of the litigants to defray the expenses of
the other, even before the final sentence—*v.g.*, where one
party has proved his allegation, at least *prima facie*, and the
other delays his answer.[6]

1205. What are the penalties incurred by ecclesiastical
judges for any injustice committed by them in the course of

[1] Cap. 6, de Dol. (ii. 14); ib. Glossa, v. Expensas.
[2] Reiff., l. c., n. 177.   [3] Schmalzg., l. c., n. 115.   [4] Reiff., l. c., n. 180.
[5] Ib., n. 191–196.   [6] Cap. 5, in 6° (ii. 14); Bouix, de Jud., vol. ii., p. 244.

the trial ?   By the law of the Church, an ecclesiastical judge, whether ordinary or delegate, who knowingly pronounces an unjust sentence, or commits some other act of injustice, in the course of the trial, whether through fear, favoritism, hatred, or hope of gain, is bound to pay the party whom he has injured all the expenses of the trial, and besides incurs suspension for a year *ab officiis divinis.*   The latter—*i.e.*, the suspension—is not incurred by bishops, as they are not expressly mentioned in the law.[1]

1206. What has been thus far said, in the present article, regarding the indemnity to be paid by the succumbing party and by the judge, applies also in the United States, both in trials before our Commissions of Investigation, and other judicial proceedings. For, apart from any positive law of the Church, the very law of nature prescribes that where an expense or damage has been wrongfully and wilfully caused by a party, it should also be made good by that party.

ART. IV.

Of Appeals.

§ 1. *Mode of Procedure in Appeals.*

1207. We have already spoken at length of appeals.[2] Here we shall add only a few remarks in regard to the mode of procedure to be followed in appeals, especially as applicable in the United States.   Every appeal, as we have seen, has three principal stages : namely, (*a*) the making of the appeal—that is, the declaration made by the appellant to the judge *a quo*, either orally or in writing, that he appeals : (*b*) the bringing of the appeal thus taken before the higher judge or superior, who is called *judex ad quem ;* (*c*) and the farther proceedings before the *judex ad quem ;* in other

[1] Cap. 1, de Sent. et re jud., in 6° (ii. 14); Schmalzg., l. c., n. 112.
[2] Supra, vol. i., n. 442–454; ib., p. 425.

words, the hearing or trial of the appeal, or the prosecution of the appeal before the higher judge.

1208. I. *First stage of the appeal.*—As to the first stage, we have already seen that both in judicial and extrajudicial appeals the appeal must be taken, and the judge *a quo* as a rule notified of it, within ten days.[1] This notification, if the appeal is made (*a*) from a definitive sentence, or (*b*) from an interlocutory sentence having the force of, and therefore equivalent to a final sentence (*sententia interlocutoria habens vim definitivae*), need contain only the simple declaration that an appeal is taken.[2] Cf. Bizzarri, Collectanea S. Sedis, p. 182.

1209. But where the appeal is from (*a*) a mixed interlocutory sentence, that is, from an interlocutory decision or decree, which, though it has not the force of a final sentence, nevertheless inflicts a *damnum irreparabile*, that is, a grievance which cannot be repaired by a final sentence, or by an appeal from a final sentence, (*b*) or from an extrajudicial gravamen,[3] the reasons for the appeal must be specifically set forth, so that the judge *a quo*, who can himself reverse such interlocutory sentence and redress such extrajudicial grievance, may be able to see whether he should himself correct his decision or not.[4] Of course, this notification should not contain anything disrespectful to the judge *a quo*.[5]

1210. We said above,[6] that the judge *a quo* must, as a rule, be notified of the appeal. This rule, like other rules, has its exceptions. These exceptions are (*a*) where the judge is inaccessible, (*b*) or where fear prevents the appellant from notifying him. In both these cases the proper course to pursue is this: The appellant can and should send his notification of appeal directly to the judge of appeal, instead of

---

[1] Supra, n. 444. [2] Reiff., l. 2, t. 28, n. 102. Schmalzg., l. 2, t. 28, n. 61.
[3] Cap. Cordi nobis 1, de Appell., in 6° (ii. 15); cf. tamen ib. Glossa, v. Vel extra.
[4] München, l. c., vol. i., p. 595, n. 7.   [5] Ib., p. 531.   [6] Supra, n. 1208.

to the judge from whom he appeals; or if this is impracti-
cable, he should protest or declare, in the presence of two or
three worthy persons, that he wishes to appeal against an
unjust sentence or gravamen, but that he does not venture
to do so.[1]   Both the notification to the judge of appeal, and
the protest in the presence of worthy persons, must take
place within the ten days allowed for appealing.[2]   If the
notification is sent directly to the judge of appeal, he may
be requested to inform the judge *a quo* of the appeal.[3]

1211. Next, the appellant should ask and receive the
apostoli from the judge *a quo* within thirty days.[4]   These
thirty days run concurrently with the ten days allowed for
appealing—that is, they begin, not at the expiration, but
with the beginning of the ten days.[5]   Hence the request for
the *apostoli* may be and is very properly made simultaneously
with the appeal itself.[6]   The appellant should make this
request humbly and urgently, though he need not make it
more than once.   The above spaces of time must be strictly
observed, both in judicial and extrajudicial appeals.   Their
non-observance is fatal to the appeal—that is, causes it to be
null.   Hence these spaces of time are called *dies fatales.*
This fatality to the appeal ensues even where the omission
or non-observance of the above days is not culpable on the
part of the appellant, being caused, *v.g.*, by error, ignorance,
etc.   The only way in which such inculpable omission can
be remedied, and the person wishing to appeal recover the
right to appeal, is by his reinstatement or *restitutio in integrum,*[7] of which canonists treat under the title *de in integrum
restitutione.*   (See Appendix XIII.)

1212. II. *Second stage of the appeal.*—According to the general law of the Church, and prescinding from the Instructions *Sacra Haec,* June 11, 1880, of the S. C. EE. et RR., and

---

[1] Cap. 73, de Appell. (ii. 28).   [2] Reiff., l. c., n. 89–93.   [3] München, l. c., p. 531.
[4] L. un. ff. (xlix. 7); Clem. 2, de Appell. (ii. 12); Schmalzg., l. c., n. 75.

Cum Magnopere, 1884, of the S. C. de Prop. Fide, the judge *a quo* should give the appellant the *apostoli* within the thirty days, as above stated, and also a certified copy of the entire trial or proceedings of the first instance. This ends the proceedings before the judge *a quo*.[1]

We say, *according to the general law*, etc.; for, the above Instructions of 1880 and 1884 enact, in Art. XXVIII., that when the appeal has been interposed, the *judex a quo* shall forthwith send (*a*) the *originals* themselves, and not merely a certified copy of the proceedings, (*b*) to the higher ecclesiastical authority or judge *ad quem*, and therefore not to the appellant.

1213. The second stage of the appeal, as we have seen, is the bringing of the appeal before the higher judge. Now, when must the appellant bring or introduce his appeal before the superior or judge of appeal? According to the general law of the Church, and apart from the above Instructions *Sacra Haec* and *Cum Magnopere*, he must certainly do so within a year from the day he made the appeal, as only a year, and for just cause two years, are granted for hearing and deciding appeals. But it is not certain at what particular time during the year this is to be done. Some hold that where the judge *a quo* does not fix the time (formerly the judge *a quo* could fix the time), it must be done six months from the day the appeal was first made.[2] The safest way is to do so as soon as possible, in order to give the judge *ad quem* ample time to try the cause.[3]

We say, *apart from the Instructions Sacra Haec* and *Cum Magnopere;* the reason is that both these Instructions ordain, in Art. XXIX., that the judge *ad quem*, having received and inspected the authentic documents or acts, shall notify the appellant to appoint within a certain time an advocate, to conduct and prosecute his appeal. The appointment of

[1] München, l. c., vol. i., p. 549, n. 12.   [2] Craisson, n. 5985.
[3] Schmalzg., l. 2, t. 28, n. 79.

such advocate seems equivalent to introducing the appeal before the judge *ad quem*.   Hence, according to the above two Instructions the judge *ad quem* always fixes the time for introducing the appeal.   Consequently, the appellant is no longer free to bring his appeal before the judge *ad quem* at any time within a year or six months from the date of the appeal.

1214. III. *Third stage of the appeal.*—The third stage refers to the admission and the hearing or trial of the appeal by the judge or superior *ad quem*.   When the judge *ad quem* has received the above *acta* or documents from the superior or judge *a quo*, and has, after inspecting them, ascertained that the appeal has been interposed (*a*) by the proper or legitimate person, that is, by the person who is entitled to appeal; (*b*) within ten days; (*c*) against a final sentence; (*d*) or one having the force of a final sentence; (*e*) or from a grievance which cannot be remedied by a final sentence or by an appeal from a final sentence, he shall forthwith admit the appeal, and that *in suspensivo*, and then notify the appellant, as we have seen, that within 20 days (with us, 30 days), he must appoint his counsel to prosecute the appeal.

1215. We say, *and having inspected them*, etc.; the reason is, that the judge *ad quem* cannot admit a suspensive appeal, unless he is certain that the case appealed to him admits of a suspensive appeal.   Now, an appeal is suspensive, a_ a rule, only when it is interposed (*a*) against a final sentence; (*b*) an interlocutory sentence which is equivalent to a final sentence; (*c*) an interlocutory decree or extrajudicial act, which inflicts an irremediable grievance.   To avoid mistakes, the law enacts that before admitting an appeal *in suspensivo*, the judge *ad quem* shall, as a rule, convince himself by an inspection of the public documents submitted to him, that the appeal belongs to one of the classes just mentioned, and therefore admits of a suspensive effect.

1216. All this is clearly laid down in the Const. *Ad*

Militantis of Pope Benedict XIV., in Art. XLIII., which enacts: "Appellationes autem non recipiantur, neque inhibitiones vigore illarum concedantur, nisi prius constiterit, quod nedum per legitimam Personam, et intra legitima tempora vere appellatum fuerit; sed etiam, quod appellatum fuerit a sententia definitiva, vel habente vim definitivae, ad a gravamine quod per definitivam sententiam reparari non possit: idque per publica documenta. . . ."

1217. What has been said applies to suspensive appeals. Consequently, before admitting an extrajudicial appeal, which has merely a devolutive effect, the superior *ad quem* should indeed be certain that the case appealed to him is one that admits of such appeal, but it is not prescribed that he must derive this certainty from the *public* or authentic acts of the case. He can, moreover, after admitting such devolutive appeal, compel the superior *a quo* to forward to him all the extrajudicial acts or records of the case, so that he may be able to adjudicate the appeal.[1]

Here we observe that whenever there is a doubt as to the admissibility of the appeal, judicial or extrajudicial, devolutive or suspensive, the appeal should be admitted by the superior *ad quem*. For an appeal is a means, nay, one of the best means, of a legitimate defence, and should, therefore, not be denied, except where it is clearly and certainly forbidden by the law.[2]

1218. *Mode of procedure before the judge ad quem.*—When the judge *ad quem* has, upon due inspection of the papers, admitted the appeal, as above stated, it becomes his right and duty to proceed to the hearing of the entire cause, as appealed; that is, to cite the appellee and appellant: to receive additional evidence, etc., and to decide the cause. For by a legitimate appeal, whether suspensive or devolutive, the whole case devolves upon him.

1219. The procedure, or the manner in which the appeal

<hr/>

[1] Conc. Trid. sess. 24, cap. 20, de Ref.   [2] München, vol. I., p. 527, n. 15.

is tried before the judge of appeal—is substantially the same
as that observed in the proceedings or trial of the first
instance, or before the judge *a quo*, though somewhat shorter
and more summary.[1] We proceed to give a brief outline
of it.

1220. As the appellant becomes the plaintiff, so far as the
appeal is directly concerned, it follows that the burden of
proof, in this respect, rests upon him. Hence, when the judge
ad quem has decided to entertain the appeal, it becomes the
appellant's right and duty to produce his proofs before the
judge of appeal within a time fixed by the latter. The mode
in which the appellant should proceed with his proofs is as
follows: First, he should draw up a written statement as
full and complete as possible of his grievances, and hand it
to the judge of appeal. Next, he should produce, one by
one, the various proofs—*v.g.*, witnesses, letters, etc.—to substantiate his written allegations.

1221. When the appellant has given in his evidence, both
in writing and orally, a copy of the appellant's allegations
and testimony, together with the minutes of the proceedings,
is given the appellee (at the latter's expense) by order of the
judge of appeal, so as to enable the appellee to prepare his
answer and submit his proofs in rebuttal. When the appellee has handed in his reply, and substantiated it by proper
proofs, the judge *ad quem* may proceed to the sentence,
unless he finds it desirable to obtain a clearer knowledge of
the case. In the latter case the appellant is given a copy
of the appellee's answer, proofs submitted, and of the minutes of the court on this head, and he is allowed to file a
rejoinder. Both parties may be confronted with the other
side's witnesses. When both parties have exhausted all
their arguments, proofs, etc., the judge, after having taken
time to weigh everything carefully, should pronounce sentence.[2] We observe here that the acts of the trial in the

---

[1] München, l. c., p. 553, n. 14.   [2] Ib., pp. 553, 554.

first instance can and should be made use of by both parties in order to establish their respective positions.

1222. We said above,[1] *so far as the appeal is directly concerned;* for so far as regards the merits of the main cause, or of the cause appealed, the burden of proof rests upon the same parties upon whom it did or would rest in the trial of the first instance. From these principles it follows that the burden of proof rests upon the appellant with regard to the lawfulness of the appeal, and also the grievances on account of which he appeals. In other words, he must prove (a) that his appeal is legitimate—*i.e.,* made in due form, (b) and that the grievances complained of have really been inflicted upon him. It follows, moreover, that so far as the cause appealed itself is concerned, the appellee, who was the prosecutor in the lower court, must prove his charges, just the same as he was obliged to do in the first instance.[1]

1223. Here it is proper to ask: Whether and how far the appellant (the same holds of the appellee) is obliged, in the trial of the appeal or cause appealed, to confine himself to the matters or grievances, and the proofs or testimony therefor, of the first trial, or trial in the first instance; or whether and how far he can allege new matters or grievances, and submit new testimony in support of such new matters or complaints? He cannot introduce an entirely new matter or grievance—that is, one which is altogether foreign to or disconnected with the cause or matter or grievance as tried in the first instance.

1224. But he has the right to bring in or submit any new matter, question, allegation, complaint, or exception whatever, and, of course, also prove it, by new testimony—*v.g.,* by new witnesses or documents—not produced at the first trial, provided it arises from, or is in any way connected with, or has any bearing upon, the cause or matter as tried

---

[1] Supra, n. 1220.   [1] Schmalzg., l. c., n. 103.

in the first instance.' The appellant may also produce additional or new proofs of matters or grievances, which were alleged indeed on the first trial, but not proven, or only insufficiently proven.' The appellee has of course the same right in his reply or defence.'

1225. Observe, however, that the above applies to final judicial sentences, or interlocutory sentences having the force of a final sentence, or inflicting a *gravamen* or *damnum irreparabile*, that is, a grievance which cannot be remedied by a final sentence, or by an appeal from a final sentence. But are the above principles applicable to extrajudicial appeals? In other words, Can the appellant (the same applies to the appellee) make use of new matter or grievances and proofs therefor, in the sense stated, in extrajudicial appeals? Two kinds of extrajudicial appeals may be distinguished: one against extrajudicial acts, in the wide sense of the term—namely, acts done indeed out of regular judicial proceedings, but yet by the judge and in connection with the trial; the other kind against acts which are extrajudicial in the strict sense—namely, acts done without any judicial proceedings, and having no connection with them —*v.g.*, appointments to parishes.

1226. Now all canonists admit that in extrajudicial appeals of the first kind the causes of the appeal or grievance must be specified, and no new allegations or grievances or matters can, as a rule, be made or proved, beside those which are expressed in the notification of the appeal as sent to the *judex a quo*.' Whether this applies also to extrajudicial appeals of the second class, seems controverted. The common opinion of canonists is in the affirmative, or, rather,

' Cap. 10, de Fid. Instr. (ii. 22); ib. Glossa, v. Hujusmodi exceptio; L. 6, Cod. de Appel. (vii. 42); L. 4, Cod. de Temp. Appell. (vii. 43); Schmalzg., l. 2, t. 28, n. 60.   ' L. 4, C. cit.   ' München, l. c., p. 556, n. 16.

⁴ Cap. 62, de App. (ii. 28); ib. Glossa, v. Dummodo haec; Clem. 5, de Appell. (ii. 12); ib. Glossa, in cas.

seems so, because they are very obscure and disappointing in the matter.[1] Those who hold the negative, contend that the texts of canon law,[2] as quoted by those who hold the affirmative, all speak of appeals from interlocutory sentences and from extrajudicial sentences of the first kind. In fact, the law is not favorable to the latter, as they simply tend to obstruct and delay judicial proceedings, which, however, is not the case with extrajudicial appeals of the second kind. The safer way is, of course, to enumerate, even in the latter case, all the grievances, and specify all the reasons and causes upon which the complaint is based.

1227. Whatever may be said on this matter, it is certain that in all extrajudicial appeals new allegations and complaints may be made, and proved by new proofs, in the following cases: 1. Where a new cause of complaint has arisen or only become known after the appeal has been lodged; 2. Where the judge *a quo* refuses to admit other causes of complaint alleged by the appellant. 3. Where an injury is to be inflicted that cannot be remedied by a final sentence.[3]

1228. What has been said will be better understood if we consider the reasons or objects for which appeals are established. These reasons are, chiefly: 1. In order to remove the grievance unjustly inflicted. 2. To correct the injustice, inexperience, want of knowledge, or other defect of the judge in the first instance. 3. To enable the litigant who either through ignorance or negligence has failed to establish his case properly in the first instance, to remedy this defect in the second instance.[4]

1229. *Q.* Do the above principles concerning the mode of procedure to be followed in the hearing of appeals apply also to appeals made in some parts of the United States, according to the Instruction of the S. C. de P. F., of July 20, 1878?

[1] Cf. Schmalzg., l. c., n. 61, 64 ; München, l. c., p. 595, n. 7.
[2] Cap. 62, de App.; cap. 1 et 3, de App., in 6° (il. 15); Clem. 5, de App.
[3] Schmalzg., l. c., n. 64.   [4] Schmalzg., l. c., n. 6.

A. They do substantially. For, as we shall presently show, the mode of hearing appeals to be followed by the metropolitan, with us, as prescribed by said Instruction, is substantially the same as the one we have above described. In fact, the Instruction says: " Si vero contingat ut a sententia in curia episcopali prolata, ad archiepiscopalem provocetur, metropolitanus *eadem methodo in causae cognitione et decisione procedat.*" [1] In other words, the metropolitan is bound to proceed, in hearing and deciding cases appealed to him, in the same manner in which the bishop is obliged to proceed in the trial of the case in the first instance.

1230. Now this mode of procedure is substantially the same as that prescribed for appeals by the general law of the Church, as already delineated. We now proceed to give a brief description of it. First, when an appeal has been made to the metropolitan, the latter upon receiving it from the appellant, and finding that the appeal has been made within the prescribed time, in due form, and in causes where appeals are not forbidden by the sacred canons, can and should entertain it. Nay, even where it is doubtful whether the appeal is legitimate or admissible, the judge *ad quem* should admit it. Hence the latter will very rarely find himself obliged to reject an appeal. For, as already shown, the right of appeal is founded in the law of nature, since it is one of the means of a legitimate defence, and a protection to innocence.[2] Consequently, where there is a doubt as to its admissibility it should be received.

1231. Before proceeding to the hearing of the case itself, it would seem proper for the metropolitan, where the nature of the case permits it, to use his good offices toward effecting an amicable settlement between the appellant and the appellee.[3] Should his efforts in this direction prove abortive, he

---

[1] Instr. cit., § 17, Si vero. [2] Schmalzg., l. c., n. 6.
[3] Cf. Instr. cit., § 1, Ad commissionem.

will proceed to convene the Commission, and place the whole case before it. Accordingly he appoints a day for the meeting of his Commission of Investigation, informing each member of the Commission, by letter, of the place, day, and hour of the meeting.[1] A citatory letter is also sent to the appellee, or diocesan promoter, acting for the bishop, informing him of the time and place of the Commission's meeting, and requiring him to be present in order to answer and combat the appeal.[2] The appellant must of course be also notified of the time and place of the meeting, and required to present his case.

1232. On the day appointed, the appellant or his advocate is first heard by the Commission. First he reads to the Commission the written statement of his cause as appealed. Next he produces his proofs—*v.g.*, witnesses, letters, the documents or acts of the first trial, etc.[3]

1233. Next the appellee—*v.g.*, bishop's official or his advocate, is given by the Commission a copy of the appellant's statement, unless this has been done already. We say, *unless this has been done already;* for where prudence does not forbid, the metropolitan should forward a copy of the appellant's statement, as sent to him in the appeal, to the appellee or bishop's curia, simultaneously with the citation.[4] Or again the appellee or bishop's curia may have been already sufficiently informed of the nature of the appeal, by the fact that the appellant, in his notification of appeal to the judge *a quo*, has enumerated all his grievances.

1234. Having been furnished with a full copy of the appellant's statements, proofs, and the minutes of the proceedings, or having been informed of them otherwise, as just seen, the appellee prepares his reply and the proofs in its support, and on the day fixed by the Commission goes before the latter body, and there reads his written answer to

---

[1] Cf. ib., § 3, Locum.
[2] Cf. ib., § 4, Per litteras.
[3] Cf. Instr. cit., § 6, Relatio causae.
[4] Cf. ib., § 4, Per litteras.

the appellant's allegations and proofs, is subject to cross-examination by the Commission, and produces, one after another, his proofs.[1]

1235. Then a copy of the appellee's answer, proofs, etc., together with the minutes of the proceedings, is given the appellant (unless the case is too clear to admit of further argument), and he is allowed to file a rejoinder; and *vice versâ*, the appellee is given the same privilege, and so on, until both parties have exhausted their arguments or proofs. The witnesses are examined as on the first trial.[2]

1236. Is it allowed in the United States to introduce new grievances or allegations, and submit new proofs therefor, in the sense stated (supra, n. 1224), in appeals from final sentences of bishops, pronounced after trial before the Commission of Investigation? It would seem that the negative ought to be maintained. For, as we have seen,[3] it is the common opinion that in extrajudicial appeals no grievances other than those expressly-stated in the appeal sent to the judge *a quo* can as a rule be submitted or proved. Now the appeals, with us, in question are extrajudicial appeals. The reason is that the trial or investigation before the Commission is not a *processus judicialis,—i.e.*, a canonical trial,—and therefore the final sentence of the bishop, as based or consequent upon such trial, is not a judicial, but merely an extrajudicial sentence.

1237. Notwithstanding these arguments, it would seem that the affirmative is the true opinion. In fact, the sentence of the bishop in the case is expressly called a judicial and definitive sentence—*sententia judicialis et definitiva*—by the S. C. de P. F., in its supplementary declarations concerning the Instruction of July 20, 1878.[4] The same Sacred Congregation expressly calls the functions and proceedings of the Commissions of Investigation judicial acts,[5] and, moreover,

---

[1] Cf. Instr. cit., § 7, Deinde.   [2] Cf. ib., § 11, 12, 13, 15.   [3] Supra, n. 1226.
[4] S. C. de P. F., Ad Dubia, § iii., Votum.   [5] Ib.

compares the members of these bodies to the synodal judges
of the Council of Trent.' Now an appeal from a sentence
which is judicial and definitive, and is therefore supposed to
have, and in fact has, been preceded by judicial proceedings,
—namely, the investigation before the Commission,—is certainly a judicial appeal, in the proper sense of the word.
For a judicial appeal is one made against the judicial acts
of the superior ; an extrajudicial, one that is lodged against
his extrajudicial or purely administrative acts.' We think,
therefore (though with complete deference to any future
decision of the Holy See), that the appeals in question are
judicial, and should be governed by the rules applicable to
judicial appeals.

1238. As to the opposing arguments above stated, we
answer : The trial before the Commission is not a canonical
trial *in the technical sense of the word*—that is, the trial is not
a canonical trial, because it need not be necessarily conducted
with the various and complex formalities prescribed by canon
law. But in every other respect it may be called and is a
canonical trial or judicial proceeding. Moreover it should be
added, that even though it were true that the appeals in question are extrajudicial, the latter are placed by some canonists
on the same footing with judicial appeals, so far as the question under discussion is concerned.

1239. What has been said here of appeals from final judicial sentences of our bishops, as pronounced after trial before
the Commission, holds also of interlocutory sentences of the
Commission of Investigation, provided they have the force
of final sentences, or inflict an injury irremediable by a final
sentence, or by an appeal from a final sentence. We observe
also that it is always best and advisable, with us, for appel-
lants to specify in their appeal as clearly and as fully as possible all grievances from which they appeal.

' S. C. de P. F., Ad Dubia, § ii., Electio.   ' Schmalzg., l. 2, t. 28, n. 4.

1240. Let us now turn to the final stage of the appeal. The Commission, after a full and fair trial or hearing of the appeal, will proceed to deliberate and make up their opinion or verdict on the merits of the cause appealed, as provided in the Instruction of July 20, 1878, § 9. These opinions, together with the minutes of the proceedings, and all the papers and documents submitted by the appellant and appellee, are then gathered together and properly arranged or filed by the archbishop's official, and delivered to the metropolitan, whose exclusive right and duty it is to pronounce the final sentence on the merits of the appeal, either confirming or modifying or annulling the sentence of the bishop against whom the appeal was lodged.

§ 2. *Effects of Appeals, also in the United States.*

1241. What are the effects of appeals? We have already substantially answered this question, in the first volume of our *Elements*, pp. 193–199, and pp. 426, 427. Here we shall merely summarize and further explain what we have there said on the matter.

1242. An appeal from a definitive judicial sentence (the same holds of an appeal from an interlocutory sentence having the force of a final sentence, or inflicting an injury irreparable by a final sentence) has two celebrated effects: one devolutive (*effectus devolutivus*), the other suspensive (*effectus suspensivus*). By means of the devolutive effect, the entire cause that has been appealed, together with all its accessories or accompaniments, devolves from the inferior judge to the superior to whom the case has been appealed, and the latter acquires, *ipso facto*, the right and power to try, or hear and take cognizance of, as also to decide or pass final sentence on, the cause.[1]

1243. The suspensive effect consists in this, that the juris-

---

[1] Cap. 55, de App. (ii. 28); cap. 59, de App. (ii. 28).

diction of the judge *a quo* is suspended, so that, pending the appeal, he cannot execute his sentence, but is bound to leave everything *in statu quo*—that is, in the same state in which it was at the time the appeal was interposed.[1] To these two effects may be added a third—namely, the remedy of attentates (*remedium attentatorum*), by which not only those acts of the judge *a quo* are to be revoked which have been done pending the appeal, or after the appeal has been interposed, but also those which took place before the appeal was made —namely, those which were attempted during the ten days allowed for appealing.[2]

1244. We said above,[3] *an appeal from a definitive judicial sentence.* It may therefore properly be asked, whether an extrajudicial appeal, or an appeal from an extrajudicial sentence or act, also has the above effects? It has, though in a slightly modified manner.[4] In other words, extrajudicial appeals, like judicial, have the suspensive and devolutive effects, as also the effect called remedy of attentates, all of which have been described.[5] Thus, speaking of the remedy of attentates, if a rector or parish priest or other ecclesiastical official, who has reason to fear that he may be extrajudicially deprived of his income or place, appeals against this proposed dismissal, but is nevertheless deprived afterwards of his position, he should before all else be reinstated.[6]

1245. The reason is, that the law of the Church forbids all changes or innovations, and that on pain of nullity *ipso jure*, not only pending a formal appeal (*pendente appellatione*), but in general pending a controversy or litigation (*pendente lite*) before the ecclesiastical judge.[7] Now, an extrajudicial

---

[1] Cap. 39. de App. (ii. 28); Schmalzg., l. 2, t. 28, n. 108.
[2] Cap. Non solum 7, de Appell. (ii. 15), in 6°; ib. Glossa, in cas.
[3] Supra, n. 1242.
[4] Cap. 51, de App. (ii. 28); ib. Glossa, v. In eum statum; cap. 10, de Elect. (i. 6); cap. 63, de App. (ii. 28).   [5] München, l. c., p. 591, n. 3.
[6] Cap. 51, de App. (ii. 28).   [7] Cap. 1 et 2, Ut lite pend., in 6° (ii. 8).

appeal, being at least a *provocatio ad causam*, induces or causes a *litis pendentia* or pendency of the litigation.[1]

1246. We said above (n. 1244), *though in a slightly modified manner ;* for there are a few accidental differences as to the manner in which these effects follow. First, as to the suspensive effect, a judicial appeal suspends the jurisdiction of the judge *a quo* in regard to the whole case and all its accessories, even though only one or two points have been appealed ; while extrajudicial appeals (at least when they are not against acts which are altogether extrajudicial and final) suspend the jurisdiction of the judge *a quo* only as to the particular matter, point, or grievance which was expressly stated in the appeal, but not to other complaints or matters of dispute. Hence, also, in judicial appeals all attentates or innovations whatever—*i.e.*, acts of the judge prejudicial in any way to the appellant—are to be revoked, even though they do not directly concern the cause appealed. But in the above extrajudicial appeals only those attentates can be revoked which are directly prejudicial to the appellant, so far as the grievances appealed are con cerned.[2]

1247. Secondly, as to the devolutive effect, in judicial appeals from final sentences (the same holds of appeals from interlocutory sentences having the force of final sentences, and, according to many, also of appeals from acts or decisions altogether extrajudicial and final) the whole case de volves upon the judge *ad quem* at once—that is, before the appellant proves that his appeal is just, or based upon good and sufficient reasons or grievances. The latter must simply prove that he has appealed with the requisite formalities —namely, within the ten days, etc. While in extrajudicial appeals, as explained, the cause itself devolves upon the judge *ad quem,* only after the reasons for the appeal have

---

[1] Schmalzg., l. c., n. 124.   [2] Schmalzg., l. 2, t. 28, n. 125.

been proved to exist and to be sufficient, by the appellant.[1]

1248. Hence, also, in judicial appeals the attentates are to be reversed by the judge *ad quem* before all else. The appellant is merely bound to prove to him (*a*) that a definitive sentence was passed; (*b*) that he appealed from it; (*c*) that attentates took place.[2] On the other hand, in the extrajudicial appeals in the case the attentates can be revoked by the judge of appeal only after he has decided that the appeal is reasonable, or after he has commanded the judge *a quo* to do nothing further in the case.[3]

1249. From this it is apparent that any innovation or change whatever, in regard to the status of the appellant, which is prejudicial to him is strictly forbidden by the law of the Church, and that in extrajudicial no less than judicial appeals. For the sacred canons expressly declare, that pending an appeal from an extrajudicial act or sentence (*pendente lite*), no less than pending an appeal proper,—*i.e.*, from a definitive sentence (*pendente appellatione*),—no change or innovation in the status of the appellant shall take place.[4] In this respect there is no difference between a judicial and an extrajudicial appeal. The difference consists simply in the manner in which attentates are revoked.

1250. We observe again, that extrajudicial appeals have the above effects as a general rule. For there are especially now, after the Council of Trent, a number of exceptions, as will be seen under Nos. 445, 446, 447, 448, where we show in what cases these appeals have at present only a devolutive, not a suspensive, effect.[5] Finally we remark, that what we have said concerning the effects of extrajudicial appeals

---

[1] Cap. Non solum 7, de App., in 6 (il. 15); Reiff., l. c., n. 260 sq.
[2] Reiff., l. c., n. 260. [3] Ib., n. 263
[4] L. Unic. ff. Nihil innovari appell. interposita. (xlix. 7).
[5] Cf. Giraldi, Expos. Jur. Pont. in l. 2, decr. sect. 308, p. 210 sq. Romae, 1829.

must be construed in the light of the remarks laid down under Nos. 1225, 1226, 1227.

1251. *Application of the above principles to the United States.*—The Instruction of the S. C. de Prop. Fide, *Cum Magnopere*, enacts that in appeals, with us, the rules laid down in the general law of the Church, as summed up by Pope Benedict XIV., in his constitution *Ad Militantis*, shall be observed in future. The words of the Instruction are: "In appellatione observentur normae expressae in Constit. Sa. Me. Benedicti XIV. *Ad Militantis* diei 30 Martii 1742, ac caeterae indictae a S. C. Episcoporum et RR. decreto diei 18 Decembris 1835, et epistola circulari diei 1 Aug. 1851."[1] This constitution points out the cases where it is allowed to appeal *in suspensivo*, or merely *in devolutive*, or only to have recourse to the Holy See. According to this constitution, appeals have a suspensive effect, when they are inter- posed (*a*) against final sentences; (*b*) or those which have the force of final sentences; (*c*) or against a gravamen which cannot be remedied by a final sentence.

However, when there is question of the appeal of a rec- tor deprived of his mission, the suspensive effect of the ap- peal has been modified by the *Third Plenary Council of Balti- more*, n. 286. Of course, devolutive appeals give the judge *ad quem* the right to admit and adjudicate the appeal; but they do not stay the execution of the sentence or decree of the judge *a quo*, pending the appeal.

---

[1] Instr. *Cum Magnopere*, Art. XXXVI.

CHAPTER IV.

OF EXTRAORDINARY CRIMINAL TRIALS IN ECCLESIASTICAL COURTS, ALSO IN THE UNITED STATES.

(De Processu Criminali Extraordinario.)

1252. By an extraordinary criminal trial or process we mean one where, by the disposition of canon law, it is not necessary to observe all the formalities of formal trials, as set forth in the preceding chapter. There are four kinds of extraordinary criminal trials approved by the sacred canons for ecclesiastical courts, namely, (*a*) The criminal trial for notorious crimes; (*b*) summary trials; (*c*) sentences *ex informata conscientia;* (*d*) trial for heresy. We shall now briefly describe each of these kinds of trials.

ART. I.

The Criminal Trial for Notorious Crimes (Processus Criminalis ex Notorio).

1253. A crime may be notorious in two ways: by fact and by law (we speak, of course, of the canon law). A crime is notorious by law (*notorietas juris*) when its notoriety arises from judicial proceedings. Thus it becomes notorious by law in these three ways: 1. By a judicial confession of guilt made by the accused spontaneously, and not through fear or force, nor revoked by him.[1] 2. By full and complete judicial proofs of guilt, provided that no proofs to the contrary are offered in evidence, and the case is closed.[2] 3. By

---

[1] Cap. Vestra 7, de Cohabit. cler. et mul. (iii.2); Ib., cap. 10.

[2] Cap. Cum olim 24, de V. S. (v. 40).

a condemnatory sentence, or a sentence declaratory of the crime, against which no appeal has been lodged, and which therefore has become *res judicata.*[1]

1254. A crime is notorious by fact (*notorietas facti*) not when it is simply public, or known to two or three or even five persons, but when it has been committed in the presence of the entire community, parish, college, town, village, etc., or at least the greater part or majority of such community, parish, etc., so that it cannot, in any way whatever, be concealed or denied.[2]

1255. We say, *not when it is simply public*, etc.; to understand this more fully, we shall briefly explain when a crime is occult, when public, and when notorious. A crime or act is occult, in the strict or proper sense of the word, when it cannot at all be established by legitimate proofs. Of crimes of this kind, the Church cannot take any cognizance whatever. To God alone belongs the right and power to punish them.[3] On the other hand, a crime is occult only in a large sense, namely, when it can be proved indeed, but only by the testimony of a few persons—*v.g.*, when it is known to two, three, or even five persons.[4] For even though a fact or crime is known to five persons, it is still occult, provided it is not made more public by being brought into court and discussed there. Crimes which are thus occult may also be, in fact are, called public, as we shall presently see.[5]

1256. *When a crime is public.*—A crime or act may be public in three ways: First, when it is only quasi-occult, as just described. This is the first degree of publicity. Secondly, when it can not only be proved, but is also known to many persons, so that there is fame or common report in regard to it. This is the second degree of publicity. Thirdly, when it is known in such a manner or so publicly that it can-

---

[1] Reiff., l. 5, t. 1, n. 246; Schmalzg., l. 5, t. 1, n. 1.   [2] Schmalzg., l. c., n. 2.
[3] Can. 11, Dist. 32.   [4] Can. 87, de Poenit., Dist. 1, § Haec ergo.
[5] Reiff., l. 5, t. 1, n. 243.

not, by any tergiversation or subterfuge whatever, be concealed or denied. This is the third and highest degree of
publicity, and is called notoriety.

1257. Now, before how many persons must a crime be
committed in order that it may be notorious? All canonists
agree that it must be known to and committed in the presence of at least six persons. For all canonists agree that a
crime is notorious only when it has been committed before
the greater number of the people composing a community.
Now the smallest community must have ten persons. A
community having a less number is no community at all.[1]
Therefore six persons constitute a majority of the smallest
possible community. Hence no crime is notorious unless
committed before at least six persons.

1258. But it is evident that a larger number is required
when the community, town, or city has more than ten persons, and where consequently six would not form a majority.
Yet it is also plain that where a place—town, village, city, or
community—is large and populous, containing several thou-
sands of people, it is not necessary that the crime should be
committed before the majority of all the inhabitants of such
place. What number, then, is required? Authors differ.
The judge seems the proper person to determine what number is sufficient in the case, considering all the circumstances.
However, it is to be observed that in the case, namely,
where the crime is committed in a large city, it is not necessary that it should be committed before the majority of the
whole city, but it is sufficient if it has been perpetrated in the
presence of the majority of the people of the immediate
neighborhood, parish, or college where it is notorious.[2]

1259. *Mode of procedure where an offence is notorious.*—
Where a crime is notorious, by notoriety of fact, the
judge (we speak always of the ecclesiastical judge) is not

---

[1] Ex can. Unio 3, C. 10, Q. 3.   [2] Reiff., l. c., n. 251.

bound to observe the ordinary formalities of ecclesiastical
criminal trials—*i.e.*, the *ordo judiciarius.* Thus the *Can. Pro-
hibentur* 14, C. 2, Q. 1, says: "Quae manifesta" (notoria)
"sunt, judiciarium ordinem non requirunt."[1]   The reason is
that the observance of the judicial forms has for its object
the ascertaining of the truth, where there is a doubt about
the guilt of the alleged offender.   Now, this object certainly
ceases to exist where the crime is notorious.[2]

1260. Consequently, when the crime is notorious, the judge
can pass sentence and inflict the proper penalty without any
previous trial whatever, so far as concerns the crime itself.
Hence it is not necessary to cite the accused for trial, to
examine witnesses, etc.   We say, *so far as concerns the crime
itself;* since the case is different with the notoriety of the
crime.   For while in notorious cases the crime itself need not
be proved,[3]—notoriety being the best proof,—yet its notoriety
must, like every other fact, be fully, clearly, and legitimately
established,[4] for instance, by the deposition of two unexceptionable witnesses,[5] who testify not only that they were themselves personally present when the crime was committed,
but also that they saw it committed in the presence of the
whole community, or at least the greater part of such community.[6]

1261. Moreover, before pronouncing the final sentence
the judge should pronounce a declaratory sentence—namely,
declaring that the crime is in reality notorious.   This latter
sentence may, however, be contained in the sentence of
condemnation, which may therefore read thus: Whereas X.
has been found notoriously guilty of the crime of drunken-
ness, we hereby condemn him to suspension for three
months.[7]

---

[1] Cf. can. 15, 16, 17, C. 2, Q. 1; cf. cap. 21, de Jurej. (ii. 24).

[2] Schmalzg., l. 5, t. 1, n. 7.   [3] Stremler, l. c., p. 81.

[4] Cap. 15, de Purg. can. (v. 34).   [5] Schmalzg., l. c., n. 16.

[6] Reiff., l. c., n. 264.   [7] Cf. Reiff., l. c., n. 264.

1262. Moreover, in order that the judge may have power to proceed without trial, the crime must be notorious, not only materially, but also formally—that is, it must be notorious not only that the crime was committed by the accused, but also that it was committed with malice, and that in such manner that in both these respects there can be no possible excuse or defence.[1] Whenever there is a doubt on any of these points, the judge must give the accused the benefit of the usual trial, and observe the prescribed judicial formalities.

1263. Accordingly, it is the advice of all canonists, that, even where the crime is notorious, both materially and formally, the judge will act wisely and prudently if he observes the usual formalities of judicial proceedings or trials—that is, if he gives the accused the benefit of the customary trial, just as in cases which are not notorious.[2] Hence the judge will do well to cite the accused for trial, hear his defences, etc.[3] For, as the sacred canons say: "Multa dicuntur notoria, quae non sunt."[4] It is, no doubt, owing to this that the law of the Church, as above explained, dispensing with trials in notorious cases, has now fallen into general desuetude, and that at present it is the universal practice of all ecclesiastical tribunals to observe the customary forms of trials in all notorious cases, even where the notoriety is clearly established. From this general custom, says Stremler,[5] it were temerity to depart.

1264. *Application of the above principles to the United States.*—What has been said above in regard to the mode of procedure in notorious cases, applies, of course, also in this country. Hence the bishop with us, where the crime is notorious, may *per se* inflict suspension and even dismissal from parish without any trial, having for its object the prov-

---

[1] Cap. fin., de Off. jud. del., in 6°; Stremler, l. c., p. 82; München, l. c., vol. I., p. 447, n. 3.

[2] Cf. Reiff., l. c., n. 265; Schmalzg., l. c., n. 16.   [3] Stremler, l. c., p. 82.

[4] Cap. 14, de App. (ii. 28).   [5] L. c., p. 82.

ing of the crime. We say, *per se ;* for, as we have seen, it is
at present, at least practically speaking, always necessary, in
view of the universal custom to that effect, to give an
accused who is notoriously guilty the benefit of the usual
trial.

Art. II.

*Of Summary Trials in Ecclesiastical Courts (Judicium Sum-
marium).*

1265. In canon law, a summary trial (*judicium summarium*)
is one in which the proceedings are conducted *simpliciter et
de plano ac sine strepitu et figura judicii.* To try summarily,
therefore, is the same as to proceed *simpliciter* and *sine figura
judicii.* But to proceed *sine figura judicii* is not to omit all
the formalities of ordinary or formal trials, but only some of
them, namely, certain accidental ones, which are expressly
mentioned in law—that is, in the *Clem. Saepe* 2, de V. S. (v. 11).

1266. A summary canonical trial may therefore be defined
that trial where, for the more speedy termination of causes
or trials, certain formalities specified in canon law, of ordinary or formal trials, may be and in fact are omitted.[1] We
say, *for the more speedy termination,* etc.; because the object
of summary trials is not to do away with the essential formalities of ordinary trials, but merely to cut short those
accidental formalities of formal trials which lead to numerous delays not only useless, but injurious. In a word, the
object of summary trials is simply to make the trial shorter
and less complicated, but not to abolish it. It may, therefore, be termed a simpler form of the ordinary trial.

1267. Hence, also, it would be a mistake to suppose that
in summary trials the proceedings may be less thorough,
less complete, or less exhaustive than in solemn or formal
trials. Much less should it be imagined that in such trials
the proofs can be less perfect or less full than in formal

[1] Bouix, de Jud., vol. ii., p. 306.

trials. No difference whatever exists in this respect between summary and formal trials.[1] Hence it may be said
that in summary trials only those accidental formalities are
omitted which unnecessarily lengthen the trial and cause
useless delays.[2]

1268. This shows also how summary trials differ from
trials in notorious causes, as explained in the preceding
article. For in trials *ex notorio* all the formalities of solemn
or ordinary trials may be dispensed with, save those which
regard the establishment of the notoriety and the citation
for the final sentence.[3] We see also how summary trials
differ from sentences *ex informata conscientia;* for in the
latter not only some, but all formalities whatever, of formal
or ordinary canonical trials, may be omitted, and they may
be wholly extrajudicial—that is, they may be pronounced
without any previous trial or judicial formality whatever.

1269. What then are the formalities of ordinary or solemn
trials that may be omitted in summary trials? It is allowed
to recede from these formalities only in the following particulars, which are expressly enumerated in the *Clem. Saepe* 2,
de V. S. (v. 11) : 1. No written charge or bill of complaint
(*libellus*) is necessary ; and the complaint may be made
orally, provided it be recorded on the minutes.[4] 2. Nor is
any formal arriving at issue, or *litis contestatio*, required.
Hence the judge, having duly cited the defendant, may forthwith on the day appointed in the citation proceed to the
taking of testimony in the case.[5] 3. The proceedings may
take place, not indeed on festivals of precept of the Church,
or on Sundays, but yet on holidays established for the benefit of the people. Such were formerly the harvest and vintage seasons in summer and fall;[6] such are at present, with

[1] München, l. c., vol. i., p. 336, n. 2.

[2] Schmalzg., l. 2, t. 1, n. 10.   [3] Cf. Schmalzg., l. 5, t. 1, n. 10.

[4] Clem. Saepe cit., § Verum quia; Ib. Glossa, v. Necessario.   [5] Ib.

[6] Ib.; cf. Ib. Glossa, v. Ob necessitates.

us, certain legal holidays, as election day, thanksgiving day, etc. 4. No peremptory citation to hear the final sentence need issue to the parties, a simple citation being sufficient. 5. The so-called *conclusio in causa* need not take place, and the final speeches or summing up by the parties or their advocates should be as short and concise as possible. 6. The judge in pronouncing final sentence need not be seated or sit solemnly in court, but may assume any proper posture he pleases—that is, he may either stand, walk up and down, etc.[1]

1270. Nothing, however, can be omitted in summary trials that is essential to judicial proceedings. Hence the following formalities of formal or ordinary canonical trials must be retained, as is expressly enacted in the *Clem. Saepe* 2, above quoted: 1. The proofs submitted by the plaintiff or prosecution in support of his case must be as full and complete as in formal canonical trials. 2. The right of defence remains unimpaired, and consequently the defendant should be given as full and free a power of defending himself as is allowed in formal trials. 3. The parties must be cited for trial. 4. The so-called articles and positions or specifications are retained as in ordinary trials. 5. Whatever petitions or proposals are made by the parties should be submitted by them, at least as far as possible, in the beginning of the trial, and should be at once spread on the minutes by the notary or secretary. 6. The witnesses must testify under oath.

1271. 7. As to exceptions and appeals, the same holds in summary as in ordinary or formal trials. For, although Pope Clement V., in his celebrated decretal *Saepe*, above quoted, which determines the formalities to be observed in summary trials, says that in these latter trials the judge should cut off exceptions, he expressly confines this to "exceptiones et appellationes *dilatorias et frustratorias*."[2] Hence

---

[1] Clem. Saepe cit. [2] Clem. Saepe 2, de V. S. (v. 11).

he forbids only such exceptions and appeals as are made maliciously and solely for the purpose of delaying and prolonging the trial and evading the ends of justice, as the *Glossa*[1] explains. Legitimate and reasonable exceptions and appeals are therefore allowed.

1272. Observe that in the cases where the trial may be summary the formalities prescribed for solemn or formal trials may nevertheless be observed in whole or in part, provided the parties or litigants consent. This is expressly stated in the above decretal *Saepe*.

1273. What causes chiefly can be tried in a summary manner? 1. All questions relating to appointments to parishes, benefices, and ecclesiastical offices in general—*v.g.*, all disputes concerning appointments; for instance, where an ecclesiastic contends that he should have received the appointment which he claims was unjustly given to another.[2] 2. All causes relating to elections to ecclesiastical offices; 3, or, to ecclesiastical tithes or contributions for the support of incumbents of ecclesiastical offices and benefices. 4. All matrimonial causes. Observe that in matrimonial causes of nullity, the Const. *Dei Miserat.* of Benedict XIV. must also be observed. 5. Finally, not only the above causes themselves, but also all other questions or causes which in any way touch upon them.

1274. These causes are expressly enumerated in the decretal *Clem. Dispendiosam* 2, de Judic. (ii. 1). Canonists commonly add the causes of persons who are poor, of orphans, widows, and the like; the causes of alimony, of spoliation; all causes of little importance; the causes of religious; those causes which on account of some imminent danger do not suffer delay. Besides, the Pope can order any cause whatever to be tried summarily.[3]

1275. Can criminal causes be tried in a summary man-

---

[1] Clem. Saepe, v. Dilatorias; Molitor. l. c., p. 194; Stremler, l. c., p. 162.

[2] Cf. cap. 8, in 6° (ii. 15); München, l. c., vol. i., p. 344; ib., p. 590, n. 2.

[3] Bouix, de Jud., vol. ii., p. 310.

ner? Apart from a special mandate of the Pope, the formalities of solemn or ordinary trials must always be observed in criminal causes, the summary trial being applicable only to civil causes of minor importance, and to the causes specified in the two decretals *Clem. Dispendiosam* and *Clem. Saepe*, above quoted.[1]

1276. That the Holy See has the power to permit criminal causes to be tried summarily, there can be no doubt. In fact, we have an instance of the exercise of this power in our very midst. For the mode of trying criminal and disciplinary causes of ecclesiastics, as ordained by the S. C. de P. F., on July 20, 1878, as also the similar mode of proceeding in dismissing permanent rectors in England, partakes of the nature of a canonical summary process or trial. We say, "partakes of the nature," not "is a canonical summary trial." For this mode of procedure differs in several particulars from canonical summary trials as above described. Thus, among other things, the formal positions or articles (*positiones, articuli*) retained in summary canonical trials are omitted in the above trials; nor do witnesses depose under oath, as they must do in summary canonical trials.

1277. Another instance is the recent Instruction of the S. C. Ep. et Reg., dated June 11, 1880, which lays down a new mode of procedure, or of conducting trials, in disciplinary and criminal causes of ecclesiastics, for those countries where canon law obtains, and which consequently are not subject to the Propaganda. The object of this Instruction is to enable bishops or ecclesiastical courts in countries not missionary, and therefore not subject to the Propaganda, to proceed in a more economical or simple manner—that is, to dispense with certain non-essential formalities of formal or solemn canonical trials—in the hearing and deciding of disciplinary and criminal causes of ecclesiastics, whenever.

[1] Stremler, l. c., p. 163; Craiss., Man., n. 6009.

owing to the condition of the Church at the present day, especially so far as concerns her relations with the secular power, it is found impossible or inexpedient to observe all the formalities of solemn canonical trials.

1278. We have just said, *whenever, owing to the condition,* etc.; for this Instruction expressly provides that wherever the formalities of solemn or ordinary trials can be freely and effectively observed, they must be observed; that only in cases where it is either impossible or inexpedient can bishops or other ecclesiastical courts proceed in the simpler and more economic manner therein laid down. Note also that bishops are simply authorized, but not obliged to proceed in this simpler form. Finally, it is to be observed that the trial, as prescribed in this Instruction, retains substantially all the formalities of solemn or ordinary canonical trials, and omits only certain non-essential forms which tend merely to prolong and delay the proceedings without any necessity, and substitutes in their place others more practical and better adapted to the wants of our time. A third instance is the Instruction *Cum Magnopere* issued by the S. C. de Prop. Fide, in 1884, for the United States. This document, which is almost an exact copy of the Instruction of 1880, prescribes the summary trial in criminal causes.

ART. III.

Sentences "ex informata conscientia," as in force also in the United States.

1279. Prior to the Council of Trent no ecclesiastic could be punished by his bishop,—*v.g.,* suspended from the exercise of orders already received, or forbidden to ascend to higher orders,—*save upon a regular or formal criminal trial, as prescribed by the sacred canons.* Hence no occult crime, in the proper sense of the word,—that is, no crime which was not provable,—could be, properly speaking, punished, no matter how enormous it was ; for the simple reason that the fact of its being occult precluded the possibility of its being proved juridically, or by such juridical proofs as are required for conviction in a formal canonical trial.

1280. This was the general law of the Church prior to the Council of Trent, and admitted of no exceptions whatever, save in the case of murder,[1] heresy, and regulars who could be forbidden by their religious superiors to ascend to higher orders, even for occult crimes, and without any trial.[2] We say, *regulars ;* for the law of the Church then in force—namely, the cap. *Ad Aures*, just quoted—clearly shows, and the common opinion of canonists (from which only a few dissent) is, that the exception did not extend to seculars, but was binding solely on regulars.[3]

1281. That the law in question was the general law of the Church before the Council of Trent is clearly expressed in the decretal *Ex Tenore*,[4] made by Pope Alexander III., in the year 1170, and the decretal *Quaesitum*, enacted by Pope Gregory IX., in 1229, and is, moreover, admitted by all canonists. Thus Stremler says : " Before the Council of Trent a bishop could not repel any unworthy candidate from holy orders, nor punish a delinquent ecclesiastic, save upon a formal or an ordinary criminal trial, as established by the law of the Church and contained in the decretals. . . . No crime could be punished, except when the delinquent had been juridically convicted, in a canonical trial conducted with the formalities established by canon law for proceedings in criminal causes."[5]

1282. The Council of Trent, in its 14th session, chapter i., de Ref., introduced in this respect a radical and complete change in the discipline of the Church as it had existed down to that time. For it enacted in that session, that in

---

[1] Cap. 17 (i. xi.).
[2] Bouix. de Jud., vol. ii., p. 317.
[3] Stremler, Des Peines Eccl., p. 310.
[4] Cap. Ad aures 5 (i. xi.).
[5] Cap. 4. de Temp. ord. (i. xi.).

certain cases bishops could inflict punishment upon their delinquent ecclesiastics without any previous trial whatever, or judicial formalities, not even those prescribed for summary trials. That this power, totally unknown, nay, unheard of, before the Council of Trent, is a very great, nay, an extraordinary, power, is admitted by all canonists. For, as we have seen, the right of self-defence is guaranteed to every accused by the very law of nature, and therefore cannot be taken away even by the Church or its head, the Supreme Pontiff.

1283. Now bishops, in virtue of the above Tridentine law, can in certain cases condemn an accused ecclesiastic without giving him any opportunity of defending himself. But it must be borne in mind that this power was given bishops only for exceptional and extraordinary cases, where the common good of the faithful required its exercise. Moreover, the right of self-defence is not taken away altogether by the above power. For the ecclesiastic who may happen to be punished *ex informata conscientia*, or without trial, can have recourse to the Holy See, where he will have the right to defend himself. Besides, as we shall see, this extraordinary power of bishops is hedged in on all sides by so many restrictions and safeguards, that the danger of its being abused is, comparatively speaking, remote. Finally, its abuse, if any exists, will bring its own correction with itself. For the Holy See has of late shown its unmistakable intention of not allowing the power to proceed *ex informata conscientia* to be extended beyond certain restricted limits.

1284. Bouix notes that the question, whether at present, considering the abuses that may have occurred in the exercise of this power, or the condition of our times, which frowns down upon anything which has even the appearance of restricting the rights of defendants, it were proper to do away altogether with the power to proceed *ex inf. consc.*, may lawfully be disputed by any Catholic, provided he does so with due submission for the authority of the Holy See.[1] That our times are no longer the same as those when the Council of Trent enacted the decree in question, seems beyond doubt. The moral depravity among no small number of the clergy in the days of the Council of Trent certainly warranted such an extreme remedy as the power conferred on bishops in its 14th session, chapter i., de Ref. At the present day this reason cannot be said to exist any longer. Moreover, the unfavorable impression which is created among non-Catholics, even by the appearance of an arbitrary procedure on the part of ecclesiastical prelates, would certainly make it advisable, especially in non-Catholic countries, for superiors to make use of this power only rarely.

1285. However, as a vindication of this power, we may be permitted to say that even civil governments have recourse at times, when an extraordinary condition of affairs requires it, to a similar power—namely, to the suspension of the *habeas corpus* act.

1286. *Nature and extent of the power of bishops to proceed "ex informata conscientia."*—How far does the power given bishops by the Council of Trent to proceed against delinquent ecclesiastics *ex informata conscientia*, or without any previous trial, extend? In other words, what kind of punishment can bishops inflict *ex informata conscientia?* Only these two penalties: 1. The prohibition to ascend to or receive sacred orders; 2, the suspension from orders already received, and also from ecclesiastical degrees or offices, and dignities or honors. That only these and no other punishments can be imposed *ex informata conscientia*, is beyond doubt, and plainly manifest from the Council of Trent, chapter i., sess. 14, which forms the foundation and is the parent of the power to proceed *ex informata conscientia.*

1287. Now, suspension from orders (*suspensio ab ordine*)

---

[1] Bouix, l. c., p. 364.

and ecclesiastical degrees and dignities is not the same as suspension from benefice (*suspensio a beneficio*),—*i.e.*, suspension from receiving and administering the income of one's benefice or office,—much less deprivation or dismissal (*privatio beneficii*) from one's benefice, ecclesiastical office, or parish. Hence bishops, also in the United States, can, *ex informata conscientia*, or without a previous trial, suspend ecclesiastics only from the exercise of the acts of the *ordo* already received, but not, at least directly, from administering or receiving the income of their parish, benefice, or office; and *a fortiori* they cannot, even with us, *ex informata conscientia* impose dismissal from benefice, parish, or office.[1] The reason is that penal laws, such as the chapter i., of sess. 14, of the Council of Trent, in question, must be strictly construed. In other words, they must be construed to impose only those penalties which are expressly and clearly mentioned. Now, the above Tridentine law does not say one word about suspension *a beneficio*. Neither suspension, therefore, nor dismissal from benefice can, even with us, be inflicted *ex informata conscientia*.[2]

1288. We said under the preceding number, *but not, at least directly*, etc. ; for an ecclesiastic suspended *ex informata conscientia* must provide the ecclesiastic who takes his place while he remains suspended with a suitable income or maintenance, the amount of which is determined by the bishop. Hence an ecclesiastic suspended *ex informata conscientia* is by this suspension deprived indirectly of part of his income or salary.[3]

1289. As the bishop has no power to punish regulars, save in certain cases, his power to proceed *ex informata conscientia* extends only to secular ecclesiastics, but not, generally speaking, to regulars. We say, *generally speaking;* for there are some exceptions. Thus the bishop, also in the United

---

[1] Our Counter-Points, n.62.
[2] Stremler, l. c., p. 314; cf. Bouix, l. c., p. 357.   [3] Ib.

States, can suspend regulars *ex informata conscientia*, and without informing them of the cause or reasons therefor, from the hearing of confessions, for a new supervening cause or reason, which concerns confessions,—*ex nova superveniente causa, confessiones concernente*,—and that even when these regulars have been approved by him for confessions without any limit of time.[1]

1290. Speaking of regulars, we observe here in passing, though this is hardly the proper place for it, that regulars, with us, who are in charge of parishes or congregations can be removed by the bishop from the parish for unfitness,—*v.g.*, illiteracy, or for crime,—not indeed *ex informata conscientia*, but yet without the trial prescribed in the Instructions of the S. C. de P. F. of July 20, 1878, and of 1884—these Instructions being only for secular ecclesiastics—or without any other trial or judicial proceedings. Nor is he bound to consult with the regular superior in doing so ; and, *vice versâ*, the religious superior can do the same without consulting the bishop.[2] Observe, moreover, that the power to proceed *ex informata conscientia* belongs also to regular prelates, so far as their subjects are concerned. Hence the Council of Trent increased the power of regular prelates in this respect. For before that Council they could only prohibit the ascent to sacred orders ; whereas now they can also suspend from orders already received, *ex informata conscientia*.

1291. The above teaching regarding the power of bishops to proceed *ex informata conscientia* applies also to the United States. Thus, first, it is certain that the power to proceed *ex informata conscientia* or without trial was not taken away from our bishops by the Instruction of the Propaganda dated July 20, 1878, or by the later Instruction *Cum Magnopere*. This is expressly stated in Art. IX. of the Instr. *Cum*

[1] Clem. X. Const. Superna, 21 Junii, 1670, § Et eos ; Giraldi, Expos. Jur. Pont., Pars ii., sect. 43.

[2] Supra, n. 256 ; Giraldi, l. c.

Magnopere, and in the answer of the S. C. de Prop. Fide, *Ad Dubia.*[1] Secondly, with us, as elsewhere, only two kinds of penalties can be inflicted *ex informata conscientia*—namely, 1, the prohibition to receive higher orders; 2, suspension from the *ordo* already received, and also from ecclesiastical degrees and dignities, but not *a beneficio*, as already explained. Dismissal, therefore, from parish, or excommunication, or interdict, or other ecclesiastical penalties or grave disciplinary corrections, such as remaining in some monastery for a time, can be inflicted with us, at present, only upon a previous trial as ordained by the Instruction *Cum Magnopere* of 1884, or by the Instruction of July 20, 1878, where the latter is still in force.[2]

1292. *Q.* For what kind of crimes can the bishop impose suspension *ex informata conscientia*, or without trial?

A. We premise: Bishops can inflict suspension *ex informata conscientia* only for crime,—*i.e.*, only upon ecclesiastics who are guilty of crime,—and not for other causes. To understand this better, we remark that the bishop may suspend an ecclesiastic from the exercise of his *ordo*, not only for crime, but also for incapacity or unfitness, and illiteracy or want of learning.[3] Now, in the latter case the bishop cannot impose suspension *ex informata conscientia*, or in virtue of the cap. i., sess. xiv., C. Trid., de Ref., so that no appeal can be taken by the person thus censured. For the S. C. C.[4] has expressly declared that from such a suspension it is allowed, not only to have recourse to the Holy See, as in the cases of suspension *ex informata conscientia*, but to appeal in the proper sense of the word, though only *ad effectum devolutivum*, and not *suspensivum*.[5]

1293. We now answer: It is certain that the bishop can impose suspension *ex informata conscientia*—that is, without any trial whatever, and in such manner as to cut off the right

---

[1] Ad Dubia, § iv. Per Instructionem. [2] Cf. Ad Dubia, § i.
[3] C. Trid., sess. 14, c. 3, de Ref. [4] In Calaguritana, 10 Maii, 1625.
[5] Giraldi, l. c.; ib., sect. xlv.; Bouix, l. c., p. 342.

of appeal proper—when the crime is occult. This is expressly stated in the Council of Trent.[1] Can he also do so when the crime is public? Bouix[2] maintains the affirmative, though he admits that the contrary is held in Rome, and adds, moreover, that it were unlawful for a bishop to impose suspension *ex informata conscientia* for a public crime, except for sufficient reasons—that is, except where the ordinary mode of procedure cannot be observed without great injury to the public or common good of the Church or faithful.[3]

1294. The negative, however, is the common opinion of canonists, is the one followed in Rome by the sacred congregations, and held there by canonists, and is therefore the more correct, nay, at present the only true and safe, opinion. That this is the opinion held by the Roman canonists, Bouix himself clearly states.[4] He says that the Roman canonists hold that, when the crime is public, the bishop cannot proceed *ex informata conscientia*, but must observe the ordinary forms of judicial procedure ; that the opinion holding the contrary is not only not probable, but is clearly against the meaning and object of the Tridentine decree, cap. i., sess. xiv., de Ref.

1295. That this opinion—namely, the negative—is, moreover, the one followed by the sacred congregations in Rome, especially at the present day, there can be no doubt. · We will give only a few decisions. The first is the decision of the S. C. C. *in S. Agathae Gothorum*, Feb. 26, 1853. The case decided is as follows: On the 13th of October, 1851, the bishop of the diocese of St. Agatha of the Goths, situate in the kingdom (formerly so called) of Naples, for "causes known to himself," suspended the archpriest, Peter D'Ambrose, *ex informata conscientia*, from the archipresbyteral dignity, the canonship, the care of souls, and the exercise of

---

[1] Sess. 14, cap. i., de Ref. [3] De Jud. Eccl., vol. ii., pp. 325, 329 sq.
[2] Bouix, l. c., pp. 343, 344. [4] Ib., p. 325.

sacred orders, for an indefinite period of time. The case was brought before the Holy See—namely, the S. C. C. D'Ambrose, or rather his advocate, impugned the validity of the censure or episcopal sentence, 1, because the alleged crime in question was not occult, but public; 2, because the censure was inflicted without any limit of time.

1296. The case, after having been argued on both sides, was formally proposed to the S. C. C. in the following manner: "An constet de validitate suspensionis in casu?" The answer or decision, as given on the 26th of February, 1853, was: "Negative, salvo jure episcopo procedendi prout de jure."[1] From this decision, then, it is evident that the bishop cannot inflict sentence *ex informata conscientia* when the crime is public, nor for an indefinite period of time, or *in perpetuum;* that, if he does so, his sentence is not only illicit and unjust, but null and void, and therefore its violation does not produce irregularity.

1297. We come now to another decision, which is of very recent date—namely, that given by the S. C. C. on Dec. 20, 1873, *in Bosnien. et Sirmien.* This decision is of the greatest weight, owing to the fact that the S. C. Ep. et Reg. itself, in its Instruction of June 11, 1880, concerning the new mode of procedure in criminal and disciplinary causes of ecclesiastics, for ecclesiastical courts or curias in countries where canon law fully obtains, refers to it by name, and lays it down officially as the rule for future cases.

1298. The case decided is as follows: On Sept. 11, 1872, a certain bishop (neither the name of the bishop, nor of the priest, nor of the diocese is mentioned) inflicted *ex informata conscientia* suspension upon a certain parish priest of his diocese. The latter had recourse to the Holy See—namely, the S. C. C. His advocate impugned the validity of the bishop's decree *ex informata conscientia*, chiefly, 1, because

[1] Ap. Acta S. Sedis, vol. vii., p. 574; Stremler, l. c., pp. 320. 639.

the alleged crime for which his client had been thus suspended was public, whereas the Council of Trent, sess. xiv.,
chapter 1, authorized such suspension only for occult crimes:
2, because the suspension was for an indefinite period of
time, whereas the S. C. C. does not allow, especially in more
recent times, suspensions *ex informata conscientia* to be in
flicted *in perpetuum* or for an indefinite period, save upon due
trial, as prescribed by the Council of Trent, sess. xxi., chapter 6, de Ref.

1299. The S. C. C., having taken cognizance of the cause,
on Dec. 20, 1873, decided as follows: "Decretum ex informata conscientia in casu non obstare quominus procedatur
in causa appellationis prout, et quatenus et coram quo de
jure." To understand this decision more fully, it is necessary to remark, that prior to the issuing of the decree *ex
informata conscientia* by the bishop, on Sept. 11, 1872, the
bishop's court or consistory (*consistorium episcopale*) had,
on July 4, 1872, given the priest in question a trial, and pronounced sentence against him. From this sentence the priest
appealed to the metropolitan within ten days. Hereupon
the bishop, foreseeing a lengthy litigation, and resolving to
suppress any scandal that might follow from such litigation,
issued the above suspension *ex informata conscientia*, so that
the priest might not be able to prosecute his appeal before
the metropolitan, since there is no appeal against sentences
ex informata conscientia.

1300. The S. C. C., however, decided, as we have seen,
that the bishop's sentence *ex informata conscientia* did not
cut off the appeal. Hence we infer, 1, that by direct implication the Holy See decided that the bishop's sentence in
the case was null and void; otherwise it would certainly
have been a valid obstacle or hindrance to the appeal.
2. We infer, moreover, that the bishop's sentence was invalid
(*a*) because the crime in the case was public; (*b*) because the
suspension in the case was for an indefinite period of time.

What makes these inferences, especially the one concerning the occult crime, perfectly certain, is the decision, above quoted, of the S. C. Ep. et Reg , given seven years afterwards—namely, on the 11th of June, 1880. In this latter decision, or rather Instruction, the S. C. Ep. et Reg. expressly refers to the above case and its decision, and declares that the rules and restrictions with regard to the exercise of the power to proceed *ex informata conscientia* as embodied in said decision and constantly followed by the S. C. C., shall serve as a rule for future cases.

1301. Lest, however, any doubt might remain in the matter, the S. C. Ep et Reg., in the same Instruction, expressly declares that suspension *ex informata conscientia* can be inflicted only for occult crimes. The words of the S. C. Ep et Reg. are : " Plenam quoque vim servat suam extrajudiciale remedium ex informata conscientia, PRO CRIMINIBUS OCCULTIS, quod decrevit S. Tridentina Synodus in ˋsess. 14, cap. 1, de Reform. adhibendum, cum illis regulis et reservationibus, quas constanter servavit pro dicti capitis interpretatione S. C. Congregatio in pluribus resolutionibus, et praesertim in Bosnien. et Sirmien., 20 Decembris, 1873." [1] This last decision in Bosn. et Sirm., here referred to, is the one just explained. Here, then, we have a clear and undoubted decision or declaration that the decree of the Council of Trent, chapter 1, sess. xiv., does not extend to public crimes.

1302. Finally, a decision given by the S. C. C. more recently still—namely, on Sept. 11, 1880—confirms the above. The case decided was this : A certain parish priest, who had made himself very odious to his people and the civil authorities, by his alleged avarice and hasty temper, was first repeatedly warned by his bishop, and finally, when the admonitions proved of no avail, suspended *ex inf. consc.* from his parochial office—" ab officio parochiali." He had recourse to

---

[1] Instr. S. C. Ep. et Reg., 11 Junii, 1873.

Rome, and impugned the bishop's sentence *ex inf. consc.* chiefly on the ground that it was inflicted for alleged crimes or acts which were not occult, but public. The decision of the S. C. C. reversed the bishop's decree, but still authorized him to proceed against the accused *ad formam juris—i.e.*, by a regular trial. The sacred congregation thereby showed that it considered the charges against the accused to be of a grave character, but yet condemned the mode of procedure *ex inf. consc.*, as the crime was not occult, but public, and therefore punishable in the ordinary way—*i.e.*, by a proper trial.'

1303. Lastly, that the negative, or opinion which maintains that bishops can proceed *ex informata conscientia* only in occult crimes, but not in public, is the common opinion of canonists, is equally certain. It is held by Barbosa,' Pirhing, Monacelli,' Pignatelli, Benedict XIV., Lucidi, and a number of others.' Space permits us to quote but one or two of them. Pope Benedict XIV., having given the Tridentine decree in question,' thus argues : " Ex quibus verbis colligitur, posse episcopum, OB OCCULTUM CRIMEN, etiam etra judicialiter cog. nitum . . . a suscepti jam ordinis ministerio eosdem" (clericos) " interdicere." ' In his Const. *Ad Militantis,* Apr. 1, 1742, he states that, among other cases, there is no appeal " adversus suspensionem ab ordinibus jam susceptis, OB OCCULTUM CRIMEN, sive ex informata conscientia, juxta dispositionem Sacri Concilii, sessione 14, de Reform., cap. 1." Here, as the advocate in the above *causa Bosn. et Sirm.* says, Benedict XIV. uses the phrases *ob occultum crimen* and *ex informata conscientia* as meaning the same thing.' Wherefore, according to him, to proceed for occult crimes is the same as to proceed *ex informata conscientia.*

1304. Lucidi,' having stated that the bishop can impose

---

¹ Ap. Acta S. Sedis, vol. xiv., p. 292.   ⁵ Ius Can. l. 1, in cap. Ad aures, n. 4.
² Form., tom. i., tit. 13, n. 29.   ⁴ Ap. Acta S. Sedis, vol. vii., p. 573.
³ Sess. 14, c. i., de Ref.   ⁶ De Syn. Dioec., l. 12, c. 8, n. 3.
⁷ Ap. Acta S. Sedis, vol. vii., p. 573.   ⁸ De Visit. SS. LL., vol. i., p. 386, n. 269.

suspension for occult crimes, and explained when a crime is considered occult,[1] when public, continues as follows : " Cavere tamen quisque debet episcopus, ne, quod publicum et notorium jam est, perinde ac esset occultum, falso sibi animo reputans suspensionem *ex informata conscientia* decernat ; hujusmodi enim decretum minime substineretur, prout evenit in *S. Agat. Gothorum,* 26 Febr., 1853."[2] From what has been said, it is plain that, according to the common opinion of canonists, sentences *ex informata conscientia,* when imposed for public crimes, are illicit, nay invalid, at least in the sense that they will be declared invalid by the S. C. C upon recourse to it. We say, *at least in the sense ;* for some canonists hold that they are *ipso facto* or *ipso jure* invalid.[3]

1305. That the power to proceed *ex informata conscientia* does not extend to public cases or crimes, seems manifest from the Council of Trent itself. For this Council, while on the one hand, in its 14th session, chapter 1, allowing of sentences *ex informata conscientia* or without any trial, on the other re-enacts and confirms, in session 24, chapter 5, the decretal of Pope Innocent III., *Qualiter et quando* 24 x, de Accus. (v. 1). Now, this latter decretal wholly excludes sentences *ex informata conscientia,* and prescribes that superiors shall in no case whatever punish their subjects, except upon a regular canonical trial. But if the Council of Trent, in its 14th session, chapter 1, de Ref., had authorized bishops to proceed *ex informata conscientia,* even where the crime was public, it would virtually have abolished ecclesiastical trials altogether, and therefore would have clearly contradicted itself.

1306. It is therefore manifest that the Council of Trent allows of sentences *ex informata conscientia,* or procedure without trial, only in rare, exceptional, and extraordinary cases[4]—namely, in occult cases, and even then, only when

---

[1] De Visit. SS. LL., vol. i., p. 387, n. 272.   [2] Ib., n. 273.
[3] Cf. Stremler, l. c., p. 319; cf. Praelectiones S. Sulpit., vol. iii., n. 692.
[4] Bouix, l. c., p. 343.

there is sufficient reason for it ; that as in the past, so in the future, the ordinary and regular mode of procedure shall be by canonical trial.[1] This is also apparent from the scope which the Council of Trent had in view in enacting its celebrated cap. *Cum honestius.* The Council did not wish to abolish, but simply to supply the defects of, trials as then in use. Now the defect was, that in occult cases there could be no trial, and consequently no punishment. Hence the Council simply intended to supply a means for punishing even occult crimes.

1307. How exceptionally and rarely the power to proceed *ex informata conscientia* should be used, also in the United States, the S. C. de Prop. Fide thus teaches, in its answer to the questions proposed by bishops of this country relative to the Instruction of July 20, 1878 : " Per Instructionem sublata non est episcopis *extraordinaria facultas* procedendi ad suspensionem ex informata conscientia, quatenus *gravissimas et canonicas causas* concurrere in Domino judicaverint, aut *gravi et urgenti necessitate,* pro salute animarum, etiam non audito Consilio, remedio aliquo providendum esse censuerint."[2]

1308. This declaration also points out plainly the nature and quality of the crimes for which suspension *ex inf. consc.* can be inflicted. First, the crime should be very grave ; this is expressed in the above passage by the words *causae gravissimae.* It should not be simply an offence of a passing character, and committed through mere frailty ; it should be such as to warrant the belief that the offender will remain addicted to it, unless punished. Secondly, that it should be occult is indicated by the words *canonicae causae.* Thirdly, it should, moreover, be injurious to the spiritual welfare of the faithful. If it were injurious only to its author, it could not be punished *ex informata conscientia.* This is also ex-

---

[1] Cf. Stremler, l. c., p. 317.   [2] Ad Dubia, § iv., Per Instructionem.

pressed in the above declaration by the words "aut gravi," etc. Fourthly, suspension *ex informata conscientia* should be resorted to only when there is no other means of remedying the evil.[1]

1309. What is here meant by an occult crime? We have already seen that a crime may be occult (*a*) in a strict sense —namely, when it cannot be juridically proved, *v.g.*, when there is but one witness; and in a wide sense—namely, when it can be juridically proved indeed, but is not known to more than two or three, or at most five persons.[2] Now, some canonists seem to mean by occult crimes for which suspension can be imposed *ex informata conscientia*, only those which are strictly occult; others, those which are occult merely in a large sense. Lucidi[3] very well says, that in a particular case the bishop is the proper judge as to whether the crime is occult or not, provided, however, he contains himself within the limits of what makes a crime occult.

1310. *Manner of inflicting sentences ex informata conscientia.* —In proceeding *ex informata conscientia* the bishop can proceed, to use the words of the Council of Trent, *quomodolibet, etiam extrajudicialiter*—that is, he is not bound to observe any judicial formalities whatever, whether of formal or summary trials. In other words, the bishop is not obliged to give the supposed delinquent the benefit of a trial, whether solemn or only summary. A suspension imposed *ex inf. consc.* is therefore the same as a suspension inflicted without any judicial proceedings, for an occult crime, which is known to the bishop, with certainty indeed, but extrajudicially;[4] from which suspension, moreover, there is no appeal, but only a recourse to the Pope.

1311. Hence the bishop need not inform the delinquent of the charges made against him, nor admonish him beforehand (*monitio canonica*), nor cite him for trial, nor hear his de-

[1] Stremler, l. c., p. 324. [2] Supra, n. 1255.
[3] De Visit. SS. LL., vol. i., p. 387, n. 272. [4] Stremler, l. c., p. 325.

fence or give him any opportunity of defending himself.   In
the sentence itself, the bishop need not state the cause or
crime for which he inflicts the suspension.   We said above,[1]
the bishop is not bound, etc. ; for he may, if he wishes, according to Bouix,[2] observe in whole or in part the judicial formalities, whether of formal or summary trials, provided he
states in the sentence that he acts by and in virtue of the
1st chapter of the 14th session of the Council of Trent, on
Reformation.   This opinion of Bouix is in harmony with his
teaching that the bishop can proceed *ex informata conscientia*
even in public crimes.   But, as we have seen, this teaching
is scarcely any longer tenable.   The bishop, therefore, must
take care not to make use of any act or judicial formalities
by which the crime will become public.   Hence if his tribunal is composed of several assessors, such as the members of
Commissions of Investigation in the United States, it would
seem at least doubtful whether he can allow the cause to be
tried by it, as by this very fact the crime would seem to become public—*i.e.*, known to more than five persons.

1312. In any case, however, the bishop will act prudently
if, wherever circumstances will allow, he will privately or
informally call the delinquent, make known to him the
charges, and hear his explanations or defence.   However,
says Stremler,[3] in the sentence itself of suspension he should
not mention this ; but should confine himself to saying that,
for causes of which he is certain, he declares N. suspended,
in virtue of the power conferred upon bishops by the Council of Trent, sess. xiv., chapter 1, de Ref.   This mention of
the Council of Trent is absolutely necessary, so that the
delinquent may be able to judge of the nature of the punishment inflicted upon him, and regulate his appeal, or rather
recourse, accordingly.[4]

---

[1] Supra, n. 1310.

[2] L. c., p. 325.

[3] L. c., p. 339.

[4] Stremler, l. c., p. 325.

1313. We subjoin from Monacelli[1] the formula for suspension *ex informata conscientia:* "Constito nobis, presbyterum N. esse reum criminis, eum ob causas quae animum nostrum digne movent, et de quibus Deo et Sedi Apostolicae, cum habuerimus in mandatis, rationem reddere debemus, et ex informata conscientia, a divinis suspendimus per sex" (tres) "menses, et suspensum declaramus, ac ei decretum suspensionis intimari mandamus.

" N. Episcopus N.,

" *N. Actuarius.*"

1314. However, from the fact that the bishop, in proceeding *ex informata conscientia*, need not give the accused any trial whatever, or observe any judicial formalities, it does not follow that he need have no certainty, and consequently no sufficient and conclusive proofs, of the crime or culpability of the person he wishes thus to suspend. For it is beyond doubt that the bishop must be perfectly certain of the guilt of the party; otherwise he would sin against the very law of nature, which forbids an innocent person, or one who is probably innocent, to be condemned. It merely follows that the proofs need not be juridical—*i.e.*, obtained in a canonical trial (with us, in a trial before the Commission of Investigation). While, therefore, the proofs in the case need not be juridical, they must, nevertheless, be sufficient to prove the guilt; in other words, they must be such as will establish with certainty and beyond any reasonable doubt the guilt of the accused, and that not only in the mind of the bishop, but also of the Holy See, in case recourse is had to it by the suspended ecclesiastic.

1315. Hence, as Bouix[2] says, the proofs should be such that, if alleged or produced in a regular trial, they would juridically prove the guilt. Otherwise, the suspension will not be sustained by the Holy See.[3] Hence the bishop should

[1] Formul. Leg. Pract., Pars 3, art. 2, form. 6, annot. 4, vol. iii., p. 205. Romae, 1844. [2] L. c., p. 348 [3] Stremler, l. c., p. 326.

not inflict suspension *ex informata conscientia—v.g.*, against Titius, even though the latter has privately and without witnesses confessed his crime to the bishop; or even where the bishop has with his own eyes seen Titius committing the crime, or even though he has the unequivocal testimony of one witness who is above all suspicion. The reason is, that these proofs are indeed sufficient to convince the bishop personally, but they are not ample enough to convince the Holy See.[1]

1316. *Q.* For what length of time can suspensions *ex informata conscientia* be inflicted ?

A. It seems certain, according to the *sententia communissima* of canonists, that at the present day they cannot be imposed *in perpetuum,* nor even for an indefinite period.[2] We say, *at the present day ;* for formerly—that is, prior to the year 1777—the Holy See—namely, the S. C. C.—seems to have held, at least in the opinion of some canonists, that suspensions could be inflicted *ex informata conscientia,* not only temporarily, but also *in perpetuum.*[3] But the Holy See or the S. C. C. has receded from this view, and now constantly follows the opposite in its decisions.[4] In fact, whatever Bouix may say to the contrary, the decisions given by the Holy See or the S. C. C. since the year 1777, as construed by Lucidi,[5] Stremler,[6] the author of the " Praelectiones Juris Can. hab. in Sem. S. Sulpitii,"[7] and other eminent canonists, clearly show that it (the Holy See) does not recognize in bishops any power to impose suspension *ex informata conscientia* " in perpetuum," or even for an indefinite period.[8]

[1] Stremler, l. c.

[2] Ib., p. 328; Lucidi, l. c., vol. i., p. 385, n. 267; Praelectiones in Sem. S. Sulp., tom. 3, n. 691, p. 97.

[3] S. C. C., 14 Julii, 1583, ap. Giraldi, Epos. Jur. Pont., Pars ii., sect. 43, p. 848. Romae, 1829.   [4] S. C. C. in caus. Lucion., 8 Apr., 1848.

[5] De Visit. SS. LL., vol. i., p. 385, n. 267. [6] L. c., p. 329. [7] Vol. iii., p. 97, n. 691.

[8] S. C. C. in caus. S. Severin., 4 Apr., 1778; in Placentina, 26 Febr., 1848; in S. Ag. Goth., 26 Feb., 1853; in Bosn. et Sirm., 20 Dec., 1873.

The reason is, that such a suspension would be practically the same as deprivation or absolute dismissal from one's office or benefice, which cannot be inflicted save upon the requisite previous warnings, and moreover a due trial, as prescribed by the Council of Trent, sess. 21, chapter 6, de Ref.[1]

1317. It seems, therefore, certain, notwithstanding Bouix's[2] opinion to the contrary, that bishops can inflict suspension *ex informata conscientia* only for a certain period of time or until the delinquent manifests sufficient signs of amendment, not *in perpetuum* or for an indefinite period. Now, for what length of time can such suspension be imposed? Stremler[3] says that no general rule can be laid down; that, however, two or three months is already a long time, and that the suspension should rarely last longer; that to allow such suspension to last more than six months, very exceptional circumstances, which can happen but very seldom, should exist.

1318. What becomes of such suspensions if the bishop who has inflicted them dies, resigns his see, or is transferred to another see? As these suspensions, unlike regular or ordinary ecclesiastical penalties, are inflicted, so to say, " per modum praecepti particularis," and not " per modum legis," they cease of themselves, and without any further formality, at the death of the bishop. For a particular precept ceases when its author dies. On the other hand, punishments which are inflicted upon due trial and the observance of judicial formalities are imposed, so to say, " per modum legis," and therefore continue in force even after the death of the judge from whom they have emanated.[4] Whether suspensions inflicted *ex informata conscientia* cease of themselves also in the case of the transfer or resignation or removal of the bishop by whom they have been imposed, is not so certain.

---

[1] Supra, nn. 1287, 1291. [2] L. c., p. 334. [3] L. c., p. 334. [4] Stremler, l. c., p. 331.

1319. Has the vicar-general power to inflict suspension *ex informata conscientia?* Stremler holds that he has not; nay, he contends that the bishop cannot even authorize the vicar-general to impose such suspension, but must inflict it in person. Monacelli holds the same. And Giraldi[1] says: "An autem competat" (facultas procedendi ex informata conscientia) "etiam vicario generali episcopi, merito dubitari posset; cum ex cit. cap." (1, sess. xiv., de Ref.) "Tridentino videatur attributa esse solis episcopis et praelatis." The reason given by Stremler[2] is, that the Council of Trent[3] speaks only of bishops. Now, the giving of such an extraordinary power as that in question is a derogation of the common law of the Church, and therefore must be most strictly construed.

ART. IV.

Criminal Trial of Heretics (Processus Criminalis contra Haereticos).

1320. Although, as we have seen,[4] the Holy See no longer sends special inquisitors through the various parts of Christendom for the purpose of trying and sentencing heretics, as was done formerly, yet it were incorrect to imagine that the discussion of the mode of procedure against heretics, peculiar to the tribunals of the Inquisition, is altogether useless at the present day. For bishops are still, in their respective dioceses, the inquisitors *ex officio (inquisitores nati)* in matters of heresy, and are bound, in their procedure against heretics, to observe the peculiar formalities or special form of procedure prescribed by the law of the Church for the punishment of crimes against the Catholic faith.[5]

1321. Moreover, a study of the subject will dispel the

---

[1] L. c., nota li.   [2] L. c., p. 327.   [3] Cap. 1, sess. 14, de Ref.
[4] Supra, n. 500, 579.   [5] Boulx, de Jud. eccl., vol. li., p. 365.

false and erroneous impressions current among non-Catholics, in regard to the working of the tribunals of the Inquisition, so much abused and perhaps so little understood by
them.   The peculiar mode of procedure against heretics is
called *inquisition;* and the tribunals established for the purpose of proceeding against them are called by the same
name, or also tribunals of the Holy Office.   There are two
kinds of inquisitors—ordinary and delegated.   Every bishop,
as we have already seen, is the ordinary inquisitor or judge
in matters of heresy in his own diocese.[1]   He has also power,
at least as delegate of the Holy See, to proceed against
exempt persons—*v.g.*, regulars—in matters of heresy.[2]   Besides, from the time of Pope Innocent III., extraordinary or
delegated inquisitors were also appointed, in the various
parts of Christendom, who had cumulative power with
bishops in this matter.[3]   By custom, only the tribunals of
the delegated inquisitors, not those of bishops, were termed
tribunals of the Inquisition or Holy Office.[4]

   1322. *Trial for heresy; or mode of procedure in causes of
heresy.*—Inquisitors, whether ordinary (namely, bishops) or
delegated, cannot pass sentence and inflict punishment upon
any person for crimes pertaining to heresy, except upon due
trial.   This trial, however, need not be a formal or solemn
canonical trial or process (*processus ordinarius*), as above
traced out,[5] but can be a summary trial (*processus summarius*),
as set forth above.[6]   "Concedimus," says Pope Boniface VIII.,
"quod in inquisitionis haereticae pravitatis negotio procedi
possit *simpliciter et de plano.*"[7]   Now, as we have shown,
speaking of summary trials, to proceed summarily or *simpliciter et de plano* does not mean to omit all the formalities
of formal canonical trials, but only some of them.

   1323. In fact, it is certain that in causes of heresy the

---

[1] Clem. Multorum 1, de Haeret. (v. 3).   [3] Cap. 9, de Haeret. (v. 7).
[2] Supra, n. 500, 579.   [4] Craiss., Man., n. 6025.   [5] Supra, n. 932 sq.
[6] Supra, n. 1265 sq.   [7] Cap. 20, de Haeret., in 6° (v. 2).

accused must, on pain of nullity of the proceedings, be cited for trial, so as to be able to defend himself. The judge must allow him full liberty of defending himself, just as in the case of other accused parties, or of defendants in causes other than those of heresy. For the Church fully recognizes the principle that the right of self-defence proceeds from the very law of nature, and cannot be restricted, much less refused, by any, even ecclesiastical judges.[1] Hence, too, the accused in the case must be furnished with a copy of the charges, specifications, proofs, and testimony submitted against him. Otherwise he could not defend himself properly, since the defence consists mainly in the refutation of the charges and proofs of the prosecution. However, the names of the witnesses need not, though they may, be made known to him. This is peculiar to trials in causes of heresy.[2] He must, moreover, be allowed the assistance of an advocate.[3]

1324. The accused cannot be condemned except upon full proof (*probatio plena*), as obtained in the course of the trial. Hence he cannot be convicted or condemned upon mere suspicions, even though violent, as is expressly enacted by Pope Innocent III.[4]

1325. The sentence must be pronounced with the advice of experts (*periti*). Otherwise the trial is null and void.[5] This is a peculiar feature of these trials. By experts are here meant theologians or canonists. The entire trial, or all the proceedings, and consequently also the defence, must be submitted to them. We say, "with the advice"; not "with the consent." Hence the judge, though obliged, and that *sub poena nullitatis*, to listen to the advice of these experts, is yet not bound to follow it in passing sentence. Finally, while the defendant cannot lodge an appeal proper

---

[1] Clem. Pastoralis 2, de Sent. et re jud. (ii. 11).
[2] Cap. 20, de Haeret., in 6° (v. 2).   [3] Bouix, l. c., p. 383.
[4] Cap. Litteras 14, de Praesumpt. (ii. 23); Leuren., For. Eccl., l. 5, t. 7, Q. 189.
[5] Cap. 12, de Haeret., in 6° (v. 2).

against the final sentence, he can have recourse to the Holy See. From all this it will be seen how unfounded are the assertions, so frequently repeated by non-Catholic writers, that persons accused of heresy have been or are denied the right of defending themselves before the tribunals of the Holy Office.

CHAPTER V.

1326. As in secular so in ecclesiastical courts or judicial tribunals, there are not only criminal, but also civil processes or causes. Now, civil causes in the ecclesiastical forum are those where there is no question of inflicting penalties for offences, but merely of obtaining something else. Thus a process or trial regarding the validity of a marriage, the jurisdiction of a prelate, or the privileges of a monastery, is a civil cause or trial.[1] Criminal causes, on the other hand, are those where crimes or delinquencies against the public order or discipline of the Church are punished. When, therefore, an ecclesiastical penalty proper is to be imposed, the cause is criminal.[2]

1327. We have already described the mode of procedure in criminal causes; it only remains to give a short outline of the mode of procedure in civil causes pertaining to the ecclesiastical forum, or of civil trials in the ecclesiastical courts. Here we may observe that civil ecclesiastical trials have many things in common with criminal ecclesiastical trials. Consequently, various questions bearing on civil ecclesiastical trials have already been sufficiently discussed by us above, under the head of criminal trials. What still remains to be said concerning civil trials in the ecclesiastical courts will be divided into two parts. The first will treat of the ordinary or formal trial or mode of procedure in civil matters (*processus ordinarius in materia civili*); the second, of

---

[1] Our Counter-Points, n. 55.   [2] Ib., n. 56.

that particular mode which is peculiar to certain kinds of ecclesiastical civil processes, especially in matrimonial causes. In the first part, therefore, we shall set forth the formalities of civil trials, as they are applicable to such trials in general; in the second, we shall discuss the formalities peculiar to certain kinds of civil processes. At the end of the first part we shall add two articles regarding appeals, complaints of nullity, and reinstatement.

ART. I.

Of the Ordinary Trial, or Mode of Procedure in Civil Causes of the Ecclesiastical Forum (De Processu Ordinario in Materia Civili).

1328. The various stages or steps in civil proceedings or trials are very much like those of criminal trials. The civil trial or process in the ecclesiastical court begins with the statement (*libellus*) or bill of complaint which the plaintiff,[1] either personally, or through his agent or attorney, presents to the judge, and in which he demands redress, or asks that something be done.[2] This bill should be clear, so that the defendant to whom it must be communicated may be enabled to deliberate whether he should yield to the demand, or rather contest the matter. As this bill constitutes the basis of the trial, and of the subsequent sentence, it should be rejected by the judge, if it is obscure or ambiguous. For further information regarding this bill, see above.[3] What is said there concerning bills or *libelli* in criminal causes, holds also of bills or *libelli* in civil causes, and therefore need not be repeated here.

1329. It is proper to observe here that what has just been said regarding the necessity of a *libellus* applies only to ordi-

---

[1] Cap. Dilecti 3, de Lib. obl. (ii. 3); cf. München, l. c., vol. i., p. 252, n. 1.
[2] Cf. Craiss., Man. n. 6041.   [3] Supra, n 989 sq.

nary or solemn trials in civil causes, of which we speak in this article; for in summary ecclesiastical trials in civil matters this bill of complaint may be omitted,[1] and the proceedings therefore need not begin with the handing to the judge of the *libellus*, as we have already shown in treating of summary trials.[2]

1330. Upon receiving and examining the bill of complaint (*libellus conventionis*), the judge, if he finds the bill legitimate, issues the citation to the defendant, so that the latter may receive due notice of the plaintiff's (*actor*) demand. The mode of issuing and executing or serving the citation, in civil causes, is substantially the same as in criminal causes, above described.[3] We shall therefore abstain from explanations on the matter.

1331. *Contumacy of the defendant.*—If, on the day appointed in the citation, the defendant—who is called *reus* in civil as well as criminal causes—does not appear, he is accused, for the first time, of contumacy on the following day, unless it be a Sunday or festival. The second and last accusation of contumacy takes place three days after the first accusation, when the defendant lives or is in the place where the trial is held; and two months if he is out of the territory of the judge; and one month, if he is indeed within the territory of the judge, but not in the place where the trial takes place. If the defendant or his attorney appears within the time fixed in the last accusation of contumacy, he is to be admitted, and the trial proceeds. But if nobody appears, the defendant is to be considered and condemned as in contempt of the court.

1332. *Effects of the condemnation of the defendant for contempt of court, or contumacy, in civil causes.*—The effects of contumacy in civil ecclesiastical causes resemble in many particulars the effects of contumacy in criminal causes. Hence we refer the reader for further information on this

---

[1] Cf. München, l. c., vol. l., p. 337, n. 2.   [2] Supra, n. 1269.   [3] Supra, n. 998 sq.

matter to what we have already said in relation to the effects of contumacy in criminal trials.[1] From the principles there laid down, it follows that in civil no less than in criminal causes, whether the civil trial is ordinary or extraordinary, the case cannot be decided against the person in contempt, solely because he is in contempt. Nevertheless as in criminal so in civil causes, the judge has a right, nay the duty, if requested, to punish the contumacious person for his contumacy. What this punishment is in civil causes is fully explained by München,[2] to whom we refer the reader.

1333. We observe here that the formal accusation of contumacy as above set forth,[3] is necessary only when the civil trial is ordinary, formal or solemn (*processus civilis ordinarius*); but not when it is extraordinary, informal or summary (*processus civilis summarius*). For in the latter case those formalities need not be observed.[4]

1334. When, however, the defendant obeys the citation, and appears in court on the day fixed in the citation, a copy of the bill of complaint is given him by the judge, and a space or term of twenty days allowed him to deliberate whether to contest the case, or rather comply with the demands of the plaintiff. To expedite matters, the judge may insert a copy of the bill in the citation itself, and require the defendant to plead when he appears in obedience to the citation.[5]

1335. The defendant's plea or general answer is the next step. However, before entering his plea, and thus effecting the *litis contestatio*, the defendant is at liberty to propose whatever exceptions he wishes to make. We remark that the same principles apply to exceptions in civil causes as in criminal causes. Hence it is not necessary to repeat here what we have already said, when speaking of exceptions in

---

[1] Supra, n. 1014–1024. [2] L. c., p. 321, n. 1–7. [3] Supra, n. 1331.
[4] Craiss., n. 6043. [5] München, l. c., p. 256, n. 7.

criminal causes.[1] We merely observe in passing, that the making of exceptions, whether peremptory or dilatory, does not at all imply any confession or admission on the part of the person or defendant making them. For a person has a perfect right to make exceptions even though he absolutely denies the position or allegations of his opponent. The law of the Church says: " Exceptionem objiciens, non videtur de intentione adversarii confiteri." [2]

1336. Again, we remark here that prescription is to be counted among the peremptory exceptions. As such, it is defined "a peremptory exception, by which the possessor in good faith, after the expiration of the time specified by law, can repel the old owner who demands back his property, or wishes to use his old right." [3] Prescription confers a valid title—that is, gives full ownership, also *in foro conscientia*— provided it has these conditions: 1. That the object be prescriptible ; 2, that there be good faith ; [4] 3, and also continued possession, 4, for the legitimate space of time ; 5, a just title.

1337. We cannot dwell on these conditions here. The reader will find them fully and lucidly explained by Schmalzgrueber.[5] We can only remark, that by a "just title" we do not mean a *true title* (*titulus verus*), because such a title is sufficient of itself, and confers ownership without any prescription.[6] A colored title is certainly sufficient,[7] but is not necessarily required. A putative title is sufficient, provided it is reasonably considered a title.[8] We remark again, that to prescribe against the real estate of churches and pious places forty years are necessary ;[9] nay, to prescribe against the real estate of the Holy See one hundred years are required."[10]

1338. The defendant's exceptions must be communicated

---

[1] Supra, n. 1026–1054.

[2] Reg. 63, de Reg. jur., in 6° (Bonif. VIII.); cf. München, l. c., p. 95.

[3] Craiss., n. 6046.   [4] Cap. 5, de Praescr. (ii. 26).   [5] L. 2, t. 26, n. 23 sq.

[6] Ib., n. 87.   [7] Cf. supra, n. 222.   [8] Schmalzg., l. c., Resp. 3.

[9] Cap. 6, 8, 9, de Praescr. (ii. 26).   [10] Cap. 13, 14, 17 de Praescr. (ii. 26)

to the plaintiff, so that he may refute them ; and, in turn, the plaintiff's answer to the defendant's exceptions is communicated to the defendant for rebuttal, and so on, till the parties have exhausted their arguments, and declare themselves ready to go on with the main cause.[1]

1339. All these proceedings—namely, the making and proving of the exceptions, as also all other acts or steps which take place prior to the *litis contestatio*—are summary, even when the trial is ordinary or solemn.[2]

1340. After these preliminary proceedings follows the plea (*litis contestatio*), or the direct though general answer of the defendant to the plaintiff's allegations. It consists in the defendant's denial, in whole or in part, of the plaintiff's bill of complaint. As the same rules govern the *litis contestatio*, both in civil and criminal causes, we refer the reader to what we have said above in regard to the *litis contestatio* in criminal causes.[3]

1341. The oath of *calumnia*, where still in use, is next administered, and that not only to the principals,—*i.e.*, plaintiff and defendant in person,—but also to their procurators and advocates. This oath, as we have seen, is no longer taken, at least in criminal causes.[4] Where it still obtains in civil causes, the judge can oblige the parties to take it only when the opposing party insists upon its being taken. [5]

1342. Next, the so-called positions (*positiones*) and answers thereto (*responsiones in jure*) are made where they are still in use.[6] For further information on this head we refer the reader to what we have already said above, as the principles there laid down apply also to positions and the answers thereto in civil causes.[7]

1343. Then follows the real trial—that is, the demonstra-

---

[1] München, l. c., p. 259, n. 9. [2] Ib.; supra, n. 1028. [3] Supra, n. 1064 sq.
[4] Supra, n. 1077. [5] München, l. c., p. 224, n. 5. [6] Ib., p. 266.
[7] Supra, n. 1070–1073.

tion or proving on the part of the plaintiff of the main cause or issue, and the rebuttal by the defendant of the former's proofs and arguments. These proceedings are therefore called probative proceedings, being held for the purpose of establishing by proper proofs the main or real points at issue, as fixed by the bill of complaint, plea, and positions. This whole procedure, therefore, consists in the judge's hearing and receiving or admitting whatever testimony or proof is produced both by the plaintiff and the defendant. As in criminal so also in civil causes, the burden of proof rests upon the plaintiff. He is therefore first called upon to prove his case. His proofs—namely, depositions of witnesses, documents, letters, etc.—must be communicated to the defendant, who is thus enabled to prepare for his defence, and to defend himself properly. As the rules which apply to the examination of the witnesses, and other proofs in civil causes, are substantially the same as in criminal causes, which we have already fully described,[1] we deem it superfluous to repeat them here.

1344. The swearing of witnesses is necessary also in civil trials (we speak, of course, always of civil trials in ecclesiastical courts). Here we may be pardoned for digressing somewhat, and asking whether, according to the civil laws of the United States, it is unlawful for an ecclesiastical judge to administer the oath to witnesses—*i.e.*, make them depose under oath in ecclesiastical trials, whether civil or criminal. We think not. We have consulted very able lawyers on this point, and their answer is, that while the State, with us, does not formally recognize such swearing of witnesses, nor give it any civil effect, yet it does not forbid it, or make the act in any sense illegal. The State, with us, simply authorizes certain persons to administer oaths. To oaths alone which are administered by such persons, it gives effect by enacting

---

[1] Supra, n. 1115 sq.

that if any person shall wilfully and corruptly swear or affirm falsely, he shall be deemed guilty of perjury and punished accordingly.[1] Hence an oath administered, with us, by an ecclesiastical judge is not illegal, but simply not punishable as perjury if taken falsely.

1345. In England and Ireland the case seems different, even at the present day. For, as appears from the testimony in the famous trial of the Rev. Robert O'Keefe, P.P. *v.* His Eminence Cardinal Cullen, the swearing of witnesses by the ecclesiastical judge seems illegal, and positively forbidden by the law of the land. Thus the Most Rev. Dr. Leahy, Archbishop of Cashel, being examined for the defence, and asked, "Now, in proceeding in canon law, must not witnesses be sworn?" answered thus: "Yes, that is one of the formalities, and it is because witnesses cannot be sworn in such a proceeding in this country that an ordinary judicial proceeding is impossible." This opinion seems to have been endorsed by Mr. Carton, the eminent lawyer who examined Archbishop Leahy. For, in the question immediately following the above, he says: "The swearing of witnesses being illegal in this country," etc.[2] Hence, also, the trial as prescribed by the First Synod of Westminster in 1852, which was taken by the Propaganda as the model for its Instruction of July 20, 1878, for this country, ordains that witnesses shall not be sworn.[3] This feature was retained in the above Instruction of the Propaganda for the United States.

1346. Let us now return to our subject. As the depositions of the witnesses for the plaintiff are made known to the defendant for his defence, so those of the witnesses for the latter are also communicated to the plaintiff for rebuttal or *repulsa repulsae;* and in turn, the rebuttal testimony of the latter's witnesses is disclosed to the defendant for his further

[1] Revision of the Statutes of New Jersey, p. 740, sec. 3. Trenton, 1877.
[2] Trial of O'Keefe *v.* Card. Cullen, p. 505. London, 1874.
[3] Coll. Lacens., vol. iii., p. 960.

defence. This is based on the general principle, that in ecclesiastical trials (as in secular trials) no *ex parte* or one-sided proceedings are allowed; but, on the contrary, each party must be fully informed of the steps, testimony, and proceedings of the other party. Of this there can be no doubt. The only dispute which exists on this head is as to how this information must be imparted. Thus, as we have seen, it may be disputed as to whether the contending parties can be confronted with the witnesses, during the latter's examination. But, in any case, all canonists agree that the party must be informed of the depositions of the witnesses, even where he is not confronted with them.

1347. Hence also in trials which take place before Commissions of Investigation, as in fact in any other judicial procedure, the same rule holds. Where therefore, also with us, a defendant, for instance, is not allowed to be present at the examination of the witnesses for the prosecution (*confrontatio personalis*), the depositions must be communicated to him in writing (*confrontatio verbalis*).

1348. When the parties have exhausted their proofs and arguments the case is closed—that is, no further taking of testimony is permitted, lest otherwise litigations become immortal and endless. Thereupon, on a day fixed by the judge, the parties either personally or by their advocates are allowed to make final speeches or to sum up the case.[1] Then the judge takes all the papers or acts and documents of the trial, —namely, the deposition of the witnesses, the minutes of the proceedings, etc.,—so that, having carefully examined and studied them, he may be able to pronounce a just sentence. A day is then appointed by the judge for the pronouncement of sentence, and the parties are to be cited to be present to hear it. Finally, on the day fixed, sentence is pronounced by the judge in the presence of the parties.

---

[1] München, l. c., p. 283.

ART. II.

*Of the Extraordinary and Summary Trial in Civil Causes of
the Ecclesiastical Forum, also in the United States (De Processu Extraordinario et Summario Ecclesiastico, in Materia
Civili).*

1349. So far we have traced out in the preceding article
the mode of procedure in ordinary or regular civil trials
(*processus civilis ordinarius seu solemnis*) in the ecclesiastical
forum. We come now to the extraordinary and summary
mode of procedure or trial in civil causes falling under the
ecclesiastical forum. It is scarcely necessary to remark here,
that, as in criminal, so also in civil causes or matters of the
ecclesiastical forum, there is both an ordinary or regular
(called also formal and solemn), and an extraordinary or summary trial or mode of procedure.[1] Nay, there are several
extraordinary and summary trials for ecclesiastical civil
causes. One is for summary causes in general, and is the one
which is ordinarily made use of when a cause is tried summarily. Of this trial we shall speak in this article. The
others are the peculiar summary modes of procedure in
matrimonial causes, the proceedings *in petitorio, possessorio,
in actione spolii*, etc.[2] Of the peculiar summary process in
matrimonial causes we shall speak below in a separate article.

1350. The summary trial, of which we here speak, and
which is the one established for civil causes in general, is
clearly explained in the *Clem. Saepe;* and the causes which
can be adjudicated summarily are set forth in the *Clem. Dispendiosam.* We have already, at length, dwelt upon these
summary trials above.[3] There we have also shown that
criminal causes cannot be tried summarily; that only certain
specified civil causes can be adjudicated *modo summario*. As

---

[1] München, l. c., p. 232.   [2] Ib., p. 345–362.   [3] Supra, n. 1265 sq.

we have already fully explained this mode of procedure, it is not necessary to repeat here what we said above.[1] However, in order to give the reader a more comprehensive understanding of the mode of procedure observed in summary trials, we shall here subjoin the text of the two constitutions issued by Pope Clement V. in 1312, and still in full force.

1351. The first constitution gives the *chief cases which allow of the summary procedure*, and is as follows: "Dispendiosam prorogationem litium (quam interdum ex subtili ordinis judiciarii observatione causarum docet experientia provenire) restringere in subscriptis casibus, cupientes; statuimus, ut in causis super electionibus, postulationibus, vel provisionibus, aut super dignitatibus, personatibus, officiis, canonicatibus, vel praebendis, seu quibusvis beneficiis ecclesiasticis, aut super decimis . . . . et eos quoque modo tangentibus, procedi valeat de caetero *simpliciter et de plano, ac sine strepitu judicii et figura.*"

1352. The second constitution of Pope Clement V. outlines the *formalities* of summary trials, and reads as follows: "Saepe contingit, quod causas committimus, et in earum aliquibus *simpliciter et de plano, ac sine strepitu et figura judicii* procedi mandamus: de quorum significatione verborum a multis contenditur, et qualiter procedi debeat, dubitatur. Nos autem dubitationem hujusmodi (quantum nobis est possibile) decidere cupientes, hac in perpetuum valitura constitutione sancimus, ut judex, cui taliter causam committimus, necessario libellum non exigat, litis contestationem non postulet, in tempore etiam feriarum ob necessitates hominum indultarum a jure procedere valeat, amputet dilationum materiam, litem quanto poterit faciat breviorem, exceptiones, appellationes dilatorias et frustratorias repellendo, partium, advocatorum et procuratorum contentiones et jurgia testiumque superfluam multitudinem refraenando."

[1] Supra, n. 1265-1279.

1353. The constitution having shown what can be omitted, now explains what formalities shall be observed. It says: "Non sic tamen judex litem abbreviet, quin probationes necessariae, et defensiones legitimae admittantur. Citationem vero, ac praestationem juramenti de calumnia vel malitia, sive de veritate dicenda, ne veritas occultetur, per commissionem hujusmodi intelligimus non excludi. Verum quia juxta petitionis formam (demand of the plaintiff or *libellus*) pronunciatio sequi debet, pro parte agentis, et etiam rei, si quid petere voluerit, est in ipso litis exordio petitio facienda, sive scriptis, sive verbo; actis tamen continuo (ut super quibus positiones et articuli formari debeant, possit haberi plenior certitudo, et ut fiat definitio clarior) inserenda. Et quia positiones ad faciliorem expeditionem litium, propter partium confessiones, et articulos ad clariorem probationem usus longaevus in causis admisit; nos autem hujusmodi observari volentes, statuimus, ut judex sic deputatus a nobis (nisi aliud de partium voluntate procedat) ad dandum simul utrosque terminos dare possit, et ad exhibendum omnia acta et munimenta quibus partes uti volunt in causa post dationem articulorum diem certum, quandocunque sibi videbitur, valet assignare. Interrogabit etiam partes, sive ad earum instantiam, sive ex officio, ubicumque hoc aequitas suadebit. Sententiam vero definitivam (citatis ad id, licet non peremptorie, partibus) in scriptis et (prout majus sibi placuerit) stans vel sedens proferat: etiam (si ei videbitur) conclusione non facta, prout ex petitione et probatione, et aliis actitatis in causa fuerit faciendum."

"Quae omnia etiam in illis casibus, in quibus per aliam constitutionem nostram, vel alias, procedi potest *simpliciter et de plano, ac sine strepitu et figura judicii* volumus observari."

ART. III.

Remedies against an unjust Sentence in Civil Causes.

1354. There are chiefly three such remedies—namely, appeals, complaint of nullity, and reinstatement. The two first are called ordinary remedies; the third an extraordinary, because it can or should be used only when the two others are of no avail.

§ 1. *Of Appeals, and the Complaint of Nullity in Civil Trials.*

1355. I. *Of appeals.*—The rules which apply to and govern appeals in civil causes or trials are the same as those which govern appeals in criminal causes. Hence what we have said above[1] concerning appeals in criminal causes applies also to appeals in civil causes, and therefore need not be repeated here. We pass on, consequently, to the second remedy—the complaint of nullity.

1356. II. *Complaint of nullity of sentence.*—Complaints of nullity, like appeals, are allowed both in criminal and civil causes. What has been remarked as to the rules governing civil and criminal appeals alike, holds also of complaints of nullity. In other words, the same rules and principles which apply to and govern complaints of nullity in criminal causes, apply to and govern complaints of nullity in civil causes. As this remedy is of great importance, and has been but cursorily and incidentally touched upon above (in the chapter on criminal trials), we shall here explain it more fully.

1357. By the complaint of nullity of sentence (*querela nullitatis sententiae*) is here meant the legitimate or proper alleging and proving that the sentence pronounced by the judge is *ipso jure* null and void.[2] Now a sentence can be void *ipso jure* in various ways, namely: 1. By reason of defects in the judge—namely, if he is publicly excommunicated; if he is infamous; if he is a layman, and the cause is ecclesiastical; if he has no jurisdiction in the case, or exceeds the limits of

---

[1] Supra, n. 444 sq.; vol. i., p 425.   [2] Reiff., l. 2, t. 28, n. 23.

his delegation, in case he is a delegated judge. 2. By reason of the litigants themselves—*v.g.*, if the sentence is pronounced on an exempt person, or on a minor (*i.e.*, one who has not yet completed his twenty-fifth year) who entered upon the litigation without the consent of his guardian ; when the sentence is in favor (not if it is against him) of a plaintiff who is excommunicated and denounced as such. 3. By reason of the place—*v.g.*, is pronounced out of the territory of the judge.

1358. 4. By reason of the time—*v.g.*, if it is pronounced at night, or on a festival, or on a day other than that appointed for the parties by the judge. 5. By reason of the sentence itself—*v.g.*, if it is neither condemnatory nor absolutory. 6. By reason of the manner in which sentence is pronounced— *v.g.*, if the judge passes sentence, not in writing ; or if he pronounces it in a standing, not a sitting posture (except where he proceeds summarily). 7. By reason of the proceedings or trial—*i.e.*, by reason of any substantial formality being omitted ;[1] *v.g.*, if sentence is pronounced against a person not cited for trial, or after an appeal has been lawfully made, or without any *litis contestatio*, in causes where the latter is required. 8. By reason of its manifest injustice—*v.g.*, if it is pronounced in express opposition to the law, or contains a clear error.[2]

1359. How is the complaint of nullity (*oppositio nullitatis*) to be made ? Considering the letter of the law of the Church, it can be addressed both to the superior or judge of appeal, and to the judge himself who passed the sentence, provided the latter is an ordinary judge. We say, *an ordinary judge ;* for a delegated judge, once he has pronounced sentence, whether right or wrong, is *functus officio*, ceases to have any further jurisdiction in the matter, and therefore cannot reverse his invalid sentence.[3] We said "considering

---

[1] Supra, n. 1170, 1186.
[2] Reiff., l. 2, t. 28, n. 23; Bouix, de Jud. eccl. vol. ii., p. 406.
[3] Cap. In litteris 9, de off. jud. del. (i. 29).

the letter of the law ;" for by custom now everywhere pre-
valent, and consequently having the force of common law,
the complaint of nullity of sentence is now to be referred to
and adjudicated upon by the judge of appeal, who, as is evident, is better qualified to reverse an invalid sentence than
the judge himself by whom it was pronounced.[1]

1360. The complaint of nullity can, as a rule, be made at
any time within thirty years from the date of sentence, but
not beyond that period, as every action or suit is prescribed
against by the space of thirty years. We say, "as a rule;"
the exceptions are : 1. If the nullity of sentence is proposed
as an exception ; since exceptions are perpetual. 2. If the act
is *ipso jure* void. 3. If the nullity proceeds from a defect of
jurisdiction or mandate. 4. Where statute or custom dis-
poses otherwise.[2] 5. Where the salvation of souls is endan-
gered.[3]

1361. *Chief differences between complaints of nullity and appeals proper.*—From what has been said, it is evident that the
complaint of nullity differs in various ways from appeals.
We shall only mention one or two additional differences:
1. Appeals can be made only ten days after the sentence ;
complaints of nullity for thirty years. 2. Again, appeals are
made against a sentence when it is *unjust*, though valid ;
complaints of nullity, against a sentence when it is *invalid*,
not merely unjust.[4] In fact, as we have already seen, when
a sentence is *ipso jure* null and void, no appeal is necessary,
since the sentence has no effect whatever, has no legal existence, and therefore need not, in fact cannot (as it does not
exist legally), be revoked upon an appeal.[5] In such a case,
therefore, it is sufficient to allege and prove the nullity of
sentence or to make the *querela nullitatis.*

1362. On the other hand, appeals and complaints of nullity

[1] Bouix, l. c., p. 411.
[2] Reiff., l. 2, t. 27, n. 115, 137.
[3] L. Si expressim 19 ff. de Appell. (49. 1).
[4] Bouix, l. c., p. 411.
[5] München, l. c., pp. 512, 586.

agree in this, that they are modes of redress, which are granted by the law, not as a matter of favor, but as a matter of right; while, *v.g.*, the *supplicatio* is a redress, granted by way of favor. Finally, we remark, that, *v.g.*, where there is a doubt whether the case admits of the complaint of nullity or of appeal, the complaint of nullity may be made conjointly with an appeal, in this manner: I charge that the sentence is null and void, and if it is perhaps valid, I appeal. In the Roman or civil law, there was no other remedy against invalid sentences than appeals; the complaint of nullity being of ecclesiastical origin.[1]

§ 2. *Supplication or Petition for a new hearing of the Cause (Supplicatio).*

1363. Against a final sentence which is pronounced by a judge who is supreme and has no superior on earth,—*v.g.*, the Pope, the entire College of Cardinals, the various Roman Congregations,[]—no appeal, properly speaking, can be made. For an appeal lies only from an inferior to a superior judge. However, while such a sentence is inappealable, yet there is, and justly so, since even supreme judges may err, a legal means of redress even against the sentences in question when the party feels aggrieved by them. This remedy is none other than a supplication or humble petition (*supplicatio*) addressed by the aggrieved party to the highest superior—to the Pope, so far as ecclesiastical causes, of which we here speak, are concerned—for a new hearing in the case.[]

1364. Hence this mode of redress, as here understood, or as applied to contentious causes, is correctly defined to be the prayer or petition of the aggrieved party addressed to the supreme judge,—namely, the Pope,—setting forth the griev-

[1] München, l. c., p. 587.   [] Supra, n. 450.
[] München, l. c., vol. i., p. 568, n. 1.

ances inflicted by the sentence, against which the ordinary remedy of appeal is of no avail, and humbly asking him, as a matter of pure favor and kindness, to review and reverse such sentence.[1] The object, therefore, of a supplication is the same as that of an appeal—namely, to obtain a new trial. In fact, while a supplication differs from an appeal, it nevertheless greatly resembles it.[2]

1365. *Principal differences between supplications and appeals.* —1. Supplications are allowed in all causes and matters, civil and criminal,[3] and, as we have seen, against sentences of the supreme judge which do not admit of appeals; whereas appeals are not so universal a means of redress.[4] 2. Appeals must be made within ten days; supplications can be made within two years from the time the sentence complained of was pronounced.[5] 3. An appeal is addressed to the superior or higher judge; a supplication usually to the same judge who passed the sentence, and who, being supreme, cannot be appealed from. 4. The appeal is an ordinary remedy, and given by the law *as a right;* the supplication an extraordinary remedy, and granted only *as a favor* by the Pope.[6] 5. Finally, in the making of appeals various formalities (already described) must be observed; in supplications the proceedings are altogether informal.[7]

1366. *Q.* What is the mode of petitioning the Sacred Congregations of Rome for a new hearing of a cause when such a cause has already been once decided by them?

A. We premise: All canonists agree that there is no appeal from a decision given by one of the Sacred Congregations at Rome—*v.g.,* by the S. C. C., or of the Council of Trent, or by the S. C. Ep. et Reg., or by the S. C. de Prop.

---

[1] Schmalzg., l. 2, t. 28, n. 2.   [2] Ib.
[3] Glossa, in cap. 68, v. De Inquisitionis (ii. 28).   [4] Reiff., l. 2, t. 28, n. 22.
[5] L. unic. C. de Sent. praef. praet. (vii. 42).
[6] Arg. l. 1, 2, 3, 4, 5, 6, C. de Prec. imp. off. (i. 19).
[7] München, l. c., p. 570, n. 3.

Fide. For these Sacred Congregations or Standing Committees of Cardinals are supreme tribunals, vested with papal
authority ; consequently their decrees are just as inappealable
as though they had been made by the Pope himself. Yet.
when there is question of decisions rendered by them in a
contentious cause or matter, these Sacred Congregations
always grant a new hearing or trial, or review of the case.
And in this new hearing, which takes place before the same
Sacred Congregation by which the first decision was given,
the parties can again submit their arguments, proofs, etc.,
just as though they were before a tribunal or judge of appeal.
Nay, these Sacred Congregations grant such new hearing
or trial not only once but several times in the same cause or
matter.[1]

1367. There are only two cases where such new hearing
is refused—namely, 1, where the request for the new hearing is manifestly based upon frivolous motives; 2, where a
Sacred Congregation adds to its decision in a case the phrase
et amplius. In this latter case it is not allowed to ask for a
new hearing of the cause, except upon obtaining from the
Cardinal Prefect of the respective Congregation a rescript
giving permission to do so. The words *et amplius* are the
first words of the formula, whose last words are *causa non
proponatur.* This latter part is always understood, though
only the first words—namely, *et amplius*—are expressed in
the decree. Hence by this phrase the Sacred Congregation
means that it has unanimously decided the matter, and so
thoroughly examined it, that it will consider any demand for
a new hearing as frivolous.[2]

1368. We now answer: The supplication for the new hearing should be made to the Sacred Congregation (with us, to
the Propaganda) by means of an humble petition, setting forth
clearly and specifically the reasons upon which the request

---

[1] Stremler, l. c., p. 424.   [2] Ib., l. c., p. 425.

is based.   The petition should be presented at the office of
the secretary of the Sacred Congregation to which the supplication is addressed.   It may also be sent by letter to the
Cardinal Prefect of the Congregation.   It should be addressed directly to the Holy Father, thus : *Beatissime Pater.*
In contentious matters, the only satisfactory way of conducting supplications, appeals, etc., is through one of the procurators who are officially recognized as such.[1]

1369. Finally, we remark, that the recourse which lies to
the Holy See against sentences *ex informata conscientia* partakes of the nature of a supplication, as here described.   For
there is no appeal against such sentences, but only a supplication to the Holy See (with us, to the Propaganda) for a
hearing of the case, and a reversal of the sentence.

§ 3.—(*a*). *The referring of a Cause by an Inferior Judge to the
Superior Judge (De Relationibus).*
(*b*). *Consultations addressed by an Inferior Judge to his Superior,
for Information to guide him in deciding a Cause—Consultations addressed by Bishops to the Holy See.*

1370. Here we will briefly explain another means, or
rather quasi-means, of redress, namely, the referring (*relatio*)
of a cause by the inferior judge—*v.g.*, bishop—to the Pope,
whenever he is in doubt as to the law applying to the cause,
with the request for information as to the law which he is to
follow in adjudicating the case.[2]   It is, therefore, a request
made by an inferior judge who is in doubt on the law applying to a case, addressed to the superior, to be instructed as to
what rules he should follow in deciding the case.   We say,
" who is in doubt about *the law ;*" for this canonical reference
or consultation can take place only when the inferior judge
entertains doubts on points of law (in our case, of canon law),
on account of its difficulty or ambiguity, but not when he is

---

[1] Stremler, l.c., p. 609.   [2] Schmalzg , l. 2, t. 28, n. 147: Reiff., l. 2, t. 28, n. 329.

uncertain as to the facts in the case; since he is bound to inquire for himself as to the truth or existence of all questions of fact in a cause. Nevertheless, he is obliged in his consultation to state the whole case, not only as to its law, but also facts, so that the Pope may fully understand the cause in all its bearings.[1]

1371. How is this consultation to be addressed by the inferior ecclesiastical judge—*v.g.*, bishop—to the Pope? 1. The inferior judge, in his request or consultation, should give a full and complete statement, either of the whole case, if the doubt extends to the whole case, or of the particular part of it which is the cause of the doubt, together with all the circumstances and facts in the case, and also the allegations of both the contending parties.[2] 2. Where the doubt is as to the whole case, the minutes and acts of the entire proceedings should be sent to the Pope with the consultation; where the doubt extends but to part of the case, only those minutes and acts which relate to such part need be sent.[3] 3. The inferior judge, before sending his consultation to Rome, must give the litigants—both plaintiff and defendant—a copy of such consultation, so that they may appeal or object against the manner in which the cause is stated; and their appeal or objections must be filed among the acts of the case and forwarded to Rome together with the consultation.[4] The object of this is to prevent the inferior judge from presenting an *ex-parte* statement, or suppressing the truth and stating untruths.[5]

1372. The effect of this formal and canonical consultation is that, pending this reference to the Pope, the jurisdiction of the judge referring the case is suspended, just as in appeals proper, so that he cannot do anything whatever in the case until the superior who has been consulted has given

[1] L. 1, C. de Relat. (vii. 61).
[2] L. Si quis 1, C. de Relat. (vii. 61).
[3] Ib., et l. 3, eod.
[4] Cap. Intimasti 68, de Appell. (ii. 28).
[5] Schmalzg., l. c., n. 151.

his reply.' We need scarcely say that this remedy obtains in civil and criminal causes.

1373. At the present day this reference of a cause is no longer in use. In its place has succeeded a simple consultation (*consultatio*). Thus, bishops and others now frequently consult the Holy See when they are in doubt as to the meaning, force, and extent of a law. However, it must be observed that this consultation must be strictly confined to questions of law, and should not extend to its application in a particular cause. For where there is question of applying the law to contending parties, the Holy See will not give an answer unless all the parties have been heard from.'

§ 4. *Of Reinstatement (De in Integrum Restitutione).*

1374. To reinstate a person (*restituere in integrum*), speaking in general, means to place him again in a former state, or restore him to a condition from which he had been displaced. By reinstatement (*restitutio in integrum*), in the stricter sense of the word, in which it is here used, is meant the extraordinary remedy of the law by which a person who has been grievously injured is, by reason of natural equity, restored by the judge to that state, condition, or right, in which he was before the injury occurred.' It is called an extraordinary remedy, because as long as an ordinary action or remedy is available reinstatement is not granted.

1375. This remedy is not given in criminal causes. For, as the Roman law says: "In criminibus aetatis suffragio minores non juvantur; etenim malorum mores, infirmitas animi non excusat."' It is therefore conceded only in civil causes.

1376. What is required in order that a party may be

---

¹ Schmalzg., l. c., n. 152.   ² Cf. Reiff , l. 2, t. 28, n. 331.
³ Cap. Auditis 3, de in integ. rest. (i. 41); Glossa, ib. in cas.; Reiff., eod. n. 3; De Angelis, eod., n. 1.   ⁴ L. 1, C. Si adv. del. (ii. 35).

entitled to or obtain reinstatement? 1. The injury complained of should be grave or notable. For the maxim of
the Roman law, as adopted by the Church, is: "De minimis
non curat praetor."   And, in fact, if reinstatement were
granted for the most trifling injuries there would be no end
to litigations.[1] 2. This grave injury, prejudice, damage, or
loss must have been inflicted by the cunning or deceit of the
opponent, or caused by the inexperience, inadvertence of
the party injured (if he is a minor), or of his agent or guardian, or in other similar ways.[2] Hence if the injury or damage happens fortuitously, reinstatement is not granted.[3]
3. The act or contract which gave rise to the injury or
damage must be valid de jure, or there must be at least a
doubt whether it is ipso jure invalid. For when the act is
ipso jure invalid, no other remedy except a simple declaration
of its invalidity by the judge is needed. 4. Finally, this act
or contract must be rescindable. For there are certain acts
which when once valid cannot be any longer revoked, as is
the case with a marriage validly contracted.[4]

1377. To whom can reinstatement be granted? 1. As a
general rule, to all minors—that is, those who have not yet
entered upon the twenty-sixth year of their age—who have
suffered a serious loss or injury.[5] The law protects them
against the effects of their youth and inexperience, which
expose them to being easily deceived. Hence, too, a minor
who shows that he has suffered loss or damage in a transaction or judicial procedure is entitled to reinstatement on
the simple ground that he is a minor. Hence he need prove
only two things to entitle him to reinstatement: 1, that he
has suffered a serious damage; 2, that he is a minor. It
matters not whether this loss or injury has been caused by

[1] De Angelis, l. c., n. 2.   [2] Ib.
[3] Ex cap. 1, de In integ. (i. 41).   [4] De Angelis, l. l., t. 41, n. 2.
[5] L. Hoc edictum 1 ff. de minor. (4. 4).

his own carelessness, or that of his parents or guardian, or through the skill and fraud of his opponent.

1378. 2. By minors are here also meant all churches, monasteries, convents, and other pious places (*loca pia*), as hospitals, orphan asylums, erected by ecclesiastical authority; also confraternities and societies established for the purpose of promoting religion and piety.[1] For all these, like minors, are not capable of governing themselves, but are subject to and governed by others.

1379. Many examples of reinstatement granted to churches on the ground that they are considered minors, are found in the Decretals. Thus Pope Alexander III. ordered that wherever a church suffered loss in selling or leasing any of its property (the same holds of course also when it buys property), it should be reinstated,[2] and that although the sale or lease was otherwise perfectly legal and properly made.[3] And to this reinstatement a church is entitled even as against another church.[4] In like manner Pope Innocent III. decided, in two cases brought before him, that where a church lost its cause in an ecclesiastical court, because of the carelessness of its procurator or the failure, even though culpable, of its agents to submit proper proofs, it was entitled to reinstatement on the ground that a church is placed on the same footing with a minor.[5]

1380. Sometimes reinstatement is also conceded to majors or persons who have completed the twenty-fifth year of their age, provided the following conditions concur: 1. That there be a just and reasonable cause for the reinstatement. apart from the injury itself; 2. that there is no ordinary remedy left to redress the injury.

1381. We have just said, *that there be just and reasonabl: cause, apart from the injury itself.* Now, what are the chie:

---

[1] Cap. 1, 3, de In integ. rest. (l. 41).   [2] Cap. 1, eod.   [3] Ib. Glossa, v. Requisivit.
[4] Ex cap. 2, 3, eod.; Reiff., l. 1, t. 41, n. 42.   [5] Cap. 2, 3 (i. 41).

causes entitling majors to reinstatement? 1. *Absence.*—By absence is here meant any lawful absence which prevented the person seeking reinstatement from being present and able to defend his rights, in consequence of which absence he lost his cause and had judgment pronounced against him. 2. *Fraud or deception.*—Thus a person is entitled to reinstatement if he loses his cause because his opponent or a third party has destroyed, forged, or falsified documents, or corrupted and bribed the judge or witnesses. For a sentence based upon corruption or fraud should not be sustained.[1] 3. *Finally, any reasonable cause .or hindrance whatever—v.g.,* fear, sickness, etc.—which prevented the party from defending his rights, or making use of the ordinary means of redress,—*v.g.,* appeal,—entitle a person of full age, or a major, to reinstatement.[2]

1382. *Differences between reinstatement granted to majors and that given to minors.*—From what has been said, it is plain that the chief differences between reinstatements granted to minors and those conceded to majors are the following: 1. A minor is reinstated wherever it is shown or proved that he has suffered loss or injury in any act, contract, or judicial proceedings, and that even though the loss or injury occurred through the minor's own carelessness or the negligence of his procurator.[3] But in the case of majors it must be proved, not only that they sustained serious losses or injuries, but moreover that they suffered these losses, not through their own carelessness or indifference, but, as we have seen, either because of lawful absence, or fraud and deception, or other just cause [4]—*v.g.,* if they were prevented by just fear or sickness from repelling the injury by an appeal.[5] For, as the Roman law adopted by the Church

---

[1] München, l. c., vol. i., p. 579, n. 12, 13.
[2] L. Hujus edicti 1 ff. Ex quibus caus. maj. (4. 6); ib., l. 2, 3, 4 sq.
[3] Cap. 2, 3, de In integr. rest. (i. 41). [4] L. 1, 2, 3. ff. de In integr. rest. (4. 1).
[5] Cap. 4 (i. 41).

says: "Non enim negligentibus subvenitur, sed necessitate rerum impeditis." [1] In minors, negligence or carelessness is excused because of their youth,[2] but not in persons of full age.

1383. 2. There is another difference between the reinstatement of majors and minors. Majors are not reinstated so long as the ordinary remedy of appeal can be made use of by them ; while minors are reinstated even when they can have recourse to appeals.[3]

1384. Speaking in general, reinstatement can be demanded in all civil (as contradistinguished from criminal) acts or transactions whatever, which though valid are yet rescindable, and by which a person has suffered loss or been injured, whether they relate to contracts, judicial proceedings, or lapses of time.[4] We say, *rescindable ;* for where a valid act is not reversible—*v.g.*, when a minor has validly contracted a marriage—it is plain that reinstatement cannot take place. On the other hand, it is evident that all judicial acts, even though valid, are, as a rule, rescindable by the superior. Hence, if a party to a trial, who is a major, is injured by a judicial sentence (we speak of sentences of ecclesiastical judges), final or only interlocutory, and has failed for just reasons—*v.g.*, out of fear of the judge, sickness, excusable ignorance of the law—to appeal within the ten days granted by law, he is entitled to reinstatement.[5]

1385. *Mode of granting reinstatement.*—This mode consists of three things—namely, (*a*) that reinstatement be demanded from the competent judge ; (*b*) within the prescribed time : (*c*) that it be asked and granted in the manner prescribed by the sacred canons. Let us briefly describe each of these formalities. First, who is the competent judge ? We premise

---

[1] L. 16 ff. Ex quib. caus. maj. (4. 6).   [2] L. Hoc edictum 1 ff. (4. 4).
[3] Reiff., l. 1, t. 41, n. 55.
[4] Cap. 2, 3, 5, de in Int. rest. (i. 41); Clem. cap. unic. (i. 11); De Angelis, l. c., n. 4.   [5] Cap. Ecclesia 1, de rest. in integ., in 6°.

with De Angelis,[1] that reinstatement may be asked (*a*) either *incidentally—i.e.*, in the course of another trial, where it comes up incidentally, (*b*) or principally—that is, directly and by itself, or separately. Now, if reinstatement is asked against a final sentence, or one equivalent to a final sentence, the universal custom is, that it cannot be granted save by the superior judge,—that is, the judge of appeal,—namely, the metropolitan or Holy See.

1386. If reinstatement is demanded against other than judicial acts, such as contracts, lapses of time, then a distinction must be made between those cases where the sacred canons expressly ordain that reinstatement shall be conceded —*v.g.*, in the case of minors, churches, etc., being injured, and those cases where this is not ordained expressly. In the first case, not only the Pope, but any ordinary judge, and consequently any bishop, having jurisdiction in the case can grant reinstatement, whether asked for principally or only incidentally.[2] A delegated judge, unless specially authorized, can do so only when it is demanded incidentally.[3] In the second case the Pope alone can grant it.[4] Hence it may be said that practically speaking, the Holy See alone can reinstate majors, unless they clearly come within the category of those entitled to reinstatement by reason of lawful absence or fraud, as above explained.

1387. Second, within what time should reinstatement be asked? Reinstatement can and should be asked within four years, as is expressly stated both in the civil or Roman[5] and the canon law.[6] In the case of minors this term begins, not from the day they suffered the loss, but from the time they became majors,—*i.e.*, from the first day of the twenty-sixth year of their age,—and lasts consequently to the first day of their

---

[1] L. c., n. 5. [2] Cap. 9, de In int. rest. (i. 41). [3] Ib.
[4] S. C. C. in Mechl., 22 Maii, 1687; S. C. C. in Herbip., 1854.
[5] L. 7, C. de Temp. in int. (ii. 53). [6] Cap. Ecclesia 1, de Rest. in integ., in 6° (i. 21).

thirtieth year.' In all other cases—*i.e.*, in the case of
churches or congregations, pious places and the like, as also
of majors—it begins to run from the day when the injury
was inflicted, or rather when it became known to the injured
party.² Here it will be observed that in this particular respect churches and pious places are not placed on a like
footing with minors.

1388. When this space of four years has elapsed, and the
injured party (whether it be a minor who has attained his
full age, or a church or pious place) has neglected, or failed
through carelessness and negligence, to ask for reinstatement
within that period, it can no longer be granted. We say,
has failed through carelessness; for where the party is prevented by some good reason—*v.g.*, by fear, sickness, or other
reasonable cause—from making the application, reinstatement is granted even after the four years have expired.'

1389. Finally, reinstatement should be granted by the
judge in the manner prescribed by the sacred canons—that
is, only upon a proper trial or hearing of the cause why
reinstatement should be granted or refused.' This trial
must, naturally speaking, take place in the presence of the
party against whom the reinstatement is demanded. Hence
he must be cited to be present at the hearing, and allowed
to submit his proofs and argue his case. If he is contumaciously absent the hearing goes on without him.'

1390. Now, what is to be proved or shown in this trial or
hearing? We must distinguish between majors and minors.
A major who demands reinstatement must, as we have seen,
prove (*a*) that he has suffered very serious loss or injury in
a transaction, judicial procedure, or other act ; (*b*) that there
is, besides, a just cause for his demand. A minor (the same

---

¹ L. 7, Cod. cit.   ² Ex cap. Ecclesia cit.; Reiff., l. 1, t. 41, n. 63.
³ L. 7, C. cit.; cap. Ecclesia cit ; Reiff., l. 1, t. 41, n. 64 sq.
⁴ L. 11 ff. de Minor (iv. 4); L. 3 ff. de in integr. rest. (iv. 1).
⁵ De Angelis, l. c., n. 5.

holds of churches and pious places) must show merely (*a*) that he has suffered serious loss or injury; (*b*) that he is a minor.[1]

1391. What is the effect of reinstatement? The effect of reinstatement as demanded, but not yet granted, is that everything should remain *in statu quo*. Hence the sentence against which reinstatement is asked cannot, as a rule, be executed so long as the request for reinstatement has not yet been decided by the judge.[2] Of reinstatement, as not only asked, but already granted, the chief effect is that each of the parties—that is, not only the party asking, but also the one opposing reinstatement—receives back what he had originally, and is consequently placed in the same condition in which he was, before the contract, act, or judicial sentence causing the alleged injury, took place.[3]

1392. *Of certain peculiar characteristics of reinstatement in spiritual causes or matters.*—So far we have spoken of reinstatement in ecclesiastical causes or matters in general. We shall now say a few words in regard to certain features which are peculiar to reinstatement in a certain kind of ecclesiastical causes—namely, in those causes or matters which are more properly spiritual in their nature. By these spiritual causes or matters we mean chiefly those which pertain (*a*) to the sacrament of marriage; (*b*) appointments to ecclesiastical offices and benefices; (*c*) and other spiritual causes of a kindred nature, such as the right to receive tithes or the offerings of the faithful, or to exercise the right of electing ecclesiastical superiors or prelates, etc.[4]

1393. Of the peculiarities of reinstatement, so far as ecclesiastical offices, benefices, and parishes are concerned, we have already spoken above.[5] As to reinstatement in spiritual causes of the third kind, such as the right of election, of

---

[1] Schmalzg., l. 1, t. 41, n. 46.   [2] L. unic. C. In integ. rest. (li. 41).
[3] L. 24 ff., § 4, de Minor (4. 4); Schmalzg., l. c., n. 47.
[4] Cf. supra, n. 1099 sq.   [5] Supra, n. 1100 sq.

receiving the offerings of the faithful or tithes, it may be asked whether the person or persons spoliated of such rights is to be reinstated before all else—that is, even before he proves that he has a legitimate title or claim to these rights? The answer is, that where the common law of the Church favors the spoliator and is against the person spoliated,—*i.e.*, where the common law vests the right or title to the object in question in the despoiler and not the person despoiled,—the person spoliated must first establish his title or claim or indult or privilege, or at least the presumption of a title, before he can be reinstated.[1]

1394. We say, *where the common law favors the spoliator;* for where it favors the person despoiled, the latter must be reinstated before he shows any title whatever. Thus a parish priest who is deprived of the income, in whole or in part, of his parish is entitled forthwith to reinstatement The reason is, that by the common law of the Church he has the right to receive this income.[2] We say, secondly, *or at least the presumption of a title;* such presumption in favor of a title would be created by a long and peaceful possession of the right in question.

1395. It now remains to say a few words in regard to reinstatement in the third kind of the above spiritual causes —namely, matrimonial causes. As a person is said to be despoiled (*spoliatus*) in property and other rights when he is unjustly deprived of them, so also is he said to be spoliated in reference to his marriage rights when he is unjustly stripped of his marriage partner. This spoliation (*spolium*) may be caused not only by a third party, but also by either of the married couple, and that chiefly in three ways: 1. When either of the pair leaves the other of his or her own authority; for the one who is thus left is unjustly deprived

---

[1] Ex cap. 2, de Rest. Spol. in 6° (ii. 5).

[2] Ex cap. 2, cit.; Schmalzg., l. 2, t. 13, n. 73.

by the other of his conjugal rights. 2. When the wife leaves her husband by her own authority, and becoming penitent wishes to return to him and is not received by him; for in this instance the husband refusing to take her back is said to despoil her of her marriage rights. 3. When the wife who is ejected by her husband, but is afterwards recalled by him, refuses to return, as in this case, the husband would be despoiled of his rights.[1]

1396. Now, in all these cases the rule is, that the ecclesiastical judge, upon due application by the injured party, should, speaking in general, forthwith decree reinstatement—that is, restore him or her to his or her conjugal rights by obliging the party that left of his or her own accord to return, unless the latter can show just cause for his or her action. We say, *unless the latter can show just cause;* that is, unless the party who left of his or her own accord can prove *v.g.,* the existence of an annulling impediment, or cruelty, or adultery, or other serious bodily or spiritual danger.[2] Hence, if, for instance, a wife who has left her husband shows that she has been cruelly treated by him, she should not be compelled to return to him, until he has given proper pledges that he will not molest her again. How reinstatement takes place, when an impediment is alleged, see Schmalzgrueber, l. c., n. 63.

[1] Schmalzg., l. c., n. 57.
[2] Cap. 8, 10, 13, de Rest. spol. (ii. 13); Schmalzg., l. c., n. 61 sq.

CHAPTER VI.

ECCLESIASTICAL CIVIL TRIALS PECULIAR TO MATRIMONIAL CAUSES, ALSO IN THE U. S.

(*Processus in Causis Matrimonialibus.*)

1397. If, after a marriage has been contracted, an annulling impediment is discovered, by which such marriage is invalid, this defect or impediment should be removed and the marriage healed, either in the ordinary way, by a dispensation, or in the extraordinary manner—*i.e.*, by a dispensation *in radice*. But if the impediment cannot be taken away—*v.g.*, where it is of the law of nature, and therefore not dispensable by the Church, or where the parties prefer to regain their matrimonial liberty rather than have the marriage healed—the cause must be submitted before, tried and decided by the proper or competent judge or tribunal. In other words, the question whether the marriage is invalid or not must be adjudicated by the proper judge. We shall, therefore, in this chapter speak, 1, of the competent forum and judge for matrimonial causes; 2, of the *personnel* of this forum or tribunal; 3, of the form of trial common to matrimonial causes in general; 4, of the peculiar mode of procedure in divorces from bed and board; 5, of the special form of trial in causes of nullity; 6, of the mode of procedure to ascertain the *status liber*. All these questions will be discussed under separate heads, and the relations they bear to our peculiar circumstances in the United States, will also be considered.

ART. I.

*Which is the competent Forum for Matrimonial Causes?—Rela-
tion of Church and State in this matter, especially in the
United States.*

1398. Among those matters which fall under the jurisdiction of the ecclesiastical forum, by their very nature, marriage
holds a prominent place. The Council of Trent has expressly
defined that matrimonial causes belong to ecclesiastical, not
to secular judges.[1] However, as Pope Benedict XIV. well
explains, not everything that relates to marriage pertains, by
that very fact, to the ecclesiastical forum.[2] For there are three
kinds of matrimonial causes or questions. First, some have
reference to the validity of the marriage contracted. That
these questions belong exclusively to the ecclesiastical forum,
no Catholic can deny. Thus the Church has the sole right to
declare whether an impediment exists or not. In like manner, it is her province to pronounce upon the legitimacy or
illegitimacy of the children, because questions of this kind
depend upon the validity or nullity of the marriage. Hence,
as it belongs to the Church to declare whether a marriage is
valid or not, so also is it her right to pronounce children
either legitimate or illegitimate, at least so far as the ecclesiastical effects are concerned.[3]

1399. Secondly, others regard either the validity of betrothments or the right of having a divorce from bed and
board. These, in like manner, because of their relation to
the sacrament of matrimony, pertain solely to the ecclesiastical forum.[4] We say, *because of their relation*, etc.; for it is
evident that betrothments are a preliminary step to marriage,
and divorces destroy the rights arising from marriage.

---

[1] C. Trid. sess. 24, can. 12, de Sacr. matr.   [2] De Syn., l. 9, cap. 9, n. 3.
[3] Cap. 1-15, Qui filii sint legitimi (iv. 17).
[4] Cap. 10, de Sponsal. (iv. 1); cap. 3, 4, de Divort. (iv. 19).

1400. Thirdly, there are those which are connected indeed with matrimony, but yet have a direct bearing only on temporal or secular matters, such as the marriage dower or gifts, the inheritance, alimony, and the like.   These belong to the secular forum, and not, at least directly, to the ecclesiastical judge.[1]   We say, *not, at least directly;* for when they come up before the ecclesiastical judge incidentally,—*i.e.*, in connection with and during the trial or hearing of matrimonial questions concerning the validity of a marriage, betrothment, or the right to a divorce a *thoro et mensa*, they can be decided by him.[2]

1401. *Relations of Church and State existing at present, especially in the United States, in regard to matrimonial causes.* —In the United States (as in most countries of the continent) marriage is regarded by the law as merely a civil contract,[3] and hence certain secular magistrates, equally with the ministers of the Gospel (we use the words of Hudson), have the right to solemnize it.[4]   The persons who are generally authorized by law in this country to solemnize marriages are, chiefly: 1. "Any regularly ordained minister of any religious society."   2. "Any justice of the peace." 3. "Any religious society, agreeably to its forms and regulations."[5]

1402. Thus in the State of New Jersey the law is: "Every judge of any court of common pleas, and justice of the peace, and mayor of a city of this State, *and every stated and ordained minister of the Gospel*, is hereby authorized to solemnize marriages between such persons as may lawfully enter into the matrimonial relation ; and every religious society in this State may join together in marriage such persons as are of the same society, or when one of such persons is of such society,

---

[1] Ex cap. 7, Qui filii sint legitimi (iv. 17).

[2] Ex cap. 1, l. c.; Bened. XIV., l. c., n. 5. Kutschker, l. c., vol. v., p. 448.

[3] Walker, American Law, p. 246, § 102.

[4] Hudson, Law for the Clergy, p. 7.   [5] Walker, l. c., p. 248, n. 4.

according to the rules and customs of the society to which they or either of them belong."[1]

1403. As will be seen from this, the civil government in the United States does not require, for the legality of the marriage, that a civil marriage or separate marriage ceremony be performed before the civil magistrate, besides that which may be solemnized by the ecclesiastical authority. On the contrary, it allows "all persons belonging to any religious society, church, or denomination to celebrate their marriage according to the rules and principles of such religious society, church, or denomination."[1] Hence also it is plain that the State, with us, is anxious not to infringe upon the liberty of conscience guaranteed by the Constitution, also in regard to marriages. It recognizes as valid and legal in the eyes of the law any marriage celebrated by a minister, priest, or other clergyman, according to the rules and principles of his church or sect. Nay, as a rule, the law in all our States is, that the parochial registers of marriages shall be admitted as evidence in all courts of law and equity.[3]

1404. Generally speaking, however, the civil government with us prescribes that the person officiating at a marriage, whether he be a minister or priest or civil magistrate, shall forward within a certain time a certificate of the marriage to the county clerk or other official designated. Thus in New Jersey the law is: " That every justice of the peace and minister of the Gospel, or other person having authority to solemnize marriages, shall make and keep a particular record of all marriages solemnized before him, and transmit a certificate of every particular marriage within six months after the solemnization thereof, to the clerk of the court of common pleas for the county in which the marriage was solemnized."[4]

---

[1] Revision of Statutes of N. J., p. 1351, sec. 1; cf. ib., p. 631, sec. 2.
[2] Cf. Statutes of Illinois, ap. Hudson, p. 29, sec. 5.
[3] Cf. Revision of Statutes of N. J., p. 633, sec. 10. Trenton, 1877.
[4] Revision of Statutes of N. J., p. 632, sec. 6.

1405. Moreover, the State with us generally requires those who solemnize marriages to use all due diligence to ascertain whether the parties are *in statu libero,—i.e.,* whether there is any impediment or disability in the way,—and authorizes them to examine the parties and also witnesses, on their oath, as to the legality of the intended marriage.[1] For further particulars concerning the relation of Church and State, with us, in reference to matrimony and divorces, see our *Notes on the Second Plenary Council of Baltimore,*[2] where we have discussed the matter in a fuller manner.

Art. II.

Organization or Personnel of Ecclesiastical Courts for Matrimonial Causes, also in the United States.

1406. The *personnel* or organization of ecclesiastical courts for matrimonial causes is, with the exception of the defender of the marriage, the same as that of ecclesiastical courts for other ecclesiastical causes, civil and criminal. The bishop may if he chooses, establish in his diocese a separate or special tribunal or court for matrimonial causes, or he may have but one and the same tribunal or court both for matrimonial causes and all other causes, civil and criminal, provided, when there is question of matrimonial causes involving the validity or invalidity of a marriage already contracted, the defender of marriage be added to the court.

1407. As a matter of fact, in many parts of Europe, there are frequently, owing to the multiplicity of these causes and their complicated nature, and for their more expeditious hearing, separate or special diocesan tribunals or courts established for matrimonial causes.

1408. Whether the ecclesiastical court for matrimonial causes is the same with that for other causes, or whether it

---

[1] Hudson, l. c., p. 100.   [2] Pp. 246–263.

is a separate tribunal, it consists, like all other ecclesiastical courts, chiefly of a judge, and a secretary, to whom in causes of nullity the defender of marriage must be added. This is, at present, the *personnel*, also in the United States, of the ecclesiastical court for matrimonial causes. For, according to the Instruction of the S. C. de Prop. Fide *Causae Matrimoniales* of 1884, and the *Third Plenary Council of Baltimore* (n. 305), the *curia*, in the United States, for matrimonial causes, involving the validity or nullity of marriages already contracted, is composed of the bishop, or his delegate, as judge; of the defender, and of the secretary. We shall therefore describe the office and duty of each of these officials in relation to the hearing or trial of matrimonial causes.

1409. I. *The judge.*—By the law of the Church, as in force at the present day, the hearing and adjudication of matrimonial causes (no less than of all other ecclesiastical causes, civil and criminal) belongs in the first instance exclusively to the Ordinary of the diocese, that is, to the bishop, *sede plena*, and to the vicar-capitular (with us, administrator), or to one delegated by him, *sede vacante*, and no longer, as formerly,—*i.e.*, before the Council of Trent,—to inferior ecclesiastics, such as rural deans and archdeacons.[1]

1410. The Ordinary may authorize or delegate his vicar-general, or any other worthy ecclesiastic, to hear and pass final sentence in matrimonial causes, and that *universally*— that is, not only in this or that matrimonial cause, but in general in all such causes. For the power of the bishop concerning these causes or matters is ordinary, and may therefore, like any other ordinary power, be delegated to others. Nay, the more probable opinion is, that the vicar-general is empowered to hear and decide or pass final sentence on matrimonial causes by virtue of his office, without any special mandate.[2]

---

[1] C. Trid., sess. 24, cap. 20, de Ref.; cf. cap. 7, de Off. ord. in 6°.
[2] Mansella, de Processu jud. in caus. matr., p. 173. Romae, 1881.

1411. However, the plaintiff (*actor*) in a matrimonial cause cannot bring such cause before any episcopal court he pleases, but only before that tribunal or court which is competent. Now, as a rule, that tribunal is competent to whose authority and jurisdiction the *defendant* is subject. Hence the axiom : " Actor sequitur forum rei." But, as we have shown above,[1] when speaking of the competency of tribunals, a person becomes subject chiefly to the tribunal or forum or judge of the place where he has his permanent dwelling-place or *domicilium*. This forum of domicile, as we have seen above,[2] is the true, natural, ordinary, and general forum or court to which a person is amenable.

1412. Hence, in order that a matrimonial cause may be brought before the proper or competent court or judge, the residence or domicile of the married couple must be principally taken into consideration. As the wife contracts the domicile, and therefore becomes subject to the forum or judge of her husband, it follows that a married couple, so far as matrimonial causes are concerned, falls under the jurisdiction of the bishop, in whose diocese the husband has his domicile or residence.[3]

1413. To this rule, however, there are two exceptions, namely, where the cohabitation of husband and wife has been broken up (*a*) by a separation *a mensa et thoro*, (*b*) by the husband's maliciously deserting the wife. In the *first* case, each party can make use of the right, which may belong to it against the other party, of asking for the annulment of the marriage, before the bishop of the diocese where the spouse against whom the annulment is asked has his or her domicile. In the *second* case, the wife who is maliciously deserted can institute her action before the bishop of the diocese where she has her domicile. For, wherever the deserting husband is, he remains subject to the bishop of that diocese where he had his domicile at the time of the desertion, since the domicile is not changed by such desertion.[4] Finally, we observe that once a party has

[1] Supra, n. 784.   [2] Supra, n. 784.
[3] Mansella, l. c., p. 174, n. 6.   [4] Mansella, l. c., pp. 172-174.

been duly cited for trial or the hearing in a matrimonial cause, it makes no difference whether he changes his domicile or not. He remains subject, so far as concerns the cause in which the citation was issued, to the bishop or judge who issued the citation.[1]

1414. The bishop is perfectly free to sit personally in court in matrimonial causes, or, as we have seen, to appoint others to do so in his stead. As a matter of fact, in the greater part of Europe, as has been already stated, bishops do not personally take cognizance of such causes, but appoint others—*v.g.*, their vicars-general, or a collective body of judges—to adjudicate upon them. Thus Cardinal Kutschker, in his celebrated work on the "Canon Law of Marriage," [2] informs us that in Austria the bishop, in the hearing and deciding of matrimonial causes, makes use of a special ecclesiastical tribunal or court, consisting of a president and of assessors, whose number shall not be less than four nor more than six, and who shall have a decisive voice.[3]

1415. The bishop is at liberty to give these delegated judges or tribunals, whether consisting of individuals or collective bodies, power either to hear and pronounce final sentence upon the case, or only to hear or try it, and to reserve to himself the final sentence. Here we may remark that these collective bodies of judges, which we have just mentioned, are greatly favored both by the letter and by the spirit of the law of the Church.[4] Thus Pope Celestine III. says: "Illa quippe fuit antiqua Sedis Apostolicae provisio, ut hujusmodi causarum recognitiones, duobus quam uni, tribus quam duobus libentius delegaret." [5] The reason is thus stated in the words immediately following the above: "Cum (sicut canones attestantur) integrum sit judicium, quod plurimorum sententiis confirmatur." [6]

1416. As in other trials or causes, so also in those relating

---

[1] Mansella, n. 7; supra, n. 1008. [2] Eherecht, vol. v., p. 482. [3] Ib., p. 485.
[4] Ib., pp. 482, 484. [5] Cap. 21, de Off. del. (i. 29). [6] Ib.

to marriages, exception can be taken to the judge, whether he be the bishop, or other person appointed by him to take cognizance of such causes. As we have already seen, when an exception is made against an ecclesiastical judge, arbitrators must be chosen to decide whether such exception has any foundation or not. Cardinal Kutschker holds that an exception taken against one of the members of a collective judicial body is decided by that body itself, and not by arbitrators.[1]

1417. *Ecclesiastical tribunals for matrimonial causes in the United States.*—Formerly, matrimonial causes, with us, even where they involved the validity or nullity of a marriage already contracted, were, as a rule, decided by the bishop or also sometimes by the rector of the parties, without any formality whatever. Only in one or two dioceses was a defender of marriage made use of, in cases where there was question of the validity or nullity of a marriage. This state of things was owing mainly to the missionary condition of the country. Now, however, that this missionary character has given way, at least in most of the Eastern and in many of the Western States, to a fuller and more perfect development of our ecclesiastical organization, which admits of a better observance of the general law of the Church, the Sacred Congregation de Prop. Fide, by its Instruction *Causae Matrimoniales* of 1884, has ordained, and the *Third Plenary Council of Baltimore*, Nos. 304, 305, has accordingly enacted, that in future, the general law of the Church, as laid down chiefly in the *Const. Dei Miseratione* of Pope Benedict XIV., shall be observed also in the United States, whenever there is question of hearing and deciding matrimonial causes, especially those which involve the validity or invalidity of marriages already contracted.

1418. Under the general law of the Church, the bishop is at liberty to hear matrimonial causes *in person*, or to ap-

[1] Canon Law of Marr., vol. v., p. 556.

point either a single person, or several persons acting as a collective body, to do so for him and in his stead. The above Instruction of the S. C. de Prop. Fide of 1884—*Causae Matrimoniales*—also enacts: " Munus moderatoris actorum episcopus vel ipse sibi assumet, vel suum vicarium gener-alem, aut alium probum et expertum virum e clero ad illud delegabit." Instr. cit. § 6; C. Pl. Balt. III., n. 305.

1419. II. *The secretary.*—In all judicial proceedings, sum-mary as well as ordinary or formal, whether in civil or criminal causes or matters,[1] and consequently also in matri-monial causes or trials, especially when there is question of the validity of a marriage already contracted, a secretary must be present, and take down the minutes of the proceed-ings.[2] These minutes should contain chiefly the names of the persons present—namely, of the judge or judges, of the defender of the marriage, of the husband and wife whose marriage is under examination ; the chief or essential for-malities of the trial, especially the documents read before or submitted to the court; the depositions of the married couple and other witnesses ; all decisions, interlocutory or final.[3] The greatest care should be taken by the secretary or notary to record accurately and *verbatim* both the ques-tions or cross-questions proposed to the married couple or the witnesses, and the answers thereto by these parties.[4]

1420. It is superfluous to remark here, that also in the United States, in matrimonial trials or processes, a secretary should be present at the proceedings, whose duty, as above described, it is to keep a careful and correct record of the proceedings.

1421. III. *Defender of marriage.*—Besides the judge and the secretary, a third official, called the defender of marriage (*defensor matrimonii*), necessarily forms part of the matrimo-

---

[1] Cap. 11 x, de Probat. [2] Cf. Instr. S. C. C., 22 Aug., 1840, § Praefinita die.
[3] Cf. cit. Instr. S. C. C.; Kutschker, l. c., p. 534.
[4] Cf. cit. Instr., § Cum itaque.

nial court in certain cases. We say, *in certain cases*—namely, in those cases where there is question of the validity or nullity of a *marriage already contracted.*[1] In other matrimonial causes—*v.g.*, where there is question of the validity of a marriage *about to be contracted*, or of separation *a mensa et thoro*, —this defender is not required. Of the rights and duties of this official we shall speak a little further on, when we come to discuss the mode of procedure in causes of nullity of marriages.

1422. All the above officials should first make the profession of faith of Pope Pius IV.,[2] as amended by Pope Pius IX. on January 20, 1877, and be also sworn.[3] The defender of marriage must be sworn not only when he is appointed to his office, but at the beginning of every matrimonial trial.

ART. III.

Form of Trial or Mode of Procedure to be followed at present in Matrimonial Causes in general.

1423. By the law of the Church, as enacted by Pope Clement V. (1312), the trial, or judicial proceedings in all matrimonial causes whatever, whether they relate to divorces from bed and board, betrothments, or even to the validity of a marriage already contracted, can be summary (*processus summarius*), and therefore need not be conducted with all the formalities of the ordinary trial, or *processus ordinarius.*[4]

1424. This law is still in force, at least, with regard to all matrimonial causes, where there is no question of the nullity of a marriage already contracted. We say, *at least;* for it is not clear whether, so far as causes of nullity are concerned, it has been altogether repealed by the constitution *Dei misera-*

---

[1] Bened. XIV., const. Dei miseratione, § 5 Quod vero.
[2] Cf. C. Trid., sess. 25, cap. 2, de Ref.; our Elements, vol. i., p. 446.
[3] Cf. Kutschker, l. c., p. 499.
[4] Clem. Dispendiosam 2, de Jud. (ii. 1); cf. Kutschker, l. c., p. 524.

tione issued by Pope Benedict XIV. on the 3d of November, 1741. It is true that this constitution prescribes many for- malities to be observed in causes of nullity of marriages which were not obligatory before that time. But apart from these special and peculiar formalities, the constitution in question nowhere states that the trial cannot be summary, so far as concerns the other parts of the trial or proceedings, which are not mentioned.[1] Hence it would seem that even matrimonial causes of nullity may at present be tried sum- marily, so far as this summary procedure is compatible with the observance of the peculiar formalities laid down in said constitution, as explained and developed by the Sacred Con- gregation of Council, in its Instruction, dated Aug. 22, 1840, on trials for matrimonial causes. We have just said *may*, not *must;* for the ecclesiastical judge not only can observe the formalities of ordinary trials, together with those prescribed in the constitution of Benedict XIV., but will, according to Bouix,[2] act more prudently and safely by doing so, as the general context of said constitution appears with sufficient clearness to suppose that the form of trial in matrimonial causes of nullity should be solemn or formal.

1425. *General form of trial for matrimonial causes in the United States.*—With us, the form of trial prescribed by the S. C. de Prop. Fide, in its Instruction *Causae Matrimoniales*, issued in 1884, and embodied in the acts of the *Third Plenary Council of Baltimore*, p. 262 sq., is obligatory at present, and that on pain of nullity, in all matrimonial causes, involving the validity or invalidity of marriages already contracted. The above Instruction is a synopsis of the *Const. Dei Miseratione* of Pope Benedict XIV., and of the Instruction of the S. C. C. issued Aug. 22, 1840; it is, therefore, a complete *resumé* of the general law of the Church on matrimonial causes, as in force at the present day.

[1] Craisson, n. 6092.   [2] De Jud., vol. ii., p. 446.

1426. *Q.* Here it may be asked whether the swearing in of the officials of the court and of the witnesses is feasible, or even obligatory, in matrimonial causes in the United States?

A. Before answering, we observe that the general rule is that all officials who take part in judicial proceedings—that is, not only the judge himself, but also the assessors, secretaries, etc.—must take an oath, when they are appointed, to discharge their duties faithfully. Thus Monacelli says: "Et est etiam generale, quod officiales in ingressu officii, jurare debeant, quamvis sint solum assessores, vel judices."[1] This holds, of course, also of officials in matrimonial causes or trials.[2] So far as the defender of marriage is concerned, the law of the Church is particularly strict on this head. In regard to the swearing of witnesses, the general law of the Church is, that they cannot testify otherwise than under oath.[3] This law is expressly declared by the S. C. C., in its Instruction of August 22, 1840, to be binding in matrimonial causes or trials of nullity.[4]

1427. We now answer. That it is feasible, with us, to administer the oath to the officials and witnesses under consideration, there can scarcely be any doubt. The only objection that could be urged would be that our civil law considered such oaths illegal, which, as we have seen, is not the case. Our civil law simply holds itself neutral with regard to such oaths, neither recognizing nor forbidding them.

1428. That it is *obligatory* at present, is undoubted. For the Instruction of the S. C. de Prop. Fide, *Causae Matrimoniales*, issued in 1884, expressly prescribes that the defender of the marriage shall take the oath. Its words are: "Defensor matrimonii antequam munus sibi commissum suscipiat, coram actorum moderatore *juramentum praestabit,*

[1] Form. Leg. Pract., tit. 7, form. 10, n. 2 (Pars I., p. 216).
[2] Kutschker, l. c., p. 499.   [3] Supra, n. 840, 841.
[4] Cf. Instr. cit., § Cum itaque.

tactis sanctis evangeliis, de munere suo diligenter et incor.
rupte adimplendo, spondens se omnia voce et scripto deduc·
turum quae ad validitatem matrimonii sustinendam conferre
judicaverit."[1]

The same Instruction also enacts, in accordance with
the general law of the Church, that the witnesses shall take
the oath. The words are: "Ab omnibus et singulis testimonium dicturis moderator actorum ante omnia *juramen-*
tum exiget de veritate dicenda, et si res ita postulet, etiam
de secreto servando, praemissa congrua monitione de juramenti sanctitate, praesertim si examinandi rudes sint et
ignari. Juramentum praestandum erit tactis sanctis evangeliis, et in singulis examinibus eodem modo repetendum."[2]

---

[1] Instr. Causae mat., § 10.   [2] Ib., § 12.

ART. IV.

Form of Trial or Mode of Procedure peculiar to Divorces "a mensa et thoro."

1431. Causes of this kind are usually introduced into the bishop's court for matrimonial causes, by the statement or report of the case sent by the parish priest or rector of the parties to the bishop. Before sending in this statement, the rector should use all the means in his power to effect a reconciliation between the married couple applying for a divorce *a mensa et thoro.* This report should summarily state the request of the plaintiff for a divorce, the grounds upon which it is based, the character of both parties, and in general all the particulars of the case.

1432. When all efforts at reconciliation have failed, the trial is begun by the citation. In other words, the defendant—that is, the husband or wife against whom the divorce is demanded—is cited by the ecclesiastical court for matrimonial causes to appear in person, on a certain day, in said court, for the trial of the cause. This citation is now usually executed or served upon the parties through their rector or parish priest. If on the appointed day the parties appear in court, the complainant—*i.e.*, the husband or wife seeking for a divorce—first states the complaint, and the defendant puts in his or her plea or general denial of the complaint, and thus the cause is said to be contested—*lis contestata.*

1433. Observe, however, that this part of the trial may also be conducted by letters. In other words, the parties, instead of appearing personally in court to lodge their complaint, may make their formal complaint and put in their plea by means of letters to the court. In this case the complainant's letter containing the charges or formal complaint must be communicated by the court to the defendant to

enable him to send in his plea. Of course in these as also in
all the other stages of the proceedings, the parties may be,
and in Europe are generally, assisted by counsel.

1434. The next step is the production of the proofs, which
is the main part of the trial. When the defendant has denied
the plaintiff's statement, it becomes the latter's duty to sustain
them by canonical proofs. These usually consist principally
of the depositions of witnesses. The manner in which these
are examined in trials for divorces is the same as that for
criminal causes, which has been already fully explained.
The defence next brings its proofs, witnesses, documents,
and the like. Finally, the counsel on both sides sum up the
case, after which the judge renders his decision, which becomes *res judicata* unless an appeal is lodged against it within
ten days.[1] From what has been said, it will be seen that the
ecclesiastical summary trial for matrimonial causes of separation *a mensa et thoro* is substantially the same with the summary trial of other causes, civil or criminal.

1435. *By whose authority and for what causes separation
from bed and board can take place.*—Divorces are of two kinds,
as we have shown elsewhere,[2] namely, (*a*) *a vinculo* from the
bond of matrimony, which totally severs the marriage tie;
(*b*) and *a mensa et thoro*, from bed and board, which merely
separates the parties without dissolving the marriage bond.
While the Church teaches on the one hand that a marriage
which has once been validly contracted and also consummated by the faithful can never be dissolved as to the *vinculum*, except by the death of one of the married couple,[3]
she also affirms on the other that a divorce or separation
from bed and board may be allowed for various reasons and
in various cases. Thus the Council of Trent expressly
teaches: "Si quis dixerit Ecclesiam errare, cum *ob multas*

[1] Permaneder, Manual of Canon Law, § 326–330.
[2] Our Notes on the Second Plenary Council of Baltimore, n. 280.
[3] Cf. Feije, de Imp., p. 452.

causas, separationes inter conjuges, quoad thorum seu cohabitationem ad certum incertumve tempus fieri posse decernit,
anathema sit." [1]

1436. As the heading of this article indicates, we shall
here confine ourselves to the latter kind of divorce—namely,
that from bed and board. It can take place, and that either
for life or only for a time, (*a*) by the mutual consent of the
married couple—*v.g.*, where both agree to embrace the
religious state, even after they have consummated the marriage, or where the party guilty of adultery, cruelty, etc.,
voluntarily assents to the separation demanded by the innocent party, without obliging the latter to have recourse to
the ecclesiastical judge to obtain the divorce ; [2] (*b*) or even
against the will of one of the married couple. Of this latter
separation we here speak. [3]

1437. *Q.* What are the causes or reasons that render a
divorce or separation from bed and board against the will of
either of the married couple lawful in the eyes of the law of
the Church ?

A. We premise : The divorce in question can take place
only for grave causes, expressed in or approved by the
sacred canons. [4] These causes are chiefly the following :
1. Adultery. 2. The falling into heresy or infidelity of the
husband or wife. 3. Danger of the soul's salvation. 3. Cruelty
or bodily danger in general. We observe, however, that
only in one of these cases—namely, in the case of adultery—
is this divorce or separation perpetual or for life. In the
other cases it is *per se* but temporary, lasting only as long
as the reason for which it was granted continues to exist.

1438. We observe, secondly, that, as a rule, the separation
should be made by authority of the proper ecclesiastical
judge (namely, the bishop to whom the couple is subject) or

---

[1] C. Trid., sess. 24, can. 8, de Sacr. matr.   [3] Feije. l. c., n. 577.
[2] Cf. Reiff., l. 4, t. 19, n. 26, 27.   [4] Cf. Feije, l. c., n. 578.

tribunal, but not by the parties themselves.[1] For nobody is a competent judge in his own cause. We say, "by authority of the proper *ecclesiastical judge ;*" for it is not permitted, at least *per se,* to have recourse to the civil or secular courts for a divorce, whether *quoad vinculum* or only *quoad thorum.* Yet, as we have shown in our "Notes on the Second Plenary Council of Baltimore,"[2] from Kenrick,[3] whose opinion is indorsed by the illustrious Feije,[4] Catholics, not only in the United States but also in Europe, may at times apply to the secular authorities for a divorce, not indeed as though they recognized in the civil power any authority to grant divorces, but simply and solely for the purpose of obtaining certain civil effects, which have been fully described in our above "Notes."

1439. It is true that in the United States the ecclesiastical judge—that is, in the first instance, the Ordinary or the tribunal, if any, established by him—is rarely invoked by Catholics for divorces *a thoro.* In most cases they either apply to the civil court or separate of their own accord. They should be instructed at least to take the advice of their rector or confessor. We think that, considering our peculiar circumstances, the permission given by the rector or confessor is usually sufficient, at least *pro foro interno.* Rectors or pastors should carefully weigh cases of this kind brought before them, consult the bishop, and, if possible, keep a record of the testimony collected by them.

1440. We now proceed to discuss the chief cases where the separation can take place according to ecclesiastical law. I. *Adultery.*—The first and chief canonical cause for which separation from bed and board may take place, and that for life, is adultery committed by either the husband or wife. This is plain from the words of our Lord himself,[5] and from

---

[1] Kutschker, l. c., p. 652.   [2] N. 284-288.   [3] Theol. Mor. Tr. xxi., n. 111, 112.
[4] De Imp., n. 583.   [5] Matth. xix. 9.

express texts of canon law.' However, in order to produce this effect, the adultery must be (*a*) formal, not merely material; (*b*) consummated; (*c*) not condoned, nor committed with the consent, express or tacit or at the instigation of the other party; (*d*) nor compensated, so to say, by the adultery of the party applying for the divorce.' Here we remark that the wife is not, as a rule, supposed to give any tacit consent to adultery committed by her husband, even when she knows for certain that he has been guilty of this crime. The reason is, that ordinarily women are afraid to reprove men.

1441. (*c*) Finally, the adultery must be *proved*, or juridically established, before the juridical sentence of separation can be pronounced by the ecclesiastical judge.' Now, as Pope Celestin III. says, the *copula carnalis*—in the present case, adultery—is proved either by eye-witnesses, or in their default, by other means, such as violent presumptions.' However, canonists commonly maintain that for the purposes of a divorce the proofs need not always be absolutely conclusive, but may be based upon vehement or violent presumptions, which must nevertheless be of such a nature as to create a moral certainty. The cap. Litteris 12, *de Praesumpt.* (ii. 23), clearly and fully explains the subject thus: " Nobis innotuit, quod . . . accusatores matrimonii produxerunt testes firmiter asserentes, quod . . . solum cum sola, nudum cum nuda, in eodem lecto jacentem, ea, ut credebant" (testes) " intentione, ut eam cognosceret carnaliter, viderunt, multis locis secretis, et latebris ad hoc commodis, et horis electis . . . Respondemus quod ex hujusmodi violenta et certa suspicione fornicationis, potest sententia divortii promulgari." Note here, that the violent indications of guilt in the case are not to be taken on mere hearsay, but must be proved to exist, by competent witnesses.'

---

¹ Cap. 4, 5, 8, ed Divort. (iv. 19). ² Feije, l. c., n. 579.
³ Cap. 27 x, de Test. et attest. (ii. 20). ⁴ Ib.
⁵ Schmalzg., l. 4, t. 19, n. 117.

1442. *Q.* Can the innocent party leave the adulterous of his or her own accord ?

A. There are two opinions. The first is absolutely in the negative, and contends that the separation can never take place, save by the sentence and intervention of the ecclesiastical court,' even where the adultery is notorious.* Thus the *can. Saeculares* expressly ordains that husbands who leave their wives without the intervention of the ecclesiastical judge shall be excommunicated.*

1443. The second opinion distinguishes thus: It is either sufficiently certain that adultery has been committed by either the husband or the wife, or it is doubtful. Where it is doubtful, the innocent party cannot separate from the adulterous of his or her own accord.* If it is certain, we must again distinguish : The certainty is either private—that is, the innocent party knows the crime, though only privately; or it is public—that is, the crime of adultery is public and notorious. In this latter case, the innocent party can leave the adulterous of his or her own accord. In the first case—that is, where the innocent party is certain *privately* of the adultery of the other party—the matter is controverted. But the more common opinion allows the innocent party to leave of his or her own accord, even in this case,* at least *pro foro conscientiae*, and apart from scandal.

1444. For the rest, it is always better that the separation should *never* take place except by the intervention of the ecclesiastical court.* We remark here in passing, that the innocent party is never *obliged* to make use of this right of separating from the guilty party, except when the correction of the latter or the avoiding of scandal makes it really necessary.'

1445. II. *Apostasy and heresy.*—According to the law of

---

[1] Cf. ib , n. 109. [2] Ex cap. 6, de Adulter. (v. 16); cap. 3, de Divort. (iv. 19).
[3] Can. Saeculares 1, Caus. 33, Q. 2.
[4] Ex cap. 9, de Sponsal. (iv. 1). [5] Schmalzg., l. c., n. 112, 113.
[6] Feije, de Imp., p. 454. [7] Ib.

the Church, as in force also with us, if either of the married couple falls from the true faith into heresy or infidelity, the other can leave him or her, and that even of his or her own accord, at least when there is *periculum in mora—i.e.*, danger to the spiritual welfare of the party from delaying the separation till the ecclesiastical judge shall have pronounced his sentence of separation.[1]

1446. III. *Incitement to crime or danger to the salvation of the innocent party (periculum animae).—*Where one of the married couple incites the other to commit crime, whether it be heresy, or any other grave sin,—*v.g.*, theft, sodomy, etc., —so that the latter cannot live with the former, without seriously endangering his or her salvation, the innocent party not only can, but is sometimes bound to separate from the guilty party.[2] This is clearly stated in the *can. Idolatria* 5, *Caus.* 28, Q. 1. The heading itself of this canon is: " Licite dimittitur uxor, quae virum suum cogere quaerit ad malum."

1447. IV. *Bodily danger (periculum corporis).—*By bodily danger we mean that which proceeds from cruel treatment. It is certain that a divorce *quod thorum* may be granted for cruelty.[3] By cruel treatment, however, we mean, not every ordinary injurious word or action, but threats to kill, frequent quarrels, blows or striking, though only if they are severe, inflicted frequently, and for slight cause. We observe that in this as well as in the foregoing case, namely, in the case of spiritual as well as bodily danger, the separation can be made only by authority of the ecclesiastical judge. If, however, there is danger in delay, a separation for a brief space of time can be made by the innocent party, of his or her own authority.[4]

1448. From what has been said it is apparent that, as far as possible, the divorce *quod thorum et cohabitationem* should

---

[1] Cap. 6, 7, de Divort.; cap. final., de Convers. conj. (iii. 32).

[2] Reiff., l. 4, t. 19, n. 34.

[3] Cap. 8, 13, de Restit. spol. (ii. 13).   [4] Feije, l. c., p. 455.

nearly always take place, not by authority of the parties themselves, but by authority of the ecclesiastical judge. However, Giraldus very properly writes : " It is true that these divorces cannot take place, except by the authority of the judge, whenever there is question of a perpetual divorce. But I believe that they can be made by private authority" (of the parties themselves) " for a time, because of some impending serious danger to the soul or body, which cannot be averted otherwise; or also for the purpose of seeing whether the party guilty of adultery will show signs of repentance ; provided, however, that the separation (by private authority) is made without scandal, and by the advice of the confessor, or some other prudent person." [1]

ART. V.

Peculiar Form of Trial in Matrimonial Causes where there is question of dissolving a Marriage, once contracted, absolutely or " Quoad Vinculum" — Processus in Causis Nullitatis Matrimonii.

§ 1. *General Features of the Law, as in force at the present Day—Defender of the Marriage, also in the United States.*

1449. In matrimonial causes of nullity there is question not merely of the rights of either of the contending married couple, but also, and that chiefly, of the marriage bond, and therefore of preventing collusion on the part of the married couple for the purpose of breaking their marriage. Hence the Church, especially in more recent times, has wisely or dained that in the hearing of matrimonial causes, particularly those involving the validity or nullity of a marriage already contracted, the mode of procedure to be followed by the ecclesiastical judge should be different from that whic'o is

---

[1] Giraldi, Expos. Jur. Pont., pars. i., sect. 734, p. 541. Roma. ·8:4.

prescribed for other causes, especially civil, falling under the ecclesiastical forum.

1450. This peculiar trial or mode of procedure, as in force at the present day all over the world, is contained in the Constitution of the great Pope Benedict XIV., beginning with the words *Dei Miseratione*, and issued November 3, 1741. This celebrated Constitution defines principally the rights and duties of the ecclesiastical judge, and of the defender of the marriage, and explains the force and effect of the sentences pronounced by the ecclesiastical judge in matrimonial causes. In order to evolve these points more fully, and particularly to point out clearly the formalities of the trial of such causes, the S. C. C. issued an Instruction, on the 22d of August, 1840, in which it lays down an accurate method of conduct-ing trials in matrimonial causes of nullity. In this admirable Instruction, the judge, the defender of the marriage, and the secretary will find their chief duties pointed out to them, and the course to be followed and the steps to be taken in the causes in question traced out and explained.

1451. These two documents—namely, the above Constitu-tion of Benedict XIV. and the Instruction of S. C. C. of 1840 —form at the present day the law of the Church concerning the trial or mode of procedure to be followed all over Chris-tendom in matrimonial causes of nullity.[1] Where circum-stances do not allow of the full and complete observance of each and every item prescribed in the above Constitution of Benedict XIV., as authentically explained by the Instruction of the S. C. C. of 1840, a dispensation can be obtained from the Pope to that effect. In fact, the Holy See frequently grants such dispensation, and permits the trial in causes of nullity to be conducted informally—that is, without the observance of all the various judicial formalities prescribed in the above documents. But the Holy See always insists,

[1] Mansella, l. c., p. 182.

even when it gives the dispensation, on the observance of the *substantial* formalities required by the above documents and especially on the presence of the defender of the marriage.[1]

1452. We shall now, before proceeding to describe the formalities of the trial in matrimonial causes of nullity, give a synopsis of the chief features of the Constitution *Dei Miseratione* of Pope Benedict XIV. In the preamble of the Constitution the great Pontiff deplores the facility and haste with which marriages were being pronounced invalid in some of the ecclesiastical courts,[2] and the scandal thus given.[3] Next, the causes of this abuse are enumerated. Among these causes the Pope points out these: (*a*) That certain ecclesiastical judges pronounce marriages invalid upon slight or no investigation; (*b*) that frequently but one of the married couple—namely, the husband or wife who demanded the nullity—appeared at the trial, the other failing to appear and defend the marriage. Whence it happened that the party demanding the annulment of the marriage easily obtained a sentence of nullity, and was thus enabled to remarry.

1453. (*c*) That even where both appeared for trial, it often came to pass that if the sentence declared the marriage invalid, neither of them appealed to the higher (ecclesiastical) court, and that either because they were in collusion with each other for the purpose of having their marriage declared invalid, or because, even where they had acted in good faith, the defendant or party that had sustained the validity of the marriage, once sentence of invalidity was rendered, failed to appeal—*v.g.*, because he or she was destitute of the money or other means of prosecuting the appeal, or also because he or she underwent a change of mind on the subject.[4]

1454. To remedy these grave evils the Pope lays down

---

[1] Cf. Kutschker, l. c., vol. v., p. 525. [2] Const. Dei Miseratione, § 1.
[3] Ib., § 2. [4] Const. Dei Miseratione cit., § 3.

the following enactments, which constitute the law of the Church in this matter at the present day, all over Christendom, and at present also in the United States: 1. Each and every Ordinary of the whole Catholic world shall appoint in his diocese a *defender of marriage* (*matrimonii defensor*), who shall, if possible, be an ecclesiastic, and skilled in canon law, and of unblemished character.[1] 2. This defender is to be regarded *tanquam pars necessaria ad judicii validitatem*, in all cases where there is question of the validity or nullity of marriages—that is, in all cases where there is question of annulling, *v.g.*, because of an alleged annulling impediment, a marriage *already contracted*, but not where there is question of the validity of a marriage *about to be contracted*. Hence all proceedings in such causes of nullity are null and void if the defender of the marriage is not properly cited to act in the case, and is therefore absent. Nay, he must be cited, not merely once,—namely, at the beginning of the trial,—but at every subsequent stage or judicial act, and any act whatever of the court to which he is not called is of no effect whatever. Thus Pope Benedict XIV. expressly says: " Quaecunque eo" (defensore) "non legitime citato, in judicio peractae fuerint, nulla declaramus."[2]

1455. 3. *Now, what are the chief duties of this defender of the marriage?* (*a*) He is strictly bound to be present at all the proceedings in the case. In fact, he is a necessary or legal co-defendant in every cause of nullity, and as such must assist at all the proceedings at which the real defendant— that is, the husband or wife against whom the annulment of the marriage is asked—has a right to assist, and that even when the latter is present in person. Hence the defender is obliged to be present at the examination of witnesses, etc.[3] But he is moreover, *ex officio*, a necessary member and official of the court itself, and as such has the right and duty to

---

[1] Const. Dei Miseratione cit., § 5.   [2] Ib., § 7.   [3] Ib., §§ 6, 7.

assist at all the sessions or meetings of the court, and to have free access at all times to the documents and testimony of either of the contending parties.[1]

1456. (*b*) He should carefully examine the facts in the case, and both orally and in writing submit to the court all possible proofs and arguments in favor of the validity of the marriage, and in rebuttal of the proofs and argu ments advanced by the party seeking to have the marriage set aside.[2] (*c*) He must, as we have seen, take an oath to fulfil his duties faithfully, and that not only when he is first appointed, but every time he acts in a cause.[3] He is appointed by the bishop, and removable by him for cause.[4]

1457. (*d*) If in the first instance the marriage is sustained as valid, he should not appeal. But if the contrary happens, he is bound to appeal, even though the party against whom the sentence was pronounced does not wish to appeal. If the court of the second instance, like that of the first, also pronounces the marriage invalid, he need not appeal again unless he thinks proper. We say, *unless he thinks proper;* for he may and should appeal a second time, namely, to the Holy See, where he believes that he cannot conscientiously acquiesce in the sentence of nullity pronounced by the court of the second instance—*v.g.*, because the sentence seems to him manifestly unjust or invalid, or because it reverses the sentence declaring the marriage valid as given in the first instance.[5]

1458. So far as the husband and wife in the case are con- cerned, whose marriage is being called in question, they are forbidden, on pain of incurring all the penalties established by the Church against polygamists and others who contract marriage against the prohibition of the Church, to consider their marriage as dissolved, and pass to a new marriage, pend-

---

[1] Instr. S. C. C., 22 Aug., 1840, § Hisce praemissis, in fine.
[2] Const. cit., § 6; Kutschker, l. c., p. 494.   [3] Const. cit., § 7.
[4] Ib., § 5.   [5] Ib., § 11.

ing any of the above appeals.[1] Only after their marriage has been declared invalid *twice*,—that is, both in the first and second instance,—can they *remarry*, provided the defender of the marriage does not appeal also from the second decision. In the latter case they must wait for the issue of the trial in the third and last instance.[2]

1459. However, it must be observed that even when the marriage has been, as above stated, twice declared invalid, and the parties have remarried, it is allowed *at any time* afterwards, no matter how many years may have elapsed, to produce new proofs (*i.e.*, proofs which have been either *newly* discovered or were not submitted in the former trials, either because of collusion, ignorance, etc.) in the ecclesiastical court to show that the marriage was valid.[3] For matrimonial causes of nullity *never* become *res judicatae*.[4] The only exception is, where both of the married couple are dead, and thirty or forty years afterwards the legitimacy of their children is impugned, on the ground that their marriage was null and void.[5]

This is a summary of the regulations made by Pope Benedict XIV., in his renowned constitution *Dei Miseratione*. Hence, whenever it is sought to have a marriage, which has been already contracted, dissolved because of an alleged annulling impediment,—*v.g.*, consanguinity, affinity,—the defender of the marriage has to be called to the proceedings, as above stated, and that on pain of nullity of the trial.

1460. The constitution *Dei Miseratione* of the immortal Pontiff, Benedict XIV., is now obligatory, also in the United States. This is expressly stated by the *Third Plenary Council of Baltimore*, n. 304, which says: "In agendis hisce causis (matrimonialibus) pro rei gravitate exacte servetur tum constitutio Benedicti XIV. *Dei Miseratione*, 3 Nov. 1741,

---

[1] Const. cit., §§ 9, 11.   [2] Ib., § 11.   [3] Ib., § 11.
[4] Cap. 7, de Sent. (ii. 27); ib. Glossa, v. Permanere.
[5] Schmalzg., l. 4, t. 18, n. 27.   [6] Supra, n. 1407, 1417.

tum Instructio a S. Congr. de Prop. Fide nobis communi-
cata, quae incipit *Causae Matrimoniales.*"[1]   The same is
manifest, also from the above Instruction of the Propaganda
mentioned by the *Third Plenary Council of Baltimore*, in the
passage just quoted.   For, this Instruction embodies in its
provisions all the enactments of the constitution *Dei Miseratione* relative to the *defensor matrimonii*, as explained
already above, n. 1452 sq.

§ 2. *Various Stages of the Trial.*

1461. Having thus far pointed out the rights and duties
of the judge, secretary, and defender of the marriage, we
shall now briefly describe the trial itself, or its various formalities and stages.   These formalities are laid down in the
above-quoted Instruction of the S. C. C., of August 22, 1840,
which is obligatory all over Christendom, and constitutes
the law at present in force everywhere.   The provisions of
the latter document are applied to the United States by the
S. C. de Prop. Fide, in its latest Instruction issued in 1884,
and beginning with the words *Causae Matrimoniales*, which
is now obligatory all over this country.   The trial for matrimonial causes involving the validity of marriages already
contracted (of which alone we here speak), as outlined in
these Instructions, is conducted in the following manner.

1462. When the ecclesiastical judge is about to take cognizance of a marriage which is alleged to have been contracted with an annulling impediment, he shall receive the
complaint or accusation of the nullity of the marriage (*accusatio matrimonii*), that is, the demand for its annulment, only
from those persons who are qualified by ecclesiastical law
to make the demand.   For, as we shall see, in the case of
some impediments the married couple alone has the right and
is allowed to demand the annulment.   In the case of others,

---

[1] Cf. Kutschker, l. c., vol. v., pp. 520, 524.

the parents and relatives, or any other persons whatever, can make the demand ; finally, in the case of other impediments, the judge himself can and is sometimes even obliged to inquire *ex officio* into the validity of the marriage. The accusation of the marriage should be made in writing, no matter whether it is made by the married couple itself, or others.[1] In receiving this accusation, the ordinary or judge should also endeavor to obtain from the plaintiff, or accusing party, a full statement of the case, together with a list of the witnesses and of the other proofs.[2]

1463. Having thus received the complaint or accusation of the marriage, the bishop appoints (*a*) another ecclesiastic —*v.g.*, his vicar-general, or some other worthy and learned ecclesiastic—to act as judge for him, unless he has already permanently appointed one beforehand, or prefers to adjudicate the cause in person; (*b*) a secretary ; (*c*) and a defender of marriage.[3] Of course, where these officials are appointed *permanently* in a diocese, it is unnecessary to make these appointments each time a cause presents itself.

1464. The matrimonial court being thus organized, the trial begins with the examination of the plaintiff and defendant, and other witnesses. The order in which these various persons are examined, as laid down in the above Instruction, is as follows : First, the plaintiff—that is, the spouse or other person who demands the annulment of the marriage or contends that it is null—is examined or heard, and that under oath, and in the presence of the judge or his deputy, the defender, and the secretary.[4] The mode of examination is this: The defender of the marriage having previously prepared written questions or interrogatories, hands them sealed to the judge or secretary in court, and in the presence of the complainant.[5] Next, at the request of the defender, the

---

[1] Instr. S. C. C., 22 Aug., 1840, § Hisce praemissis.   [2] Mansella, l. c., p. 184.
[3] Supra, n. 1421.   [4] Instr. S. C. C. cit., § Praefinita.   [5] Ib., § Cum itaque.

judge, or by his command the secretary, opens them, and puts them one by one to the plaintiff. The judge himself, as also the defender, may *ex officio* add other questions in the course of the examination, as he sees fit. The secretary or notary will carefully write down, and that *verbatim*, both the questions and the answers thereto.[1]

1465. When the examination is over, the secretary will read aloud, in a clear and intelligible voice, the deposition or answers of the plaintiff, and the latter shall have the right to change or explain his answers as he pleases. Then he shall again swear that he has told the truth, and that he will not divulge either the interrogatories put to or the answers given by him before the publication of the proceedings.[2] Finally, he shall sign his deposition, and if he cannot write, put a cross (+) in the place of his name. Afterwards the judge, the defender, and the secretary affix their signatures.[3]

1466. The plaintiff should in his examination give a clear and full *exposé* of the case, or of the grounds of his demand for the annulment of the marriage, indicate the various kinds of proofs by which he believes he can sustain his demand, state all the circumstances which he either knows of his own personal knowledge or has heard from others, and if he affirms that he can prove his assertions by the testimony of witnesses, he should name them, and they should afterwards be examined. Whether one of the married couple demands the annulment, or none of them, both must always be cited and heard during the trial, in order that they may defend their rights, and rebut any proofs brought against them.[4]

1467. The spouse or plaintiff thus examined can, either immediately after his or her examination, or later on in the course of the trial, though before the publication of the proceedings, submit interrogatories to the judge, on which the defendant or spouse against whom the annulment of the mar

[1] Instr. S. C. C. cit., § Interim.
[2] Ib., § Si examen.
[3] Mansella, l. c., p. 186.
[4] Ib.

riage is sought shall be examined by the judge, in the presence of the defender of the marriage. And if, in turn, the defendant wishes also to submit questions to be put to his or her spouse who is the plaintiff, the judge shall receive them, and put them to the plaintiff, in the presence of the defender.[1] This mode of examination is to be observed in all the other examinations of witnesses. All the persons in the case— that is, the married couple as well as the witnesses—are examined apart from each other and under oath.[2]

1468. After the examination of the plaintiff or spouse who seeks the annulment of the marriage follows that of the defendant—that is, of the spouse against whom it is sought to have the marriage declared invalid. This examination is, as we have seen, conducted in the same manner with that of the plaintiff above described. The questions put to the defendant may be either the same with those put to the plaintiff, or others, as the defender of the marriage may see fit.[3]

1469. Next comes the examination of the witnesses. The witnesses for the plaintiff are examined first; those of the defence afterwards. The mode in which the witnesses are examined is the same with that of the plaintiff and defendant as described above.[4] The married couple shall be free to produce any witness of good character they choose. When the witnesses have all been examined, and the other proofs, such as instruments,—*v.g.*, parochial registers, private letters, etc.,—submitted, the publication of the proceedings takes place.[5] The defence may then submit new proofs and arguments.[6] Finally, the parties—the plaintiff and defender— sum up the case, and the judge, after consulting canonists and theologians, pronounces final sentence.[7]

1470. Whether this trial or mode of procedure can be

---

[1] Instr. S. C. C., 22 Aug., 1840, § Poterit.   [2] Mansella, p. 185.

[3] Instr. cit., § Expleto. [4] Ib., § Deinde procedendum. [5] Cf. supra, n. 855.

[6] Cf. supra, n. 856-859.   [7] Instr. cit., § Locus erit.

conducted in a summary manner, so far as this is compatible with the above formalities, we have seen already.[1] We also observe that the trial as above described may and usually is preceded and inaugurated by a preliminary investigation. The object of the latter is to ascertain as far as possible all the facts in the case, and thus to enable the judge to know whether he is justified in going on with the trial or hearing of the case.

1471. This preliminary trial usually consists in the informal examination of the married couple, of the witnesses on both sides, and of all the other evidence bearing on the case. We say, *informal*, etc.; for the proceedings are informal, and the judge is not bound to observe any judicial formalities. The minutes of the proceedings, however, should be carefully kept by the secretary. Generally, the judge does not conduct this preliminary examination in person, but commissions some other person to do it and to report to him.[2] As in the preliminary trial for a simple divorce *a mensa et toro*, so also in the preliminary trial for the annulment of the marriage, the parish priest or rector of the parish of the parties whose marriage is being called in question is requested by the bishop's court for matrimonial causes to forward a statement of the case to the court.

1472. As a rule, a similar informal preliminary trial (*processus informativus*) takes place, as has been shown, also in causes of divorce *a mensa et toro*. However, the effect of such preliminary investigation is sometimes different in causes of nullity from its effect in causes of mere separation *a mensa et toro*. For in the latter case, if the judge discovers sufficient evidence on the preliminary trial, he may forthwith pronounce sentence; whereas in the former case—*i.e.*, in causes of nullity—the real or formal trial, as traced out above, cannot be omitted.

---

[1] Supra, n. 1424.   [2] Card. Kutschker, l. c., vol. v., pp. 763, 765, 767.

§ 3. *Formalities to be observed in regard to the Annulment of a Marriage which is ratum not consummatum.*

1473. A marriage, though validly contracted, if not yet consummated, can be dissolved in two ways: (*a*) by one of the parties entering a religious community approved by the Holy See, and taking solemn vows;[1] (*b*) by dispensation of the Supreme Pontiff.[2] Here we observe with Bouix, that petitions are not unfrequently addressed to the Holy See for such dispensations.

1474. For the *validity* of the dissolution of the marriage in the case, whether by religious profession or papal dispensation, it is necessary that the marriage has not been consummated.

1475. Now what is the mode of procedure in dissolving a marriage which is *ratum,* but not yet *consummatum ?* In both cases—namely, whether the dissolution takes place by religious profession or pontifical dispensation—the non-consummation must be fully and canonically *proven,* and therefore the mere assertion or confession, even though confirmed by oath, of the married couple, is of itself insufficient. Hence, in the case of the dissolution of the marriage by religious profession, the married couple cannot separate of their own accord, but must apply to the ecclesiastical court of the diocese to which they belong, whose right and duty it is to examine the case, by a trial or judicial proceedings, and pronounce sentence.[3]

1476. Moreover, in the case of the dissolution of the marriage by papal dispensation, a sufficient cause should be alleged, apart from the non-consummation. Hence, in the petition for such a dispensation, two things must be clearly shown: *First,* that the marriage was not consummated;

---

[1] C. Trid., sess. 24, can. 6, de Sacr. matr.; cap. Verum, de Convers. conjug.; Bened. XIV., de Syn., l. 13, c. 12.

[2] Const. Dei Miseratione cit., § 15.　[3] Kutschker, l. c., vol. i., pp. 283, 284.

secondly, that there is just cause for the granting of the dispensation. Unless both these things be proved, the dispensation will not be granted. These two conditions, however, are required only for the licitness of the dispensation. For the dispensation would be *valid*, though illicit, even though the non-consummation of the marriage were not *proved*, provided it really were a fact.' For the causes which are usually considered sufficient for such a dispensation, see Cardinal Kutschker.'

1477. The married couple can send their petition to Rome themselves, though it is much better to do so through the Ordinary. The petition, which should be addressed to the Pope himself, should state all the facts and circumstances of the case, the causes upon which the request for the dispensation is based,' the names of both of the married couple, their residence, the parish and diocese to which they belong, the priest before whom their marriage was contracted.' Here it is necessary to observe that the Pope grants such a dispensation only when the petition therefor emanates from at least one of the spouses themselves, but not when it comes from others.'

1478. The Holy Father, upon receipt of the petition in the case, submits it to one of the sacred congregations,—generally to the Sacred Congregation of Council, whose duty it is, not indeed to grant the dispensation,—for this is reserved exclusively to the Pope,—but to examine all the facts in the case, and advise the Holy Father whether, in view of the facts ascertained, the dispensation should be granted or refused.'

1479. In order that the S. C. C., when such a case is referred to it by the Pope, may be able to give the Holy

' Bouix, de Jud., vol. ii., p. 455.   ' L. c., vol. i., p. 312 sq.

' Kutschker, l. c., p. 317.   ' Bened. XIV., Const. Dei Miseratione, § 15.

' S. C. C. in Agrigent., 15 Martii, 1727; cf. Kutschker, l. c., p. 316.

' Bened. XIV., Const. cit., § 15.

Father its advice or consultative vote on the petition for the dispensation, it usually writes to the Ordinary of the parties for his opinion and for further information—*pro voto et informatione.* It then becomes the bishop's duty to institute a canonical summary trial for the purpose of juridically ascertaining the non-consummation of the marriage, and the existence of legitimate causes for the dispensation.[1]

1480. *Q.* Is the S. C. C., and the bishop to whom it writes for information, bound, in verifying the non-consummation of the marriage and the existence of legitimate causes for the dispensation, to proceed in the manner prescribed by Pope Benedict XIV. in his constitution *Dei Miseratione,* especially so far as making use of a defender of marriage is concerned?

A. Cardinal Kutschker[2] seems to hold the affirmative, so far as the bishop is concerned, and therefore by implication also in relation to the Sacred Congregation of Council. Bouix maintains the negative. His reasoning is substantially as follows: The formalities prescribed by Benedict XIV. are binding only on judges *who are to pronounce upon the validity or invalidity of a marriage.* Now, in the case under discussion, no such sentence is or can be pronounced, as the marriage is supposed to be, and always to have been perfectly valid, though not consummated. Moreover, the dispensation in a marriage which is *ratum* not *consummatum* is reserved exclusively to the Pope, and cannot be granted by the Sacred Congregation of Council, much less by any bishop. Hence the Sacred Congregation's duty consists simply in *advising* the Pope as to whether the dispensation is to be granted or not. So also the bishop to whom the S. C. C. writes for information cannot proceed to declare the marriage null. His duty is simply to report to the Sacred Congregation whether the marriage has been consummated or not, and whether there are legitimate reasons for granting the dispensation.[3]

[1] Kutschker, l. c., p. 317.   [2] L. c., p. 317.   [3] Bouix, de Judic., vol. ii., p. 458.

1481. Whatever may be said on this head, practically speaking it will always be safer for the bishop to make use of the defender of the marriage, as prescribed by Benedict XIV. Thus the S. C. C. is accustomed to appoint and hear this defender in the causes here under consideration.[1]   In regard to the special mode of procedure, when either or both of the married couple demand the annulment of the marriage because of alleged impotence, see the Instruction of the S. C. C., August 22, 1840, above quoted, and also the Instruction of the Supreme Congregation of the Holy Office, both of which documents we shall give in the Appendix.

§ 4. *Judicial Proofs in Matrimonial Causes of Nullity.*

1482. *Judicial proofs in these causes, in general.*—Once a marriage has been contracted in due form, or as canonists say, *in facie ecclesiae,*—that is, with the prescribed formalities, —the presumption is always in favor of its validity.[2]   Hence, whoever wishes to have a marriage, once it has been contracted, annulled, must *clearly* and *fully* prove its nullity.   In other words, he must show, by proofs which are canonically and juridically full and complete (*probatio plena*)—*v.g.*, by the testimony of two unexceptionable witnesses—that the marriage is invalid—*v.g.*, because of an annulling impediment existing at the time of its solemnization.[3]   Hence also, when a marriage is contested as invalid before the ecclesiastical court, by either of the married couple or by others, and the ecclesiastical judge, upon due trial or investigation, finds that the invalidity is not fully and completely established, but that a doubt remains as to whether the alleged impediment exists or not, he must pronounce in favor of the validity of the contested marriage.[4]

1483. Consequently, whenever it is asserted by one of the

---

[1] Bouix, de Judic., vol. ii., p. 457.
[2] Cap. 5. de Eo qui cogn. (iv. 13); cap. 22, de Test. (ii. 20).
[3] Arg. cap. 1, de Consang. (iv. 14).   [4] Reiff., l. 4, t. 19, n. 17, 21.

married couple that an annulling impediment exists by which the marriage is null and void, it is incumbent upon this party to prove fully and beyond a doubt that such an impediment really does exist. Here we observe with Cardinal Kutschker. that where there is question of a double marriage—namely, where a party has married a second time, while the spouse of the first marriage is still living—the presumption is in favor of the first marriage, not of the second. Consequently the second marriage, even though contracted *in facie ecclesiae*, —*i.e.*, in due form,—must be presumed null and void until the first marriage is *clearly proved* invalid.[1]

1484. From what has just been said, it will be seen that it may happen that a married person may be perfectly certain personally of the nullity of his or her marriage (*v.g.*, if he knows that an annulling impediment existed at the time the marriage was contracted), and yet be unable to prove it *juridically* or *canonically*. What is to be done? It is certain that such a person cannot ask or render the *debitum maritale*; otherwise he would be acting against his conscience. He is, moreover, bound to separate from the other spouse, unless he can live with her, or she with him, as brother and sister. It is true that *in foro externo* the ecclesiastical judge would have to compel them to live together as a married couple, there being no juridical proof of the invalidity of the marriage. But the person in the case would be obliged to disobey this judicial mandate.[2]

1485. *Judicial proofs in matrimonial causes of nullity, in particular.*—Having given certain general principles concerning the proofs in question, we now proceed to touch upon each kind of proofs in particular. As we have already discussed the nature and force of the various kinds of judicial proofs, as admissible in criminal and civil ecclesiastical trials in general,[3] and as the proofs in matrimonial causes or trials

---

[1] Kutschker, vol. v., p. 832.   [2] Reiff., l. c., n. 22, 23.   [3] Supra, n. 814 sq.

partake in general of the same nature, and are governed by the same principles, we shall only say a few words in regard to each of these proofs.

1486. The chief kinds of proofs in matrimonial causes are the confession or deposition of the married couple itself; instruments; the testimony of witnesses; the inspection and testimony of experts; the oath.   1. *The confession of the married couple.*—We have seen above, that a judicial confession constitutes full proof, nay, the strongest of proofs.[1]   This rule, however, does not hold in causes of nullity of marriages. In these causes the confession, admission, or testimony of either of the married couple, or even of both, as against the validity of a marriage contracted by them, has of itself no force, even when it is corroborated by rumor among the neighbors.[2]   This is expressly enacted by Pope Celestine III., as follows: "Propter eorum" (conjugum) "confessionem tantum, vel rumorem viciniae separari non debent."[3]

1487. The reason of the inadmissibility of the confession of the married couple lies in the evident danger of collusion on their part.   For it is plain that if married people who are tired of their marriage, and anxious to break it, knew that the ecclesiastical judge would dissolve their marriage on the strength of their confession alone, they would readily agree with each other that one of them should affirm the existence of an annulling impediment (though it does not really exist), and that the other should corroborate this false statement either expressly or at least tacitly—*v.g.*, by not saying anything at all, or by not appearing in court, when cited, to defend the marriage.[4]   This reason is thus set forth by Pope Celestine III.: " Cum quandoque nonnulli inter se contra matrimonium *velint colludere*, et ad confessionem incestus" (or

[1] Supra, n. 823.   [2] Reiff., l. 4, t. 19. n. 16; Permaneder, l. c., § 331.
[3] Cap. Super eo 5, de eo qui cogn. (iv. 13).
[4] Kutschker, l. c., vol. v., p. 845.

of some other impediment) " facile prosilirent, si suo judicio crederent, per judicium ecclesiae concurrendum."[1]

1488. It is partly also owing to the fear or danger of collusion in the married couple that the malicious and wilful disobedience to the citation for trial, on the part of either of the married couple, is not at all to be taken as proof against the validity of the marriage. This contumacy, as we have shown in the case of criminal and grave civil causes, has simply this effect, that the cause or trial may now go on *in the absence* of the contumacious party as though he were present ; and sentence may be pronounced against the absent party, though only if the testimony as brought out during the trial is clear and complete.[2] Observe that in these causes the defender of the marriage is always the *ex officio* co-defendant, and it is his duty to supply the place of the party contumaciously absent.

1489. Of course, where either of the married couple is absent indeed from the trial, but not wilfully or maliciously, the trial cannot go on, and the cause must be left *in statu quo* until he or she either appears, or undoubted proof of his or her death is obtained.[3]

1490. We said above,[4] that the confession of the married couple had of itself no force as against the marriage. Observe the words *of itself*. For, taken in conjunction with other proofs, this confession or statement of the married couple may be of considerable importance, and enable the judge to arrive at a better knowledge of the facts in the case. Hence also, as we have seen, both the husband and wife whose marriage is being called in question should be examined, and that before any one else, at the trial. It is for the judge to weigh their evidence or statement, and to decide whether it is based on truth or collusion and fraud.[5]

[1] Cap. 5 cit.; Glossa, ib. v. Confessionem.
[2] Cap. 5, § Porro specialis, ut lite non cont. (ii. 6); cap. 10, de Sent. (ii. 27), S. C. C. in Cajet., 2 Oct., 1728, et in Milev., 1821; Kutschker, l. c., p. 775.
[3] Cap. 5 (ii. 6).   [4] Supra, n. 1486.   [5] Mansella, l. c., p. 187.

1491. 2. *Instruments as proofs in matrimonial causes.*—The principles laid down by us above,[1] concerning the various kinds and the force of instruments, apply here also. We merely observe that matrimonial registers are considered public instruments in matrimonial causes, and consequently constitute of themselves full proof. Nay, a single document of this or a similar kind has of itself greater force than the testimony of two unexceptionable witnesses. Hence the following axiom of law : "Contra authenticum litterale instrumentum, humanum non admittitur testimonium."[2] The meaning of this axiom is not that such instruments can never be overthrown by proper evidence, but simply that they can be shown to be false only by *clear and manifest proofs* to that effect.[3]

1492. 3. *Witnesses as proofs in matrimonial causes.*—The third kind of proofs in matrimonial causes is the deposition of witnesses. Of this kind of proofs we have already spoken at sufficient length.[4] Here we shall subjoin but a few words, specially applicable to the causes under consideration. As in other causes, so in matrimonial causes of nullity, two witnesses who are above all suspicion are, as a rule, required and sufficient to prove the invalidity of a marriage. We say, *as a rule ;* for when there is question of establishing the impediment of sexual impotency for the purpose of annulling a marriage already contracted, and the inspection or examination of the sexual organs of the married couple by experts —*i.e.,* physicians for the husband, and midwives for the wife —does not give a certainty but a mere probability of the existence of impotency,[5] then it becomes necessary for the spouses to swear that they cannot consummate the *copula,* and for *seven (septima manus)* relatives or neighbors, or in their default seven other reliable persons, to swear that they

---

[1] Supra, n. 864 sq.
[2] Cf. cap. 10, de Fide instr. (ii. 22).
[3] Phillips, Comp. § 263.

[4] Mansella, l. c., p. 188.
[5] Supra, n. 825 sq.

believe what the spouses affirm under oath to be true.' By
custom, however, where seven such persons cannot be had
a less number is sufficient.

1493. The questions to be put to the witnesses in matrimonial causes are, as in other causes, general and particular.
The general questions are the same for nearly all matrimonial causes. They are chiefly these: What is your name,
age, religion, condition or station in life, residence? Do you
know the married couple, their parents, relatives, etc.? Are
you a relative of theirs? In what degree, etc., etc.? Please
state the facts in the case as you know them? It is well to
allow the witness to tell what he knows in his own way.

1494. Next, the particular questions are to be asked.
They are to be taken from and based on the statement or
testimony of the married couple, and all other facts and
arguments submitted to the court. They are framed by the
defender of the marriage.' Of course, these particular questions vary considerably according to the various kinds of
annulling impediments which are alleged against the validity
of the marriage. Specimens of such questions are given by
Mansella,' to whom we refer the reader.

1495. 4. *Corporal inspection by experts* is the next kind of
proofs in matrimonial causes. This means is employed
under certain conditions, as we have already intimated,' in
those cases where the marriage is impugned because of
alleged impotency or the physical inability to consummate the
copula, or in order to prove that a *matrimonium ratum* was not
consummated.' Concerning this corporal inspection by experts, see the Instruction of the S. C. C. of August 22, 1840,
and the Instruction of the Congregation S. O., both of which
documents lay down the mode in which it is to take place.

1496. 5. *The oath as a proof in matrimonial causes.*—As we

---

¹ Instr. S. C. C., 22 Aug., 1840; Instr. S. C. Off. de imped. impot.
² Mansella, l. c , p. 198.   ³ Ib.. p. 199.
⁴ Supra, n. 1492.   ⁵ Mansella, l. c., p. 203.

have seen,, not only the spouses themselves, but also all the witnesses, must depose under oath. Otherwise their testimony is of no force whatever. Hence it will be seen that the oath adds great weight to the testimony, and is therefore a necessary part of the proofs in matrimonial as in other causes.[1]

§ 5. *What Persons are qualified by the Law of the Church to act as (a) Plaintiffs and (b) Witnesses in Matrimonial Causes.*

1497. *Q.* What persons can and should be admitted to object to or contest a marriage (*accusare matrimonium*)? In other words, what persons can be *plaintiffs* against a marriage?

A. We premise: We are speaking here not of marriages *about to be contracted.* For all persons whatever who know of an impediment existing between persons about to be married can, nay, even if they are unable to prove its existence, are bound, if they can do so conveniently, to make it known, so as to prevent the marriage from taking place.[2]

1491. We speak, therefore, only of marriages *already contracted*, both so far as the separation from bed and board and the dissolution of the *vinculum* itself are concerned. Now in these cases not all persons are promiscuously admitted as plaintiffs. What persons, therefore, are admitted by the law of the Church, as in force also in the United States, to demand the separation *a mensa et toro*, or the annulment of the marriage? *First*, when there is question of separation *a mensa et toro*, only the innocent spouse can act as plaintiff —that is, demand the separation. The reason is, that the right of complaint or asking for such divorce is granted in favor of the innocent party, who has a perfect right to condone the injury and thus relinquish the right of preferring the complaint.[3]

---

[1] Mansella, l. c., p. 205.   [2] S. Alph. l. vi., n. 995; Konings, n. 1541, q. 3.
[3] Ex cap. 5, de Procur. (i. 38); cap. 4, de Adult. et stupr. (v. 16).

1499. This, however, is to be understood only of a *civil* action for such divorce—that is, only of an action instituted before the ecclesiastical judge solely for the purpose of obtaining the separation. Therefore it does not extend to a *criminal* action. Hence when there is question, not simply of obtaining a divorce, but rather of *punishing* the adulterous spouse, any person whatever can make the complaint—that is, act as accuser or plaintiff, provided he be a male and twenty-five years old.[1]

1500. *Secondly*, when there is question of dissolving the *vinculum* of a marriage already contracted, it is necessary to distinguish between three kinds of annulling impediments, on account of which the demand for the annulment of the marriage is made. The first kind comprises those which arise from a defective consent—namely, the impediments of fear and error. The second kind are the impediments of public. propriety (*publica honestas*) and of consanguinity and affinity *ex copula conjugali*. The third includes all the other impediments—*v.g.*, the impediment of *ligamen*.

1501. Now the dissolution or annulment of a marriage contracted with an impediment of the first class can be demanded only by the married couple itself. The reason is, that if the couple is willing, either expressly or tacitly, to ratify or renew their consent given under grave fear or substantial error, and thus make the marriage valid, they can do so, and no one else has a right to interfere or complain.[2] Nay, the law of the Church presumes that the married couple in the case does actually ratify the marriage, if after becoming aware of the impediment they nevertheless know each other carnally.[3] Hence if in the latter case the married couple nevertheless wished to have their marriage annulled, they could not be heard.

1502. The impediment of impotency is placed on the same

---

[1] Schmalzg., l. c., n. 13.
[2] Schmalzg., l. c., n. 15.
[3] Cap. 4, Qui matr. acc. (iv. 18).

footing with those just described, so far as the right to act as plaintiff or accuser against the marriage is concerned.[1] For the married couple can, if they choose, live together as brother and sister, notwithstanding the *impedimentum impotentiae.*[2]

1503. In the second case,—that is, in the case of the impediments of public propriety and of consanguinity and affinity,—those persons are admitted as plaintiffs who usually are best acquainted with the facts. Such are evidently, besides the married couple itself, their parents, next their brothers and sisters and other relatives ; then neighbors; finally, in default of the foregoing, all others who may have a knowledge of the facts.[3]

1504. In the third case, not only the married couple itself, but all persons, as a rule, who are cognizant of an impediment, are allowed to contest the marriage and demand its annulment, especially when their interest is concerned in the matter, provided, of course, they are of a good character and worthy of belief.[4] We observe that in the case of impediments of the second and third class the ecclesiastical judge may and sometimes should himself proceed *ex officio* against the marriage if the other parties fail to do so.

1505. What persons, in particular, are chiefly excluded from acting as plaintiffs against a marriage ? All those who are not above suspicion, and therefore not worthy of belief. Hence the following persons are chiefly excluded as plaintiffs : (*a*) Those who accept money for acting as plaintiffs, or exact money for desisting from acting as such.[5] (*b*) Those who neglected to reveal the impediment at the time the publication of the banns took place, prior to the marriage, unless they prove under oath that owing to absence, sickness, and the like they were ignorant of the publication of the banns,

---

[1] Mansella, p. 179.
[2] Cap. 4, 5, de Frig. et malef.
[3] Cap. 3, Qui matr. acc. (iv. 18); Mansella, l. c., p. 180.
[4] Mansella, l. c., p. 180.
[5] Cap. 5 , Qui matr. acc.

or that they did not become aware of the impediment any sooner.[1] (*c*) As a rule, those who impugn the marriage merely by letter, without being present personally.[2] The object of this law is to prevent calumnious denunciations, which would occur frequently if the complaint or accusation could be made by an absent person. Hence a person who demands the annulment of a marriage must, as a rule, present this demand in person to the judge, and that in writing.[3]

1506. *Q.* What persons are admissible *as witnesses* in matrimonial causes of nullity? In other words, who can *testify* for or against the validity of a marriage?

A. All those who have a knowledge of the impediment objected by the plaintiff, and are otherwise worthy of belief.[4] Hence even parents, brothers and sisters, and other relatives of both sexes, are competent witnesses in these causes, at least where there is question of dissolving the marriage on account of an impediment of consanguinity or affinity, or public propriety.[5] The reason is, that they are not only better acquainted with the degree of relationship existing between the married couple, but are believed, moreover, to be opposed to incestuous marriages, as bringing disgrace upon their family.[6] From what has been said, it will be seen that while parents and relatives are not usually admissible as witnesses in other civil causes, nor in criminal causes,[7] they are competent witnesses in the causes under consideration.

1507. In certain circumstances, however, the testimony of parents and relatives may become suspected, and consequently inadmissible—*v.g.*, where they testify in favor of sustaining the validity of a marriage contracted by a poor female relative with a rich, noble, and powerful man. For

---

[1] Schmalzg., l. c., n. 19.   [2] Can. 5, C. 2, Q. 8; cap. 2 (iv. 18).
[3] Card. Kutschker, vol. v., pp. 522–525.
[4] Arg. cap. 47, de Test. et attest. (ii. 20).   [5] Cap. 3, Qui matr. acc. (iv. 18).
[6] Schmalzg., l. c., n. 22.   Supra, n. 527, 528.

the presumption in this and similar cases is, that the advantages of such a marriage are so great as to warp their judgment and render them incapable of giving impartial testimony.[1]

1508. Who are inadmissible as witnesses in matrimonial causes? Chiefly these persons: 1. Those who are induced by money to testify or not to testify.[2] 2. Those who testify only by letter, without being personally present in court. For a witness must be personally present in court, and give his testimony in person.[3] 3. Those who impugn the marriage—that is, those who are the plaintiffs in the case; on the general principle that a person cannot at the same time be plaintiff and also witness. This rule, however, admits of exceptions.[4] Thus plaintiffs can be also witnesses when the judge proceeds *ex officio*.[5]

1509. *Remedies against a sentence pronounced by an ecclesiastical judge in matrimonial causes.*—As we have seen above, after the case has been tried and the parties rest their case, the ecclesiastical judge proceeds to pronounce sentence, and that in writing, stating distinctly and clearly the reasons upon which it is based, and declaring the marriage either valid or not valid.[6] As we have seen above, the sentence in matrimonial causes of nullity never passes into *res judicata*, and consequently a new trial can be demanded at any time,[7] where sufficient reasons warrant it—*v.g.*, when new evidence of a grave character is discovered.[8]

1510. The remedies against a sentence in matrimonial causes are the same with those in other causes—namely, complaint of nullity of the sentence, appeals, and reinstate-

---

[1] Schmalzg., l. c., n. 23. [2] Cap. 5, Qui matr. acc. (iv. 18).

[3] Cap. 2, eod.; L. Testium 3, § 3 idem ff., de Test. et. attest.

[4] Schmalzg., l. c., n. 25; Mansella, l. c., p. 180.

[5] Arg. cap. 4, de Test. (ii. 20); cap. 27, de Sponsal. et matr. (iv. 1).

[6] Mansella, l. c., p. 211. [7] Cap. 7, de Sent. (ii. 27).

[8] Phillips, Lehrb., § 280, p. 703.

ment. The application, however, of these remedies in matrimonial causes has certain peculiarities. Thus the complaint of nullity (*querela nullitatis*) may be lodged against the sentence when either some essential formality of the trial is omitted, or the defender of the marriage has not been called to the proceedings.

1511. In regard to appeals in the causes under consideration, we observe, that when the judgment of the court in the first instance is in favor of the validity of the marriage, the plaintiff, or the one who has demanded its annulment (*accusator matrimonii*), has the right to appeal. If he appeals, and the validity of the marriage is again sustained in the second instance, or if not in the second at least in the third instance, the plaintiff or accuser has no further appeal. Where, on the other hand, the marriage is declared null and void by the ecclesiastical judge of the first instance, the defender of the marriage not only *can* but *is bound* to appeal; and if, thereupon, the marriage is again declared invalid also by the judge in the second instance,[1] he can indeed, if in conscience he thinks proper, appeal again, but he is not obliged to do so.[2] We conclude this second volume in the words of the *Glossa in Clem.*, cap. 2, lib. 5, tit. 11, v. Irritandus: "Natura vero naturans, cum ad illam redibimus, per intercessionem Virginis gloriosae, nos collocet cum electis."

[1] Bened. XIV., Const. Dei Miseratione, §§ 8, 9.   [2] Phillips, l. c., p. 704.

FINIS.

APPENDIX.

I.

INSTRUCTIO

S. CONGREGATIONIS DE PROPA-GANDA FIDE

DE MODO SERVANDO AB EPISCOPIS FOE-DERATORUM SEPTENTRIONALIS AMER-ICAE STATUUM IN COGNOSCENDIS ET DEFINIENDIS CAUSIS CRIMINALIBUS ET DISCIPLINARIBUS CLERICORUM.

1512. Quamvis Concilium plenarium Baltimorense II., ab Apostolica Sede recognitum, certam quamdam iudicii formam iam antea a concilio provinciali S. Ludovici sancitam, in criminalibus clericorum causis ab ecclesiasticis curiis dioecesium Foederatorum Septentrionalis Americae Statuum pertractandis servandam esse decreverit, experientia tamen compertum est, statutum iudicii ordinem haud undequaque parem esse ad querelas eorum praecavendas quos poena aliqua mulctari contigerit. Saepe enim postremis hisce temporibus accidit ut presbyteri iudiciis ea ratione initis latisque sententiis damnati, remoti praesertim ab officio rectoris missionarii, huc illuc de suis Praelatis conquesti fuerint et frequenter etiam ad Apostolicam Sedem recursus detulerint. Dolendum autem est, non raro evenire, ut in transmissis actis plura, eaque necessaria, desiderentur atque perpensis omnibus, gravia saepe dubia oriantur circa fidem documentis hisce in causis allatis habendam vel denegandam.

INSTRUCTION

OF THE SACRED CONGREGATION DE PROPAGANDA FIDE

ON THE MODE OF PROCEDURE TO BE OBSERVED BY THE BISHOPS OF THE UNITED STATES OF NORTH AMERICA IN TAKING COGNIZANCE OF AND DE-CIDING CRIMINAL AND DISCIPLINARY CAUSES OF ECCLESIASTICS.

1512. Although the Second Plenary Council of Baltimore, revised by the Holy See, enacted that a certain kind of judicial form, already sanctioned by the Provincial Council of St. Louis, should be observed by the ecclesiastical courts of the dioceses of the United States of North America in criminal causes of ecclesiastics, nevertheless experience has shown that the prescribed form of trial is not quite sufficient to prevent complaints on the part of those who happen to be visited with punishment. For of late it has often happened that priests condemned by judicial trial and sentence of this kind, especially when removed from the office of missionary rector, have complained in various quarters of their prelates, and have also frequently had recourse to the Apostolic See. Now it is to be regretted that not seldom it happens that in the papers or documents transmitted to us many and, it must be added, necessary items are wanting, so that, upon examination of the whole, serious doubts frequently arise as to the credit to be accorded or refused to the documents brought forward in these causes.

1513. Quae omnia S. Congregatio fidei propagandae praeposita serio perpendens, aliquod remedium hisce incommodis parandum ac ita iustitiae consulendum esse censuit ut neque insontes clerici per iniuriam poena afficiantur neque alicuius criminis rei ob minus rectam iudiciorum formam a promerita poena immunes evadant. Quod quidem facili pacto obtineret, si cmnes praescriptiones a sacris canonibus sapienter editas pro ecclesiasticis iudiciis praesertim criminalibus, ineundis et absolvendis servandas omnino esse praeciperet. Verum animo reputans, in praedictis Foederatorum Ordinum regionibus id facile servari non posse, ea ratione providendum esse duxit ut saltem illae de admisso crimine accurate peragantur investigationes quae omnino necessariae existimantur, antequam ad poenam irrogandam deveniatur.

1514. Itaque SSmo Domino Nostro Divina Providentia PP. Leone XIII. approbante, in generalibus comitiis habitis die 25 Iunii 1878 S. C. decrevit, ac districte mandavit, ut singuli memoratae regionis sacrorum Antistites in Dioecesana Synodo quamprimum convocanda quinque, aut ubi ob peculiaria rerum adiuncta tot haberi nequeant tres saltem presbyteros ex probatissimis et quantum fieri poterit in iure canonico peritis seligant, quibus consilium quoddam iudiciale, seu, ut appellant, Commissio investigationis constituatur, eidemque unum ex electis praeficiant. Quod si ob aliquam gravem causam Synodus dioecesana statim haberi nequeat, quinque vel tres prouti supra per Episcopum interim ecclesiastici viri ad munus de quo agitur deputentur.

1513. The Sacred Congregation charged with the Propagation of the Faith, having seriously weighed all this, has resolved that some remedy must be provided for these troubles, and the ends of justice attained in such a manner that innocent clergymen may not be punished nor the guilty escape with impunity, through any defective form of trial. All this could be easily effected if the Sacred Congregation were to command that all the provisions wisely established by the sacred canons for conducting (from beginning to end) ecclesiastical trials, especially in criminal causes, should be unfailingly observed. But the Sacred Congregation, taking into consideration that in the aforesaid country this cannot be easily carried out, has determined to make provision that there shall be at least such careful inquiry into the party's alleged guilt as is absolutely necessary before punishment may be inflicted.

1514. Wherefore, with the approval of our Most Holy Father, by Divine providence, Pope Leo XIII., in a general meeting held on the 25th day of June, 1878, the Sacred Congregation has decreed and strictly commanded that each bishop of the above country, in diocesan synod, to be convoked as soon as possible, shall select five, or, where by reason of peculiar circumstances so many cannot be had, at least three of the most worthy priests, and as much as possible those skilled in canon law, who will constitute a sort of judicial council, or, as they say, a Commission of Investigation, over which he shall appoint one of their number to preside. But if for any grave reason a diocesan synod cannot be held immediately, five or three ecclesiastics, as stated above, shall be named meanwhile by the bishop to the office in question.

1515. Commissionis ita constitutae princeps erit officium criminales atque disciplinares presbyterorum aliorumque clericorum causas iuxta normam mox proponendam ad examen revocare, rite cognoscere ac ita Episcopo in ipsis definiendis auxilium praebere. Satagant propterea oportet ad hoc munus electi, ut accuratae fiant investigationes, ea proferantur testimonia atque a praesumpto reo omnia exquirantur quae ad veritatem eruendam necessaria censentur ac ad iustam sententiam tuto prudenterque ferendam certa vel satis firma argumenta suppeditent.

1516. Quod si de alicuius Rectoris missionis remotione agatur, nequeat ipse a credito sibi munere deiici nisi tribus saltem praedictae commissionis membris per Episcopum ad causam cognoscendam adhibitis, eorumque consilio audito.

1517. Electi Consiliarii in suscepto munere permanebunt ad proximam usque Dioecesanae Synodi celebrationem, in qua vel ipsi confirmentur in officio vel alii designentur. Quod si interim morte, aut renuntiatione vel alia causa. praescriptus Consiliariorum numerus minuatur, Episcopus extra Synodum alios in deficientium locum prout superius statutum est, sufficiat.

1518. In causis cognoscendis, iis praesertim in quibus de rectore missionario definitive a suo officio amovendo agatur, iudicialis commissio hanc sequetur agendi rationem.

1515. Of the Commission so constituted, the principal duty shall be to inquire into, and take due cognizance of, criminal and disciplinary causes of priests and other ecclesiastics, according to the mode of procedure given below, and thus to assist the bishop in deciding the same. Hence those chosen for this office must take good care to make diligent inquiry, to bring out the testimony, to interrogate the defendant on all points that may be deemed necessary to elicit the truth, so as to furnish certain or sufficiently strong grounds for safely and prudently pronouncing a just sentence.

1516. Whenever there is question of the removal of a rector of a mission, the same cannot be ejected from the office committed to him unless the bishop shall have previously engaged three members at least of the abovementioned Commission to take cognizance of the cause and shall have listened to their advice.

1517. The councillors chosen shall remain in office until the celebration of the next diocesan synod, in which they will either be confirmed in office or others appointed in their stead. But if, in the meanwhile, the prescribed number of councillors be lessened by death, resignation, or other cause, the bishop shall extra-synodically fill the vacancies, as above provided.

1518. In taking cognizance of causes, those especially where there is question of the absolute removal of a missionary rector from his office, the judicial Commission shall observe the following form of procedure:[1]

---

[1] This mode of procedure is substantially the same as that existing in England, and also recommended by the late Synod of Maynooth for Ireland, though its application is much wider with us than in England. In England this method was established in 1853 in the following manner: A committee of bishops was appointed in the First Provincial Council of Westminster, held July 6, 1852, for the purpose of preparing a mode of procedure

1519. 1. Ad commissionem investigationis non recurratur, nisi prius clare et praecise exposita ab Episcopo causa ad deiectionem finalem movente, ipse rector missionarius malit rem ad Consilium deferri quam se a munere et officio sponte dimittere.

1520. 2. Re ad Consilium delata, Episcopus vicario suo generali vel alii sacerdoti ad hoc ab ipso deputato committat, ut relationem causae in scriptis conficiat, cum expositione investigationis eo usque peractae, et circumstantiarum quae causam vel eiusdem demonstrationem specialiter afficiant.

1521. 3. Locum, diem, et horam opportunam ad conveniendum indicet, idque per litteras ad singulos consiliarios.

1522. 4. Per litteras etiam Rectorem missionarium, de quo agitur, ad locum et diem constitutum ad Consilium habendum advocet exponens nisi prudentia vetat, uti in casu criminis oc-

---

1519. 1. It shall not be allowed to have recourse to the Commission of Investigation unless the bishop beforehand shall have stated in clear and precise terms the nature of the cause calling for final removal, and the missionary rector shall have chosen to have the matter referred to the Council, rather than to resign of his own free will.

1520. 2. The matter having been laid before the Council, the bishop shall charge his vicar-general, or other priest deputed for this purpose by himself, to draw up in writing a statement of the case, with an account of the investigation as far as it has gone, and of the circumstances that may have a special bearing on the case or its establishment.

1521. 3. He shall appoint a suitable place, day, and hour for the meeting, and notify the same by letter to each councillor.

1522. 4. He shall also by letter summon the missionary rector in question to appear at the place and time appointed for holding the meeting of the Council, stating in detail—except

---

to be followed in deposing a missionary rector from his parish. The method agreed upon by this committee was submitted by Cardinal Wiseman to the Sacred Congregation of Propaganda, and approved by this Congregation by decree of August 4, 1853. (C. Prov. Westmonaster. I. apud Coll. Lac., vol. iii., pp. 925, 960.)

A comparison of the two documents shows that the S. C. de P. F. took the English document as the model for ours. For the latter is almost word for word the same with the former. The following are the only points of difference: According to the English document, it is necessary that two thirds of the Councillors should agree on a verdict or opinion; according to ours, it is sufficient that a bare majority should agree. Then again, § 8, *Si contingat;* § 16, *Omnia acta;* § 17, *Si vero contingat,* of our Instruction are omitted in the English mode of procedure.

But apart from the form of trial, there are substantial points of difference as to its application with us and in England. In the latter country, at least by virtue of the First Provincial Council of Westminster, the benefit of the prescribed trial need be accorded only in the case of the final removal of a missionary rector from his parish. In the United States this trial must be given a defendant, not only where a rector (and with us all duly appointed pastors are rectors, whereas in England only a few pastors—namely, those of the principal parishes—are rectors) is to be dismissed, but also where a censure or an ecclesiastical punishment or a grave disciplinary chastisement is to be inflicted upon an ecclesiastic, whether he be a rector, or merely an assistant; whether he be a priest, or only a deacon or sub-deacon, etc.

culti, causam ad delectionem moventem per extensum, monensque ipsum
rectorem ut responsum suis rationibus
suffultum ad ea praeparet in scriptis,
quae in causae expositione vel iam
antea oretenus, vel tunc in scriptis
relata fuerint.

1523. 5. Convenientibus consiliariis
tempore et loco praefinitis, praecipiat
Episcopus silentium servandum de iis,
quae in Consilio audiantur; moneat
investigationem non esse processum
iudicialem, sed eo fine habitam, et eo
modo faciendam, ut ad cognitionem
veritatis diligentiori qua poterit ratione
perveniatur, adeo ut unusquisque consiliarius, perpensis omnibus, opin-
ionem de veritate factorum, quibus
causa innititur, efformare quam accurate possit. Moneat etiam ne quid in
investigatione fiat. quod aut ipsos, aut
alios, periculo damni vel gravaminis
exponat, praesertim ne locus detur
actioni libelli famosi vel alii cuicumque
processui coram tribunali civili.

1524. 6. Relatio causae legatur coram Consilio ab Episcopi officiali qui
etiam ad interpellationes respondebit
a praeside vel ab aliis consiliariis per
praesidem faciendas ad uberiorem rei
notitiam assequendam.

1525. 7. Deinde in Consilium intro-
ducatur rector missionarius, qui responsum a se confectum leget, et ad
interpellationes similiter respondebit,
facta ipsi plena facultate ea omnia in
medium afferendi, intra tempus tamen
a Consilio determinandum. quae ad
propriam defensionem conferre possunt.

where prudence forbids, as in the case
of occult crime—the cause that calls
for his dismissal, and warning him
further to prepare a written answer,
supported by proofs, to the charges
and evidence so far given, and which
had been already communicated to
him orally, or were now (in the
bishop's letter citing the rector) being
set forth in writing.

1523. 5. When the Councillors assem-
ble at the time and place set apart
beforehand, the bishop shall enjoin
secrecy upon all matters brought before the Council; he shall further warn
them that the investigation is not a
judicial process, but undertaken for
the purpose, and to be conducted in
such a manner as to ascertain the
truth with all possible care and diligence; so that each Councillor, having
duly weighed all things, may be able
to form an accurate opinion of the
facts on which the case is based. He
shall also warn them against anything
during the investigation which might
expose themselves or others to injury;
above all, that no occasion be given
for a libel suit or other action before
a civil tribunal.

1524. 6. The written statement of the
case shall be read before the Council
by the official of the bishop, who will
also answer all questions put to him
by the president, or by the other
Councillors through the president, in
order to get at the full truth of the
matter.

1525. 7. The missionary rector shall
then be introduced into the Council,
and read the answer he has prepared,
and reply to all questions put as above
stated. He shall, further, have full
liberty to produce, yet within a period
of time to be determined by the Council, whatever else may serve to his de
fence.

1526. 8. Si contingat rectorem missionarium de cuius causa agitur, nolle ad Consilium accedere, iterum datis literis vocetur, eique congruum temporis spatium ad comparendum praefiniatur, et si ad constitutum diem non comparuerit, dummodo legitime praepeditus non fuerit, uti contumax habeatur.

1527. 9. Quibus omnibus rite expletis Consiliarii simul consilia conferant, et si maior pars consiliariorum satis constare de factis arbitretur, sententiam suam unusquisque consiliarius in scriptis exponat rationibus quibus nititur expressis; conferantur sententiae; acta in Consilio ab episcopi officiali redigantur, a praeside nomine consilii subscribantur, et simul cum sententiis singulorum in extenso ad Episcopum deferantur.

1528. 10. Quod si ulterior investigatio necessaria vel congrua videatur, eo ipso die vel alio ad conveniendum a Consilio constituto, testes vocentur, quos opportunos Consilium iudicaverit, audito etiam rectore missionario de iis quos ipse advocandos esse voluerit.

1529. 11. Singuli testes *pro causa* seorsim et accurate examinentur a praeside et ab aliis per praesidem, absente primum rectore missionario. Non requiratur iuramentum, sed si testes ipsi non renuant et se paratos esse declarent ad ea quae detulerint iuramento data occasione, confirmanda, fiat adnotatio huiusmodi dispositionis seu declarationis in actis.

1530. 12. Consentientibus testibus,

1526. 8. Should it happen that the missionary rector, who is on trial, refuses to appear before the Council, he shall be summoned a second time by letter, and a suitable space of time fixed for his appearance. Should he fail to appear on the day appointed. unless he can plead a legitimate excuse, he shall be considered contumacious.

1527. 9. After all this has been duly done, the members of the Commission shall take counsel together, and if the greater number of the Councillors think the facts sufficiently proven, each Councillor shall state in writing his opinion, with the reasons on which it is grounded. The opinions shall then be compared. The acts of the Council shall be arranged or filed by the bishop's official, and signed by the president in the name of the Council, which, together with the opinions of each Councillor in full, shall be laid before the bishop.

1528. 10. Should further investigation be deemed necessary or opportune, on the same day, or another day fixed by the Council for reassembling, those witnesses shall be called whom the Council may deem suitable, the missionary rector having also been heard as to the witnesses he may wish to have summoned.

18. 11. Each witness for the prosecution shall be carefully examined, apart from the rest, by the president, and by the other Councillors through the president, and that first in the absence of the missionary rector. No oath shall be required, but if the witnesses themselves be willing, and declare themselves ready, if opportunity be given, to confirm by oath their testimony, a note of this disposition or declaration shall be made in the minutes of the proceedings.

1530. 12. Should the witnesses give

et dirigente prudentia Consilii, repetatur testimonium coram rectore missionario qui et ipse testes si voluerit interroget per praesidem.

1531. 13. Eadem ratione qua testes *pro causa*, examinentur testes *contra causam.*

1532. 14. Collatis tunc consiliis fiat ut supra n. 9.

1533. 15. Quod si testes nolint aut nequeant Consilio assistere, vel eorum testimonium nondum satis luculentum negotium reddat, duo saltem ex Consilio deputentur, qui testes adeuntes, loca invisentes, vel alio quocumque modo poterunt, lumen ad dubia solvenda requirentes, relationem suae investigationis, ad Consilium deferant, ut ita nulla via intentata relinquatur ad verum moraliter certo cognoscendum antequam ad sententiae prolationem deveniatur.

1534. 16. Omnia acta occasione judicii in medium allata accurate in Curia Episcopali custodiantur, ut in casu appellationis commode exhiberi valeant.

1535. 17. Si vero contingat, ut a sententia in Curia Episcopali prolata ad Archiepiscopalem provocetur, Metropolitanus eadem methodo in causae cognitione et decisione procedat.

Datum Romae ex aedibus prefatae S. Congregationis die 20 Iulii anni 1878. IOANNES CARD. SIMEONI
Praefectus.
IOANNES BAPTISTA AGNOZZI
Secretarius.

their consent, and should the Council deem it prudent, the testimony shall be repeated in presence of the missionary rector, who shall have the right of questioning, if he choose, the witnesses through the president.

1531. 13. The witnesses for the defence shall be examined in the same way as the witnesses for the prosecution.

1532. 14. The Council shall then deliberate, and act as provided above in No. 9.

1533. 15. Should the witnesses be unwilling or unable to appear before the Council, or their testimony throw insufficient light on the case, two members at least of the Council shall be deputed, who shall endeavor by every means in their power to clear up the doubts in the case, going to the witnesses, visiting the localities, and who shall submit to the Council a report of their investigation, so that nothing be left untried to discover with moral certainty the truth before sentence shall be pronounced.

1534. 16. All the records and documents of the trial (namely, the minutes of the proceedings, the various steps taken by the Council, the documents submitted both by the prosecution and the defence, etc.) shall be carefully kept in the (archives of the) episcopal court, so that they may be produced without difficulty in case of appeal.

1535. 17. Should it happen that an appeal be taken from the judgment pronounced in the episcopal court to that of the archbishop, the metropolitan shall proceed in the same way in the trial and decision of the cause.

Given at Rome, from the house of the aforesaid Sacred Congregation, the 20th day of July, in the year 1878.

JOHN CARD. SIMEONI, *Prefect.*
JOHN BAPTIST AGNOZZI, *Secretary.*

II.

AD DUBIA CIRCA MODUM SERVAN-
DUM AB EPISCOPIS FOEDERATO-
RUM SEPTENTRIONALIS AMERICAE
STATUUM IN COGNOSCENDIS ET
DEFINIENDIS CAUSIS CRIMINALI-
BUS ET DISCIPLINARIBUS CLERI-
CORUM.

II.

(ANSWER OF THE SACRED CONGRE-
GATION DE PROPAGANDA FIDE)
CONCERNING QUESTIONS (PRO-
POSED BY BISHOPS OF THE UNITED
STATES) IN REGARD TO THE MODE
OF PROCEDURE TO BE FOLLOWED
BY THE BISHOPS OF THE UNITED
STATES OF NORTH AMERICA IN
TAKING COGNIZANCE OF AND DE-
CIDING CRIMINAL AND DISCIPLIN-
ARY CAUSES OF ECCLESIASTICS.

1536. Instructio diei 20 Julii 1878
lata est de casibus, in quibus ecclesiastica poena seu censura sit infligenda,
aut gravi disciplinari coercitioni sit
locus. Hinc Concilii plenarii Balti-
morensis II. decreta N. 125 quoad
naturam missionum, NN. 77, 108
quoad juridicos effectus remotionis
missionariorum ab officio nullatenus
innovata seu infirmata fuerunt.

1536. The Instruction of July 20,
1878, applies to cases where an ecclesiastical punishment or censure is to
be inflicted, or where there is room for
a grave disciplinary correction. Hence
the decrees of the Second Plenary
Council of Baltimore, No. 125, so far
as regards the character of the missions (congregations), and Nos. 77,
108, so far as concerns the juridical
effects of the removal of missionaries
from office, have in no wise been
changed or annulled.

1537. Episcopi vero curent, ne sac-
erdotes sine gravi et rationabili causa
de una ad aliam missionem invitos
transferant. Quod si de alicuius Rectoris definitiva remotione a munere in
poenam delicti infligenda agatur, id
episcopi executioni non mandent nisi
audito prius Consilio.

1537. Let bishops, however, take
care not to transfer priests against
their will from one mission to another
without grave and reasonable cause.
But when there is question of definitively removing a (missionary) rector
from his office in punishment of a
crime, the bishop shall not make such
removal save upon having beforehand
listened to the advice of the council.

1538. 2. Electio consiliariorum facienda est in synodo ad instar deputa-
tionis, seu canonicae electionis judicum
synodalium, qui non a clero, sed ab
episcopo eliguntur, audito quidem consilio clericorum in synodo, *etsi ex
causis sibi notis illud amplecti postea
episcopus noluerit,* ut bene observat
Benedictus XIV., *De Syn., lib. IV.
cap. V. num.* 5. Hinc absonum est,
ut in casu quo agit Instructio, horum
consiliariorum electio ad clerum per-
tineat.

1538. 2. The election of the councillors must take place in (diocesan)
synod, like the appointment or canonical election of synodal judges, who are
chosen, not by the clergy, but by the
bishop. The latter (bishop) shall indeed, before making the appointment
of these synodal judges, take the advice of the clergy assembled in synod,
*though, for reasons known to himself
he may not be willing afterwards to
follow this advice,* as Benedict XIV.
well remarks in his work De Syn.,

lib. v., cap. v., num. 5. Hence it is
incorrect to say, that in the case of
which the Instruction treats the election of these councillors belongs to the
clergy.

1539. Extra synodum electio absolute ad episcopum pertinet, quem
decet, ut votum audiat reliquorum Consiliariorum in casu subrogationis alicuius qui defecerit, prout episcopus in
casu deficientis judicis synodalis debet
*exquirere capituli consilium, sed illud
sequi non tenetur.*

1539. Outside of the synod, the appointment belongs absolutely to the
bishop, although it is becoming that
he should, in filling any vacancy which
may occur in the Council, take the advice of the remaining councillors, just
as the bishop, in the case of a vacancy
occurring among the synodal judges,
should indeed, before filling such vacancy, *ask the advice of the chapter,
though he is not bound to follow it.*

1540. 3. Votum a consilio datum
est semper consultivum, et sententia
definitiva episcopo est reservata;
quando enim canones dicunt aliquid
ab episcopo de capituli vel cleri consilio agendum esse, non propterea ne-
cessitatem ipsi episcopo inducunt illud
sequi, nisi expresse id cautum sit.
Hinc recte dicitur in Instructione, hos
consiliarios *episcopo in causis definiendis
auxilium praebere,* minime vero ipsos
decidere. Sed inquisitionis acta, et
opinio pandita a Consiliariis est semper inserenda processui.

1540. 3. The opinion given by the
Council is always consultative, and
the final sentence is reserved to the
bishop; for, when the canons say that
something is to be done by the bishop
with the advice of the chapter or clergy,
they do not thereby impose upon the
bishop the necessity of following such
advice, except where this is expressly
declared. Consequently the Instruction rightly says, that these councillors
aid the bishop in deciding causes, but
not by any means that they themselves decide. However, the acts of
the investigation and the opinion
rendered by the councillors must
always be inserted in the process.[1]

1541. Ex quibus patet officium consiliariorum judiciale qudem esse, cum
instructio sit iisdem commissa, ac tamquam adsessores episcopo adsistant:
sed patet etiam judicialis et definitivae
sententiae prolationem episcopo esse
unice reservatam.

1541. From this it is evident that
the office of the councillors is judicial
indeed, since the hearing of the cause
is committed to them, and they assist
the bishop in the capacity of assessors;
but it is also apparent that the passing
of the judicial and final sentence is
reserved exclusively to the bishop.

1542. 2. Per Instructionem sublata
non est episcopis extraordinaria facultas, procedendi ad suspensionem ex

1542. 4. The Instruction does not
deprive bishops of the extraordinary
power of inflicting suspension "ex in-

[1] Consequently the above acts and opinions
must always be preserved, as essential parts
of the whole trial.

informata conscientia, quatenus gravissimas et canonicas causas concurrere in Domino judicaverint, aut gravi et urgente necessitate pro salute animarum, etiam non audito Consilio, remedio aliquo providendum esse censuerint.

1543. Liberum cuique rectori est alium sacerdotem ab episcopo approbandum secum habere coram consilio siv· ad simplicem dsistentiam sive ad suas animadversiones aut defensionem exhibendam.

Ioan Card. Simeoni,
Sacr. Cong. Praef.

I. B. Agnozzi,
Secret.

formata conscientia," if in the Lord they come to the conclusion that most grave and canonical causes exist therefor, or if they believe that, owing to grave and urgent necessity, provision must be made for the salvation of souls, by some extraordinary remedy, even without having previously heard the advice of the Council.

1543. Every rector is free to have with him before the Council another priest, who must be approved by the bishop, in order either to simply assist him (the rector), or to make remarks, or to conduct the defence.

John Card. Simeoni,
Prefect of the Sacred Congregation.

J. B. Agnozzi,
Secretary.

III.

THE CANONICAL TRIAL ADAPTED TO THE WANTS OF THE PRESENT DAY—INSTRUCTION OF THE S. C. EE. ET RR. AUTHORIZING ORDINARIES IN COUNTRIES NOT SUBJECT TO THE PROPAGANDA, TO CONDUCT ECCLESIASTICAL TRIALS, WITHOUT OBSERVING, IN CERTAIN CASES, ALL THE FORMALITIES PRESCRIBED BY CANON LAW.

Instructio pro Ecclesiasticis Curiis quoad modum procedendi oeconomice in causis disciplinaribus et criminalibus clericorum.[1]

1544. *Die* 11 *Iunii* 1880.—Sacra haec EE. et RR. Congregatio, mature praesenti Ecclesiae conditione perpensâ, quae pene ubique impeditur, quominus externam explicet suam actionem super materias et personas ecclesiasticas, et considerato quoque defectu mediorum aptorum pro regulari Curiarum ordinatione, constituit facultatem Ordinariis locorum expresse concedere, ut forma· magis oeconomicas adhibere valeant in exercitio suae disciplinaris iurisdiction;· super Clericis. Ut autem tota iustitiae ratio sarta tectaque maneat, ser vveturque processuum canonica regularitas et uniformitas, opportunum censui: sequentes emanare normas, a Curiis servandas.

[1] This Instruction is of great practical importance also for this country, since its provisions tend manifestly to explain the Instruction of the S. C. de P. F., of July 20, 1878. Cf. supra, n. 1512 sq.; Acta S. Sedis, vol. 13, p. 324 sq.

1545. I. Ordinario pastorale onus incumbit disciplinam correctionemque Clericorum a se dependentium curandi, super eorumdem vitae rationem vigilando, remediisque utendo canonicis ad praecavendas apud eosdem et elimi nandas ordinis perturbationes.

1546. II. Ex his remediis alia praeveniunt, alia reprimunt et medelam afferunt. Priora ad hoc diriguntur ut impediant quominus malum adveniat, ut scandali stimuli, occasiones voluntariae, causaeque ad delinquendum proximae removeantur. Altera finem habent revocandi delinquentes ut sapiant reparentque admissi criminis consequentias.

1547. III. Conscientiae et prudentiae Ordinarii horum remediorum incumbit applicatio, iuxta canonum praescriptiones, et casuum adiunctorumque gravitatem.

1548. IV. Mediis quae praeservant praecipue accensentur spiritualia exercitia, monitiones et praecepta.

1549. V. Has provisiones praecedere debet summaria facti cognitio quae ab Ordinario notanda est, ut *ad ulteriora* procedere, quatenus opus sit, et certiorem reddere queat superiorem Auctoritatem, in casu legitimi recursus.

1550. VI. Canonicae monitiones fiunt sive in forma paterna et secreta (etiam per epistolam aut per interpositam personam) sive in forma legali, ita tamen ut de earumdem executione constet ex aliquo actu.

1551. VII. Quatenus infructuosae monitiones evadant, Ordinarius praecipit Curiae, ut delinquenti analogum iniungatur praeceptum, in quo declaretur quid eidem agendum aut omittendum sit, cum respondentis poena ecclesiasticae comminatione, quam incurret in casu transgressionis.

1552. VIII. Praeceptum intimatur praevento a Cancellario coram Vicario Generali; sive coram duobus testibus ecclesiasticis aut laicis probatae integritatis.

§ 1. Actus subsignatur a partibus praesentibus et a praevento quoque, si velit.

§ 2. Vicarius Generalis adiicere valet iuramentum servandi secretum, quatenus id prudenter expetat tituli indoles, de quo agitur.

1553. IX. Quoad *poenalia* media, animadvertant reverendissimi Ordinarii, praesenti instructione haud derogatum esse iudiciorum solemnitatibus, per sacros Canones, per Apostolicas Constitutiones et alias ecclesiasticas dispositiones imperatis, quatenus eaedem libere efficaciterque applicari queant; sed oeconomicae formae consulere intendunt illis casibus Curiisque, in quibus solemnes processus, aut adhiberi nequeant, aut non expedire videantur. Plenam quoque vim servat suam extraiudiciale remedium *ex informata conscientia* pro criminibus occultis, quod decrevit s. Tridentina Synodus in *Sess.* 14 *cap.* I. *de Reform.* adhibendum, cum illis regulis et reservationibus, quas constanter servavit pro dicti capitis interpretatione s. C. Congregatio in pluribus resolutionibus, et praecipue in *Bosnien.* et *Sirmien.* 20 Decembris 1873.[1]

1554. X. Quum procedi oporteat criminaliter, sive infractionis praecepti, aut criminum communium, vel legum Ecclesiae violationis causâ, processus confici potest formis summariis et absque iudicii strepitu, servatis semper regulis iustitiae substantialibus.

---

[1] Cf. Acta S. Sedis, vol. VII. pag. 569.

1555. XI. Processus instruitur ex *officio* aut in sequelam supplicis libelli et querelae, aut notitiae, alio modo, a Curia habitae, et ad finem perducitur eo consilio, ut omni studio atque prudentiâ veritas detegatur, et cognitio tum criminis, cum reitatis aut innocentiae accusati exurgat.

1556. XII. Processus confectio committi potest alicui probolat que idoneo ecclesiastico, adstante Actuario.

1557. XIII. Unicuique Curiae opus est Procuratore fiscali pro iustitiae et legis tutela.

1558. XIV. Quatenus pro intimationibus aut notificationibus, haud praesto sit opera Apparitorum Curiae, suppletur exhibitione earumdem explendâ per qualificatam personam, quae de facto certioret; sive eas transmittendo, ope commendationis penes tabellariorum officium, illis in locis in quibus hoc invaluit systema, exposcendo fidem exhibitionis, receptionis aut repudii.

1559. XV. Basis facti criminosi constitui potest per expositionem in processu habitam, authenticis roboratam informationibus aut confessionibus extra-iudicialibus, vel testium depositionibus, et quoad titulum transgressionis praecepti constat per novam exhibitionem decreti et actus indictionis, perfectorum modis enuntiatis Art. VII. et VIII.

1560. XVI. Ad retinendam in specie culpabilitatem accusati opus est probatione legali, quae talia continere debet elementa, ut veritatem evincat, aut saltem inducat moralem certitudinem, remoto in contrarium quovis rationabili dubio.

1561. XVII. Personae, quas examinare expediat, semper audiuntur separatim.

1562. XVIII. Testes ad probationem, aut ad defensionem, quoties legalia obstacula haud obsistant, sub iuramento audiri debent, quod extendi potest, si opus sit, ad obligationem secreti.

1563. XIX. Testium absentium, aut in aliena Dioecesi morantium exposcitur examen in subsidium ab Ecclesiastica loci auctoritate, eidem transmittendo prospectum facti; et Auctoritas requisita petitioni respondet, servando praesentis instructionis normas.

1564. XX. Quoties indicentur testes ob facta aut adiuncta essentialiter utilia merito Causae, qui examini subiici nequeant, eoquod censeatur haud convenire ut vocentur, aut quia vocati abnuant, mentio eorumdem fit in actibus, et curatur supplere eorum defectui per depositiones aliorum testium, qui de relato aut alia ratione, noverint id quod exquiritur.

1565. XXI. Quum collectum fuerit quidquid opus sit ad factum et accusati responsabilitatem constituendam, vocatur iste ad examen.

1566. XXII. In indictione, nisi prudentia id vetet, exponuntur ei per extensum accusationes adversus eum collatae, ut parari valeat ad respondendum.

1567. XXIII. Quando autem ob accusationum qualitates, aut ob alia adiuncta prudens non sit in actu intimationis eas patefacere, in hac solum innuitur eumdem ad examen vocari ut sese excuset in Causa, quae ipsum respicit uti accusatum.

1568. XXIV. Si iudicio sistere abnuat, iteratur indictio, in quo eidem praefigitur congruum peremptorium terminum. eique significatur quod si adhuc obedire renuat, habebitur ceu contumax; et pro tali in facto aestimabitur, quatenus absque probato legitimo impedimento, istam quoque posthaberet intimationem.

1569. XXV. Si compareat, auditur in examine; et quatenus inductiones faciat alicuius momenti, debent istae, quantum fieri potest, exhauriri.

1570. XXVI. Proceditur inde ad contestationem facti criminosi, et conclusionum habitarum, ad retinendum accusatum criminosum lapsumque in relativis poenis canonicis.

1571. XXVII. Quum accusatus, tali modo, habeat plenam cognitionem eius quod in actis extat contra se, ultra quod respondere possit, iure se defendendi a semetipso etiam uti valet.

1572. XXVIII. Potest quoque, si id expetat, obtinere praefixionem termini ad exhibendam defensionem cum memoria in scriptis, praecipue quando ob dispositionem *Art. XXIII.* nequiverit paratus esse ad responsa pro sua excusatione.

1573. XXIX. Expleto processu, actorum instructor, restrictum conficit essentialium conclusionum eiusdem.

1574. XXX. In die qua Causa proponitur, est in facultate accusati faciendi se repraesentare et defendere ab alio Sacerdote aut laico Patrocinatore, antea approbatis ab Ordinario.

1575. XXXI. Quatenus praeventus constituere defensorem renuat, Ordinarius consulit constituendo aliquem ex officio.

1576. XXXII. Defensor caute notitiam haurit processus et restricti in Cancellaria, ut paratus sit ad defensionem peragendam, quae ante'propositionem causae exhiberi potest in scriptis. Ipse quoque subiicitur oneri secreti iurati, quatenus Ordinario videatur indolem Causae id expostulare.

1577. XXXIII. Transmittitur dein Procuratori fiscali processus et restrictus, ut munere suo *ex officio* fungatur; uterque Ordinario traditur qui plenâ Causae cognitione adeptâ, diem constituit in qua disceptanda et resolvenda sit, curans ut accusatus certior de hoc fiat.

1578. XXXIV. Die constituta proponitur Causa coram Vicario generali, interessentibus Procuratore fiscali, Defensore et Cancellario.

1579. XXXV. Post votum Procuratoris Fisci et deductiones defensionis profertur sententia, dictando dispositivam Cancellario, cum explicita mentione, in casu damnationis, canonicae sanctionis, accusato applicatae.

1580. XXXVI. Sententia indicitur praevento, qui appellationem interponere potest ad Auctoritatem Ecclesiasticam superiorem.

1581. XXXVII. Pro appellatione servantur normae statutae a Constitutione *Ad militantes* s. m. Bened. XIV. 30 Martii 1742, aliaeque emanatae ab hac s. Congregatione Decreto 18 Decembris 1835 [1] et Littera circulari diei 1 Augusti 1851.

---

[1] En in commodum lectorum decretum huiusmodi. Haud referimus litteram prolixam diei 1 Augusti 1851, quoniam praecipuae eiusdem praescriptiones in praesenti Instructione relatae nobis videntur.

DECRETUM PRO CAUSIS CRIMINALIBUS. Non ita pridem a. s. Congregatione negociis, et consultationibus Episcoporum, et Regularium praepositae nonnullae regulae praescriptae fuerunt pro recta, et expedita definitione causarum criminalium, quae a Curiis Episcoporum, vel Ordinariorum ad eamdem s. Congregationem in gradu appellationis deferuntur. Quas quidem praescriptiones, quoniam impedimenta sublata sunt, quae aliqua ex parte earum executioni interposita fuerant, visum est Eminentissimis Patribus in Conventu habito xv. Calend. Januar. MDCCCXXXV. uberius explicare, et cum assensu, et approbatione S. D. N.

428 *Appendix.*

1582. XXXVIII. Comparitio pro appellatione facienda est infra terminum decem dierum a notificatione sententiae; quo termino inutiliter èlapso, sententia ipsa in executionis statu reperitur.

1583. XXXIX. Interposita appellatione infra decem dies, Curia absque mora remittit ad Auctoritatem ecclesiasticam superiorem, apud quam appellatio facta est, omnes actus Causae originales, idest processum, restrictum, defensiones et sententiam.

1584. XL. Auctoritas ecclesiastica superior, captâ cognitione actus appel-

GREGORII XVI. iterum promulgare, ut ab omnibus, ad quos pertinent, accuratissimae serventur. Sunt autem quae sequuntur.

I. Reis a Curiis Episcopalibus criminali iudicio damnatis spatium dierum decem conceditur, quo ad s. Congregationem Episcoporum, et Regularium appellare possint.

II. Decem dies numerari incipient non a die, quo sententia lata est, sed a die, quo reo vel eius defensori per Cursorem denunciata fuit.

III. Eo tempore elapso, quin reus vel eius defensor appellaverit, latam a se sententiam Episcopus exequetur.

IV. Interposita intra decem dies appellatione Curia Episcopalis acta autographa totius causae ad s. Congregationem continuo transmittat, nempe
    1. *Processum* ipsum in Curia confectum.
    2. Eius *restrictum*, seu compendiariam expositionem eorum quae ex eodem processu emergunt.
    3. Defensiones pro reo exhibitas.
    4. Denique sententiam latam.

V. Ipsa Curia reo, eiusque defensori denunciabit, appellationem coram eadem s. Congregatione prosequendam esse.

VI. Si nemo compareat, aut si appellationis acta negligenter vel malitiose protrahantur, congruens tempus a s. Congregatione praefinietur, quo inutiliter elapso, causa deserta censeatur, et sententia Curiae Episcopalis executioni mandetur.

VII. Reo, aut illi, qui eius defensionem suscepit, tradendus est *restrictus* processus, qui a Iudice relatore conficitur.

VIII. Allegationes, seu defensiones Eminentissimis Patribus distribuendas typis non committantur, nisi Iudex relator imprimendi veniam dederit.

IX. Causa definietur stata die ab Eminentissimis Patribus in pleno Auditorio congregatis.

X. Eidem Congregationis Procurator Generalis Fisci, et Iudex relator intererunt.

XI. Iudex relator de toto statu causae ad Eminentissimos Patres refert, et Procurator Generalis Fisci stabit pro Curia Episcopali, suasque conclusiones explanabit.

XII. Post haec Eminentissimi Patres iudicium proferent, sententiam Curiae Episcopalis aut confirmando, aut infirmando aut etiam reformando.

XIII. Prolata Sententia una cum omnibus Actis causae ad eamdem Curiam Episcopalem remittitur, ut eam exequatur.

XIV. *Revisio*, seu recognitio rei iudicatae non conceditur, nisi eius tribuendae potestas a Sanctitate Sua facta fuerit, et subsint gravissimae causae, super quibus cognitio, et iudicium ad plenam Congregationem pertinet.

XV. Sciant denique Curiae Episcopales per novissimas leges, quae ad investiganda, et coercenda crimina pro Tribunalibus laicis promulgatae sunt, nihil detractum esse de formis, et regulis Canonicis, quas proinde sequi omnino debent, non modo in conficiendo processu, ad quem spectant haec verba Edicti die 5 Novembris 1831 - *Nihil innovetur, quantum ad iudicia ecclesiastica pertinet* - verum etiam in poenis decernendis, quemadmodum in appendice eiusdem Edicti ita cautum est - *Tribunalia iurisdictionis mixtae Clericos, et Personas ecclesiasticas iis poenis mulctabunt, quas secundum Canones, et Constitutiones Apostolicas Tribunal Ecclesiasticum iisdem irrogaret* -.

J. A. CARD. SALA PRAEFECTUS.
I. Patriarcha Constantinopolitanus Secr.

lationis, intimare facit appellanti, ut infra terminum viginti dierum Defensorem constituat, qui approbari debet ab eadem superiori auctoritate.

1585. 41. Decurso dicto termino peremptorio absque effectu, censetur appellantem nuncium misisse appellationis beneficio, et haec consequenter perempta declaratur a superiori auctoritate.

1586. 42. Quum appellatio producitur a sententia aliculus Curiae episcopalis ad Metropolitanam, Archiepiscopus pro cognitione et decisione Causae sequitur normam procedendi in hac instructione traditam.

1587. 43. Si contingat quod Clericus, non obstante fori privilegio, ob crimina communia subiiciatur processui et iudicio laicae potestatis, Ordinarius, hoc in casu, summariam sumit criminosi facti cognitionem, atque perpendit an ipsum, ad tradita per sacros canones, locum faciat infamiae, irregularitati, aut alii ecclesiasticae sanctioni.

§ 1. Donec iudicium pendeat, aut accusatus detentus sit, prudens est, quod Ordinarius sese limitet ad media provisoria.

§ 2. Expleto tamen iudicio, et libero reddito accusato, Curia iuxta exitum informationum ceu superius assumptarum, procedit ad tramites dispositionum praesentis instructionis.

1588. 44. In casibus dubiis, et in variis practicis difficultatibus, quae contingere possint, Ordinarii consulant hanc s. Congregat., ad vitandas contentiones et nullitates.

Ex Aud. SSmi. diei 11 *Iunii* 1880.

SSmus Dñus Noster LEO div. prov. PP. XIII., audita relatione praesentis Instructionis ab infrascripto Sacr. Congreg. Episcopor. et Regularium Secretario, eam in omnibus approbare et confirmare dignatus est.

Romae die et anno quibus supra.

I. Card. Ferrieri Praef.

I. B. *Agnossi Secretarius.*

IV.

CONSTITUTIO

BENEDICTI PP. XIV.

In qua praescribitur ordo et forma in iudiciis Causarum matrimonialium super matrimoniorum validitate vel nullitate declaranda servandus.[1]

BENEDICTUS

EPISCOPUS

SERVUS SERVORUM DEI AD PERPETUAM REI MEMORIAM.

1589. Dei miseratione, cuius iudicia incomprehensibilia sunt, et viae investigabiles, in suprema Ecclesiae specula immerentes constituti, ut super universum Dominicum gregem excubias sedulo agamus, ad commissum pastoralis officii munus pertinere dignoscimus subnascentes ex infernalis hostis astutia, et hominum malitia abusus, quibus et animarum saluti pernicies, et sacramentis Ecclesiae iniuria infertur, radicitus evellere, et potestatis Nobis desuper traditae operam interponere, ut et humana cohibeatur temeritas, et veneranda divinae legis servetur auctoritas.

1590. § 1. Siquidem matrimonii foedus a Deo institutum, quod et quatenus naturae officium est, pro educandae prolis studio, aliisque matrimonii bonis servandis, perpetuum et indissolubile esse convenit; et quatenus est catholicae Ecclesiae sacramentum, humana praesumptione dissolvi non posse, Salvator ipse ore suo pronunciavit dicens: *Quod Deus coniunxit, homo non separet;* ad aures Apostolatus Nostri pervenit, in quibusdam ecclesiasticis Curiis inconsulta nimis iudicum facilitate infringi, et temere atque inconsiderate de eorumdem matrimoniorum nullitate latis sententiis, potestatem coniugibus fieri transeundi ad alia vota. Quos sane improvidos iudices humanae naturae conditione et voce ipsa quodammodo admoneri oportebat, ne tam praecipiti audacia sanctum matrimonii nexum frangerent, quem perpetuum atque indissolubilem primus humani generis parens praemonuit inquiens: *Hoc nunc os ex ossibus meis, et caro de carne mea,* et illud additum est: *Quamobrem relinquet homo patrem suum et matrem, et adhaerebit uxori suae, et erunt duo in carne una.*

1591. § 2. Huiusmodi autem abolendae pravitatis notitia diversis ex partibus Nobis delata est, atque etiam indicata sunt exempla nonnullorum virorum, qui post primam et secundam ac tertiam, quam duxerant, uxorem ob nimiam iudicum praecipitantiam in nullitate matrimoniorum declaranda, adhuc illis primis uxoribus superstitibus, ad quartas contrahendas nuptias devenerant; et similiter feminarum, quae post primum, secundum et tertium maritum, quarto etiam, illis quoque viventibus, se iunxerant, non sine pusillorum scandalo, et bonorum omnium detestatione, qui sacra matrimonii vincula ita contemni, et temere per-

---

[1] Nearly this whole constitution is taken up in defining the duties of the judge, of the defender of the marriage, the force and effect of sentences in matrimonial causes. Cf. supra, n. 1450, sq.

fringi dolebant. Nos autem, his intellectis, gravi affecti dolore, intimo animo ingemuimus, et non praetermisimus apostolicae nostrae sollicitudinis partes in Domino adimplere. Siquidem primo Pontificatus nostri anno ad Episcopos illarum partium, in quibus praedicta acciderant, plenissimis datis literis, graviter conquesti sumus de huiusmodi pravitate, quae in Ecclesia Dei tolerabatur, et ad eam abolendam eorum animos erigere, et pastoralem zelum accendere curavimus: quod etiam egimus cum aliis aliarum regionum Episcopis, ubi huiusmodi pravum dirimendorum matrimoniorum usum irrepsisse cognovimus.

1592. § 3. Verum Nobis responsum est, id saepe contingere partim ex culpa illorum Iudicum, quibus vel in prima instantia, cum causa coram Iudice ordinario ex aliqua legitima causa cognosci nequit, vel in secunda, cum in partibus nullus adest Iudex, ad cuius tribunal causa in gradu appellationis devolvatur, vel si adest, iusta de causa coram eo disceptari nequit, causae matrimoniales huiusmodi a Sede apostolica committuntur, qui vel ob inscitiam, vel ob malam voluntatem procliVes sunt ad matrimonia dissolvenda, atque eadem matrimonia, levi vel etiam nullo habito examine, irrita ac invalida declarant; partim etiam ex facto coniugum super nullitate suorum matrimoniorum litigantium, cum frequenter unus tantum eorum, qui dissolutionem matrimonii postulat, in iudicio compareat, et sententia, nullo contradicente, secundum sua vota obtenta, ad alias nuptias convolat; vel ambobus coniugibus in iudicium venientibus, alter qui pro matrimonio, alter vero qui contra agit, sententia de nullitate matrimonii prolata, nullus est, qui ad superiorem Iudicem appellationem interponat, vel quia litigantes in specie quidem discordes, re vera inter se concordes sunt, et invicem colludentes, contractum matrimonium dissolvi cupiunt; vel quia pars, quae pro validitate matrimonii stabat, eiusque nullitatem acriter contra adversarium impugnabat, lata a Iudice sententia contra matrimonium, mutat voluntatem, vel pecunia sibi ad sumptus litis non suppetente, vel aliis deficientibus auxiliis ad litigandum necessariis, et incoeptum opus ac causam post primam sententiam deserit. Quo fit, ut deinde ambo coniuges, vel unus eorum ad aliud contrahendum matrimonium se conferat.

1593. § 4. Quod autem ad Iudices pertinet, quibus extra romanam Curiam pro litigantium commodo causae matrimoniales committuntur, paterna illa vigilantia, qua de iustitia unicuique integre sapienterque administranda solliciti esse debemus, encyclicis literis ad venerabiles fratres Patriarchas, Primates, Archiepiscopos et Episcopos scriptis vicesima sexta augusti anno secundo Pontificatus nostri, providere curavimus, in quibus ea praescripsimus, quae sacris Canonibus, et Concilii tridentini decretis consona, si diligenter, ut speramus, serventur, in posterum causae non nisi personis congrua iuris peritia et necessario probitatis spectataeque fidei munitis praesidio committentur. Insuper ad ea, quae in iisdem encyclicis literis constituta sunt, id etiam in praesenti adiungimus; quod, quamvis Concilii tridentini decretum, quo causae matrimoniales subtractae fuerunt Decani, Archidiaconi et aliorum inferiorum iudicio, et Episcoporum tantum examini et iurisdictioni reservatae, dumtaxat procedat de Archidiaconis, Decanis, aliisque inferioribus, qui in eadem dioecesi constituti, vel privilegio aliquo vel praescriptione, saltem in visitatione, causarum matrimonialium cognitionem sibi adrogabant; ac idcirco minime obstet commissionibus, quae pro iisdem causis matrimonialibus definiendis a Sede apostolica alicui eorum in secunda instantia fierent; nihilominus praecipimus ac mandamus iis, ad quos huiusmodi commissionum seu delegationum expediendarum cura pertinet, ut in futurum causarum matrimonialium cognitionem non committant nisi Episcopis praesertim vicinioribus, vel si nullus sit Episcopus, cui ex legitima causa commode committi possit, tum commissio et delegatio dirigatur uni ex iis, qui secundum ordinem et modum a Nobis in praefatis encyclicis literis praescriptum pro Iudice idoneo ab Episcopo cum consilio sui Capituli nominatus fuerit.

1594. § 5. Quod vero ad ordinem, et seriem iudiciorum in causis matrimonialibus pro debita et congrua earum terminatione servandum spectat, motu proprio, certa scientia ac matura deliberatione nostris, deque apostolicae potestatis plenitudine hac nostra in perpetuum valitura sanctione constituimus, decernimus ac iubemus, ut ab omnibus et singulis locorum Ordinariis in suis respective dioecesibus persona aliqua idonea eligatur, et si fieri potest, ex ecclesiastico coetu, iuris scientia pariter et vitae probitate praedita, quae matrimoniorum defensor nominabitur, cum facultate tamen eam suspendendi, vel removendi, si iusta causa adfuerit, et substituendi aliam aeque idoneam et iisdem qualitatibus ornatam, quod etiam fieri poterit, quotiescumque persona ad matrimoniorum defensionem destinata, cum se occasio agendi obtulerit, erit legitime impedita.

1595. § 6. Ad officium autem defensoris matrimoniorum huiusmodi, ut supra electi, spectabit in iudicium venire quotiescumque contigerit, matrimoniales causas super validitate vel nullitate coram legitimo Iudice disceptari, eumque oportebit in quolibet actu iudiciali citari, adesse examini testium, voce et scriptis matrimonii validitatem tueri, eaque omnia deducere, quae ad matrimonium sustinendum necessaria censebit.

1596. § 7. Et demum defensoris huiusmodi persona, tanquam pars necessaria ad iudicii validitatem et integritatem censeatur, semperque adsit in iudicio sive unus ex coniugibus, qui pro nullitate matrimonii agit, sive ambo, quorum alter pro nullitate, alter vero pro validitate in iudicium veniant. Defensor autem, cum ei munus huiusmodi committetur, iuramentum praestabit fideliter officium suum obeundi, et quotiescumque contigerit, ut in iudicio adesse debeat pro alicuius matrimonii validitate tuenda, rursus idem iuramentum praebebit: quaecumque vero, eo non legitime citato aut intimato, in iudicio peracta fuerint, nulla, irrita, cassa declaramus, ac pro nullis, cassis ac irritis haberi volumus, perinde ac si citata et intimata non esset ea pars, cuius citari intererat, et quam iuxta legum et canonum praescripta ad legitimam iudicii validitatem citari aut intimari omnino necessarium erat.

1597. § 8. Cum igitur coram Ordinario, ad quem causas huiusmodi cognoscere pertinet, controversia aliqua proponetur, in qua de matrimonii validitate dubitabitur, et existentibus in iudicio vel uno ex coniugibus, qui pro nullitate matrimonii, vel ambobus, quorum alter pro validitate, alter vero pro nullitate actionem intendat, defensor matrimonii partes omnes officii sui diligenter adimpleat. Itaque si a Iudice pro matrimonii validitate iudicabitur, et nullus sit qui appellet, ipse etiam ab appellatione se abstineat: idque etiam servetur si a Iudice secundae instantiae pro validitate matrimonii fuerit iudicatum, postquam Iudex primae instantiae de illius nullitate sententiam pronunciaverat; sin autem contra matrimonii validitatem sententia feratur, defensor inter legitima tempora appellabit adhaerens parti, quae pro validitate agebat; cum autem in iudicio nemo unus sit, qui pro matrimonii validitate negotium insistat, vel si adsit, lata contra eum sententia, iudicium deseruerit, ipse ex officio ad superiorem Iudicem provocabit.

1598. § 9. Appellatione a prima sententia pendente, vel etiam nulla ob malitiam vel oscitantiam vel collusionem defensoris et partium interposita si ambo vel unus ex coniugibus novas nuptias celebrare ausus fuerit, volumus ac decernimus, ut non solum serventur quae adversus eos, qui matrimonium contra interdictum Ecclesiae contrahunt, statuta sunt, praesertim ut invicem a cohabitatione separentur, quoadusque altera sententia super nullitate emanaverit, a qua intra *decem dies* non sit appellatum, vel appellatio interposita deserta deinde fuerit; sed ulterius ut contrahens vel contrahentes matrimonium huiusmodi omnibus poenis contra poligamos a sacris Canonibus et Constitutionibus apostolicis constitutis omnino subiaceant, quas in eos, quatenus opus sit, motu, scientia ac potestate simili rursus statuimus, decernimus ac renovamus.

1599. § 10. Posteaquam vero appellationis beneficio ad alterum Iudicem causa in secunda instantia delata fuerit, omnia et singula quaecumque coram Iudice in prima instantia servanda praefinita fuerunt, etiam coram altero in secunda exacte ac diligenter custodientur, citato in quolibet iudicii actu defensore matrimonii, qui voce et scripto matrimonii validitatem strenue ac pro viribus tuebitur, et si Iudex in secunda instantia fuerit Metropolitanus, aut Sedis apostolicae Nuncius, aut Episcopus viciniór, matrimonii defensor sit qui ab ipsis fuerit deputatus, quemadmodum ipsis deputare mandamus, ut quae a Nobis superius constituta sunt, peragere possit; si autem Iudex in secunda instantia erit Iudex commissarius, cui a Sede apostolica causae cognitio demandata sit, et qui tribunal et iurisdictionem ordinariam non habeat, et propterea careat defensore matrimonii, volumus, ut illo defensore matrimonii utatur, qui constitutus fuerit ab Ordinario, in cuius dioecesi causam cognoscet, etiam si idem Ordinarius sit, qui primam sententiam in eadem causa pronunciaverit.

1600. § 11. Instructo autem in hunc modum iudicio, si secunda sententia alteri conformis fuerit, hoc est, si in secunda aeque ac in prima nullum ac irritum matrimonium iudicatum fuerit, et ab ea pars vel defensor pro sua conscientia non crediderit appellandum vel appellationem interpositam prosequendam minime censuerit, in potestate et arbitrio coniugum sit novas nuptias contrahere, dummodo alicui eorum ob aliquod impedimentum vel legitimam causam id vetitum non sit. Potestas tamen post alteram sententiam conformem, ut supra, coniugibus facta intelligatur et locum habeat, salvo semper et firmo remanente iure seu privilegio causarum matrimonialium, quae ob cuiuscumque temporis lapsum nunquam transeunt in rem iudicatam; sed si nova res, quae non deducta vel ignorata fuerit, detegatur, resumi possunt, et rursus in iudicialem controversiam revocari. Quod si a secunda sententia super nullitate vel altera pars appellaverit, vel huiusmodi sit, ut ei salva conscientia, defensor matrimonii acquiescendum non putet, vel quia sibi videtur manifeste iniusta vel invalida, vel quia fuerit lata in tertia instantia, et sit revocatoria alterius praecedentis super validitate in secunda instantia emanatae, volumus, ut firma remanente utrique coniugi prohibitione ad alias transeundi nuptias, quas si contrahere ausi fuerint, poenis, ut praefertur, a Nobis constitutis subesse decernimus, causa in tertia vel quarta instantia cognoscatur, servatis diligenter omnibus, quae a Nobis in prima et secunda instantia demandata fuerunt, nempe in quolibet iudiciali actu citato et audito defensore matrimonii, qui a Iudice tertiae instantiae deputatus fuerit.

1601. § 12. Defensor autem matrimonii, quem ad munus suum gratis obeundum pro amore Dei, et proximi utilitate, et Ecclesiae reverentia in Domino exhortamur, si operam suam sine mercede aut salario aliqua ex causa exhibere recusaverit, ab ipsius causae Iudice ei constituatur, et ab ea parte, quae pro validitate matrimonii agit, si ipsi facultas sit, solvatur, sin minus a Iudice primae vel secunda vel tertiae instantiae respective subministrabitur, qui pecunias ex mulctis suorum tribunalium redactas vel redigendas, et in opera pia erogandas, in huiusmodi sumptus insumere poterunt. Cum vero iudices causae erunt Iudices commissarii, qui neque forum habent, et consequenter neque pecuniam ex mulctis collectam, volumus ac mandamus, ut defensori matrimonii satisfiat ex pecunia mulctarum illius Episcopi, in cuius dioecesi Iudex commissarius iuxta Sedis apostolicae mandatum iudicium exercebit.

1602. § 13. Hactenus quidem quoad causas matrimoniales, quae extra romanam Curiam pertractantur. Quoad causas vero, quae Romae disceptandae sunt, cum earum cognitio in prima instantia ad S. R. E. Cardinalem in praefata Urbe, eiusque Suburbiis et districtu Vicarium nostrum in spiritualibus pro tempore spectet, mandamus ac iubemus, ut omnia et singula, quae in aliis causis extra romanam Curiam pertractandis praescripta fuerunt, nempe ut iudicium peragatur citato et audito defensore matrimonii ab eodem Cardinali Vicario deputato, aliaque ut supra omnino serventur, tum etiam in aliis causis, quae in prima instantia ex consensu partium, vel in secunda per appellationem ad Sedem apostolicam, omisso medio, interpositam, vel in tertia Romam deferuntur, quas omnes iudicari volumus vel in Congregatione S. R. E. Cardinalium super interpretatione et executione Concilii tridentini, vel in causarum Palatii nostri Auditorio, dummodo Nobis et romano Pontifici pro tempore iustis ex causis non videatur particularis Congregatio S. R. E. Cardinalium, vel romanae Curiae Praelatorum deputanda. Cum autem causa super matrimonii nullitate agitabitur in dicta Congregatione S. R. E. Cardinalium Concilii tridentini interpretum, defensor matrimonii a Cardinali Praefecto eiusdem Congregationis, si vero in Palatii nostri Auditorio, ab Auditore decano praefati tribunalis, si demum in Congregatione particulari, a persona eiusdem Congregationis digniore deputetur.

1603. § 14. Unica quidem resolutio pro nullitate matrimonii emanata, si causa in Congregatione Cardinalium Concilii tridentini interpretum, vel in Congregatione particulari deputata cognoscatur, et similiter in Palatii nostri Auditorio, unica sententia super eadem nullitate pronunciata minime sufficiat ad tribuendam liberam coniugibus facultatem novas nuptias contrahendi, sed si causa in praefata Congregatione Cardinalium tridentini Concilii interpretum introducta fuerit, rursus in eadem ad defensoris matrimonii instantiam reproponatur; si vero Congregationi particulari commissa fuerit, ad petitionem eiusdem defensoris altera etiam particularis Congregatio deputabitur; si vero in Palatii nostri Auditorio iudicata sit, a praefato defensore appellatione interposita, ab aliis Auditoribus iuxta ordinem in gyrum seu turnum definiatur; si autem causa universo tribunali commissa fuerit, ob omnibus Auditoribus rursus examinabitur nolentes omnino, ut nullo in casu matrimonii vinculum dissolutum censeatur, nisi duo iudicata vel resolutiones aut sententiae penitus similes et conformes, a quibus neque pars, neque defensor matrimonii crediderit appellandum, emanaverint; quod si secus factum fuerit, et novum initum matrimonium, nostrae voluntatis huiusmodi transgressores poenis a Nobis ut supra statutis submittantur.

1604. § 15. Et quoniam saepe apud Sedem apostolicam preces porrigi solent pro dispensatione matrimonii rati et non consummati, quae ut plurimum pro voto consultivo ad Congregationem S. R. E. Cardinalium Concilii interpretum, vel nonnunquam ad aliquam Congregationem particularem deputatam a romanis Pontificibus pro tempore remitti solent, ut huiusmodi instantiae ordine ac rite procedant, volumus ac mandamus, ut supplex libellus Nobis vel romano Pontifici pro tempore exhibeatur, in quo plena et accurata totius facti species contineatur, causaeque omnes in eo exprimantur, quae ad obtinendam petitam dispensationem conducere posse a supplicante censentur, ut romanus Pontifex, eo lecto et mature considerato, secum deliberare possit, an petitionem reiiciat, vel eius examen alicui ex dictis Congregationibus committat, a qua posteaquam suum votum consultivum editum fuerit, a Secretario eiusdem Congregationis totius negotii series exacte romano Pontifici pro tempore referatur, qui pro sua prudentia iudicabit, an Congregationis resolutio sit approbanda, vel potius totius causae examen alteri Congregationi vel tribunali, prout eidem Pontifici videbitur, rursus committendum.

1605. § 16. Demum volumus ac decernimus, easdem praesentes literas semper firmas, validas et efficaces existere et fore, suosque plenarios et integros effectus sortiri et obtinere, ac ab illis, ad quos spectat, et pro tempore quandocumque spectabit, in omnibus et per omnia plenissime et inviolabiliter observari. Sicque et non aliter per quoscumque Iudices ordinarios et delegatos, etiam causarum Palatii apostolici Auditores, ac eosdem S. R. E. Cardinales, etiam de latere legatos, et s. Sedis Nuntios, aliosve quoslibet quacumque praeeminentia et potestate fungentes et functuros, sublata eis et eorum cuilibet quavis aliter iudicandi et interpretandi facultate et auctoritate, ubique iudicari et definiri debere, *ac irritum et inane*, si secus super his a quoquam quavis auctoritate scienter vel ignoranter contigerit attentari. Non obstantibus praemissis ac constitutionibus et ordinationibus apostolicis, nec non quibusvis etiam iuramento, confirmatione apostolica vel quavis firmitate alia roboratis, statutis et consuetudinibus, privilegiis quoque, indultis et literis apostolicis sub quibuscumque tenoribus verborum et formis, ac cum quibusvis etiam derogatoriarum derogatoriis, aliisque efficacioribus et insolitis clausulis irritantibusque et aliis decretis etiam motu, scientia et potestatis plenitudine paribus in genere vel in specie, seu alias quomodolibet concessis, confirmatis et innovatis. Quibus omnibus et singulis etiam si pro illorum sufficienti derogatione de illis eorumque totis tenoribus specialis, specifica, expressa et individua, ac de verbo ad verbum, non autem per clausulas generales idem importantes, mentio, seu quaevis alia expressio habenda, aut aliqua alia exquisita forma in illis tradita observata eisdem praesentibus pro expressis et insertis habentes, illis alias in suo robore permansuris, ad praemissorum effectum hac vice dumtaxat expresse derogamus, caeterisque contrariis quibuscumque.

1606. § 17. Volumus autem, ut praesentes literae in valvis Ecclesiae lateranensis et Principis Apostolorum, nec non Cancellariae apostolicae ac in acie

436 *Appendix.*

Campi Florae de Urbe, ut moris est, publicentur et affigantur, sicque publicatae et affixae, omnes et singulos, quos illae concernunt, perinde arctent et afficiant, ac si unicuique eorum nominatim et personaliter intimatae fuissent; quodque earumdem praesentium transumptis seu exemplis, etiam impressis, manu alicuius Notarii publici subscriptis, et sigillo alicuius personae in dignitate ecclesiastica constitutae munitis, eadem prorsus fides tam in iudicio, quam extra illud ubique adhibeatur, quae ipsis praesentibus adhiberetur, si forent exhibitae vel ostensae.

1607. § 18. Nulli ergo omnino hominum liceat hanc paginam nostri decreti, statuti, constitutionis, prohibitionis, revocationis, annullationis, declarationis, mandati ac voluntatis infringere, vel ei ausu temerario contraire. Si quis autem hoc attentare praesumpserit, indignationem omnipotentis Dei ac bb. Petri et Pauli apostolorum eius se noverit incursurum. Datum Romae apud s. Mariam maiorem tertio nonas novembris anno Incarnationis dominicae millesimo septingentesimo quadragesimo primo, Pontificatus nostri anno secundo.

D. CARD. PASSIONEUS.

Visa de Curia
N. Antonellus

X. Sub-Datarius.

Loco ✠ Plumbi.

I. B. Eugenius.

Anno a Nativitate D. N. IESU CHRISTI MDCCXLI. Indictione quarta, die vero 29 novembris, Pontificatus autem SSmi in Christo Patris et D. N. D. BENEDICTI divina providentia PP. XIV anno secundo, supradicta Constitutio affixa et publicata fuit ad valvas Basilicae lateranensis et Principis Apostolorum, nec non Cancellariae apostolicae, Curiae generalis in Monte Citatorio, in Acie Campi Florae, ac in aliis locis solitis et consuetis Urbis per me Ioannem Triselli apost. Curs.

Nicolaus Cappelli Mag. Curs.

V.

Instructio edita a s. Congregatione Concilii die 22 augusti 1840 pro confectione processus in causis matrimonialibus.[1]

1608. Cum moneat Glossa (*in cap. fin. de frig. et malef.*) in causis matrimonialibus omnem cautelam esse adhibendam propter periculum animarum, quod et docuit Sanchez (*de matrim. lib. 7. disp.* 107) et Card. Argenvilliers (*in dissert. matrimonii relat. inter vota Constantini P.* 5. *vol. ult. n.* 16) plura hinc a sacris Canonibus sancita sunt, ut tutum ac rectum iudicium efformari queat. Ad removendas vero fraudes, quae coniugum malitia vel collusione saepe oriebantur, s. m. Bened. XIV (in Constit. *Dei miseratione*) processum conficiendum esse praecepit sub poena nullitatis omnium actorum, ut probationibus undequaque

[1] This Instruction, as its heading indicates, lays down in detail the formalities of trials in matrimonial causes of nullity, and is of the greatest practical importance also in this country. Cf. supra, n. 1451, sq.

accuratissime cumulatis in causis huiusmodi omnium gravissimis, in quibus agitur de sacramenti validitate vel nullitate, ac de dissolvendo vinculo matrimoniali, iudices in proferendo iudicio tuti conquiescere possent. At quia saepe in hoc difficillimo processu acta minus recte et apte ad veritatem eruendam conficiebantur, s. Congregatio saepius instructiones edidit, ac normam praescripsit quam Episcopi sequerentur.

1609. Cum itaque in huiusmodi causis non de iure alterutrius partis tantum, sed praecipue de sacramentali vinculo dissolvendo agatur, processus acta non ad instar aliorum iudiciorum, praesertim civilium, sed iuxta ss. Canones, citatam s. m. Bened. XIV Constitutionem, et praesentem instructionem erunt efformanda. Ea itaque non vernaculo sed latino sermone erunt conscribenda, exceptis tamen excipiendis, nimirum articulis, interrogatoriis, responsionibus ad ea, et peritorum relationibus; praesertim vero decreta et sententia, quae iuxta priscos mores erit conficienda, latina lingua exarabuntur. Praeterea cum a sacro Conc. trid. (*sess.* 24. *cap.* 20. *de ref.* § *ad haec*), ac etiam a s. m. Bened. XIV (in cit. Constit. *Dei miseratione* § 4.) causarum matrimonialium cognitio quibusvis iudicibus inferioribus, non obstante quovis privilegio ac praescriptione, fuerit sublata, ac Episcoporum tantum examini et iurisdictioni reservata etiam prae Abbatibus vere *Nullius*, licet cardinalitia dignitate fulgentibus iuxta s. Congregationis resolutiones, hinc tutius erit, ut nedum sententia proferatur, sed etiam acta processus per Episcopum vel per ecclesiasticam personam specialiter ab eo delegandam conficiantur.

1610. Hisce praemissis, quoties aliquis ex coniugibus instantiam in scriptis porriget super nullitate matrimonii, Episcopus Iudicem, si velit, delegabit, deinde ipse vel iudex delegatus citari mandabit Defensorem matrimonii, quatenus in Curia episcopali iam deputatus existat, sin minus, idoneum virum deputabit iis qualitatibus praestantem, quas superius memorata Constitut. s. m. Benedicti XIV requirit, eumque citari mandabit. Defensoris matrimonii erit praefixa die accedere ad praestandum iuramentum, se munus suum diligenter et incorrupte expleturum, et omnia voce ac scriptis deducturum, quae ad validitatem matrimonii sustinendam conferre poterunt. Praeterea hic Defensor matrimonii *citandus erit ad quaelibet acta, ne vitio nullitatis ipsa tabescant.*[1] Ipsi, qui pro sacramenti validitate stat, semper et quandocumque acta processus, etsi nondum publicati, erunt communicanda, semper et quandocumque eius scripta erunt recipienda, ac novi termini eo flagitante erunt prorogandi, ut ea perficiat et exhibeat.

1611. Praefinita die in citatione comparebit instans pro nullitate, et tunc Defensor matrimonii tradet interrogatoria clausa et obsignata Cancellario seu Notario, aperienda, illo postulante, ex Iudicis decreto in actu examinis, super quibus interrogandus erit coniux instans pro nullitate. Iis ea addet etiam in actu examinis ex officio Iudex, quae ex responsionibus magis apta conspiciet ad veritatem eruendam sive in declarationem responsionum datarum, sive super novis circumstantiis resultantibus, quod erit intelligendum etiam de aliis interrogatoriis, super quibus ceteri omnes de re instructi erunt examinandi.

1612. Cum itaque advenerit statuta dies pars nullitatem matrimonii allegans comparebit ut supra dictum, coram Iudice, adstante Defensore matrimonii et

[1] Ex cit. Const. § 7.

Cancellario. Iudex deferet parti examinandae iuramentum de veritate dicenda, et deinde reserabit interrogatoria exhibita, ut supra dictum est, a Defensore matrimonii, eaque singulatim proponet, audiet responsiones, easque dictabit Cancellario.

1613. Interim dum pars erit examinanda ipse Cancellarius exscribet in processu primam interrogationem, et deinceps singulas ex ordine, post quas scribet responsiones a Iudice dictandas. Si quod interrogatorium, ut superius monitum est, addatur ex officio a Iudice vel a Defensore matrimonii, Cancellarius interrumpet ordinem progressivum, et adnotabit *interrogata ex officio;* et scripta interrogatione et responsione, reassumet ordinem progressivum interrogationum exhibitarum a Defensore matrimonii.

1614. Si examen una sessione absolvi non poterit, Iudex illud suspendet, ac destinabit etiam diem et horam pro reassumptione et prosecutione iisdem modo ac forma facienda, ut supra dictum est. Absoluto examine Cancellarius leget clara et intelligibili voce responsiones datas, facta examinato facultate variandi et declarandi datas responsiones, prout ei libuerit. Tandem Iudex deferat iuramentum eidem coniugi, se vera dixisse, atque nunquam ante publicationem processus se evulgaturum sive interrogationes propositas, sive responsiones datas. Deinde ipse subscribet, et si fuerit illiteratus per signum Cru†cis; dein Iudex et Defensor validitatis matrimonii apponet suam subscriptionem, et Cancellarius de actu rogabit.

1615. Poterit pars examini subiecta vel illico post examen, vel etiam deinceps antequam publicetur processus, si velit, articulos proponere, super quibus etiam, citato Defensore matrimonii, erit examinandus alter coniux, et quatenus etiam ab hoc articuli proponantur, erit iterum citandus coniux, qui primus fuerat interrogatus, et adstante Defensore matrimonii, super articulis ab altero propositis audietur.

1616. Haec norma quae data fuit pro instantis examine servanda erit, congrua congruis referendo, in quovis alio examine.

1617. Expleto examine illius coniugis qui actor fuit in promovenda nullitatis querela, sequitur examen alterius coniugis, quod erit conficiendum iisdem prorsus methodo ac lege, quae praescriptae fuerunt in praecedentibus paragraphis, ac sub iisdem interrogatoriis actori propositis, vel aliis additis, vel novis confectis prout Defensor matrimonii in Domino censuerit.

1618. Deinde procedendum erit ad examen *septimae manus,* hoc est septem propinquorum ex utroque latere ad formam text. (in cap. *litterae vestrae, de frig. et malef.*). Ut id facilius exequi Iudex valeat, Defensor matrimonii citabit partem actricem, ut indicet septem sibi sanguine vel affinitate coniunctos, si fieri possit, sin minus septem vicinos bonae famae. Singuli, audita prius lectura examinis, seu confessionis coniugis eos inducentis, erunt interrogandi, utrum perspectam habeant religionem et honestatem illius coniugis, ut propterea sibi verosimile sit, ac credant eum vera dixisse. Similiter instante Defensore matrimonii citandus erit alter coniux, ut etiam ipse indicet septem propinquos vel affines, iisque deficientibus, septem vicinos bonae famae, qui ut supra dictum est deponant; seorsim erunt hi quatuordecim conflantes septimam manum examini subiiciendi, designatis diebus et horis, delato prius iuramento singulis. Defensor matrimonii interrogatoria clausa exhibebit, ut superius dictum est.

1619. Liberum erit coniugibus testes bonae famae ac de re instructos inducere, qui omnes seorsim et methodo hactenus praescripta erunt examini subiiciendi.

1620. Si alios etiam Defensor matrimonii ex actis iam confectis deprehendet de re instructos, hos etiam citabit, ut examini subiiciantur. Si qui forsan absentes noscantur, qui commode ad civitatem accedere nequeant etiam ob distantiae sumptus, vel ad partis instantiam, vel, ea silente, ad instantiam Defensoris matrimonii erunt ab Episcopo illius dioecesis, in qua morantur, examinandi iuxta interrogatoria ab eodem Defensore conficienda, ac clausa et obsignata transmittenda, deputato ab eodem Episcopo altero idoneo viro, qui praes:et requisitis in Bulla saepius laudata s. m. Bened. XIV praescriptis, quique expleat munus Defensoris validitatis matrimonii, et examini adsit.

1621. Omnes vero testes, congrua congruis referendo, rogandi erunt, praesertim quando initum fuerit matrimonium: utrum inter coniuges mutui amoris et benevolentiae signa intercesserint; quamdiu in eadem domo vel civitate cohabitaverint; utrum innotuerit, eos consummationi operam dedisse; an inde matrimonium consummatum censeretur; de causis consummationem impeditivis; de conquestionibus, quando et cum quibus factis, et cur nolint amplius in matrimonio permanere.

1622. Si querela super impotentia versetur, interrogandi erunt Periti physici, quos coniuges consuluerunt.

1623. Praeterea quatenus querela super nullitate ex iis sit, ut solvi possit matrimonium, si coniuges illud non consummarunt, tunc procedendum erit ad inspectionem corporis coniugum seorsim sequenti methodo perficiendam, instante praesertim Defensore matrimonii.

1624. Iudex praefiget terminum tam utrique coniugi, quam Defensori matrimonii ad exhibendas notulas Peritorum Medicorum et Chirurgorum confidentium et diffidentium pro utriusque coniugis inspectione, congrua congruis referendo.

1625. Exhibitis notulis a partibus, Iudex eliget quinque Peritos, tres scilicet Medicos et duos Chirurgos ex his, in quibus partes consentiant, sin minus ex officio eos, qui tamen partibus non sint rationabiliter suspecti, deputabit; atque curabit, ut deputatio cadat super celebrioribus civitatis tum quoad scientiam tum quoad religionem et honestatem, atque his Peritis facultatem dabit recognoscendi corpus viri, adhibitis *honestis mediis* ad explorandam ipsius potentiam, nec non facultatem, quatenus non conveniant in prima inspectione, iterum accedendi. Atque in eodem decreto diem, horam et locum destinabit, in quibus Periti accedent, ut inspectionem perficiant.

1626. Designata die et hora, ad locum accedent Iudex, Defensor matrimonii, Cancellarius ac Periti. Singuli ex Peritis ac seorsim corpus viri inspicient ea qua fieri poterit decentia, et factis experimentis, quae iuxta artem, *non tamen illicitis*, opportuna iudicabunt, singuli scriptam emittent relationem.

1627. In inspectione et relatione haec praecipue investiganda et referenda erunt.

1628. An adsint signa physice certa impotentiae deducta ex conformatione partium, aut ex aliquo vitio quod apparere poterit. An adsint signa, quae moralem certitudinem inducant impotentiae, et quatenus existant, quae sit huius impotentiae causa, utrum sit impotentia perpetua insanabilis ac praecedens matrimonium, an signa impotentiae sint dubia vel aequivoca.

1629. Peracta relatione a singulis seorsim, Defensor matrimonii exhibebit interrogatoria clausa, sigillata, super quibus fieri debet examen Peritorum, sibique reservabit ius addendi alia interrogatoria, ac iterum ea ad examen revocand . Si examen singulorum Peritorum eadem die perfici nequiverit, iudex aliam diem designabit, ut illud prosequatur. Uterque ex Peritis tum ante examen iuramentum praestabit de veritate dicenda, tum post examen iuramento dicta confirmabit, sese propria manu subscribens, Iudex, Defensor validitatis matrimonii et Cancellarius se subscribent, qui actum rogabit.

1630. Procedendum etiam erit ad inspectionem corporis mulieris. Iudex, ut supra dictum est de Peritis, tres saltem Obstetrices deputabit, quae a duobus saltem Peritis uno Medico, et altero Chirurgo, ut supra seligendis, sedulo erunt instruendae de recognoscendo visu et tactu in muliebrium inspectione. Statuta autem huius inspectionis die mulier erit traducenda ad domum honestae Matronae pariter a Iudice deputandae pro infrascripta praestanda personali adsistentia, atque adstantibus semper tribus Obstetricibus et Matrona, immergenda erit in balneo aquae tepentis a Peritis prius recognoscendo, quod sit aquae purae, quo in balneo per spatium saltem trium quadrantium horae unius permanere debebit; quo tempore transacto, adstantibus semper et praesentibus Matrona et Obstetricibus, statim, ne ullum spatium aut momentum temporis mulieri detur, quo ad arctandum vas ullo medicamento aut aliqua fraude uti queat, ad ipsius corporis inspectionem a singulis seorsim deveniendum erit, adstante semper et praesente Matrona; qua in re prospiciendum etiam, ut haec recognitio fiat tempore tantum diurno et in cubiculo luminoso, ut ex inspectione huiusmodi utrum mulier virgo sit, an violata et corrupta, adhibitis artis regulis, exactius deprehendatur.

1631. Iudex, Defensor matrimonii et Cancellarius cum Peritis, ut supra ad domum Matronae accedent. Peracta hinc recognitione, seorsim singulae Obstetrices referent de virginitatis aut corruptionis indiciis ab inspectione resultantibus, an certa et qualia supersint signa et argumenta intemerati aut corrupti claustri virginalis, et an ulla fraus ad virginitatem simulandam adhiberi potuerit. Deinde super his magis praecise deponent in responsionibus ad interrogatoria, quae clausa et obsignata exhibebit Defensor validitatis matrimonii. Deinde formali examini erunt subiiciendi Periti, quorum iudicium erit exquirendum super relatis et depositis ab Obstetricibus. Tandem examen subire debebit quoque Matrona quoad praestitam toto balnei et recognitionis tempore adsistentiam, servatis quoad examen iis omnibus, quae superius dicta sunt, congrua tamen congruis referendo.

1632. Quatenus Defensori matrimonii nulla alia probatio exquirenda videatur, nullamque putet aliam Iudex prae sua diligentia assumendam, finis imponetur probationum collectioni et publicabitur processus, edito super hoc decreto a Iudice, factisque subscriptionibus ab eo, a Defensore matrimonii et a Cancellario. Haec habenda methodus. Quae in actis continentur nemini, nec ipsis quidem coniugibus eorumque defensoribus erunt communicanda ante processus publicationem, uno excepto Defensore matrimonii, cui libera semper et quandocumque erit actorum inspectio et examen.

1633. Locus deinde erit defensionibus. Liberum etiam erit Defensori matrimonii post processus publicationem novas probationes exquirere, cum agat favore sacramenti, et numquam bina sententia nullitatis conformis transeat in rem iudicatam, ac reassumi caussa possit etiam post initas novas nuptias a partibus iuxta Constitut. saepius citatam *Dei miseratione.*

1634. Omnibus absolutis, et cum nil amplius deducendum censuerit Defensor matrimonii, sententiam proferet Episcopus.

1635. Si hac matrimonii nullitas decreta fuerit, debebit Defensor matrimonii appellare iuxta citatam Constitutionem, nec poterunt coniuges ad alia vota transire nisi post obtentam alteram sententiam conformem super nullitate, sub poenis contra polygamos constitutis in citata Constitutione *Dei miseratione.* Deinde transmittenda erunt acta ab Episcopo ad Iudicem, ad quem provocatum fuit, in copia authentica, soluta per partem diligentiorem competenti mercede Cancellario

---

VI.

Instructio supremae Congregationis S. O. sequenda in conficiendo processu super viri impotentia, et non secuta matrimonii consummatione, accedente summi Pontificis dispensatione ab accurata observantia praescriptionum Bullae Benedicti XIV " Dei miseratione" servata tamen in substantialibus.

1636. Iudex ad hoc deputatus prae oculis habeat quod examina quaecumque illa erunt, fieri debent sub iuramenti fide, et Cancellarius Curiae episcopalis vel altera persona deleganda, interrogationes, responsa et quaelibet acta scripto tradet, facta prius annotatione mensis, diei, anni, loci et personae iudicis coram quo conficiuntur acta, nec non cuiuslibet testis examinandi.

1637. Testes singillatim audiantur, et in fine examinis se subscribant proprio nomine, vel cum signo crucis quatenus sint illiterati.

1638. Primus ille coniux audiatur qui Actor est in causa. Interrogationes Iudicis arbitrio, prudentiae et sagacitati relinquuntur, attamen pro eius commoditate sequentes traduntur, quibus alterae addantur prout melius in Domino iudicaverit ad factorum veritatem magis magisque eruendam, nimirum:

1639. A quanto tempore sese cognoverint sponsi ante matrimonium; an parentum consensu, sponte et mutua voluntate illud inierint; an in sequenti nocte in eadem domo, eodemque cubiculo et toro cubaverint, officiisque coniugalibus ultro libenterque operam dederint; an matrimonium consummaverint; an ipse examinatus cognoscat vel suspicetur causas propter quas consummare nequiverint, licet iteratis vicibus etiam in sequentibus noctibus ausi fuerint; an id contigerit ob nimiam angustiam cunni mulieris, vel ob immodicam sui penis crassitudinem, aut propter debilitatem ita ut nulla vel parvi momenti fuerit erectio; an, quae et quanto tempore adhibita fuerint medicamenta, et quinam fuerint effectus; quamdiu simul vixerint et condormierint; quis primus alterum coniugem deseruerit, et an etiam aliae causae accesserint; an et quibus parentibus, amicis vel vicinis secreto manifestaverint quod matrimonium non fuerit consummatum, eosque singillatim nominet.

1640. Haec vel similia etiam ab altero coniuge requirantur, ut an inter se apprime conveniant dignoscatur.

1641. Deinde testes. qui ab ipsis coniugibus fuerint recensiti, seorsim examini subiiciantur. Prius vero eorumdem parentes audiantur, uti praesumptive magis informati; postea vero famuli et viciniores. Si quis illorum obierit, vel longinquas regiones petierit, in actis innuendum erit. Interrogationes autem sequentes proponuntur, sed immutandae pro rerum adiunctis

1642. An cognoscat coniuges de quibus sermo; an sciat utrum libenter mutuoque affectu sese copulaverint, condormierint, et matrimonium consummaverint; an sit instructus quibus de causis consummare nequiverint, et an, et quid ad illas amovendas experti fuerint; utrum, et quae conquestio inter ipsos extiterit; quaenam sit fama tam apud se, quam apud alios de hac praetensa non consummatione.

1643. Singulorum testium absoluto examine, duo saltem ex celebrioribus civitatis Physici medicinam et chirurgiam callentes seligantur corpus viri inspecturi super eius potentia ad coeundum cum muliere maxime virgine, nec ille Physicus praetereundus qui forsan antea fuerit adhibitus ad viri incommoda medenda. Animadvertendum autem ut *mediis* utantur *licitis et honestis*, et perscrutandum praecipue utrum illius virilia sint iuxta naturae leges accurate conformata; nimirum an penis naturalem habeat dimensionem, promptamque erectionem ad coeundum necessario duraturam; an aliquo morbo fuerit affectus, a quanto tempore, et cuiusnam characteris; an fibrae compactae et consistentes, seu potius flaccidae, lassaeque sint; an testes sani naturalisque magnitudinis, et utrum aliquo vitio laboraverint, vel adhuc laborent; quo in casu morbi characterem et causas investigabunt; an vetus vel recens, naturalis vel acquisitus, et an curabilis nec ne absque salutis periculo.

1644. Quibus omnibus diligenter inspectis, singula sub iuramento scripto tradent, et quid ipsi sentiant de viri impotentia an acquisita vel ingenita, absoluta vel relativa tantum, ingenue fateantur, nullaque relicta ambigendi ratione.

1645. Corpus insuper mulieris, sed maxime illius genitalia membra a duabus saltem Obstetricibus in arte et praxi peritioribus ac bonis moribus imbutis inspiciantur, adhibito prius mulieris balneo si necessarium praemittendum Physici et ipsae iudicaverint. Accurate observabunt signa integritatem mulieris constituentia, nimirum conformationem partium, iuncturam, duritiem, rugositatem et colorem; an hymen sit integer, vel confractus in totum vel in parte; hoc in casu an et qua naturali causa, seu potius e congressu extranei corporis contigerit; an myrtiformes carunculae inveniantur, earumque magnitudinem, numerum, et conformationem, aliaque signa ab arte tradita integritatem aut corruptionem mulieris constituentia sedulo inspiciant. Deinde unaquaeque seorsim singula quae repererit sub sacramento Iudici, et a Cancellario scripto fideliter tradenda, distincte exponat, et quid ipsae sentiant de illius integritate declarent.

1646. Earumdem depositiones praedictis Physicis examinandae tradantur, ut decernant num mulier adhuc integra habenda sit, atque matrimonium non consummatum iudicandum.

1647. Verum si aliquod dubium adhuc explicandum supersit, opportunis ab ipsis Physicis concinnatis interrogationibus, iterum Obstetrices examinentur, et si nihilominus anceps Peritorum iudicium permanserit, corpus mulieris ab ipsis inspiciatur, adstante vero Matrona antiquae virtutis, nullique exceptioni obnoxia, et ab Ordinario designanda; expleta inspectione iudicium dabunt Physici singulasque proferent rationes quibus ipsorum sententia innititur.

1648. Praetereunda tandem non erit investigatio super qualitate testium audito eorumdem parocho, vel alia proba et apprime instructa persona utrum ipsi sint bonis moribus imbuti, ac plenam mereantur fidem illorum depositiones.

1649. Omnibus superius recensitis diligenter ab Ordinario collectis, illa ad s. Congregationem mittere festinabit decretorio eius iudicio subiicienda.

VII.

Instructio de Iudiciis Ecclesiasticis Circa Caussas Matrimoniales.

PARS PRIMA—DE PROCESSU MATRIMONIALI.

§. 1. Caussae matrimoniales ad iudicem ecclesiasticum spectant, cui soli competit de validitate matrimonii et obligationibus ex eodem derivantibus sententiam ferre. De effectibus matrimonii mere civilibus potestas civilis iudicat.

§. 2. Coniuges in caussis matrimonialibus subsunt Episcopo in cuius dioecesi maritus domicilium habet. Exceptioni locus est si coniugale vitae consortium aut per separationem a thoro et mensa, aut per desertionem malitiosam a marito patratam sublatum sit. Priori casu quaelibet pars ius accusandi contra alteram ipsi competens coram Episcopo dioecesis, ubi haecce domicilium habet, exercere debet. Posteriori casu uxor apud Episcopum, intra cuius dioecesim domicilium eius situm est, actionem instituere potest. Postquam citatio iudicialis intimata est, mutatio quoad coniugum domicilium facta mutationem respectu iudicis competentis minime operatur.

§. 3. Ut in tribunali ecclesiastico caussa aliqua matrimonialis tractanda suscipiatur, necesse est ut contra matrimonium regularis et iuridica accusatio praecesserit; quae nunquam erit admittenda, nisi proficiscatur a persona vel personis, quae communi iure habiles ad accusandum habeantur. Etenim in quibusdam impedimentis ipsi coniuges tantum uti accusatores admittuntur, in aliis qui sunt iisdem sanguine propinqui, vel etiam quilibet de populo, ac tandem ex officio etiam inquisitio fieri potest, et quandoque debet, quando praesertim contra alicuius matrimonii validitatem simplex denunciatio facta fuerit, aut fama fundamentum veritatis praeseferens de alicuius impedimenti existentia divulgata sit.

§. 4. Ista accusatio coram legitimo Ordinario ecclesiastico fieri debet, et quidem in scripto: si oretenus facta fuerit, iudicialis reddenda erit iuxta regulas communi iure traditas, scilicet efficiendo ut accusator eam repetat coram tribunali, et a cancellario in actis redigatur.

§. 5. In ea, praeter accuratam facti expositionem, enarranda erunt omnia adjuncta necessaria, et omnia indicia concurrentia; indicandi et nominandi testes de re instructi, ut hoc modo fundamenta accusationis cognoscantur, et via tribunali sternatur veritati detegendae.

§. 6. Accusatione sic recepta, munus moderatoris actorum Episcopus vel ipse sibi assumet, vel suum Vicarium generalem, aut alium probum et expertum virum e clero ad illud delegabit. Similiter alium virum designabit, qui cancellarii officio fungens quidquid ad caussam pertinet in acta referat, ac nominatim interrogationes examinandis faciendas, eorumque responsiones scripto consignet.

§. 7. Praeterea ipse Ordinarius omnino tenetur deputare alium virum ecclesiasticum iuris scientia et vitae probitate praeditum, qui matrimonii defensor existat. Eum vero suspendere vel removere, si iusta caussa adfuerit, et alium substituere iis qualitatibus ornatum Ordinario semper fas erit.

§. 8. Praedictae deputationes et delegationes in scriptis ab Ordinario fiant, et earum authentica documenta vel saltem mentio in actis prostent.

§. 9 Moderatoris actorum erit tribunal convocare, partes et testes citare ut in iudicium compareant; terminos dilationis concedere, quoties rationabiliter ab iis qui ius habent petantur; edere decreta et ordinationes pro regulari et recta actorum compilatione. Quae omnia scripto erunt exaranda, et in actis ipsis recensenda.

§. 10. Defensor matrimoni antequam munus sibi commissum suscipiat, coram actorum moderatore iuramentum praestabit tactis Sanctis Evangeliis de munere suo diligenter et in corrupte adimplendo, spondens se omnia voce et scripto deducturum quae ad validitatem matrimonii sustinendam conferre iudicaverit. Hic matrimonii defensor a moderatore actorum citandus erit ad quaelibet acta, ne vitio nullitatis concidant; eidem semper et quandocumque acta processus, etsi nondum publicati, erunt communicanda, semper et quandocumque eius scripta recipienda, atque novi termini, eo flagitante, prorogandi, ut ea scripta perficiat atque exhibeat.

§. 11. Quod si ob peculiares circumstantias matrimonii defensor singulis actis interesse nequiverat, absoluto processu eadem ipsi tradantur, ut eas exarare queat animadversiones quas tuendae matrimonii validitati necessarias iudicaverit; si alia acta suggesserit, haec conficienda omnino erunt; si ex iam confectis deprehenderit alias adesse personas testimonio ferendo idoneas et opportunas nondum examinatas, has examini subiiciendas proponet.

§. 12. Constituto tribunali, haec actorum conficiendorum ratio tenenda erit. Ab omnibus et singulis testimonium dicturis moderator actorum ante omnia iuramentum exiget de veritate dicenda, et si ita res postulet, etiam de secreto servando, praemissa congrua monitione de iuramenti sanctitate, praesertim si examinandi rudes sint et ignari. Iuramentum praestandum erit tactis Sanctis Evangeliis, et in singulis examinibus eodem modo repetendum.

§. 13. Qui examini subiiciendi suut, seorsum semper audiantur. Porro cancellarius adnotabit diem, mensem, et annum cuiuslibet examinis, nec non singulorum nomen, cognomen, aetatem, conditionem, statum, et patriam, et etiam quod iuramentum revera praestiterint.

§. 14. Post quodlibet examen, etiamsi eadem persona pluries illi subiicienda sit, cancellarius clara et intelligibili voce coram eadem legat interrogationes et responsiones, facta eidem facultate variandi aut declarandi quidquid ei visum fuerit: deinde ipse examinatus subscribat, et si fuerit illiteratus, faciet hoc signum Cru✠cis; ac denique moderator actorum et defensor validitatis matrimonii apponent suam subscriptionem, et cancellarius de actu rogabit.

§. 15. Si aliquando contingat examinandos apud exteras et forsan longinquas regiones versari, nec tribunali se sistere posse, a moderatore actorum accurata factorum et circumstantiarum, quarum cognitio et confirmatio requiritur, expositio erit facienda, quae concinnatis opportunis interrogationibus, de sententia quoque defensoris matrimonii, et indicatis examinandorum nomin.bus, ad Ordinarium loci, in quo commorantur, mittatur, ut ille sive per se, sive per suum vicarium generalem, sive per alium virum probum et expertum e clero eligendum, eos examini subiiciat iuxta datas interrogationes, requisito prius iuramento de veritate dicenda, et caeteris servatis quae supra praescripta sunt.

Si vero contigerit aliquem examini subiiciendum e vita migrasse, mortis documentum inter acta recenseatur.

§. 16. Quoad singulos in iudicium vocatos vel vocandos actorum moderator inquirere debebit probitatem et credibilitatem, et ad hoc curabit, ut ab eorum parochis, sin minus a personis fide dignis, litterae testimoniales exhibeantur, quae etiam in actis erunt referendae.

§. 17. Inter examinandos primo loco venit ille qui accusationem contra matrimonium movit. Ab isto exquirendum erit, ut clare distincteque exponat accusationis titulum; facta omnia fideliter et religiose enarret, eorumque probationes afferat; circumstantias omnes et indicia exponat quae vel ex propria scientia cognoverit, vel ex aliorum relatione didicerit; et denique nominet testes quos de re instructos sciverit, vel saltem reputaverit.

§. 18. Secundo loco veniunt coniuges ipsi, qui semper, et seorsum audiri debent, ut unusquisque sua iura tueri, et rationes, deductiones, ac facta allata aut reiicere, aut explicare queat. Quaelibet pars examini subiecta poterit vel illico post examen, vel etiam deinceps, antequam processus claudatur, proponere, si velit, articulos, super quibus alter coniux sit examinandus; et quatenus etiam ab hoc articuli proponantur, erit iterum citandus coniux qui primus fuerat examinatus, ut super articulis ab altero propositis audiatur. Iuxta casuum diversitatem a coniugibus inquirendum erit, ut si quae documenta habeant ad suum·matrimonium, vel ad coniugalem vitae consuetudinem spectantia, ea exhibeant, in acta recensenda. Quae documenta cuiuscumque generis sint, et a quocumque exhibeantur, semper erunt recipienda; et cancellarius adnotare debebit diem, mensem, et annum, nec non nomen illius a quo exhibita fuerunt.

§. 19. Si ambo coniuges concordes in depositionibus fuerint, moderator actorum et defensor matrimonii sedulo inspiciant utrum inter eosdem collusio intercesserit. Hoc in casu singula argumenta contra eorum depositiones ex processu resultantia die l icte iisdem obiiciantur, ut fraude, si qua fuerit, detecta, veritas, quoad fieripo ssit, dilucide appareat.

§. 20. Post coniuges citandi erunt testes inducti, servata eorum examinandorum ratione superius descripta, et exquisitis ab iisdem iis notitiis, de quibus instructi existimantur. Interrogationes singulis faciendae, prout accusationis titulus, aut allata factorum et circumstantiarum congeries, vel ipsa testium indoles atque capacitas requirere videatur, sagacitati atque prudentiae moderatoris actorum et defensoris vinculi relinquuntur qui illas concinnare, augere aut imminuere poterunt, dummodo tamen semper ea omnia inquirantur quae ad rectum proferendum iudicium aut necessaria aut opportuna censeantur.

§. 21. Quae in actis continentur, nemini, ne ipsis quidem coniugibus eorumque defensoribus, erunt communicanda ante processus publicationem, uno excepto matrimonii defensore, cui liberum erit semper et quandocumque acta inspicere et examinare.

§. 22. Quatenus vero actorum moderatori aut defensori matrimonii nulla alia probatio requirenda videatur, finis imponatur probationum collectioni, et processus publicetur, edito hac super re decreto ab ipso moderatore, a defensore matrimonii, et a cancellario subscribendo.

§. 23. Publicato processu, locus fiet defensionibus quas partes ad sua iura tuenda voluerint allegare, facta iisdem facultate adhibendi eos defensores quos maluerint; imo praemonendae erunt de hoc iure, ut lata sententia, iniustae contra eam incusationi aut reclamationi aditus praecludatur. Allegationes autem si ab iisdem oblatae fuerint communicandae erunt defensori vinculi matrimonialis, ut eas expendere, et quatenus matrimonii validitatem impugnent refutare valeat.

§. 24. Omnibus ut supra peractis ad sententiam pronunciandam veniendum erit. Quod ut ab Ordinario seu eius delegato rite fiat, in primis a defensore matrimonii exquiri debet declaratio, sibi nihil amplius deducendum aut inquirendum superesse; deinde integra causa duobus aut tribus viris peritis, si haberi possint, examinanda subiiciatur, et nonnisi audito eorum voto sententia proferatur.

Haec in scriptis erit exaranda, in eaque rationum momenta, quibus innititur, ex processu deprompta exponantur, surcincte quidem, sed ita tamen, ne quidpiam essentiale omittatur. Sententia subscriptione iudicis et secretarii, nec non sigillo curiae episcopalis munita partibus erit notificanda per curiae apparitorem, relicto iisdem illius exemplari, de quo in scripto fides erit facienda.

§. 25. Iudex si pro validitate matrimonii sententiam dixerit, et nemo ex coniugibus contra eam appellaverit, neque defensor matrimonii appellabit, et caussa finita censeatur. E contra si matrimonium nullum fuisse decreverit, quamvis coniuges iudicio Praelati acquieverint, defensor matrimonii appellationem facere debebit, et novam sententiam ab alio tribunali postulare; quam appellationem primus iudex impedire nulla unquam ratione poterit. Interim nullatenus permittetur partibus novas nuptias inire.

Quamvis appellationi interponendae nulli fatales dies vinculi defensori statuti sint, curandum tamen ut quantocius id fiat. Quod si defensor ipse hoc munus neglexerit, compelli ad id poterit vel a suo Episcopo, vel etiam ab illo, apud quem de iure appellatio esset facienda.

§. 26. Ordo appellationis erit prout sequitur. Si prima sententia a curia Episcopali lata fuerit, appellatio fiet ad curiam Metropolitanam; si vero a curia Metropolitana ea prodierit, appellabitur ad curiam Metropolitanam viciniorem. Ad S. Sedem appellatio erit semper facienda, quoties primae duae sententiae inter se conformes non fuerint, nisi partibus placuerit caussam ad ipsam S. Sedem ab initio et immediate deferre.

§. 27. Facta appellatione, Episcopus seu Ordinarius qui primam sententiam protulit, eam remittere debebit una cum integro processu, caeterisque omnibus ad caussam iterum iudicandam pertinentibus, ad tribunal ad quod appellatum est.

§. 28. Hoc autem omnia a primo tribunali peracta diligenter examinabit, atque ea omnia peraget quae necessaria videbuntur, ut defectus suppleantur, dubia elucidentur, et errores corrigantur. Hunc in fidem, praesente semper vinculi defensore in curia constituto vel specialiter delegato, coniuges examinabit, investigationes instituet circa documenta priori tribunali exhibita, testes, a quibus novae informationes hauriri possint, iterum audiet. Imo poterit etiam praescribere, ut novus processus ex integro conficiatur.

Verum quatenus validae desint rationes novum processum exigendi, consultius erit, praesertim si personarum et locorum circumstantiae id suaserint, ut processu iam expleto utatur, indictis tamen ulterioribus investigationibus quas necessarias iudicaverit.

Quod si novum processum faciendum esse censuerit, methodus supra descripta servanda erit. Si vero aliqua tantum nova acta adiungenda, vel novi aliquid investigandum censuerit, semper tamen defensor matrimonii adesse debebit, vel saltem nova haec eidem communicanda erunt, ut pro munere suo ea expendere, et quatenus opus esse duxerit proprias animadversiones illis apponere valeat.

§. 29. Expleto examine primi processus, et imposito fine novis investigationibus, iudex appellationis debebit exquirere a defensore matrimonii, utrum aliquid adhuc habeat deducendum aut inquirendum; et quatenus se nil amplius habere dixerit, auditis prius, modo quo supra declaratum est, aliquibus viris in scientia iuris peritis, sententiam pronunciabit, omnia servando quae pro tribunali primae instantiae praescripta fuerunt.

§. 30. Quando utraque sententia conformis pro validitate coniugii pronuntiata sit, sciat tamen pars impugnans matrimonium, sibi adhuc omnino patere appellationem ad Apostolicam Sedem. Si porro in secunda aeque ac in prima sententia nullum ac irritum matrimonium iudicatum fuerit, et ab ea pars vel defensor pro sua conscientia non crediderit appellandum, in potestate et arbitrio coniugum sit novas nuptias contrahere, dummodo alicui eorum ob aliquod impedimentum vel legitimam causam id vetitum non sit. Potestas tamen post alteram sententiam conformem, ut supra, coniugibus facta intelligatur, salvo semper et firmo remanente iure seu privilegio caussarum matrimonialium, quae ob cuiuscumque temporis lapsum numquam transeunt in rem iudicatam; sed si nova res, quae non deducta vel ignorata fuerit, detegatur, resumi possunt et rursus in iudicialem controversiam revocari. Quodsi a secunda sententia super nullitate vel altera pars appellaverit, vel defensor matrimonii ei salva conscientia acquiescendum non putet, quia sibi vel manifeste iniusta vel aliunde invalida videatur, re tota ad S. Sedem delata, interim firma remaneat utrique coniugi prohibitio ad alias transeundi nuptias.

PARS ALTERA—DE REGULIS SERVANDIS IN TRACTANDIS CAUSSIS MATRIMONIAL-
IBUS IN SPECIE.

Praeter hactenus recensitas regulas in omnibus caussis matrimonialibus generatim servandas ut iuridica illis stet validitas, quaedam etiam speciales prae oculis habendae sunt iuxta peculiarem impedimentorum naturam et indolem quae iudicio occasionem praebuerunt. Quare de his singulis, saltem quae frequentius occurrere solent, aliqua speciatim animadvertenda sunt.

Articulus I.—De Impedimentis Cognationis Carnalis, vel Spiritualis, et Affinitatis.

§. 31. Si matrimonium impugnetur ob assertum impedimentum cognationis carnalis aut spiritualis, vel affinitatis, facile erit eiusdem existentiam detegere ope authenticorum documentorum. Etenim cognatio carnalis, et etiam affinitas, quae ex praecedenti matrimonio processerit, dignoscuntur ex arbore genealogica utriusque familiae, conficienda ex regestis matrimoniorum, et ex libris etiam baptizatorum, in quibus notata esse debent nomina non modo coniugum, et eorum qui baptizati sunt, sed horum etiam parentum. Similiter ex libris baptizatorum et confirmatorum aperte eruitur cognatio spiritualis, quia in illis una cum eorum qui baptizati vel confirmati fuerunt, nomina quoque recensita esse debent sive patrinorum sive matrinarum. Talia documenta in forma authentica ex dictis libris erunt haurienda opera parochorum vel curiae, una cum testimonio de eorum identitate cum respectivis particulis in libris extanti- bus; imo si a parocho testimonium datum fuerit, opus erit ut eiusdem parochi obsignatio a curia Episcopali authentica declaretur.

§. 32. Quod si aliquod oriatur dubium circa documenta praedicta vel circa eorum veritatem, in iudicium vocandi erunt et iuridice examinandi consanguinei, affines, propinqui, quibus origo eorum de quibus agitur nota sit aut nota esse possit, ut ex horum depositionibus gradus consanguinitatis vel affinitatis clarius valeat determinari. Non levi fundamento huic rei esse potest etiam publica fama, de qua ratio erit habenda; eius tamen sedulo consideranda erit origo et rationes quibus innititur. Caeterum iudex semper prae oculis habeat, his quaestionibus dirimendis praecipuum fundamentum praebere documenta au- thentica, et numquam licere contra eadem iudicare, nisi ex certis et evidentibus argumentis constiterit ipsa vitiosa aut falsa esse. Ac proinde locorum Ordinarii sedulo curabunt ut libri baptizatorum, confirmatorum, et matrimonio copulatorum, nec non defunctorum a parochis diligentissime exarentur et accurate custodiantur.

Articulus II.—De Impedimento Publicae Honestatis.

§. 33. Quoties aliquod matrimonium impugnatur ob impedimentum, quod publicae honestatis nominatur, in primis accurate statuendum erit, utrum illud originem duxerit ex matrimonio simpliciter rato, an ex sponsalibus.

In priori casu ad impedimentum adstruendum proferantur documenta matrimonii praecendentis celebrationem comprobantia, quae documenta facile suppeditabunt vel libri matrimoniorum a parocho servandi, si matrimonium coram Ecclesia fuerit celebratum, vel regesta existentia penes ministros haereticos, si apud eos matrimonium contractum affirmetur. Quamvis documenta vel a sola civili potestate, vel ab haereticis manantia, vim habere possint aliquando ad factum de matrimonio celebrato extraiudicialiter confirmandum, tamen iudex catholicus, qui de existentia vel de non existentia impedimenti sententiam laturus erit, curabit ut in iudicium compareant partes, testes qui matrimonii celebrationi interfuerunt, propinqui eorum qui contraxerunt, nec non omnes quos sciverit de re instructos, ut omnia possint cognosci quae ad factum rite iudicandum conducere poterunt.

§. 34. Quod si praedictum impedimentum ortum asseratur ex sponsalibus cum persona alteri parti consanguinea in gradu impedimentum constituente contractis, ad iudicium proferendum duo erunt inquirenda, videlicet utrum revera asserta sponsalia locum habuerint, et utrum valida in sensu canonico haberi possint. Primum deducendum erit ex partium confessione, dummodo hae exceptiones minime patiantur, ex documentis si habeantur, ex testium fidem merentium depositionibus, nec non ex indiciis quae iudex peritus et expertus deducere poterit ex circumstantiis quae facta exposita aut praecesserunt aut subsecutae sunt. Ad secundum probandum, utrum videlicet asserta sponsalia valida fuerint in sensu canonico, plura erunt sedulo perpendenda. Ante omnia iudex prae oculis habeat, quod ex usu et consuetudine fere in singulis locis speciales aliquae formae pro solemni sponsalium celebratione inductae reperiuntur, quae communiter et regulariter ab omnibus servari solent. Itaque inquirendum erit, utrum istae formae fuerint, nec ne, servatae; si primum, praesumptio pro sponsalium valore aderit, contra quam nunquam erit iudicandum, nisi ex certis et evidentibus argumentis sponsalia nulliter contracta fuisse constiterit; si secundum, inquirendum erit, qua de causa consuetae formae fuerint omissae, et utrum pro personarum, locorum, et consuetudinum circumstantiis sponsalia nihilominus valide fuerint contracta, eo quod utrimque voluntas sese obligandi vere intercesserit, atque ita ut ex iure impedimentum constituant. In hunc finem praeter alia quaerendum est, quibus verbis, vel factis sibi futurum matrimonium promiserint; utrum promissio ab utraque parte processerit; et si ab una tantum, utrum alia eam acceptaverit sive verbis, sive factis, sive signis aequivalentibus; utrum post datam promissionem praetensi sponsi reputaverint sese matrimonio contrahendo obligatos, an liberos. Erit quoque inquirendum de sponsorum conditione, utrum scilicet ea talis sit ut praesumi non possit veram in ipsis voluntatem sese mutuo obligandi adfuisse.

§. 35. Quatenus casus exigat, inquirendum etiam erit, qua aetate praetensi sponsi sibi invicem matrimonium promiserint. Etenim sponsalia ab infantibus, vel a maiori cum infante contracta, ipso iure nulla sunt, et impedimentum publicae honestatis gignere non valent. Quare in hoc casu inquirendum erit de aetate legitima eorum, a quibus sponsalia fuerunt contracta, quod facile fiet petitis documentis ex libris baptizatorum atque ex testimonio parentum, sive aliorum, qui personas, de quibus agitur, cognoscunt. Si constiterit in aetate adhuc infantili sponsalia inita fuisse, investigandum erit utrum post septennium fuerint renovata, aut saltem ratificata.

Articulus III.—De Impedimento Vis et Metus.

§. 36. Circa impedimentum quod vis et metus dicitur, ante omnia advertendum occurrit, neminem a iure admitti ad matrimonium ex hoc capite impugnandum nisi qui violentiam et coactionem passus dicitur, reiici vero eum, qui per longum tempus in matrimonio vixerit, dummodo eidem libertas et opportunitas reclamandi non defuerit; ita ut si liber iam a metu sua sponte in coniugali domo perstiterit, matrimonialia officia non detrectaverit, audiri amplius non debeat. Etenim qui liber a coactione metuve, facultate et opportunitate reclamandi non utitur, censetur consentire, et ratificare quod antea invitus atque adverso animo fecerat. Unde in primis erit inquirendum, utrum accusatio tempore, uti dicitur, utili facta sit; et si hoc iam fluxerit, quaerendum erit quanam de causa hoc acciderit, ut iudicari possit utrum accusatio admittenda an reiicienda sit. Secundo prae oculis habendum erit, solummodo metum gravem, qui nempe in virum constantem cadat, matrimonium dirimere, et consequenter ad hunc metum exquirendum omnes sive moderatoris actorum sive defensoris matrimonii investigationes esse dirigendas. Porro gravitas timoris oritur ex natura minarum, ex qualitate tum eorum a quibus illae proficiscuntur, tum eorum qui eas passi dicuntur. Ista tria itaque erunt praesertim investiganda.

§. 37. Circa primum sedulo inquirendum, utrum qui de adhibita coactione accusantur, ita consueverint agere cum persona quae coacta dicitur, ut gravem atque molestam eidem redderent domesticam et familiarem cohabitationem; quaenam fuerint in specie molestiae eidem illatae: utrum verba gravi indignatione plena adhibita, intentata haereditatis privatio, eiectio e paterna domo, an addita etiam verbera.

Circa secundum considerandum est, utrum qui de illata vi metuve accusantur, patria potestate et auctoritate polleant, an qui vim metumve passi sunt, nullatenus iisdem subiecti fuerint; quae ratio vis inferendae, magna ne ex matrimonio propriae domui utilitas, aut decus obventurum? quae indoles vim inferentium, quae conditio, qui mores; qua ratione familiam regere consueverint; utrum ad iracundiam et violentiam ita essent proclives, ut facile quod minabantur perficerent, et animo ita essent duro atque obstinato, ut a nemine sibi contradici aut consiliis suis impedimenta obiici paterentur.

Quoad tertium ratio habenda erit primum sexus personae quae violentiam passa dicitur; facilius enim animus puellae commovetur, quam viri; deinde aetatis, educationis, indolis, utrum nempe mitis ac timida fuerit, an fortis et constans; qua ratione in familia vivere consueverit, utrum sub custodia et vigilantia parentum, ita ut ab eorum imperio semper et in omnibus penderet, an aliqua libertate frueretur ut et propria sensa exponere, et iuxta propriam voluntatem operari potuerit; an parentes ita eam segregarint, ut omnis consilii expetendi facultas eidem adempta fuerit, nec cuiquam eiusdem alloquendae copiam tribuerint, nisi quos de matrimonio ineundo consilia praebere posse iudicaverint.

§. 38. Praeter ista inquirendum erit, utrum qui de illata vi conqueritur, aliquando relationem habuerit cum eo cum quo postea contraxit; et utrum aliquando propositum habuerit cum eodem contrahendi. In casu affirmativo inquirendum, quas ob causas voluntatis mutatio contigerit; a quo tempore consilium fuerit mutatum, utrum nempe antequam parentes propriam voluntatem ostenderent, an postea; et utrum ex praecedenti relatione aliqua exorta sit suspicio contra decorem vel ipsius personae vel familiae, a qua parentes moveri potuerint ad matrimonium exigendum tamquam remedium bonae famae recuperandae. Etiam investigandum, quid haec persona fecerit ut a coactione parentum sese liberaret: utrum preces adhibuerit, utrum usa fuerit opera aliorum ad parentes a proposito dimovendos, utrum et quomodo propriam aversionem et contrarietatem in illud matrimonium significaverit, utrum et quomodo altera pars operam dederit ut matrimonium revera concluderetur. Considerandum erit, utrum quando contractus matrimonialis erat signandus, libenter et sine ulla protestatione id praestiterit, utrum aliqua fraus adhibita ad talem obsignationem obtinendam; quomodo sese gesserit, sive quando necessaria pro matrimonio parabantur, sive quando ad consensum promendum adducta fuit, sive quando post datum consensum festum nuptiale celebrabatur, utrum nempe his omnibus hilaris, prompte, et laeta adstiterit, an secus. Consideranda quoque eius agendi ratio erga alteram partem, et erga eiusdem familiam; utrum nempe benevola et affectuosa, utrum libenter et sine oppositione ad oficia matrimonialia sese exhibuerit, an eisdem obstiterit, ea praesertim de caussa quia matrimonium nullum putaverit, atque ut melius tueri posset propriam libertatem. Ad hoc postremum factum probandum considerari debet, utrum hac de caussa inter coniuges ipsos ortae sint lites et contentiones, utrum hoc factum manifestaverint, et quibus, a quo tempore post matrimonium istae querimoniae inceperint, et ex qua caussa vel ratione, utrum ad tales lites et dissensiones tollendas adhibita fuerint consilia, hortationes, et in casu affirmativo, a quibus et quo exitu.

§. 39. Ad praedicta cognoscenda in iudicium vocandi erunt ambo coniuges. eorumque parentes, illi praesertim qui de coactione adhibita accusantur, et opportune interrogandi de facto ipso, de modo, de animo, et de fine ob quem ad vim adhibendam ducti fuerint. Item vocandi propinqui et familiares violentiam accusantis, et interrogandi de omnibus quae vel ad parentes, vel ad filios referuntur; utrum quidquam eorum quae in actis habentur viderint aut audiverint, quidve norint accidisse ad rem pertinens, sive antequam matrimonium celebraretur, sive tempore cohabitationis, sive post coniugum separationem, si haec locum habuerit. In hisce examinandis iudex diligenter invigilet, utrum aliqua collusionis suspicandae caussa subsit, et curet, ut quoad singulas personas parochorum testimonium obtineat de ipsarum probitate atque credibilitate. Post istos vocandi parochus vel alius sacerdos, qui matrimonio adstitit; illi qui eiusdem celebrationi et festo nuptiale interfuerunt, ut referant praesertim de modo quo persona contra matrimonium reclamans in illis circumstantiis se gesserit; aliae personae inductae, illae speciatim quae adhibitae fuerunt vel ut consiliis et hortationibus reclamantem ad matrimonium inducerent, vel ut excitarent ad officia matrimonialia praestanda, ab iisque quaerendum, quid egerint, quibus argumentis usae, quidve consecutae fuerint.

§. 40. Caeterum in hac re iudex sciat, matrimonium esse per se factum quoddam solemne et publicum, quod semper validum censeri debet, nisi evidentes rationes eiusdem nullitatem demonstraverint. Ideo curandum quidem omni studio atque diligentia, ut rationes istae colligantur, sed iudicium contra matrimonium nunquam erit pronunciandum, nisi earum complexio omne prudens dubium de existentia impedimenti excludat.

Articulus IV.—De Impedimento Ligaminis.

§. 41. Vinculum praecedentis matrimonii, quod ad posterius connubium impugnandum adducitur, repetendum asseritur vel ex matrimonio, catholico modo a catholicis celebrato; vel ex connubio ab haereticis aut iuxta diversarum sectarum instituta contracto, et postea per sententiam talium tribunalium dissoluto; vel ex contractu inter infideles, qui postea rescissus, aut nullus fuerit declaratus. Diversorum istorum casuum possibilitas, aut etiam frequentia manifesta est, cum in regionibus Americae catholici commixti vivere cogantur cum haereticis, et infidelibus. Quaedam pro singulis casibus adnotanda sunt, quia diversis legibus reguntur.

§. 42. Ad primum casum quod attinet, doctrina catholica est matrimonium baptizatorum rite celebratum et consummatum aliter solvi non posse, nisi per mortem unius coniugis; et ideo locum non esse eiusdem dissolutioni declarandae in iudicio, nisi de morte alterutrius coniugis constiterit. Ut autem de hac constare dicatur, non sufficit rumor aut fama quaecumque, neque solae praesumptiones, sed requiritur certus de ea nuntius, aut saltem concursus talium rationum, quae certo nuntio aequipollentes omne de illa dubium excludant. Ideo in hoc casu iudex ante omnia exigere debebit, ut prioris matrimonii documentum authenticum proferatur, atque, si opus fuerit, alias probationes colliget, quae praedicti prioris matrimonii existentiam demonstrent; similiter exquiret documenta vel probationes de secundo matrimonio contracto; quae omnia documenta facile haberi poterunt ex libris matrimoniorum in parochiis asservatis. Post haec exigenda erunt a competentibus parochis authentica documenta de praetensa morte alterius coniugis, et in defectu poterunt eadem requiri ab auctoritate civili, si suos libros habuerit, in quibus adnotentur. Quae comparari debebunt cum documento secundum matrimonium comprobante, ut cognoscatur, utrum secundum hoc matrimonium contractum fuerit ante, vel post prioris coniugis mortem; atque ita iudicetur utrum secundum matrimonium validum, an nullum fuerit.

§. 43. Quando ad mortem prioris coniugis probandam praesto non sunt neque esse possunt haec authentica documenta, aliis argumentis et aliis probationibus opus est, quae a iudice sedulo erunt colligendae. In primis argumentum desumi potest ex depositione testium fidem merentium, si ipsi de visu mortem illius, de quo agitur, revera accidisse affirmaverint, aut idem asseruerint ex auditu, dummodo non ex vaga aliqua relatione, sed a personis minime suspectis proprias informationes se hausisse testentur. Isti testes erunt interrogandi, utrum bene cognoverint quem mortuum asserunt; quo tempore, quo loco mors acciderit, qua de caussa, ubi cadaver sepultum, utrum adsint et ubi commorentur alii qui de hoc facto instructi sint aut esse possint. Ab illis vero qui ex aliorum relatione deponunt, erit quoque inquirendum, a quibus tales hauserint notitias, a quo tempore fama de morte vulgari coeperit, et quid ipsi sentiant de probitate et credibilitate eorum qui primitus de re ista sunt loquuti; utrum isti peculiarem aliquam rationem habuerint aut habere potuerint ut talem notitiam evulgarent. His cognitis in iudicium vocandi erunt testes inducti, et eodem modo examini subiiciendi, ut tandem aliquando vel ad testes de visu, vel ad certa documenta obtinenda perveniatur. Animadvertat iudex, ne admittat eos qui sponte ad examen accesserint, quia mendaces praesumuntur; et si requisiti fuerint, quaerat ab eis, a quibusnam, ubi, quando, quomodo, coram quibus, et quoties fuerint requisiti; utrum pro hoc testimonio ferendo fuerit ipsis aliquid datum, promissum, remissum, vel oblatum a personis interesse habentibus, vel ab aliis eorum nomine. Similiter advertat, non esse admittendos testes qui personas, de quibus agitur, plene non cognoscant; et consequenter extraneos non esse testes idoneos, nisi a longo tempore in loco fuerint, aut ex peculiaribus circumstantiis appareat eos cognitionem habere potuisse de iis quae enarrant. Quod si testes sive de visu, sive de auditu haberi non poterunt, considerandae erunt circumstantiae omnes in facto concurrentes, et diligenter ponderandae, ut videatur, utrum ex illarum complexu exurgere possit moralis illa certitudo quae necessaria est ut iudicium proferatur. Porro circumstantiae istae praecipuae sunt: aetas personae quae mortua dicitur, utrum senior, an iunior fuerit; tempus eiusdem discessus a patria et familia, utrum longius an brevius, locus vel loca, ad quae se contulerit, utrum valitudini corporali noxia, an et quibus vicissitudinibus subiecta fuerint, ex. gr. num ibidem bella, vel pestilentiae saevierint; eiusdem personae physica constitutio, utrum sana et robusta, an debilis et infirma. Erit similiter perpendenda caussa quare e propria discesserit domo, utrum nempe ad negotium vel ad artem aliquam exercendam, an potius ut coniugem derelinqueret. Haec cognosci vel deduci poterunt ex benevolis, aut contrariis relationibus, quas vel coniuges habuerunt inter se, durante eorum contubernio, vel ille qui discessit continuavit cum altero coniuge sive per litteras sive per nuncios; si enim constiterit, ad tempus talem epistolarum sive relationum consuetudinem adfuisse, et postea cessasse, quin cessationis caussa aut ratio appareat, gravis de morte obita praesumptio habebitur; si e contra constiterit eum qui discessit nunquam epistolarum commercium habuisse cum sua familia, aut cum propinquis et amicis, indicium mere negativum nullam probationem facere poterit. Ponderandum quoque erit genus vitae, quod discedens in aliena regione amplexus fuerit; si vitam et artem militarem exercendam elegerit, vel arti nauticae aut servitio alicuius navis sese addixerit, et cognoscatur in quo exercitu militaverit, aut in qua navi servierit, inquisitiones erunt faciendae penes duces exercitus illius, et penes gubernatores vel officiales navis. Si cognita fuerint loca, in quibus commoratus est, in singulis locis, et praesertim in illo in quo commorabatur, quando eius indicia perdita fuerunt, investigationes erunt faciendae. Ad has tribunal adhibebit idoneas personas, si praesto sint, vel etiam civiles auctoritates, ab iisdem postulando ut, quibus pollent modis, de illo opportunas investigationes faciant, atque etiam in subsidium vocentur publica diaria cum indicatione nominis, cognominis, patriae, professionis, et conditionis illius, de quo quaeritur. Item si fieri possit, tribunal curabit, ut in locis in quibus idem commoratus fuerit publica edicta affigantur, et singuli excitentur, ut notitias, si quas habent, velint suppeditare. Si omnibus istis adiumentis adhibitis nihil omnino poterit reperiri, et si omnes circumstantiae ad mortem prioris coniugis ante secundas nuptias, de quarum valore agitur, adstruendam conspiraverint, iudex sententiam proferre contra secundum matrimonium non poterit; non enim constaret de eius nullitate. Quod si de matrimonio contrahendo agatur, hoc permitti numquam poterit, donec de morte prioris coniugis certo constiterit.

§. 44. At si non ex isto capite, sed potius quia primum matrimonium in haeresi contractum, rescissum fuerit ob aliam caussam, specialia quaedam erunt observanda. Et primo advertendum est, Evangelicam et Apostolicam doctrinam esse, matrimonium valide celebratum solvi non posse propter adulterium, vel propter molestam cohabitationem, aut longam et affectatam coniugis unius absentiam, aut propter aliud quodcumque motivum ab haereticis confictum. Quare si constiterit, a tribunalibus haereticorum ob aliquam ex istis rationibus praecedens matrimonium dissolutum fuisse, caussa in favorem secundi matrimonii a tribunali catholico ne admittenda quidem seu introducenda erit. Si vero eiusdem dissolutio fuerit decreta ob alium titulum a iure canonico recognitum, sciendum est, acta a tribunali haeretico confecta valore iuridico carere, et ex ipsis solummodo iudicium proferre catholico iudici minime licere. Quare tunc caussa ex integro erit instituenda, et iuxta ss. canones pertractanda. Vetitum tamen non est, imo aliquando expediet, ut acta tribunalis haeretici requirantur, quo plenior factorum et circumstantiarum cognitio attingatur. Imo si huiusmodi documenta a partibus fuerint exhibita, dummodo nihil aliud obstet, poterunt adhiberi, atque ex illis indicia colligi. Partes tamen erunt semper audiendae, nec non, quatenus fieri poterit, etiam testes singuli iterum in iudicium vocandi, et interrogandi ad normam harum regularum. Neque omittenda aliarum personarum iuridica depositio si adesse cognoscantur; sicut neque alia acta, quae vel moderator vel defensor matrimonii necessaria reputaverint. Si perpensis omnibus iudex censuerit, sententiam edicendam esse conformem sententiae a tribunali haeretico prolatae, numquam tamen istam sententiam tamquam sui iudicii motivum invocare debebit; neque ullo modo post eam existimandum erit, duas adesse sententias conformes, a quibus necesse non sit appellare.

§. 45. Quoad matrimonia in infidelitate contracta, si haec dissoluta dicantur per sententiam editam vel ab auctoritate civili, vel a quovis tribunali haeretico, eadem erunt servanda quae dicta sunt de matrimoniis baptizatorum resolutis per sententiam tribunalis saecularis, nempe caussam admittendam non esse, si rescissio proclamata fuerit ex titulo ab Ecclesia non agnito, vel servatis servandis esse ex integro instituendam, si contrarium contigerit. Si vero coniugum separatio acciderit absque ullo iudicio, observandum utrum pars quae coram tribunali catholico agere intendit, secundum matrimonium contraxerit post baptismi susceptionem, an ante. Si matrimonium acciderit cum parte catholica post baptismi susceptionem, erit inquirendum, utrum praecesserit coniugis adhuc infidelis canonica interpellatio, aut saltem a legitima potestate fuerit super eadem interpellatione dispensatum. Quatenus constiterit de facta interpellatione aut de illius dispensatione, primum matrimonium nequit amplius constituere vinculum secundum connubium irritans; quatenus vero neque interpellatio neque eiusdem dispensatio praecesserit, primum matrimonium obstabit quidem secundo, sed Ordinarius iudicium suspendere debebit, et casum cum omnibus suis circumstantiis ad S. Sedem remittere, quae ipsi Ordinario quid faciendum sit, indicabit. Ad probandum vero, utrum interpellatio vel eius dispensatio intercesserit, consulendi erunt libri matrimoniorum, vel etiam regesta curiae, in quibus haec accurate erunt semper recensenda. Quod si secundum matrimonium contractum fuerit etiam in infidelitate, praesumendum quidem erit quod, antequam persona, de qua agitur, ad baptismum admitteretur, servata fuerint omnia quae ss canones pro his casibus statuunt; sed si institutis opportunis investigationibus adhuc dubium subsit, ad S. Sedem erit recurrendum.

Articulus V.—De Impedimento Impotentiae.

§. 46. Ad impugnandum ex capite impotentiae matrimonium solummodo coniuges admittuntur, quia ipsis solummodo hoc factum cognitum esse potest, et ipsi tantummodo de hac re solliciti esse debent. Ut autem impotentia matrimonium contractum irritet, necesse est ut sit antecedens atque perpetua, quae scilicet naturalibus atque licitis remediis tolli non possit. Ista impotentia si fuerit absoluta, seu talis ut omnino impossibilem reddat coniugalem copulam, matrimonium dirimit semper, et cum qualibet persona contractum; si vero relativa tantum, matrimonium dirimit solummodo cum illa ad quam impotentia ipsa refertur. Ita igi'ur in causis huius generis investigationes erunt dirigendae, ut tandem deveniatur ad adstruendam vel excludendam assertam impotentiam antecedentem et perpetuam, sive absolutam sive saltem relativam.

Hunc in finem prae oculis habenda erit instructio supremae Congregationis S. Officii.

§. 47. Quod si casus occurrat, cui in instructione hac provisum non sit, ad iuris communis normam pertractetur, ac decidatur oportet.

VIII.

Testimony of Singular Witnesses in Causes of Solicitation.

[Supra, n. 833, p. 83; n. 851, p. 98.]

1650. We say above,[1] that in criminal causes two concordant and unexceptionable witnesses are always required for conviction; that singular witnesses, no matter how numerous, do not constitute full proof in such causes.[2] We here add, that when there is question of proving the crime of *sollicitatio,* singular witnesses are indeed sufficient to prove the guilt, provided, however, other presumptions and signs of guilt corroborate the testimony of such witnesses. Thus the Congregation of the Holy Office, in its Instruction of 1867, says: "Sollicitationis crimen ut plurimum secreto perpetratur; hinc privilegium est, ut in causis, quae contra hoc crimen instituuntur, ad plenam probationem faciendam *attestationes etiam singulares admittantur.* At in memoratis SS. Pontificum constitutionibus praescribitur, ne cum testibus singularibus procedatur, *nisi praesumptiones, indicia et alia adminicula concurrant.* Pondus igitur cujusque denuntiationis qualitates et circumstantiae serio accurateque perpendendae sunt, et antequam contra denuntiatum procedatur perspectum exploratumque judici esse debet, quod mulieres vel viri denuntiantes sint boni nominis neque ad accusandum vel inimicitia vel alio humano affectu adducantur. Oportet enim, ut testes enim, ut testes hujusmodi singulares ab omnibus privatis affectionibus sint immunes, ut ipsis integra fides haberi possit."[3]

1651. It will be seen from this quotation that the testimony of singular witnesses is not only not sufficient of itself in causes of solicitation,[4] but that, moreover, the greatest care should be taken to find out whether they are above all suspicion. Hence the Sacred Congregation ordains that when a denunciation has been received, the ecclesiastical superior shall not proceed forthwith against the accused, but shall first inquire carefully whether the person who makes the denunciation is worthy of belief. Hence the parish priest and other reliable persons should be examined in regard to the character of the denouncer. Nay, the above Instruction says: " Ea est hujus supremae Inquisitionis consuetudo, ut post unam alteramve denuntiationem rescribatur, quod denuntiatus *observetur,* ita videlicet super delato crimine suspectus habeatur, ut quum primum per

---

[1] Supra, n. 833.
[2] Instr. cit., § 10, apud Konings, vol. i. p. lxiii.
[3] Supra, n. 851.
[4] Cf. Reiff. l. a, t. 20, n. 312.

novas denuntiationes res explorata erit, in judicium vocandus sit. Ut plurimum nonnisi a tertia denuntiatione procedi solet." [1] All this shows plainly enough with what diffidence and circumspection the testimony of singular witnesses should be admitted even in causes of solicitation.

IX.

Is the administering of an Oath by the Ecclesiastical Judge or Superior, as such, to Witnesses or other parties, forbidden by the Civil Law in England, Ireland, and the United States?

[Supra, n. 1344, 1345, pp. 344, 345; n. 1426, pp. 379, 380.]

1652. I. *Illegality of these oaths in England and Ireland.*—It seems certain, as we have already shown,[2] that the swearing of witnesses or other parties by the ecclesiastical judge or superior, as such, is positively forbidden by law in England and Ireland. Here is the law: "Whereas a practice has prevailed of administering and receiving oaths and affidavits voluntarily taken and made in matters not the subject of any juridical inquiry, nor in anywise pending or at issue before the justice of the peace or other person by whom such oaths or affidavits have been administered or received; and whereas doubts have arisen whether or not such proceeding is illegal; for the more effectual suppression of such practice and removing such doubts, be it enacted, That from and after the commencement of this act it shall not be lawful for any justice of the peace or other person to administer, or cause or allow to be administered, or to receive or cause or allow to be received, any oath, affidavit, or solemn affirmation touching any matter or thing whereof such justice or other person hath not jurisdiction or cognizance by some statute in force at the time being." [3]

1653. Mr. Justice Coleridge, in 1843, in Regina *v.* Nott, decided that the administering of an oath in an ecclesiastical judicial inquiry was contrary to the above statute, and consequently illegal.[4] It should be, however, observed that the statute just quoted does not make the administering of the oath contrary to its provisions a penal offence, but simply declares it unlawful, without decreeing any penalty for its violation.

1654. II. *The swearing of witnesses or other persons in the ecclesiastical courts of the United States.*—In the United States this administering of the oath is not illegal, as we have already shown.[5] At our request, Mr. E. Stevenson, the public prosecutor of Passaic Co., New Jersey, made a thorough inquiry into the question. He informs us that he has looked up all the available laws and authorities on the matter, and that he cannot find any prohibition whatever against administering the oaths in question; that it is the universal opinion of lawyers and competent judges that no such prohibition exists with us; that it is the general practice of Protestant denominations, with us, to administer oaths in their ecclesiastical courts.

---

[1] Instr. cit., § 11. [2] Supra, n. 1315. [3] 5 and 6 Will. 4, c. 62, s. 13.
[4] Regina *v.* Nott, 1 Carr and Marsh. 285 (41 E. C. L.). [5] Supra, n. 1344, 1426.

X.

Force of the Confession or Statement of the Married Couple, concerning Clandestine Marriages, especially with us.

[Supra, n. 1486–1491.]

1655. We say above (n. 1486) that *the confession of either of the married couple, or even of both, as against the validity of a marriage contracted by them, has of itself no force.* Here then it is proper to ask: Is this rule applicable also to clandestine marriages contracted in so secret a manner as not to be susceptible of proof? Before answering, we remark that we speak of clandestine marriages as contracted in those places where the Tridentine decree *Tametsi* does not obtain. For where it is in force clandestine marriages are null and void, and consequently there can be no question of proving the validity of such marriages. The question therefore has reference to clandestine marriages as contracted in the greater part of the United States, where the Tridentine decree is not promulgated. We observe in passing that as these marriages are valid if contracted solely by the consent of the couple, without the assistance of a priest or of witnesses, it must often become very difficult to prove them.

We now answer: The above rule is not applicable in the case of clandestine marriages under consideration. Hence, if both or even one of the couple alleged to have been clandestinely married denies the marriage, they are not to be compelled to cohabit and regard each other as married; nay, they should be separated, and their alleged marriage regarded as no marriage. But if both affirm the existence of their marriage, their confession or statement constitutes full proof of the marriage, and such a marriage must be accepted and approved by the Church, as though it had been contracted from the beginning *in facie ecclesiæ?* [1]

XI.

Compulsory Appointment of Procurators.

[Supra, p. 47.]

Q. Can a person be sometimes compelled to appoint a procurator to represent him in judicial proceedings?

A. We premise: It is certain that a litigant who is willing to appear in person cannot be compelled to appear by a procurator. For every one has the right to appear in his own cause. The question therefore relates only to the case where one of the contending parties is hindered from appearing in person by sickness or some other similar obstacle.

[1] Cap. 1, 2, de Cland. desp. (iv. 3); Schmalzg., l. 4, t. 3, n. 249.

Having premised this, we now answer: If the obstacle is permanent or likely to last long, v.g. for two or three months, the party so hindered can be compelled by the judge to appoint a procurator, lest otherwise the interests of the opposite party should be injured. If the impediment is merely of short duration, and the case can be delayed, he cannot be compelled to appoint a procurator.[1]

Observe also that in disputes or causes between bishops and their priests it is more in keeping with the dignity of the bishop to appoint a procurator to conduct his case before the ecclesiastical judge of appeal.[2]

XII.

Ocular Inspection on the part of the Judge.

[Supra, n. 968, 992; pp. 162, 176.]

In order to gain a clearer and fuller knowledge of the facts in a case, it becomes at times necessary, or at least useful, for the judge to make a *personal* or *ocular inspection.*[3] In criminal ecclesiastical causes, this inspection is called *visitatio corporis delicti;* in civil ecclesiastical causes, it is styled simply *inspectio ocularis.* It may of course take place in civil and criminal causes. It consists in the judge's visiting and personally viewing the scene or place where the alleged crime occurred, or the disputed object is situate.[4]

Q. How is this inspection to be made?

A. The judge or superior may of course make this inspection extrajudicially and privately. But this private inspection will have no judicial effect. In order that it may have any judicial value this inspection should be ordered by the judge in his judicial capacity, and made in the following manner: the judge himself or his delegate repairs with the secretary to the place or person where or upon whom an offence has been committed, or where the object in dispute is located, or also he orders portable things, such as instruments, clothing, etc., to be produced before him. Two witnesses should also be present. The minutes of the inspection are drawn up and signed by the secretary, the witnesses, and the judge.[5] They are then communicated to the defendant. The reason is that this inspection is a species of judicial proof, and should therefore, like every other proof, be made known to the adverse party. The ocular inspection can be made, in criminal causes, either during the informative process and prior to the citation of the accused, or afterwards.

However, as Cardinal De Luca says, when the judge cannot conveniently visit the place and make the ocular inspection, it is customary to replace the visit by geographical maps or charts made especially for the occasion by order of the court. These charts should outline the place, location, etc., so as to give the judge a clear and full idea of the facts and circumstances in the case.[6]

[1] Cap. 2. 9, de proc. (i. 38); cap. 6 de dol. et cont. (ii. 14); Schmalzg. l. 1, t. 38, n. 8.
[2] De Angelis, t. 2, t. 7, n. 10. [3] Bouix de Jud., vol. ii. p. 519.
[4] Soglia-Necchiotti, vol. ii. p 293. [5] München, vol. i. p. 182.
[6] Card. De Luca, l 15, de Judic. Disc. 24, n. 8.

In our secular courts, such maps or charts are now usually made and set up in the court-room in all important cases. However, not unfrequently the judge and the jury make the ocular inspection.

XIII.

Expenses of Ecclesiastical Trials.

The impartial administration of justice, and the confidence which all should be able to have in courts of justice, seem to require that judicial proceedings should be conducted free of all costs to the litigants. In fact, it is to the interest of society, ecclesiastical as well as secular, Church as well as State, that justice shall be fairly and impartially administered, in criminal and civil matters, to all its members. Consequently it would appear just that society itself should defray all the expenses consequent upon litigation.

On the other hand, it will also be readily seen that in many cases great evils would flow from the application of this principle. Numbers of people, knowing that it would entail upon them no cost whatever, would rush into court without any cause whatever. Besides, natural equity dictates that the person who seeks redress, and who is therefore directly benefited by judicial proceedings, should also bear the expenses, labor, and loss of time occasioned by them.

Of course there are certain expenses which society itself—the Church or State—will always be obliged to bear in the interests of a fair and impartial administration of justice. Thus, by the law of the Church (the same is enacted by secular governments for secular judges) all ecclesiastical judges, ordinary and delegated, should be, and in fact are, paid wholly by the diocese, etc., where they act as judges.[1] The reason is that they should be completely independent of the litigants, and entirely uninfluenced by their liberality.[2]

Then again, especially in criminal causes, where the accused is too poor to pay his own expenses—for instance, those of an advocate, or of the witnesses in his behalf—it is evidently the duty of society—i.e. of the Church or State—to pay these expenses for him, lest he should, by reason of his poverty and consequent inability to provide the means of defence, be condemned, even though innocent,[3] or deprived of his just rights.

Q. What are the various kinds of expenses of ecclesiastical trials, civil and criminal, which are to be defrayed by the litigants themselves?

A. Chiefly the following: 1. Those which are incurred by each party—namely, plaintiff and defendant—in prosecuting or defending the case. Such are the expenses of witnesses, of the advocate, of travelling, etc. 2. Those incurred by the court itself, excluding always the judge, who is paid by the diocese. Such are, therefore, (*a*) fees paid to the secretary for writing out copies of decrees and orders of the court; (*b*) fees paid to the messengers of the court for serving citations and other messages of the judge. 3. Those which come under the head

---

[1] Bonifac. VIII. anno 1302, cap. Statutum 11. § 4, de Rescr. in 6° (l. 3).
[2] München, vol. i. p. 218. [3] Arg. Cap. Statutum cit. § 4.

of damages, namely, pecuniary compensation for the annoyance, loss of time, money, and good name caused by the litigation, apart from the direct expenses of the proceedings.[1] For the present we shall speak merely of the first and second kind of expenses.

Q. How are the expenses to be defrayed by the contending parties during the progress of the trial and before the final decision of the judge?

A The rule is, that in the beginning and during the progress of the proceedings, civil or criminal, and until the final decision of ·the judge is given, each party must bear (*a*) his own expenses,[2] v.g. for the advocate, witnesses produced by him, etc.; (*b*) also half the costs, v.g. of the instruments made out by the secretary, when they are common to both litigants; (*c*) the entire cost of any paper written out by the secretary for him solely. The costs of these writings should be, however, very moderate, and taxed by the judge.[3] The costs of the court procedure proper are borne by the court until the end of the proceedings.

The reason why each party is obliged before the final decision to pay his own share of the expenses is that at this stage the law presumes that each party has entered upon the proceedings in good faith, i.e. with the honest and reasonable conviction tnat he has justice on his side.

We have said, *the rule is;* for there are chiefly two exceptions, namely: 1. Where a litigant—plaintiff or defendant—is notably poor. Notable poverty exempts a litigant from all expenses, especially in criminal trials. But if such a poor litigant is found to have entered upon the proceedings either unadvisedly or even maliciously, he can, at the discretion of the judge, be condemned, for such conduct, to punishments other than pecuniary fines.

2. Where a litigant—plaintiff or defendant—becomes, during the proceedings, wilfully and culpably—that is, without a legitimate excuse—disobedient to the orders of the judge—v.g. not appearing in court, either personally or through a procurator, on the day appointed in the citation ;[4] or interposing frivolous and dishonest exceptions to delay the proceedings, and thus causing unnecessary delay, and therefore additional expenses to the opposing party, the judge can, and if asked should, at once, and without waiting for the final sentence, and that both in civil and criminal causes, condemn the party disobedient or guilty of trickery as above stated to refund to the opposing party all the expenses entailed upon it by the delay, and that from the time the citation which was disobeyed was issued.[5] Nay, if the party *repeats* this disobedience, and becomes therefore not merely culpably disobedient, but moreover contumacious or stubbornly disobedient, the judge can proceed, both in civil and criminal causes, to hear, try, and decide the case in the absence of the contumacious party.

We have said, *either personally or through a procurator.* For in civil causes falling under the ecclesiastical forum, both of the contending parties—namely, the plaintiff and the defendant, and in appeals the appellant and appellee—can appear in court by proxy as well as in person. Nay, where a party is unable to appear personally, either by reason of illness or other legitimate cause, he is

---

[1] Arg. Cap. Statutum cit. §§ 4, 5, 6.   [2] Alez. III. cap. 11, de accus. (v. 1).
[3] Bonifac. VIII. cap. Statutum 11, §§ 4, 6, de Rescr. in 6° (t. 3).
[4] Innoc. III. cap. 5, 6 de dol. et cont. (il. 14); Innoc. IV. cap. 1 de dol. et cont. in 6° (il. 5).
[5] München, vol. i, p. 225.

obliged, and can be compelled by the judge, to send a procurator to act for him, except where the case is of great importance and therefore requires the *personal* attention of the principal, and the impediment, v.g. illness, is of very short duration. But even in this case a procurator should be appointed if the cause of delay is or will be of long duration, v.g. two or three months.[1]

Here it is to be remembered that bishops, in disputes between them and their subjects, are not supposed to appear personally, as plaintiff or defendant, appellant or appellee, in ecclesiastical courts of appeal, but generally appear by proxy or by the diocesan procurator. And in fact it would seem incompatible with the high dignity of a bishop that he should personally descend to the plane of defendant or plaintiff in the cases referred to.[2]

Q. How are the expenses of ecclesiastical trials to be defrayed by the parties after the trial is over ?

A. When the trial is finished, and the final decision is pronounced, the rule of law is that, both in civil and criminal ecclesiastical causes, the succumbing or defeated party is to be condemned by the judge, and that in the final sentence, to pay the entire costs, namely, not only his own, but also those incurred by his opponent and by the court itself.[3] The reason is, the law justly presumes that the litigant who has entirely failed to prove or establish his case, and has therefore been completely defeated, entered upon the proceedings, whether as plaintiff or as defendant, either (*a*) rashly (*temere*), that is, carelessly and thoughtlessly, and without due consideration or regard for the rights of the opponent, or (*b*) maliciously (*dolo malo, calumnia*), that is, in bad faith, from ill-will, chicanery, and trickery, and is therefore bound to refund the expenses caused by his rash or malicious conduct.

We have said, *the rule is.* The exceptions to this rule are: 1. A defendant in a criminal cause, at least when there is question of a serious punishment to be inflicted upon him, is not considered rash for defending himself.[4] Hence he cannot be condemned to pay the costs of the court or of the opposite party. We say *a defendant*, for the case is different with the *accuser*, private or official, who, if he fails altogether to substantiate the charges preferred by him, is considered guilty of having carelessly or even knowingly and wilfully preferred wrong or false charges, and should therefore be condemned by the judge to pay the costs also of the defendant, unless it appears from the acts of the informative process that there was at least half proof of guilt.

2. Next, the above rule does not apply when it appears that the succumbing party had a just or probable cause for entering upon the proceedings, and therefore acted in good faith.[5] In this case, the judge should oblige each party to pay his own expenses, that is, he should assess the costs equally upon both litigants (*compensare expensas*). Consequently the defeated party is not in this case compelled to pay also the expenses of the victor. For he has done no injustice as yet to the latter. He simply sought redress in a proper manner and for good reasons.[6]

[1] Glossa in cap. 6 de dol. et cont. v. responsalem ; Schmalzg. l. 2, t. 38, n. 8.
[2] Novella 7, cap. i.; Schmalzg. l. c.
[3] L. 3, C. de fruct. et lit. exp. (vii. 51); Reiff. l. 2, t. 27, n. 205.
[4] L. 1 ff. de bonis eorum qui ante sent. (48, 21); Reiff. l. 2, t. 27, n. 177.
[5] Reiff. l. c. n. 178; Card. de Luca, lib. 15, de Judic. disc. 39, n. 10, 11, 12.
[6] München, vol. 1, p. 218.

Now, a defeated party is regarded as having had a just cause for entering upon judicial proceedings, (*a*) when he has produced half proof, v.g. one good witness, in support of his cause ; (*b*) when he has a probable opinion in his favor, etc. In general, it is left to the discretion of the judge to determine, from the nature of the case, the condition of the persons, and the surrounding circumstances, whether the defeated party acted in good faith and from sufficient motives or probable cause.[1]

From this principle it will be seen that when the prosecution, under the Instruction *Cum Magnopere*, fails, in criminal and disciplinary causes, to substantiate its charges, this fact constitutes *presumptive* calumny. That is, the law presumes or infers that a false accusation has been made. But this presumption is overcome if it appears from the acts of the informative process that there were *prima facie* good reasons or proofs, v.g. one good witness for each charge. When the acts of the informative process do not overthrow the presumptive calumny, then the latter becomes true calumny (*vera calumnia*), and the prosecution is to be condemned to pay to the defendant the costs and damages.

Q. How should the judge proceed in condemning the defeated party to pay the costs of the opponent and of the court?

A. We premise : We have already seen that, except in the case of delay of the proceedings caused by the disobedience or trickery of one of the litigants, the costs cannot be assessed upon either of the contending parties until the trial is over and the final sentence is being pronounced. Up to that time each party must bear his own expenses.

We now answer : 1. It is certain that the ecclesiastical judge is bound to condemn the defeated party who entered upon the trial carelessly or even maliciously to pay the expenses incurred by the opponent when the latter so asks either expressly or impliedly, v.g. by the phrase "Hoc et omni alio meliori modo." Otherwise the judge is obliged to pay these expenses himself.

2. But if no such request is made, the judge can indeed, *ex-officio*, condemn the rash litigant to refund the expenses incurred by the opposite party, but he is not bound to do so.[2]

Q. What rules govern the amount of the expenses to be refunded to the victor?

A. The defeated party can, as a rule, be condemned by the judge to refund to the victor only those moderate and necessary outlays which were made directly on account of the judicial proceedings, such as a moderate and reasonable fee to the advocate, the necessary and moderate expenses of the witnesses.[3] He cannot, therefore, be condemned to pay liberal and unnecessary outlays, such as a very generous fee to the advocate, etc.[4]

Q. Can the judge, in condemning a party to pay the expenses of the other litigant, do so in a general manner, or is he obliged to specify the amount of costs?

A. 1. He is not bound to specify the precise amount in his sentence, but may simply word the part of the sentence referring to the costs thus : We condemn Titius to pay costs.[5]

[1] Schmalzg. l. ii. t. 27, n. 117, 118.   [2] Reiff. l. c. n. 192.
[3] Cap. 5, 6 de dol. et cont. (li. 14); Reiff. l. c. n. 196.
[4] See our Elements, vol. ii. n. 1902.   [5] Reiff. l. c. n. 207.

2. When a party has been condemned to pay the expenses of the other, the victor is obliged to exhibit to the judge an itemized bill of his expenses. The judge should then revise this bill, rejecting those items which are unnecessary and cutting down those which are immoderate.[1] Only those expenses which are thus approved need be refunded.

Q. When can a defeated party be condemned by the judge to pay to the victor not only the direct judicial expenses (*expensas*), as seen thus far, but also damages (*damna*)?

A. A defeated party cannot be mulcted in damages except (*a*) when he has entered upon the proceedings, not simply through carelessness or want of thought, but through malice or ill-will and chicanery (*calumnia*); (*b*) when he has unduly retarded the proceedings by dishonest and tricky exceptions, or by disobedience to the citations of the judge. The damages are to be taxed or fixed by the judge.[2]

Q. Is it allowed to appeal from the decision of the judge imposing costs to be refunded to the victor?

A. 1. It is. In fact, the right of appeal belongs both to the party who is condemned to refund costs and damages, if he thinks the assessment is unjust or exorbitant, and to the party to whom the costs were adjudicated, if he considers the amount too small.[3] *A fortiori* can the victorious party appeal, and that both in civil and criminal ecclesiastical causes, when no costs at all, expenses or damages, are adjudicated to him by the judge.

2. However, as we have already shown, the judge may impose the costs upon one guilty of delaying the trial, through disobedience or dishonest exceptions, by an interlocutory decision, and consequently before the final sentence. Against such an interlocutory decision the first remedy is recourse to the judge himself who gave it, for he can correct his interlocutory sentences. If he does not correct it, the remedy is an appeal to the higher judge. In all other cases the expenses are to be assessed or imposed only by and in the final decision, but not before. In this case the appeal is the only remedy, since the judge cannot revoke or correct his final sentence.

Q. Who is obliged to bear the expenses occasioned by judicial proceedings in ecclesiastical courts of appeal?

A. 1. As in the courts of the first instance, so also in appellate courts, the rule is that during the progress of the appeal, and until the appellate judge pronounces his final decision, each party must, as a rule, pay his own expenses. The reason is that at this stage it is presumed that each party is in good faith.

We say, *as a rule;* for where, in the course of appellate proceedings, either litigant causes unnecessary delays, either by disobeying the citations of the judge or by interposing frivolous exceptions, such litigant can and should be condemned at once, and prior to the final decision, to refund to the opposite party all the expenses and damages caused directly by the delay.

2. At the end of the appellate proceedings, the judge of appeal can, and, if requested, should, in his final decision, condemn either the appellant or the appellee to pay the other's costs and the costs of the court only when it appears

[1] Ib. n. 208.　　　　　　　　　　[2] Schmalzg. l. ii. t. 27, n. 129.

[3] Schmalzg. l. c. n. 130.

that he has entered rashly, inconsiderately, and without probable cause upon the appeal, whether as appellant or as appellee.[1] Now, an appellant, at least in civil ecclesiastical causes, is regarded as having appealed rashly when, having been defeated in the first instance, he is defeated again in the court of appeal. This is, however, merely a presumption which, like other presumptions, may be and is overthrown by the appellant if he shows that he acted in good faith and from probable cause. Hence an appellee who was victorious in the first instance but is defeated on appeal is considered as a rash litigant, not when he is defeated on account of new allegations and new proofs submitted for the first time on appeal, but only when he is defeated on the acts and proofs of the first instance.[2]

We have said, *at least in civil causes;* for in criminal causes of ecclesiastics, also as conducted under the recent instruction of the S. C. de Prop. Fide, *Cum Magnopere*, it is doubtful whether an appellant who is found guilty and condemned in the court of the first instance, and who on appeal is again found guilty, is regarded as a rash litigant. For every one feels that a person cannot be blamed for appealing to save his honor and good name and to escape punishment by all lawful means of redress, such as appeals. Thus the Roman law, as adopted by the Church, enacts: " Nam ignoscendum censuerunt ei, qui sanguinem (honorem, etc.) suum, qualiter qualiter redemptum voluit."[3]

NOTE.—The expenses or damages need not be refunded by one litigant to the other until the sentence of the court has become *res judicata*."[4]

XIV.

Has the accused the right to be present at the examination of the witnesses produced against him?

[Supra, n. 838, 839.]

A number of canonists affirm, as we have seen above, n. 839, that in ecclesiastical trials, civil or criminal, the accused or defendant has a right to be present during the entire examination of the witnesses produced against him, and to cross-examine them. Thus Todeschi writes :[5] "On doit d'ailleurs citer le competiteur [the person against whom the witnesses are to testify] contre lequel les temoins sont produits, afin que, s'il veut, il puisse *assister a leur examen*, et objecter tout ce qu'il croira necessaire et opportun, ou contre les temoins eux-mêmes,

---

[1] Cap. 59, de appell. (ii. 28); Glossa. ib. v. *in expensis.*
[2] Reiff, l. c. n 209 sp.; Schmalzg. l. c. n. 191, 192. .
[3] L. 1. ff. de bonis eorum qui ante sent. (48, 21). •
[4] Card. de Luca, de Judic. disc. 39, n. 1.
[5] L. 2, t. 20, n. 3.

ou contre les articles, et provoquer des éclaircissements sur leur reponses." In support of this teaching he quotes the Cap. 2, de test., and the Nov. 90, cap. 9.

Craisson, Man. n. 5714, after having spoken of the opinion of those canonists who hold that the party against whom the witnesses are produced need not be allowed to be present at their examination, says : " Sed res aliter se habet coram tribunalibus nostris civilibus, quibus se conformarunt quaedam officialitates in Gallia, veluti nostra Valentinensis. Etenim juxta art. 73, Codicis . . . a judice informante primum testes seorsim audiuntur, absente reo ; postea vero coram tribunali interrogantur quidem seorsim non audientibus caeteris testibus nondum interrogatis, sed tamen *coram reo, ut iste respondere possit.* Hic autem modus non videtur contrarius Decretalibus modo citatis. Etenim decretales *Inqui-sitionis* et *Venerabili* supponunt quidem audiendos esse testes secreto vel sigil-latim, sed hoc, ut explicat Glossa, ut sibi invicem convenire nequeant de modo uniformi deponendi. Porro ad hoc non requiritur ut testes interrogentur *in absentia rei*, sed sufficit ut seorsim ab aliis testibus, singuli (testes) interrogentur, qui modus conformior videtur Decretali *In nomine* juxta quam adversarius *ad audiendos* testes venire debet. S. Liguorius huic modo interrogandi sat con-formis videtur."

Devoti, l. 3, t. 9, § 18. writes : "Interrogationes testium plerumque *ab adver-sario proponuntur,* QUO PRAESENTE interrogandi sunt testes, quae civilis[1] et ca-nonici juris[2] disciplina est." Then, having mentioned the custom or usage which had crept into ecclesiastical courts, of examining witnesses in the absence of the accused, he says of this practice, in note 7 : " Error interpretum, maxime vete-rum, hunc morem induxit ; error autem processit ex prave intellecta Zenonis Constitutione in L. 14, c. de test. (iv. 20). In ea quidem scriptum est *intrare testes judicantis secretum.* Verum, ut bene monet Polletus. *Hist. For. Rom.,* l. 5, c. 12, secretum est tribunal ac judicii locus ; non autem haec verba signifi-cant, quod putarunt interpretes, testes secreto interrogandos atque examinandos esse."

The examination of witnesses in the presence of the party against whom they testify has been sanctioned by the Holy See for this country, as also for England, Ireland, Scotland, etc. Thus the Instr. *Quamvis* of the S. Congr. de Prop. Fide, July 20, 1878, enacts in n. 12 : "Consentientibus testibus, et dirigente prudentia consilii, repetatur testimonium coram rectore Missionario, qui et ipse testes, si voluerit, interroget per praesidem Commissionis Investigationis."

This mode of examining witnesses has been found to be the only satisfactory way of arriving at the truth. Hence it is now universally made use of in all the civil tribunals both here and throughout the world. Chitty[3] writes : "When the witness is thus duly sworn, he must . . . deliver his testimony in the presence of the accused. For the law regards the *viva voce* examination of witnesses in open court, where the manner may be observed, as well as the substance scrutinized, and where apt and sudden questions may be asked, for which the witness could not be prepared, and where he may be confronted with other witnesses, and *where the defendant may have the benefit of cross-examination* and of instant

---

[1] L. 15, C. de test.; Novella 90, cap. 9.   [2] Cap. 2, de test.
[3] Criminal Law, vol. I. p. 617 sq.

inquiry, to be the most satisfactory mode of ascertaining the credit which they deserve.

"When the witness (against the accused) is thus sworn and present, he is examined by the counsel for the prosecution. . . . When the examination-in-chief of the witness is concluded, the prisoner or his counsel has power to cross-examine him as to every part of his testimony."

Walker[1] also writes : "The party who calls a witness first examines him ; and this is called *examination-in-chief.* . . . The *cross-examination* (which follows) by the adversary may be by leading questions, and as searching and particular as he pleases ; for this is often the only way to detect a false witness."

Thus it will be seen that the practice introduced into some of the ecclesiastical curias of Europe, of excluding the accused or party against whom witnesses testify from their examination, is not founded in the law of the Church, but owes its origin to an erroneous interpretation of the law ; is inadequate and unsatisfactory; may have been adapted to former ages, but is behind the present age, which has made steady and enlightened progress in the administration of justice.

In the Church judicial proceedings are not nearly as frequent as in the State. Consequently, while in secular courts constant progress and improvements take place in the manner of administering justice, in the Church little or none occurs. Hence, as in the early ages the Church adopted in her judicature most of the forms and proceedings of the secular Roman law, so also it is not out of her sphere and custom to follow and adopt useful modes of procedure now in vogue in our secular courts.

Besides, in the details of judicial proceedings it is the practice and rule of the Church to allow a considerable latitude. Hence the customs and practices of a particular country, concerning the details of judicial proceedings, are to be generally followed, even though they differ from those which obtain at Rome.

XV.

The oath. Its use at the present day, especially in judicial proceedings.

[Supra, n. 885 sq.]

Above (n. 885 sq.) we have spoken of the oath, upon which is staked the whole issue of a controversy, and which is therefore called the decisive oath (*juramentum litis decisorium*). We shall here briefly add some explanations both in regard to this decisive oath and other oaths, in general, taken in or out of judicial proceedings.

Q. What is an oath ?

A. It is the calling upon God to be the witness of something. Santi thus defines it . "Juramentum est invocatio divini nominis in testimonium alicujus rei."[2]

Q. How many kinds of oaths are there ?

---

[1] American Law, p. 633.   [2] Lib. 2, t. 24, n. 2.

A. 1st. While the oath is in its substance always one and the same—namely, a calling upon God as a witness—yet it takes different names from the various occasions or circumstances under which it is taken.[1] Now these occasions on which the oath is taken may be divided into two classes, namely, those where a person either (*a*) *asserts*, (*b*) or *promises* something. Accordingly all oaths are in a general sense either *assertory* or *promissory*.[2] The assertory oath (*juramentum assertorium*) therefore is the calling upon God to be witness of the truth of an assertion, statement, allegation, or affirmation made by a person. The promissory oath (*juramentum promissorium*) is a calling upon God to be a witness of a promise, agreement, stipulation, or contract made by a person or persons. It will be seen that the words *assertory* and *promissory* are here taken in their broadest sense.

2d. Both the assertory and promissory oath may be taken in judicial or extrajudicial matters and proceedings. In other words, God may be and is called upon to be a witness (*a*) of the truth of assertions or statements made, (*b*) and of the sincerity of promises given, both in judicial matters and in extrajudicial affairs. Accordingly, assertory as well as promissory oaths are subdivided into *judicial* and *extrajudicial* oaths.[3]

3d. Now, in judicial proceedings or causes, the oath may be taken (*a*) by witnesses before they testify ; (*b*) or by the litigants ; (*c*) or by the officials of the court, namely, the judge (if he is delegated), the secretary, the fiscal procurator, etc. The *witnesses* swear that they will tell the truth ; hence their oath is called *juramentum veritatis dicendae*. Can this oath be administered also to the principals or litigants themselves, in case they wish personally to make statements in court in their own behalf? In criminal causes, which are being criminally tried, the *juramentum veritatis dicendae* can no longer be administered in ecclesiastical courts to the accused when he is examined or makes statements in his own behalf.[4] In other causes of the ecclesiastical forum the principals may be allowed to depose under oath. In matrimonial causes of nullity, the husband and wife must take the oath before making their statements in court.

The *litigants*, namely, the plaintiff and defendant, their agents, procurators, or representatives, swear, at least according to the older practice, that they believe they have a good cause and that they will not use dishonorable means to gain their case. Hence this oath is called *juramentum calumniae et malitiae*. Whether and how far this oath is still in use in ecclesiastical courts, we shall see further on. Furthermore, the litigants or their representatives may take the oath for the purpose of staking upon it the whole case (*juramentum litis decisorium*), or of supplying the absence of full proofs (*juramentum suppletorium*), or of proving their innocence (*juramentum purgatorium*), as we have shown above, n. 886 sq.

The *officials* of the court swear that they will discharge their respective duties conscientiously and faithfully. Consequently this oath is called *juramentum fidelitatis.*

4th. In extrajudicial matters the following oaths occur : (*a*) *juramentum fidelitatis*, that is, the oath taken by officials to discharge the duties of their office

---

[1] Card. De Luca, l. 15, de Jud. disc. 25, n. 5. [2] Devoti, l. 3, t. 9, n. 23.
[3] Santi, l. 2, t. 24, n. 3. [4] Bened. XIII., in Conc. Rom. ann. 1725, tit. 13, cap. 2.

faithfully and conscientiously. This oath is taken by the Pope, the Cardinals, Bishops, Synodal examiners. Parish Priests, etc.[1] (*b*) *Juramentum confirmativum* or *promissorium*, that is, the oath taken by a person that he will keep his promise, agreement, etc. (*c*) *Juramentum assertorium*, or the oath to tell the truth, outside of judicial proceedings. (*d*) *Juramentum litis decisorium*, namely, when contending parties, in extrajudicial matters, stake the controversy upon the oath. (*e*) *Juramentum suppletorium* and *purgativum*, that is, when persons in extrajudicial matters agree to supply the want of sufficient proof by the oath.[2]

Q. What is the force of the oath, especially in judicial matters and proceedings?

A. The oath is simply a corroboration, but not a proof, of the existence of a fact or of the truth of a statement, allegation, etc. Thus a witness swears that he will tell the truth. This oath, however, is not a proof of the truth of what he says, but simply adds a presumption to his truthfulness.[3] Only in the case of the *juramentum litis decisorium*, and partly also in the case of the *juramentum suppletorium* and *purgativum*, does the oath itself take the place of proof proper.

Q. What is at present the policy of the Church with regard to oaths, especially in judicial proceedings?

A. In former days the oath was held in the highest esteem and inspired the greatest awe. It was taken but rarely, for great cause, after mature deliberation, and with impressive solemnity. Persons who were convicted of false oaths were visited, both in the ecclesiastical and secular tribunals, with the severest corporal punishments, in some places with amputation of the right hand. Perjurers were regarded with horror and aversion by everybody. Consequently the force and weight of an oath were very great.[4]

But the times, manners, and feelings of the people have undergone no small change in this respect. The oath is now administered in very trivial affairs, and that not infrequently in so irreverent, careless, and nonchalant a manner that many who take it do not know or advert to what they are doing ; often they think they commit no sin whatever if they swear falsely. Perjuries are so frequent that scarcely any abhorrence is felt against them.[5] Besides, in the Church there is at present scarcely any way of punishing perjury.

When the oath had thus lost the great weight attributed to it in former times, it naturally fell into gradual disuse. Thus the oath which is called *litis decisorium* is now completely out of use. Likewise the *juramentum purgativum* and *suppletorium* may be said to have disappeared in criminal causes, since in these causes the guilt has to be fully proved ; and where it is not fully proved, the accused is either absolved unconditionally, or is absolved *ex hactenus deductis*, or *novis non supervenientibus indiciis*. The decisive and supplementary oath is at present used, at most, in civil matters of small consequence.[6]

Card. De Luca states that, owing to the reasons given above, the *juramentum calumniae et malitiae* is also frequently omitted in ecclesiastical trials, and that it should be abolished altogether.[7]

The only oaths which are still in full force and obligatory in the Church at

[1] Card. De Luca, de Judic. disc. 25, n. 19, 20.   [2] Card. De Luca, l. c., n. 5.
[3] Santi, l. 2, t. 24, n. 1.   [4] Card. De Luca, l. c., n. 1, 2.   [5] Ib. n. 3, 4.
[6] Card. De Luca, l. c., n. 7, 8.   [7] Ib. n. 16, 17, 18.

present are (*a*) the *juramentum veritatis dicendae*, as taken by witnesses in judicial proceedings, (*b*) and the *juramentum fidelitatis*, by which officials, v.g., Pope, Bishops, Judges, etc., swear that they will faithfully discharge the duties of their respective offices, judicial or extrajudicial.[1]

From the above it will be seen that the law and practice of the Church is at present opposed to persons taking the oath when they testify or make statements in their own behalf, especially where these statements involve considerable interests. For it is evident that these persons would be greatly tempted to swear falsely, and would, as a matter of fact, frequently perjure themselves. The same does not apply to witnesses. These are third persons, and disinterested, who make statements which regard not themselves, but others. Consequently witnesses have not the motives which affect the litigants or principals to commit perjury.

XVI.

Delays fatal to appeals, especially extrajudicial (FATALIA APPELLATIONUM).

[Suprá, n. 1211.]

By days or times fatal to appeals (*fatalia appellationum, dies fatales*) are meant those spaces of time which, if allowed to go by without being made use of, either preclude or extinguish the appeal. According to the law of the Church, as in force at present also with us, there are three spaces of time fatal to appeals, namely, (*a*) the time to make or interpose it before the judge or superior *a quo ;* (*b*) the time to introduce it before the superior *ad quem ;* (*c*) the time to prosecute and finish it. Formerly there was a fourth fatal time, namely, that of asking for and of granting the *apostoli*. This term no longer exists, as the *apostoli* have gone out of use. We shall here speak merely of the first of the three fatal terms, namely, that of making the appeal, or of the *fatalia appellationis interponendae.*

Q. Within what time should the appeal be made?

A. Within *ten days*, and that whether the appeal is from a judicial or extrajudicial grievance or act, from a final or an interlocutory sentence or decision. Consequently, where a person allows these ten days to elapse, he loses the right of appealing, although he may use other remedies granted by the law of the Church to obtain redress. We have said *judicial grievances :* this is clear from the general law of the Church,[2] and also, so far as this country is concerned, from the S. C. de P. F. Instr. *Cum Magnopere*, art. 37. We have also said *extrajudicial*, etc.: this is evident from the decretal *Concertationi*, 8, de appell. in 6°, of Pope Boniface VIII. (1298), which is as follows: "Concertationi antiquae finem imponere praesenti constitutione volentes: Statuimus, ut ab electionibus, postulationibus, provisionibus, *et quibuslibet extrajudicialibus actibus*, quisquis ex eis gravatum se reputans, per appellationis beneficium gravamen illatum desideraverit revocari, *intra decem dies* (postquam sciverit) si velit, appellet : post decendium vero eidem aditus non pateat appellandi. Sed si per contradictionem debitam, vel alia juris remedia petierit revocari gravamen ei (dummodo medio

[1] Card. De Luca, l. c. n. 19, 20.   [2] Cap. 15, de sent. et re jud. (II. 27).

tempore his non consenserit) lapsus decendii non obsistat." This constitution is still in force, also among us.

Q. When do the ten days granted for appealing begin to run in the case of judicial appeals?

A. They begin to run, not from the day on which the sentence was pronounced, even though the appellant was present when it was being pronounced, but from the day or time the sentence was delivered to him in writing. Thus the decree of the S. C. EE. et RR., issued Dec. 18, 1835, for criminal causes enacts, in art. II.: "Decem dies numerari incipient non a die, quo sententia lata est, sed a die quo reo vel ejus defensori per cursorem denuntiata fuit." Likewise the S. C. de Prop. Fide, Instr. *Cum Magnopere*, art. 37, decrees: "Intra terminum decem dierum *a notificatione sententiae*, interpositio appellationis fieri debet, quo elapso tempore, sententiae executio locum habet."

Q. When do the above ten days begin to run in extrajudicial appeals?

A. We must distinguish between the case of a grievance *already* inflicted and one *not yet inflicted*, but about to be inflicted. Where the grievance is not yet inflicted a person may appeal against it at any time, from the day he began to be afraid of its being inflicted until it is actually inflicted.[1]

Where the grievance is already inflicted, the ten days, speaking in general, begin to run, not from the time the grievance was inflicted, but from the time it became known to the party aggrieved, and that not only in general, but as a grievance to him in particular. We say, *speaking in general:* since the application of this rule in a particular case is sometimes beset with difficulties.[2] For it is frequently hard to know when an extrajudicial act or grievance is *merely begun*, or is in *progress*, or is *completed*. Now, it is certain that when the grievance is *continuous*, a person can appeal also after the lapse of ten days from the time it was first inflicted; in other words, he can appeal as long as the grievance lasts.[3] Where it is doubtful whether the injury or grievance is *completed* or not, the benefit of the doubt is to be given to the appellant. For, on the one hand, the appeal is a benefit, which is therefore to be amply construed; and on the other, in extrajudicial acts or grievances there is frequently no formal sentence or decision, but merely informal acts, of which it is sometimes difficult to know whether they are final, or only tentative and incipient. Hence, too, the law of the Church does not define the precise time when the ten days run in extrajudicial appeals, but simply enacts, in a general way, that they shall run from the time a person has obtained due and certain knowledge of grievances extrajudicially inflicted. In judicial appeals the case is different. For they are made against a formal decision, which constitutes a supposed full, complete, and determinate grievance. Hence the law of the Church determines the precise time when the ten days begin to run in such appeals, since it is easy to know when the sentence was pronounced, and when it was delivered to the party.

Again, it may be here remarked, that when a person feels aggrieved by some extrajudicial act, he can first request the Superior inflicting it to redress or revoke it; and that the grievance may be said to be complete only when the Superior refuses to revoke it.[4]

[1] Glosse, in cap. *Concertationi*, 8, in 6°, v. *gravatum*. [2] Cf. Santi, l. 2, t. 28, n. 32.
[3] Schmalzg., l. 28, n. 73. [4] Cf. Glossa, in cap. 8, de sent. in 6°, v. *gravatum*, in marg. c.

CONTENTS.

CHAPTER IV.

CHAPTER V.

CHAPTER VI.

APPENDIX.

I.

II.

Contents.

III.

IV.

V.

VI.

VII.

VIII.

IX.

www.ingramcontent.com/pod-product-compliance
Lightning Source LLC
Chambersburg PA
CBHW030040130726
47901CB00005BA/1176